Sultana: Two Sisters

By Lisa J. Yarde

Sultana: Two Sisters
Copyright © Lisa J. Yarde 2013

ISBN-10: 1939138132
ISBN-13: 978-1939138132

This is a work of fiction. The names, characters, locations, and
incidents portrayed in it are the work of the author's
imagination, or have been used fictitiously.

www.lisajyarde.com

Cover Artwork
Aimée, a Young Egyptian, Emile Vernet Lecomte 1869
http://commons.wikimedia.org/wiki/File:Vernet-Lecomte_2.jpg

Beauté Orientale, Emile Vernet-Lecomte 1869
http://commons.wikimedia.org/wiki/File:Vernet-Lecomte_5.jpg

Cover design and Alhambra Press logo by Lance Ganey
www.freelanceganey.com

Also by Lisa J. Yarde

On Falcon's Wings (2010)

Sultana (2011)

Sultana's Legacy (2011)

Long Way Home: A novella (2011)

The Burning Candle (2012)

The Legend Rises - HerStory anthology (2013)

Sultana: Two Sisters (2013)

Dedication

For Butayna, Maryam, Shams ed-Duna, Zoraya, and countless
other unnamed women sold into harems across medieval Muslim
Spain and North Africa,
I dedicate this novel to your courage and perseverance as
captives, slaves, mothers, and wives.

Acknowledgments

Many writers often refer to their novel as their baby. Like any baby, a new novel needs a little help coming into the world.

My enduring thanks to members of the Historical Fiction Authors Yahoo critique group, especially Jen Black, Anita Davison, Carolyn Heinemann, Cori Houser, Mark Patten, Mirella Sichirollo Patzer, Katherine Pym, and Rosemary Rach, who helped me shape the first draft of this work.

I am indebted to Siobhan Daiko, Melissa Mahan, Ginger Myrick, Mirella Sichirollo Patzer, N. Gemini Sasson, and Julia Try, the intrepid and patient group who agreed to become beta readers.

To my editor, Jessica Lux, thanks for saving me from myself and for taking such good care of my baby.

Foreword

Sultana: Two Sisters takes place in fourteenth-century Moorish Spain, during the reign of Sultan Abdul Hajjaj Yusuf I of Granada. It is a fictional account of his two wives, Butayna and Maryam. Both women endured lives as slaves in Yusuf's harem before they became his constant companions and the mothers of his heirs. My understanding of the achievements of Yusuf's reign, the political landscape of medieval Spain, the impact of the Black Death on the population, and the lives of captives like Butayna and Maryam could not have occurred without reference to the following sources:

The Alhambra by Robert Irwin (Harvard University Press – 2004)

The Alhambra: Volume I – From the Ninth Century to Yusuf (1354) by Antonio Fernandez-Puertas (Saqi Books – 1997)

The Black Death 1346 – 1353: The Complete History by Ole J. Benedictow (The Boydell Press - 2004)

The Gibraltar Crusade: Castile and the Battle of the Strait by Joseph F. O'Callaghan (University of Pennsylvania Press – 2011)

Arab Women in the Middle Ages: Private Lives and Public Roles by Shirley Guthrie (Saqi Books – 2001)

Captives and their Saviors in the Medieval Crown of Aragon by Jarbel Rodriguez (The Catholic University of America Press – 2007)

A History of Medieval Spain by Joseph F. O'Callaghan (Cornell University – 1975)

Jewish Life in the Middle Ages by Israel Abrahams (Dover Publications, Inc. – 2004)

Las Siete Partidas: Volume II – Medieval Government: The World of Kings and Warriors, translated by Samuel Parsons Scott, edited by Robert I. Burns, S.J. (University of Pennsylvania Press – 2001)

Las Siete Partidas: Volume IV – Family, Commerce and the Sea: The Worlds of Women and Merchants, translated by Samuel

Parsons Scott, edited by Robert I. Burns, S.J. (University of Pennsylvania Press – 2001)

Las Sultanas de la Alhambra: Las grandes desconocidas del Reino Nazari de Granada (siglos XIII-XV), by Barbara Boloix Gallardo (Patronato de la Alhambra y del Generalife Editorial Comares – 2013)

Under Crescent & Cross: The Jews in the Middle Ages by Mark R. Cohen (Princeton University Press – 1994)

Characters

The Peralta Family

Esperanza Peralta / Butayna, daughter of Efrain Peralta
Efrain Peralta, a physician from Talavera de la Reina

The Alubel Family

Miriam Alubel / Maryam, Esperanza's friend, wife of the Jewish goldsmith Gedaliah Alubel
Palomba Alubel, daughter of Miriam and Gedaliah Alubel
Gedaliah Alubel, a Jewish goldsmith

The Nasrids

Abdul Hajjaj Yusuf I ibn Ismail of Gharnatah, the seventh Sultan of Gharnatah (r. AD 1333-1354 or 733-755 AH), son of Abu'l-Walid Ismail I ibn Faraj and Safa bint Yusuf

Fatima bint Muhammad, paternal grandmother of Abdul Hajjaj Yusuf I ibn Ismail of Gharnatah

Safa bint Yusuf, mother of Abdul Hajjaj Yusuf I ibn Ismail of Gharnatah, widow of Abu'l-Walid Ismail I ibn Faraj of Gharnatah

Leila bint Ismail, eldest daughter of Abu'l-Walid Ismail I ibn Faraj of Gharnatah, sister of Abdul Hajjaj Yusuf I ibn Ismail of Gharnatah

Ismail ibn Ismail, second son of Abu'l-Walid Ismail I ibn Faraj and Arub bint Muhammad, brother of Abdul Hajjaj Yusuf I ibn Ismail of Gharnatah

Muhammad ibn Yusuf, son of Abdul Hajjaj Yusuf I ibn Ismail of Gharnatah and Butayna
Aisha bint Yusuf, daughter of Abdul Hajjaj Yusuf I ibn Ismail of Gharnatah and Butayna

Ismail ibn Yusuf, eldest son of Abdul Hajjaj Yusuf I ibn Ismail of Gharnatah and Maryam
Fatima bint Yusuf, eldest daughter of Abdul Hajjaj Yusuf I ibn Ismail of Gharnatah and Maryam

Qays ibn Yusuf, second son of Abdul Hajjaj Yusuf I ibn Ismail of Gharnatah and Maryam

Khadija bint Yusuf, second daughter of Abdul Hajjaj Yusuf I ibn Ismail of Gharnatah and Maryam

Shams bint Yusuf, third daughter of Abdul Hajjaj Yusuf I ibn Ismail of Gharnatah and Maryam

Mumina bint Yusuf, fourth daughter of Abdul Hajjaj Yusuf I ibn Ismail of Gharnatah and Maryam

Zoraya bint Yusuf, fifth daughter of Abdul Hajjaj Yusuf I ibn Ismail of Gharnatah and Maryam

Muhammad the Red, son of Ismail ibn Muhammad, cousin to Abdul Hajjaj Yusuf I ibn Ismail of Gharnatah, betrothed to Fatima bint Yusuf

Courtiers, Ministers, and Aides

Abu'l-Nu'aym Ridwan, the chief minister to Abdul Hajjaj Yusuf I ibn Ismail of Gharnatah and head of the Sultan's chancery (AD 1329-1340 or 729-741 AH and from AD 1354 or 755 AH), the chief royal tutor

Abdullah Hisham, chief eunuch in the harem of Abdul Hajjaj Yusuf I ibn Ismail of Gharnatah, brother to Abu'l-Nu'aym Ridwan

Ali ibn al-Jayyab, the chief minister to Abdul Hajjaj Yusuf I ibn Ismail of Gharnatah and head of the Sultan's chancery (AD 1340-1349 or 741-749 AH)

Lisan ad-Din ibn al-Khatib, chief secretary to Abdul Hajjaj Yusuf I ibn Ismail of Gharnatah

Muhammad al-Shaquri, chief personal physician to Abdul Hajjaj Yusuf I ibn Ismail of Gharnatah

Al-Hasan ibn Muhammad ibn Hasan al-Qaysi, a doctor from Malaga

The Marinids

Abu'l-Hasan Ali ibn Uthman, the Sultan of the Marinids (r. AD 1331-1351 or 731-751 AH)

Fatima bint Abu Bakr, daughter of Caliph Abu Bakr of the Hafsid Dynasty, first wife of Abu'l-Hasan Ali ibn Uthman

Umm Alfat, sister of Abu'l-Hasan Ali ibn Uthman

Abu'l-Fadl ibn Abu'l-Hasan Ali, a son of Abu'l-Hasan Ali ibn Uthman

Abu Salim Ibrahim ibn Abu'l-Hasan Ali, another son of Abu'l-Hasan Ali ibn Uthman

Shams ed-Duna, favorite concubine of Abu'l-Hasan Ali ibn Uthman

The Castillans

Fray Rufino Del Moral, a Dominican friar, Esperanza's childhood tutor

Fray Antonio Navas y Montilla, a Trinitarian friar

Retainers, Slaves, and Others

Ahmed al-Qurtubi, a slaver
Fadil al-Qurtubi, nephew of Ahmed al-Qurtubi

Juan Manuel Gomero, a Jewish slave merchant
Sadiya, the favored French slave of Juan Manuel Gomero
Binta, a Nubian slave in the service of Juan Manuel Gomero

Pero Ruiz, a former Christian captive, the captain of Muhammad ibn Yusuf's eunuch guards
Alfonso Ruiz, a former Christian captive and brother of Pero Ruiz, the captain of Butayna's eunuch guards

Mufawwiz, the chief steward of Abdul Hajjaj Yusuf I ibn Ismail of Gharnatah

Ifrit, the favored body slave of Leila bint Ismail

Zarru, a stewardess in the service of Leila bint Ismail
Sut, a seamstress and laundress in the service of Leila bint Ismail, Zarru's younger sister

Amat, mistress of wardrobe in the service of Leila bint Ismail

Hamduna, a *henna* artist in the service of Leila bint Ismail

Rima, the kitchen maid of Leila bint Ismail

Nazhun, a body slave of Safa bint Yusuf

Asiya, Fatima bint Muhammad's maidservant

Jawla, a servant of Butayna
Hafsa, a servant of Butayna

Bilal as–Sudan, a stableman
Al-Sagir, the brother of Bilal as-Sudan, a groomsman

Ramadi, a cat in the harem

Chapter 1
The Raiders

Esperanza Peralta

Castilla La Mancha, Kingdom of Castilla-Leon
January 18, AD 1336 / 3 Jumada al-Thani 736 AH / 4th of
Shevat, 5096

Esperanza Peralta snuggled closer to Miriam Alubel and clutched
hands so unlike her own—weathered and careworn with small,
brown burns earned in the service of Miriam's goldsmith father.
Miriam's fingers appeared as those of a woman twice her age of
nineteen, with livid veins visible beneath pale, coarse skin. Yet,
Esperanza found comfort in the familiar touch.

Wintry air intruded into the wooden horse litter. Faint streaks
of sunlight peeked through thin seams. The chill seeped within
the woolen blanket, folds of linen, and *cendal,* even the leather of
Esperanza's *zapatas.* She wriggled her pinched toes in the ankle-
length boots. The litter swayed and wobbled on the poles. Its
panels scraped against her back.

Miriam murmured, "Try to sleep, *mi querida.*" Her chafed lips
pressed against Esperanza's forehead. "The cold would not
trouble you then. Shall I sing to you as I do with my daughter?"

At the velvety tone of her friend, spoken in their shared
Castillan tongue, Esperanza patted Miriam's hand. "Did I
awaken you? I cannot sleep, not while I am aware of the daylight.
Papa said we would arrive at the next town soon. That was hours
ago. I am sorry to complain."

"You will be sorrier if your father should find us bundled so
close together."

"Why? In your state, you fare better in a litter than upon
horseback. Papa may not have encouraged my friendship with
you, but he has never denied me your company. He even offered
you and Palomba comfort at my side."

"Doctor Peralta tired of your insistence. You can be forceful
when you wish. Your father should have taken the trouble to
check your willfulness or ensured your *duenna* did so."

Esperanza giggled. "He tried." Not even he or a succession of
governesses had improved her fractious nature.

1

"You must never again impose your will upon him in regards to me. Be grateful he allowed my presence on this journey. He needed Gedaliah, not me."

"Papa is a courteous man, not given to the usual prejudices against Jews. Besides, your husband should have you at his side. You could not abandon your daughter. Gedaliah may be gone for at least three months."

Esperanza released Miriam and cupped the woman's rounded belly instead. The child nestled inside stirred with furtive movements.

"What if your baby arrived early? A father should be present once his child enters the world. I could not bear it if Gedaliah missed the opportunity now, since he was absent for a month after Palomba's birth."

Miriam nuzzled Esperanza's brow. "The babe always turns at the sound of your voice. He recognizes you."

"He?"

"Gedaliah thinks it is the son he has prayed for and I share his belief."

"Hmm, a son I shall never know. I envy you, Miriam, for you will return home."

"I have never held any attachment to Talavera de la Reina. Jews can never call any of the kingdoms of Spain their homeland."

"But in Talavera's *aljama*, everyone showed you great respect as the daughter of the foremost goldsmith in the community and the wife of his best apprentice." Esperanza had visited Talavera's Jewish quarter once. She stayed long enough to understand the respect the Alubel name commanded in the community.

"*Sí*, among the *kehilla*, my family has achieved merit. To Christians, however, we will never be more than the Jews they have tolerated. I have accepted this fact. You must do the same. Our religions divide us, as do other circumstances. We will never share the same course in life. Our destinies are different. At times we travel in the same direction, but it is always along separate paths."

A trace of bitterness lent a raspy tone to Miriam's otherwise smooth voice.

She fingered a gold brooch inlaid with carnelian and sardonyx, which fastened her woolen mantle at the neck. Miriam had given it to her. "Even in marriage we do not tread the same course. I must wed a stranger my father has chosen, while you have known and loved Gedaliah for all your life."

Miriam whispered, "Never loved."

Esperanza raised her head and allowed a scant distance between them. "You have never loved your husband? Not even once in these two years you have been wed."

"Your artlessness loses its charm with such questions. You must know a contract served as the basis for my marriage, as with yours. Do not expect love in marriage for it is a rare blessing. Instead, find your joy in the children born from such a union."

Miriam reached for the ink-black hair of the daughter who nestled at her left. With hands clasped in sleep, Palomba wriggled and murmured before she settled into deep even breaths again.

Esperanza smiled at the tenderness Miriam displayed. "I remember when Papa was so gentle with me."

"I'm sure he still is."

"He is distracted. Thoughts preoccupy him. Though he will not speak the words, he is troubled."

"The Cerdas have done him an injustice. Doctor Peralta shall survive this time of trouble. He has always persisted against the world's adversities. This time shall be no different."

With a wearied sigh, tendrils of white vapor from Esperanza's lips curled and dispersed. Would Miriam's words prove true? After long years of service to the Cerdas to recommend him, her father believed another wealthy patron would secure his services as a physician. Esperanza prayed no one would inquire as to why he sought another employer now.

He had contracted a betrothal arrangement within five months of his discharge. The prospective groom had visited within a month, his parents at his side. They signed the betrothal documents, while Esperanza gave quiet assent to the barter of her life to strangers. The end of their two-week journey eastward into the Levant meant she would never see Talavera de la Reina again. At the coastal town of Alicante in the old kingdom of Valencia, her future husband and his mercantile relatives expected her arrival.

She smiled at her foolish, fanciful thoughts. Rather, their hosts awaited the delivery of her extravagant bride price. She recalled her future husband, a sallow-faced young man with golden curls who had shamed her with his lascivious demands. The memory of his Christian name eluded her, but perhaps it would come to mind before she reached the destination. Mere months could not have altered his haughty disposition or the dour expressions of his parents. She faced a precarious future among those who would tolerate her because of the generous dowry her father offered.

Miriam asked, "Do you consider your betrothed, Esperanza?"

"I think of the future and how life in Alicante may be."

"I do not doubt you shall know the usual comforts. Consider yourself fortunate. You will have servants and charge of a household, at least when your husband's mother is absent. Once you are in control, rabbit stew will never appear at your table unless you wish it."

Esperanza giggled at Miriam's reference to the tiresome meal. Throughout the journey, they often lodged for the night at the guesthouse of an isolated Cistercian or Benedictine chapter house and the rare inn. Gold *maravedies* did not guarantee any variety at dinner. No matter where they went, stringy stewed rabbit flavored with herbs, garlic, and onion became the staple. Thank God, they would eat no meat on the morrow, as custom dictated on Fridays.

Miriam continued, "What do you anticipate this future will hold?"

Esperanza frowned until her forehead hurt. "I don't imagine any prospect in particular."

Miriam sniggered. "You must learn to be a better liar once you are wed, *mi querida*. Otherwise, your new family may discern your thoughts. Your gaze reveals all, hope coupled with resentment."

"My views upon this marriage are plain. Why should I act as if it pleases me? For Papa's sake? He must know the hastiness of my betrothal requires time before acceptance comes. What do I care for the opinions of the haughty boy I must marry or his parents?"

"You may when you realize this new life is dependent on their good graces. You should seek to please them though it may be difficult. Indeed, they may look at you and wonder if you are female at all. There have been fourteen summers since your birth, though no one would know it for you are straight as a stalk."

Esperanza pressed her lips together. After the disastrous first encounter with her betrothed, her hopes for happiness withered like summer buds at the change of season. Youthful optimism would fade soon under the burdens of marriage. Did Miriam also have to remind her of the bitter truth? Esperanza had not bled, still did not possess hips to stir a man's ardor or breasts to suckle his children. Her last governess had warned her, a woman in childbirth needed generous hips. She often despaired of Esperanza's future as a mother.

"Papa has cautioned me not to worry. He says I need more time to blossom."

Miriam snorted. "Pray your flower blooms long before your husband's mother clamors for grandchildren!"

"I trust Papa's word. He is a fine doctor. The Cerdas thought so."

"*Sí!* At least until they dismissed him!"

A tingling sensation swept up the back of Esperanza's neck and she looked away. The bitter truth of her father's losses left them without supporters except the kind Peralta wealth could buy, like the strength of Gedaliah Alubel's mercenaries. Esperanza reached for the neckline of her layered garments. She grasped the precious rosary worn against her skin. Until her betrothal, she had never believed any of the words Fray Rufino compelled from her. Where she had once mocked the Dominican, prayer became her refuge from panicked thoughts of the future.

Her personal shame magnified as she glanced at Miriam. Did she know the truth behind what had happened between Efrain and Don Alfonso de la Cerda? Were there secrets to which Miriam's husband might have been privy? Efrain might have confided in the goldsmith and secured his daughter's bride price at the cost of great mortification.

"Miriam, do you know why the Cerdas released Papa from their service?"

"I have oft told you I do not, *mi querida*. Why do you question my word again? Have I ever given you reason to doubt me?"

Under her white *toca* and the veil worn with the headdress, Miriam's eyebrows arched. Esperanza discerned the challenge in Miriam's hardened gaze darker than indigo and in the firm set of her thinned lips.

Miriam demanded, "Well? Have I?"

"You have not. Still, I feel there are certain truths I have not discovered."

"If so, then you should ask your father, if you dare provoke him again with your impertinent questions. You do remember what happened last time?"

The flesh on Esperanza's cheek tingled. Unbidden, the memory of a slap across her face came to mind. She avoided Miriam's pertinent stare afterward.

Palomba stirred. Her eyelashes fluttered against plump, dewy cheeks. A soft whimper escaped her. Miriam turned her attention to her daughter. She cradled Palomba's head with one hand and untied the cords, which held Miriam's mantle closed at the neck. The woolen cloth pushed aside, she loosened the threads at her back. Palomba whined while her mother pulled her slender arms from the sleeves of the fitted *saya* and unlaced the wrists of the linen *camisa* worn with her robe. Miriam bunched these garments around her prominent belly. She bared her rounded shoulders and breasts engorged with milk. White fluid dribbled from her nipple down to her stomach, where a faint brown line trailed to her navel. When Miriam grasped her full breast without any sign of embarrassment, Esperanza bit her lower lip.

Miriam fitted her little girl against her in a tight embrace. "My Palomba, come nurse."

She cupped the child's head and sang to her. With a wriggle, the child latched on to the pebbled nipple, evidenced by Miriam's sudden wince.

Esperanza pressed against the wooden beam behind her. "Does it hurt when she nurses?"

"She has a few teeth, which can leave their mark."

"Then why do you endure her at your breast?"

Miriam raised her dark eyebrows. "Gedaliah never wished for another woman to feed our child. I was not fortunate to hire a wet nurse after Palomba's birth, unlike your mother."

Esperanza sighed. "You remark on the differences between us at every opportunity."

"I tell truths you must never allow yourself to forget, for both of our sakes. When you birth your husband's babies, other women shall attend them. A *duenna* shall raise your children."

While Miriam sang to her daughter in a hushed, evocative melody of Ladino, Esperanza joined in the song. For a brief instant, their voices blended, Miriam's rich husky tone coupled with Esperanza's dulcet one. At a sharp glance from Miriam, Esperanza lapsed into silence again.

Miriam sniffled. "Why do you persist? You shall never have the talent for song as I do."

"Then why did you take the trouble to teach me if you believe it was a wasted effort?"

"You should forget those lessons. Your husband's family would not welcome a daughter who would fill their grandchildren's ears with Jewish lullabies. Do not arouse their concerns."

"Why should they be concerned?"

Miriam did not answer. She resumed her tune alone.

Esperanza lowered her gaze. The future seemed so uncertain. Still, she stared hard at Miriam's abdomen. Would her husband's children delight her with the same joy as Palomba brought to her mother? She considered Miriam's earlier advice. In truth, she might never love the young man who awaited her in Alicante. She did not doubt her ability to love any children she bore him. Her mother had enriched Esperanza's childhood with steadfast care and never left her daughter in doubt of her adoration. Esperanza would do the same with her children.

She murmured, "I suppose my father was wrong."

Miriam paused in the midst of her song. "About what?"

"Before we left Talavera, I shared my concerns about the travail of childbirth with Papa. He said my husband would have to wait until after I bled to try for children. Father also suggested women who nursed for at least a year between each ordeal would not conceive soon afterward. You have nursed Palomba since birth for eighteen months. Yet, you are with child again."

Miriam laughed. "What can men know of women's bodies?"

"My father is a learned doctor with many years of training!"

"I do not deny this fact. As mothers themselves, midwives understand a woman's travail best, which is why they attend the delivery of children."

"Last winter, your cousin's husband summoned my father to Talavera's *aljama* when his wife endured a difficult childbirth."

"I remember you went with him. As I recall it, you insisted on the journey to a place no well-born Christian girl would enter."

"He could not leave me alone in our house, without a *duenna* or anyone to ensure my safety in his absence."

"But for Avram Alubel's miserly ways, his wife would not have needed a doctor's care. Avram hired the services of an inexperienced midwife because he is a close-fisted, youthful fool. He jeopardized the lives of his wife and babe for a few *maravedies*."

"Papa saved the boy and his mother."

"A breech birth would not have caused difficulty for an expert midwife."

Palomba raised her tiny head and turned an almost severe glare on Esperanza. The child possessed prominent eyes, the irises a deep shade of smoky blue. Thick black hair framed her face in an imitation of her mother's features.

Miriam kissed Palomba's curls before she dressed herself again. She laced the *saya* again, which gaped and revealed the *camisa*. Esperanza's last governess had often warned against poor or indecent women who wore a robe and undergarment without the *pellote*. Esperanza suspected the hard-faced woman would not have thought well of Miriam's current attire.

"You should not look upon me with such reproof in your stare, Esperanza. Heed my experience in such matters for I am a woman who has had children. Remember I am older than you."

"By five years!" Esperanza met the sharp glint in Miriam's dark eyes, almost indistinguishable from the black pupils at their center. The length of her neck evoked memories of elegant swans along the banks of the Tagus River.

Dimples indented the soft curve of Miriam's florid cheeks and her brows flared again. "Your mother's temper shows itself."

"What do you know of it?"

"The good Doctor Peralta often surrendered to it to keep the peace of his house. You are more like your mother than him."

Esperanza bowed her head. "I'd rather be like Papa. I wish we could have stayed in Talavera. All of his friends there abandoned him and I still don't know why."

Miriam draped an arm over her shoulder. "Not all of his associates. My husband has not turned from him. Do not tell me you care about the sentiments of those old fools and drunkards in Talavera? For years, they had the honor of a noble physician in their midst."

"A short time after Papa helped deliver Avram's boy, our neighbors muttered 'Cristianos Nuevos' at our backs whenever we went out. Papa told me to ignore them. I could not. Why did they call us New Christians?"

Before Miriam could answer, the horse litter lurched. Its wooden walls shuddered. From outside, the loud snorts of the Peralta horses vied with a deep rumble in the ground.

Esperanza plucked the string of jet rosary beads worn next to her skin. Her father had brought the gift from Santiago de Compostela for her first Communion. "*Dios mío*! Is it an earth tremor?"

While Palomba whimpered and buried her plump cheeks against her mother's arm, Miriam cocked her head. "Earth tremors have not troubled La Mancha for several generations."

"Papa told me one collapsed the house of his grandfather Esteban and killed him."

"This is no tremor. The horses and pack animals would have grown restless long before midday."

Before Esperanza could ask how Miriam knew, their conveyance came to a sudden stop. Palomba slipped from her mother's lap with a loud wail. Esperanza slammed the back of her head against the wood. Tears clouded her vision. Her fillet secured a gauzy, white veil over the dark brown hair she wore loose. With a deep inhalation, she pressed against a sore patch of her skull. Her hand came away bloodless. She heaved a deep sigh.

Miriam gasped and hugged a frightened Palomba against her body. "Hush, my sweet one, hush! Your father's men shall protect us."

"Protect us against what?" Esperanza demanded. She and her father depended on Gedaliah's men, who protected the Peraltas' property in their strongboxes. Would the men guard her family as well?

"Moors! To arms!"

The terror laced in the voice from outside left Esperanza aghast. Her fingers tightened on the rosary until the golden cross cut into her palm. Moors in La Mancha! They had received no word of a renewal of the ageless conflicts between the Christians of Castilla-Leon and the Mohammedans with their false religion, who kept a tenuous hold on southern Spain from their stronghold at Granada. Her father would never have risked the arduous journey given any advanced knowledge. The danger their party faced now derived from the frequent raids, with which the Mohammedans drove terror into the hearts of Christians. How had they crossed *la frontera* between their kingdom and the towns at the outskirts of Castilla-Leon without detection?

"The men must protect us. Your husband has twenty in his pay for our protection."

Miriam sneered. "And if the Moorish number is greater?"

"Then, *Dios mío* help us."

"You may wait upon heaven's grace. I intend to save myself and my child." Miriam unlatched the bolt over the shuttered doors.

Esperanza grabbed her shoulder. "No, you can't leave!"

Miriam shrugged her off and clambered down with Palomba perched on her hip. A streak of burnished orange blazed across the evening sky. Shadows darkened the rough-hewn walls of Alcaraz, their destination.

Esperanza hung back for a moment before she followed Miriam into the crisp, dry air. The tip of her boot stubbed against a low bar and plunged her into the dirt. Dazed, she pushed herself up on her palms and knees. Her fingers fisted in mounds of sienna-colored earth.

"Esperanza! Get up now!" Efrain Peralta steadied his skittish mount and reined in the horse near her, before he dismounted. His sharpened gaze glowed, his eyes the color of burnished brass. He flung the folds of his rust-colored mantle behind his left shoulder and revealed a green samite *pellote* slit up to the inner thigh, worn with a gold belt and a dagger in a scabbard at his hip.

A sinewy man, Efrain Peralta shared the diminutive stature of his daughter. Late evening sunlight framed him in a golden-orange glare as he strode toward her. Spurs affixed to his *zapatos* drew furrows across the soil. Lines etched in his olive-brown features betrayed a year's worth of misfortune. The dark brown hairs atop his head had lost their luster and begun a steady retreat from his sloped forehead. A full beard with flecks of gray almost hid the creases around his mouth. At fifty-six years old, his gnarled fingers and gangling arms coupled with a receded hairline gave him the appearance of a man burdened by age. His prideful bearing and a strident tone hinted at the strength he retained.

She scrambled to her feet and clutched his arms. "Papa, what are we to do?"

He clasped her to him for the space of a heartbeat. "You must flee!"

She warbled, "Where, Papa? Where can I go? I won't leave without you or Miriam!"

The first haven along their route might have been at Montiel. They had avoided the castle there, because the Cerdas held sway over its inhabitants. Most of the sparse settlements across La Mancha crowded around fortified defenses. Set on a wide plateau, Alcaraz abutted a rugged hill. Her father had hoped to reach the township this evening. The Mohammedans had held Alcaraz until a century ago, when the tide of the *Reconquista* under Alfonso VII of Castilla-Leon swept over the town and its castle. It could not offer refuge from the attackers, not when they approached from the same direction.

Gedaliah's men had closed ranks and surrounded their charges. More than half the men brandished swords, while six others drew their crossbows. Before the Mohammedans could close another third of the distance, a lethal volley of bolts cut down three men in the lead. The Jews cheered, but a slight decline in the enemy numbers would not be enough.

Miriam stood silent beside her red-haired husband's horse with Palomba. Their mutual gazes took in the approach of the Mohammedans, who drew their swords and whooped in spiteful glee. They showed no interest in minor losses and left the bodies where they fell. Faded light clung to the edges of their long, curved blades.

Esperanza strained for the sight of someone at the ramparts of Alcaraz. No denizen appeared at hand to witness the drama south of the township. Unimpeded, the formidable band of dark-clad Mohammedans drove their mounts across the *meseta*, the tableland of La Mancha.

Chapter 2
Taken

Esperanza Peralta

Castilla La Mancha, Kingdom of Castilla-Leon
January 18 - 19, AD 1336 / 3 - 4 Jumada al-Thani 736 AH / 4th
- 5th of Shevat, 5096

Esperanza surveyed the scene in mute horror. The pious Fray
Rufino del Moral knelt in the dirt beside his donkey. The priest
wore a frayed white habit paired with a shorter black cloak, his
scapular. Wooden rosary beads trembled between fat fingers.
With his beady eyes closed, the Dominican muttered a fervent
prayer. Beads of perspiration set his tonsured head aglow. His
pathetic state stirred not a shred of pity within Esperanza. His
cruelty would have never ceased if Miriam had not spoken of his
excesses to Esperanza's father. The memory of Fray Rufino's
chastisements summoned a dull ache in her muscles.

Efrain grasped her arms and shook her. "This is no time for
your stubbornness. You are my child and I will not lose you!" He
released her and grabbed the reins. "Get on the horse. Ride west
now, the evening sun ahead of you. At night, you will look for the
North Star on your right. Do not stop until you reach the safety
of Valdepeñas, where we departed from yesterday. Valdepeñas
belongs to the *caballeros* of the Order of Calatrava. The
Cistercians shall protect you for my sake."

He drew his dagger and cut the strings, which secured a
weighted pouch to his leather belt. He shoved the purse filled
with coins into her hand. "For your care and comfort."

She clutched the sack. "You want me to ride off alone into the
darkness? Papa, I can't reach Valdepeñas!"

"You can and you will! You have spent more time with horses
than I ever did, since you were four years old. I do not ask you to
ride on without me. I am telling you! Get on the damned horse! I
will not see your life ended by a Mohammedan's blade. Greater
peril may lie ahead, but you will make the attempt to escape."

He considered failure a possibility, yet held hope for her
against the obvious threat. Such words gave a clear indication of

his resolve and the graveness of their state. Still Esperanza stood catatonic. Her gaze watered.

He captured her face between his withered hands and pressed his lips to her cheeks and forehead in turn. "My most precious life. I beg of you, please go. Do not let me live my last moments with the knowledge of your failure to try. Whatever happens, you must survive. If I can, I will come for you at Valdepeñas. Wait for me there."

"Papa, no—"

"I'll go with her." Miriam joined them. "We'll keep each other safe."

Gedaliah had abandoned his mount and given orders to his men to stand firm. He never spared a backward glance for his wife or child. Esperanza could not fathom how his last exchange with Miriam might have affected both of them.

Efrain regarded Miriam. "Protect yourselves if you can. My daughter is all I have."

She gave a stiff nod and ran to Gedaliah's horse. She grasped the reins her husband had discarded and tugged the mare behind her.

Efrain kissed both of Esperanza's hands. "Promise me you'll survive."

"I will, Papa, I will. We'll see each other soon at Valdepeñas."

He said no more and led her to his horse. He helped her to mount astride the animal. Then he offered to take Palomba. Her mother hesitated. Then, she nodded and handed him the child. Settled astride the saddle with her *saya* bunched up to reveal her booted feet, Miriam reached for Palomba and secured her with a hand around the toddler's waist.

With a slap on the rump of both their horses, Efrain urged their departure. Esperanza's mount bolted straightaway, Miriam's own beside them. Esperanza gripped the reins and pressed her knees against the mare's sides.

"There is always hope, *mi hija!*" Efrain's shout echoed across the plateau.

The full force of the Mohammedan charge clashed with Gedaliah's company. The screams of men and horses reverberated across the plain. Her face awash with tears, Esperanza peered behind her although Miriam yelled, "You'll break your neck! Do not look back! We cannot help them now. Do as your father said. Survive."

Esperanza refused to abandon him to his fate as Miriam had done with her husband. Another brief glance showed Gedaliah had ducked his head and avoided a blow, while he slashed upward at the same time. His sword cleaved his attacker's chest before the man sprawled backward on his horse. Then Esperanza's father gripped his side just after a rider clad in white rode past him.

"Papa!"

Esperanza relaxed her thighs. She grabbed the mare's mane and loosened her hold on the reins. The horse slowed in response while Miriam's mount shot past them.

"Esperanza! What are you doing?"

She did not answer the furious demand in Miriam's voice. Instead, she slowed her horse to a canter and circled the ground. Darkness had almost consumed the evening. The combat in the distance threw up spirals of dust and almost obscured her vision. She found her father. He knelt beside a supine body garbed in grayish-white. Efrain pressed his hand to his side. Blood seeped between his fingers while a crimson blotch extended across his tunic.

Miriam snatched the reins from Esperanza's hands. "You cannot help your father. He would never forgive himself if you died trying to save him."

Although Gedaliah's men fought on, more of their dead littered the ground. Among them Gedaliah rested facedown. His flame-colored hair rippled in the wind. Miriam's audible gasp warned of her awareness.

Another flurry of dust rose up. Out of the spiral, four pairs of riders sped across the ground. Men slung a wide net between their horses.

Miriam screamed. "It's a raid! The Moors have come for captives. We must flee."

Esperanza blinked as her father sagged to the ground. He did not move. Esperanza could not tear her eyes away from the scene.

Miriam snagged her arm. "Damn you! Do not linger here. He is dead! Do not dare to make his sacrifice a vain one! You promised him you would survive. We have to leave now! We must live to have our vengeance another day."

At Miriam's prod, both horses sped away again. A brusque wind ripped away Miriam's *toca* and it tumbled across the *meseta*. The veil remained affixed with pins. Her thick dark hair streamed from it like spilled ink. The clash of swords resounded from behind them. This time, Esperanza did not look back. Tears blinded her as she dwelled upon loving memories of the father who had cherished her and given his life to save hers. She must repay him and live as she had sworn.

She and Miriam flew through tortuous turns and bends in the long pass at dangerous speeds. The labored snorts of the horses and shouts from the men behind them became louder, grew closer. Esperanza leaned forward. Her mare stretched her neck. Her dark mane flowed on the wind. Still, the riders gained on them. As they emerged at the base of another plateau, the first two riders flung their net, which sailed through the air and missed their targets.

"Look ahead! Christians!" Miriam cried.

Two large bands of men who brandished swords and torches sped toward them. The riders wore hooded white mantles with scarlet crosses. Their white *pellotes* billowed and revealed blackened armor underneath.

Tears almost blinded Esperanza and she shouted to Miriam, "It's the *caballeros* from the Order of Calatrava. We are saved!"

A smaller group on mules crested the rise, Cistercian monks. She could not fathom why the group traveled so late in the evening, but sent silent thanks heavenward for their arrival. Swords upraised, they charged down the slope and readied to defend Esperanza and Miriam from their pursuers. Castillan *ballesteros,* with their crossbows at the ready, aimed and fired on the Mohammedans.

As they neared, Esperanza looked over her shoulder. A Mohammedan with a large nose drew abreast of her. His ragged breaths came closer. Puffs of air billowed from his gray horse's reddened nostrils. She dug her heels against her mount. Desperation overwhelmed her. His companions aimed for Miriam, who held on to a tear-stricken Palomba. The girl wailed and wriggled against her mother. When they flung the second net, the mesh ensnared horse and rider. Miriam's scream pierced the evening.

The Mohammedan beside Esperanza swooped in and dragged her on to his horse. He lifted her through the air and slammed her into the saddle. His action left her breathless for a moment. In the next instance, she reared her head back and bashed it against the bulbous nose of her captor. He grappled with her. He forced her wrists together with one hand against the pommel until she swore he must have broken the bones. Even as she wriggled, he retained firm control over her and his horse. He wheeled his horse in the direction they had come. Miriam's screams and the squeals of her horse echoed behind Esperanza.

"Miriam! Miriam! Where are you?"

A quarrel shot by a Castillan *ballestero* whizzed past Esperanza's cheek. Her Mohammedan captor drew a knife and pressed it to her side. He growled unintelligible words in her ear. Without the benefit of the knowledge of Arabic, she perceived he warned her to be silent. The last promise she had sworn to her father kept her silent. She would do what she must for survival. Her captor kept her on his mount and plunged into the darkness.

***

On a moonless evening, the stranger dragged Esperanza from the gray stallion. He shoved her next to a large rock beside a desiccated stump, the sole evidence of trees in the barren landscape. Her elbow banged against the stone so hard, tears pricked her gaze. She hung her head and bit her lip. She stifled a cry. She would never give her abductor the satisfaction of the resultant pain displayed in her features.

He cocked his head as if he studied her. His stubby nose at the center of a pockmarked face disgusted her almost as much as the jagged scar, which rippled across his left cheek. On the furious ride, he had snatched the sack of coins from her grasp. The red strings, which secured the money inside, looped around his leather belt. Now, he knelt at her feet and reached for the fasteners of her *zapatas*.

She kicked him straight in the chest. "Do not touch me, you ugly savage!"

He scrambled and regained his foothold. The knife he had pressed to her ribs earlier reappeared in his copper-colored hand. She shrank against the stone as he raised the blade.

"*La!*" A gruff tone echoed in the night. Thick leather boots emerged from the shadows. Esperanza's gaze traipsed up the length of them. They reminded her of similar expensive pairs she had seen on the feet of the Cerda men. The boots rose to the wearer's knees and vanished at the hem of a voluminous white cloak. Hooded dark eyes peered at her from a weather-beaten craggy face. Other men followed the stranger until at least twenty of them stood over her.

She drew her knees up to her chest and averted her gaze. The stranger dismissed the man with the knife and took his place. Thin olive fingers went for her chin. She slapped his hand away and seethed at his presumption. Those around him stepped back or focused murderous glares on her.

A chuckle rumbled through the stranger's barrel chest before his stare darkened. His palm swung wide and connected with her cheek. Sudden tears fell.

He stood. "I have no wish to hurt you. Never do that again, *mi querida*."

If he had said anything else in the Castillan tongue, except for the cherished term Miriam had long favored her with, she might have shown no reaction to his silver-tongued tone. Now, she might never see her dearest friend again. She would never know

15

of her fate or if the *caballeros* had intercepted the Mohammedans. Had Miriam and Palomba escaped? The weight of her present misfortune, the loss of her father, and the uncertainty of Miriam's circumstances stirred Esperanza. This man, the clear leader among his companions, had ruined all their lives.

She raised her chin and spat in his face.

He did not hesitate. His thick fingers clenched her veil and ripped it along with the fillet from her head. He wound a haft of her locks around his hand and pulled hard. A fire flared across her scalp. Hair tore from the roots. He delivered two more fierce slaps to her cheeks. She bit her tongue and shuttered her gaze.

He pushed her against the rough rock face and loosened his hold. Shards of stone dug into her back through her dirtied clothes.

The young man with the knife and a vicious scar etched in his cheek returned. He offered her his profile. Guttural sounds enveloped his exchange with the white-cloaked leader. Esperanza shuddered each time he stabbed a finger in her direction. At one point, he made as if to grab her again. The other man at her side shoved him back and berated him until he backed away.

The leader pointed at the purse of stolen coins affixed to the young man's belt. His counterpart clutched his gains against his hip. He shook his head and stalked off, though his commander issued terse shouts.

Snorts and whinnies echoed. Esperanza peered into the dimness. Had the knights of Calatrava found them at last? In the same instance she readied to let loose a shrill scream, the cloaked man knelt. He covered her mouth with his hand and choked off the sound. At a silent wave from him, his men melted into the shadows as if she had imagined them there. Eight riders cantered in a line toward the remnant of the tree.

Esperanza could have wept for a mix of bitter sorrow and relief. Miriam sat atop the last horse. Palomba clung to her mother. Miriam had strapped her daughter to her with her veil. The little girl's bloodshot eyes, with swollen and puffy circles beneath them, revealed her torment and fear. Her mother clambered down from the horse, at a prod from one of the Mohammedans. He shoved her toward the rock. Miriam kissed Palomba's head and soothed the child.

The man behind Esperanza released his hold and she rolled toward Miriam. "I thought you had gained your freedom! I was certain the *caballeros* saved you."

"They were too far away and the Moorish crossbows countered theirs. If you had ridden off, as I told you and not worried for your father, the *caballeros* would have rescued us. Now, we belong to these Moors to do with as they will."

Esperanza drew back. A heavy weight settled in her stomach. Her wet gaze watered again. "How can you blame me for concerns about my father?"

"Because he told you not to worry! He warned you to get away, to survive. You have made a mockery of your promise to him."

"So, I should have abandoned him as you did Gedaliah? Have you shed one tear for the father of your children? When you told me you did not love him, I never imagined you would have left him to die in La Mancha!"

"Tears are for fools! Will tears change our circumstances now? Gedaliah is dead. Your father is dead. We are captives along the frontier."

"Not forever!"

"No one knows where we are. Our lives are altered evermore because of your stupidity and stubbornness," Miriam accused.

The stranger in his white cloak intruded on their exchange with a husky laugh. "Listen to you foolish women! You bicker amongst yourselves when you should have concerns about the future."

With a final shake of the dark curls stop his head, he turned away and strode among the men who had just returned. Two pairs of them hefted the Peraltas' strong boxes. They placed them on the ground. Two others wielded iron bars against the locks. They pried the caskets open. Their leader knelt and plunged his hands into the bolts of *cendal* in each wooden box. From one, he withdrew two small bags. He delved inside them with rapacious speed. His gleeful cry rent the silence. He pulled out a fistful of gold coins and showed them to those of his company. His companions gathered around, patted each other on the backs, and laughed at their ill-gotten gains.

The leader searched the other chest. A frown marred his brow as he drew out a rolled parchment. The thick sheepskin bore a red wax seal. He opened it and read in silence. His gaze fell on Miriam and Esperanza, who turned her face away from the spectacle, while the rest of the marauders rummaged through her dowry.

She muttered, "We are not without hope. The Cistercians have seen us. They will not halt the pursuit, especially if there are tracks in the dirt to follow."

Miriam answered, "You believe they can see pathways in darkness? Even if they have torches, the *caballeros* would not wish to stray far from protection. If they wait until morning to resume the search, the wind will have obliterated the tracks the Moorish horses left behind."

"Then the Order will stop at Alcaraz and tell of what they have seen. There must be a garrison to send word of our capture across La Mancha and warn about the raiders. At least, they will find my father's body and the others slain upon the ground."

A lump swelled inside Esperanza's throat and she swallowed with difficulty. The weight of her loss settled upon her shoulders. She did not cry. Perhaps Miriam was right. Tears would gain her nothing now.

"What chance awaits us then, eh?" Miriam hugged Palomba against her body and kissed the child who still whimpered. "Do you know what Moors do to their captives? To women without protection?"

Esperanza closed her eyes. "I won't let them hurt any of us. The promise of ransom must be enough to convince them to leave us untroubled. Before we left Talavera, I worried for our safety. Papa assured me the current truce between the Mohammedans and Castilla-Leon would ensure our safety—"

"He did not consider raiders who have little concern for treaties between kings."

"He could not have anticipated this attack! It is a crime to take captives when there is peace between Christian and Mohammedan. Why do you think they brought us here so fast, if not to escape detection by any trackers from Alcaraz? These are greedy men. They have seized a little of Papa's wealth and will wonder if there is more. They will ask for ransom. My father told me of such transactions, where the *alfaqueques* of the Cerda court organized aid and brought captives out of bondage, even from across the Mediterranean Sea."

"How can any exchange occur? Are you blind or just stupid? These Moors have stolen everything you held of value. You have nothing with which to repay the fee of one *maravedi*, which an *alfaqueque* would demand. Even if the Moors believed your claim, to whom would they send word of our capture? Would you have our captors write to Alicante and your dear betrothed's family instead?" Miriam's snort echoed on the wind. "The moment they received word of your capture, the wool merchant and his wife would have cause to rescind the arrangement. If they have any reason to suspect our captors abused you or placed you in a Moor's bed, your betrothed's parents would find an untainted bride for their prideful son and leave you to your doom."

"You still have relatives at Talavera de la Reina! We will tell these wretches of the Alubel clan and they will submit demands for payment."

"You think my kinfolk have the wealth to purchase freedom for me and my child? Would you see them beggared, reduced to penury?"

"If their sacrifice saves your life and Palomba's own, then so be it!"

Miriam's shoulders sagged. Even as her chin trembled, she laid it against her child's brow. "My relatives will not risk the attempt. They will abandon me as well. Fate has consigned us to lives as captives and slaves until we die."

"I will never be a slave! There is no one left of my family at Talavera de la Reina, but I shall make my own appeal to the mendicant orders. The Franciscans or the Trinitarians will help."

"For once in your life, think, Esperanza! When the mendicants attempt their rescue, they seek to secure more than a few meager lives. They would never choose you, a female with no wealth or skills to enrich their coffers. Shall you sing to them at mealtimes or sew their frayed vestments? Those embroidery lessons with your *duenna* shall not avail you."

"My father's good name still means something."

"Not without the Cerdas' patronage. Give up this foolish expectancy of liberation. Better the Franciscans or Trinitarians should spend hard-won gold on a royal official, a nobleman, a soldier, or a master mason than a mere girl."

"All life is valuable."

"*Sí*, a sentiment the Moors would appreciate. They have no trouble assigning value to the life of each captive sold into bondage."

Esperanza buried her face in her hands. It could not be as hopeless as Miriam described.

A moment later, another squabble erupted, again from the copper-colored youth with the fearsome scar.

"That one has demanded his share of the spoils now, including you," Miriam muttered.

"What?" Esperanza lifted her head as he motioned to her again. "You can understand them? You speak Arabic. Why have you never told me before now?"

Miriam rolled her eyes. "Did you think my father and husband dealt with just Christians in their business? *Sí*, I can understand the Moors. Big Nose with his scarred face wants you as part of his reward."

"He cannot have me."

"How would you stop him if he truly intended it? The man in the white cloak, who the other one refers to as 'Uncle Ahmed', says the same. He says you are likely a virgin. He says even if you are not as beautiful, as the black-haired woman, *muger fermosa*, your innocence alone will fetch a high price. The younger one, who Ahmed has named as Fadil, will not listen. He demands a woman for his pleasure tonight. Fadil says he deserves a reward after the risks they have taken. It seems his father has contributed horses and financed their raids. He says if his father were here, he would deny him nothing."

Miriam leaned closer, intent on their conversation. "Ahmed says it is good his brother is dead. Otherwise, he would know he had sired a lustful fool for a son." She paused and then added, "He chides his nephew for his selfishness. The other men just escaped the Castillan knights with their lives and all Fadil can think of is a woman. One among them says he should wait to quench his fires among whores. Fadil insists he will not wait. Now their leader says, he declares—"

Miriam fell silent. She pulled Palomba impossibly closer and her pained stare fell to the ground. Esperanza prodded her. "What does he say? Please tell me."

Miriam replied, "Their leader says Fadil may have me tonight instead since I am no virgin."

Palomba whimpered and covered her ears against the argument. Esperanza understood what the men intended for Miriam and wished she might avoid their cruel words as the child did.

Instead, Esperanza cried, "My family will pay a fine ransom for our return!"

The leader sniffed the *cendal* fragranced with dried orange peels for the last time. He stuffed the fabric into the strongbox again.

In a hushed tone, Miriam demanded, "What are you doing? A lie will gain us nothing!"

"It might save you from the lust of our captors," Esperanza muttered. She inhaled as the man strode toward them.

He asked, "What did you say?"

Esperanza tilted her chin a little. "My father is a wealthy man, a doctor in the household of the Cerdas, the old princely household of Castilla-Leon. He has traveled on ahead of us to meet with the relatives of my betrothed in Alicante. You must send word of our fate. In return you will receive a reward, if you do not mistreat us."

He shook his head. "I guessed right. This wealth," he said, as he gestured with a wide sweep of his hand to the chests, "belonged to Castillans of great means. Your father must indeed be a rich man to provide such a dowry. The offer of fine cloth meant you must be a bride on your way across La Mancha for your wedding." His gaze shifted to Miriam. "Who is this woman with you?"

When neither she nor Miriam gave an answer, he turned to Esperanza again. "What is your name?"

She answered with her Christian name and he nodded. "*Sí,* you would be the little hope of your father, would you not? Perhaps a fortunate alliance awaited you in Alicante, eh?"

"It still does, as does your reward."

"Tell me about the woman and her child."

"She is my *duenna* and she travels with me to my new home."

"A youthful woman to occupy the vaunted position of governess in your home. It is possible her skin, soft as a flower petal kissed by morning dew, deceives me about her age." He crouched and grabbed Miriam's hand. He pressed his fingers against her palm. She remained silent although her nostrils flared.

"These dry, coarse hands do not lie. They have known greater toil than any rich Castillan's governess ever could. Where I am taking you, they do not care so much for the touch of a woman, just what she can do with her other parts."

When his hold slackened, Miriam pulled away from him and wiped her palm on her skirt.

He shoved the parchment at her. "Read this to me."

She glared at the paper. His hand struck her cheek. "I said read it, damn you! Now!"

Esperanza clutched Miriam, who shook off her hold.

He asked, "You are a Jewess and her friend, are you not? A Christian girl and a Jewess who have traveled the *meseta* in a caravan loaded with a fortune in precious fabric. Should I still wonder at your presence here? Tell me how these words pertain to you."

Miriam's fearless silence challenged him. Her scrutiny flickered from the smooth sheepskin to his face. "They do not. If you are so eager to know the letter's contents, you should find someone to read it."

"I have. You! The words are Ladino. Isn't that what you Jews speak? What is this?"

Miriam's mouth moved, but the words remained inaudible. Esperanza leaned into her and hoped to catch some meaningful phrase. Miriam lifted her gaze. "*Al-suftaja.*"

Esperanza questioned her, "What are you saying?"

Miriam flicked a sharp glance in her direction. "It is a letter of credit my husband granted your father. Upon arrival, the bearer, Efrain Peralta, or his representative should present the missive to a Mattai ben Tsevi in Alicante. Ben Tsevi holds a sum equal to the claim submitted here for my husband's sake. A normal custom."

Esperanza drew back. "My father took money from your husband? Why would he need it?"

Miriam snapped, "How else did you expect him to provide for you? He could not travel with all he valued—"

The man before them growled, "Enough! I tire of your arguments." His somber stare met Esperanza's own again. "It seems I have ruined all of your prospects. It was not to be, *querida.*"

"It can still be if you would listen. What of my father and the reward I have promised? There is greater wealth in Alicante than you have found among our coffers."

Miriam pinched her hip for the brazen lie. Esperanza ignored her. Perhaps the family of her betrothed would take pity on her when they received the request for ransom. They could not know the misfortunes befallen her father. They would pay for her release in anticipation of recompense. Then together, she and Miriam would prevail upon the Jew in Alicante to render his obligation to Gedaliah's heirs. The grand scheme unfolded in Esperanza's mind. She would worry about the consequences of her lies later, if she managed to gain freedom for her and Miriam. Freedom for her, Miriam and Palomba mattered.

The Mohammedan leader scratched his tangled beard before he stood. "There might be more coin for me elsewhere, but I'm uncertain it lies within the old kingdom of Valencia." He reached within a fold in his cloak and withdrew a long curved blade with woven bands along its surface. He pointed the sword at Esperanza, who shriveled against the rock.

"You see this, little hope? The finest steel from Damascus. I took this from the first man I slaughtered more than twenty years ago. It has never left my hands since then. I remember each person it has killed. I have never beheld another blade of the same quality and craftsmanship, until today."

He pulled another weapon from within the cloak. The jewel-encrusted handle glittered in the darkness. Esperanza shuddered as he held up the dagger she had last seen in her father's hands. A gift from the Cerdas, he had treasured the weapon with its golden handle encrusted in sapphire, emerald, amber, and opal gemstones.

The Mohammedan continued, "My sword sliced open the man who carried this weapon. It left a grievous wound in his side. You remind me of him, a man who wore green silk. He stood about your height, his eyes the color of a newborn fawn. He fought with valor and killed three of my men before I was compelled to end his life." Her gasp did not stop him. "I believe he was your father. Now, he lies dead on the *meseta* of La Mancha. He does not await you in Alicante, nor does the value of this letter of credit. Whoever your betrothed may be, he shall have to find another rich bride to wed. Your future lies elsewhere."

As her father's killer turned and walked away from her, Esperanza shook with fury. She scrambled to her feet and lunged at him. Her momentum shoved him face down in the dirt, unprepared for her assault. She pummeled his back.

"Murderer! I hate you."

Two of his men dragged her off him and held her from him, though she kicked at the air. He rose on his hands and knees. A white blob from his lips landed in the dirt.

His gaze met hers. "There is fire inside you. I would hate to extinguish it forever."

Tears streamed down her cheeks. She maintained her struggle against the steadfast hold of her captors. One said something to his companion, who laughed and nodded.

Their leader stood and brushed the topsoil from his ruined cloak. "My men say you are a hellion and they pity the man who tries to tame you. I say it shall never occur. I am not the man to try."

His nephew brushed past him. He sneered at the younger man before he tended to the strongboxes.

The ugly youth knelt at Miriam's feet and grabbed her leg. Over his shoulder, his uncle shouted. Two others restrained Esperanza and dragged her away. She struggled against them. "No! Let me go! Miriam! Let me stay with Miriam."

Across the encampment, Miriam put up one hand and warded off the intent of the one who wished to claim her. Esperanza could not understand their exchange. A note of desperation shattered Miriam's voice. Her hands shook as she unraveled the knot in the veil, which secured her hold on Palomba. The child wailed and screeched, terrified by the proximity of the strange man.

He slapped Miriam with an open palm and pulled out his knife. He sliced through the veil and grabbed Palomba by the leg. She dangled in his grip, her screams almost animalistic. Esperanza kicked and clawed the men who held her back, while

Miriam sobbed and held her arms out for her child. Her abuser gave a maniacal chortle and swung Palomba toward the rock.

Chapter 3
A New Master

Miriam Alubel

Andalusia
January 24, AD 1336 / 9 Jumada al-Thani 736 AH /10th of
Shevat, 5096

The raiders took a southward track through crystalline rock
passes and skirted weathered limestone formations. In the
daylight hours, they retreated into large caverns, which
concealed their horses as well. At night, they traveled and
crossed the low-lying Guadalquivir River without incident. The
fourth day of captivity ushered a change in the terrain. A
labyrinth of ravines and gorges gave way to the first carobs,
myrtle trees. Lavender and oleander bushes grew in thick
clusters. Dense clouds hung heavy in the sky. The vista might
have been a welcome sight after the arid, sienna-colored plains of
the *meseta*. How could Miriam gain any pleasure from her
environs?

Later, the raiders skirted a large town in the darkness. She
had not recognized the place. Its extensive wheat fields hid her
captors' movements. As the next morning dawned, most of
Ahmed's men dismounted when he called for a respite from their
journey.

He said, *"Al-Qal'at ibn Zaide* is far behind us now."

Miriam assumed he meant Alcala la Real, the northern town
she had last seen. If any world-be trackers had followed them
into Andalusia, the men were safe from justice on this side of the
buffer zone. They found shelter from the glare of midday under
rows of shady carob trees set on the southern edge of a wide
plateau. Their leader did not join them. He ordered four of his
companions to remain on horseback, while he shepherded
Esperanza to the center of the encampment.

Miriam sighed for he had not included Fadil in his company.
The youth idled beside his horse, his possessive gaze on her.

Meanwhile, Ahmed shoved Esperanza to her knees and
repeated the same pronouncement he often made whenever they
stopped. "The first man to touch this one will see me slice off his

25

balls and his manhood. I will feed those parts to the fire before staking out any such fool in the noonday sun to suffer in agony. Keep far from the girl. She is the prize."

Although she could not have understood the extent of his protection, Esperanza buried her face in her hands and wept. Miriam turned away. A solitary golden eagle nestled in the canopy above her head. A hare darted between petals of cistus shrubs. Miriam's mouth watered. Would she ever taste fresh meat again, instead of the stale bread her captors offered at times?

After Ahmed mounted his horse again, he gave the order to ride out. Hooves thundered in a descent from the highland. The wind rattled carob pods, the color of dried blood. Miriam closed her eyes and inhaled the resin from the evergreen leaves of the cistus.

"Come, my beauty. This time I will have you on your hands and knees. You will be the mare to my stallion."

She shrugged off Fadil's hold and Ahmed's men laughed. Fadil jerked her against him and swung her around in the iron circle of his arms. "Or not. Either way, I shall have you again!"

She wrenched an arm free from his hold and slapped him. He released her and returned the gesture with remarkable force. She hit her head against a rock shingle and sprawled at his feet. She clutched her cheek. The bezel of his ring had broken the skin. He pounced on her. His hands tugged her ruined skirt. Esperanza's sobs echoed and grew more bothersome while Miriam fought in vain. She scratched and spat at him. Her curses went unheeded as he kneed her legs apart. Deep inside, she maintained her vow. No matter how many times he took her, she would never submit.

***

Later, Miriam endured the Moor's leisurely touch, almost a gentle caress. She stared into the depths of Fadil's dark-eyed gaze. Disheveled hair hung in disarray over her shoulders. A purple blotch marred her face on the right.

The Moor's forefinger traced a line along the curve of her left cheek. Dried blood flaked off a thin laceration of the skin. "It will be a match for my own scar. I never desired it, my beauty."

She slapped his hand away. "Do not touch me, you swine!"

"You must know I do not seek to alter your loveliness." Despite the insult, her rapist's voice never rose above a whisper in a mockery of a lover's tenderness. "Let me be kind to you. Why must you continue to fight me so? I would give you anything in the world if you asked for it with some courtesy."

She raised her chin a notch. "Would you free me from your hold?"

"I cannot. Such is beyond my means now."

As his onion-scented breath stirred a new wave of nausea in the pit of her stomach, Miriam kept her features impassive. What could he perhaps offer her of value? Could he give her Palomba back, the life of the daughter he had so destroyed on a whim? Could he grant her fervent wish for justice and meet his slow death at the end of his blade?

He cupped her chin with a free hand with potent energy. A lesser woman would have winced or cried out. She did neither.

He asked, "Does the cut hurt? I do not want to be the cause of your pain. Instead, I could give you joy your husband never did."

"You know nothing of my husband."

"True. If you would submit, you would enjoy my loving."

His loving? Is that what he called rape? Did the fool assume she had learned to enjoy his brutish rutting atop her each day and evening? A few nights ago, he had dashed Palomba against the rock and ravaged her mother beside the spot where the murdered child's blood seeped into the earth.

Now, the man who had murdered her child and raped her had grown attached to his prize. Miriam wished she could have laughed in his ugly face and skewered him with the weapon at his hip. Instead, she pushed at his shoulders and sat up. She rejected his vile attempt at a lover's intimacy. "Get me water to wash your seed away. It defiles my body, as does the stench of your mouth upon me."

He cocked his head and laughed. Food remnants filled the gaps between his yellowed teeth. "Careful, woman, I will not bear much more of your viper's tongue. Besides, you forget who holds authority here. Shall I remind you again?"

Aware of his sentiment toward her, Miriam perceived the balance of power between them. She maintained a level gaze with him. His lips parted somewhat as he sucked in a breath and exhaled, captivated. She could bind this one body and soul to her if she wished. Perhaps when the opportunity arose, she would peel away the layers of flesh with his blade and discover whether a heart dwelt underneath, something which held compassion for others.

When he touched her shoulder, she rebuffed him with a hand. "You said you would give me anything in the world. I asked for water from the stream."

Frigid air swept a shudder through her frame and gooseflesh pimpled her skin. She sucked the cold air into her chest and hoped her fearlessness would deter his interest.

Fadil's gaze dipped to her bared breasts. The flesh from the tattered *camisa* he had torn in his haste on the first night. He sucked in his breath and reached for her. This time she slapped his fingers away. "Get the water! I will not ask again."

His nostrils flared. His gaze lingered on her exposed skin. She returned his stare without fear and did not attempt to cover herself. When he clenched his teeth together, the scar along his ruined cheek rippled.

He rose and swiped the dust from his knee-length tunic. "You do not command me, woman." He pitched his voice low so the others could not hear.

Still, he spun on his heels as she expected and went to his horse. He untied one of the saddlebags, which swayed in the afternoon breeze from his pommel. A gourd in hand, he sauntered through lone clumps of sage grass to the nearby *arroyo*.

A cramp rippled across her lower abdomen. She stifled a sob and stared at her stomach. "Please, no."

Another painful spasm followed. She groaned and lifted her head. She glared in Fadil's wake and spat into the dirt twice. Nothing she could do would rid her of the taste of his foul breath in her mouth. When she scanned the encampment, vacant or indolent looks met hers. The men lounged in idle contemplation, heedless of the deaths they had caused and the lives they had ruined. Now, Miriam studied the features of each and memorized all she could of them. Several returned her determined stare with impertinent leers. One nudged another and they both laughed. None dared move toward her.

Esperanza huddled, her chin on her knees. Her sobs had dissolved into hiccups by now. Miriam shook her head at the young girl's misery. Did she cry due to the cold or hunger, or did she just bemoan the loss of the shoes their captors had taken so she could not run away? Whatever the reason, tears would not help her. She should consider herself lucky. She had lost a father, while Miriam endured the murders of her child and husband. Even in their current circumstances, Esperanza fared better. She did not face the threat of rape.

Fadil thwarted Miriam's contemplation, for he returned in haste and flopped on the ground. Water sloshed from the gourd and fed the parched and broken earth.

The careless fool grinned at her in his idiocy. "I have decided you will be mine. My uncle can have my share of the spoils. All I want is you. After you have delivered of this babe, I shall put another into your belly, one whom my uncle cannot sell as a slave. If you obey me, I shall be generous to you. Any children I sire upon you may have their freedom."

She snatched the vessel from his grasp, tore a strip from the hem of her tattered *saya,* and wadded the cloth. Then she dipped it into the water. She shoved aside her grief and sang for the tender child ripped from her clutches, a sonant melody about a mother and daughter in preparation for the *Shabbat* meal. She used to sing it for Palomba, in days when Miriam imagined how her child might carry on the traditions of their faith. Now Palomba would never grow to womanhood or teach songs to children of her own, because of the devil beside her mother.

The muscles in Miriam's battered body throbbed with a deeper intensity than the heavy ache in her throat, the pain of tears she refused to shed. She scoured her face and arms, which bore dappled marks where Fadil had seized her on the previous night. Fresh bruises from the morning's violence marred her skin. She could count the layers of scratches, discolorations and scabs if she wished, each a reminder of when her captor had gripped her hard, or shoved or slapped her. She would never forget his cruelty.

Each of the Moors sat silent, even Fadil, captivated by the sound of her voice. Even Esperanza had roused herself from her petulant mood. Childlike eagerness warmed Fadil's stare even now, turned soft and doe-like. How pathetic. He did not fool her for a moment. She knew the capricious brutality he could inflict. Someday, he would comprehend her true nature just before she ended his life.

He captured her chin again and forced her to meet his regard. "What do you think of our future together, my flower?"

For her part, she had ignored his ruminations. She halted her song and asked, "Does my opinion matter to you?"

His hold on her fell away along with his enraptured stare. "You are a captive, after all, so I suppose it does not. I should not discuss such plans without the knowledge of what my uncle will say. I must speak to him as soon as he returns." Then he scrutinized her again. "I must tell him before he decides to sell you. I could not bear it. You must be mine. You are mine!" His fingers closed on her wrist.

She glared at him in silence until he removed the offensive hand. Her voice filled the air again. Her throat swelled so much it required brief pauses between verses before she could resume. She sang for her beloved Palomba, gone from her arms forever, because of a boy who pretended to own a man's lusts and appetites.

She hitched her skirts to her upper thighs and ran the wet cloth down her legs. Lascivious sniggers and whistles followed. She ignored Ahmed's men. A smear of blood on the rag sent a shudder through her.

Beneath lowered lids, she took full measure of Fadil instead. He reminded her of Gedaliah with his gangling limbs and elongated fingers. His movements were awkward and erratic, as if uncontrolled impulses raged through his body. Gedaliah's ambitions had accounted for his nervous energy. Therein lay the one similarity between her husband and the impetuous fool at her side. She guessed he might be her age or even a year or two younger.

Despite his youth, he possessed the temperament of a man accustomed to obedience from others. Where had this Moor gained such confidence? Those whom he could not compel, he would kill. Did he presume she would submit to his willpower in due course? A soundless chortle escaped her at the thought.

"Why do you laugh? Do you delight in my company at last?"

She soothed the dull throb at the soles of her feet. Their captors had removed her shoes on the first night. "Does it please you to assume so?"

"It does." He reached for the strands of hair, limp on her shoulder. He cradled the length of her neck. "You please me."

The wind brought the snorts of horses before the earth rumbled. Fadil and his company sprang to their feet with swords drawn and crossbows at the ready. From a thick cloud of dust, Ahmed emerged on the crest of the plateau. He returned with double the entourage of men.

He spoke with his nephew first. "Get the captives ready. We ride for the city now."

"*La!* Not until we speak of my woman."

Ahmed threw back his head and laughed in Fadil's face. "Who is your woman? I do not recall when you captured any other besides the two I have taken. Where is the female you would claim? Bring her out so we may all see her."

"I meant the one with the black hair. You know I captured the other on my own."

"Then you should have kept her for yourself! Instead, you brought her into my camp. Your error, not mine. Be satisfied with the meager pleasures you have attained with a woman who fights you at each chance. Take your gold and go home. Enjoy the comforts of all your father bequeathed you, including a house filled with female slaves. They are not as pretty, but they are good-natured."

Loud guffaws and vigorous nods of agreement followed. Ahmed turned and spoke with one of those who had accompanied his return to the camp, a man Miriam had not seen before. A Moor who stood closest to Fadil clapped his back and urged him to forget the woman, especially when he would find a compliant whore in the city or even in his own house. The youth growled low in his throat and shrugged off his companion's hold.

"Uncle, you will give me the woman I have claimed. Take my share of the spoils. I care nothing for coin or expensive fabric." He pointed at Miriam. "I want her."

Ahmed turned from his conversation with raised eyebrows as if surprised by his nephew's defiance. His gaze alighted on Miriam. "You cannot have her. I have already promised both of the Castillans to Juan Manuel. He is their master now."

Who was this Juan Manuel, whom Ahmed had mentioned often in the last two days? What new uncertainties might she face with a stranger than with these others?

Fadil's lower lip quivered. Miriam suppressed a smile. He was little more than a boy in a man's guise after all. His bright stare remained on her. She stood and eyed him. Did he possess the courage to hold the tears back? He did. Desire coupled with determination hardened his gaze and stilled the quivers of his mouth. His next move proved more unexpected.

He drew the knife worn at his hip. With a snarl, Fadil aimed the weapon for his uncle's stomach. Shouts of dismay and outrage arose. Even Esperanza emerged from her torpor. Her horrendous scream echoed across the plains. At the same time, Ahmed realized his nephew's intent and grabbed the blade. His jaw line tightened. Blood seeped between his fingers and dotted the once pristine cloak with rich flecks of red.

Fadil screeched and the dreadful scar twitched in his fury. His uncle's viselike grip on the blade held. Without warning, Ahmed twisted it. Fadil cried out. Ahmed raised his leg and kicked his nephew in his stomach. In the instant Fadil tumbled backward, Ahmed leapt from his horse. He flung Fadil's knife to the ground. Ahmed delivered another swift blow to the young man's groin and did not stop.

Fadil's groans matched each powerful wallop against his stomach and ribs. Bloodied spittle dribbled between his lips. Perspiration dotted Ahmed's brow. His heavy booted feet landed with forceful precision. His men stood idle, their expressions aloof. A heavy grunt escaped Ahmed before he ceased the relentless kicks and staggered away from the battered body of his nephew. Ahmed sagged on his knees in the dust, exhausted from his exertions.

Miriam hefted her threadbare skirt and edged a little closer. Fadil's chest still rose and fell, though his breaths grew labored. Each intake and exhale must be agony for him. He cupped between his legs and hitched his knees up to his chest. The tears he had kept at bay a moment ago now trickled across the ridge of his nose and pooled below his ragged cheek.

A deep sigh coursed through Miriam's body. Fadil's pitiable state was not enough. Sunlight glinted off the edge of his blade, discarded near his uncle's feet. Ahmed still gulped mouthfuls of air. The bout had depleted his last reserves of energy.

Miriam darted one last glance at him before she eyed the weapon. Fortune might never offer her this opportunity again. It would be quick, a better end than Fadil deserved. His uncle would kill her, but then she would be with Palomba again in death. She took a step forward.

"*La!*" The resolute command in Ahmed's voice halted her at once. He switched from Arabic to the Castillan tongue in the next breath. "You will not kill him. Not today."

Her stare fixed on him. He grasped the blade in his crimson-stained hand and staggered to his feet.

Miriam ground her teeth together and tossed her hair. "He murdered my daughter, a sweet babe. She never harmed him. I live by the words of my people and my faith: life for life. He forfeited his when he stole my Palomba from my arms and dashed her against a rock for the sake of fickle whim alone."

Ahmed shook his head. "Your daughter's life was not the first Fadil has ever taken. It will not be the last. Nothing can ease your pain except time. My nephew's death will not bring your daughter back. Accept her loss."

"I will never forget my daughter. Her blood cries out for justice. She shall have it."

He ignored her and called for two ropes. One of his men obeyed. Ahmed approached Miriam, the rough hemp coiled in his hands. He held out his hands and awaited her acquiescence. Miriam stared hard at the rope and then into his eyes. He drew back for a moment as though startled by what he must have seen.

"Listen and understand me well, woman," he whispered. "Fadil is impetuous and vicious. He is still my kin."

"I will have my vengeance against him regardless," she insisted.

"I do not permit it! I cannot surrender my duty as his uncle to mold Fadil in the image of my brother, into a man worthy of his heritage. We were not always thus. Along the banks of the Guadalete River, below the banners of the conqueror Tariq, my ancestors routed the armies of Roderick. My great-grandfather struck the deathblow against Pedro Arias, master of the Order of Santiago, on the plains of Tolosa a century ago. Fadil is all I have left of a once illustrious clan. I cannot allow you to injure him for the sake of the brother I shall love until my last breath, the man who was his father."

"You dare speak of family and duty? I do not care for your proud origins or your sentiments, slaver! You have taken everything from me. Why should I care for your misfortunes as the guardian of this wretch? After the harm he has done, he deserves death. You will not deny me."

"I must. Do not gainsay me. His punishment is not for you or me to decide. He will earn the fate he deserves. His end shall not come at your hand or my own."

"You almost kicked him to death because he attacked you. You could have killed him. He is mine. He owes me a large debt, one he must settle with blood. He has stolen more from me than he can ever repay. One day, he shall give me his worthless life in exchange. I swear it."

"Not on this day." He grabbed the hands she would not offer and tied them at the wrists. Turbulent heat spread across her belly. When he secured her bonds, she bit back a wince just before he met her gaze again. He did not flinch as before.

He muttered, "Beautiful women make fools of all men. Fadil shall soon count himself among the fortunate who escaped your clutches."

"Not for long."

Ahmed glared at Miriam and tugged the rope. She raked her blistered feet across rough pebbles and shards of sandstone. Each footfall left a thin trail of bloodied smears. Her gaze focused on Fadil, who cradled his stomach and rolled in the dirt. Soon, she stood beside Esperanza.

Their captor wrenched the girl to her feet. She batted at his hands. Dirt mired her ruddy cheeks and clung to the dark ringlets of hair tipped with fiery ends, one of her two favorable physical attributes, the other being the eyes inherited from her mother. Her skin remained pallid, even in summer. Her cheeks proved too gaunt. A narrow face with large eyes gave her an almost rodent-like appearance. She would never be a beauty like Miriam.

Despite Esperanza's protests, the slaver secured her hands with the other end of the rope, which already bound Miriam. At least their travail had not diminished her companion's spirit. She would need her strength for the trials ahead.

Ahmed directed his men, who fanned out and stripped the low-hanging pods from the carob trees before they stuffed them into sacks. "We'll feed our pack animals later," their leader said.

Someone retrieved Fadil's gourd and shoved it into the injured youth's satchel. "What do we do with him?"

Ahmed brushed his mare's dappled sand-colored coat. He refused an answer. Another of his followers dared make the same inquiry and earned an angry scowl for his trouble.

Miriam flicked a glance over her shoulder. "You cannot abandon him." She would never have her revenge if Fadil died on the plains.

Ahmed strode toward her and halted at less than a pace between them. His hot gaze seared her own, as he strove for the truth of her soul. "You wanted him dead earlier, woman! Now you think he should live."

"You said his life was not yours to take. Instead, you would assure his death if you left him here to rot. Can your heart bear the loss? Do you even have one?"

His weathered features contorted in a horrid mask. When he raised his hand, she cupped her abdomen and met his stare. "After the trials I have suffered, what is one more beating? Strike me down if you must, Moor. You will regret it one day."

He fisted his fingers in the dirtied cloak and spat into the dirt. "Empty, vain promises. You are not worth the effort. I knew you would be trouble from the moment you entered our encampment. I wish Juan Manuel joy of you. I doubt he shall find it."

He whirled from her side, though her voice chased him. "What of Fadil?"

Silence answered her. He grasped the rope again and dragged her with Esperanza toward his horse. He looped the second length of hemp with the first and gripped the rope. Miriam jerked against her restraints while he mounted.

Ahmed growled low in his throat. "Cease your struggles, woman! I will drag you behind the damned horse whether you will walk or not!"

"I will not leave this place until I know what you intend to do about Fadil."

He chuckled. "By the Prophet's beard, you are a strong-willed bitch! I had thought you hated my nephew's attentions. Perhaps you offered a ruse. Are you one to deny a man with a lie on your lips while your body betrays the lustful truth?"

She knew he spoke in Arabic for the benefit of everyone around them, so they might enjoy her humiliation. The men laughed while Miriam glared at his back.

He turned in the saddle and rubbed a hand over his craggy face. "Someone, get the simpleton whom I must call my nephew slung over the back of his horse. Be careful now! I want him to live to see a doctor."

Two of his men hefted Fadil, while one removed the saddle on the youth's horse and threw a blanket over the animal's back. Fadil's breath escaped him in a pain-filled wheeze. The men fastened him to the horse with leather straps around his torso. A hideous shriek from him scattered hares through the brush. Ahmed's followers left his limbs to dangle on either side of the mount. At some point, his head hung limp as he fainted.

Satisfied, Miriam nodded. Ahmed's jaw tightened and he jerked the rope. She tripped and abraded her toe against a sandstone shard. Pain shot through the soles of her feet. She suppressed a moan and followed her captor in silence.

Wisps of distended clouds raced across an azure silk sky and wove bands of shadowy blotches across rugged hillocks and the lustrous red and green *vega*. The horses dipped down an inclined track from the plateau to a wide plain below, encircled to the east and south by mountain peaks shrouded in pristine snow. At the epicenter of the wooded valley, the rust red walls of a city rose from the earth blanketed in a coat of white.

Miriam inhaled. "The Damascus of Andalusia. *Gharnatah*."

Beside her, Esperanza asked, "What are you saying?"

The girl's voice croaked from disuse and the misery she had endured. These were the first words they had exchanged since their initial captivity. For the most part, Fadil's lust and Ahmed's insistence upon Esperanza's isolation had kept them apart.

"We are in Granada, or as the Moors say it, *Gharnatah*. My father often spoke of this city. He was born here."

"You never told me so. Why did you keep it a secret?"

Miriam countered, "Why should I have told you? When we were children, a small, spoiled child as you had little reason to care for my family's origins." She paused when Esperanza frowned at her. "I never thought I would see this place."

"You sound almost pleased," Esperanza murmured.

"My feet still tread this earth. What greater pleasure do I have than my life?" Miriam could not resist a taunt. "Are you so eager to be with your Jesus? Fray Rufino should have lived to witness this newfound faith."

"At least if I had died, I would be with Papa." Then Esperanza raised her chin a notch. "Still, I will keep my promise to him. I must live."

The riders approached the northern gate of the city. Traders of every sort and origin rode or walked the dirt track. Ahmed waited for his turn among them.

"Ah, it is Ahmed al-Qurtubi. The slaver scum has returned." A bad-tempered guardsman with a bedraggled beard peered behind Ahmed's mount. "Best take this scruffy lot to the public baths before sale. No one will thank you if lice spread through the city."

The sentry's reed-thin companion chuckled. "The taller one with the dark hair holds promise, after a bath." He approached and fingered the thin abrasion on Miriam's cheek. She endured his intrusive attentions. "The other is younger, but plain-faced. I do not like them so small and scrawny. Nothing except skin stretched over bones."

Esperanza stared at the ground, oblivious to the insult. In the past, she had demonstrated an aptitude for Catalan and Latin, under Miriam's impromptu instruction. For the first time, Miriam regretted her failure to tutor the girl in some Arabic. After all, she deserved to know what others spoke of her. Why should Miriam possess the brutal knowledge alone?

The guard rubbed several strands of Miriam's hair between his thumb and forefinger. He glanced at Ahmed. "How many *dinars* do you want for this one?"

Ahmed shook his head. "She has already been sold. I must deliver her to her new master."

The man grunted. His companion slapped his hand away. "You have a wife with a child on the way. Find someone else to slake your lust, better than this dirtied whore."

The sentries demanded payment of the tax required of all traders for entrance into Granada. Then they ushered Ahmed and his company inside. Stalls lined the grounds of the city's fortifications and bustled with activity. Ahmed cursed a camel boy who did not move his beast in haste.

The horses clattered along a narrow, cobblestone street. A gutter bisected the road, through which all manner of human and animal filth oozed in a thick sludge of discarded food, excrement, ashes, sodden straw, fetid water, and oils. While Esperanza raised a hand to her nose, Miriam trudged behind Ahmed's mount in strained silence.

On both sides of the filthy street, people bargained for leathers and cotton, knives, kitchen pots and utensils. The stalls of food vendors beckoned with a tantalizing variety of odors. Miriam's stomach rumbled in response. In the hustle and bustle of the marketplace, a red-faced fruit seller lobbed a rotten pomegranate at a street urchin. The emaciated boy, dressed in rags, scampered down a darkened alley. Guards brandished long scimitars with curved blades as they chased him. The men shoved aside anyone unfortunate enough to dawdle in their path. Glares from unfamiliar faces surrounded Miriam. The proximity of every stranger threatened her well-being and sanity.

They passed through a horseshoe archway, which gave entry beyond a secondary wall. Here, buildings abutted each other. Slate roofs jutted and almost blotted out the sky. The city's denizens rambled across the narrow pathway or lingered over a variety of wares. Women haggled over precious silks and a large selection of red, yellow, and green spices, while men visited the armories and blacksmiths' stalls.

The rectangular grid of streets gave way to another section. Miriam's knees almost buckled. She clutched the ragged folds of her bodice and swayed at the grim sight of miserable captives clustered beneath the thatched roof of an open stall. At the forefront of two rows, a young man stood at auction. Ragged in appearance, he clutched the hand of the female companion just behind him. Three small children huddled with the couple. The woman cradled the youngest child against her thigh. The little boy wept as would-be buyers pawed and inspected him. Miriam closed her eyes and blotted out the sight of another family soon to be torn asunder by the Moors.

To live now, she must surrender to another person's whim. She gritted her teeth, nauseated at the thought of fate's caprice. She would have to survive by her wits alone.

She opened her eyes again and forced herself to witness the wretched scene behind her. Coins exchanged hands and rattled in the weighing pan of a brass scale. Soon a pot-bellied man dragged the mournful boy from his parents. Miriam shuddered. At least her Palomba had escaped such cruelty.

Ahmed rode on, oblivious to her distress. He led her with Esperanza under another carved arch, his men at the rear. They ascended an incline shaded by myrtle trees. The cobblestones smoothed and followed distinct pattern. A cool breeze descended upon the shrouded walkway. The furor of the marketplace retreated. Whitewashed structures clung to the right of the hillside. The occupants of the houses remained hidden behind shuttered windows. Through the gaps in the trees on the left, Miriam discerned the rocky façade of a gorge. Water cascaded nearby from some imperceptible source.

Where the street intersected a narrower road, Ahmed slowed his horse. He patted the mare's neck and murmured to her before he dismounted. Miriam sneered. He demonstrated more fondness for an animal than he showed for people. He went to an ornate wooden door. Iron rivets jutted from the door, interspersed between the exterior latticework. Sculpted of rough-hewn stone, the entryway rose above walls of the same material on either side of the wood.

Before the slaver put his hand to the brass knocker in the shape of a lion's head, a tall fair-skinned man with shoulder-length, light brown hair emerged from the entryway. He closed the door behind him. Brown spots dotted his pale, weathered hands and speckled his cheeks.

"You have returned to my house." He spoke the Castillan tongue with the ease any native of the country might have.

"As I promised, Juan Manuel Gomero." Ahmed offered a stiff bow. "You awaited me? How else could you have anticipated my arrival?"

"You presume much. I wish to know whether your boastful words are true. Let us hope you have not wasted my precious time. I'll see your offer now."

Miriam eyed the stranger. He smoothed the folds of his brocaded *pellote* colored a garish orange. He circled Miriam and Esperanza, before he paused beside the latter. She held the appearance of quiet reserve. His clean-shaven face colored a little for some imperceptible reason. He cast a sidelong glance at Ahmed before his stare alighted on Esperanza again. He tapped a forefinger against his lips. A ruby set in gold surrounded by lustrous pearls glinted on his hand and caught Miriam's eye.

He reached for Esperanza's bedraggled curls. The spiteful glare she offered must have jolted him from his presumption. He stumbled and almost fell. Ahmed righted him. A gust of wind whipped through the street and revealed the girl's stick thin form through her clothes.

"You see, my friend?" Ahmed waved at Esperanza. "She is silk and fire."

"You mean once my Sadiya washes the dirt away," the buyer mused. Both men chuckled. "*Sí*, this captive may have some worth, though perhaps not the full value you have demanded. You shall not cheat me this time. Although she is thin and a little boyish, I admit her thick hair and the fire in her gaze would stir anyone. Hmm, young and tender. She is a virgin?"

"I have no doubt she remains unspoiled."

Juan Manuel grunted. "Humph. Your assurances offer little comfort. I will have the proof myself."

Miriam darted a glance at Esperanza, who appeared uninterested. How could she remain impassive while these men decided her lot in life? Miriam would not submit without a fight.

She would master her own destiny, no matter where fate consigned her.

"Then we have an agreement?" Ahmed asked.

"Not so fast! You remain too hasty for my pleasure." Juan Manuel's stare lingered upon Esperanza as he noted, "For once, Ahmed, your liar's tongue may not have boasted. Her features are more angular than I would have liked. No, I have chosen the wrong word. Rather, her face is delicate, fine-boned."

When Miriam snorted, she received a quizzical glance from the man before he added, "With *kohl* for her eyes and some color on her lips, she shall reveal her true worth."

Ahmed winked. "You have boasted your Sadiya could work miracles."

"Indeed, she can." Juan Manuel approached Miriam. He scrutinized her with a frown and then lifted an eyebrow. "You have spoiled this one, Ahmed. Look at these scars and the bruise. What of this cut on her face? My patrons have specific desires. All of my stock must be beautiful and free from blemish. You never mentioned she was pregnant either. I bargained for a midwife to attest to the younger one's virginity, not for the sake of a woman with child! Take this one away and make what profit you can in the market."

Bitterness assailed Miriam. How dare this egotistical peacock dismiss her, especially after he had shown excessive reflection on Esperanza's bland appearance?

Ahmed clasped his hands together. "I thought you would be pleased to know she is fertile. I could sell the mother and the unborn child for fifty *maravedies* less than the agreed upon price. You would gain two captives at a bargain."

"Fifty gold coins less? Bah! You presume I still wish to buy her. You do not fool me when it's clear you are eager to rid yourself of the woman."

"You mistake me. She is yours. Do not quibble over a few scratches. They will fade."

"In a month? I expected to auction both females then."

Miriam sucked in her breath. Juan Manuel's home would not be their final destination.

Ahmed rubbed his crinkled brow. "My fool nephew is to blame for her flaws. As you must guess, I had to correct his wayward expectations."

Juan Manuel glanced at the prone body draped across the horse before his stare returned to Miriam. His stare, the warmth of amber, assessed her. She had seen this honey-gold color suffused with brown undertones in only Esperanza's gaze. Did the girl even notice the similarity she shared with a stranger?

Miriam pushed aside thoughts of her, as he intended to buy the girl. She forced her lips to form a smile and hoped he would not discern the charade. He returned the gesture with candid appreciation in his gaze.

When he stroked the tip of his finger down her nose, she steeled herself not to recoil. She must appeal to him or suffer Fadil's continued abuses.

He murmured, "She is well-proportioned. The face is rather exquisite, even with the marks on her. These ink-black eyes also intrigue me. What other talents does she possess beyond the ability to stir your nephew's lust, Ahmed?"

"She is a goldsmith's daughter. She can also sing. No other voice can equal hers."

As one, Ahmed, the buyer and Miriam gaped at Esperanza, who continued, "Miriam is my friend, the last I have left in this world. Please do not part us, señor. These men have taken everyone else I have ever cared for from me. If you will claim her, I shall be forever grateful."

Ahmed chuckled. "Forgive the little one. She still thinks she can make demands. Just needs a lesson or two in humility."

"You are not the one to teach her. Just be quiet," Juan Manuel admonished. When he leaned closer, Esperanza stiffened.

"What could you offer, *niña*? What do you possess which I cannot call my own?"

"You want my obedience." He smirked as Esperanza continued, "Take Miriam into your household and you shall have it."

"You will yield, even if I must compel you!"

"You plan to sell me in a month. Are you so certain you can if I choose not to submit? Would a disobedient captive interest your patron?"

When his jaw tightened, Miriam could have almost cast an appreciative smile at the girl, if Esperanza's entreaty had not prickled her. She needed no one's help to survive.

Ahmed interjected, "A female's pride, eh. Do not listen to her foolish boasts."

Juan Manuel's gaze darted between Esperanza and Miriam before his features relaxed. "She charms me with her loyalty and courage, both commendable traits. Her attributes have engaged my interest." He cupped Miriam's ruined cheek. "This one remains unbroken and unbowed. She must be a remarkable woman to have beguiled your nephew. I will examine her also before the final choice is made."

He released Miriam and rubbed his hands together. "You are all lucky to find me in a generous mood."

Ahmed's shoulders sagged in obvious relief. "You bless us with your favor."

"I am a tolerant man, but you must not test my nature. Now, you and yours must share a meal with me. Allow me to escort the captives to my Sadiya first. I will summon a physician to attend Fadil." Juan Manuel waved his bejeweled hand toward the house.

Miriam turned from him. A deep throb radiated from the epicenter of her abdomen. A warm, sticky wetness seeped between her thighs. She blinked back the tears and glared at Fadil. She prayed to meet him once more, when she would recoup her losses.

One of his companions laughed. "Fadil, awaken! Your beautiful flower wishes to say farewell. Look at her watery eyes. She will never forget you."

Miriam ignored his derisive slander. She made a silent, solemn vow on the life of the child stolen from her and the one she appeared fated to lose. The youth Fadil would see her again, just before he drew his last breath.

Chapter 4
The House of Myrtles

Esperanza Peralta

Granada, Andalusia
January 24 - 25, AD 1336 / 9 - 10 Jumada al-Thani 736 AH /
10th - 11th of Shevat, 5096

Esperanza opened her eyes to a cold, darkened room. She fought against a wave of confusion. The stupor within her mind dissipated. As awareness returned with frightful clarity, the memories from the earlier day consumed her. The Castillan had brought her downstairs and pushed her through the sole wooden door, before he closed it on her cries. She did not know where he had taken Miriam.

Tears coursed down her cheeks. Perhaps she wept for her father and the absence of Miriam, or for the uncertainty of her fate, or the loss of freedom in this strange land of the Mohammedans. With a last sniffle, she rubbed her abraded wrists and stretched her cramped legs. Although the muscles in her calves flared in a heated protest, she forced herself upright from her position. The ruined soles of her feet ached. She faced a barred window, shuttered against the outside world. A chill breeze rustled her hair.

With a slight hobble, Esperanza turned and gripped the edge of the sill on tiptoes. She threaded thin fingers through the bars and pushed at one of two carved wooden panels. It remained fixed until she gave a hard shove. Dense bushes greeted her, as they jutted from the ground coated with a thin pristine layer of snow. She must be on a level below the street. The evening wind rustled the bushes. Slivers of moonlight pierced thin gaps between them and filtered to the floor below.

She turned from the sight and glanced over her shoulder. Swift prickles darted up her spine and a moment's fear of the shadows jolted her heart. She gathered the folds of her ruined mantle closer. Her murky gaze traced the lapis blue, green, and white tiles, which crisscrossed the floor in a haphazard pattern to the darkened recesses of the room. She was no longer a child who dreaded the darkness or shied away from imagined terrors.

The Mohammedans had shown her the true nature of horror. Youthful nightmares paled in comparison.

She slumped underneath the window and fingered the gold brooch inlaid with stones. With a deft hand, she unpinned it from the mantle and recalled the day she received the gift. Her breaths slowed as thoughts of the past drifted. How far off those memories seemed. She would never recapture those tranquil days of Miriam at her side, the affection and patience of her father. She would never see the familiar environs of Talavera de la Reina again.

Of these memories, the specter of a rapport with Miriam remained. The raiders had kept her from Esperanza, with Miriam left to suffer foul abuses and Esperanza forced to watch what no tender young woman should have seen. In her despair, Miriam had lashed out at everyone including the girl who idolized and trusted her. Esperanza would forgive her once they saw each other again. Miriam could not have meant those bitter words spoken in the wake of Gedaliah's death and the loss of Palomba. The child's final scream would haunt Esperanza until her death.

Her hands cradled the consolatory weight of the gold, carnelian, and sardonyx. Her father once called it a fine piece, lavish beyond her ability to appreciate. She had refused to return it because Miriam's kindness meant so much. Now the expensive jewel might secure her future. Could the trinket buy her freedom? If the man agreed to release her, what would be Miriam's fate? Esperanza could not hope the golden brooch would also secure freedom for both of them.

Her shoulders quaked and her chest ached. Were her circumstances so fraught? Would she have to surrender the lone symbol of an enduring bond? If she gained her liberty, could she leave Miriam behind? She knew the answer even before the question plagued her. She would never abandon her friend, not after all she had undergone. Whatever path lay before them, they would follow its course together.

"How beautiful. It is a pity the master will not allow you to keep it."

From the shadows, a young woman materialized as though plucked from the air. She crept across the tiles on bare feet and unfurled the other shutter. Then she opened the door, stepped out into the hall and returned with a torch. In a brilliant flare, she brought beacons to life around the room before she returned the fiery brand to its place.

Esperanza tightened her hold on the brooch while the stranger closed the door, returned to her and sat down cross-legged. Her attractive features were in stark contrast to

Esperanza's plain-faced appearance. Pale yellow curls shimmered like gold with an almost iridescent glow. Almond-shaped eyes sparkled like emeralds against a face the color of heavy cream, coupled with a thin nose and lips upturned in a smile. A scant distance separated them. How long had this woman waited in the shadows, quieter than a mouse?

"You did not understand me? My master said you spoke his native tongue. You are in the home of Juan Manuel Gomero, the House of Myrtles, within the city of Granada. All here live by my master's command, including you. He will take the brooch away. You cannot keep it."

Esperanza realized Castillan was not the woman's natural language. While she spoke well and without hesitation, her high-pitched nasal tone betrayed a heritage far beyond Esperanza's birthplace.

The young woman cocked her head. "Those slavers must have frightened you out of your wits. No one will hurt you now. My master would never permit it. Why do you not speak? Are you afraid of me?" A playful laugh bubbled up and softened the glow of her acute gaze.

She mistook the reason for Esperanza's silence. Rather, her physical appearance caused more uneasiness than her unexpected presence. The moonlight fell on voluminous fabric, which exposed rather than concealed the skin. Layers of a gauzy floor-length tunic suggested the curves behind the cloth. The garment fastened from the neckline to the waist, with wide sleeves sewn with tiny pearls at the wrists. Esperanza discerned a gold tunic layered under a white one, which skirted her generous hips. Neither garment obscured the woman's rounded breasts or the rose-colored circles around each nipple, protruding from the cloth. The pale pink material on each leg disappeared below the shorter tunic. Small pearls encircled her throat and ankles. For all her finery, she might as well have gone naked.

"I am the slave Sadiya—"

"A name from the Mohammedan tribes. You are not one of them, not with your yellow hair."

Sadiya clapped her hands. "You speak at last! I feared the worst. Ahmed of Cordoba is a proud, gruff man, but better than most of his ilk. You have suffered and survived him. By this means, you have discovered a measure of your own strength, which God has granted."

"I don't know this god you worship."

"I serve the same as you for I am a Christian. Muslims do not subjugate those who share their faith."

"You call yourself a slave. You have embraced another name, forsaking the one your parents gave at birth."

"Sadiya is the name I shall ever answer to until my death. I claim it because I have accepted this life. Since you know my name, please tell me yours."

Esperanza did not reply.

"Perhaps you will share it later, after you have eaten. I was once like you, a captive brought to this land. I learned the lessons you must accept. Forget the past. You cannot cling to it. My master will not allow you to keep the brooch. You must surrender the tokens of your former life and acknowledge your fate."

"This is not fate!" Esperanza's nails bit into her palm.

They lapsed into a strained silence. Then an unexpected cry penetrated the walls and shattered Esperanza's composure. Her gaze darted everywhere and sought the source of the noise. Then the melodic song of a man's voice followed.

Sadiya chuckled. "It is the Muslim call to prayer for *Salat al-Maghrib*. When I first came to Granada, it frightened me. You will grow accustomed to the sound. It occurs five times throughout the day and evening."

Esperanza sniffed and crossed her arms over her chest. She tucked the brooch against her body. "I do not intend to remain in this city forever. Summon your master. I must speak to him about ransom."

Thin creases furrowed beneath the fringe of Sadiya's yellow hair. "No one summons the master. You mistake his purpose. You reside in his house so he can judge your value. If he decides to buy you, there will be no ransom. For now, you are a captive, soon to become a slave like me."

"I am not a slave! I will never be anyone's slave!"

"You must yield to the Moors." With a sigh, Sadiya rose and bowed. "It is time for you to eat. I will return soon with food."

"Wait!" Esperanza stood as well. "There was another brought with me to this place. May I see her?"

"You will see her if my master permits it."

Alone again, Esperanza worried after Miriam's fate and the welfare of the child she carried. She pinned her brooch on the mantle again and vowed to keep the gemstones safe in her clutches. A long interval passed. She did not know the hour, but she must have sat alone in slivers of moonlight for some time.

Even more troublesome, a flurry of footsteps and gruff voices echoed from the floor above her. Faint dust caked her hair whenever the floorboard creaked. Esperanza stared at the timbered rafters and sought the source of the tumult. She dared hope for Miriam's escape. Perhaps she had found a route to freedom and the household's occupants searched for her. Esperanza did not doubt Miriam's wits or purpose. If her friend had gained her liberty, Esperanza prayed for guidance far from this savage land and its cruel people. Still, a little tear trickled down her cheek at the thought. Without Miriam, she would have to face the danger on her own.

She must have dozed again. Later, a hand pressed against her shoulder stirred her from a fitful slumber, remembrances of Miriam's accusations at the start of their captivity.

Sadiya awaited her, a round wooden platter heaped with food between them. A linen cloth and a small sack sewn with coarse white and gray hairs were adjacent to a ceramic bowl of warm water. Crushed red petals and green herbs floated on the surface. Curled tendrils of vapor rose from the vessel. The odor of garlic and onions wafted from thick-sliced meat, pink at the center. The piece of bread resembled a flattened sphere. Some green olives, three figs, and a pomegranate accompanied the meat. While Esperanza stared at the food, more than she had eaten in several days, her stomach clenched and rumbled with hunger pangs.

"Why do you wait? Would you have me believe you are not hungry?"

Esperanza raised her chin and resisted the impulse to devour the meal. "I will not eat until I know what has happened to Miriam. Where is my friend?"

"Ah, so she is Miriam. She refused to speak her name. I shall bring her a meal after I have finished here. You may eat after you have washed your hands."

Heat flushed through Esperanza's body. Despite her hunger, she had not forgotten her courtesies, learned at Efrain Peralta's table. The mere thought of him ripped at raw wounds, unable to heal at the loss of her father. She had helped celebrate his natal day twenty days before at Valdepeñas. She still could not believe he was gone from her life forever.

Esperanza choked back her misery and reminded herself of her last promise to him. She would need to eat. Food meant life and a means of escape.

"Give me your hands. I will wash them with the rosewater." Sadiya did not seek permission as she grasped Esperanza's right hand and dribbled tepid water over it, slick to the touch. Then Sadiya slipped her hand into the sack and rubbed away the dirt with it.

More than a week's worth of grime disappeared from Esperanza's fingers and palm. She could not hold back a sigh of delight while Sadiya kneaded her flesh, before she attended to the left hand. Esperanza dried her fingers in the nearby cloth. She grasped the coarse bread and bit into the crust. She restrained another ragged sigh and kept the depths of her hunger and gratitude hidden from the woman.

She reached for a piece of meat next while she clutched the last morsel of bread. Sadiya slapped her fingers away. "Never eat with your left hand! The Moors deem it unclean."

"You have just washed my hands! How can one be considered unclean?"

"I speak of ritual and beliefs the people of this land hold sacred. Unless you wish to offend, you will heed my advice."

Esperanza glared at her for the space of several breaths and finished the bread before she took the meat. The soft and tender lamb tasted of spices on her tongue. The olives and fruits followed. Afterward, she wiped her hands on the linen.

"It will please my master to know you have enjoyed the meal."

Esperanza spat the last of the olive pits on to the salver. "I did not eat to please him."

"There is no cause for your resentment, when he has provided good food."

"I know why your master wants me to eat. If you think I feel grateful to a vile man who intends to sell me as one would sell an animal at market, you have a fool's hope. I am little more than a lamb he prepares for the slaughter."

"How ignorant you are of your own value. He would never harm you, unless you provoked him. He would not destroy his own property—"

"I am not his property!"

"You will learn otherwise with time." The slave pinched the bridge of her nose and closed her eyes for a moment. Then she placed the water bowl on the platter, covered it with the dirtied linen, and stood.

She walked toward the door, pale skin revealed with each movement. "You have eaten well for tonight. On the morrow at dawn, you shall visit the bathhouse. The bath area is called the *hammam*."

"I do not care what Mohammedans call the place! I care for my freedom."

An impatient snort escaped Sadiya before she glanced over her shoulder. "The Moors do not worship Muhammad. He was their prophet. You will never secure your freedom with ignorant assumptions. You have chosen the wrong path again. If you demand your release or seek to bargain with my master, your petitions shall go unanswered."

Esperanza threw up her hands. "What will work? What is this path you would have me seek?"

Sadiya gave a half-hearted shrug. "You must find it. This is your journey."

***

The next morning and the slave's return came sooner than anticipated, before dawn. Sadiya wore an opaque, unadorned black robe paired with brown leather sandals. Esperanza prayed never to witness the shameful display of the previous evening. Sadiya offered her more fruits, pomegranates, oranges, and grapes, along with a warm drink of mint leaves. Esperanza sipped a little before she set the cup aside.

Sadiya chided, "You must finish the tisane before we go to the *hammam*."

Although grateful for another meal and relieved at the prospect of a bath, Esperanza had a much more dire need. "I can't! I must, that is, I need to relieve myself!"

"Why did you not say so when I arrived? Come now. The latrine, or *al-bayt al-ma'* in Arabic, is next to the *hammam*."

Esperanza rose on unsteady legs and followed. The presence of guards at the four corners of the tiled room beyond the door halted her. Transfixed, she gripped the doorpost. The men were silent sentinels against the walls, hands on the hilts of sheathed daggers. Esperanza gulped and her muscles tensed. "What are these men doing here?"

"Isn't it obvious? Did you think my master would not ensure your security or my own?" Sadiya halted and eyed her. "He has no reason to trust you. You would seek to escape given the least autonomy. These men protect you against your own impulses."

As they resumed the walk, a little trickle ran down Esperanza's leg. She hurried along the long wide corridor to the left and found more guards at either end of it. Just beyond a stone arcade and through a door, she reached a rectangular alcove. Instead of a chamber pot, a rounded hole cut into cream-colored stonework rested on a plinth of the same stone. Linen cloths occupied the floor. In a recessed area of the wall, a large ceramic jar emitted a heady aroma through multiple gaps the size of coins. The tiny window above it reached the ceiling. Iron bars covered the small aperture. A small fountain near the door bubbled up water into a basin, perhaps intended for a wash. Torches in ornamental brackets lit the room.

With a gesture, Sadiya said, "I will wait outside. There is no means of exit except through the door. Do not try any tricks. Do not waste your time or mine."

When Esperanza realized she needed to do more than urinate, she also discovered the purpose of the cloths scented with an odor similar to the water from last night. Sadiya had called it rosewater.

A knock at the door quickened her heartbeat. What should she do with the dirtied material?

Sadiya's husky voice echoed through the olive wood. "The *bayt al-ma'* is over a pit dug deep into the earth. At night, we dump the burnt incense from the jars you see into the pit and cover it with leaves. Then they burn the latrine's contents."

Esperanza cast the linen into the pit and washed her hands. More of the fragrant red petals from her meal skimmed the basin. She scanned the room in a futile search for some hidden exit. Perhaps if she placed the wooden stool against the ceramic jar and reached for the window. Then she sighed. The height of the stool would not permit her to get to the ledge. Besides, steam vented from the holes and warned her of furious heat within the jar.

She sighed. Even without the bars, the aperture would be too small. If she escaped through it, she had no idea where it led. When chance arrived, her departure must come by other means. She opened the door.

Sadiya awaited her. "You will find the Moors emphasize a certain cleanliness of the body which Christian priests still forbid. In my little village, we did not wash except on feast days. The Moors of Granada bathe at least twice a day. It took me some time to accept this practice."

"I enjoyed a bath at home each week. A regular wash would not trouble me. You should not assume anything when you do not know my past or me."

"You judge my master and me, although you discern little about us."

As Esperanza rolled her eyes, Sadiya's laugh mocked her and echoed through the alcove. They found the entrance to the bath through a door opposite the latrine. The room within corresponded to the size of the latrine stood bare, but for wooden pegs and an overhead lantern.

"This is *al-bayt al-maslakh*. We must remove our garments and hang them up. There would be bath attendants here to aid you by custom. I suggested and my master agreed the presence of others would unsettle you. It is also the reason he provides a solitary cell for you, when he could have placed you alongside other captives. It is a kindness."

Esperanza whimpered. "There are others here, besides Miriam and me?"

Sadiya's brow crinkled. "What an odd question to ask in the house of a slave merchant. Do you think my master affords his apparent wealth by the sale of one or two captives per year?"

She discarded her black robe and hung it. As she moved, her thick blonde hair shone against her back. She wore no other garments. All the curves hinted at by her clothes on the previous day were on display. If she experienced any concern or embarrassment now, it did not show.

Esperanza bowed her head. Her knees locked together. She struggled to swallow, embittered at the thought of her nakedness revealed to a stranger.

Sadiya cupped her elbow and jerked her from a stupor. "Do you need help?"

Esperanza wrenched away from her grasp. "It is shameful for you to see me so! I once had a servant girl who attended me and saw me unclothed, but you are a stranger."

"Think upon me as her," the slave offered in a conciliatory tone while she stroked Esperanza's arm. "I would never seek to cause you further shame."

"You must make an allowance for my pride. Let me remove my garments in private."

Esperanza's cheeks warmed under scrutiny, but then Sadiya inclined her head.

"I shall await you in the next room. Do not tarry. You have no other place to go. The guards remain in the corridor. They will stop you if you attempt to leave here without me."

She disappeared around the corner. Esperanza's shoulders sagged. With unsteady fingers, she unpinned her brooch and fastened it at the neck of the mantle again. Her watery gaze found a wooden peg here she hung the garment. After a long exhale, she unlaced the sleeves of the *saya* and removed the garment. A shiver coursed through her body. She tugged at the corded neckline of her linen *camisa*. Lastly, she removed her rosary beads.

Naked now with two long plaits against her shoulders, fat tears trickled down her cheeks. She cupped a hand over her mouth, stifled a cry of frustration, and swiped at her tears. After she regained her composure, she crossed an arm over her small breasts with a hand pressed against the apex of her thighs. With a last deep breath, she crept across icy multicolored tiles into the next room.

Sadiya sat unabashed on one of a pair of low wooden stools. Large tiled slabs bounded the chamber on all sides except for a plastered wall. Linens were stacked to the height of her shoulders behind the stool. In the corners, more of the pottery

jars as the one found in the latrine emitted the same perfume.
The slave inspected two curved metal implements with wooden
handles, one thinner than the other. Then she removed the
stoppers of four ceramic vials and sniffed the contents. She
placed everything in a woven basket already filled with rough-cut
bars at her dainty feet. An empty, wooden pail abutted the
basket.

Esperanza hugged her body. "Where am I to bathe? What
about my clothes?"

"Do not worry for your garments. We will wash in the next
room." Sadiya pointed to the vacant wall and the door at its
center. "Sit and allow me to unbraid your hair. It is almost as
filthy as your hands were last night."

Esperanza slunk into the other seat. A slight jerk pulled the
weight of her plaits away from her shoulders and neck.
Gooseflesh pimpled her skin and the heated flush on her cheeks
spread.

"Your eyes are red," Sadiya observed. "There is no shame in
the display of our bodies. How can anything the Lord has made
cause such embarrassment?"

Esperanza's panicked thoughts warred with reality. She could
not fathom how she had arrived at this disgraceful end.

"Perhaps someone taught you to be ashamed of your own
form?"

Esperanza would not confirm the truth. If her governess had
remained with the family, the woman would have died of
mortification by now. Her past reproaches about maidenly
modesty weighed upon the present.

"Your ways are revealed to me." Sadiya's voice pulled her from
reverie. "You do not respond when you wish to be stubborn or for
fear you might be wrong."

Esperanza turned and fixed her with a baleful stare. Her
pleasant, beatific expression set Esperanza's blood afire. She
ignored the impulse to strike the woman. She would never
achieve her freedom except if she outwitted the Mohammedans.

Chapter 5
Unbroken

Granada, Andalusia
January 25, AD 1336 / 10 Jumada al-Thani 736 AH / 11th of
Shevat, 5096

Sadiya raked her fingers through Esperanza's hair. "Even the
dirt cannot hide this lustrous color, dark at the roots. Look at
these flecks of red fire at the tips. Your hair must lighten and
appear like copper in the summer sun. There are women in
Andalusia who spend their husband's fortunes on *henna*, wigs,
and false tresses of dyed flax and cotton just to achieve what you
have."

"I do not care for the heathen practices of Andalusia."

Sadiya's soft chuckle followed. "You reject my every attempt
at pleasantry. Must you be insolent?"

"If I am, perhaps captivity does not suit me. Your master
should let me go."

"You know he will never release you." The slave heaved a
weary sigh. "You are not alone. Every captive in the cities of
Andalusia has shared your plight."

"I do not want or need your pity. It is meaningless from one
whose master has robbed me of freedom. Spare me your
sympathy! Do not speak such words to me again. Why must you
speak at all?"

"If we did not converse, you would be left alone to your
misery."

"Why do you care?"

"I appreciate your circumstances." Before Esperanza could
turn on her, she added, "I have finished with your hair. Stand
now. There is one more task before we go to *al-bayt al-barid* and
then *al-bayt al-wastani*, the first and second bath areas. No one
uses the third, which in Arabic is called—"

"Please stop! I cannot understand all of these words."

"You must hear them and begin to comprehend. How else
shall you endure in this land if you do not know the language of
its people?"

While Esperanza remained seated, bewildered by her lack of discernment, Sadiya came around her and knelt with one of the vials cupped in her hand. She removed the glass stopper and took up the thinner piece of metal. She dipped it into the vial. A chalky white paste clung to the tip.

"It is called *nura*." At Esperanza's harrumph, she rushed on, "I do not know the word in your language. It keeps the skin hairless for at least a month. There is danger in this mix of water, lime, and arsenic. If *nura* remains on the skin for too long, it will burn and eat at the flesh."

Esperanza stared open-mouthed until Sadiya frowned. "I will demonstrate and ease your fears."

She spread the hair remover with the flat side of the metal across fine hairs under her arm. "Stand before me and lift up your arms. I will be careful. Trust me. I have applied *nura* many times before. Please, you must do this."

Esperanza's hands twitched. She clenched her fingers together. "Why must I?"

"Arab women brought the practice to this land. I must remove all bodily hair, lest it catch and hold perspiration. The removal with *nura* keeps our bodies clean."

A dry mouth and tightened throat plagued Esperanza. She rose on spastic limbs and shuffled forward. A chill from the tiles seeped through the soles of her feet. At Sadiya's gesture, she unclenched her fingers and lifted her arms. The cold paste covered her skin. Then the slave bent and smeared a thin layer from Esperanza's ankles upward.

As Sadiya reached the apex of her thighs, Esperanza drew back. "What are you doing? You cannot touch me there!"

"I must remove all the hair, including the thatch on your pubic mound. Do you not see how I have done the same for myself?"

Esperanza stared in full for the first time at her counterpart. "I refuse. Your master bears a Castillan name, but he lives among the Mohammedans and practices their barbaric customs. How can any Christian do such a thing?"

"I never said my master was a Christian. He told me to acquaint you with all manners and customs in Andalusia. This is just one among them. It is natural and expected of all women. If you are embarrassed for a stranger to touch you in an intimate way, I could let you put on and remove the *nura*. There is the chance your ignorance and shame would result in harm. Would you rouse my master's displeasure at the sight of your skin so blemished?"

Esperanza grumbled, "Oh, of course not! He values me. He cannot have his property tainted."

Sadiya's smile beamed. "You understand at last!"

"I do not understand nor do I accept any of this." Exhaustion weighed down her limbs. She slumped upon the wooden stool. Her shoulders hunched, she stared at the tiles.

"Will you allow me to continue?"

"No." When spots of red dotted Sadiya's cheeks, Esperanza rushed on, "I have endured too much already."

"I accept your answer, for today. I will ask again on the morrow."

"I make no promises about what I may say then!"

Sadiya chuckled. "I would expect nothing less." She reached beneath the stools and pulled out leather sandals Esperanza had never seen before, the soles affixed to two wooden bars the width of a finger. "Take the *qabqab*. You are to wear them into the next rooms."

"They don't look comfortable. They are too high."

"The tiles can be slippery. Sometimes a careless bath attendant spills unguents on the floor. The sandals protect us from injury."

With Sadiya's help, Esperanza slipped on the strange footwear. Sadiya donned her own pair, before she placed four linen bolts and smaller squares atop the basket. She took everything and guided Esperanza to the next chamber. When Esperanza stumbled, unaccustomed to the height of the shoes, the slave helped her regain her foothold.

They entered a narrow area twice the size of the latrine. Water spilled into a shallow basin from some unseen source, underneath an arch carved in the style Esperanza recognized as a feature of Mohammedan design.

"Is my skin meant to tingle this much?"

"*Nura* prickles as hair loosens at the root."

At the edge of the basin, Sadiya removed her sandals. She cupped a hand in the liquid and splashed some on her leg. Her fingers smoothed over the skin while she examined it.

"Perfect. I must ensure all traces are gone from your skin."

Esperanza took off her shoes. "How would you know if any hair remover remained?"

"Your skin would burn." Sadiya tended to Esperanza before she washed and wiped her skin free of the paste with ice-cold water from the basin. The filmy liquid ran off into a channel and disappeared under the floor.

Sadiya said, "I could apply some *henna* to your underarms later to ease the sensation. It will pass with each successive use. You must wear the sandals again."

In the next chamber, vapors rose from the long channel. Grateful for the protection of the high footgear, Esperanza swiped at beads of sweat across her forehead. Her hair clung to her skin. She fanned herself with a limp hand and studied the wide room. Overhead, circular vents permitted the steam's escape. Torchlight reflected in the water basins, which encircled a central fountain. It connected to a channel through which runoff drained. Plaster covered the high walls and four slender columns on stone plinths at each corner of the room. On the wall opposite the entryway, the wall became a stone sculpture. Esperanza discerned leaves, birds, and flowers incised into the masonry, with little gaps between the intertwined figures.

She pointed. "What is behind there?"

"The stone latticework conceals a third bath area even hotter than this. My master had it walled up as you see years ago."

Sadiya plunged her hand into the water. Waves rippled. She peeked at Esperanza and then flicked some droplets at her with a girlish squeal. "Shall I bathe you?"

"I can do it for myself."

"If it is your wish." Sadiya reached into the basket and handed Esperanza a green-tinged, square-shaped bar, the weight of a brick. "My master's favorite soap, made with olive and sesame oils. Rub it on the soaked linen and wash your skin."

"I know how to use soap! Miriam always gave me some on my birthday."

"Her family traded with Moors?"

Esperanza answered, "They must have," although she did not know.

She soaked the cloth and washed herself beside the fountain. The water sluiced down her body and flowed into the channel.

"Your hair must be cleansed."

Esperanza ignored Sadiya. Then the sensation of some watchful gaze swept over Esperanza. It could not have come from Sadiya, who enjoyed her bath with the gaiety of a little girl at play. Esperanza scanned the room. Annoyed at her childish uncertainties, she rinsed and asked for time to soak her sore feet.

Sadiya reminded her, "We cannot leave until I have washed your hair."

The scented soap coupled with long fingers through her locks and against her scalp stirred a pleasure-filled sigh from Esperanza's lips, a joy that caused no embarrassment even after the slave laughed at her. After Sadiya rinsed the aromatic soap, she washed her own hair while Esperanza waited.

Something about the lattice drew her gaze again and she peered into its depths.

Sadiya interrupted her reverie. "I must also scrub your hands and the soles of your feet." She took the second of the vials and poured into her palm a pulverized mixture. She rubbed it on Esperanza's palms and kneaded her heels, arches, and toes with it.

Afterward they washed off and wrapped their bodies in the larger linen squares, Sadiya bound their heads with the rest of the cloth and slipped into her shoes again. Esperanza mimicked her. Esperanza focused a hard gaze on the wall of carved stone, before they retraced steps through the previous chamber. The strange sensation of a presence behind the wall returned. It mystified rather than frightened her.

Sadiya urged her along. "We must cool ourselves in the previous chamber."

As they lingered, Sadiya chattered until she noticed how Esperanza shivered against the cool tile. In the changing room, Sadiya spread another long sheet of cloth over a stone slab. "Remove the bath towel and rest on your stomach. I will massage your skin with rose and argan oil."

Esperanza mumbled, "Bathing takes a long time in this land."

"The Moors spend several hours at the public baths. There are many in Granada, close to any *masjid*, the Muslim houses of worship. Those who attend prayers must cleanse themselves beforehand. Communal bathhouses are larger than this one."

"I have seen four rooms now. How could any other bathhouse be larger? Is so much space required?"

"They are communal baths, where all classes of men and women congregate at separate times." While Esperanza took in this information, Sadiya asked, "Would you like to apply the oils to your front first?"

"If I must."

Sadiya held out a third vial from the basket. She took the moist linen and held it up before Esperanza, who was grateful for a measure of privacy while she rubbed the fragrant mixture on her slick skin. Afterward she reclined and pressed her stomach to the stone. Heat emanated from it as well.

She rested her chin against her forearms. "How long have you been a slave?"

Sadiya sat next to her and poured the oils into a cupped hand. "For ten years, since I reached the age of seven. After weeks of passage across the mountains of Navarra, my parents sold me in Pamplona."

Esperanza lifted her head. "Your parents. How barbaric!"

"When one daughter is married, another belongs to the church, and a third remains to attend the household and her parents, the last must have seemed needless."

"Pamplona is a Christian city. How could the sale of captives occur there?"

"You must know Christians trade in captives and slaves as well as Muslims?"

"Humph. Where did you come from?"

"My poor family lived in a little hamlet south of Toulouse in the kingdom of France. My parents descended from Cathars. Our neighbors always looked upon us with suspicion of heresy, though they could never find proof. The burden became too much for my father. He left my mother and remaining sister at Pamplona. He and I followed the pilgrims' road west to Santiago de Compostela. Juan Manuel purchased me, although my father had some reservations about the sale. Juan Manuel brought me into Andalusia. I have lived here for more than half of my life. I learned to yield for the sake of survival."

Esperanza whispered, "I cannot."

Sadiya kneaded her back and soothed her skin until she relaxed against the tiles again. "Then you will die in this land. Submission is required of us all. Even the noble Sultan who rules this land must surrender to the dictates of God. Muslims believe the faithful must defer to the will of Allah. The same god whom Christians worship and the Jews of Spain call *El Dio* in Ladino. Let me teach you all you need to know of Andalusia and its people."

"You admire the Mohammedans."

"I respect Moorish dedication to study and perfection. Their enjoyment of life's beauties. Their conviction. Your spirit is like theirs, strong, not broken by adversity. Remember the tree that does not bend to the force of the wind will crack at its base."

"You have had many years to grow familiar with this life. You want me to accept a horrible future in as little as a few days. I refuse to deny who I am, to submit, and surrender my past. I promised my papa I would survive captivity. Freedom will be mine again."

"If you cannot accept this life, permit me to be your friend. Let me help you."

Esperanza raised her head and glanced over her shoulder. "I cannot think of you as a friend, not yet. I will try to be less bad-tempered with you though."

Sadiya smiled. "Will you indulge me in a final courtesy? Tell me your given name."

"It is Esperanza Peralta."

Sadiya spread more of the oils over Esperanza's back. The massage drew further sighs from Esperanza, who closed her eyes, her body made languid by each caress. When the slave's fingers smoothed over her buttocks and down her thighs and calves, Esperanza did not even lift her head.

Afterward, Sadiya removed the towel and twisted Esperanza's wet hair in her hands. Sadiya rubbed a cloth against the tresses, until mild dampness remained. She opened the last vial, poured the contents into her hand, and threaded long strokes through the hair.

"This is almond oil, meant to sweeten and strengthen."

Esperanza's eyelids grew heavy. Sadiya's last murmur soothed her to sleep. "Your body and soul are weary of trial and dangers. Rest now for you shall emerge stronger from these experiences."

***

When she opened her eyes, Esperanza first became aware of the unusual tiles of the floor, another random design. Then she realized the brown-haired man who had inspected her the day before now sat on the stool.

She sat up, grabbed the damp linen Sadiya has used for her hair and pressed it to her torso, though the cloth provided scant coverage. "What are you doing here?"

He put up his hands and leaned forward. As his chest rumbled, a throaty laugh filled the air. "You are like a little hare afraid of the pot. I am master of the house and all who dwell herein, *sí*. My coin built this bathhouse, provides the comforts you have experienced within its walls."

His elbows pressed against his knees and his fists propped up his chin. He wore a black silken *pellote* trimmed with gold braid. Under the loose surcoat, the fitted sleeves of a green tunic almost covered his fingers.

A chill ran through her and gooseflesh pimpled on her arms. "You should leave. You should not be alone with me."

"Why? I am a purveyor of fine flesh, a slave merchant. Do you think yours is the first naked body I have ever seen? You showed intelligence when we first met, enough to know the possible value of your friend's musical talent. Do not pretend to be a lackwit now. What is your age?"

"I have lived for fourteen years."

"Tell me, is your full name Esperanza Peralta?"

She should have expected the man's slave would reveal anything told to her. "It is."

His gaze probed her face. A strange and unexpected regard glinted in his honeyed look. She thought she recognized sympathy, but his intent regard for her suggested another elusive emotion. Pleasure perhaps. She did not doubt it. He thought himself master of one at the mercy of his whims. She would teach him otherwise.

He mumbled, "*Sí*. I should have known you by your features.

Her temple pulsed and her breath quickened. "Why? You have never met me before now. My father never traveled to Andalusia."

"Perhaps everything is not as you believe. Did he ever tell you how he came by the Peralta name, its origins?"

"If he knew, he did not say."

"I suppose not. And you were born in Castilla-Leon?"

"At Talavera—"

"De la Reina, *sí*." he finished for her. "I should have guessed. Did your father have an occupation, a trade?"

She lifted her chin. "He was a doctor in the household of the Cerdas."

"He served the *Infantes* of Castilla-Leon? A man of some means and importance then." He reached within the surcoat and pulled out her father's dagger. He held it up to the light. She gasped and his stare skimmed over her face. "I assume this belonged to your parent. When I dined with Ahmed, he claimed it as his, but he forgot it in the furor of his hasty departure."

"The slaver lied. The weapon belonged to my father, granted to him by the hands of Alfonso de la Cerda. I want it returned."

With a nod, he tucked the weapon back into the sheath at his waist. "We all desire much beyond our grasp, *niña*. Did your father provide for your education? Can you read or write?"

She frowned at his refusal to return the stolen blade, but responded, "I can read from the Psalter. My father arranged reading lessons with a Dominican friar, Fray Rufino del Moral. He traveled with us across the *meseta*." She did not mention his brutal death. Reflection on the events of her capture would lead to tears she could not permit.

"Was Fray Rufino a good teacher?"

"He was ardent and took to his duty with vigor. I once bore bruises on my knuckles to prove it."

Something in Juan Manuel's almost indulgent smile triggered powerful remembrances of her father. She could not bear the kind regard reflected in his gaze, particularly when he held her in captivity.

59

Instead, she blinked and looked away. "My father provided instruction in Latin and Catalan. He also taught me to speak and read some Greek. No one taught me to write. My wits led me to copy from the Psalter onto parchment."

"What else did you learn?"

"No more. Fray Rufino insisted a lady should read from the Book of Psalms, if she needed lessons in more than household management. Of that, my *duenna* taught me to sew."

The last governess her father had employed taught embroidery as well, but Esperanza was not about to reveal the knowledge. She abhorred long hours spent at embroidery and if the opportunity presented itself again, she would never take up the task. Absorbed in her thoughts, she lapsed into silence until she remembered the merchant's presence.

While he mused upon her and indulged in a satisfied smile, she scooted back on the tiles and drew her legs up under the short linen.

His grin widened. "Why do you hide from me? There is nothing of you I have not seen in these past hours."

She rubbed at her exposed forearms and pressed her knees together. Had he touched her while she remained insensible and unaware? An uncomfortable knot filled her throat. "How long was I asleep while you watched me?"

"You relaxed for an hour. I admired you before this while you enjoyed your bath."

"How were you able to see me?" The answer came to her in an instant. Still, she needed him to say the words.

He obliged her. "The stone latticework in the bathhouse concealed my presence. Your hot stare fell upon me many times though you could not have known. Some strange sense must have warned you. You intrigue me, as does your intuitive mind, *sí*. When I first saw you, I never knew hatred could light a spark in the gaze of one so young. It is natural for you to despise me, as I have claimed your liberty."

Her jaw tightened. "So your Sadiya has told me."

"You do not believe this, hmm?"

"Nothing stays the same forever. I shall regain what I have lost."

"But not all things?" His query hinted at some awareness of her circumstances. "Such spirit. *Sí*, I shall enjoy your presence. You have not disappointed me thus far. As much as I admire fortitude, your true worth lies in your body, a pearl. When you let Sadiya remove the little thatch of hair between your legs, you will be perfect. For now, I am delighted to find your skin is unblemished. Your arms are long, the breasts firm like ripened pomegranates. You have soft and rounded shoulders. The ribs poke out a little. Your captors must have offered meager ration. I shall never understand a slaver's mentality. Fine fare encourages a robust appetite and lessens susceptibility to all manner of sickness. However, I am not concerned, for the rich foods of Andalusia will fill you out. Your belly remains flat, as a maiden's should.

"Your future master will take great pleasure in those long legs, for the flesh is supple. The feet are larger than I would like, but do not detract from an otherwise admirable appearance. Most satisfactory. Others would look upon your face and consider you plain, of little beauty. Large almond-shaped eyes are common among captives in Spain, but not these like amber stones with flecks of cinnamon. No one who could ever question your worth has ever beheld the rest of your exquisite form, more graceful and slender than the branches of a willow tree. I suspect if the slaver Ahmed knew of your perfection, he might have kept you for himself. Greed outweighed his other interests. When the auction occurs, I would not have Sadiya mar your features with cosmetics of any kind. You need no further enhancements. You are a lithe and energetic young woman and shall bring joy to your eventual master, both within and outside his bed."

Her stomach fluttered. His frank speech should have rendered her dumbstruck, mortified at his shameful description of her attributes. He had lied, of course, for her governess often remarked she had the body of a boy.

She pressed against the wall and eyed him. "If you think I shall go to the bed of any man who would dare call me his slave, you are wrong."

"Husbands rule wives in their bedchambers. How do you suppose life as a Moor's pleasure slave would be different?"

"No one will ever touch me in the manner reserved for a husband, except a husband!"

"Then you should be forewarned. Among the Moors, the men take concubines before they choose wives. You must do much to endear yourself before you are wed." He paused and offered an enigmatic smile. "If this is *El Dio's* plan for you, why do you fight against it? He has brought you to this moment."

"God did not intend for me to remain captive."

"The Arabian ancestors of the Moors believe in predestined fate, which they say is *qadar*. You are here because *El Dio* has willed it. A fool fights destiny." He stood and brushed a wrinkle from the *pellote*. "You promised obedience for the sake of your friend, Miriam. Do you remember?"

"I do. I will keep all of my vows, chief among them my quest for freedom."

"You may regain it in time. For now, I expect your obedience. No more talk of escape. My Sadiya indulged you. I will not. You must follow her commands as if they were my own. If you do not, your friend will bear the penalty for your offenses. It would pain you if she suffered in your stead, *si?*"

When she nodded, he said, "I am not so certain she deserves your loyalty. In these two days, she has not asked after your welfare, while I have heard you wished to see her. She has caused me some trouble. I ordered Ahmed of Cordoba from my house because of her and had to send for the midwife during the night, at great expense and inconvenience to myself."

He walked away from her while she shouted, "A midwife? What has happened to Miriam? What of her baby?"

Alone with him in the room where she had changed, she demanded an answer again. He turned to her. "If you do all I have asked, I will allow you to see her in a few days. She might benefit from your comfort."

The prospect of a reunion buoyed her spirit. Nothing could please her more than to be at Miriam's side again. Perhaps they could offer reassurance in each other's presence. She reached for her garments and found empty pegs on the wall. "Where are my clothes? What of my rosary beads?"

His cool regard coupled with a slight smile. "I had the rags burned. Such a delectable form as yours deserves attire that is more suitable. You do not need rosary beads either. Captives in this household do not keep the symbols of Christian life. It does not aid their acceptance of the inevitable future."

She lunged at him. Her fingers scrabbled at braided embroidery. "You had no right! No matter what you do, I shall remain a Christian until my death. Give me back my things!"

He gripped her wrists with rigid strength and stilled her rage in an instant. His warm gaze met hers. Cinnamon scented his ragged breath. Something hard and metallic in his palm pressed against the back of her hand. He released his hold and held up her brooch to the light.

"That is mine!" she insisted.

"You are mine! You are no different from this trinket, crafted by the expert hands of a master Jewish goldsmith. When you are long gone from my house into the service of your new master, I shall keep it as a reminder of you and the debt you owe." He spoke with cold finality. "I have saved the Jewess' life as a boon to you, for your comfort. I will not grant this favor again. Your attachment to her mystifies me. I perceive your lot and hers remain entwined. You shall live to be a comfort for her much as for your own foolish hope for freedom."

She gulped ragged breaths long after his departure. What had Miriam endured while they remained separated?

Chapter 6
The First Betrayal

Esperanza Peralta

Granada, Andalusia
January 26 - February 1, AD 1336 / 11 - 17 Jumada al-Thani
736 AH / 12th - 18th of Shevat, 5096

The day afterward, Juan Manuel informed Esperanza of his expectations. He did not permit captives to while away the hours in idleness. He sent Sadiya to her in the evening with armfuls of crinkled, tattered garments. Mounds of cloth soon littered her cell each night. When Sadiya often fetched them at daybreak, Esperanza revealed her fingertips, dappled with needle pricks.

Sadiya rolled her eyes. "Be thankful it is not summer, or you would find yourself out in the sun, mired in the heat of the master's garden each day. Finish what he has sent. There will be another set in the morning. My master provides new garments to those whom he will sell to a rich buyer. Other captives must wear what they have on their backs. Much of their clothing needs repair."

The week dragged on, longer than any other did in Esperanza's memory. True to her master's word, Sadiya escorted Esperanza to Miriam's cell days later, when a new month began. Esperanza rose from her pallet and clutched the folds of a gossamer tunic overlaid against a more fitted, opaque one. She had received a change of vestments mid-week, after Sadiya and the laundress came to remove the plain robe she had donned after the first visit to the baths. In leather sandals, she followed Sadiya out and to the right through a warren of corridors. The exterior of the House of Myrtles hid a complex of rooms at the lower level. Behind eight other doorways, the cries and sniffles of other unseen captives echoed. Esperanza scowled at Sadiya's back and wondered how she ignored their misery.

After a sudden right turn, Sadiya gestured to the two sentries who stood beside the tenth door. One man grimaced, his thinned lips tight in displeasure. A long scratch raked across his right cheek and a reddened bruise dotted the other side of his face. His counterpart grunted. He stabbed a bony pale forefinger at the door. Blood seeped through a linen bandage wrapped around his fingertip. Whatever answer Sadiya gave barely mollified him, but he took the brass key she proffered and opened the portal just a crack.

Something crashed and splattered against the wood inside. He drew back, pulled the door closed and locked it behind him.

Esperanza gasped and covered her mouth with shaky fingers. What had Miriam done to cause the sentry's reaction? Then a stream of words echoed beyond the room, a garbled jumble of Arabic mixed with a smattering of Ladino and Hebrew, shattered the din.

Sadiya pinched Esperanza's forearm. "Speak to your friend. Let her know you are here and no one will harm her."

Esperanza eyed the wary sentry. "Are you so certain?"

Sadiya nodded. "No one will touch the master's property, despite all provocation."

Esperanza rapped at the wood. "Miriam! Will you please let me in...?"

"*El Dio!* If those bastards come near me again, I'll cut something else off!"

While Miriam spewed her fury at the minions of their captor, part of Esperanza experienced some relief to know she was not alone in her resistance. Still, concern for Miriam's well-being must govern her actions. She glanced at the guardsman with the bloodied finger and asked no one in particular, "Did Miriam attack anyone?"

"She did. Several persons." Sadiya replied. "On the day of your arrival, my master put the woman into a room with three other women. I brought your companion food. The others had eaten earlier, but they tried to take her rations. She fought them off and smashed one's head against the wall." Despite Esperanza's gasp, she continued, "The woman will live. My master would have been displeased if she did not. One of his men intervened in the fight. Your friend kicked him between the legs and bolted from the cell. The others stopped her and summoned my master. I noted the blood on her legs."

"Why did Miriam bleed?"

She continued as if Esperanza had not spoken. "My master summoned a Jewish midwife, though your companion fought her at every instance. When these men brought in the morning meal today after the dawn prayer, she bit one's hand. She also scratched and slapped the other man before both subdued her. Your friend has attacked everyone who sees to her. She blames us for her loss."

"What loss?" Esperanza's pulse hammered for she already anticipated the slave's response.

"You should go to her and offer familiar comfort."

When she spoke to the doorkeeper again, he shook his head and edged away. With a frown and a sigh, she snatched the key from his grasp and pushed it into the lock.

Esperanza breathed a ragged sigh. "Miriam? I am coming in. Please don't be frightened." The cautionary words suited her better. Still, she pushed at the handle. The door swung open with a creak.

Inside a bare room similar in size to where Juan Manuel had consigned Esperanza, remnants of stale food and cracked wooden vessels littered the floor. Adjacent the door, on a whitewashed wall mired with various stains, a deep crimson fluid dribbled and pooled. The discarded, broken cup leaked the rest of the wine into furrows between the tiles. At the opposite wall, Miriam crouched on the floor. Unlike the pallet Esperanza had received, Miriam sat on a straw mat. Her black hair streamed like spilled ink around her face and shoulders. The remnants of her ragged garments hung in tatters and revealed bruises. Had she not bathed since their arrival?

"Can you understand me?" Esperanza crept toward her.

Miriam stared from sunken eyes as though purblind. Then she cackled as recognition brightened her gaze. "Do my eyes deceive me? Have you become a Moor? Look at the clothes you wear."

"Never," Esperanza swore. She knelt at Miriam's side and reached for the strands of dirtied hair plastered to her brow. A whiff of the unkempt strands warned her of the rest of Miriam's disheveled state, but Esperanza would not recoil now.

Miriam slapped her hands away. "Do not touch me! I know why you have come. To gloat over my wretched state because I blamed you for it. You show me how you will live, a dalliance for these Moors, while I shall die in this place, alone—"

"Stop it! I would never wish for your death or hold trivial resentment against you. We have known each other for too long. Desperation governed your mood then. I forgive you, Miriam."

Still, Miriam wrestled with her. Skeletal fingers scrabbled and twitched within Esperanza's hold. The roughened texture of the flesh brought fresh tears to Esperanza's eyes, for the agony Miriam endured was almost unbearable. She held on until Miriam's struggles wavered and kissed the chapped hands, tears the lone balm she might offer.

A year ago, the same hands stilled Esperanza's shoulders after her father had announced his removal from the post of physician to the princely household of Don Alfonso de la Cerda. Miriam lingered while Esperanza questioned her father. She once suspected he hid more than he revealed about the dismissal. Esperanza's accusatory tone had earned her a slap across the face, which rendered her father almost as shocked as her. Miriam had embraced her afterward and whispered words of solace. Miriam encouraged her to believe the sudden loss of his post soured her father's usual indulgent moods. Much could happen in a year. For now, she hastened to return Miriam's past gestures of kindness.

Esperanza whispered, "You will not die! I will not allow it."

"You think you know the will of *El Dio*? Then ask Him why he has taken my children from me, my Palomba, my boy. Was it not enough for Him to claim the girl? If I am mother to no one now, what else remains for me?"

Esperanza lifted her gaze to Miriam's stomach, still rounded as if life dwelled within. The savagery of the Mohammedans saw two children taken from this world. Was it better they had not lived to share in their mother's fate? Esperanza would never know the answer. She clung to the chance of a better existence, far from these dreadful circumstances. The memory of her father's last cherished words buoyed her spirit. "There is always life. There is always hope."

"Is such prattle meant to reassure me or you? You never believed it before when Rufino tutored you."

"He brought the lash alone, not the commandments of a merciful Father in heaven. God does not speak to me. Perhaps I have forsaken Him too often in the past. I seek Him now in these dark days for your sake and mine."

Miriam shrugged off her hold. "You should go and leave me be! If there is mercy in heaven, I shall die and be with my children again. They are all I have ever loved in this life."

"No. You will learn to love again so other children might call you mother. I shall help you regain your strength." Esperanza stood and yelled for Sadiya.

At her summons, Sadiya peeked around the doorway. Miriam's chin jutted, a feral awareness glittered in her sharpened gaze as she focused on the intruder. Esperanza bent again and clutched Miriam's arms, even as tremors coursed through her.

"Will you bring some of the chicken broth you gave me earlier? Miriam needs food."

Sadiya scanned the dirtied floor. "My master offered it. She threw all of the food at the sentries!"

"Please! Whatever she has done, I promise she will not repeat it now if you will fetch her something to eat. Also, send a little water for her wash in a basin."

Sadiya bowed. "As you wish. The door stays locked until I come back."

Esperanza gathered Miriam's frail body against hers. The woman's shoulder blades poked through the ragged skin draped across her bones.

Her low chuckle rumbled against Esperanza's chest. "Already, you think to rule this place. A slave does as you bid although you rank no higher than she does. You even seek to control me. Shall you govern my will and whims?"

Esperanza kissed Miriam's forehand and soothed her. "You will not be here forever. Neither will I. Do not give into despair. We must remain watchful for opportunities to gain our freedom. I will never abandon you, not ever. We will survive and leave this place together soon. I promise."

"How do you intend to accomplish this escape?"

With a sigh, Esperanza loosened her hold and rested her palms in her lap. She flicked the tip of her tongue over dried lips. "Well. We should not devise anything until you have regained your strength. We could try for escape together."

Miriam stiffened and lifted her head. Her jaw line twitched before she spoke. "You have no plan as I suspected! If we are to find our way beyond these walls, I believe the yellow-haired slave will play a role, if you can gain her confidence. She allowed you here and followed your command. Has she offered friendship?"

"She has done so to lure me into an acceptance of her lot in life."

"At least you have the good sense to foresee the trap. Let us hope you can avoid it. Speak to me of this woman. She looks to be the same age as you, perhaps a little older. What is her role in this house? How are her relations with her master? Does she share his bed?"

An ache stirred in Esperanza's throat. "I don't know where she sleeps. I do think—"

Miriam's hand sliced through the air. "That is your problem! You never think! Left to your impulse and wits alone, our escape would never happen."

"You're being cruel and unfair!"

"Life is much the same. Haven't our experiences taught you a lesson yet?"

Loss had not dulled the sharp edge of Miriam's tone. If anything, she appeared more spiteful with each day.

With a stifled sob, Esperanza shrank away from her while Miriam sneered. They lapsed into silence and awaited Sadiya's arrival. When she returned with a hot bowl of broth and a piece of the flatbread Esperanza did not like, her master followed.

A distinct shudder quaked within Miriam's body. Esperanza huddled closer and stilled her. She did not doubt Miriam would have attacked the man if she could.

Sadiya set the food near Miriam's feet and edged away. Her persistent gaze remained fixed on Miriam, who asked, "Are you so afraid I would kick a wooden bowl at your precious face? You should fear me."

"*Sí*, but not because of your disruptive behavior," Juan Manuel chimed in. With a wave of his hand, he ushered Sadiya toward the exit. As she bypassed him, he cupped her elbow. His reverent touch lingered on the silken sleeve. She smiled and leaned into him before he released her. She left and closed the door behind her.

Esperanza stared in her wake. She held little doubt of the nature of their relationship. Juan Manuel trusted his slave and Sadiya would do nothing to alter his sentiment. Esperanza glanced at Miriam and hoped she had witnessed their byplay as well. A heavy knot tightened in Esperanza's stomach at the thought of any scheme where she might inveigle the woman into a false sense of comfort. No matter how Sadiya played a role in Esperanza's continued captivity, she did not deserve to be misused.

Her master crisscrossed the short length of Miriam's cell twice. The hem of his black silken *pellote* grazed knee-length, red leather boots. He stroked a hand over his brown hair before he halted at the center of the room.

"You." He pointed at Esperanza with a forefinger weighted by a large ruby set in gold. "I have come to understand you well. The desire for freedom is paramount for now. You seek stability and security above all else. You place equal value upon the same happiness for your friend, *sí*. Selfish motive does not rule you. Instead, you express genuine concern and care for the well-being of others. Whatever is good and fair in life, you would have for your friend. You have a remarkable, generous nature. I fear for your survival. Others do not share your temperament. The world outside these walls will hold unpleasant surprises for you."

She met his stare. "And I shall endure and survive them, whatever their nature."

He nodded. "As you say. Whether your character shall remain untainted is a mystery time shall resolve." Then he glanced at Miriam. "But you? You are unpredictable. Fickle women are dangerous. It has never been so hard for me to detect the needs of others."

Miriam tensed further and Esperanza's hold tightened. "Perhaps you should not try with me. You would make a game of pretending to know my wishes. You cannot know my heart. The loss of my children has killed it."

"I do not believe so. Their deaths have not deprived you of foolhardy courage, or so my guards tell me. No, some measure of the woman who survived cruel rape across the *meseta* gives strength to your voice and limbs still."

When she recoiled, he rushed on, "*Sí*, the midwife verified what I could not have guessed of your experiences. Other women would have long surrendered to despair, but not you. This ability to survive intrigues me. It is part of why you are still in my house rather than sold at a loss to the first buyer who would have you and your troubles."

Esperanza gasped. "Please, do not send her away!"

He shook his head. "Such a tender heart. It shall suffer grievous wounds before life's end. My dismissal of your friend will not be among them."

His stare returned to Miriam. "I pride myself on an innate talent for knowing what people want long before they ask for it. How else could I gain success as a purveyor of the finest slaves in Andalusia? My patrons trust me to anticipate their needs. I perceive the truth hidden behind base desire. For instance, Ahmed of Cordoba, who gives the appearance of a man concerned with coin alone. No, wealth is one means to achieve his true purpose. He would use the money to buy back the prestige his family once held. His nephew Fadil thought he wanted you. Instead, he desired to govern your will and think himself powerful by mastery of one such as you. So tell me, woman, what is it you want?"

Miriam declared, "I wish for the lives of the children stolen from me! Can you give me the daughter ripped from my grasp or the stillborn son torn from my body?"

He crouched over the bowl, his face level with hers. "Authority over life and death is not mine to grant. I do not have such power, much to my regret. As the Moors say, *al-mulk li-llah*. Power belongs to *El Dio*."

The hitch in his voice appeared genuine. Had he known some terrible grief in the past?

Esperanza put aside her rumination, while he addressed Miriam again. "Is power what you want?" When she did not answer, he chuckled. "Have I stumbled upon the truth at last?"

He rose and retraced his earlier steps once more before he regarded both of them. "What if I told each of you I could grant your heart's true desire?"

Miriam spat on the floor next to the broth, which grew ever colder. "I would govern my own will and desires. What is the resolve of a slave compared to the whim of her master? *Diablo*, you have no answer! You are no better than a filthy slaver. You seek to cajole with soft words instead of the lash."

As if she had not insulted him, he continued, "Your sweet friend told me you are a singer. Do you know the worth of a well-trained songstress to the Moors? If her claim is not exaggerated, you could find yourself well situated with a bright future before you. Would you like such an opportunity? I can offer both of you futures you have never dreamed of, the comfort of home with children at your feet and power above others amid opulent splendor. Beyond these walls, in palaces of marble with sun-shaded porticoes and gardens of fragrant flowers, new lives await you in the harem of the Sultan of Granada. Does such a prospect appeal?"

Miriam laughed. "I am not a fool, held in the sway of your lies. I would still be the property of Granada's ruler."

"For a bondwoman blessed with a biddable master, the boundaries between such divisions often blur. What man's lust does not stir at the sight of an attractive female? Does he not worship at the temple of her beauty? Does his pride not soar when such a woman presents him with an heir? For the mother of this boy, life would hold limitless possibilities and pleasures."

Miriam murmured, "As it would for the one who brought such a woman to the attention of the Sultan."

He stroked his beard and mused, "If such is the will of *El Dio*." He turned from them, headed for the door. "Think upon your futures for the Sultanas of Granada arrive within the month. Impress these women with your worth, your wit, and your adaptability. You may find great reward and ascend heights few attain. Perhaps one or both of you may claim the heart of a Sultan. You may share his bed and his life."

Esperanza said, "A life of sloth and sin, imprisoned at the mercy of one man. How would such be any different from our miserable existence with you?"

He paused and gripped the olive wood with bejeweled fingers. His faraway look lingered on her face. "Bedding me would not grant you a son fit for Granada's throne. It would not gain me favor with the Sultanas either. Prepare yourself and your friend. She is your responsibility. Your failure shall cost her. Ensure she takes in the broth. I will send no water for her wash. Let her prove her mettle and find her way to the bath."

Esperanza protested, "She might not have the strength to walk there."

Juan Manuel answered, "The weak need to be coddled, not the strong."

Miriam loosened herself from Esperanza's hold and reached for the wooden bowl at her feet. She brought it to her lips and sipped. After she swallowed a mouthful of broth, she proclaimed, "I may yet surprise you both."

Juan Manuel's raucous laugh pealed through the corridor. "I do not doubt it."

***

February 15, AD 1336 / 2 Rajab 736 AH / 2nd of Adar II, 5096

In silence, Esperanza padded in leather sandals, which slapped against the titles. Her feet tugged at the hem of a floor-length pink tunic of linen. The entire length of the heavy material fell open. It revealed a thin cotton blouse tucked under an embroidered girdle paired with white, linen trousers, which tapered to the ankles.

Under Sadiya's supervision and with the constant guards in attendance, Juan Manuel permitted continued visits with Miriam every morning. He still restricted the interactions among friends. He would not allow them to attend the bath together or sleep in the same room. Even if his Sadiya had grown less cautious, he never would. For the success of Esperanza's endeavor today, he must remain true to the traits he had exhibited. Most of all, she depended on his care for Sadiya.

Rampant thoughts blazed a bright path in Esperanza's mind. She once again considered her desperate ruse, formed in these two weeks after her reunion with Miriam at the House of Myrtles. The ploy required the perfect convergence of events and more audacity than she once thought she possessed. She had never before faced such fraught circumstances. To succeed, she would have to maintain the facade of meek compliance, adopted to gain Sadiya's trust. To that end, she had submitted to the shameful touch of the midwife between her legs, who sought the proof of her virginity. She listened while Sadiya dispensed repeated instructions about the proper stance, appearance and deference a slave should show.

In her heart, Esperanza rejected the yoke of captivity and slavery, while she adapted to the food and dress of the Mohammedans. In the final humiliation, she had even permitted Sadiya to remove her bodily hair. Grave scruples about her choices, including sudden duplicity, plagued her each night she returned to her isolated cell. Esperanza could not turn from her goal now. Freedom for her and Miriam beckoned.

Unfathomable as it appeared, Miriam now seemed less interested in escape than when she first accused Esperanza of having no plan. Since then, Miriam never mentioned a desire for liberty again. While she still resented Juan Manuel's dominion, her resistance ebbed with each day. Had the length of their captivity dulled Miriam's hopes?

Esperanza could not fathom the act of surrender. How could anyone just give up? Let the Mohammedans keep their belief about the will of fate. She would make her own destiny. She had kept the scheme to herself, lest Miriam berate her for it. Although Esperanza could not quite bring herself to admit the truth, the gulf between her and Miriam widened every time they met. Perhaps Miriam understood the truth better than she did and the division between them had long existed. They had never quarreled about obvious differences except after their captivity. If she succeeded, perhaps they might heal the rift and recapture old sentiments, fractured by the losses of their loved ones and captivity among the Mohammedans. They might learn to forgive each other.

Beside her, Sadiya huffed and halted. The pair of escorts also stopped. The woman waved them away, though they did not go far.

"You're pensive again, Esperanza. Why should you be so sad still? I should be mournful for your sojourn here will be over within a day."

Esperanza could not suppress a rueful chuckle. "You cannot expect me to believe you shall miss my sullen sighs and stubborn behavior."

Sadiya patted her forearm, familiarity Esperanza would have rejected weeks ago. She allowed it. The act served the higher purpose of freedom. In truth, she missed the similar gestures Miriam once made.

"When the Sultanas take you away to the Sultan's palace, I may never see you again. We are not friends, perhaps we could never be. Your determination to regain all you have lost stirs my sympathy and respect. Your future shall be bright. I will never witness the outcome—to my regret. Still, my heart is joyful for my part in it and for having met you. Pity softens your gaze whenever you look at me these days. Do not be sad for me. I have the life I want. May you also find what you seek."

Esperanza blinked and her stare wavered. Despite her resentment, she bore no ill will against the woman and did not wish her any harm in the attempt at escape. Sadiya would soon lose the admiration in her gaze.

The slave pressed her further. "Did you imagine your father again last night?"

"How did you know I have dreamt of him?"

"You called out his name while you slumbered after your bath last week. You whispered it in your sleep just before I woke you yesterday."

It would be useless to deny it, but Esperanza hesitated to share the painful recollections. Each night she thought of her father before she closed her eyes and awoke with swollen eyelids, her cheeks dampened by tears. She missed him so much. Her last vow bolstered her, gave her the will to endure each wretched day trapped in the House of Myrtles. If he had lived, would he be proud of her?

She admitted, "I think of him often. His death seems an impossible nightmare. In the past, I never imagined life without him."

With a sigh, Sadiya whispered, "Your father is not dead. He lives here," she pointed her index and middle fingers at Esperanza's head, "and here." She tapped Esperanza's chest, just above the heart. "Those whom we love can never die if we remember them."

They resumed the walk, Juan Manuel's sentinels at their backs. With every step, a heavy weight settled upon Esperanza's limbs, made her gait sluggish. Every exhalation wrenched from her body caused her chest to tighten. Her nails raked along the adjacent wall.

Sadiya slowed and touched her arm. "How do you fare? What ill befalls you?"

The lump inside Esperanza's throat stifled her breathing. She must summon some answer before she stirred the slave's suspicions. Worse, Sadiya might insist they return to the cell. This one chance loomed, freedom more precious than any other desire she once held.

She gasped and cast a cautious glance at the men just behind them. Their slight, wiry frames and relaxed stances encouraged her reckless thoughts. Indeed, they appeared bored and idled in the passageway again, less concerned with their duty to keep watchful gazes on her. There would never be a better time.

Esperanza pressed her back against the wall and raked her moisture-laden palms across it. "I don't know if I can do this."

A frown crinkled Sadiya's brow. "Do what?"

"This." Esperanza turned and aimed a swift kick at the apex of the first guardsman's trousers. His howl of outrage shattered the virtual silence before he buckled and clutched himself between his legs. Esperanza ducked and snatched his blade from its sheath. His companion's apathy dissolved into confusion. He bent and offered aid to the man before he realized Esperanza held a weapon. Sadiya stood catatonic, her stare bewildered.

Then Esperanza touched the blade to the smooth, slim column of her throat. "Take me to Miriam. Open the door and let us go free. If you do not, I will have to hurt you and take the key myself."

"You would kill me after all I have done for you? You would make a mockery of all we have shared?"

"You did nothing without your master's command! Do not bandy words with me when you have already admitted the truth. We could never be friends. Miriam is the one person outside my family who has ever cared for me, not you."

"Then it appears you do not understand the true nature of friendship."

Esperanza's hand shook. Still, she dug the blade a little deeper.

Sadiya winced and said, "I shall take you to the woman you believe is a friend, but I beg you to consider what happens afterward. My master enjoys substantial protection. Have you thought of how you will get out of here without recapture?"

"I have thought of little else. Your master will allow no harm to you. For your sake, he shall let me go with Miriam, unmolested by his men. Now, stop wasting time! Lead on."

The uninjured sentry rose from his companion and growled something at Sadiya. She answered him with a curt, one-worded response, which Esperanza had heard among the slavers on the *meseta. La.*

Esperanza ordered, "No more talk! If you speak at all, ensure I understand. What did you say to each other?"

Sadiya grumbled, "He said he could try to disarm you. I told him no."

"Good. Now go."

When Sadiya turned, Esperanza dug the pointed end of the blade into the slave's back. A tiny slit rent the silk. Sadiya whimpered as Esperanza urged her onward. Sadiya took furtive steps, while Esperanza kept her grip on the weapon steady. She often cast a glance over her shoulder at the two men until she and Sadiya rounded a corner and stood outside Miriam's cell. From inside her voice echoed, raised in song. Esperanza frowned at the door.

75

The men stationed on either side of the door straightened. They showed no signs of heightened awareness. Esperanza could not depend on their inattention for long. The key rattled in the lock. Anticipation swelled inside of Esperanza as the door swung open.

Sadiya said, "I have done as you asked. What more would you have from me?" Her tone wavered. A fresh pang of regret budded inside Esperanza. The path to liberty awaited bold and decisive action. Esperanza could not turn away now.

"No sudden moves. If you remain calm, this will be over soon. Once Miriam and I leave Granada, you will never need to consider me again."

"You are wrong. I shall think of you forever with some regret."

"Step just inside the doorway. Slowly now."

"As you wish," the slave murmured.

Sadiya did so and Esperanza moved with her. With the tip of her toe, she pushed the wood back on its hinges. One of the sentries gasped and drew his sword. His sudden action caused the same behavior from the other man. Both shouted at Sadiya, who stayed silent.

Esperanza looked past Sadiya's shoulder to Miriam, who sat on her mat. She sang at full volume and spooned a thick, light-brown paste onto a slice of flatbread. She bit into it with a deep-throated sigh and chewed. The past two weeks of regular baths and hearty meals had enhanced her appearance. Perhaps her general disposition could improve as well. Today, her cheeks glistened with a pink glow and her hair spilled in black waves around her shoulders. A thin tunic of flimsy material revealed her form.

"Get up. We must leave this place at once," Esperanza urged.

Miriam's ever-present frown greeted her. A tic pulsed along the thin scar on her cheek. "Where will we go?"

A heady rush overcame Esperanza. Her gaze swerved twice between Miriam and the men at the door. She did not doubt they would try to overpower her given the opportunity. With her back against the doorpost, she fiddled with the key. "Miriam, do not delay! Don't you want to be free of this place?"

"It would seem her fate lies upon a different path."

Esperanza gulped at Juan Manuel's swift entry, unnoticed in her attempt to gain Miriam's compliance. Of all the times she might choose to be difficult, why this one? She could not worry for Miriam's idiocy now, when Juan Manuel leaned against the opposite doorpost. One of the men who had escorted Esperanza earlier stood at his back, while the pair outside Miriam's door awaited instructions from their master.

Deep within, Esperanza's stomach roiled. She had not expected a confrontation with Juan Manuel so soon. The sudden arrival of the inevitable moment left her resolve unaltered. "Tell your guards to withdraw, with orders to prepare three horses at once."

Juan Manuel cocked his head. "Three horses?"

"Sadiya comes with us to the northern gate of Granada. When we are outside the city, I will let her go. She may return to you and her wayward life."

When he said nothing and made no gesture to his men, she switched the dagger to the base of Sadiya's throat. The slave flinched. Her shoulders shook and a whimper escaped her lips.

Esperanza held back a desperate cry. "Please, I don't want to harm her."

Although Juan Manuel smiled, his expression lacked genuine warmth. "Always, you reveal the truth of yourself. You would no more hurt Sadiya than abandon the woman there who refuses to be a part of your misguided attempt. I have told you my gift of perception never fails. Once she revealed her true desire, I knew her aims differed from yours. She wants power and thinks to find it in the bed of the Sultan of Granada. You should not have placed your faith in her."

The breath caught in Esperanza's throat. She glanced at Miriam, who tossed her head and returned the stare with a narrowed gaze. Was Juan Manuel right about her? Had Miriam lost all hope because she thought life as a Sultan's concubine would suit her better? Would she abandon the past for such a desolate future?

Juan Manuel interrupted their silent rapport. "Whether you yield now or continue with this reckless farce, the result will be the same. You will come to regret this day's madness."

Her chest constricted with each breath. How had her design come undone so soon? Her peripheral gaze on Miriam, her eyes watered at the woman's disloyalty.

Juan Manuel's hand closed with unanticipated strength on her wrist. He squeezed without mercy until she cried out. The weapon clattered on the tiles. He kicked it away and wrenched her toward him. The fiery depths of his stare burned into hers.

Sadiya buried her moist face in her hands. Juan Manuel released his grip on Esperanza, who stumbled backward and gripped the doorpost with clenched fingers.

He enveloped Sadiya in his arms and kissed her brow. "Sweet child, are you hurt? Do not be frightened, you are safe again."

Despite her humble status, Juan Manual treated her as a treasured companion. Esperanza flattened her palm against her breastbone, the skin clammy. Recriminations flooded her and bound her stomach into tight knots. Memories of her beloved father and similar comforts stirred tears. Her turbulent emotions did not stem from bitter desire for the past alone. She had wronged Sadiya and betrayed her kindness.

With the edge of his tunic sleeve, Juan Manuel dabbed at a little spot, which welled within the thin cut at Sadiya's throat. When he looked up again, his glare rendered Esperanza speechless. She could not bear the hateful glint in his look and peered at the floor instead.

"Take her to the courtyard." The cold menace of his tone chilled her heart.

Two of his men seized her by the wrists, while the third kept his sword level with her stomach. She offered no resistance. Instead, she raised her head and peered at Miriam serene and at ease on her mat. She licked paste from her fingertips.

Esperanza demanded, "How could you betray me like this? We are friends. We have been for years! How can you just sit there and do nothing?"

Miriam lounged against the wall. "I have done something. I have preserved my life. You are responsible for our current circumstances. Concern for your father's well-being outweighed other interests, including freedom and safety. You have brought us both to this end. Your stupidity will not imperil me again, especially in this ill-starred scheme. My destiny remains in my hands alone. Whatever befalls you now derives from your own recklessness, *mi querida*."

Esperanza's heart lurched at Miriam's use of the once tender endearment. In the face of her wrath, the words became nothing more than a mockery of their assumed friendship. From now on, no ties would bind her to Miriam, a loss almost as painful as the deaths upon the plains.

Chapter 7
The Sultanas

Esperanza Peralta

Granada, Andalusia
February 15 - 20, AD 1336 / 2 - 7 Rajab 736 AH / 2nd - 7th of
Adar II, 5096

Sunlight blazed across the sky and cast its unrepentant glare on
Esperanza's face. After two weeks spent indoors without the
benefit of natural light, she emerged into the open air of a garden
courtyard. Morning dew and a thin layer of frost coated the
shrubs. Myrtle trees encircled the space. Elegant stone columns
ringed the shrubberies. Juan Manuel's men dragged her across
the grounds to the center of the garden. Four metal pegs affixed
with rings stabbed the earth. Fibrous rope looped through each
ring.

Esperanza's heart thrummed. They would tie her down,
staked out in the frigid morning air. The pair who held her now
shoved her onto the frost-covered grass between the pegs. One
grabbed her left wrist and the other held her right foot. She
kicked and clawed with her free limbs until the third man, who
had held his sword at her waist throughout their ascent from the
flight below, pressed the blade point against her neck. She
winced and shuddered. Her struggles subsided. The men who
knelt beside her tied the ropes at her wrists and ankles. They
wrenched her arms and legs apart with sharp tugs. A heavy
weight settled on her chest as it rose and fell with every ragged
breath.

Other sentries filed out into the daylight, almost fifty by her
count. Fifty guardsmen. The rashness of her enterprise filled her
thoughts with more reproaches. How could she have ever hoped
to escape from this place, under the protection of such a force?
Several of the sentries led, prodded, or forced a bedraggled lot of
unfortunates between the columns, three men, ten women, and
a child who appeared half of Esperanza's age. These were the
individuals whose desperate cries she had overheard each
morning while she visited Miriam. Miserable, fellow captives who
awaited any fate Juan Manuel would decree, just as she did.

He exited the whitewashed house and approached with hands clasped behind his back, a grim-faced expression for all those assembled. Sadiya did not reappear at his side. Had she frightened her more than she intended? Esperanza had acknowledged an inability to take the life of Juan Manuel's slave. Now, she would never leave this house except by his command. The truth damned her and revealed the idiocy of her ruse. She did not possess Miriam's cold prudence.

The woman had turned on her and still blamed her for their predicament. Their relations would never be the same after today's betrayal. Doubts often tormented Esperanza in the desolate dark of her cell at night and they returned now, most prominent among them the fear of some truth in Miriam's accusations. If so, then Miriam had cause to hold her responsible for their enslavement. Blame over the deaths of the child Palomba and Miriam's baby belong to Esperanza as well. How could she ever soothe those losses?

A moment's defiance reared up in the midst of her recriminations. Was her loss any less painful than Miriam's own? Her father's body lay abandoned on the plains of the *meseta*. All of their possessions were scattered to the wind, an easy prize for any passersby. Had the people of Alcaraz at least given her father a Christian burial? Had they perceived the scale of his valiant struggle? He had fought in vain for his child's one chance at escape and died in defense of her. By her inaction today, Miriam had made a mockery of Efrain Peralta's death and the murder of Miriam's own husband. Now, she sealed their fates as slaves forever lost in the heathen Mohammedan lands. Esperanza's heart beat a furious tattoo at the thought. She would not reconcile herself to a life in purgatory. Whatever her future beheld, she would have to find her own path to freedom, without Miriam.

Juan Manuel towered over her, his expression devoid of any sentiment. She gazed into the depths of his eyes and pressed her lips together. She refused a display of her turbulent emotions. Had she not promised him to survive against all the odds? Her father had held her to the same pledge. The memory strengthened her, even as he unclasped his hands. He hefted a rod twice the length and half the thickness of his forearm. Sinewy fibers bound the edge of the wood where he grasped it.

He turned from her and strolled around the courtyard. "I am a patient man. I reward good behavior with generosity and punish those who do not obey." He thumbed the wood in Esperanza's direction. "This captive sought flight from me and threatened the life of my favored servant in the process. I have called you here to witness this punishment and the extent of my mercy. Observe and learn. While I do not like to repeat lessons, I will do so again out of necessity. There is no escape from this place for any captive. To leave these walls with your lives intact, you shall depart as the property of another."

He switched from Castillan into Catalan. Then he repeated the same words in Latin, all for the benefit of those assembled in the courtyard. Some of the captives shrank whenever he approached. One woman even wept into her hands. All averted their stares from him. Although gladdened by her ability to understand him, each short speech heightened the enormity of the plight Esperanza shared with the others. If she had escaped, these unfortunates would have remained behind. She could no more bear the thought of their plight than the punishment her captor would dispense. No one deserved to live as a captive.

Juan Manuel returned to her side, his features impassive. She held her breath, poised for his punishment. He squatted at her side and touched the wooden truncheon to her cheek. She flinched, unable to stifle the instinctive response. The ropes at her wrists and ankles scraped and burned the skin.

"I am certain you have never witnessed the use of a bastinado before now. I take no pleasure in your punishment. You must learn your hopes are in vain."

She spat at him, "I will keep them! Nothing you can say or do will ever change me. Do what you must. One day, you shall regret your wicked ways. I'll make certain of it."

He ran the roughened tip of the wood along the curve of her flesh in a subtle caress. She jerked away from his touch and waited for him to prove himself as cruel as the Mohammedans who had stolen her future. A sigh whistled between his lips. He stood and moved to her feet. She held her breath and eyed him beneath lowered lids. Her cheeks warmed despite the chill in the air. Perspiration glided along her temple.

At a gesture from him, two of his men loosened the ropes, which immobilized her legs. A shudder suffused her. Each of them grasped her ankles and suspended her feet. Her stomach tightened. What monstrous torture followed?

The first heavy wallop of the wood against her bare sole drew a guttural yell from Esperanza, a cry of astonishment rather than hurt. Before she drew the next breath, the rod fell a second time. She pressed her lips together and jerked against the iron grasp of her captors. Tears spilled as the next whack jolted the breath from her body. Pain shot through her right foot. Soon, she lost count of the blows. Her shrieks descended into whimpers.

***

A fog of agony reduced Esperanza to a shell of her former self. She reclined on her side within the dank loneliness of her cell, a limp hand on her belly. Someone had closed the shutter and blocked out the sunlight. Her sobs subsided with each moment until the breath no longer hitched inside her chest at every intake. Juan Manuel's men returned her to confinement. She remained alone, until the cell door creaked and a torch illuminated the bleak chamber. Leather sandals slapped against the tiles.

"Sadiya?" Esperanza croaked as she raised her head. Her vision swam, unfocused while she peered in desperation at the blurred form before her.

Callused fingers on her ankles warned another had taken Sadiya's place. She pulled away from the unwelcome touch. A firm grip held her fast. Instead of Sadiya's velvet purr, a gruff tone followed. She could not understand a word. She gave up and shrank against her pallet. Liquid sluiced over her battered feet followed by the scrape of cloth. She bit her lower lip until she tasted blood on the tip of her tongue. Time passed outside of her full awareness. She winced when cloth bandages wound around her feet. Her gaze sharpened on the sour-faced woman with charcoal colored skin, as she hefted the basin of water tinged pink and left the room without another word. The sentinels just inside the doorway followed her from the room. The door closed with a resonant bang and jarred Esperanza. A sharp tremor spiked at the base of her neck. She surrendered to the darkness.

Days and nights blurred together, stillness shattered by calls to prayer. The same woman returned with food, evidencing no care or concern as the meals went untouched. In those cold moments, Esperanza regretted Sadiya's absence. She might never see her again. Aches throbbed through the soles of her feet and penetrated Esperanza's awareness. She roused herself once, reaching for a bowl of congealed stew and vegetables, yellowed grease floating in globs on the surface. Dots floated across her gaze. She squeezed her eyes shut before she opened them again. Her attempts hurt too much. With a groan, she reclined on her back and drifted to sleep.

A sharp pinch on her hip stirred her. The rough-skinned woman, who still had not revealed her name, knelt at her side. She thumbed Esperanza's chest and gesticulated at the door with a tone almost as coarse as her touch. Still, one word became clear with each strident pronouncement from her fleshy lips. "*Hammam.*"

Then the woman went out and returned with the sentries in tow. Both men reached for Esperanza and dragged her to her feet. Panic rose and ebbed in an instant, as hellfire licked at the bottom of her feet. The men half-dragged, half-carried her down the corridors. Her screams echoed against the walls. They cast her into the changing room, where three male bath attendants swarmed around and removed her clothes. She batted at their hands and warded them off. When she broke free and skidded on the tiles, a red blotch smeared across the floor. The slaves restrained her again. She still fought, while they stripped her of the same garments she had worn in the garden courtyard. They bore her through the rooms of the bathhouse and washed her body, despite all protests.

At the end of the ordeal, they deposited her on a stone slab, naked and wet with hair pasted on her back. Juan Manuel waited on the seat opposite her. She dragged a long linen cloth over her torso and glared at him. He waved away the men, even as one reached for a damp cloth and wiped at the bloodstain.

Juan Manuel drew Esperanza's attention. "The fire in your gaze reminds me of another who belonged to me."

"Did your slaves also abuse her?" She shivered and draped the material over her legs. "Did she have to endure the intimate touch of strange men?"

"They are not men. They are eunuchs."

She gave a slight shake of her head. "I do not understand what that means."

"No man keeps other men around the women in his household, if he wishes to assure himself of their purity. *Sí*, he relies upon eunuchs, boys and men who have been castrated, their sexual organs removed."

She froze, robbed of her speech.

"All of the guards and the male attendants you have encountered here are eunuchs. How else might I ensure captives are not raped by my own household servants?" When she remained silent, he went on, "The one I spoke of, she understood the role of eunuchs for she lived in Byzantium before her capture and sale. I found her tractable. You are not. In time, she endeared herself to me. I would not part with her. I held too many excuses to delay or put off a sale. My devotion stirred the envy of a former steward. He thought I held an unnatural infatuation for the captive and drowned her in the bath. I had the place walled up afterward, my steward sealed alive behind the masonry. One day, his screams stopped. The more superstitious among my household say his specter haunts the house. It does not trouble me. Instead, I often recall the girl's bright, bold gaze."

She stared in silence. Why had he chosen to tell her this tale of woe?

"Have I shocked you?" He leaned forward and rested his chin on clasped hands.

"After your cruelty of days past, you can do nothing to surprise me."

His gaze tracked the crimson trail from the entrance to the changing room, across the tiles and to the chamber beyond. In a sudden movement, he rose and crouched in front of her. She winced and kept her limbs rigid. His feather-light touch probed her swollen feet. She tugged at her lower lip with her teeth.

He murmured, "*Sí*, no broken bones. Good, for I did not intend to leave you enfeebled."

"A crippled captive would cause you no further trouble."

His laughter pealed. "You acknowledge your state as a captive then?"

She closed her eyes and blotted out the hateful sight of him.

"No, you would never admit how your condition has altered. You yearn for freedom, impermissible within these walls. Will you wait here and let me return with a fresh poultice and bandages for your feet?"

"Do I have a choice?"

"You do not. Still, I would prefer it if you did not seek to leave. The welts would bleed again. Await me. No one shall trouble you here, not even the bath attendants."

She pressed her back against the wall. His footfalls departed. The stillness of the room lulled her. Even the intense throbs in her soles ceased. When a doorway creaked, she opened her eyes again. Juan Manuel returned alone. He bore crisp linens and a bowl. The scent of juniper and mint wafted from the vessel. He knelt at her feet once more and attended her. He patted and dried the skin before he applied the warm poultice. How odd. The man responsible for her agony sought to soothe her.

"Where is Sadiya?" she asked.

His movements stilled. "Do not think of her further."

"You must believe me. She must. I never meant to hurt Sadiya—"

He jerked to his feet and mashed his hand against her mouth. His action silenced a sudden cry. He shook his head. "Do not. Do not speak her name. You could never understand my regard for her. She is the daughter I shall never have. You cannot know how I have cherished her or the number of times I have granted her freedom. She has refused each time and pleaded to remain with me. She should marry and have children of her own. She does not desire such a life. Surprise colors your cheeks. Did you think I held some perverse intention toward her? You assumed I bedded my slave?"

He loosened his hold a little, enough to permit a shake of her head.

"*Sí*, I love her, but in the manner a father reserves for his child. I could have killed you for your attempt. Do you understand my affection for Sadiya? Even a would-be father would do anything for his child."

When she nodded, his hand fell away.

She glared at him. "My father held the same love for me. The Mohammedans destroyed it when they killed him and left his body without the benefit of burial."

He bandaged her feet without comment before he answered, "No one can alter the bond between parents and their children. It endures beyond death."

He stood. "Now, you must wait here again. I shall send a servant to massage you, dry and dress your hair. You will also have fresh garments. Your days here are almost at an end. The Sultanas come at midday on the morrow."

She stiffened. "So soon?" Had the week come and gone with such haste?

"*Sí*, so you must eat well today. Your ribs are poking out again, too much for my liking. *El Dio* reveals your fate, whether you shall find a place within the Sultan's household or not."

"This is not my fate, but your desire," she muttered.

He reached for her chin and held it between his thumb and index finger. When she recoiled, his hold tightened. "No matter where life may take you, our destinies are now intertwined. I shall be the better for your residency here, Esperanza Peralta."

She jerked away from his touch. "I cannot say the same. You've stolen my dreams and ruined my future."

He replied, "Or, I have set you on the path to a brighter one revealed with time. Meet the future with the same fortitude with which you have endured the House of Myrtles. I do not doubt your destiny shall be great."

***

Dawn broke and cast its pale pink hue over the sky. Esperanza reclined on her pallet in the center of the cell. Her gaze tracked the light as it intruded and traipsed along the wall to the floor. The ever-present call to prayer stirred her from sleep. Her stiff muscles refused to move. A tender throb still pierced her soles, but had subsided to a dull ache in the night, with the aid of Juan Manuel's poultice. No such a balm existed to soothe her wearied soul and ease her mind, fraught with visions of a dreadful life among the Mohammedans. She did not welcome sunrise, not when its arrival heralded greater uncertainty.

Instead of the recalcitrant slave who brought her meals and ushered her to the bath, Juan Manuel opened her cell door. Resplendent in a red *pellote* with gold embroidery at the hem and wrists, a lengthy stride in his leather boots brought him to her.

"A glorious day. Did you sleep well, Esperanza?" He crouched and cupped her cheek.

She stifled a natural instinct to pull away.

He murmured, "You did, though not as well as I would have hoped. There are dark circles under your eyes. Never mind them. Sadiya will erase such faults from your fine skin."

With a gasp, she sat up.

He said, "*Sí*, she will come for you. You shall not speak to her nor trouble her for any reason. Do you understand me?"

She swallowed and nodded. Sadiya would never forgive the betrayal.

Juan Manuel lifted her chin and framed her face between his long fingers. "I require perfection from you today, for the Sultanas. Can you do this?"

Esperanza answered his question with her own. "Who are these women?"

"They are the relatives of Sultan Yusuf, the Sultana Safa, and the Sultana Leila. Both share equal power in the harem. If the gossip is true, theirs is a tenuous peace. The harem can be a dangerous place for those who are not careful. Captives who pass beyond the walls remain there at the mercy of the royal women, for it is their domain. Believe me when I say these women possess power over life and death. With a few words, they can change your circumstances for better or worse in an instant. You must be cautious and clever. Subdue your impetuous nature and learn from them, if you hope to survive."

"What will they want from me?"

He shrugged. "They will accept nothing less than your obedience at the start. Perhaps in time, they will demand an heir for Yusuf. The possibilities are limitless, as you shall discover."

"Who is this Yusuf?"

"He is a son of the Sultan Ismail, a proud and cultured man assassinated by his kinsmen almost eleven years ago. Yusuf is much like his father. He is the seventh ruler of Granada from his family line, the Nasrids. He became the sovereign when his elder brother Muhammad was also murdered, two years past."

Esperanza sucked in her breath. "You expect me to live among such barbarous people."

Juan Manuel's mouth twisted into a wry smile. "I suggest you temper those misguided words. The Nasrids do not forgive too soon and none would relish your opinion of them. They have been among my benefactors since the time of Yusuf's grandmother. Theirs is an illustrious heritage."

"One also mired in blood."

He mused, "Perhaps. Perhaps more than their fair share. So, I ask you, tread with caution among these Nasrid Sultanas. They are women of influence and advantage, whose collective will dominates the existence of everyone in the harem. The one person they do not exercise authority over is the Sultan, the master of all."

Her heart pounded. Was this to be her final fate, subjected to the whim of these women and their master forever?

"Put aside the past and accept the destiny before you. There is no escape as you envision it. The life you have lived, the person you once were is gone forever. There is no one named Esperanza Peralta from Talavera de la Reina in this new existence. Just the woman she may become. When the Sultanas arrive at the auction, each shall bid upon you. The winner shall be your mistress. Once you enter the harem, she shall grant you a new name. Embrace it. If you heed my admonitions, you may find what you seek in Yusuf's palace. Think of all the potential paths you may find to your heart's true desire there," he cajoled.

She snorted and glared at him. "I am to gain my liberty among the women you have described? I should submit to a Mohammedan and cavort in his bed? You mistake me for Miriam if you believe I would want such a life."

Juan Manuel settled beside her on the pallet. She drew up her legs with a wince. He rubbed a hand over his long face and regarded her.

"The Jewess has disappointed you—"

"You know nothing of my relations with her! As you would have me keep silent about your slave, do not speak to me of Miriam!"

She blinked back the tears. The wound of betrayal, still too fresh, ached deep within. He kept silent while she stared at a vacant spot in the corner of the room.

Then she said, "I do not accept this life you would have for me. You can keep me here and beat me for stubbornness or barter me to these women, I shall cling to my hopes for better."

He rested his fingers atop hers. The tips skimmed her flesh. She allowed the gentle gesture. She grew tired of the resistance against his attempts at intimacy and a rapport between them.

He told her, "I was once like you, idealistic and naïve. I believed myself the ruler of my own fate. *El Dio* had other plans for me. He often leads us along unexpected paths to find what we need."

"You and I do not serve the same god. Sadiya led me to believe you are not a Christian. Have you embraced the Mohammedan god, as you have accepted their ways?"

"Esperanza, Moors, Christians, and Jews serve the same master in heaven. We each call Him by a different name. Sadiya has not deceived you. I am not a Christian, nor am I a Muslim. I am a Jew, like your Miriam. My mother's people suffered tragedy at the court in Toledo more than a hundred years ago, after King Alfonso's loss at the battle of Alarcos. In my boyhood, my mother often told stories of this ruler and his tragic love for Rahel Esra, *la fermosa* to her lover. Less pleasant were tales of the near annihilation of our bloodline. My great-grandfather Naphtali, younger than you at the time, escaped into Granada with his younger brother Simeon. But not before both boys witnessed their own father and aunt, Rahel *la fermosa,* murdered along with the remainder of their relatives."

She regarded him again. Why had she dismissed his references to God as *El Dio* before? Miriam often used the same term. "Your ancestor found a haven among the Mohammedans."

"*Sí,* for a time, he practiced the Jewish religion without fear of papal bulls. The Church has always forbidden our public processions, even at funerals. They even forced us to don yellow badges on our clothes. The Moors still abide by the Pact of Umar, who was one of their first rulers. They would not let my people construct new synagogues either. At least they permitted repairs to the ones we had established and did not destroy them. I have always assumed my line would end with me. I have never discovered another whom I wanted more than the captive girl that I loved and lost to my steward's treachery."

Her vision misted. She could have pitied him, if not for his part in her miserable condition.

Juan Manuel continued, "I speak to you of my heritage and the experiences of my family because they should be examples for you. You have lost your father and freedom. In the midst of tragedy, *El Dio* often reveals the path before us. Who are we to go against His will?"

***

Sadiya came as her master commanded. He remained in the cell when she brought flatbread, goat cheese, and dates. A cup brimmed with snow colored a pale red. Esperanza peered into the vessel and looked at him. A charmed countenance greeted her.

"It is *sharbah,* a delight even in the wintry months. From the mountains around Granada, the Moors bring donkeys laden with snow packed into wooden crates. Here is a blend of pomegranate and crushed rose petals. Taste it."

Under his watchful gaze, Esperanza ate everything. Afterward, she accompanied a silent Sadiya to the bath. A filmy mixture of rosewater, melon juice, and milk coated her face before an attendant rinsed it away. Then Esperanza cleaned her teeth with a paste called *ghasul* applied to a fibrous stick with a pungent odor, the *miswak.* She spent the rest of the morning in the usual ritual of hair removal, scrubs, and washes, followed by a massage with almond oil until her skin glistened.

Sadiya issued terse commands to the other slaves. No resentment altered her emerald gaze, but it never softened as in the past. Esperanza resigned herself to Sadiya's mere tolerance and tried to let the attendants do as they willed.

One who applied a creamy mixture of ground chamomile, powdered almonds, and honey to the corners of Esperanza's eyes raked her nail across tender skin. Esperanza pulled away. She earned the woman's ire and a slap.

Sadiya pushed her fellow slave aside. "*Idiota!*"

A terse exchange followed between Sadiya and the attendant, soon dismissed in favor of another who proved more patient. Esperanza would have thanked Sadiya for her intervention but the slave motioned for her to sit on a heated stone slab. Courage fled in the next breath.

Sadiya twisted and braided Esperanza's hair with strands of pearls. More of the translucent pink stones wound about her throat, wrists and ankles until they weighed upon her. Sadiya pinched her cheeks none too hard and made her press her lips together.

"For color," she said in the first words spoken to Esperanza since their reunion.

At Sadiya's beckon, Esperanza stood and slipped an almost sheer lavender robe over her head. Citrus peel suffused the loose silken garment. Her eyes watered at the shameful display of flesh. She blinked back the tears and gulped several breaths. She calmed with each exhalation. A braided belt with pearls at the tip wound about her waist and kept the robe closed.

From a glass vial, Sadiya dabbed a musky fluid at her neck and between her breasts, her wrists, and ankles. A second application of the mint and juniper poultice eased the dull ache in her soles. Bandages wound around her feet before Sadiya offered kid slippers dyed pristine white. Esperanza slipped her feet into them, grateful for the padded comfort. For the first time in a few days, she relied upon her own strength to stand and walk unaided.

In silence, Esperanza followed Sadiya from the bath and through the corridor. At a corner where they would have returned to her cell, the slave opened a door and revealed stairs, different from the ones Esperanza had climbed on the morning Juan Manuel's eunuchs escorted her to the courtyard for punishment. Near the top of the steps, they walked down a short corridor. At its end, Sadiya pushed aside the bright orange door curtain and stepped inside. Esperanza trailed her.

Juan Manuel awaited them within the chamber, as did Miriam. Sunlight peeked through the arched window at her back, pierced a gossamer black robe, and revealed the flesh. Her breasts heaved as she drew breath. Faint shadows encircled the nipples made visible through the gauzy cloth. Inky hair fell on either side of her face and curled at her hips in thick ringlets. Golden beads shimmered on several strands and created a dramatic effect.

A full month after the abuses she had endured at the hands of the Mohammedan Fadil, the restoration of her full beauty staggered Esperanza. There was no trace of Miriam's former scars and bruises. A heavy gold necklace adorned her. Its oval obsidian pendant hung between her breasts. A disk of gold affixed with the same obsidian jewels at the center dangled from each earlobe, suspended from thin gold wire, which perforated the flesh. Miriam must have allowed the piercing days ago, for Esperanza had never seen her with earrings. Bracelets, anklets and a belt festooned with gold completed her finery. No shoes covered her feet, the toenails colored red. A ruby flush colored her cheeks and red pigment stained her lips. She wore *kohl* around her eyes like Sadiya. Her harsh squint intensified and became fixated on Esperanza.

Miriam's mouth fell open and her fingers, painted with dark circles and dots, touched her parted lips. Her eyebrows flared and then she lowered her hand. Juan Manuel blocked Esperanza's vision of her as he moved between them. He grasped Esperanza's shoulders. His gaze traipsed over her form from head to toe. She focused on his face and ignored the heat on her cheeks, which crept down her neck. Her chest rose and fell with each ragged breath, audible in the stillness of the room.

He uttered a deep-throated sigh and his hold tightened. "You are perfect."

Miriam's short, disgusted snort echoed behind him. Both he and Esperanza glanced at her with frowns. Then Juan Manuel said, "Stand beside the Jewess, *niña*. The midday prayer finished an hour ago. I anticipate the arrival of the Sultanas at any moment. Have courage."

He loosened his hold and waved Esperanza forward. On wooden legs, she joined her counterpart who stood with an unpleasant, twisted mouth. Even if Miriam had spoken the first words since her betrayal, Esperanza doubted her ability to answer. Her throat tightened and her hands curled into little fists at her side. Nails scored her palm.

She ignored Miriam's presence and instead studied Sadiya and Juan Manuel, who exchanged a few murmured words. Then the slave bowed and crossed the room in anticipation of her master's leave-taking. She sat near the entryway against a pile of cushions with her legs drawn up beneath her. He paused in the doorway and offered long stares to Esperanza and Miriam, whose sharp chin jutted.

A covered ceramic inkpot, a thin wooden reed, and a brass scale were beside Sadiya's feet. More cushions lined the walls, except the area adjacent Miriam and Esperanza. Here, a stone dais rose one level above the floor. Another carpet covered all except the edges and two wooden, high-backed chairs fronted a latticework partition. On a round table between them, steam rose from a glass pitcher surrounded small cups. One roll of sheepskin rested alongside the vessels. Braziers emitted a heady white vapor. The scent of camphor vied with some other sweet odor. Brass lanterns affixed to the walls illuminated the recesses.

"No amount of perfume or fine clothes shall change you for the better."

Esperanza held her breath despite Miriam's caustic remark.

"Do you intend to ignore me now? We stand here because of you."

"No!" Esperanza's vehement whisper shattered the din. "You have chosen this moment. You made your decision in the days beforehand to accept life among the Mohammedans, when we could have aided each other in escape. I shall never forgive you for your part in our misery. Do not blame me, not when your selfish aims have forced us upon this path together."

She lifted her chin and returned Miriam's glare. "Say what you will of my recklessness in our circumstances. You have done nothing to help. Your disdain for my feelings has revealed your true nature. I cannot believe how you deceived me all these years. I thought we were friends."

"A foolish error of the past forever removed from mind, Esperanza."

"Now I know better."

"Nothing stays the same. I have long recognized from girlhood, we could never be constant friends. We shared a companionable relationship, little more. We are not and could never be equals. Your future shall differ from mine, one I intend to find in the bed of this Yusuf of Granada. Perhaps I shall even occupy his heart in time. Do what you must to survive. I will not let you impede my plans again."

"I want nothing to do with your schemes. You may have this Yusuf. I shall have my heart's desire."

The pair lapsed into silence. Esperanza kept the stupid tears at bay and ignored Sadiya's watchful gaze. Nothing could assuage her gloom, not even the commiseration of another. How could Miriam have undone the past and broken with her so soon? Could their experiences with the Mohammedans have ruined and scarred them forever? Perhaps, Miriam might be right. The boundaries between them had always existed, a rift neither could bridge.

She glanced at Miriam again. "You used to call me '*mi querida*' in pleasurable days before this nightmare engulfed both of our lives. Did you once mean the endearment? Was there ever a time when our differences did not govern your feelings? Have you cared for me at all?"

Miriam sniffed and stared straight ahead. "If you need to ask, even after all I have said, then you will never accept the truth. For a time, my father and later my husband secured patronage through your father. When we were children, relations between the men inspired a semblance of companionship between us."

"Just a semblance?"

Miriam glanced at her. "These three men are gone as are the bonds between us, Esperanza. We must each make our own way in the world. The moment arrives in which you should choose to learn this final lesson."

The rumble of Juan Manuel's voice warned of his approach. He led his guests and at the door hanging, he ushered them ahead of him. Two women strolled into the room, their footfalls in unison. Even if Esperanza did not already possess some familiarity with their identities, she would have known them for royal women anywhere. The pair took their seats on the high-backed chairs. Female slaves arranged themselves upon the dais, arrayed in bright silks with their faces uncovered, unlike their mistresses. Whereas the royal women dazzled in fine jewels, thin blackened metal collars encircled the left ankle of each bondwoman.

The slender woman closest to the doorway raised bejeweled, creased fingers painted with intricate patterns in *henna*. She loosened the white gossamer folds of the veil and tugged it below her pointed chin. Prominent blue veins ridged the back of her hand. Her thin eyebrows arched like crescents over large brown eyes, crinkled at the corners. High cheekbones flared in a narrow face. The yellow light cast by braziers caught and reflected in her stare, which flitted to her companion, who also removed an opaque indigo veil from the lower half of her face. The material on her head slipped a little and exposed dark brown, coiled tendrils at her forehead.

She appeared younger than her counterpart did. Her heavy-lidded gaze, lined with thick *kohl*, fell on Esperanza and the eyes widened. Her tapered brows rose for an instant before she leaned forward. Voluptuous lips parted and curved in a smile. Dimples appeared and her olive-brown cheeks became flushed. The elder woman beside her with her sharp features in profile now followed the direction of her stare.

Esperanza peered at the base of the carpeted dais, but not before she marked a sudden exchange of glowers between the women. Had the younger woman's obvious interest sparked some jealousy?

A harsh breath escaped Esperanza's lips. She fisted her hands in the folds of her delicate robe. Juan Manuel's caution regarding a possible rivalry between the Sultanas raised concerns. Life among such women would be dangerous. If power resided with them, when they conspired against each other, neither woman would consider the consequences for the harem's occupants—least of all Esperanza.

She focused on the present moment and took in their rich garments. Black ankle-length leather boots peeked out from their clothes. Brocaded robes covered them from the neckline downward. Gold thread shot through the blue-green material of the younger Sultana's dress, dotted with turquoise, emerald and gold beads in bird motifs. The other royal woman wore a dusky silken robe, turned back to display a red damask lining edged with gold filigree. Where their robes parted at the knees, the same gauzy trousers as Sadiya often donned also covered their lower legs to the top of their footwear. All of Juan Manuel's finery paled in comparison to their attire.

He bowed and spoke with the women in their native tongue. Both responded, the elder in a husky tone, the younger Sultana with a sonant, amused lilt in her voice. Again, Esperanza regretted her inability to understand their exchange. She did not dare ask Miriam about the conversation. She might refuse to convey the words or lie about their import. How had trust dissolved so soon between them?

Juan Manuel approached them and rounded Miriam. He still spoke words Esperanza could not understand. She relied upon on his actions and the almost whimsical speech he adopted for cues. She guessed at how he extolled Miriam's virtues, his hand first upon her chin and then her rounded shoulder, before he lifted her arm. Even the brown blotches and old scars earned in her father's trade appeared less prominent in the daylight. Her skin glowed with vitality and good health.

Miriam's present disposition made it impossible to consider her as another lamb doomed for slaughter. Still, Esperanza could not avoid the comparison. Between the trio, Juan Manuel and the Sultanas, they would now decide Miriam's fate. Esperanza's bitterness did not recede even when she acknowledged Miriam wanted the life the women offered.

With a wave of her hand, the elder woman halted the barrage of conversation. She spoke and Juan Manuel nodded an acknowledgment, before he whispered in Miriam's ear. She responded with a stark gaze for the space of several breaths. His nostrils flared and a mottled hue colored his cheeks. Then her hands went to the golden belt.

He released an audible sigh before he glanced at Esperanza. "Move back against the wall beside the window, if you please. The Sultana Safa wishes to examine your companion."

"Examine her?" Esperanza's voice echoed in the stillness of the room.

The other Sultana looked at her with dark eyes, sea green to match the color of her robe. The corners of her mouth upturned in a preoccupied smile, she stared almost in a daze.

Esperanza averted her gaze and brushed against the wall behind her. Miriam's garment pooled at her feet. Naked, she stood with her hands clasped behind her back. Although Esperanza wished for an escape, her peripheral gaze revealed how Miriam remained stiff while both women approached her. A flurry of words passed between the pair and Juan Manuel, who gestured for Miriam to turn. When she did so, her breasts swayed. With slits for eyes, her unrepentant stare challenged Esperanza's own again.

The Sultanas circled Miriam and scrutinized her form, predators committed to the kill. The elder woman lifted her brows, her lips pursed. She pinched the alabaster flesh on Miriam's arm and provoked a bold and direct stare. A lesser woman might have shriveled. Though Miriam stood taller than she did, the woman showed no sign of intimidation. Rather, her face colored and deep lines crinkled her forehead. Her lips compressed in a thin line before she raised her hand and slapped Miriam across the cheek.

Flushed, Miriam recoiled. The Sultana grasped her arm and kept her still. Rounded nails colored a deep red dug into the skin. Juan Manuel clasped his hands together and addressed his guest. While the woman issued some terse words, she kept a tight hold. Her companion took in the scene with a close-lipped smile. Then she sought Esperanza's regard again before she took her seat again. The elder Sultana joined her thereafter.

Esperanza released a pent-up breath, before Miriam's stony expression alighted on her again. A scarlet mark blossomed on her cheek. Juan Manuel cupped her elbow while he spoke in a low tone. She turned her malevolent glare on him and shrugged off his hold before she faced the women again, her back rigid.

Juan Manuel rubbed his hands together and approached his guests. He bowed low before the elder of them. She leaned aside and spoke to the woman closest to her, who addressed Juan Manuel in a sharp tone. He nodded and gestured to the other Sultana, who also had one of her servants make a reply.

While this strange method of communication continued, Esperanza surmised how the offers became fervent. The strident tone of the older Sultana vied with the delighted voice of her companion. When the clash of voices ceased, the crooked grin on the elder Sultana's lips and the glitter in her eyes conveyed triumph. Her counterpart gave Miriam a squint-eyed glance before she shrugged. A thin crease between her brows relaxed. She said something to one of her slaves, who poured a warm brew from the pitcher into a cup and placed it in her mistress' hands. The Sultana tilted her head and took the drink. As she sipped, her forehead crinkled again before she imbibed more.

Juan Manuel retrieved the parchment from the table. He crouched and whispered to Sadiya, who reached for the ink and reed. Soon, its tip scratched across the page. At a gesture from Juan Manuel, Miriam pulled on her robe and belted it. He waved her to the far corner.

Tremors coursed through Esperanza's body. Perspiration trickled down her back. Her robe clung to her skin. She shook her head, a scream trapped in her throat. Could Miriam's life have altered in one moment? Once, she had known another existence as a daughter, a wife, and mother. Now she would be nothing: the property of another. The same fate awaited Esperanza.

Chapter 8
Sold

Esperanza Peralta

Granada, Andalusia
February 20 - April 19, AD 1336 / 7 Rajab – 7 Ramadan 736 AH
/ 7th of Adar II - 7th of Iyar, 5096

Juan Manuel touched Esperanza's shoulder. She flinched. His grip tightened and he steadied her. "They will ask you to disrobe, the same as they have done with Miriam."

She groped at the smooth *cendal* of his *pellote*. "I don't think I can do this."

He offered her a small smile and stroked her upper arm. His whisper washed over her. "*Sí*, you can. You have survived the Moors and my commands. You will endure the demands of these Sultanas, of this new life."

Without another word, he left her. She peered at Miriam, whose tight-lipped sneer and lowered brows made her appear an older woman. Esperanza pressed her palms against the wall behind her and drew deep breaths, while Juan Manuel addressed the Sultanas again. Within moments, he beckoned Esperanza with a crooked finger. She took the first agonized step, her limbs heavy.

He instructed her, "You will remove your robe now."

With her hand pressed against her waist, she fingered the tassels of the belt affixed with pearls. She shook and sought to loosen the knot. All her efforts were in vain. Her fingertips would not cooperate. A little cry escaped her.

Sadiya set aside her implements and stood. She offered her master a slight bow and he returned a nod. She clasped her hands together and approached Esperanza. Sunlight revealed the discolored nick at her throat.

Her hands covered Esperanza's own. "This will soon be over. Do not dwell upon this moment. It is one in a lifetime, meant to test your mettle. You have shown my master courage, but let me aid you."

Esperanza whispered, "You shouldn't want to help me again after what I did."

"You did what you felt was necessary, as we all must do in life."

Sadiya brushed her fingers aside and worked at the knot. The belt slid away. The slave slipped her hands inside the robe. Her hands skimmed Esperanza's taut abdomen and ascended to her shoulders. Sadiya spread the edges of the garment and pushed it off Esperanza's shoulders. When she would have covered whatever she could of her exposed parts, Sadiya shook her head and stepped aside.

Esperanza shivered as cool air intruded from the window. Her knees knocked together. A chill swept through her and little bumps pimpled her arms. Her bottom lip trembled. She kept the tears at bay. Instead, with her gaze on the floor she focused on one point as a wave of nausea threatened. When a quick, disgusted snort from Miriam echoed from the corner, she still did not look up.

What began as a throaty chuckle and developed into full-blown laughter made her raise her head. The elder Sultana pressed a hand to her belly and almost doubled over with peals of delight. Juan Manuel's gaze darted to her. His features remained impassive. Then she spoke to him in a rich, husky tone and waved a dismissive hand in Esperanza's direction. One of the women seated at her feet offered her a small square of cloth with which the Sultana dabbed at her cheeks. Her mirth soon subsided.

Lethargy seeped through Esperanza's limbs and she staggered. Sadiya's sudden grasp at her elbow caused her to flinch. The slave steadied her. Esperanza repressed the cry in her throat. The tightness across her chest increased.

The younger Sultana rolled her eyes before she stood. With nimble steps, she withdrew from the circle of her entourage and approached. She halted less than an arm's span away from Esperanza. They stood the same height.

Without preamble, the Sultana asked, "Why are your feet in slippers?"

A crisp tone and easy use of the Castillan language startled Esperanza. Before she could summon an answer, the Sultana turned to Juan Manuel. "Is it your custom, señor Gomero, to pamper a captive? Your merchandise always appears in suitable attire, but this one received a little more attention. Why does she wear shoes while the other in the corner does not?"

He began, "A good question, my Sultana." A hitch in his voice, he ran long fingers over his hair.

"It is why I asked it," she snapped. Her enigmatic stare met Esperanza's own again. "Remove them and show me your feet."

Esperanza looked beyond her to Juan Manuel, his mouth in a wide O before he closed it and backed away to the wall behind him. Sadiya released Esperanza before she bent and did as instructed. She revealed her bandaged feet, still somewhat swollen. At a gesture from the Sultana, she removed the linen wrappings.

"Now, lift one of your feet so I may view the underside."

Esperanza did so, a little unsteady on one leg. The Sultana whistled at the purple crisscrossed lines visible through the mashed juniper and mint concoction. "Lower the leg. You have been scourged with a bastinado in recent days. The resultant welts and bruises are more vivid than those left by a simple rod. You are healing well. Why were you beaten?"

Esperanza's gaze fled to Juan Manuel again. The Sultana grasped her chin and held her gaze. "You will regard me when I address you. Unlike some," her sidelong glance darted to the left where the other Sultana sat, "I require my slaves to look me in the eyes, for I desire the truth. The eyes reveal much. Yours fill with fright and despair. Why are you afraid? Do you think to hide the reason for your reprimand from me? Are you a liar by nature?"

"It is no trait of mine! Earlier this week, I tried to escape and in doing so, threatened the life of this favored slave at my side. Her master punished me."

"He has not subdued you, has he? There is something else behind these eyes, a refusal to submit."

Her lips pursed, the thin line between the Sultana's brows reappeared. She tapped a forefinger against her mouth before she spoke again. "Bodily imperfections can be overlooked, such as a stick-thin form or feet larger than most, if other attributes recommend a captive. A defect I cannot overlook is of the mind, which can lead to rash thoughts. Dangerous musings expose others to peril. I'll say this—you have courage beyond your youthful years." Then she turned to Juan Manuel. "She remains too reckless. I will not buy her today either."

His widened gaze matched the other Sultana's own. The young woman returned to the table and downed the contents of the glass. "Thank you for the tea, señor. The best I have ever tasted. It rivals anything brewed in the harem." She traded a knowing glance with her counterpart. "At least your time was not wasted, Safa. Shall you formalize the sale so we can return home? I remind you of Yusuf's invitation to share his meal this evening. I would rest before dinner."

Esperanza's watery gaze slid to the floor. She covered her pubis with her hands, unable to fathom the afternoon's events.

Miriam sold into Granada's royal harem, while Esperanza would remain behind subject to an unknown fate, still captive in the House of Myrtles.

Juan Manuel ordered Sadiya to take Miriam back to her cell, where she could change into other attire for the journey. "Return soon with the Sultana's slave, sweet child."

Miriam's new owner snapped, "How much longer must I wait? I would conclude our business and leave this place." She cast a glare around the room, as if she had noticed the decor for the first time and found it unacceptable. As if she had not spent her last moments humiliating Esperanza with her laughter or abusing Miriam upon a whim, before she subjected her to a life of servitude.

"But a moment, I promise, o queen of queens," Juan Manuel assured her.

While Sadiya led Miriam from the room, one of the elder Sultana's women, frail and haggard in appearance, brought forth a small bag tied with a red string. From within, she produced a handful of gold coins and leaned toward the brass scale's weighing pan.

Esperanza closed her eyes and blotted out the sight. She could not drown out the repetitive clink of metal against metal. The final coin added equated to the value of Miriam's life, in the view of her new mistress. These Mohammedans set the worth of a person with no care to an individual's past or desires for the future. Tears squeezed under Esperanza's lashes. Why had God abandoned her in such a desolate place, condemned to uncertainty among these vicious barbarians?

She opened her eyes again at the velvet purr of Sadiya's voice. Miriam stood just beyond the door curtain, the redness on her cheeks dissipated a little. She wore black again. A voluminous robe fell from her neckline to her feet, where the tips of her toes peeked out. Her thick braid hung over her right shoulder.

Esperanza peered at her and willed Miriam to do the same. She would not comply. After the exchange of coins and the sale document, to which Juan Manuel had affixed his signet in red wax, the elder Sultana shoved the sheepskin at the same person who carried the moneybag. Then the Sultana stepped out into the corridor. Her narrowed gaze reviewed Miriam's form. Creases deepened in the ridges of the old woman's forehead and her mouth crimped. She beckoned her retinue with a crooked, whippet-thin finger.

Miriam fell into step among the Sultana's servants. She would leave without a word in final farewell or even a last glance. A knot burgeoned in Esperanza's throat and kept her silent when she would have called out instead. The edge of Miriam's robe disappeared around the corner, gone from sight forever. Esperanza bowed her head. They would never see each other again.

The younger Sultana trailed behind the other women. Just at the doorway, she ushered her entourage ahead of her and turned around. Her enigmatic gaze swept over Esperanza, her features impassive. Then she gave a slight nod in Esperanza's direction before she departed from the room.

When only Juan Manuel, Esperanza, and Sadiya remained, the slave approached. She retrieved Esperanza's robe and ushered her into it. "Would you catch your death of cold? Come now."

Juan Manuel leaned against the wall and stared hard at the gold coins in the weighing pan. Then he knuckled his forehead. "How can this be? I deemed it certain Sultana Leila would have preferred you."

Sadiya patted Esperanza's shoulder and turned to him. "Do not blame her, master. She did her best under difficult circumstances."

"I do not doubt they were difficult! Life is brutal or have you forgotten?"

At his harsh irritated tone, she bowed her head. Her lower lip trembled. He raked his hands through his hair and crossed the room to envelop her in his arms. She leaned against him.

With a light kiss on her brow, he crooned, "Forgive me, sweet child. No one is at fault here. I had anticipated a different result, both of the females gone and myself a richer man. *Sí*, I am well rid of the Jewess to be sure, but it is a great shock to find Sultana Leila's predilections changed after some years. I thought I knew her preferences."

He lifted his head and looked at Esperanza. She swallowed and met his stare. "What is to become of me now?"

Juan Manuel did not answer. Instead, he pressed his lips to Sadiya's cheeks. "Return her to the cell. Do not dally. Send food for her. Then join me for a meal in my counting room so we may discuss her future."

"I shall do as you've bid, master."

When he released her, she tugged at Esperanza's fingers. Esperanza would not budge, despite Sadiya's prod. "Come with me now. Your ordeal is over. I'll send Binta with food."

"Is she the sour-faced Nubian woman who has brought me meals in days past?"

A dimple indented Sadiya's cheek and Juan Manuel gave a hearty chortle. "You surmised her origins with ease. I did not keep Binta for her soft moods. She follows orders well." He offered Esperanza a little nod and wink. "As you should learn to do. Obey me. Go with Sadiya as I have commanded."

"I will not."

"*Niña.*" A dire rebuke laced the one word.

She shook her head. "I have borne your worst and can do so again if necessary. I will not return to my cell while you and Sadiya ponder my fate. At every moment in life, someone else has made decisions for me, while I have borne the consequences. My father's wishes alone decided my life for the last fourteen years. Now you seek to supplant him in the determination of my path." She lifted her chin. "If it is the will of God, as you believe, for me to remain in this land then I want to know more of its customs and the language, its people and their faith. I came here in ignorance of such and I can no longer wallow in this state. Teach me what I must learn to endure this place. God alone shall lead me to my destiny, armed with the knowledge you would grant."

He cocked his head and glanced at Sadiya. She nodded and squeezed Esperanza's hand. "There are other places for a young, desirable female of some intelligence or skill, master. Consider other possibilities, with patrons just as rich as the Sultanas."

Juan Manuel scratched his chin. "My sweet child, no one is as rich as the Sultanas of Granada, except perhaps Yusuf. However, there are the governors of Andalusia, Yusuf's uncles or brothers. One of them might be more amenable, such as the young Prince Ismail. *Sí.*"

He reached out and cupped Esperanza's chin. She no longer flinched at his presumption.

"Tell me, what brought about this abrupt desire to adapt? This morning, you vowed never to accept life as a slave. Sadiya has told me of how you disdained the few Moorish words she has tried to impart. You believe Muslims are heathens who do not worship the same deity as Christians and Jews. You will not keep your beautiful head atop those shoulders for long with such misguided beliefs."

Esperanza answered, "Then inform me. I do not accept a life of servitude, but if I reject the knowledge of this land and its customs, freedom will never be mine. If I remain uneducated, I shall never find my own way among these people."

His grasp fell away. "*Sí*, a journey we must all undertake. Have you any talent yet unrevealed to me? Sewing does not count."

"My father taught me to play music, the lute, the flute, and harp, though Fray Rufino deemed the lessons a sin of idleness and pleasure. Papa did not teach me songs of praise as the Dominican wished. Rather, they concerned lost love, or lovers reunited. He also sang of battles against the Mohammedans... I mean, the Moors."

Juan Manuel nodded in approval of her usage of the term.

"Did your father encourage you to sing as well?" When Esperanza did not answer straightaway, he added, "I have often heard your voice drift beyond the bath, even before Sadiya remarked on the pleasant sound as one of your best attributes. The Moors prize excellence, in appearance and artistic forms. I have such an instrument as you have studied. You will learn the *oud* after the meal and sing for us."

She raised her head. Heat flared across her cheeks. "Sadiya exaggerated—"

The pair laughed at her. He said, "You dare call my favorite a liar to her face."

"I would never say such a thing! She is as trustworthy as may be." She paused and cast a glance at Sadiya before she continued, "Still, in this case, she was wrong. I am no songstress. Miriam possessed the talent. I told you once of her beautiful voice." One Miriam had often extolled while she dared Esperanza to match her. Miriam's obvious talent often rendered Esperanza incapable of an answer to the challenge.

"*Sí*, a voice I rarely heard except when she called down vile curses upon my head or anyone of my household who dared approach her. Until now, I have ignored your talent for languages. Did Miriam teach you the Hebrew tongue as well?"

She lowered her gaze. "Why must we speak of her now? She is gone from my life."

"True, she is no longer here to rival you, but the memories of her will linger. Embrace them because they will not fade. Never be afraid to confront the past. Learn from it. Besides, I still believe fate shall bring you and the Jewess together again. Your recent experiences with her will have strengthened you for future encounters. I ask again of what she taught you."

"Her Hebrew lessons hardly aided me. She provided what little she could so my father would not know. He never approved of our friendship. He was polite to her and to her family. Nothing more than common civility required."

"*Sí*, I suspected such."

"Whenever I speak of my father, you act as if you could have known him. You did not. I wish you would not talk about him either."

"Perchance I can discern something of the proud and incisive man he may have been through his daughter. A purposed and

strong-willed person would have raised someone such as you."
He scratched his cheek. "I have decided. I will test your abilities
to read and study languages. If I find you have not been boastful,
I shall tutor you in Arabic and Hebrew myself. Perhaps Persian
as well and some of the Berber tongue. You can never anticipate
necessity. Come, we go to the counting room. You shall play for
us and sing." He nodded to Sadiya. "Find Binta and have our
meal brought there. Bring the *oud* as well."

"As you command, master."

When Sadiya departed and Esperanza stood alone with Juan
Manuel, she looked around the room and smiled. "I did gain one
last valuable lesson from Miriam before her departure."

He arched his eyebrows. "What was it?"

"She taught me to never rely upon the motives of anyone. I
must trust myself."

Juan Manuel nodded and offered her his arm. She hesitated
for too long to take it and he rescinded the gesture. "It is a harsh
lesson, *niña,* but an important one for you to comprehend.
Adhere to it and you shall fare well in this land of the Moors."

***

When Juan Manuel determined Esperanza had not bragged
about her talent, her language lessons began in earnest. From
dawn until two hours after sunset, with intermittent breaks for
baths, meals and prayer, she studied with him. They began with
Arabic numerals, days of the week, months, and colors. Soon,
she discovered words for everything within his household. She
absorbed the knowledge with ease, which spurred his efforts.
Interspersed among his instructions were the basic tenets of
Islam, the concepts of belief, prayer, almsgiving, fasting, and
pilgrimage. Her reticence with Juan Manuel dissipated. There
were times in which she could almost pretend they were equals,
particularly when she debated with him on the religious virtues.

On a quiet afternoon she asked, "Would you have me think
all Muslims adhere to these rules? What of those wretched men
who kidnapped me?"

"The principles of Islam offer guidance. You would not have
me think all Christians turn the other cheek as Jesus preached.
Each of us struggles with the precepts of our faith. Take heed
and do not judge a religion by the actions of a few. Islam may
hold the path to your liberty. Muslims do not make slaves of
those who share their religion. Their holy book forbids it."

She listened, yet rejected the temptation to become an
apostate for the sake of freedom. The Church would never accept
her into the fold again if she forsook Christian beliefs. A little
knowledge of the Moorish faith could not hurt and might aid her

efforts. Still, she resolved to recite the Pater Noster in the solitude of her cell each night.

After two weeks, Juan Manuel added elements of the Hebrew and Persian languages to her repertoire. Often, the glint in his eyes hinted at pride in her aptitude. At least he proved better company than the slave Binta, who continued to wear her perpetual frown. Whenever Esperanza remarked upon it, Juan Manuel laughed at her expense.

"*Sí*, I recall your fixed nature when first we met. You're a fine one to complain about Binta."

"Would it harm her to be even a little pleasant? Surely not."

Once, in their hours alone, she found the courage and asked after Sadiya.

"I told you not to worry for her." Juan Manuel glanced at her from his seat beside a shuttered window. The wooden screens almost kept out a blast of frigid morning air. Bundled in layers of cotton and woolen clothes, a shudder coursed through him.

"How can you demand I do so? I need to know if she will ever forgive me."

"Why? Her opinion of you has no value. It will not influence your fate."

"Her thoughts matter to me. The reasons are mine alone."

"Your explanation is not good enough."

Icy fingers held in a tight fist, she pounded the low table between them. The glass cups of warm mint tea shook on a gilt tray. "Why must you keep us apart? You cannot believe I would ever attempt to harm her again."

His loud sigh filled the room. "I do it as much for your sake as hers. It is the same lesson you must discover, *niña*, one of self-reliance. You tread the path, but there is still a struggle to find your own way. Do not waver now. Attend to my teachings and leave Sadiya be."

She said nothing further.

He leaned forward and tapped the salver between them. "Remind me, what is this again?"

She rolled her eyes heavenward. "Do you wish for me to say it in Arabic, Hebrew, or Persian?"

He offered her a generous smile. "In Arabic, if you please."

She gritted her teeth for a moment. "*Al-tabaq.*"

In rare moments of solitude, she often pondered Miriam's fate and her choices. The Moors had dashed her expectations of the future also. They bore direct responsibility for the death of her husband and one child. They also bore some blame for the loss of Miriam's unborn son. What would Esperanza have done under the same circumstances? Would she have sought a new opportunity among the same people who ruined all hopes?

Esperanza's adaptations made it harder for her to judge Miriam each day. Soon, the rituals of the bathhouse and the alterations in her food and manner of dress became familiar, as though she had maintained them all her life. The affinity between her and Juan Manuel grew. She could no longer judge him as cruel captor or dismiss the solicitude he offered as insincere. Still, she underwent great distress in their quiet moments, where she looked up from the *oud* and found his contemplative gaze upon her. Even worse were the times when she drifted to sleep near the end of a long day of study. His gentle touch upon her shoulder always awoke her. While he chided her laziness and distraction, his indulgent smile often favored her before they parted. Her father had once done the same.

At the end of the sixth week since her tutelage started, Esperanza came to understand short phrases, which allowed her to exchange proper greetings and farewells with Juan Manuel in all of the new languages. They moved on to short conversations. Then two weeks later came a morning when he did not summon her.

Had she done something to displease him the night before? She recalled the evening meal, where she sat beside him with Sadiya at her left. Both had favored her with glances of approval in their rapt expressions while she strummed the musical instrument and sang another of her father's favorites, of lovers reunited. Nothing strange had occurred, so Juan Manuel held no reason to ignore her now. Afterward, when she had returned to her cell, she wept at the vivid memories of her beloved parent and woke with dampened cheeks. Juan Manuel could not have known of her misery.

She paced her cell for two hours after the dawn prayer had shattered her fitful slumber. The edge of her wrinkled yellow robe grazed the floor at each footfall. She kneaded a dull ache in her back through the linen. Where was Juan Manuel? How dare he keep her so idle? She paused at the center of the room. Had some ill befallen him? Would she remain trapped inside the small room forever? Her breaths devolved into short, shallow pants. A chill seeped into her bones and froze her in place.

The cell door creaked. As if drawn by her imagination alone, he stood there. Hands clasped in front of him, circles shadowed his eyes. He offered a slight nod. "*Al-salam 'alayka*. Did you sleep well?"

The familiar salutation did not ease her agitation. "You wish me peace after causing such concerns? Where were you? I have been awake since dawn, awaiting your arrival. I feared I had displeased you or something untoward had occurred. You must never frighten me so again, do you understand?"

He smiled and shook his head. The irony of her commands and solicitude for the one who kept her captive was not lost on her either.

"There was no cause for such anxiety. Important matters required my attention. Take a last look at this room for you shall leave it forever. You have been sold."

She stopped in her tracks and pressed a hand to her breastbone. "To whom? One of the Sultanas?" When he nodded, she released a sharp breath. "But, the elder of the two, she laughed at me. The other thought me too foolhardy. What caused one of them to change their opinions?"

"I do not know, niña. All bills of sale indicate a slave is the property of the lord of Granada, Sultan Yusuf. For your sake, I hope it is Sultana Leila who has bought you rather than Safa. Do not doubt me when I say both of them are dangerous women. You will never fathom the motives of either woman, so do not try. Now come," he said as he ushered her into the corridor, "you must not dally here."

She followed him out of the room, where sentries stationed at two corners watched her every move. "How do you know so much about the royal women of Granada?"

"I pay well for information from within harem walls. How else could I anticipate the needs of my patrons? The harem's occupants can be deceitful. You must be vigilant at every hour of the day and even in the night. Some of the captives Safa purchased in the past did not serve her for long."

"Why?"

"If they became sources of aggravation, she had them killed. I assure you, her means are inventive, more so than an assassin with a knife or a silken cord in the night. One girl had her flesh eaten away by what she thought to be a hair remover. Others ate cakes slathered in honey or drank bitter teas, which hid the poison well. All dead because they did not please Sultana Safa, or perhaps, pleased the Sultan too well. Safa does not welcome rivals who might usurp her influence over Yusuf. Sí. She would rid herself of Leila if she could."

Esperanza clenched her fingernails on his silk-clad forearm. "Why have you thrown me into this pit of vipers?"

He sighed and turned to her. His speckled hand covered hers. "I warned you of the dangers of the harem. You must outwit the

Sultanas and others among Yusuf's women, if you mean to live. You have wit and courage in abundance. These assets will aid you. I have told you the Sultanas will want your obedience, but they desire more from every captive. They shall strive to govern your thoughts and volition as well. Do not let them. You can be stubborn. Survive these women by whatever means you have at your disposal. Do not let them alter who you are within your mind and heart. That is all the advice I can give. Hurry, please. We cannot keep the chief eunuch of the harem here overlong. He has come to fetch you."

He urged her toward the stairs. The soft moans and miserable cries of her fellow captives filtered through bolted doorways. She hesitated at the base of the steps.

He chided, "Your heart is too tender. Come, you can do nothing for them."

She nodded. "Not now. When I am free, God shall grant me the strength to aid others so afflicted. I swear it."

"It is hard for me to doubt your conviction."

He took the stairs two at a time with the vigor of a much younger man. She matched his frantic pace. "Who is the chief eunuch? What role does he serve in the harem?"

"His name is Abdullah Hisham, quiet and observant to all outward appearances. He is a clever predator. Always watching and waiting for an opportunity to advance himself or initiate the downfall of a rival. His enemies and even some of his compatriots call him the Sultan's Shadow, a term he deserves for more than one reason."

"To whom does he owe loyalty, the Sultana Safa or Leila?"

"You ask the right question and it is an easy one to answer. The chief eunuch is loyal to himself. Somehow, he has managed to serve the interests of all others. He does nothing without an assessment of the costs and benefits to himself. When Yusuf's brother died, the chief eunuch's star rose alongside his elder brother's own, the Sultan's *hajib*."

"*Hajib*. Unlike *hijab*, the veil. *Hajib*. What does it mean?"

"It is one of the titles borne by the chief minister of the Sultan's court. When Abdullah Hisham became the chief eunuch of the harem, his brother Abu'l-Nu'aym Ridwan became the chief minister. In his capacity, Ridwan directs the course of government and carries out the duties and laws the Sultan makes. Other ministers hold sway at court. He is foremost among them. Do you understand the power Ridwan and Hisham can exert?"

"I do. In his lifetime, my father's service to the disinherited princes of Castilla-Leon introduced me to such concepts. Papa took me to court twice, first when I was nine years old and then at twelve. He introduced me to his patrons, who maintained courtly functions. The chief eunuch sounds like the *mayordomo* in the Cerdas' household." As they reached the landing and exited into a short corridor, Esperanza mused, "Here, one of the brothers controls the court and the other the harem. Together, they influence public life and activities within the home. What power does this Yusuf exercise if others govern his household and courtiers?"

"*Sí*, you have already begun to grasp the nuances of royal life in Granada. A little power can be a heady experience, especially for those who come to it young, as did Yusuf. At the age of fifteen, he became the master of us all. These three years of his reign have been troubled. He cannot oversee every aspect of the Sultanate. The powerful brothers who serve him are apostates, former Christian captives who embraced Islam as boys during the reign of Yusuf's father. You will remember what I told you of conversion to Islam."

She mumbled, "It doesn't seem like much of a choice, to give up one's faith and accept another, or remain enslaved forever."

He laughed and patted her fingers again. "I shall miss your perceptive mind most of all."

They reached a doorway, the one Esperanza first entered almost two months before. A row of varied shoes and boots lined either side of the walls, beneath several dark cloaks. All the rest of the passageway remained in darkness, except for an oil lamp set in a wall bracket just above the lintel. The low light flickered.

Juan Manuel released his hold on Esperanza. Then he bent and grasped a pair of ankle boots trimmed with brown fur. He urged her to place her feet in them. "It is a blessing you and Sadiya wear the same size."

"These are hers?" At his nod, she slipped them on. "I shall treasure them."

He draped a black woolen cloak around her shoulders and tied the strings at her neck. "Your new mistress will not let you keep anything. It is why I took your brooch. I shall keep your father's weapon as well. If your destiny is as great as I have perceived, perchance there shall be a moment where I may return such valuables to you."

Miriam's gift represented a lie. Esperanza would not ask after it again. Her father's dagger represented a treasured memento of the past. She hated to part with it.

Juan Manuel assured her. "Both items shall remain safe with me. No harm shall ever befall them."

"Please let me say farewell to Sadiya. Have you told her of my leave-taking?"

"Nothing passes in the House of Myrtles of which she is unaware. I trust her in all things. She wept when Abdullah Hisham came because she knew his intent as soon as he appeared. She returned to her room in misery. Your arrival stirred something she has had little remembrance of, a desire for friendship with others like her. She has depended on my poor company for too long. She forgot what it was like to have a female companion. I do not wish to extend the burden of your farewell for her sake. You have awakened long-buried memories of her sisters."

"I did?" Esperanza's stomach roiled and she blinked. "I never had any sisters. Well, I once thought so, but I was...."

When she trailed off, he ran the back of his hand across her cheek and cupped her chin. He drew her stare again. "You know you may see the Jewess again, if she has survived Sultana Safa's excesses. You will need to be careful with Miriam. Old ties to the past cannot bind you in the future. Miriam wants the power attainable by a favorite at the Sultan's side. If you do anything to interfere with her plans for Yusuf, she shall strike out at you with unimaginable fury. Her ambition knows no bounds. I admire the trait, but she may prove a greater nemesis than Sultana Safa ever could. The Jewess knows you and your weaknesses."

His caution was unnecessary. She welcomed it all the same at this moment of farewell. Though his hand should have repelled, it offered comfort. She leaned into his palm with a soft sigh. His touch induced powerful memories of her father's indulgences. How could she seek relief from the man who had forced her on this hazardous path?

He drew closer. "Promise me you shall survive them all, Miriam included."

Tears welled as his words evoked the last her father had spoken. A lump swelled in her throat and prevented any reply for a moment. Then she raised her head. "I shall remember you, Juan Manuel Gomero. I will never cease to think of the valuable lessons revealed in the House of Myrtles."

"And I shall never forget you, Esperanza Peralta. Keep my warnings about the harem foremost in your mind. If you ever have need of me, I will know it."

"How? Who is your spy?"

His dimpled smile warmed her. "Who told you there is just one?" Then he bent and grasped her hands in his, before he pressed his lips to each in turn. "It has been my honor and privilege to know you. Now go with *El Dio* and find what you seek outside of these walls."

He released her for a final time. Her hand on the doorknob, she pulled it inward. The wood creaked. She stepped out into a morning as pale as her garment. She had not left the confines of the property for almost two months. She fingered a diamond-shaped niche covered by iron latticework on the right side of the wall. Behind the grille would be the *mezuzah* of Juan Manuel's house, similarly placed as the vellum at Miriam's home. Even the briefest memory of life at Talavera de la Reina troubled her, but encumbrances of the past would fade with time. She peered into the courtyard, shrouded in a layer of morning mist.

A shiver, not caused by the cold temperature, ran through her body. When she would have turned to the door again, it closed behind her. She pressed back against the portal and sheltered below the lintel. One man garbed in pallid white sat atop a dun-colored horse with a black mane. His shaved head appeared too small to sit atop such wide shoulders. Fifteen green and blue-robed guardsmen on foot encircled him. Did the chief eunuch's status necessitate such protection? Were so many required for her cooperation?

She willed courage into her heart and moved toward the band. Closer inspection revealed the lone rider's eyes as the dull gray of a dove's breast. Nothing soft or muted filled his expression. His crystalline gaze peered from a pale, narrow face. She had never seen anyone so fair, with pale yellow eyebrows. The tight slash of his lips across haggard, whitened features and the crinkles of his brow suggested more than displeasure at the sight of her. She perceived how the Sultan's Shadow suited him, for he appeared in the morning mist like a ghost.

She peered at the crinkles across her skirt. Perhaps she appeared shoddy in his estimation. Then Juan Manuel's admonitions echoed in her mind, the proper acknowledgment a Moor would expect from her. She gritted her teeth at the requirement, but performed her bow. Unbound hair fell over her eyes and on either side of her head. She held the position and awaited his command. It never came. She dared look up.

He snapped, "Eyes down!" Although she comprehended the command spoken, she did not comply straightaway. With hands gloved in white silk, he maneuvered his mount through the circle of his companions, each of whom carried a large curved sword at their sides.

"Eyes down, I said." His natural ease with Castillan betrayed his origins. After she followed his command, he snorted and spat in the dirt between them. "Ignorant girl, no better than a newly acquired savage kept in the *corrals*. I should not have presumed a worthless Jew would have bothered to teach you the language of your master."

She saw no reason to correct his misguided opinion, although the comment about Juan Manuel rankled as much as his derision of her. There might be some advantage for her if she kept her knowledge of Arabic a secret for now. If she would observe and learn in secret, perhaps she might ferret out a means of escape.

The chief eunuch's mount nickered and tossed its head. The rider jerked the reins and the animal snorted. Its nostrils flared with puffs of white smoke.

Long weeks had passed in which Esperanza never thought to see a horse again. This high-strung one evoked remembrances of her mother's mare. She reached for the muzzle. "*Tranquilo, tranquilo.*"

"Fool! Would you risk your fingers?" He fought for control as the horse whinnied and crabbed sideways. He snapped his riding crop across the animal's flank, which agitated the beast further. "My horse should have bitten you and taught you a good lesson! You are just a stupid girl. Why the Sultana thought you merited her interest escapes me."

She ignored his insult. "Which Sultana?"

He never answered her and instead concentrated on his difficult mount. At length, he calmed the animal. His murky gaze found her again. "Until your new mistress grants you a name, you shall answer to the title slave. On our journey to the Sultan's harem, you will speak if I require it. When you do so, you shall address me as 'my lord' and you will keep that rebellious gaze upon the ground at all times. Otherwise, I shall have your fiery eyes plucked out. Do you understand me, slave?"

She bit back a sharp retort. "*Sí*, my lord."

He summoned one of his protectors, who stepped forward and produced iron manacles from the folds of his robe. She drew back. The stern, unrepentant stare of the chief eunuch pinned her in place. The enormity of their intention sent a wave of dizziness in a spiral through her body. She recalled the ropes the slavers tied around her and Miriam's hands. The fibers had burned and shredded her skin. Before she could move, the guardsman pushed aside the cloak and encased both her wrists. She jerked away, but his hold tightened.

"Please, this is unnecessary!"

The chief eunuch thrust out his chest and fisted a hand on his hip. "Hush, foolish girl! Did you think we would allow you to stroll through the streets unchained?"

Despite her fervent struggles, the first of the iron restraints closed around her wrist with a loud clink. A lengthy chain linked it to the other shackle, which soon imprisoned her. She stared at her hands.

A final, malignant glare fell upon her. "Now come. I have lingered too long in the stink of the Jewish quarter."

He spurred his horse on. The sentry tugged the chain and propelled her forward. He and the other men who accompanied the rider now coalesced around both of them with tight-lipped expressions. Each bearded man wore a white tunic with fitted sleeves under his blue or green outer tunic. Each man radiated a formidable appearance with the sword belt on the right and a curved dagger tucked into it. The warriors also carried shields, each of which bore the shape of a hand in white. How could she ever hope for an escape from them?

Esperanza's gaze watered, but she vowed never to shed tears in their midst. No one would gain the enjoyment of her misery. Chin held high, she left the confines of the property. Just outside the wall, she viewed the horseshoe arch and iron-riveted door. A dull ache spread across her belly. Perhaps the sensation warned this would not be the last time she might ever stand before the House of Myrtles.

Chapter 9
The Riddle of the Harem

Esperanza Peralta

Granada, Andalusia
April 19, AD 1336 / 7 Ramadan 736 AH / 7th of Iyar, 5096

The chief eunuch's horse moved through the streets at a brisk trot. Its iron-shod hooves struck the cobblestones. Even at such an early hour, Granada's denizens stirred from their whitewashed homes and went about their business. Most descended the incline shaded with myrtle trees as Esperanza did and headed for the marketplace. The chain, slung low between her wrists, jangled across the paving stones. If the *Granadinos* noticed, none displayed an interest in her plight. What was one more slave to these people, who prospered by the subjugation of others?

Before the chief eunuch reached the carved passageway, which demarcated the entry into the market, he urged his horse left at a stone bridge. Sentries protected access, garbed in similar fashion the others around her. River water rushed down a slope and disappeared under sharp gray rocks. Wind stirred the trees at either edge of the rock face. Esperanza's cloak and robe billowed, as she plodded across the long bridge with her head bowed. The pathway led through olive groves and ended with a sudden right turn, which brought her up a low, paved ramp. She raised her head when the horse slowed and swished its thick tail. At a great distance, a whitewashed building with a northern tower loomed.

Visitors who had preceded them now stood aside and hugged the redbrick walls at her right. The company thinned into a line as the route narrowed. The left side revealed a precarious drop into the gorge below and the city as it sprawled across the plains on the adjacent riverbank. Dawn's light glinted off tiled roofs in a golden pink haze and shimmered within water fountains. Just ahead, the tower door creaked and revealed a deep chasm. The chief eunuch urged his mount and men onward into the darkness.

Trapped in their midst, blackness engulfed Esperanza. A moment's fear surged through her heart. As she emerged into daylight again, the myriad faces of lookouts posted on the sentry walk met her gaze. She swung to the right and entered a courtyard, which bustled with activity. Sentinels on foot demanded taxes from merchants with their horses, pack animals, and wares. One seller led a bedraggled lot of six men in chains with collars linked to the manacles. Threadbare garments offered little protection for them against the morning chill. At the sight of them, so gaunt and pallid, Esperanza stumbled on one of the larger paving stones and righted herself in an instant. One desolate figure exchanged a dejected glance with her. Then he bowed his head, encumbered by his own misery.

"Eyes down! Don't make me tell you again, slave!"

The chief eunuch's frigid stare froze her for a moment before she complied. She followed the clip-clop of his horse's iron shoes across the courtyard. From her peripheral gaze, she took in the long redbrick wall on the right, which blocked her view of the structures beyond it except for a tower. Had she seen the same earlier? A wave of disorientation muddled her mind. She could not gain her bearings. The horse traversed a covered gateway topped by a windowed second storey, set inside the boundary wall on the left. Hemmed against the edge by the chief eunuch's escort, Esperanza breathed a sigh of relief as golden light beckoned. A glance behind her revealed a shallow ravine.

She reached an intermediate courtyard of yellowed stone, separated from another by gardens of shrubs. Water bubbled up from innumerable fountains within the precinct. Two men crossed Esperanza's path. They wore long white robes decorated with silver swirls at the neckline and breast. They carried scrolls bundled under their armpits. Both men slowed and nodded to the chief eunuch. He inclined his head and turned, as though his gaze followed the pair. They disappeared behind a marble edifice bounded on the left side by a wide garden and stone benches. The hills of Granada rose to the north.

The chief eunuch dismounted and tossed the reins to a young groom, another slave, his status denoted by the collar secured around his neck. Did the people of Granada have nothing but slaves in Granada to serve them? With a harsh ragged breath, he spoke for a short time. His tone of supplication and the inflection held a question.

"*La!*" The chief eunuch boxed the boy's ear.

With a snap of his fingers, he signaled for the key to her manacles. When he had it, he grasped the middle of Esperanza's chain and tugged the iron restraints. As though he led a beast of burden, he pulled her with outstretched arms through the quiet streets. She passed by houses with stables and orchards. Outside a door shaded by one myrtle tree, a girl who appeared similar to Esperanza's age swept dust from the stairway. An iron cuff fastened at her ankle. She paused in regard of Esperanza and rubbed the middle of her back, until the chief eunuch stared at her. The slave dashed into the house.

The outskirts of a building offered cool shade. Across the narrow street, the boundaries of a garden extended southward. Groves of almond and olives swayed in the cool breeze. White marble canopies rose above clumps of rosemary and cistus. Esperanza counted eleven funerary stones before the chief eunuch quickened his pace. The shackles raked against her tender flesh. Oblivious to her agony, he dragged her along. When she could not bear another moment, she jerked hard against his hold. He gave a satisfactory yelp. In an instant, he turned and swung his riding crop at her head. She ducked and the would-be blow whistled less than a hand's width from her cheek. He aimed again.

A rumble of laughter echoed behind him. He paused, the crop held in mid-air. Esperanza looked up. A dark-skinned young man stood in their path. Thick strands of almost black hair curled at his shoulders and framed his broad face. Large and limpid brown eyes scanned her from head to toe before his gaze darted to the chief eunuch's own.

Was this the ruler of Granada? If he reigned, no finery or emblems marked him as Sultan. In a land where even favored slaves like Sadiya donned expensive fabrics, she could not always be certain of anyone's status. Juan Manuel had described the monarch as a man some four years her senior. The stranger suited the age of eighteen.

The chief eunuch lowered his hand and bowed, despite the obvious youth of the other man. As the stranger spoke in a husky voice, a broad grin emphasized the high cheekbones. Garbed in brown from a robe, tunic, and trousers to the snug leather boots, he stood taller than Juan Manuel did. Despite the young man's amused tone, the chief eunuch's clipped retorts did not offer an address in kind.

This could not be the Sultan, for he should not have permitted such a derisive attitude from a minion. Their rapid exchange left Esperanza oblivious to the content, except for two words, *jariyu* for female slave and the harem.

Then the young man looked at her again. "*Al-salam 'alayka.*"

The chief eunuch laughed in a shrill and derisive tone. Whatever he said next, Esperanza guessed he told of how she would not have understood the words of peace bestowed upon her. In his view, she remained an uneducated savage.

He tossed aside the chain and turned to her. "You will follow me, slave. If you attempt to run, the executioner will have you for his amusement long before noonday."

With another bow, he approached sentries who barred an ornate door. The young man's stare returned to Esperanza. She stood still for a moment, startled by the small smile he offered. No one had shown any kindness since she left the House of Myrtles. He tilted his head in her direction. He greeted her again with the peace of God.

She whispered, "*Wa-'alayka*," and in the next breath, chided herself for the stupid impulse to wish him the same peace.

His soft chuckle rumbled behind her. Would he reveal her secret to others?

The patrol at the entryway stood aside now with their eyes averted. She crossed the threshold behind the chief eunuch and after a right turn, walked past a bare wall. She emerged at the edge of a shaded marble portico, protected on either side by a pair of black-robed sentinels.

A slender dark-skinned woman stood beside an enclosed arch the width of three men. A thin metal collar wound around her neck. With hair close-cropped to her skull, she held the appearance of a boy except for generous breasts, which rose and fell at each breath. Her gauzy yellow robe with wide, elbow-length sleeves fell open to her knees. The gap revealed a short cotton shirt dyed indigo-blue and the familiar trousers paired with leather slippers. As the chief eunuch neared, she clasped her long fingers together, bowed, and greeted him. Behind her, two lengths of indigo damask curtains fluttered on a breeze between massive wooden doors.

Feminine giggles pealed, joined by a chorus of voices from behind the door hanging. The woman outside held a portion of the woven silk aloft and ushered the chief eunuch in. Before she lowered her hand, her stare pinned Esperanza in place. "Just him for now. You will wait with me until we are summoned, *señorita*."

Esperanza studied the woman's delicate features. Something appeared familiar about the fleshy mouth. The lower lip jutted. Perhaps Esperanza had seen her before at the House of Myrtles with the Sultanas. Which one? Muffled conversation broken by occasional titters offered no clues.

Esperanza turned away and studied the spacious courtyard. Flower and bird motifs covered the capitals of slender columns. Before now, she once thought the beautiful castles of the Cerdas outshone all others. The Moorish palace exceeded her imagination. Several pillars linked three other galleries, guarded in similar fashion. Faint light cascaded into the center of the space, where spring flowers bloomed beneath orange trees. Then her stomach soured, at the thought of the slaves she had seen earlier. Had their hands created such beauty? How many of them labored now at its upkeep?

"My Ifrit? Bring the new slave to me now." A clear, authoritative tone pierced the drapery.

A knot tightened and rippled across Esperanza's belly at the summons. The woman, whom Esperanza assumed bore the name, waved her inside. She entered the doors and walked under the archway. A narrow corridor led to darkened marble stairs on both sides. Beyond another sculpted entrance, numerous tiles scaled the lower half of the walls, while carved plasterwork rose to the ceiling.

Metal links rattled when Esperanza dragged the chain across the marble. The chief eunuch's inscrutable stare greeted her. He stood in a square chamber surrounded by young women in simple robes of diverse colors. Two sat on large square cushions along a tiled southern wall. The olive-skinned pair who resembled each other occupied spaces between windows covered in wooden latticework, which faced the street Esperanza had just traveled. Layers of cloth splayed across their laps. A low table between them and the chief eunuch supported a bronze lamp. Small stained glass cups surrounded a platter of dried figs and the lamp. Beside the table, a large red-gold jar caught the edge of the light.

Carpets covered the floors raised on the right and to the left, where three other women encircled the final occupant. Ensconced within the columned recesses between a stone brazier and perforated incense burner, none among the trio regarded Esperanza at first. With a smile etched on her lush lips, a yellow-haired young woman twiddled the tip of a thin brush in an inkpot set in a metal stand. A dark orange stain clung to the bristles. The second, darker skinned than Juan Manuel's slave Binta, lifted a lid from a ceramic pot. She added a pinch of small, gray-brown seeds, which reminded Esperanza of fennel. She ground the contents with a pestle. The third woman, with little brown burns on her fingers, displayed a tunic trimmed with silver braid for the one she and the others surrounded. A shimmer of recognition lit the eyes of this last woman.

The young Sultana who had rejected Esperanza in the House of Myrtles hushed her companions with a wave of her hand. Seated cross-legged on a long cushion edged with gold filigree, with pillows strewn around her, she lowered her upturned hand. Rust-colored swirls and dots crisscrossed her skin.

"Kneel before your mistress, the Sultana Leila bint Ismail." The slender black woman pushed Esperanza. She cried out and fell forward. The flat of her hands braced her. A chill from the marble seeped into the flesh. Some of the women tittered behind their hands, but the Sultana chided them.

She leaned forward. "How awkward you are, as if Allah made your limbs too long. Now, sit back on your heels and raise your head. Good, now look at me. Let me see the spark in those eyes again."

Curiosity overwhelmed Esperanza. "Why did you bring me here? Did you think another two months in the House of Myrtles would have improved the defects of my mind?"

Leila clapped her hands. "Obviously not, for you are still as reckless as ever! I shall enjoy your training." Her laughter echoed in the chamber. Her companions stared in wide-eyed shock.

The chief eunuch raised his riding crop.

Leila sobered in an instant. She stood and placed herself between him and Esperanza. "I did not give you the authority to discipline my slave, Hisham. You would not dare make the attempt without my permission."

With a ragged breath torn from his lips, he lowered his arm. "Someone must take the trouble to teach the slave good manners before her betters."

"As her mistress I intend to do so. A duty I will not defer. She is mine, no matter what the bill of sale might indicate. Never forget." She clasped her hands and peered at Esperanza. "Anyone among my servants would tell you I am a fair mistress. The first offense does not demand a punishment, just correction. Ignorance is permissible for one who is new to my household. I grant one opportunity to correct errors. There is no mercy for a second offense. So, understand me well. You will never question me again. If you do, I shall have your tongue cut out."

Esperanza sucked in her breath at such casual cruelty. She never flinched or lowered her gaze.

Leila said, "I perceive your understanding, but the fire in your regard has not dulled. Good. I bought you to replace one who died in childbirth. Gomero offered a better price than the other merchants did. Nothing more. Everyone in this room has a purpose. You shall discover yours as well."

She waved to those seated beside the windows. "Sut is my seamstress and laundress. Her sister Zarru is my stewardess and keeps the inventory of all household items, including the linen and cotton. She is meticulous. She will notice if even one article is missing. Are you a thief, slave?"

Esperanza stiffened, opened her mouth, and then stopped short. "As I am not a liar, I am also no thief."

"I hope for your sake this is true. We cut off the hands of thieves in this land." She turned and patted the hand of the woman who pounded the mixture in the mortar. "Rima prepares my meals. Hamduna keeps me beautiful with her *nura, henna* and ointments, while Amat ensures I am always dressed as befits a Sultana. Ifrit has been my body slave since childhood. I am seldom without her company. Among her responsibilities, she attends me in the bath.

"The loss of Ishraq has placed an undue burden upon the rest of my household. Your duty, in Ishraq's absence, is to tend to this hall and my room upstairs. You must clean the floors each day. You will empty the chamber pot as often as required. I need fresh water each morning and evening from the cistern. Ifrit can show you the place. Dirtied or torn garments and linens must go to Sut. Nothing of use is ever wasted in my household when a little care and upkeep is needed."

The furious rhythm of Esperanza's heart froze for a moment. Then blood rushed and pulsed against her temple. She closed her eyes against a rush of bewilderment. Her fingers twitched. Reduced to a menial life, how would she survive?

Leila crouched beside her and lifted her chin. "You will need a new name, for I cannot call you 'slave' forever. You are just as Gomero described. Strange, for he is often given to exaggeration in the sale of captives. From this day onward, you shall answer to Butayna, for one who possesses a young and tender body."

Esperanza gazed into Leila's sea-green eyes. "That is not my name. I am Esperanza Peralta, the daughter of Efrain Peralta. You can claim my life, but I shall never answer to any other name until I die."

Leila cocked her head and smiled. "Many things await you within these walls, but I doubt death is among them. Not yet." She rose and turned to the chief eunuch. "Remove the chains."

"From a slave lately acquired? You cannot trust her, my Sultana."

She sidestepped him and resumed her seat. She held out her hand for the one called Hamduna, who continued her artistry with the brush. Then Leila replied, "It is not a matter of trust. The chains are impractical. Butayna cannot fetch water from the cistern without making a racket. Better you remove the chains than her clumsiness with them slow her down."

119

Esperanza blinked back tears and looked up. Did God see her misery? Did He care? The honeycombed ceiling above, shaped as a six-pointed star, shone in brilliant blues, yellows, reds and greens, interspersed with white. Heaven's beauty must shine in the same manner. For now, this place became her personal hell.

***

After the dismissal of the chief eunuch, Sultana Leila remained below with most of her entourage while Esperanza followed Ifrit's wordless beckon. Esperanza rubbed her wrists, free of the chains. Ifrit led her from the chamber along the wall and down a short flight of steps, which she had not noticed. The wall above hid a wide cistern, shrouded in darkness. Two warriors stood on either side of the clear water. They hefted spears the height of most men.

Ifrit said, "Each morning and before sunset, you will fetch water for the Sultana's tea and other needs. Zarru shall give you a wooden pail or basin and ewer with which to draw the water. You will fill the lusterware jar on the ground floor of the Sultana's room. Now come."

Esperanza retraced her earlier steps. The sentries in the courtyard increased as they changed the watch. She shook her head at her earlier ruminations. The gilded walls and columns of her prison could crumble to dust for all she cared.

At the entrance, Ifrit turned to her. Her gaze wandered from Esperanza's shoulders to her feet. "Remove the cloak and those boots. I will not have you trekking the dust of the city through the harem."

Esperanza untied the strings and took off the footwear.

Afterward, she went with Ifrit up the narrow marble stairway and entered the first of several doorways on the right. Arches of paneled red wood led to two small alcoves furnished with carpets and heavy damask drapery across the windows. Fabric spilled from ornate niches along the walls from the ceiling to the top of the tiles. Chests lined the bases of the first room. Several pairs of shoes littered the floor of the second chamber. In the next room, scattered garments hung over every surface. Linen and samite covered the bed comprised of two long cushions piled high in the central chamber. Other clothes strewn on the carpets, cast on a low wooden stool at the foot of the bed, and tossed over a small chest bore crinkles and smudged stains. A stiff breeze blew in through three north-facing windows, their lattice covers opened and latched against the adjacent walls. A burnished lantern hung from an iron hook, trussed up by iron links. The hook whirled each time the wind gusted.

Ifrit directed Esperanza, "You are to arrange the garments in the niches. Then fold the laundered items on the bed and place them with the other clothes. If there is anything that cannot fit, place the remainder in the chests." She disappeared into a fourth room and shoved a woven basket into Esperanza's arms. "Take this. Be sure to add the orange and lemon peel inside to the base of the chest before you put any clothes into them. The rest scattered here, you must gather up and take to Sut for the washing."

Then Ifrit indicated two pairs of embroidered slippers beside the bed. "Those go to the second alcove. You will ensure the shoes are each a matching set. Can you do that?"

Esperanza stifled a groan. Did the woman expect her to answer such an idiotic question? Any fool with a pair of eyes could complete the task. "I can."

Ifrit's dark eyes flitted over her face. "The Sultana shall provide all you need. For now, you may keep that yellow robe until the Sultana orders Zarru to give something else. My mistress despises slovenliness and is quick to notice its appearance."

Esperanza looked around the disheveled chamber. That statement could not be so true if the woman cared so little for the state of her rooms.

Ifrit scowled at her. "Attend to your duties."

As Esperanza did so, Ifrit's hot gaze followed her throughout the chamber. After some time, she left Esperanza alone. Although occasional laughter rang through the glazed flooring, Esperanza never overheard any conversation. Her fingers snapped the folds of cloth and shoved each layer into a niche, until the sight of the crumpled fabric caused her concern. Leila could punish her for carelessness. Thereafter, she took greater care with her task.

The door below creaked. She looked up from the floor where she gathered the slippers, intent on taking them to the second alcove. With a pair in hand, she crept to the window and looked into the courtyard below. She spied no one and with a sigh, returned to her assigned duty. She muttered to herself all the while. How many pairs of shoes could one woman need?

She squealed once a cascade of mouse droppings spilled from an overturned boot. When she finished cleaning the floor of the rank pellets and completed her task with the shoes, her attention turned to the piles of dirtied clothes. With a bundle in hand, she made for the stairs. The laundress must allow a question about what Esperanza should do next.

At the landing, she sucked in her breath. No one remained in the room. Further within, the recesses held the carpets, brazier and incense burner. Even the cloak and boots Juan Manuel had provided were gone. She dropped everything on the floor with a loud huff.

The closed door scraped again and she whirled. The young man who had greeted her in peace outside the harem stood at the entrance. She bowed. The dull ache across her back lingered.

He spoke to her in the same amused tone he had adopted with the chief eunuch.

She whispered, "I can't understand you, my lord."

He chuckled, a husky rumble unexpected at his obvious age. When he advanced into the room, she backed until her calves bumped against the table. She turned and ensured the cups did not fall.

"Ah, the girl who pretends she cannot speak a word of Arabic. At least not within the chief eunuch's hearing."

"I know a little of the language! A few phrases, the words of a proper greeting and such."

He put up his palms. "Have no fear. I will not reveal your secret to Hisham. He would be most displeased if he discovered you sought to hide the truth from him. I presume my sister does not know either?"

"Your sister, my lord?"

"The Sultana Leila. She is my sister."

Esperanza sighed. At last, some part of the mystery of the harem began to unravel. If this was the Sultana's brother, what relationship did Leila share with the Sultan? Was she a wife? Esperanza wished Juan Manuel had spent more time on the relationships within the Sultan's palace. No matter. She would discover them on her own.

He asked, "Is my sister still abed? That's not her custom."

She answered, "The Sultana is not here. I do not know where–"

"Then she's gone to the bath early."

Esperanza's stomach rumbled. She had gone without food or drink since the previous night. How would she eat today?

The young man inquired, "Are you hungry?"

She clasped her hands in front of her. "No, my lord." The gurgle in her stomach became audible and he laughed.

He reached for a fig and handed it to her. "Sit and eat, I command it. As you have acknowledged, I am a lord. You cannot ignore my command."

When she followed his order, he rested his back against a pillar. "This is the month of fasting. All believers take no food or drink during the daylight hours. Slaves are under no such obligation."

The dark purple fig eased her stomach's gurgles. When she finished it, little pitted seeds and all, she stared at the floor.

He studied her and said, "I am Prince Ismail. Tell me your name."

She recalled mention of him in the House of Myrtles. Juan Manuel had considered selling her to the same individual among a choice of Yusuf's uncles or brothers.

She looked up, into his expectant gaze. "I am Esperanza Peralta."

He shook his head. "What name has my sister granted you? You must know slaves do not keep ties to their pasts."

"She has called me Butayna, my lord. A name I shall never answer."

Up close, his broad grin revealed a slight gap between his even teeth. "A pity for it is well deserved. Hmm, young and tender." He perused every aspect of her shape, as though he could see through the pale yellow robe. She clutched the folds of it.

"Have no fear. I do not intend to claim you for my own. Besides, I prefer red haired women."

"Does everyone here speak the Castillan language?" She blurted the question, relief embedded in her tone. Then she clapped a hand over her mouth. "Forgive me, my lord. I forgot I could not ask questions. The Sultana Leila said so."

"I would suggest you remember my sister's admonitions for she never repeats them. Even so, I shall answer. My maternal grandmother was a Castillan slave. She ensured my mother Arub learned the language against her master's objections. Later, I studied in the princes' school and reinforced the teachings with my mother's help. I should say we aided each other."

He rose from the cool tiles. "Tell my sister I still struggle with the duty to fast during the daylight hours, but I thank her for the figs."

When he winked at her and waved to them, she frowned. Why would he choose to lie for her if slaves did not have to observe the period of starvation Moors inflicted upon themselves?

"You make a remarkable gesture for a stranger, one you do not have to do."

He nodded and chortled again at her bold speech.

When would she ever learn to subdue her forthright nature among these Moors? Life and death were uncertain. She must learn to be more circumspect.

"Despite your audacity, I am glad to know you, Butayna. The peace of Allah be with you."

"And with you, my lord."

He left her alone again. She reached for another of the fragrant figs.

Just as she finished the third piece of fruit, a hoarse cry emanated from the top of the stairs. "Leila? Are you here?"

Esperanza froze as another person she did not know inquired after the Sultana. Near silent footfalls shuffled across the floorboards. She released a pent-up breath and hoped whomever this stranger might be, a swift departure would follow, if only so Esperanza might hide the evidence of the fruits she had pilfered.

The raspy, yet clearly feminine voice, continued in Arabic. "Where is she? I need Leila!"

A lisping answer from another woman followed, one Esperanza barely understood. The words issued in a soft undertone sounded like the cascade of a waterfall. Of the phrases, Esperanza remained ignorant of all, but the beginning. "My Sultana, I am here for you...."

The pair, perhaps a member of Leila's family and her slave most likely, continued their conversation from above stairs. The first voice Esperanza had heard became increasingly insistent and strident over the second, before a quavering plea echoed. "My Sultana! Please, be careful on the stairs!"

Esperanza stood and eased beside the pillar within the recesses of the alcove. A foolhardy attempt, as if she might conceal herself behind its slender length. Even she was not so thin. She hugged the column and waited for the encounter.

Ragged breaths preceded the faltering steps of an aged woman. Her feet, painted in dark orange-stained swirls, peeked beneath a simple lavender robe. A younger female in white cotton followed the woman. Both were of a similar height and shared the same slight build as Esperanza.

The elder lady stood straight-backed and unyielding like one of the orange trees in the palace's garden courtyard. Thick, silver hair framed her face and trailed to her hips. Deep-set eyes, yellowed around the centers, peered out from wizened features. Brown spots on her hands and feet were interspersed with blue-black veins.

She sniffled before her glassy stare focused on Esperanza. "You are not my granddaughter. Where is Leila? You will answer me now."

Esperanza fell to her knees and gulped mouthfuls of air. Her heart raced. Something in the old woman's demand hinted at a power not evident in her frail appearance. The desperate need to keep her furtive understanding of Arabic a secret did not compel Esperanza's silence. She found herself reduced to a quiver solely by the presence of this regal woman.

"Who are you?" The Sultana's aide crossed the room and stood before Esperanza. "Can you understand what I am saying?"

She nudged Esperanza with toes covered by black slippers. "Do not be so frightened. Would it be better if I spoke in Castillan?"

Esperanza raised her head as her familiar mother tongue spilled from the stranger's lips. The woman extended her honey-colored hand and Esperanza accepted the aid as she stood. She stared into the stranger's almond-shaped eyes with a few crinkled lines at their corners, but kept her face averted from the Sultana's pertinent stare.

The Sultana's companion stated, "I am Asiya, a servant of this household."

A servant, not a slave, also evidenced by the lack of a collar around her neck. Black hair peeked beneath her sheer veil of the same color.

"And you are?"

Esperanza murmured an introduction and gave her Christian name. At an audible intake of breath from the Sultana, Esperanza added, "I... serve the Sultana Leila now. I do not know where she is. There was a man earlier, Prince Ismail, who said he was the Sultana's brother. He was also looking for her and thought she had gone to the bath."

The elderly woman cocked her head, as though she studied Esperanza. Then she turned and mounted the stairs again with a grunt. Her servant followed.

"Wait, please!" Esperanza came out of the alcove and called to the younger woman. When Asiya halted, Esperanza pitched her voice low. "Who is she?"

The servant looked up the marble steps as her mistress neared the landing. "She is Fatima bint Muhammad, the noble grandmother of Sultana Leila and her brothers Prince Ismail and our great Sultan Abdul Hajjaj Yusuf. Bint means 'daughter of' in Arabic. You will have to learn it and much more to serve your Sultana well."

"Were you a captive brought to this land like me?"

Asiya chuckled. "I have served the Sultana Fatima since childhood, born of a favored servant in her house. I do not know the captive or a slave's lot in life. My Sultana has never treated me as less than a treasured attendant. Thus, I have devoted my life to her. Did you think there were only former captives and slaves here?"

Without awaiting an answer, she rushed and rejoined the Sultana Fatima at the top of the stairs. Leila's grandmother glanced at Esperanza a final time before she retreated from view with her servant at her side.

Esperanza sighed, the riddle of the connections between family members resolved at last. She had survived her encounters with three of the Sultan's relatives. Would she meet him also? Would he be as perplexing as his siblings and his grandmother?

***

Leila and her women did not return until late evening. Their laughter and footfalls on the stairs jarred Esperanza from a miserable slumber. Shoulders hunched and her hair spilling over her shoulders, she sat on a rug at the end of the bed with her feet curled up under her. Cold air drifted through the opened windows and chilled her to the bone. She roused herself, stretched, and yawned. Then she rubbed her stomach and her arms through the sleeves.

Leila entered the bedchamber with two of her women in tow, Ifrit and the stewardess.

"You've slept, I see. At least you carried out your duties in my absence. You should be invigorated now."

As she spoke, she strolled through the room and stripped off her garments. The gauzy scarlet veil floated to the floor, soon joined by the gold cloth fringed with tassels around her hips. She removed a brocaded red and green robe last. The undergarments fitted her curves. Thick dark ringlets tumbled down her back to her hips. She kicked off her boots in a corner. She sat on the bed with one knee drawn up under her, while Ifrit retrieved the brush set on a low table and began to brush her mistress' hair.

Her servant Zarru glowered at Esperanza. "Well, pick them up! Do you have to be told?"

Esperanza bent and retrieved each article. Then she remembered the first visitor. "Your brother, Prince Ismail, stopped by this morning. He thanked you for the figs."

Leila chortled. "Ah. So, he ate three of them." She reached for Ifrit's arm. "See, my loyal one, you were wrong to suspect Butayna."

Ifrit said nothing. She glanced at Esperanza before she returned to her task. Esperanza lowered her gaze, her lips compressed together. Had they intended for her to starve all day without a moment's concern for if she ate or drank anything?

"There was also a second person, the Sultana Fatima, who came with her servant."

The brush in Ifrit's hand hovered against her mistress' hair. Zarru paused in mid-step. Esperanza's gaze flitted between them as she pondered their reactions.

Leila gestured for Ifrit to continue with the brush. "Thank you for telling me, Butayna."

Zarru fastened the shutters. "Shall I light the lamps for the evening, my Sultana?"

"Please, Zarru. Butayna, did you not realize you should have closed the *shimasas* over each window? Now there is a chill in the room. I will not remind you in the future."

The stirring notes of some instrument like a lute reached the second floor. Esperanza raised her head at the sound.

"Do you recognize it, Butayna? Can you play the *oud*? Hamduna tries, but she should attend to her *henna* brushes instead."

With the clothes clasped against her chest, Esperanza said, "I learned to play it a little in the House of Myrtles."

"My Sultana!" Ifrit hollered. "When you answer our mistress, you will always say 'my Sultana' as a sign of the respect her position commands."

Leila patted her slave's arm. "Be at ease, my Ifrit. Butayna does not know our ways as yet." A smile curved her lips as she gazed at Esperanza. "You will study our customs in earnest, won't you?"

A promise implicit in her words suggested there would be repercussions if Esperanza did not do as expected.

"I shall try." When Ifrit's stare flicked again to hers and hardened, she added, "My Sultana."

She went to the corner and retrieved the Sultana's boots. When she turned, the smile on Leila's visage had disappeared. "What is that red stain on the back of your robe?" She looked down at the red, blue, and black carpet. "Are you bleeding?"

Perplexed, Esperanza set the clothes on the floor and tugged the back of her robe around to her hip. A dark blotch almost the color of russet marred the garment, just under her buttocks.

"Have you had your show of woman's blood before, Butayna?"

She turned at the sudden proximity of Leila, who had left the bed and stood before her. Wordless, she shook her head. A fat tear splashed on her cheek.

"There is no need to be frightened. It is but one of the trials of womanhood." She pressed a hand to Esperanza's arm. "Zarru, escort her to the baths. Give her several of the cotton bands and a change of clothes."

"At once, my Sultana." Zarru bowed and went into the first alcove. She opened up a cupboard covered by latticework at the base of the wall. Esperanza had not noticed it. What other secret enclosures did this palace hold?

Leila patted her arm. "Have you experienced any discomfort today?"

"There is an ache across my back and tightness in my belly, my Sultana."

"All expected. Leave my clothes here. I will summon Sut. Go to the bathhouse with Zarru. After you have attended to your needs, return here. You shall fetch fresh water from the cistern for my evening tea and you may eat with us. We are having roasted kid to celebrate the breaking of this evening's fast. This is the month of Ramadan, in which Muslims observe the fast. You and my other slaves may have fruits, water, juices, and breads during the day. We will feast together each evening."

Esperanza looked at the ground again. "It is Friday, my Sultana. I do not eat meat on this day."

"Then you will starve for there is nothing else. Come now, you must be hungry."

"I cannot permit you to tempt me to break my vows. I do not think my lord Jesus–"

A stinging slap from Leila cut her off. Esperanza clutched her cheek, stunned into silence.

Leila grasped her chin and raised it. The talon-like nails dug into Esperanza's skin until she winced. Leila's sea-green eyes sparkled in the lamp light.

"You do not think, Butayna. You do not feel. You do not disobey. You are a slave of this harem. Slaves have no thoughts or wishes contrary to those of their master or mistress. Slaves live to serve the commands of the Sultan and his family."

With a throaty sigh, she released Esperanza and waved her away. "Go with Zarru now."

After her easy dismissal, she beckoned Ifrit. "Fetch my blue robe, the one with the yellow stars."

Esperanza padded across the floor. At the edge of the first alcove, she paused and looked over her shoulder.

Zarru snapped, "Do not linger!"

Across the expanse, Esperanza met Leila's stare. "I won't be a slave forever, my Sultana."

"I see one lecture is not enough to subdue your insolence, Butayna. You will have harsh lessons to learn in this harem. Now go. I will not tell you again."

Into the passage and down the stairs in bare feet, Esperanza followed Zarru. The watchful gazes of the women in the chamber below followed. Sunset set the evening sky ablaze in burnished brass and fiery orange. Esperanza took the path the stewardess determined. Together, they crossed the marble walkway and stepped down into the center of the courtyard. Shaded by the orange trees and surrounded by verdant bushes and countless petals, Esperanza turned right and walked along a lengthy corridor. Torches illuminated the faces of stalwart sentries positioned at intervals along one wall.

Chatter greeted them before a procession of women appeared on the stairs at the end of the passageway.

"Stand aside and turn your face to the wall," Zarru ordered before she hastened to do the same.

A sweet, yet musky scent heralded the women before the one who led them spoke. "Hurry, my girls. We must make this *jarya* beautiful for Yusuf tonight."

Though she kept her gaze averted at Zarru's command, Esperanza could not deny herself a glimpse of the Sultana Safa, in white brocade, trimmed with gold ribbon. Little metal balls sewn at the wrists of her garment tinkled as she strode past. Her train of women scurried after her, the tallest among them, Miriam.

Esperanza's gasp echoed the length of the corridor. A dazed look overcame Miriam's dark gaze. Then she hastened to keep pace with the others.

Chapter 10
The Sultan's Bed

Granada, Andalusia
April 19 - 25, AD 1336 / 7 - 13 Ramadan 736 AH / 7th - 13th of
Iyar, 5096

After the final prayer of *Salat al-Isha*, Maryam stood trapped in a circle of Sultana Safa's slaves, who poked and prodded her in turns. She gritted her teeth and permitted them to do as they willed. What other choice did she have? Safa had decreed the name Miriam Alubel no longer belonged to her and she would be Maryam ever after. The Moors had taken her children and husband, her former existence away. One factor remained within her control.

The women pinned her hair up off her shoulders in waves of black curls. She stifled a screech as another silver gilt pin stabbed at her scalp. At the neckline, the slaves tied the strings of a shimmery *qamis* made of linen so sheer, she might as well have gone without the tunic. The white *sarawil* which tapered to her ankles were little better. Not even the red embroidered belt, the *tikka*, with its fringed edges suspended at her right hip made her feel less exposed. A good stiff breeze would reveal her body.

All the while, Safa strolled around the room within her apartment where she often took her morning meal. She inspected Maryam with pursed lips. The tiny crease etched between Safa's brows deepened. Had she already found something else she disliked? Would this require a third change of garments? Maryam stifled a yawn at the possibility. Another pin dug into her scalp. She glared at the slave who carried them until the woman backed away.

Maryam sighed deeply. Why, on one of the most important evenings in her life, had *El Dio* revealed Esperanza's presence here? When had she arrived? Maryam had never encountered her during the communal bath hours, so she could not have entered the palace of *al-Qal'at al-Hamra* before the week began, perhaps even as early as this afternoon. Why had she come now?

"That frown will not endear my son to you," Safa observed.

How dare the haggard crone interrupt her ruminations? The temptation to scratch Safa's dark eyes from her face stirred such joy in Maryam, she bit the inside of her cheek and kept the laughter at bay. Instead, she allowed herself the indulgence of a smile, the one Safa desired. She would discover the circumstances of Esperanza's intrusion later.

As she anticipated, Safa crossed her arms over her bosom and nodded. "Now, bring the rubies and gold!"

Safa's servants affixed ruby earrings to her lobes, which dangled almost to her shoulders, along with gold bracelets and anklets. A necklace of rubies set in gold with a pendant the size of an egg went around her neck and dangled at her waist. Nothing as fine as crafted by the expert hands of her father or Gedaliah, but Maryam knew better than to tell Safa so.

"You should feel quite honored, slave. These trinkets were but small portions of my bridal gifts, granted by my dear husband Ismail, Allah preserve his memory. If even one piece of jewelry is unaccounted for after tonight, I will not waste time with a summons for the executioner. I'll strangle you myself," Safa promised.

The lantern light cast a glint upon her eyes. They sparkled with malice and some other indiscernible emotion.

Maryam did not doubt Safa's vow. She had witnessed the cruelty of Yusuf's mother to slaves in the two months she had resided in the harem. Maryam refused to become the next hapless victim.

Safa ordered, "All of you, away." As her slaves withdrew to the fringes of the room, she approached Maryam. "Hold out your hands."

Maryam displayed the *henna* painted on her fingers and palms three days before.

"There is a smudge just below your wrist," Safa muttered. She glowered at Maryam before her bellow echoed. "Nazhun!"

If she wished, Maryam could have pitied the stunted slave who shuffled forward on pudgy legs, her back bowed and bent by possible years of abuse and torment in the service of a tyrant. She stood half the height of every other woman in the room. Her deformity was one of many defects. Hanks of garish orange hair hung on either side of Nazhun's narrow face and concealed sunken cheeks with the ash gray freckles Safa criticized so much. The other slaves affirmed Nazhun's age as five more than Maryam's own. Otherwise, she would have thought the beleaguered handmaid older than the Sultan's mother. Nazhun possessed a child's form. Her red-rimmed gaze, always puffed below the eyes, focused on the floor even as Safa berated her.

"Useless fool! Did I not tell you to ensure the *henna* dried before you removed the cotton bands?"

Nazhun whispered, "I did, my Sultana."

Safa grasped her chin and upturned her bulbous features to the light of the brass lantern. "You think so, eh?"

When she released her, nail marks indented Nazhun's skin. Safa grabbed Maryam's right hand. "What does this look like to you, Nazhun? It would appear you removed the cloths too early, wouldn't it?"

"As you say, my Sultana."

Safa cast aside Maryam's hand and stabbed a fingertip at the slave's temple. "As I say, indeed. Another of your foolish mistakes. Why do I keep you here? I should have had you flayed to the bone and left to die years ago, dwarf. You are nothing! Do you hear me, Nazhun?"

How could she not hear with Safa bellowing in her ear, flecks of spittle flying?

"I do, my Sultana. Please forgive me for my many offenses."

"I should not, but you'll live another day. Make the same error again and I may change my mind. Now get out of my sight!" Safa shoved the slave to the ground.

Nazhun's head hit the low table at Maryam's feet with a heavy thud. The servant groaned and clutched her skull. When she lifted her fingers, a little bloodstain dotted the tips.

"I said go!" Safa kicked her in the stomach. Nazhun doubled up and held her stomach, before she crawled on pudgy limbs across the carpet and into the next room.

Maryam studied the averted gazes of the other women, some whose lower lips trembled. Others idled and stared at some indeterminate spot in the room. All of them shook with fear. Safa inhaled almost as if she thrived on the trepidation of her women.

A sentry called at the door just beyond the room with gilded walls. Safa ordered someone to attend to him. One of the slaves scrambled. She returned soon, her head bowed. "My Sultana, the chief eunuch is here to escort Maryam to the Sultan's bedchamber."

"He will wait until I say the *jarya* is ready. More *kohl* for her eyes! Make her as beautiful as the *houri* of Paradise."

Maryam endured the application of thin lines of the dark powder, made from charred frankincense. Then another slave brought forth a ceramic pot pierced at the top. Fragrant vapors vented through the holes.

Safa barked, "Spread your legs and stand over the pot! Let the musk, sandalwood, rose, ambergris, and lemon infuse your clothes, your skin. Then go to my son's bed. May you bring him great joy."

With a nod, Maryam followed her commands. She left the chamber and passed beneath the sheer, red curtains. She intended to do more than grant the Sultan joy on this night. She would give him an heir.

The ghostlike Abdullah Hisham awaited her. At the first sight of him upon her arrival at *al-Qal'at al-Hamra*, bathed in the mid-afternoon sunlight, she thought a specter haunted the palace. The chief eunuch proved flesh and blood, but his albino features seemed ghostlike. He inspected her from head to toe before he escorted from the harem without a word.

She followed him out into a cool night. Innumerable stars twinkled like gold in the curtain of the heavens. A glimpse of the quarter moon disappeared behind a canopy of dark leaves and branches interlocked like a spider's web. A four-winged structure, with walls covered in a pattern of six-pointed stars opened to the south via an enclosed and guarded arch. The old palace offered scant protection, yet according to Safa, her son often retreated here for a sentimental connection to his ancestors.

The pathway encompassed a wide canal, reflected the torchlight stationed on poles around the complex. Under a pavilion, ten eunuchs stood at even intervals between five columns. Two other sentries guarded the door on the left. At a wave from the chief eunuch, Maryam pulled the handle. An ornate lantern with jade colored glass diffused an eerie green light. Multicolored tiles set within a wooden paneled framework covered the walls. She traversed the stairway and entered an attic-like chamber.

In the shuttered room of scant furnishings, a young man with dark, straight hair reclined on a yellow damask coverlet. She had seen him several times in the last two months, when he visited Safa on every second and fifth day of the week before public audience, or if he dined with his mother in her chambers. She doubted he noted her among Safa's slaves. Tonight, she would change his regard. He always appeared so serious. She would make him laugh before she exited this room.

His long feet angled away from the pillows, his head at the opposite end. He held a scroll in one hand and a thin reed in the other. His olive-brown fingers dipped the reed into an inkpot on the floor next to a pair of brown ankle boots. Soon the tip scraped across the parchment. By the blessings of *El Dio*, he did not favor his mother's overweight appearance. The shadows of a beard and mustache framed his cheeks and lips. Long limbed and of a lean build, he stretched out in a white linen *qamis* and opaque *sarawil*. In his nonchalant appearance, he could have been anyone except the sovereign. A table up by the pillows on the bed held a lantern, which provided a light source.

Maryam drew a deep breath and slid to her knees. She pressed her forehead to the floor and waited, just as Safa had trained her to do. She kept the old hag's admonitions uppermost in mind. She would not raise her head or speak unless Sultan Yusuf spoke first. She would do nothing until he acknowledged her.

For a time, his furious scribbles became the sole audible sound in the din. What words held him so absorbed? Safa claimed her son was a learned man, unequaled among his brothers and sisters. He excelled at his lessons and did not rely upon his ministers for letters of state. Such power possessed by someone at his age, a year younger than her, must be an enormous burden. He needed a companion, an equal to match his handsome form and his keen mind, with whom he could share his thoughts and troubles. A man of such capabilities would not be satisfied with a woman who pleased him just in the privacy of his bedchamber.

She suspected therein lay the reason for Yusuf's apparent lack of interest in his bevy of girls and women, for one went each week to his chamber, always a different *jarya* than the last. Maryam had seen them all, for Safa inspected each slave beforehand. Whether tall or short, thin as bowstrings or shapelier than the imagined *houri* in Paradise, his mother's offerings never stimulated Yusuf's fascination. Slaves with red, black, yellow, or brown hair, their skin whiter than alabaster marble or browner than the cedar panels of the harem's doors, went into his bed. All became disappointed when he did not summon them a second time.

Maryam would outdo them all and accomplish what they could not. She would make him hers. To do so required an appeal to his intellect as well as natural desires. His heart and mind must become and remain enthralled. Still, he was in the prime of his youth. What man of his age could resist the appeal of a beautiful woman?

He would have to lift his gaze from the task in order to view her charms. As far as she could tell, he had not looked up from the parchment. How much longer would she have to hold this position until he noticed her? He must have observed her intrusion by now. The perfume alone should have alerted him. Perhaps it was a game of wills he played with his *jawari*, where he sought to discover the limits of women's patience.

She smiled at the thought. He did not know her, but soon he would discover she held the forbearance of the Talmudic Job. She intended to gain much from a union with the Sultan. She had yielded so much in the last few months against her own will. A place at Yusuf's side would allow her to recoup those losses.

"So, you're the newest one my mother has sent." His withering exhalation and smooth tone warned her there would be no easy seduction. The scribbling had not stopped. "Look at me when I speak."

When she raised her gaze to his, the movement of his hand did halt. He sat up and planted his soles on the wooden floor. She suppressed a girlish giggle and settled with her legs drawn up under her.

His large, dark eyes roamed over her. "You don't appear any different from the others trained by my mother in ways she thinks will please me. What can you do, which the other *jawari* have not?"

"I can entertain you, my Sultan, both in and out of your bed."

He set the reed down on the sheepskin. "How do you propose to do that? How would you know what I find entertaining?"

She inhaled, followed by a deep sigh, and knew by the way his stare narrowed that he watched the rise and fall of her full breasts. "I am told you are an educated man of good taste and discernment. I can sing and dance for you, if you wish. Shall I recite the letters of the caliph's daughter Wallada and her lover Ibn Zaydun, whom I am told are among your favorites? My joy would be found in pleasing you, my Sultan."

He leaned forward. "Would you have nothing in return?"

"Whatever you desire to offer, my Sultan."

Yusuf's throaty chuckle resounded and he threw back his head. She smiled along with him for appearance's sake, though in truth she could not fathom what he found so funny. At least, she had accomplished one goal tonight.

When he sobered, he said, "Perhaps I was wrong about you." He placed the calfskin and other materials on the low table. Then he patted the space beside him. "Come, *jarya*. Take your place here with me."

She would ensure he always remembered she belonged at his side. With another deep sigh, she padded across the room in the soft kid slippers dyed a deep red, which Sultana Safa had provided. She sat beside him and looked down at her fingers clasped in her lap. Outside, the light patter of raindrops hit the roof.

"Don't be coy with me now." His firm grip on her chin raised her visage to his before he cupped her cheek. Up close, his teeth sparkled behind a wide grin. His fingers splayed on her flesh, he stroked the curve down to her lips with his thumb.

"So soft. So fair. My mother trained you well. What has she named you?"

"Maryam, my Sultan."

"And your name before you became a slave here?"

Why must he bring up the past in their first meeting? "It was Miriam Alubel, my Sultan."

He chuckled. "Not too inventive of my mother. She is often more thoughtful."

The last thing she wanted to talk about was Safa. "Was I misinformed, my Sultan? Are Wallada and Ibn Zaydun's verses not among your favorites?"

He countered with a question of his own. "Is that why you learned them? To please me. To take joy in my delight, as you repeat everything my mother told you to say. Are you nothing, but a mindless sycophant?"

When she drew back and stared at her clasped fingers, his hand fell away. She said, "I studied the poets at my mother's knee. She aspired to write verses herself, my Sultan, but the wife of a Jewish goldsmith has few choices in life. I do nothing just to please anyone. As I have said, there must be joy in it for me as well."

He leaned closer. "Affronted, are you? Have I undone your bold plan to seduce me with more than your body? You will learn, *jarya*, I do not give in so soon."

Her stare flicked to his again. His forehead wrinkled. Something flickered within the hardness of his gaze. The same rapacious look other men often granted her. He would be no different, but if he proved to be, she would thrive on the challenge.

She inclined her head toward his and inhaled the scent of orange peel from his clothes. "Nor do I, my Sultan."

Yusuf twisted his body toward hers and sat cross-legged on the bed, which groaned as he shifted his weight. An intent look from him raked over her face as if he searched for something elusive. Then his callused hand clamped on the back of her neck. A lesser woman would have quaked with fear. Instead, she admired the strength inherent in his sinewy grasp, the touch of one accustomed to the grip of hard leather in his hands. His fingers cupped her nape and then slid away. Then they rose to her hair. One by one, he removed the pins and tossed them away.

She hid her smile at his unhurried gestures. Safa had demanded the return of her jewels. She had said nothing about the pins. Tendrils fell around Maryam's shoulders at first, followed by a cascade of her black hair. He ran his hand through the length of it, weighed the silken feel, and brought a coil to his nose.

His nostrils flared. "Jasmine oil. My favorite. She did not miss a thing."

Maryam guessed his displeasure at his mother's meticulous instructions dissipated now, as he followed the path of the curls to one curved at her breast. His hot gaze lingered there for so long, her skin turned balmy in a flush of heat and her nipple tightened. He raised his hand as if to cup her skin through the cloth. Then he seemed to think better of it. Instead, he swiped her hair back along her shoulders. His fingers closed on her arm and stroked the sheer linen. He even drew little circles with the pad of his thumb. His breath grew heavy, the scant space between them warmer with each passing moment.

She had anticipated his arousal, but also found her own mirrored his. After the violence her body endured, she once believed she would never crave a man's touch again. Yusuf's proximity awoke her natural instincts. For the first time in the months since Gedaliah's death and after the abuses she suffered among her captors, the stirrings of desire thrummed through her veins again. She wanted this man, not for his power, but for himself. He was wrong. Safa had missed one thing in her instructions. She never warned Maryam of how she might respond to Yusuf. She drew deep, even breaths and stilled the flutters of her heart. She could not lose sight of the ultimate goal so soon, no matter how her body betrayed her.

He moved closer and silky hair fell over his eyes. His fleshy lips parted. She smiled and smoothed away his forelock, his brow feverish against her fingertips.

He turned his head and nipped her wrist. "You are indeed a mystery. Why do I feel you can make a man believe anything, yet never reveal the truth of yourself?"

She kissed his smooth forehead and nuzzled his cheek. Her mouth hovered against his. "You have more than this night to know me, my Sultan. You have all the time in the world."

In the instant their lips met, the delicious warmth stirred by her triumph coiled in her abdomen and spread. The first taste of his mouth proved sweeter than honey, softer than silk. His fingers quested, gripped her hips through the cloth, and lifted her until she sat astride him. Her legs splayed on either side of him, she bucked against the hardness between his thighs. When he cupped her bottom with a ragged groan, she melted against him. She framed his face in her hands. Rough stubble scraped her palms, but she cared little. Too much time had passed since she knew a man's desire for her and experienced the same yearning. She moaned into his mouth, her arms draped around his shoulders. She had almost forgotten the simple pleasures of a kiss. His heart vied in a taut rhythm with hers.

A wave of dizziness overcame her as they pulled apart. Yusuf's fingers unlaced the strings of her *qamis*. She gloried in his haste and heated touch. She tugged at his neckline. Their mutual eagerness made a mockery of earlier vows barring an easy surrender. He tugged the tunic up and bade her raise her arms. As he wrenched the linen over her head and flung it aside, he stared down between their bodies. He hefted the necklace and threw it on the ground.

"Let me see you." His voice had grown hoarse.

She leaned back and let him have his fill of the prospect of her. An enflamed stare traveled up the line etched from her stomach to her breastbone. He followed the curve of each breast to her rounded shoulders and long neck.

"By Allah's grace, you are the most beauteous creature I have ever seen."

He lowered his head. The quick flicker of the tip of his tongue against her nipple knotted her stomach. The thought of little Palomba at her breast intruded, but she banished the image of her sweet girl from mind. No one, not even this proud man, could ever make her forget her beloved children. If she achieved her intent, one day, both would have the justice they deserved. Until then, Maryam could not dwell in the bitter past. The future with Yusuf mattered.

He cupped both breasts in his hands and suckled each of them in turn. The contrast of his darker fingers against her smooth skin sent a shiver through her. Then he drew a line with one fingertip down to her navel, the same path soon followed by his lips.

"You are no virgin. No woman untried could stoke a man's fires as you do."

She stiffened for a moment. Her belly was neither rounded nor maidenly flat. Could he discern the difference in a woman who had borne a child from others brought to his bed in the past? If he could, the fact left him untroubled. Without awaiting any comment from her, he gripped her waist with both hands. His tongue returned to her nipples, where be laved the buds until they stung. All of her senses were ablaze. She ground her hips against his and leaned back. Her nails delved through his hair and raked his scalp.

Yusuf held her taut as a bowstring and raised his head. He gazed into her eyes. "Do you want this? Not because my mother ordered you into my bed, but because you wish it?"

"*Nam*, my Sultan." She tugged his head down and prayed he believed in her desire.

He pressed her against the end of the bed. The coverlet bunched her around her hips and slid to the edge of the mattress. Her hair brushed the floor. His hands made short work of the knot in the *tikka*, lifted her legs, and jerked the *sarawil* down. He scooted back, his hands tight fists at his hips. He sucked in his breath.

She studied his narrow, handsome face. He hid none of his emotions from her. His brows lifted and his eyes widened at first. A deep rose flush blossomed across his cheeks. Lines furrowed his brow while he took in the curve of her ankles, the length of her legs and the hairless triangle between her thighs. Then he removed the bracelets, anklets, and earrings until she wore no adornments.

He whispered, "Allah, preserve me."

Her throaty giggle echoed. "I want you naked as well, my Sultan."

A strangled moan escaped his lips. He took off his clothes faster than he had removed hers and hovered over her trembling body. She palmed the pelt of fine hairs, which branched out across his chest and tapered to a thin line just above his navel. The hair matched those on his lean forearms. She grasped both and tugged him closer. Her lips sought his again. He obliged her and covered her mouth. With his hands underneath her thighs, he molded her flesh before he rolled and placed her atop him. The hair on his chest tickled her nipples, already turned into hard little peaks.

He broke the kiss, nibbled her earlobe and neck. He inhaled the fragrance of her as though he could not get enough. She laughed and sat astride him, her thighs on either side. Her forefinger smoothed over his lips. He bit and suckled the tip of her finger.

"What did you say earlier, my Sultan, about not surrendering so soon?"

He cupped between her thighs. His thumb glided over her flesh. Sparks shot through the epicenter of her body and she lifted her hips. His chest rumbled. "I recall you spoke much the same words."

"Mm. I may have. I'm h-h-having some difficulty, mmm, with my memory, my Sultan."

He clutched her hips and raised himself up. His kiss pressed between her breasts before he looked up at her. "As fickle as your mind may be, I recall the words. I must say, you are more ambitious than most of my women."

"Then perhaps... my Sultan cares little... for whether I am a virgin?"

"Indeed, I do not care."

She moved her hips in slow, tight circles. "H-how am I different from the others, my Sultan? Don't they all... make an attempt... to satisfy you?" His thumb proved distracting. Twinges of delight shot through her body.

He stilled her motions and withdrew his light touch. "None have ever delighted me as much as you tonight."

She held his regard and lowered her hips. His groan erupted. She pressed her body down and took in the full length of him. He bowed his head and kissed her neck. Both hands tightened at her waist and pressed her to him. She clung to his shoulders, her soft cheek against his silky hair.

Maryam breathed in his ear, "Oh, my Sultan, your pleasure has just begun."

***

In the dimness of Yusuf's room, his fingers stroked her forearm. "Were you married before entering the harem?"

The rumble of his voice stirred her from drowsiness. She stretched and pressed her bottom against his hip. His hand stilled her. "Do not seek to distract me. Answer the question."

With her back still to him, she pouted and pillowed her head in silken comfort. "I was married, my Sultan."

"What happened to your husband?"

"He died in the same raid which brought me to *al-Andalus*, my Sultan."

His fingers slid across her side and cupped her lower abdomen. Despite the lingering pulses between her thighs, she shifted her legs and opened them.

He ignored the hint. "Did you have a child for him? Where is this child?"

She made no reply and blinked back a sudden rush of tears. The silence stretched for the space of several breaths, while she fought for composure. His hand glided up her arm and cupped her cheek. "Who were these men who took the life of your husband and child?"

Maryam stiffened. "I never knew their names, my Sultan."

No one would deny her the chance for revenge. If she shared every agonized moment she had endured on the *meseta*, Yusuf would not seek Ahmed and Fadil al-Qurtubi on her behalf. His desires satiated, he might give no more thought to her than the next *jarya*. No, before she revealed the truth, she must have his heart and mind as well. Besides, the justice she craved was not his to extract.

"Forgive me. Difficult memories are fresh and painful, like a wound for which the best balm is time and healing." He pressed a kiss at the curve of her shoulder.

She swallowed. "You have not disturbed me, my Sultan. Your care emboldens me to think I have pleased you so well, you are attuned to my moods."

When he laughed, she rolled on her back and kissed him, a languid intertwining of their lips and tongues. He pulled back and placed his firm lips in turn against her wet eyelashes, his fingers on the curve of her cheek.

How had he learned to be such a tender, but demanding lover? Her sensual match in every way. She could lose sight of her aim in the comfort of his arms. Still, she must never surrender in full, not even if Yusuf did.

"Do you wish me to leave now?" She opened her eyes and caressed his cheek with a fingertip. "Your mother explained the custom. No one except a *kadin* or your wife is allowed to remain in your bed overnight."

He gathered her close to him. "Stay with me a little longer."

A thrill rippled through her abdomen, while his hand skimmed the surface and delved lower.

Later, when the sentries called the midnight watch, Yusuf kissed Maryam's brow. "I should let Hisham get some sleep at this late hour."

She nipped his jawline. "Is it true he lingers outside your door to escort a *jarya* back to the harem no matter the time?"

"He is dutiful."

She noted the information and extracted herself from his clutches. Even then, he reached for her. She avoided his hands. Instead, she stood with a loud yawn and stretch. While she crouched and picked up every pin he had scattered, she also offered him the full view of her curvaceous backside. His resultant groan stirred a deep sigh of satisfaction within her. While she dressed, he reached for the parchment and his writing implements.

Maryam eyed him over her shoulder. "Shouldn't you be resting, my Sultan?"

A grin softened his angular features and lent him a boyish appearance. "I find myself refreshed and exhilarated."

She joined him in a hearty laugh before she asked, "What words do you compose?"

"No poetic verses, I can assure you. Nothing to please the recipient of this missive. I am replying to the demands of King Alfonso of Castilla-Leon. He reminds me of our treaty signed three years ago in which I promised to release Christian captives from the *corrals*."

"Do you intend to do so now?"

"*La*. I will not until Alfonso grants the freedom of the Muslim captives he promised by the same treaty.

She shook her head and turned to him, once again attired in the clothes and jewels. He reached for her hand again, but she ignored the gesture and bowed in the same manner as earlier. At his command, she stood.

"*Al-salam 'alayka*, my Sultan."

"*Wa-'alayka*, Maryam."

She strolled to the door with a slight sway of her hips. His laughter rumbled again.

When she went down the stairs and emerged into the night, the chief eunuch stood beneath an almond tree. Puddles gathered on the tiles around him, evidence of the earlier rainfall. An expectant gaze flitted over her face. Without a word, he retraced the steps to the harem and she followed, skirting the pools of rainwater.

The tangy saltiness of Yusuf's skin lingered on Maryam's tongue. She licked her lips and smiled at the prospect of many more days and nights with him.

***

Seated at a low table beside the window in the hour after *Salat al-Fajr*, Sultana Safa accepted the *nakhwa* and black seed Nazhun had brewed. Her silent slaves waited in the fringes of her reception room, among them Maryam. The Sultan's mother drank the bitter beverage without any sweetener every morning. A platter held two slices of warm flatbread, baked with sumac, sesame seeds, and dried thyme. Safa dipped the first in olive oil and chewed with obvious enjoyment.

Bleary-eyed, Maryam's stomach gurgled. She leaned against the wall with a sigh. Hunger dogged her each morning and night. Safa did not believe slaves required much nourishment and would never permit hers to eat at her table. Her women must wait until she finished.

Safa peered down into the courtyard and grumbled, "What is he doing here at this time of the morning?"

The doorkeeper announced the chief eunuch's arrival. Safa finished her meal before she permitted his entry. She brushed her hands free of crumbs and washed her fingers in a rosewater bowl.

Hisham bowed three times as he entered the chamber and greeted Safa. Her almost imperceptible nod acknowledged him.

"How unfortunate you have just arrived now! I have already finished my morning meal. I would have saved a little of the flatbread for you, had I known."

Hisham's baldpate glistened when sunlight broke through the clouds again and filtered through the lattice window. "You are most kind, my Sultana."

From the voluminous brocaded sleeve of his *jubba*, he withdrew a packet wrapped in muslin and tied with yellow ribbon. He set it on the table. "I bring gifts from the Sultan."

Safa's rapacious grasp closed on the package, before she peered at Hisham. "How kind! Why did Yusuf not bring this himself?"

"He is with the *Diwan al-Insha*. The ambassadors from Aragon have returned with King Pedro's counteroffer."

She pursed her lips. "Which is...?"

"An extension of the truce enjoyed with his father, for another five years."

"Does Ridwan believe we should accept the terms? It is little better than our four-year treaty with Castilla-Leon. What is the opinion of other influential ministers among the council members?"

"My Sultana, I do not know what my brother will suggest, nor am I privy to the opinions of others among your son's council of ministers."

"Little liar!" She snorted and opened the packet. Inside, a beautiful necklace of black opals, pale pink pearls, and gold beads rested on a leather-bound book. Safa frowned at the latter, but she picked up the jewelry and admired it in the natural light. "Oh, how exquisite!"

"Your son thought you might be pleased with his offering. He means it as a testament of his everlasting love and devotion to you."

"He has forgotten I do not share his fondness for reading."

"The book is for the slave from last night. Maryam."

Maryam perked up when the chief eunuch mentioned her name. He beckoned her with a crook of his thin finger. She crossed the room and sank into a deep bow.

"She does that well, my Sultana," he remarked.

Safa ignored his comment. "Why does Yusuf send her a gift, Hisham? Will he claim the slave as his *kadin* so soon?"

"The Sultan has not informed me of his intention." He paused and tapped Maryam's shoulder. When she lifted her gaze, he slapped the book into her hands.

Safa watched her. "Well, what sort of book is it?"

Maryam opened the crisp pages at random and bit the inside of her cheek, as she stifled a cry of joy. She avoided the pertinent stares from Safa and Hisham. "It is a book of poetry. The Sultan's thoughtfulness and generosity is unexpected. May I keep it, my Sultana?"

Safa rolled her eyes and waved her away. Then she bellowed for Nazhun, who removed the leftovers of the meal.

The chief eunuch would not be disarmed without some inquiry. "Why did my master give you poetic verses? Did you speak of poetry with him last night?"

"I did, my lord."

He snatched the book from her and frowned at the words written in Ladino. "What is this Jewish gibberish? Why would the Sultan possess such a book?"

"Give it back to her. She is a Jewess and I presume she can read. Leave it to a useless slave to bore my son with talk of poetry. You had better have not lied to me, slave, when you said Yusuf enjoyed your visit. Now come, Hisham, I would observe his discussions with the *Diwan al-Insha.*" Safa rose and looked around the room for her stewardess, before she flung the necklace at her. "Put this among my other jewels and see my women to their tasks in my absence. Upon my return, I expect the rooms tidied and everything in readiness for the *hammam.*"

Maryam expected to undertake duties as well. The Moors held no respect for her Sabbath. She clutched the book against her thigh after Safa and the chief eunuch departed. Where could she hide it from prying eyes?

***

A vicious slap stung Maryam's cheek. Where Safa's ring scraped her, she clutched the skin and prayed it remained unbroken.

Safa crouched above her, arm upraised again. Spittle flew as she vented her wrath. "Filthy Jew! You went to my son's bed, told me he was well pleased with you and then this? Why could you not capture his seed? Are you barren?"

She flung her hand at Maryam, who clutched the apex of her *sarawil.* Her woman's blood tainted the fabric. Six days after she first went to Yusuf's bed, the proof of her failure damned her.

"I am not barren!"

"Then you should have produced proof you could carry a child. You will not make a fool of me again. I shall send another to Yusuf this week."

Maryam's heart pitched. It did not seem possible for her plans to be undone so soon.

"You're not the one to give him heirs. Get the cotton bands from my stewardess and go the *hammam*. Clean yourself up. You are a disgrace!"

When Safa left her with a disgusted snort, Maryam reached under her straw sleeping mat, where she kept the book of poetry hidden. Her fingers opened to the start of a favorite stanza, one she could not read with her bleary eyesight. Three centuries before, Wallada had composed the words for her lover after an evening of pleasure. Maryam recited them in her mind.

'The nights now seem long to me, and I complain night after night. That only those were so short, which I once spent with you.'

Chapter 11
At the Sultan's Pleasure

Esperanza Peralta

Granada, Andalusia
August 3, AD 1336 / 24 Dhu al-Hijja 736 AH / 25th of Av,
5096

When summer baked Andalusia in shimmering heat, the close
family members of the Sultan's household escaped to the *Jannat
al-'Arif*, the whitewashed summer palace built on a hillside
across from *al-Qal'at al-Hamra*. Esperanza had seen it in the
distance on the morning of her arrival. Seated alone on the floor
beside a window grille, she folded the laundered garments Sut
had brought up in the morning. The call to noonday prayer
occurred earlier and Leila would be with her relatives. They
observed the ritual invocation five times a day in the eastern
oratory atop a hillock at the *Jannat al-'Arif*. Solitude often eluded
Esperanza, except for rare moments like this one where the ever-
watchful Ifrit accompanied her mistress and the rest of the
slaves busied themselves with their duties in the tower.

With a sigh, Esperanza swiped tendrils of hair pasted to her
temple and leaned her feverish head against the cool masonry.
From the window, she looked north beyond the central courtyard
with its pool, the tiled roofs of the arcaded gallery and the
expanse of green boughs and terraced orchards. She wished
herself far from this place.

Sultan Yusuf's great-grandfather Muhammad II ordered its
construction, with changes made during the reign of Yusuf's
father Ismail. Fig trees and laurels, abundant roses and white
petals of jasmine lined the route to the summer palace. Leila and
her retinue lodged in two rooms to the northeast apart from the
southern pavilion, where Sultana Safa resided. In the newer
rooms above the northern pavilion, the Sultan dwelled. He
emerged in the Royal House of Felicity at rare instances to
welcome his two brothers or ministers when they visited.

Her fourth month of residence among the household of the
Sultan revealed much about the indolent lives of the Moors. They
took great pleasure in food and drink, in the natural beauty of

146

their surroundings, while they ignored the plight of so many who toiled for their purposes. Invisible chains bound her in service of a mercurial Sultana, so cruel and kind by contrasts Esperanza often despaired as to the mood she might find Leila in each day.

In the warmth of the afternoon, a sudden gust of wind streamed hair away from her face and off her shoulders. She raised her features to the welcome breeze. Modesty had compelled her to tie the strings of the lavender colored cotton *qamis,* with its embroidered neckline of flowers slit to the valley of her chest. Thin *sarawil* belted with a *tikka* covered her legs. While she toiled, she sang a *cantiga* of a valiant *caballero* who rescued a maiden from the Moor who kept her imprisoned in his castle.

"I believe you have the second verse incorrect. At first, the girl longs for her father's rescue. When she sees a white mount on the horizon, she thinks it is his, not the horse of the *caballero.*"

When she turned at the intrusion, Sultan Yusuf stood in the doorway. His shoulder pressed against the post. He held a gray and white kitten in his arms, which he set on the floor.

Esperanza scrambled and spilled all the folded clothes from her lap. She bowed before him, her forehead pressed to the cool marble.

Leila often spent time with her brother when duty or other visitors did not occupy him, but Ifrit always accompanied her on those visits. Esperanza had been in Yusuf's presence once, three weeks ago when the family gathered in the garden between the two pavilions in celebration of Prince Ismail's birthday.

His red leather sandals slapped against the floor and halted at her side. She quivered as his hand settled on her shoulder. "You may rise."

When she raised her head, he stood over in similar modest dress, except the round neck hole of his white *qamis* opened wider at the shoulder. The kitten nipped at his sandals and rubbed his fur against Yusuf's ankle. Then he scurried into the corners as if he chased some imaginary rodent. Yusuf's stare followed the kitten's erratic movements, while Esperanza looked on in amazement at the Sultan's softened, almost blissful features.

At her first sight of him in a brocaded midnight blue *jubba* shot through with silver threads, his elegant and pristine manner made him stand out among all others. Now, he might have blended in among his slaves. No rings adorned his hands. Dark hair curled at his ears and a beard covered his cheeks.

He looked at her just then, as if he caught her staring too long. "I thought Leila returned here after prayers. Perhaps she has gone to the baths, though it is unlikely since my mother is there at this hour. Do you know where my sister went?"

Her eyes averted, she shook her head. "I do not, my Sultan."

He crouched at her side. "The rest of her women are with her, for I have seen no one else. Why did they leave you behind?"

Why must he ask questions to which she did not know the answer? The lack of knowledge must make her appear inept in his opinion.

"I do not know, my Sultan."

He frowned. "Are you always thus? Quiet and sullen like a little brown-haired mouse?"

Before she could offer an answer, his fingers grasped her chin and raised her face for his inspection. She could not have avoided his rapt gaze if she tried. Dark circles shadowed his reddened eyes. Was he ill? She peeked at his brow, which did not appear feverish.

"Though no mouse would ever possess eyes like amber stones," he whispered before his hand fell away. He stood and brushed the same fingers over the left leg of his *sarawil*.

Was his touch upon her skin so abhorrent, he had to wipe it away? She never asked for his attention. With a groan, she picked up the scattered clothes. If he had not entered, she would be half finished by now. Instead, she must start the task again. Why did he loiter in the room, hovering over her? His presence offended more than Ifrit's own. He must have something else to do, a guard or eunuch to command, or a girl to take to his bed. She frowned at the course of her thoughts. Why should she care how the greatest slave master in Andalusia spent his day?

Contrary to her wish for his departure, Yusuf crossed the room. He sat on one of two cedar wood chairs beside a small chest where his sister kept her jewels. The kitten slinked around Yusuf's feet and stretched out. He licked the large white patches on his paws.

Yusuf said, "You will sing for me."

She jerked her gaze away from the kitten. "What?"

His rich, throaty laughter startled her, coming from such a grim-faced visage. She had never seen him smile on the night of his brother's birthday, while he mingled among the guests. He appeared so serious at the celebration, she thought it impossible for him to show amusement. He did, as he leaned forward with a grin, his chin propped up on his fist.

"You forgot to say 'my Sultan' as is customary address. I will not remind you again. Do you often wear these frowns in Leila's presence? She must grow tired of your sighs and sadness."

She snapped, "I am held in bondage! It is not my lot in life to be happy, my Sultan."

His brows lifted and his nostrils flared wide. She clapped a hand over her mouth, astonished at her own audacity. The piles of cloth tumbled again as she rushed to his side and collapsed at his feet. She clasped her thin fingers together.

"Please, my lord, I mean, my Sultan, forgive me! If the Sultana Leila ever knew—"

His gaze narrowed. "You presume my sister cares for your feelings. If you are so miserable here, perhaps Leila should end your misery at once. She would do well to summon the executioner—"

"No, my Sultan, please! I do not want to die. I have to live."

He tugged her chin again and this time, his touch lingered. A dark-eyed gaze bored into hers, coupled with a tight-lipped smile. "Then do not give in to such despair. Life is a trial for all, even for a Sultan. You must do as I have. Live and find your happiness wherever you may."

She doubted he could ever understand her losses. She withdrew and returned to her duty. His keen stare remained on her. She obliged him and started another tune, a *cantiga* of lovers separated by frontier wars, both with a promise to remain faithful in the absence of the other.

> '*Sweet noble knight, how I long to see you again,*
> *For love of you, my heart forever faithful,*
> *The pain I shall learn to bear, until your return,*
> *Do not forget me, or my devotion to you.*
>
> '*Think only of me, never choose another,*
> *For if you leave me forever, I shall surely die,*
> *Let my eyes see you again in this life,*
> *For without you, there shall be no joy for me.*

When she would have taken up the next verses, meant for the *caballero* to his lady, the rich timbre of Yusuf's voice matched hers. She lapsed into incredulous silence and sat back on her heels, while he sang:

> '*Sweet noble lady, I shall never be untrue*
> *There is no joy in your absence.*
> *Never give your heart away to another lover,*
> *For without you, I would die.*
>
> *However far you may be from me, have faith.*

Your love has ruined me for another.
God in heaven, never let me leave this life,
Ere I see your sweet, fair face again.

Her heart raced. Then she questioned him, "My Sultan, how do you know the *cantiga?*"

"When Leila and I were children, our grandmother provided for our educational needs with the help of tutors. She personally taught us many things about Christians, including your languages and customs, and some of your songs and poems. She believed knowledge would arm us with a better awareness of our foes. There is much to admire about Castillan verse and song. *Cantar de mío Cid* is still one of my favorites. Do you know it?"

"My father taught me." When the kitten mewled, she asked, "Is he yours, my Sultan?"

"No, a gift for Leila. Her chamomile tea aided me in previous seasons. I came to find more. I thought the pet would be fair recompense for—"

"Yusuf!" The object of his discussion strolled into the room, Ifrit and Sut at her heels.

She looked from her brother to Esperanza, before she bowed. "Yusuf, what drew you from your pavilion at midday? I thought you would have slept after *Salat al-Zuhr.*"

"I could not find comfort in my bed. I came to you for chamomile tea."

She peered at the kitten who slumbered at his feet. "And you thought to bribe me to have Rima prepare the brew?"

A sheepish grin suffused his face in a rose pink flush. He offered his hand.

She clasped his fingers and pressed her lips to the olive-brown skin. "I thank you, but the gesture was unnecessary. I would do anything for you, dear brother."

While Leila sent word to Rima via her stewardess, Esperanza bent her head to her task. Having witnessed their bond, she thought herself an interloper, in part, because she understood every word of their exchange.

Since her arrival at *al-Qal'at al-Hamra*, she had listened and grasped the nuances of a new language. At night when Leila dismissed her women to their floor mats, permitting just Ifrit at her side, Esperanza did not seek her rest. In her mind, she repeated all the words and phrases learned throughout the day. She risked discovery by surreptitious exchanges with slaves in the gardens. Without practice, she would never achieve her aim. When Leila gave her other slaves instructions, Esperanza heeded the words and responses until she achieved more than a general perception. Thus far, no one had detected her duplicity.

She wished to leave, but both Yusuf and his sister would not take a kind view of her interruption now. They behaved as though she was not present.

Leila took the chair opposite her brother. The hem of her *rida* trailed to the ground, the voluminous robe dyed in expensive saffron, with a *qamis* worn next to her skin.

Her brother inquired, "Where did you go after *Salat al-Zuhr?*"

With a downturned mouth, Leila uttered, "I went to see our grandmother at *al-Qal'at al-Hamra.*"

The same aged Sultana whom Esperanza had met upon her arrival in the harem. Yusuf sighed. "Was she better today than in recent weeks?"

"She was. Perhaps she is improving at last."

Yusuf shook his head. "You always say so and then suffer the disappointment."

"I have to believe it can be otherwise!"

"I understand your struggle. This is a very difficult time for all of us, her especially. My doctor says old age is the culprit, nothing more. I have never imagined a life without her, but each day I see how she is slipping away from all of us. You must accept it, Leila! Something has changed inside her. Even she acknowledged it when she ceded control of the harem to my mother."

When she would have interrupted him, he held up his hand and she clamped her lips together.

He said, "I do not say these things to be cruel. I have never found much use for pretense and I cannot allow it now. Why do you torture yourself so, Leila? You take pains each day to talk with her of things she will never recall on the morrow. She is mired in the past."

"You want me to help her forget these recent years?"

"You know I do not desire the impossible. Whenever you return after an encounter with her, your saddened demeanor is inescapable. It pains me! You have to acknowledge the changes in her, sister."

"Why should they be permanent? She would never have given up on any of us. I will not give up on her!" Leila's sharp voice rang through the room.

Esperanza's heart thudded, but she kept her gaze averted lest Leila guessed at her secret understanding of the evident pain inside.

Leila's lips quivered while she stared at the floor. "Forgive me, Yusuf. It is... difficult to see how... different she is."

151

Yusuf's hand covered hers. "She will never be the same woman she once was, Leila. She possesses a strong heart and great courage, but she will never again be the person we knew in our childhood."

Leila murmured, "When our cousins murdered our father, she became mother and father to me. She has been our support for so long, yours especially."

"Did she ask after me?"

"She never fails to mention you, brother. She said you must not trouble yourself to visit each day, especially when your duties as Sultan demand your attention. At least she remembered you have ascended the *kursi al-mulk* this time."

Esperanza nodded to herself. *Kursi* meant seat and Juan Manuel once said the Arabic word for power was *al-mulk*. Seat of power. Leila referred to the throne.

Yusuf had seemed so filled with admiration of his grandmother, yet Sultana Fatima was not among any of the occupants of the family rooms here. If Leila spoke with such devotion, why had her brother left an old woman behind while he and the rest of his family dwelled in the summer palace?

Leila continued in a dull monotone, "Seven days ago, she wondered when our brother Muhammad would return from Malaka. She worried after his well-being in the company of Uthman ibn Abi'l-Ula. I could not remind her of Muhammad's cruel death at Uthman's once trusted hands."

Yusuf responded, "When I visited in the same evening, the memory returned to her as soon as she saw me. She wept in my arms afterward. Sometimes, I wonder if it would not do her well to forget the past. Think of all she endured until my reign, Leila."

"I try not to. The murders of our father and our brother Muhammad would have destroyed a lesser woman, but not her. She survived."

He squeezed her fingers. "She taught us to do the same, to preserve this family and its proud name. For a time, she has been our sole strength. We honor her life by living ours to the fullest. We cannot dwell in the past. In her more lucid moments, she would have told us, 'Look to the future.' She did so for our sakes. For this and much more, I will honor her all the days of my life. I shall visit with her this evening, even if she will not remember it in the morning."

After a long sigh, Leila nodded. He smiled at her. "Whenever I see you, I imagine the beauty of Sultana Fatima in her youth. You should have married, sister. You can still make someone a fortunate husband. After the boy in Qirbilyan died of the pox, why did you not ask our brother Muhammad to arrange another union?"

"I did not wish it. Dear Muhammad, Allah preserve his memory, consented." She looked up as Ifrit brought a tray of glasses and offered them the lemon-colored *sharbah* inside. "Do not worry for me, dear brother. I have everything I desire here."

Leila lifted the glass to her painted lips and peered at her slave before saying, "What of you, dear brother? Shall you ever marry? Will your mother offer up an endless supply of *jawari* who occupy your bed for one night? They return to the harem to face her wrath."

He sipped the *sharbah*. "There was one who charmed me more than the others."

"Ah! I had not heard you had chosen a *kadin*. Your other *jawari* must be so disappointed and ready to claw your favorite's eyes out. Don't become too attached."

"Thank you for the advice, but I have not picked a favorite, sister."

"What of the *jarya* whom you just mentioned? Has she been poisoned already?"

"I do not believe so. *Ummi* sent her to me months ago. I would have summoned her again, but when I asked for her, *Ummi* said her woman's blood made a return to my bed impossible. Since then, al-Maghrib el-Aska has occupied my concern."

"You remember the *jarya* now. She must have been rather skillful."

He chuckled. "Oh, she was, sweet sister."

Esperanza did not wish to listen as Yusuf extolled the virtues of his bed slave. She did not have to guess what he thought those might be. His casual talk disgusted her. How could a man, who must have bedded countless women each month regardless of their wishes to the contrary, speak with such ease of his encounters? His women meant nothing to him. She doubted they felt the same way about him.

She would not listen any further. She gathered the bundles of cloth and stacked them in neat folds within three chests Leila brought from *al-Qal'at al-Hamra*. With any luck, she would be finished soon and could escape downstairs.

To her horror, he continued, "I have never beheld a woman as sensuous as she. Tall and black-haired, her eyes a deep shape of indigo. More than her beauty intrigued me. She challenged me in ways no other *jarya* would have dared. I delighted in her body and mind in equal measure. It was almost as if she was there right beside me, but still I could not touch the deepest part of her." When his sister sniggered, he also laughed. "I do not mean that, Leila! She was a mystery, elusive. She gave with passion and took the same without hesitation."

"She does not sound like the usual frightened virgin your mother offers."

"She was not. She lost her husband and child in a raid across the border. It has been four months, but I recall every detail of one night with her."

Leila still smirked. "Including her name?"

"*Nam*, even that. She was Maryam the Jewess."

The lid of the chest slammed with a loud bang, despite Esperanza's desperate attempt to keep it open with her free hand.

Yusuf eyed her with a frown, but Leila's smile widened. Her ardent gaze sparkled as she focused on Esperanza and pinned her to the spot with one look.

Then she declared, "*Idiota!* Butayna, have a care with my caskets. If that wood splinters, I shall drive the shards up your nails myself. *Sí*, you understand threats well."

Her brother stilled her. "You can always buy another chest."

"That is not the point, Yusuf. The cedar wood is an heirloom our grandmother gave me, part of her *addahbia*. Butayna knows the care I require, don't you, slave?"

Esperanza nodded. "*Sí*. Forgive me, my Sultana. I shall be more cautious."

While the brother and sister resumed their conversation, Esperanza returned to her work, but her movements were sluggish compared to the flurry of thoughts within her head. It could not be coincidence. Four months ago, she entered the harem and encountered Miriam coming from the baths. Had the Sultana Safa prepared her then to bed the Sultan?

Esperanza had not seen her since then, not even at Prince Ismail's birthday. The physical description and personality traits Yusuf indicated and the circumstances of the *jarya*'s placement in the harem matched. Although his pronunciation of the name was not quite right, he must have meant Miriam Alubel.

Yusuf finished the *sharbah* and stood. His movement stirred the kitten, which raised its head, peered around, and closed its eyes again.

"I have bored you with my exploits for too long, sister."

"I'll send Rima to you when the chamomile tea is ready, brother."

He went to the doorway and then paused beneath it. When he turned, his gaze found Esperanza. "Send your slave Butayna with the tea instead."

She turned her face to the wall and clutched the last of the cotton tunics tight against her chest. If Leila noticed any change in her appearance, she would discover Esperanza's secret. Worry festered inside her. What did Yusuf want from her? He could not desire to bed her as he had done with Miriam. Esperanza would die from humiliation before she surrendered to such shameless behavior.

Behind her, Leila said, "Not Rima? Yusuf, this is my maid—"

"Do calm yourself, Leila! I do not want her in my bed. My mother has arranged for a Frankish girl tonight. I am to meet with Ibn al-Khatib within the hour, so send two cups with the teapot. When your slave arrives, she can entertain my minister and perhaps sing me to sleep this evening."

***

Esperanza balanced the steaming ceramic pot and two glazed glasses on a wooden tray, as she headed north through the arcaded gallery. Behind her, Ifrit's steady gaze bored into her back, but rather than cast the slave a glare over her shoulder, Esperanza concentrated on her task. Ifrit would report if even one drop spilled to her mistress.

She exited an opened door and entered the courtyard. Climbing roses stretched along the adjoining eastern wall. The walkway paved with cobblestones in fish and flower figures ran the length of a garden quartered into sections. A central fountain spilled water into a circular basin of stone. Bees and butterflies flitted between oleander bushes, rose leaves, thyme, aromatic lantana shrubs, bluebells, and lilies.

Tinkling laughter warned her exit into the garden court became the subject of observation. She turned and looked to the south, where two women lingered on the belvedere to the south. She did not recognize them, but by their silken dress and the little eunuchs in attendance, they appeared to be the guests of Yusuf's mother.

She hurried across the pavement and kept to the shadows of the building on her right. At the end of the bed of flowers and herbs, the gallery sheltered Yusuf's protectors. Suspended on poles in brackets, banners of scarlet *cendal* fluttered on an inward breeze. Each silk standard fell from the wooden ceiling to the floor and bore the Nasrid court of arms, a red shield stitched with transverse gold letters. *Wa-la ghalib illa Allah.*

She whispered the translated words, "Only God is the victor."

The captain of Yusuf's guard, distinguishable from the eunuchs by the ceremonial dagger he carried along with two swords, ordered her to halt at the wider central arch. As she obeyed, her fingers twitched and the teapot rattled. He lifted the lid with dark, almost womanly fingers and sniffed at the honey-sweetened brew, flavored with lemon balm and sage. His ovoid gaze swung back to hers and for the space of two breaths, he just looked at her. Then with a nod, he turned aside and ushered her within the portico. She removed her leather sandals.

A group of five young men and older boys bent over slabs of wood on their laps. Each wrote in cursive Arabic script on smooth parchment. None looked up as she traversed the space between them and headed for the stairs.

At the top of the landing, ringed by a wooden banister, Yusuf sat near the opened window of the tower on a red and gold mat. A small round table of ebony covered the six-pointed star centered in the woven rug. Yusuf leaned against the cushions behind him, his hand shading his shimmery brow. Beside him, a young man of similar age with thick, curled black locks spoke in a hushed tone.

"My Sultan, you are the *Amir al-Muslimin*, it is your duty to defend the faithful."

Yusuf grunted. "Would you have me wait, Ibn al-Khatib, until Sultan Abu'l-Hasan Ali rides at the head of his two hundred thousand warriors to the gates of *al-Qal'at al-Hamra*, before I make a decision? I have no choice except to support the Marinids in this ill-starred enterprise."

"There are always choices, my Sultan, with little difference in meaning except the consequences."

"Don't spout maxims to me as if I were one of your *talibs* in the hall below! I am no ignorant, green boy you can lecture. A thing Ridwan seems to have forgotten as well."

Yusuf's companion averred, "I am, but one of your faithful *katibs*, my Sultan."

"Then as part of my secretariat and as my friend since boyhood, advise me!"

"I have gained much in the service of you, my Sultan. My honored father and brother have achieved exalted positions because of your recognition. Despite many years of your generous favor, you know I am not afraid to tell hard truths. Are you willing to be on the losing side for now, to change the future balance of power between this Sultanate and the Marinid kingdom?"

"You think pride holds sway over me? Do I strike you as a vainglorious fool? I did not gain the Sultanate of my ancestors to watch it crumble to dust underneath Marinid ambitions! I am willing to take a calculated risk. My concern is for my people. How do I protect them against the determination of the Marinids to conquer this land as their forbearers did? The treachery of their rebellious princes took the life of my brother, possibly that of my father as well."

"Something the Sultana Fatima always suspected."

"My grandmother was right to question the loyalties of the Marinid rebel princes. Are you aware of the defection of Uthman ibn Abi'l-Ula's son, Suleiman? I should have killed him! He has returned from exile in al-Tunisiyah and found a place in the Castillan court."

"I have heard, my Sultan. Ridwan has dispatched agents, who... monitor Suleiman's activities."

"Better they should slaughter him outright," Yusuf grumbled.

What sort of brutal tyrant ruled Granada, one who could advocate the callous murder of someone? Esperanza's fingers shook and the glasses clinked together. The one closest to the tray's edge now slid and shattered into jagged fragments.

Yusuf and his secretary stared at her, the latter's face frozen in slack-jawed shock. Yusuf stood and stepped back from a large shard of glass at his feet. Heavy footfalls on the staircase announced his guards before their captain rushed to the landing with swords drawn. Yusuf waved his men away and then his fist tightened. His lips became a thin seam of displeasure.

Esperanza drew back a step. Her calves bumped against the balustrade.

Yusuf muttered, "See to the clean-up. Now!"

Her knees quivered and locked together, as she blinked. "Of course, my Sultan."

With a breathless shudder, she forced her limbs to cooperate and placed the tray on the table. She looked around her, at anything other than the minister or Yusuf and his three henchmen. What was she expected to tidy the floor with, some sort of rag? The larger, broken pieces of glass would be easy to retrieve. What of the other shards?

A hearty chuckle rumbled through the chest of Yusuf's minister. "She's quite afraid of you, my Sultan. I have never seen a slave so terrified. At any moment, she will run."

"She won't do that."

Yusuf rounded the table. His hand clamped on Esperanza's wrist. She jerked away, but his hold tightened. "You will come with me."

Dios mío! Did he intend to see her punished for such a minor infraction?

"Please, my Sultan, do not...."

He took the stairs and dragged her in his wake. She had no choice except to follow him down to the first floor and out into the blazing sun. The guards stood at attention as he marched her barefooted past them.

"Wait! My sandals, I need them!"

Esperanza stumbled as Yusuf almost wrenched her arm in his haste. By the mercy of God, the women whom she had spied were not on the southern balcony to witness her shame. In the afternoon heat, everyone had retreated indoors.

"Please, my Sultan, forgive my clumsiness. I swear I shall never do it again!"

He forced her along the path, his grip merciless. She whimpered as he took her down a flight of steps at the southern end of the garden courtyard. Around the bend and a shorter series of six steps, she arrived with him outside a large storeroom.

The slaves who packed firewood and hemp satchels inside the building halted their work. All fell to their knees on the gravel walkway.

Yusuf demanded of the assembly, "Where is Mufawwiz?"

Esperanza sobbed. Her fingers covered her mouth. Would he summon an executioner to kill her over a broken glass?

A pale overweight man with receding yellow hair scrambled from the storeroom on spindly legs. He bowed before Yusuf. A substantial belly spilled over his *sarawil*. "I am your faithful chief steward, my Sultan. How may I aid you?"

Yusuf said, "There is broken glass in my chamber. I need another cup to enjoy my tea with Ibn al-Khatib. First, see to the removal of the fragments before anyone cuts a foot on them."

Esperanza lowered her hand from her parted lips.

Yusuf urged her forward. "This is my household steward, Mufawwiz," he introduced, switching from Arabic to Castillan with ease. "He is the caretaker of the Royal House of Felicity. If accidents occur in the future, such as earlier in my room, find my chief steward in this vicinity at any hour and he will assign a slave. The steward's quarters are on the level below."

While she nodded, still incredulous, Yusuf spoke to his steward again. "This is the slave Butayna, who is new to my sister Leila's household. It was time for you two to meet. She hails from your land."

Mufawwiz offered her a broad smile and tilted his head. "It is always an honor to meet a fellow countrywoman." Then he regarded Yusuf. "Your servants shall attend to your need at once, my Sultan."

With a snap of his fingertips, he barked orders to two eunuchs, who went into the storeroom and reemerged with bundled twigs interspersed with rushes. Another disappeared inside the adjacent building. Both bowed at Yusuf's side and then took the path Esperanza trod.

She gaped in their wake and when she turned, found Yusuf staring at her with lifted brows.

He stated, "Let us leave Mufawwiz to his duties."

Yusuf clasped his hands behind his back and left the storage area. Esperanza glared at his back until he paused and looked over his shoulder. "Did you intend to remain?"

She sighed and followed him. Halfway past the first of the western garden beds, she muttered, "You let me think the worst of you, my Sultan. I believed you would have me executed for my transgression."

His laughter echoed on the hot wind. "I may be the Sultan, but even I cannot govern the direction of your mind, Butayna. As it is, your thoughts fascinate me. You presumed the most extreme behavior because you expect the worst of Moors."

She halted. "I have no reason to think otherwise."

He stopped in the shade afforded by a central kiosk. "You should not judge a people by singular experience."

"You know nothing of what I have endured, nor would you care if you did."

He cocked his head and offered a little indulgent smile. "How would you surmise this as fact?"

"Do you ever concern yourself with the lives of your slaves? How long has your steward Mufawwiz served here? Do you know anything of him?"

Yusuf crossed his arms over his chest. "Mufawwiz was cut when he was seven, a captive taken from Alcala la Real. At the age of twenty, he began his apprenticeship in the shadow of my father's chief steward. Thirteen years later when that man died, my brother Muhammad appointed Mufawwiz to the high position. He is dutiful, though sometimes the gout makes his tasks arduous. He has been seen by my trusted doctor many times and always received the same advice, but my steward's love of our savory food keeps him fat."

Her cheeks burned. She lowered her gaze.

He grasped her chin. "Look at me, Butayna." When she did, his fingers splayed across her cheek. "I am not heartless. I take an active interest in the lives of everyone in my household, including the slaves. I am no tyrant who would order a girl's head lopped from her shoulders because of a broken glass. You possess many improper notions beneath this pretty head of hair. It is time you corrected them."

She eyed him. "My misguided assumptions aside, you forget neither of us can deny our states. In your view, I am a slave and you are my master. In my heart, I long for freedom, to reclaim my life and will as my own."

His smile broadened. "We cannot resolve all of these quandaries now. Come, my tea will be cold and I still expect you to sing for me.

***

After Ibn al-Khatib's departure with a bow and flourish to both Yusuf and Esperanza, the Sultan placed an *oud* in her hands, similar in design to Juan Manuel's own with three carved rosettes. He demanded she practice with it each day, starting in his room, while he accompanied her on another version of the instrument. He laughed at her protests and urged her on. When her voice grew hoarse, he sent word to Leila for more chamomile tea.

He attended prayers twice and went to the *hammam*, all while leaving strict orders for her to stay. By the evening, Esperanza remained in Yusuf's chamber alone and strummed the pear-shaped *oud*. The sun began a slow descent below the horizon. She sat on cushions aligned along the western wall with a laurel wood table at the center. When slaves had brought a dish of lemon chicken cooked with rice, garlic and olives earlier, Yusuf offered her a portion of his meal. Now a eunuch returned and removed the remnants.

She shook her head. Yusuf proved just unpredictable as his sister, sympathetic and harsh by contrasts. A man who spoke of murdering his family's betrayers, but offered the services of a doctor to a trusted steward. One who left her alone in his personal quarters, his bedchamber left open to her perusal. Did she dare cross the threshold and peek inside?

Esperanza set the instrument aside and gathered her courage. She tiptoed across the gallery in bare feet, unsure whether the occupants of the southern pavilion might see her. She wiped her soles on the woven mat at the threshold and stepped inside the small room. Her fingers pressed against the door of paneled wood decorated with interlaced stars. The bed occupied the center of the room, pillows buttressed against the whitewashed wall. Chests lined the floors, except for the northeastern corner where a perforated incense burner released fragrant myrrh.

"The women found in this part of the chamber take their place in the Sultan's bed."

She whirled as Yusuf came up behind her. He had shed the simple garments from earlier in the day for an embroidered *jubba*. Black songbirds with opals for eyes and butterflies with wings stitched in silver thread shimmered on the surface of the

160

cloth. Yusuf had turned the neckline back and revealed the red brocaded lining underneath. His silky hair glistened with oil.

She dropped to her knees, her stare fixed on the woven carpet. "Forgive me, my Sultan, I had no right—"

He bent and offered his hand. "No, you did not."

She accepted his touch and he propelled her to her feet. He contemplated her in silence and did not release her fingers.

"If you wish, my Sultan, I will leave you now." She recalled his mention of the yellow-haired slave who would come to his bed tonight. She hoped he would dismiss her before then.

"I do not wish it. You will remain until I say you can depart. Play for me again." He waved her away, turned aside, and beckoned a eunuch who hovered outside the door. The young man rummaged in a small chest at the window and pulled out a vial.

Esperanza clasped her fingers together and drew deep breaths. Yusuf could not be serious. Did he expect her to stay? Besides, Leila would be furious at her long absence and find some inventive means to punish her.

He swerved. "Did you hear what I said? Play, Butayna."

She bowed. "*Sí*, my Sultan."

Seated across from him in the gallery, she seethed inside at his demand. The strings of the *oud* rippled in discord. He peered out past the door at her, until slaves climbed up the stairs with his evening meal. She ignored the scent of roasted lamb sprinkled with mint and the resultant growl in her stomach. This time, he ate alone. At *Salat al-Isha*, he disappeared for the fourth time.

Resentment soured her stomach. She set the instrument aside, her arms crossed over her chest. How dare he leave her again? He had not even concerned himself with whether she was hungry or not. She peeked into the gallery. The slaves had not removed the food. She scrambled for a slice of flatbread and chunks of lamb. Grease coated the pieces, but she crammed two into her mouth. She also chewed the tough bread. A glass decanter held pomegranate juice, but Yusuf had used the sole cup. With a groan she poured a little of the liquid inside. The small repast would have to be enough. She dashed back to the cushion and stared with longing at the trays, until his servants took them.

He returned soon afterward. He held the hand of a willowy young woman in his. She wore an opaque girdle slung around her hips, but the gossamer cloth of her *qamis* and *sarawil* revealed the skin. Silver glittered at her earlobes. More jewelry wound around her wrists and neck. Yusuf led her into his bedchamber.

Esperanza gaped. He could not expect she would remain while he cavorted with one of his slaves! She understood what occurred between a man and woman in bed from frank discussions with Miriam and her father. To be a silent witness of Yusuf's exploits would embarrass her too much.

Over his shoulder, he commanded, "Play!"

Esperanza obliged him with a groan and prayed he would close the door.

He did not. When he tugged the woman to the bed, her soft giggle urged him on, as did her limbs snaking around his neck.

A shudder passed through Esperanza and she concentrated on the laurel wood table. Such beautiful workmanship, she could not deny the Moors' abilities. Her father would have admired the handicraft. If he had lived to see it—no, he would be mortified now, if he knew of her circumstances and the shameful display Yusuf forced her to endure. Try as she might, she could not dismiss the view of Yusuf and his bed partner from her peripheral gaze.

Yusuf unlaced the tunic and pushed it off the slave's angular shoulders. When he bent his head to the *jarya*'s rounded breast, Esperanza squeaked. He never noticed, just transferred his attention to the other pert nipple. His hands tugged aside the waist wrapper and delved below the *sarawil*. His companion panted underneath him and bared her throat.

Esperanza pushed the *oud* from her lap. She did not care whether she stirred Yusuf's wrath, but she could not remain a moment longer. With a hand over her mouth, she fled the alcove and raced down the steps.

Yusuf's voice chased her into the bleak, balmy night. "Butayna!"

She could not return to Leila. If Yusuf searched for her, he would go to his sister first. Leila would do nothing to protect Esperanza.

She plunged down the steps set near the southern pavilion and down to the next level, where Yusuf had told her the chief steward lived. The stench of horse manure assailed her, but she went for the door to the stable.

Two dark-skinned eunuchs reclined just inside the doorway on the straw. One draped his arm around the shoulder of a smaller boy, whose lower lip drooped. He drooled in deep slumber. His companion sat up. His bulging stare took her in.

She begged, "Please, let me stay here just for tonight."

The older eunuch reached behind him and she shrank back. He drew out one of two woolen covers underneath his head and tossed it at her.

"*Nam.* You may sleep here if you wish, but you should take this. Sometimes, the nights can get cold. I am the stable boy, Bilal as-Sudan." He jerked his chin to the one who slumbered beside him. "This is my brother, al-Sagir. He helps me sometimes."

With a sigh of exhaustion, she settled across from them and almost smiled. Al-Sagir, meaning 'the little one'. The name suited the snoring boy.

"Thank you for the blanket, Bilal."

He nodded and closed his eyes. Within moments, she did the same.

Chapter 12
Fever Dreams

Esperanza Peralta

Granada, Andalusia
January 22, AD 1337 / 18 Jumada al-Thani 737 AH / 19th of
Shevat, 5097

Almost every night of the summer and after Yusuf's return to *al-Qal'at al-Hamra*, he demanded Esperanza's presence in his chambers. Whether he entertained guests or women in his bed, or dined alone and found his rest afterward, the strains of her *oud* filled his room. She played long into the night after the sentries called the midnight watch and awaited his dismissal. Neither of them spoke of the first night, in which she had run from him. In the next instance where he brought a woman to his bed, a closed door or heavy curtains spared her the sight of his fornication, if not the sounds.

Light snow covered the orange trees and marked a full twelve months of Esperanza's wretched existence in Andalusia. She hid her sighs and teary eyes in the company of others. At night, she often dreamt of her father and his last moments on earth. She kept her promise to him and endured each trial yet every day brought increased concerns for the future. Would she ever return to her former life?

She dunked her spoon in a half-finished bowl of lentils. Ifrit shoved a piece of flatbread, warm and slathered in butter at her. She took it and chewed out of habit more than hunger. Leila's women gathered as they always did at crowded mealtimes. In the depths of winter, Leila retreated to the warmth of her chambers, where she dined and entertained at times when her younger sisters visited Granada.

During the midday meal after *Salat al-Zuhr*, Esperanza often averted her gaze when Leila looked her way. Lines crisscrossed the Sultana's brow at each instance, as if she found something to displease her. Esperanza stopped her earlier attempts to understand the vagaries of the princess' moods. She recalled Juan Manuel had told her not to try. Leila remained as difficult and severe as her brother.

When the rest of the slaves finished the food, Rima cleared the table with Zarru's aid.

Leila beckoned Ifrit closer and spoke to her in a low whisper. The body slave nodded and retreated to the alcoves. She returned with two fur-lined cloaks and boots. She gave the one set to Leila and shoved the other into Esperanza's hands.

The Sultana stood. "Butayna, you will accompany me to the *rawda*."

In twelve months, Leila had never made the demand for her to join in such excursions.

"Shall I come with you as well, my Sultana?" Ifrit clasped her hands under her chin and offered a questioning gaze. "Please?"

Leila said, "You may not. If I desired it, I would have asked you."

Ifrit's long arms fell to her sides and she balled them into fists. She bowed her head. "As you wish, my Sultana."

A look passed between Sut and Zarru before the seamstress announced, "I'll check on this morning's washing." The sisters left the room together and went down the stairs.

Esperanza stood and slipped on the warm cover and knee-length boots Ifrit thrust at her. She followed Leila outside. A sensation of warmth tingled along her spine. She did not doubt Ifrit glared at her in the usual fashion.

The Sultana acknowledged the nods of greetings of nameless concubines and slaves. Snowdrifts scattered and piled according to the wind patterns. Pristine white flakes floated around Esperanza's head. On a childish impulse, she stuck her tongue out and caught a fleck of ice at the tip. Two women paused in observance, pointed and laughed behind their hands. Leila glared at them, before she peeked over her shoulder with upraised brows. When she resumed the walk, Esperanza trailed her in silence.

They proceeded into the space reserved for the burial of Nasrid dead. The tombstones of Leila's ancestors lined up in neat rows and reflected attentive care, freed from an overgrowth of weeds.

Leila paused beside a vault. "This is the burial site of my father Ismail. Our cousins, the sons of the governor of Algeciras, stabbed him to death over a slave girl in the months before my wedding should have occurred. When my father perished, I wanted to join him."

Esperanza looked at the marble slab. "I'm sorry for your loss, my Sultana. No one deserves to lose a parent to violence."

"My mother died in childbirth twenty-nine years ago, so I never knew her."

Esperanza shook her head. The similarities she shared with Leila were unexpected.

Leila continued, "My sister Fatimah and I lived here for a time in the old palace of Sultan Muhammad, the third of his line, until our father brought us to the coast at Malaga. Then we resided with my grandparents, the governor, Abu Said Faraj, and his wife. My grandmother cared for us, even after the death of our father.

She paused and turned to Esperanza. "When you lose someone so dear, it is such a deep wound and you think it will never heal. The pain lessens with time and you learn to survive."

Esperanza blinked back tears and nodded, though she could not agree so soon. Her lips parted, but no sound came out. She bowed her head.

A sigh whistled between Leila's lips. "Ask your questions. I will allow them."

Ponderous weight settled on Esperanza's chest. She rubbed at an imaginary ache and clasped her frigid hands together. "How do... how do you find the courage, my Sultana, to relinquish the past and live for the future when everyone you once loved is gone?"

Leila knelt in the snow and brushed a thin coat of white from her father's monument. "Love never leaves us, Butayna, not real love. Sometimes, one has little choice except to go on after a painful loss. Circumstances beyond our control often force us to surrender old ideals and wishes. We can also learn from adversity. In our loneliest moments Allah reveals the strength, which dwells in all of us, power summoned by the deepest sorrow."

She stood and strolled to the adjacent gravesite. "My great-grandfather Muhammad the Lawgiver is buried here beside my father." She lifted her hand and pointed to another row. "My grandfather Faraj rests just there. Both were men betrayed by their sons. The heir of my great-grandfather poisoned him with a honey cake and left him in terrible agony to die a cruel death. My father locked his own father in a dungeon for years. When Faraj died, my father brought his bones to rest here, in the place where he grew to manhood and married my grandmother."

She paused and turned to Esperanza. "We Nasrids are a proud clan. Sometimes, pride can lead us to disregard the importance of those whom we love, to be cruel in our neglect, but the ties between our family members remain strong. They transcend heartbreak and betrayal. Blood binds us together in a common cause. The preservation of the Sultanate is all that matters."

Esperanza shook her head. "Why did you bring me here to tell me this, my Sultana?"

"It is important to me for you to understand the Nasrids, the motives that drive our actions. At times, they will seem unclear. Now, you have had five months to become acquainted with Yusuf. What do you think of my brother?"

"The Sultan is... complicated, my Sultana. He is unlike any other man I have ever known. There are times when he can be almost kind, but then in the next instant—"

"He is cold," Leila finished for her. "Even vicious. *Sí*. Do you enjoy your time spent with him? I need the truth, Butayna."

Esperanza licked her dried lips. "It is hard to say. Sometimes, I think he likes it if I am uncomfortable when he is with his concubines. He wants acceptance from me of a way of life I find disturbing. He is the most observant man I have ever known. I can hide little from him. He always knows when I am sad or displeased, so I do not try to pretend otherwise. He perceives my moods and things I will not say to him. Even more, I think my awareness of him improves in each encounter."

Her heart raced and she turned away from Leila for a moment. Why had she revealed herself in such a way? The impulsive truth seldom aided her in the past. She always felt compelled to speak it, even at cost to her pride. Perhaps she longed for someone who shared her perspective on Yusuf and might understand him better than she ever could. Perchance she wanted someone who would listen. Since Miriam's abandonment, Esperanza had no friend left in the world.

She chided herself for her foolery. The Sultana Leila would never view her as an equal, one entitled to an opinion of her brother. She threatened Esperanza day and night with promises of punishment for the smallest infractions, though by God's grace alone, Leila never acted upon any of her impulses. Esperanza could be grateful if she wished, but if her luck expired, on whom could she rely? Exposed and vulnerable, she hugged her body against the cold.

Leila's soft touch landed on her shoulder. "The profundities of Yusuf's heart and mind are as the depths of the Mediterranean Sea, difficult to fathom. Two men dwell inside of him. One is Yusuf the second son of Ismail, beloved of his grandmother Fatima, a youth who grew to be a fine man. Ingenious, perceptive and thoughtful, blessed with wondrous intellect and sound judgment. The other is the Sultan Abdul Hajjaj Yusuf, the prince of the faithful. A ruler molded in the image of his great-grandfather Muhammad the Lawgiver, but mired in the brutal history of his ancestors. To know Yusuf is to discern the demons inside him, which can vie for a man's soul and bring about his ruination. It would take a strong companion in life, a woman who is his equal and knows him better than any other, to guide him on the path away from destruction."

With a gasp, Esperanza locked gazes with her. "Is this why you brought me here, my Sultana, to be your brother's companion in life?"

Leila smiled and patted her arm, but never answered. She ambled through the gravestones of her ancestors and left a trail of footprints in the pristine snow.

***

On wooden legs, Esperanza left Leila's chambers in the early evening and ambled through the shadows. Ramadi, Leila's cat, had followed her to the doorway and yowled as she departed. At the sun's fiery death, darkness encroached on *al-Qal'at al-Hamra*. Sentries stationed along the wall looked straight ahead, while Esperanza's stare remained on the marble floor. She no longer marveled at its immaculate beauty, as familiar to her as the clothes on her back or the shoes.

Outside the doorway of the oratory, where the royal women prayed each day, a eunuch stepped out of her path. "My lady."

When he spoke and inclined his head, she returned the nod, but kept her even pace. When she reached the next pavilion, his deference troubled her. Why would he bow to someone from Leila's retinue? Why had he referred to her as 'my lady' when she did not warrant the title?

She arrived at the Sultan's pavilion. Yusuf's captain acknowledged her with little more than a grunt and waved her between the pillars toward the door.

Her fingers hovered over the handle at the entrance. "My Sultan?"

"Come, Butayna!" Yusuf's voice echoed from within.

The wood creaked when she pushed at it. She stepped inside and found Yusuf seated in the center of his three-chambered residence. A frown marred his brow while he studied a rounded object with bronze bands across its circumference.

Yusuf's slaves fanned out and brought the lanterns in his room to life. They tended to the braziers in each alcove. Warm ambergris and frankincense wafted from the incense burners. He occupied one of two chairs placed before a central alcove. He draped his arms over the support covered in leather. His clothes were a palette of red, gold and black, the colors of his banners unfurled around the harem.

She offered him the customary bow and waited for his acknowledgment.

"Oh, do stop that! Come here. This is an astrolabe. I have never seen its equal."

She removed her footwear, unable to subdue a wry smile. "You should surrender the throne, my Sultan. Why not pursue your other interests?"

He raised his head for a moment. "You're in a playful mood. I expected you to greet me with the usual sighs and frowns. I like your smiles better."

When she approached, he tugged her beside him and placed her fingers on the globe. His hand covered hers. "Feel the smoothness of the brass."

The contrast between the colors of their skin mesmerized her instead. The callus on his palm proved he was not just an indolent, pampered ruler, who idled his time away at pleasurable pursuits.

He leaned forward and his brow pressed against the wide sleeve of her *misha*. The heightened warmth of his skin penetrated the long housecoat to the cotton *qandara*, a short shirt, worn underneath.

"Are you ill, my Sultan?"

A noisy sigh escaped him. "A little tired, nothing more. My duties are ample. I enjoy moments like this one, where I may relax. Thank you for coming to me."

"Did I have a choice, my Sultan?"

"If I gave in to your preference, would you visit me every evening?"

The silence hung heavy between them. He released her and she stepped away.

He said, "I have a present for you. At the end of this evening, I am giving you the *oud*, which my grandmother gave to me."

"You should not, my Sultan."

"I may grant gifts as I please. Your skill is greater than mine, though I believe you have benefited from some lesson I never had. Admit it. You played before the summer where I introduced the *oud*."

"Another man in addition to my father taught me the lute, my Sultan."

He glanced at her again. "Is it the latter who occupies your morose thoughts of late?"

She rubbed her arms and looked at the carpet. He gestured to the opposite seat.

When she took it, he set aside the astrolabe and leaned toward her, his chin propped up on his hand. "As you know by now, I lost my father to violence. You've never spoken of your own, but I sense there is tragedy involved."

"Do you want to hear the tale, my Sultan?"

"I will listen if you wish to tell me."

While she spoke to him of the band of Moors who set upon them on the *meseta*, her words held him in rapt attention. She avoided his gaze and stared out beyond the door into the frozen garden. She talked of the death of her father in a low monotone. More slaves entered with Yusuf's dinner, which they took into the alcove behind the chairs. They had finished the table settings by the time she stopped.

He commented, "Raids occur often throughout Andalusia. In the past, my father and my elder brother had men who tracked and killed slavers, anyone who took captives during the treaty years. The raid that altered your life took place during a period of truce. It did not occur during *de bona guerra,* as your people would say. I am sorry."

She snapped, "Cold comfort to my father murdered on the plains!"

He eyed her. "I never intended to justify his death. Do you think you have suffered losses alone? There are as many Muslim slaves burdened by service to Castillans, Valencians, and Galicians."

"You could outlaw the practice altogether here."

He waved a hand through the air. "The slave trade is too lucrative. The slavers earn a good profit from the merchants, the merchants from the buyers–"

"And the Sultanate collects taxes at each exchange." She pressed against the high-backed chair and glared at him.

He did not shrink away under her scrutiny. "You are correct. My government takes its share, one-fifth of the price upon each captive's head, whether sold or ransomed. You would have me alter a way of life, which has existed for centuries."

"You are Sultan! Don't you make the laws of your own country?"

"Butayna, do not be foolish! You must know nothing is ever so easy as you may imagine."

She crossed her arms over her chest and ignored him. They sat in tense silence.

Then he stated, "You loved your father."

A bitter laugh bubbled up inside her. "You seem surprised. Don't all children love their fathers, my Sultan?"

"No, not all children."

When he spoke, she recollected the calamities Leila had mentioned in the *rawda,* of sons imprisoning and killing their own fathers. What world of misfortune had she found herself placed, where the most violent acts occurred between people who claimed to love each other?

He stood and held out his hand. "Dine with me."

She stared at his fingers. "It would be wrong for me to sit and eat at your table as a guest, my Sultan. As you and your sister sometimes like to remind me, I am a slave."

"You have partaken of my meals many times before, here and at the *Jannat al-'Arif.*"

"Will you... have other... company this evening, my Sultan? You know the presence of your women makes me uncomfortable. You take joy in my distress."

"That is a bold claim, which is also untrue. I have told my mother not to send me any other women tonight. I prefer not to be disturbed."

"Then I should go—"

"Why are you in such a hurry to leave me?" His warm gaze, enlivened by the lamplight, pierced hers.

She looked at the ground again. "Perhaps it is for the best, my Sultan."

Yusuf threw up his hands. "Best for whom, Butayna? By the Prophet's beard, you are the most contrary female I have ever met."

She peered beyond him through the doorway. "Then I should leave, my Sultan. Then my presence would cease to be a trial for you."

"No, you should remain! You are difficult, but you have also charmed me with your wit and songs. I wish for a quiet evening with you, a gesture of my goodwill. You resent your status as a slave. Can we not put our roles aside and take enjoyment in each other's company?"

"We cannot. You will always be the Sultan."

"You have sworn never to remain a slave. If such alteration is possible for you, then I can change as well."

She laughed aloud at him and clutched her belly. "Nonsense!"

He flung his arms wide. "You see? Who else would dare find amusement in your lord and master?"

She sobered and shook her head. "What I can see is how ill-suited you would be to ordinary life, my Sultan. You say you would change, but in the next instance speak of yourself as my lord and master. Please, let me leave you."

"I do not wish it! Besides, it has been a little while since you scowled or upbraided me with your hot gaze for my perceived arrogance."

"Well, you are arrogant and strong-minded, my Sultan."

"You find just those two traits disagreeable?"

"Shall I tell you of the others?"

His mouth tightened. "Your bold nature amuses me often, but do not speak above your station. Still, if I am all you say and more, there is little hope of changing your opinion. Therefore, I shall be a willful tyrant. I am dressed for dinner. In my arrogance, I presumed you would dine with me. My indomitable wish is to have you sit at my table. As you reminded me, I am the Sultan. I shall have my way."

"I suppose it is good to be the sovereign. You can make others do as you please at any time."

"*Sí*, there are some advantages."

"Some, my Sultan?"

"If one is your compliance, I shall be lucky." He extended his fingers for her grasp again. When she placed her hand in his, he hauled her up and led her to the table.

The slaves revealed the contents of the platters set between them on the table. Then the eunuchs stepped back into the shadows of the alcove. Yusuf devoured one after another of chicken livers fried in sesame seed oil and the date balls, fresh-baked flatbread and a lamb stew of almonds and chickpeas. Esperanza adjudged the best dish to be an eggplant dip on the flatbread and sliced eggs, their yolks mashed into a paste with coriander, crushed onions, and garlic. The eggs were the most delicious dish she had ever eaten, at least until she ate *zirbiya* for the first time. The doves tasted of cinnamon and saffron, cooked in a sweet, thick paste of mashed almonds soaked in rosewater.

Seated beside her, Yusuf looked up from the last of his stew. "Is your appetite always so poor, or is the food not to your liking?"

She sipped a cold lemon *sharbah* and looked at the rest of three dishes still untouched.

His hand closed on her wrist. "I can feel the bones. You are as thin as a delicate bird. Eat some more. Try the dish in the red pot. It is *'tharid*, made from lamb. My grandmother's favorite. It was my special request for tonight."

She looked into the bowl of thick yoghurt broth, swimming with meat, small garlic bulbs, and sprigs of mint. Then she glanced at him. "Is it the Sultan who orders me to eat because he thinks I am too scrawny?"

"No. One who worries for your appetite and would not have you wither away. You must keep up your strength, so we may continue these arguments."

She reached for the flatbread and spooned the *'tharid* on to a slice. "When the raiders held me captive, I grew accustomed to rations and never knew when another meal would arrive. Then I resented the slave merchant's attempts to fatten me, as one prepares a calf for slaughter."

His hand covered hers. "You will never have to worry for food or other comforts here."

When she ate, he joined her. Soon less than a third of the bowl remained.

She rubbed her abdomen. "My Sultan, I could not eat a thing more."

He leaned toward her. "What is your opinion?"

She shrugged. "The dish you called '*tharid* was good, but I still liked the *zarbaya*–"

"*Zirbiya*," he corrected.

"*Sí, zirbiya.* I liked it best of all, my Sultan."

"Your pronunciation improves. Soon, you will speak as one of us. You should practice with my sister's slaves."

Yusuf veered close to the uneasy truth she tried to hide. "They do not have time for me, my Sultan. Since each one of them speaks my mother tongue, I have little reason to try."

He nodded and signaled the unobtrusive eunuchs, who brought rosewater bowls with towels and removed the meal. They closed the doors behind them.

Then Yusuf said, "I must perform my ablutions and pray within my private oratory."

"Then I should leave you, my Sultan."

"You do not have my permission to go. You shall remain. I like having you near."

When she sighed and rolled her eyes, he smiled in a broad grin before he withdrew.

She looked to the *oud*, propped in a corner of the room where they had dined. He might find the noise intrusive, so she left the instrument where it stood. He had not given her permission to touch the astrolabe again.

He crossed her line of vision again as he retreated into the alcove in the southeast. He no longer wore the red and silver *jubba* or his black indoor slippers. Steam floated into view before water splashed. Did Muslims need to wash themselves each time they communed with God? The call to prayer no longer startled her. It became familiar to her as the clothes she donned each day, the food, and the once bizarre words she often practiced in private.

At his return, in bare feet, she asked, "Shall I play for you tonight, my Sultan?"

He did not answer. He dropped on to his side and placed his head in her lap. His dark hair shone against the pallid material of her *sarawil.*

She gasped. "What are you doing? This is improper."

He yawned behind his hand. "You reminded me there are benefits to my position in life. I can say what is proper and what is not. You will sing to me now. Your voice comforts me."

With a low sigh, she assented. He did not seem to notice the little quaver in her voice while she sang.

He burrowed his head deeper and closed his eyes. His sigh of contentment made her recall the day they first met, when he had joined her in the *cantiga.* Strange impulses governed the man.

She considered Leila's words spoken earlier in the *rawda* about the dual personality inside Yusuf. She had seen the evidence for herself. He possessed two sides, the young man who took delight in all manner of things, and the Sultan, who had no time for pleasures.

He muttered something unintelligible. At the end of the song, she peered at his face. Deep, even breaths betrayed how soon he had fallen asleep. In repose, his angular features relaxed. He possessed dark, long lashes, almost a woman's own.

They fluttered now, as he murmured, "Sing, Butayna."

She shook her head, but continued.

At some point, she must have drifted asleep. She raised her head, groggy at first. She looked around in time and caught sight of a mouse. The creature snatched a crumb of flatbread from the table and scurried away. She released an uneven breath and pressed her hand to her breastbone. Her heart thumped furiously.

The change of watch echoed in the night and stirred Yusuf as well. He opened his eyes and stared at her with a frown as though unfocused. "Help me to my bedchamber."

She raised her eyebrows. "I doubt the Sultan needs any assistance to find his bed."

"Still, you will do as I wish."

She gritted her teeth together as he raised himself up. When he stumbled a little, she stood and bolstered him with her arm around his waist. "Did you do that just for your benefit, my Sultan?"

His laughter rumbled. She offered him her meager support and took him into the next room, dominated by the bed. Accustomed to his austerity from her many visits, she brushed past one chest and maneuvered him to the bed. As soon as she accomplished the deed, he pulled her down atop him and rolled with her.

She slapped his chest. "Let me go, Yusuf! I am not one of your concubines!"

His stare found hers in the dying light of the lantern above. "Yusuf, is it? I did not give you permission to address me as anything, but the Sultan. You forget the rules of the harem." He buried a yawn in her curls. "I find I like the sound of my name upon your lips."

Her jaw tightened. "My Sultan, please release me."

"I do not wish it." His mouth brushed her ear.

"Life does not always accommodate our wishes," she muttered.

He stretched out beside her, his arm an iron band around her waist. She wriggled, but his hold tightened.

She pushed at him. "You have no right to keep me here against my will! Must I remind you of your own customs? You do not permit anyone except a favorite or your wife to share your bed. I am neither!"

He nuzzled her hair. "Butayna, for once, do not fight me. Just go to sleep...."

Afterward, she watched the lantern as it swayed on the slight breeze. Then she closed her eyes, exhausted.

Yusuf thrashed sometime in the night and roused her again. Bleary-eyed, she stared at her small fists curled against his chest. He no longer held her, but had draped his leg over hers.

"*La!* Muhammad!" He flung an arm across the pillow beneath her head.

She tried to roll away from him, but his forearm pulled on her hair. She cupped his feverish brow while he called out the name again.

"My Sultan? Yusuf! You are having a–"

A guttural growl filled his throat. He reared up and forced her back against the pillow. The hilt of the dagger in his hand gleamed at her throat.

"*Min fadlak!*" She winced and cried out at the slight sting. "*La!* Yusuf!"

His ragged breath washed over her face. He shook his head, squinted, and blinked at her. "Butayna? By the Prophet's beard. What are you doing here? What hour is it?"

She gulped a mouthful of air. The blade pressed against her skin. He looked down at it, as though seeing the weapon for the first time. He flung the glittering handle across the room and gripped her shoulder. She blinked back tears and returned his stare.

Then he gasped. "Allah! I've cut you."

175

He shuffled from the bed, his footfalls silent as he crossed the long chamber. She did not move until he returned with a wet rag and placed it at the apex of her shoulder and neck. He lifted the cloth and blood tainted it. He pressed it to her flesh once more.

She demanded, "Wha-what demons haunt you, which require you to sleep with a dagger... under your pillow?"

He shook his head. "The past never leaves us."

After he had staunched the bleeding, he said, "It is a thin scratch. I do not believe it will scar."

He sat up and she joined him. His fingers aligned with hers. "The weapon belonged to my great-grandfather, Muhammad the Lawgiver. Seventy years have not dulled the blade."

She pressed a hand to the sting at her throat. "As I have realized."

"I could have killed you! I'm so sorry. Please believe I never meant to harm you."

She nodded. "I believe you, my Sultan. In your sleep, you called out a name. Muhammad."

His shoulders slumped. "He was my brother. He died at eighteen, betrayed like my father by the same clan of Marinid rebel princes, who lived in exile in Andalusia. The traitors pierced his body with lances. I dream of his death almost every night. It is one reason I prefer to sleep alone. What just happened... if you had not...."

She whispered, "I am sorry for your loss, my Sultan."

He swung to her and his fingers delved into her hair. His gaze locked with hers. "You addressed me as Yusuf sometime earlier tonight. I told you I liked it."

"A mistake, which will never happen again, my Sultan. I should have refused your demand and never come to your bed. It was madness."

"Uh-hmm. For both of us."

He brushed his lips against her brow, his touch softer than a feather. At first, she thought she had imagined it. Her heart pulsed in a furious rhythm. He nuzzled her temple and placed a kiss there as well, then one at her earlobe. She closed her eyes for a moment and breathed an uneven sigh. It would be easy to forget he sanctioned a vile practice, which resulted in more than her father's death. To surrender to his touch, to be one of those women he pleasured. The possibility did not frighten or shame her, as it should have.

His lips pressed against her jaw line, warm breath at her neck. "Butayna?"

She shuddered and murmured, "My Sultan?"

His thumb trailed along the corner of her mouth. "Unless you wish me to keep you here forever, you should go."

He released her. She shied away and slid from the bed. She crept from his bedchamber to the central room.

"Do not forget the *oud*. I meant it as a gift. You will take it."

She shivered at his low tone. "Thank you, my Sultan." She bent and scooped up the instrument. The cords vibrated against her fingertips. She found her shoes in the darkness.

Just at the entrance, he called to her again. She paused and gripped the door handle. Her heart hammered. "My Sultan?"

"When I pressed you into the bed, you spoke almost perfect Arabic without hesitation. I was not so groggy as to mishear. You said *'min fadlak'*, which means 'please' in general terms, except the intonation changes if you address a man or woman. Then you said no after the dagger slipped."

Esperanza pressed her forehead against the wood, weary of the charade and the turbulent emotions he roused within her. "May I go now, my Sultan?"

"You may leave me. Shut the doors behind you."

She left his apartment and stepped into the night. Silent sentries lined the wall. Moonlight tracked her progress. She hurried into Leila's chambers. What would happen when Yusuf revealed the secret Esperanza had kept?

Esperanza climbed the steps, picked her path through the crates and shoes in the alcoves, and crept across the floor into the bedroom. Snorts and sleep-induced mutters filled the air while Leila's women slumbered on their mats. Esperanza found hers and laid the *oud* against a wall beside her.

Ramadi stared up at her with his yellow-green eyes aglow. She crouched and petted the cat, who rubbed his head against the softness of her palm.

"Butayna? Are you well?" Leila's voice pierced the darkness. She propped herself up on her elbows.

Esperanza rested on the mat. "I am well, my Sultana."

When Ramadi purred and nosed her arm, she picked up him and laid him on her chest as had become customary. She stroked his gray fur. In time, his snores vied with the others in the room. Sleep did not come to Esperanza.

Chapter 13
The Accord

Maryam

Granada, Andalusia
February 26 – March 1, AD 1337 / 24 - 27 Rajab 737 AH / 24th -
27th of Adar, 5097

An hour before midday, Maryam hugged the recesses of the gallery and peered over the balustrade to the *hammam* below. The bath superintendent remained after almost every slave had retired. Now, he spoke with one of Sultana Leila's slaves, the yellow-haired one with the dull, simpering look on her face. Then Esperanza emerged from the changing room. A drab, brown robe clung to her stick-thin form. She balanced well on the *qabqab* sandals before removing them in favor of leather slippers. Maryam gritted her teeth and waited.

Soon, footfalls on the landing marked the progress of one pair of feet up the first level of the staircase, then the second. The bath superintendent inclined his head to the Sultana's slave and disappeared inside the *hammam*.

Maryam held her breath as the footfalls drew closer. She sprang from the shadows when Esperanza appeared and hauled her up by her neckline. Maryam shoved her against the adjacent tiled wall. The girl's head made a satisfying thud on the hard wall.

"Did you think I would let you ruin my life again?"

Esperanza screamed. "Get off me! Hamduna!"

Maryam clenched her hands around the girl's neck. "The Sultana's slave can't help you now. You have stolen from me–"

Esperanza dug her nails into Maryam's flesh, but she had suffered too much from Esperanza's idiocy to let a few scratches stop her.

"Your stupidity robbed my daughter of her life! I shall have yours in return–"

"Let her go!" The other slave reached the top of the landing.

"I'll choke the life from her if you take another step toward us," Maryam promised. She screeched and jerked as Esperanza raked her nails across her eyes.

"Hamduna... help!"

"*Sí*, Butayna! I'm going to fetch the Sultana!"

Maryam tightened her hold even as the slave's voice echoed. "Sultana Leila! You must come. The woman has gone mad! They are fighting...."

"Ah, but she is so wrong! I am not mad. My purpose is very clear. Somehow, you have bewitched Yusuf. What did you do to him to make him summon you every night? Has he bedded you? Why then does he not name you as his favorite? No matter how you may delight him in bed, never forget I had him first. You will not take him from me. I shall ruin you first!"

Esperanza pried at Maryam's hands still, but the girl's grip slackened. Her eyes bulged and the whites around the irises reddening.

Maryam whispered, "The daughter stolen from me, the son I lost. Even Gedaliah's death I can lay at your feet. You will not take my chance to have what I desire. I will never stop, Esperanza! Every happy moment you may ever discover shall be mine! Do you hear me? I will never rest until I have ruined you. You owe me for all I have suffered. It is your fault! Your fault!"

A cacophony of shouts and footfalls reverberated through the passage. Strong hands clamped on Maryam's shoulders and hauled her backward to the balustrade.

"*La!* Stop! I will have her life. You cannot stop me."

Even a vicious backhand from Yusuf's mother could not halt her tirade. Safa bellowed, "Control yourself, slave!"

Maryam struggled against the bath superintendent's clutch. She stretched her arms and clawed the air. Esperanza stood close in a circle of Leila's slave women, cradled against Yusuf's sister, who demanded, "Safa! Restrain your hellcat!"

"Do not tell me what to do, Leila. Take your scraggy slave and go!"

"When I do, Yusuf shall hear of this!"

"Do you think my son cares for trivial squabbles? He is engrossed with events in al-Maghrib. Of what import is this little fight between two slaves when the Marinids prepare to shift the balance of power in their favor?"

***

Maryam entered the Sultana Safa's bedchamber at her summons later in the evening. The glow of sundown set the tiles ablaze. Yusuf's mother sat cross-legged on a stool, a hookah beside a bowl of dates on the ebony table beside her. She gestured to an empty cushion at her feet. "You did a very foolish thing today."

"That is your opinion, my Sultana."

"Sometimes, personal beliefs matter more than the truth. Opinions can direct the course of history. You would do well to remember this fact. You moved against Butayna too soon. Leila pretended not to want her in the House of Myrtles. She thought to deceive me, to place the girl in Yusuf's bed and have her win his heart through song and verse. If her slave gives Yusuf an heir, Leila will believe she has won. She shall learn otherwise, with your help."

Maryam's pulse throbbed. Still, she sniffed, lifted her chin, and feigned nonchalance. "What does your rivalry with the Sultan's sister have to do with me?"

"Oh, you mindless woman, it has everything to do with you!" Safa's broad smile exposed her dimples and the gaps between her yellowed teeth. "Leila made it so, by her choice of your companion in the House of Myrtles as a rival for Yusuf's attention. Do sit! You're making my neck hurt."

Maryam joined the Sultana. Safa pushed the white bowl with blue flowers in her direction, but Maryam declined with a shake of her head.

Safa shrugged. "As you prefer. Shall I tell you where your recklessness lies?"

"I did not ask."

Safa continued as if Maryam had not spoken. "You attacked without forethought and gave the girl a chance to summon help. You must learn to be subtle, to move in shadows. The blade in the back, the slow poison is the best approach. Never reveal the intent before you strike at your enemy."

Maryam bit down on the inside of her cheek and subdued a smile. The truth would be the woman's undoing. The old harridan sought aid against her nemesis. In doing so, she revealed the depths of her wiles. She had forgotten an important maxim. Never disclose the depths of one's true self before any would-be ally. A friend in the daylight hours could be an enemy by nightfall.

"Now, tell me all I wish to know of this slave," Safa ordered. "Begin with her life before she entered the harem."

Maryam gritted her teeth. More than a year ago, she would have deemed any truthful response to this request from the Sultana as a betrayal. Even then, she owed Esperanza nothing, but after the raid changed both their lives, the girl owed her everything. Maryam would recoup her losses and learn all she could of vengeance from Safa.

Maryam said, "The slave you know as Butayna was born fifteen years ago at Talavera de la Reina in the kingdom of Castilla-Leon. I knew her from girlhood, for I was born five years earlier. Her father Efrain Peralta gave her the name Esperanza at birth, meaning hope. He was a prominent doctor in the service of the dispossessed heirs, the family of the Cerdas. He often spent time away from his household, returning each year to sire another child on his wife's body. She disappointed him with stillbirths until the last pregnancy claimed her life and that of the son she should have delivered. By that time, his one living child had reached the age of fourteen. Afterward, the troubles began."

"What troubles?" Folded skin around Safa's eyes tightened.

"The Cerdas discovered uncomfortable truths about Peralta's heritage and of his wife's origins. The Peraltas converted to Christianity a century ago, after they fled Toledo in a purge of the Jews. Until then, they had been Jews like me. An ancestor, some five generations before Esperanza, moved to Talavera in his manhood. He discarded his Jewish identity as one sheds a cloak indoors and took the Peralta name forever. The Cerdas believed, as do other ignorant people, that Jews practiced witchcraft and blood magic in their healing arts."

"The Castillan princes must have found it difficult to maintain the association. They killed Butayna's father?"

"*La,* nothing so extreme. They dismissed him from court, but his heritage was not the sole cause of their shame. They had also learned Peralta's wife was a former Jewess, an apostate who converted before her marriage."

Blood colored the surface of the crone's sallow skin and gave the flesh a ruddy glow. "Then Butayna has Jewish ancestry on both sides of her family. Does she know?"

"Her father kept it a secret from most, but he failed."

"How did you learn the truth?"

"My father introduced Efrain Peralta to his future wife. Her father suffered from pus-filled boils, which he needed a physician to lance. No Jewish doctor would treat him, but my father inquired with Peralta, a young man sympathetic to the plight of any patient who would pay. In his youth, he treated anyone who would support his growing practice. He offered his services and grew to love the old man's daughter. By then, Peralta also enjoyed the patronage of the Cerdas. He knew he could not have a Jewess for his wife if she practiced her religion. When her father died, at Peralta's behest, she became a Christian. He kept her away from court, but the Cerdas discovered the truth."

"You knew and still concealed Butayna's heritage from her. Why?"

"The knowledge was not mine to share."

181

Safa smiled. "This is not the time to dissemble."

Maryam pressed her lips together before she released a pent-up breath. "My father made me swear an oath during his lifetime. His death released me from it."

"You hate the girl. I sensed this from the moment both of you stood together in the House of Myrtles."

"She is the harbinger of all my misery."

"How so?"

"In the months after his wife's death and the dismissal from court, Efrain contracted a marriage for his child with a Castillan merchant's son in Alicante. Efrain offered most of his possessions to the husband I once had, in return for a *suftaja*. My husband also provided guards as the Peraltas left Talavera. None of us counted on the raiders. Efrain begged us to get away, but Esperanza would not leave him behind. I blame her for the deaths of my daughter and the son I carried within me. I will never forgive her for those losses. Even if it takes an entire lifetime, I shall have my due."

Safa grasped the end of the water pipe and inhaled. "We are alike, you and I."

Maryam snorted. "I don't think so."

"Believe what you like, but we are the same. You need to develop patience and further skill." When Maryam would have interjected, the Sultana put up a hand and called for silence. "You have a strong heart and an energetic spirit, but more is required. Your next move must be a delicate dance between your inclinations and resolve. Master the will and achieve your aims. If you can govern your impulses, I shall help you destroy this girl."

"Why do you care?"

"I have waited almost a lifetime for my own revenge. We can aid each other."

"Why would you help me, a filthy Jew? Or don't you remember what you called me after Yusuf never summoned me again?"

Safa sighed. "A poor choice of words. Like you, I once suffered under a much more powerful woman. For the last seven years of my husband's reign, the eight of his eldest son's rule and the first year of Yusuf's own, his grandmother Fatima ruled this harem. She possessed an iron will and did not hesitate to eliminate anyone she deemed a threat. In the last year of his life, my husband Ismail, Allah preserve his memory, became infatuated with a girl from Martus. His jealous cousins murdered him because one of them wanted the slave for himself. Fatima's first act after Ismail's murder was to have her chief eunuch poison the girl. I have lived in Fatima's shadow and bided my time until opportunity arrived."

Maryam leaned forward. "You have chosen an interesting expression, opportunity. Did you give the Sultana Fatima some poison to affect her mind? I have glimpsed her on brief occasions, shuffling around the harem at all hours. Sometimes, she calls for a Sultan Muhammad; I do not know which one, or Sultan Ismail. Then the servant who is always with her reminds her of the deaths of these men. Does she suffer these lapses in memory because of you?"

Safa's widened eyes and raised brows did not fool Maryam for a moment. She inquired, "Would you have me believe that you have never thought of killing Fatima?"

"It is all I have thought of since my son ascended the throne! The woman is old, but she had formidable resources. If anyone discovered a plot against her, Fatima would not hesitate to strike at her enemies. She is a true Nasrid, vicious and willful."

"You fear her still."

Yusuf's mother did not deny Maryam's observation. Instead, she said, "When Fatima acknowledged the changes in her mind and formally rescinded her power as the *Umm al-Walad,* my life did not change as I once expected. That is what I meant by opportunity. Allah has addled her mind. She remembers events of the past, but cannot tell anyone what she wore or whom she spoke with yesterday. Her presence divides this harem, even if the *jawari* follow my dictates rather than hers. Her influence has guided Yusuf into manhood. She molded him in the image of her father. Even worse, his sister Leila took Fatima's place and became his confidante. Leila is the same as her grandmother. Now, Leila uses sentiment and attachment to manipulate my son's interest in Butayna. I would put an end to Leila's schemes."

Maryam nodded. "What is to be my role in this intrigue?"

Safa plucked a few dates from the bowl. "It has been too long since my son last saw you. I should not have kept you far from him. He asked after you for a time or two. I always told him your monthly link with the moon prevented another encounter."

"Did you?" Maryam clasped her hands under the table and stilled a tremor within her fingers. Safa would come to regret her choice one day.

"A foolish lie, I admit that as well."

Maryam bit back her silent rage. "His infatuation with the girl deepened as a result."

"Then it is time you reminded Yusuf there are other women in the world. Then Leila will discover she cannot hold sway over him forever. Do you know Butayna shall perform with the *oud* for the entire harem in four days? She will play at Yusuf's request to honor his beloved father, Allah preserve his memory, who died twelve years ago this month."

"I am aware. What can we do to thwart or embarrass her?"

"We? There is no 'we' until I have your oath. Will you help me destroy Leila, if I guide you to a position at Yusuf's side and ruin Butayna's hopes? Do we have an accord?"

Maryam did not hesitate. "*Nam.* We do."

***

Wisps of ambergris, aloe wood, and aromatic frankincense floated in gauzy clouds from incense burners stationed at each corner of the harem's courtyard. Torches lit the garden while braziers warmed the guests. Eunuchs and handmaidens served trays of *hais*, pastries filled with ground almonds, and pistachios, dusted with crystalline sugar. A saffron-colored, twisted *dafair* loaf fell on the floor and rolled into the bushes, but Maryam doubted anyone else noticed it. She followed Safa's lead and picked her way through the crowded and noisy patio, while she carried a glass of *sekanjabin*. A yellow-haired *jarya* dressed in gauzy fabrics jostled her arm.

Maryam's gaze leveled with the slave's own. "If you had made me spill even one drop, you would have lapped it up like the peasant dog you are!"

The slave colored and drew back into the circle of her companions.

Ahead of her, Safa trilled a high-pitched laugh. "You still reject my lessons, Maryam. Leave the fool girl alone! Your aim is accomplished and the girl shall fear you from now on. Come, Yusuf awaits us."

Maryam glared at the *jarya* for a final time and finished the glass of *sekanjabin*. She slapped it on a tray of others held aloft by a passing eunuch, before she fell into step behind Safa again. Together, they arrived at the outskirts of the pavilion where Yusuf sat with his sister Leila on stout chairs with leather-covered arms.

On a plush cushion between them, dressed in lavender, brown, and gold, Esperanza tuned the strings of an *oud*. Gold dust speckled her skin, though not quite enough to cover the fading purple bruises at the base of her throat. She looked up and her nostrils flared.

Maryam turned her attention to Yusuf, who spoke with Leila, until his mother cleared her throat. His *jubba* fitted him well. Her hearted fluttered at the majestic sight of him.

"*Ummi*, I wondered when you would join us." He reached for Safa's hand.

"You have allowed too many *jawari* tonight, my Sultan."

"There is no such thing as too many women." A young man who resembled Yusuf strolled through the forecourt. He hugged red-haired twins close to him.

When he bowed, Yusuf nodded. "Ismail. I wondered when I would see you."

The prince peered around. "It is a wonder you can find anyone in this crowded courtyard." Then he looked down at Esperanza. "My lady, my noble brother has oft mentioned your charming voice and skill with the *oud*. I look forward to your performance."

She lowered her lids and said nothing.

Yusuf scowled at his brother. After another obeisance, the prince withdrew with his women.

Safa took the seat reserved for her at Yusuf's right. "*Nam*, I have often heard the noise coming from my son's chambers at late hours. How fortunate we both are, my Sultan, to have acquired talented slaves who can sing and play. Do you remember my Maryam? She is a songstress who could rival Leila's Butayna."

While a well-practiced smile pasted on her lips, Maryam executed a deep bow. Her waist-length hair fell on either side of her face. At the Sultan's command, she raised her head.

Yusuf leaned forward. "I do remember her. Eyes like indigo."

Beside him, the strings of the *oud* vibrated in a sharp ripple. Leila turned to Esperanza and inquired about her well-being in Castillan.

Beneath hooded eyelids, Maryam watched her. Could it be possible, even after more than a year, Esperanza still did not understand Arabic and required translated words?

Safa's booted foot nudged a silk pillow. "Sit here beside me, dear Maryam."

With a demure nod, she joined the Sultana. Yusuf's gaze flitted between her and his mother, before he attended to the low conversation between his sister and Esperanza.

Safa leaned forward. "This slave is familiar to me, as one I once saw when I purchased Maryam. Could it be the same skinny girl, Leila?"

Esperanza lifted her chin, her gaze hot as she flicked a narrowed stare at Yusuf's mother.

Maryam concealed her smile. The girl attempted to deceive the Moors, yet she must have understood every word.

Leila muttered, "You know who she is, Safa."

"How would I? Do you think I remember every malnourished captive who has crossed my path? I recall her because I had never seen one so wretched before, the ribs poking from the flesh. Ugh!" Safa shuddered and beckoned a eunuch who held glasses of lemon syrup diluted with water.

While she sipped the hot drink, Leila's eyes narrowed to slits and her lips tightened.

"Butayna has no cause to worry for food here," Yusuf commented. His hand pressed the girl's shoulder and she gazed up at him.

Maryam's jaw tightened. The dazed look on Esperanza's face mirrored the taut, shining appearance of Yusuf's own. Both of their lips parted. They would have kissed each other if they wished in the presence of everyone.

Her stomach in a taut knot, Maryam turned to Safa and shot her a bold, direct stare.

The Sultana nodded and pecked at her son's sleeve. For the space of three full breaths, his focus dawdled on Esperanza.

Then he gave an annoyed huff and glanced at his mother. "What is it?"

Unaffected by his abrupt tone, she said, "You are such an honorable man, my son, always so kind and solicitous to slaves. It is a wonder we have any who fear us at all."

He replied, "I don't believe slaves deserve contempt, *Ummi.*"

"As you say, but I would never have allowed even the finest musician access to the prized *oud* your grandmother gave you as a boy. Why, she is even dressed in Fatima's favorite color, purple. How has this girl bewitched you, Yusuf?"

His sharp glance met his mother's own. "She has not, *Ummi.*" He ground out the words, his color heightened.

Safa covered his olive-brown hand with her jeweled fingers. "Forgive me, my Sultan. I worry for your tender heart. No one should take advantage of your kindness. Let us all here this accomplished musician. Why keep anyone in suspense for much longer?"

With a mollified sigh, he spoke to Esperanza in a hushed tone.

Then, silence fell over the courtyard. The guests gathered at the entrance to the harem parted. Maryam stood, as did the rest of the Sultan's household, for a glimpse of the Sultana Fatima while she strode the length of the garden with her constant companion.

Maryam took in her first full view of the shriveled woman who had reared Yusuf after the death of his father and once ruled this harem. She did not seem so powerful, rather like a little girl.

Gray silk swirled around her and silvery hair floated at her back like wisps of clouds. Yet Maryam knew outward appearances never told the full truth of a person. She would have to learn more of Fatima, even as immediate observation revealed important details.

Yusuf indulged his grandmother's rejection of the *hijab*, which told Maryam of his love and reverence for the old woman. The wide grin splayed on his face suggested he cared more for her than a lack of decorum.

The Sultana focused on the family who awaited her, but every person in the courtyard from the lowliest *jarya* to the most stalwart guardsmen bent low as she entered their midst. Maryam smiled as her understanding increased. No one had bowed or even acknowledged Safa when she appeared in the courtyard, despite the fact that she held the official title of the Sultan's mother. Safa could presume whatever she wished of her control over the harem, but its occupants still recognized Fatima's latent supremacy.

"What is she doing here?"

Safa's shrill voice pierced Maryam's awareness. When she turned and viewed her, Safa's hands had curled into fists. She tugged at her lower lip, gone almost as pale as her ashen face. Her chest rose and fell rapidly beneath her *jubba*. Fury and fear vied for control of her.

Maryam pushed aside her earlier premise about Fatima. Safa would only display such emotions in the presence of one who deserved a formidable reputation. Maryam tapped her fingertip against her mouth. She perceived she had chosen the right alliance. Still, if Fatima held sway over Yusuf, could she undo Safa's plans for Leila? She would not stand idly by while Safa removed her granddaughter from a position of influence. Maryam would have to maneuver carefully in matters affecting the old Sultana's interests.

Yusuf left his family and approached Fatima at the center of the courtyard. When he bowed before her, his sister and Butayna followed the gesture. Maryam gaped. She never thought the Sultan would bow before anyone.

At a sharp glance from Leila, Safa's jawline tightened and she returned her rival's glare. The silent battle of wills between the women continued, until Safa bent her back and snapped at Maryam to do the same.

Then Yusuf uttered, "Grandmother, I did not think you would remember the performance tonight."

"I am an old woman, Yusuf, and I cannot sleep with all this noise in the harem!"

His chuckle indicated he only half-believed her protest. "Still, your presence honors this assembly. Come and sit with me." He turned and waved his hand over the guests. "You may all rise."

The din of conversations resumed. Yusuf tucked Fatima's hand in the crook of his arm and led her under the pavilion. A eunuch brought another chair, but Yusuf demanded, "Put that down! Move my mother's seat back a pace first."

The slave hastened to do his mater's bidding. While Safa scowled as expected, Maryam nodded. Yusuf had chosen to place his grandmother directly on his right instead of his mother, but Esperanza remained in place on his left. She had bewitched him, just as Safa claimed. Maryam glared at the girl, who idled beside Yusuf's sister until the latter stepped forward.

Leila bowed again, grasped Fatima's thin shoulders and kissed the woman's leathery cheeks. "I'm so glad you're here."

No formal titles between them then. The Nasrids could be quite cruel to each other, but their blood bonds remained strong, evident in the regard Yusuf and his sister held for their grandmother.

Fatima rasped, "My dearest girl, as lovely as the day we sewed *tiraz* bands for your wedding."

Leila colored and ducked her gaze. "A union that was not meant to be. It has been a long time since then."

Fatima shook her head. "Not for me." She turned and stared at Maryam, who stood to Safa's right. "I do not know you."

Then Fatima peered up at Yusuf. "She is not the slave who will sing tonight?"

Maryam took a step forward, ready to proclaim herself a better songstress than Esperanza. Safa clapped a hand on Maryam's wrist so hard that she feared the bones would break. She swallowed a wince and steadied herself.

Safa released her and cleared her throat. "This is Maryam, a slave of mine. She would be unimportant to you, my Sultana."

Fatima lifted her chin. Although the fleshy wattle beneath it jiggled, something in her timeworn features gave way to the beauty she must have once held. "Do not presume to tell me who may be important or unimportant in the harem, Safa. My mind is not so addled that it cannot discern truth."

As a flush crept across Safa's rounded cheeks, Fatima's murky gaze swiveled back to Maryam. She studied her in silence far longer than propriety allowed. Then her thin lips pursed and her brow crinkled as if something vexed her.

Yusuf patted her hand. "Come and let me introduce you to Butayna instead."

Maryam's teeth ground against each other as Esperanza executed a simpering bow and kept her eyes averted before the old queen. Fatima stared at her for a lengthy period before she took her seat. Her servant joined her, resting at the woman's feet.

Yusuf bent and spoke in a whisper to Esperanza again. Whatever he said made her wan cheeks brighten a deep shade of pink. She nodded and picked up the instrument. Then she held it before Fatima and bowed. The Sultana nodded and waved her away.

Esperanza turned and focused on Maryam with a tight-lipped sneer on her lips, before she strode underneath the orange trees. She stood with her head bowed in the center of the garden while Yusuf called for silence.

A hush fell over the guests when Esperanza plucked the instrument's strings. She closed her eyes and her fingers flowed across the cords. She played an old ballad of Castilla-Leon, the *cantiga* of a wounded knight who traveled homeward at the end of his life to die in his son's arms. Even without the words half of the attendees would have understood, the tune conveyed a somber, even wistful mood. At the fringes of the court, more than one *jarya* brushed at her wet cheek before the song ended. Even the Sultan swiped his eyes, likely in memory of his own father.

Cheers erupted and Yusuf jerked to his feet, the nosiest among his household. Esperanza bowed and a tight smile upturned the corners of her mouth. When she strummed the *oud* again, quiet descended and the Sultan resumed his seat.

Safa leaned toward Maryam and cleared her throat. "Is she as good as you remember from your childhood together?"

Maryam nodded. She would never underestimate her adversary again. "Better! I am amazed and filled with admiration for her talents."

Leila's sharp intake shifted Maryam's regard. Yusuf's sister frowned. She had not informed him of the fight just outside the *hammam.*

He chewed slices of orange and washed his fingertips in a proffered bowl of rosewater. "You knew Butayna outside of the harem?"

Maryam favored him with a wide smile. "We grew up together as children in Castilla-Leon. We were still with each other when the raiders captured us and brought us into *al-Andalus*, my Sultan."

He directed a frown at Esperanza. "I wonder why she has never told me there was anyone else with her except her father."

189

Maryam sighed. "A captive's life can be so uncertain in those first few days. I thought Butayna and I would have clung to each other, but she cloaked herself in bitter grief and despair over her loss. After your honored mother the Sultana brought me here, I thought I would never see my dear friend again. Now, it is as if we are strangers. Perhaps, I remind her of the difficult past we have shared."

"*Nam*, still it displeases me that I would have never known of the connection if you had not told me," Yusuf muttered.

Safa interposed, "I wonder why the girl hid the truth from you, sweet son."

His sister rubbed his arm. "We cannot know the experience of captivity and should not judge anyone's conduct after such horrid conditions."

In a moment, the creases across his brow relaxed. "You are right, of course, sweet sister. I will ask Butayna of her past. Has she told you nothing?"

Leila said, "Butayna has shared little of her life before the harem because I have never encouraged it. Why should I care for the history of former captives? Butayna's relations with Maryam remain a mystery, but my slave is not the cause of any discord. A few days ago, my Sultan, Hamduna fetched me to stop a vicious argument between the pair. Butayna had nail marks on her throat."

An audible growl in Safa's throat rose above Esperanza's soaring voice.

Before his mother spoke, Yusuf's fierce glower returned, this time to Maryam. "When I questioned Butayna last night, she refused to tell me how she suffered those bruises, even when I threatened to have Hisham beat her for defiance. What did you do to her, slave?"

Maryam's heart thudded. She shuddered at the demand in his wintry, clipped tone.

With a tight smile, Leila settled back against her chair and sipped pomegranate juice with crushed rose petals. Safa summoned a slave for a *dafair* loaf. Fatima sipped a cup of tea and accepted half of a sugarcoated pastry.

The Sultan's scrutiny deepened and Maryam whispered, "I confronted Butayna about the estrangement between us. Her abandonment of our friendship almost ruined me. I would not let her leave the *hammam*. My anger overrode good judgment and I attacked her."

Then Safa swallowed a piece of bread and added, "I have punished my slave for her stupidity, my Sultan. This is the first night in four where anything but spittle has passed between her lips."

Leila scowled at both of them, but Safa raised her eyebrows. Her measured look dared the Sultan's sister to contradict her.

Yusuf turned to Leila. "Where were you when this argument occurred?"

She jerked at his severe tone. "I did not send Butayna to the baths alone and defenseless! Hamduna was with her and returned to fetch me."

Safa said, "It no longer matters, at least not to my Maryam. I have an idea. I would love to hear them as a duet. If Leila's slave has no lingering bitterness over the incident in the *hammam*, I am sure she would be amenable to the suggestion. Let us see them side by side. We may gain assurance whether there will be further trouble."

Yusuf scratched his trim beard. "You are possibly right."

When Esperanza finished, another round of ovations arose. Yusuf stood and raised his hands in a bid for silence.

"As a final act, the slaves of my sister Sultana Leila and the *Umm al-Walad* shall entertain us together, Maryam in song and Butayna with the *oud*." He repeated the words in Castillan.

Before he did, Esperanza stood in the shade of an orange tree, her crestfallen features illuminated by torchlight, her mouth in a wide O.

When Sultana Fatima stood with her half-empty cup in hand, Yusuf turned to her. "Are you well?"

"I am," Fatima replied. Her gaze flicked over Safa's face and Maryam's own before she regarded her grandson. "I have had enough entertainment for one evening."

Yusuf's cheeks colored. "But, there is only one more song we shall hear. Surely, you don't mean to leave so soon."

"I do. Come, Asiya." She beckoned her servant, who stood beside her. The young woman took the cup and placed it on a tray held by a eunuch.

Yusuf raked his hands over his hair. "Very well. Thank you for coming tonight. I hope you enjoyed Butayna's performance."

Fatima glanced at Esperanza in the center of the courtyard. "She is a rare find in this harem, a *jarya* whose talents extend beyond your bedchamber. Enjoy her."

She tossed her long hair back and swept from the courtyard with the trusted servant at her side.

Maryam scowled. How dare the old crone leave at such a moment? Whether or not she intended an insult, she made it seem as if Maryam's talent did not warrant her interest. A stupid slight Maryam would never forget.

She breathed a ragged sigh and bowed her head. "I do not think Butayna and I should sing together. I doubt she has forgiven me."

Safa thumped her shoulder. "Her prideful wishes do not matter! My son commands it. Forget Sultana Fatima and your silly misunderstanding with Butayna. Sing!"

Maryam nodded and rose. She ambled to Esperanza's side. They stood several hand spans' apart. Maryam's chest rose and fell, each breath stolen. To stand so close to the wretched girl who had changed her fortunes forever and maintain this farce proved a great trial.

Esperanza muttered something unintelligible under her breath before she touched the cords. She chose a familiar tune.

Maryam smiled and sang of a Christian knight and a Moorish cavalier, who battled for the love of a Castillan lady. Enraptured gazes remained on her as she circled her rival and then strolled through the garden's quadrants, her melodious voice carried on the wind. When she finished, the guests clamored for more. Maryam sank into a deep bow directed to the Sultan.

Safa approached her and addressed the assembly. "Have you ever heard such wondrous talent?"

A chorus of cheers acknowledged the truth of her words.

Yusuf stated, "I believe she changed the few last lines. As I once heard in the original version, the Moor lost the battle for his Christian lady's love."

He remained seated, his chin propped up on his fist. His rapt gaze veered between Maryam and Esperanza, as if he found himself befuddled by the differences between them.

When the moon rode high in the starlit heavens, Safa begged Yusuf's indulgence despite his protests. "I am an old woman and must retire."

He peered at Maryam before he addressed his mother. "Do you have to leave so soon?"

"Perhaps if we have another evening such as this one, Maryam and Butayna might entertain us again. Sleep well, my dear son."

She bowed before him and beckoned Maryam, who also made her obeisance before she followed Safa. As she departed, the sensation of heat swept up her back. She peeked and found both Esperanza and Yusuf observed her progress out of the garden courtyard.

On the upper floor of Safa's apartment, Maryam peered out through the *shimasas* at the festivities below. If she had been in Talavera's *aljama* almost two weeks ago, she would have joined her family in the celebration of *Purim*, the escape of the Jews from the cruel Persian vizier Haman. Now, Maryam would devise her own deliverance from the clutches of her enemies in the harem. She would deal with Butayna's treachery first, but Safa's day would come as well.

The Sultan's mother joined her with her fat fingers clasped together. "The trick with my son, as with all men, is to keep him desirous. Familiarity offers ease and comfort, but men crave what they cannot often have. Long before he tires of Butayna, you will claim him as yours."

Maryam did not turn from the window. "Did you practice these wiles on your husband? Did you not say he died because of a slave woman preferred by all others?"

"Do not ask me questions!" Safa snapped. "Go to your pallet. Now."

Maryam bowed. "As you wish, my Sultana."

Chapter 14
A Night's Consideration

Esperanza Peralta

Granada, Andalusia
March 30 – April 17, AD 1337 / 26 Sha'ban – 15 Ramadan 737
AH / 27th of Nissan - 15th of Iyar, 5097

Esperanza dipped a corner of the flatbread into the congealed *zabarbada* of goat cheese. A gooey pale string of the melted cheese clung to the pot and then broke as she brought the bread to her mouth. Yusuf reclined on cushions next to her, his head braced upon his hand. He had finished the meal long ago, but as usual encouraged her to eat more. While she chewed, his concentrated stare lingered on her face. Her cheeks warmed underneath his examination.

"I wish you would not look at me so, my Sultan."

He drawled, "You wish I would not find you desirable, a woman whom I want in my bed?"

Her heart thumped and she rubbed at her breastbone under the *misha*. The action served to draw his gaze there. An uneven breath filtered through his lips.

"*Si!* You should not say such things to me, my Sultan."

"Why, when you prize truth above all else? I have yearned for you for some time, long before we returned from *Jannat al-'Arif* at the end of last summer. How could any man not want you after he has gazed for months upon a face as fine-boned as yours, touched the underside of your arm, as soft as silk, watched that delectable mouth as you chewed or stared into those eyes of fire? Why do you think I have rejected the women my mother sends to me each week? I dine with you instead because you are all I desire. I wish to burn in the heat of your eyes filled with equal passion for me and stir the embers deep inside you, until your fires consume me. The first time I touched you, your skin burned my fingertips."

Esperanza dragged her gaze from his and gripped the edge of the table.

His long fingers covered hers, the skin heated. His fingertips traced the curve between her thumb and index finger before he joined their hands and drew hers to his lips. He upturned the wrist, nipped, and kissed the pale flesh there.

She heaved a ragged sigh and stilled the tremors in her body with deep breaths. "You may claim me if you wish. Your own laws say I am your property to do with as you will."

He released her. "You think I want a slave who does as she's told in my bed?"

She bowed her head. "I cannot yield to you, my Sultan. What you believe is the natural yearning of a man, I consider it a sin without the benefit of marriage. How can you ask me to set aside my Christian beliefs? They are part of who I am. I have given up so much already in these last fifteen months. Do not tempt me to abandon the tenets of my faith, my Sultan."

He sat up and reached for her chin, drawing her regard to him again. He caressed the curve of her cheek. She leaned into his touch and closed her eyes, the warmth of her breath reflected from his palm.

"Yusuf. I have told you to call me Yusuf. Our laws permit marriage to a Christian woman after she has borne me a son. You believe I look at you and see a slave meant for my pleasure. You have so much more to offer any man who takes the chance to know you as I have. In a world of liars and half-truths, you speak what is in your heart, so it is often the truth. There is little artifice in you, not like these women whom my mother trains and sends into my arms. I have bedded them and never found one to hold my heart, until you. You are my match in every way, one who tests and excites me, who stirs my heart and passions."

When she opened her eyes and stared at him in full, he drew away with a sigh. "I will not take what you will not give. You will come to me in the time of your choosing, or not at all. I refuse to accept anything less than the truth, the whole of you. If you come to my bed, it will be because you want me as much as I want you."

She blinked back tears. Why did he have to be so honorable? If he had demanded her surrender, she could have at least despised him for it. His reluctant acceptance of her hesitancy made her quandary even more difficult.

In choosing him, she would have to put aside her diminished hope of escape. She would have to accept his way of life and share his bed outside the bounds of a marital union. His religion allowed him to bed other women with impunity. Could she accept his behavior? Would she lose the last remnants of her former self in the process?

She struggled each night with her prayers, unable to focus whenever Yusuf's shining visage encroached on her thoughts.

Did God even hear her supplication anymore? Had He abandoned her at last, knowing lust for Yusuf lurked in her heart? If she surrendered to his desire, what would become of her? Esperanza Peralta would no longer exist, just the slave Butayna as Juan Manuel once predicted. Could she let go of the past and her true self?

The ignominy of Yusuf's blatant attentions aside, she could not deny the certainty in her heart. She wanted him, not because he was noble or handsome. From the beginning, he challenged her as well, to accept life's disappointments, and learn and grow from them. He introduced her to so much and opened her eyes to the simple beauties of a world she once scorned. When he touched her skin, her soul sang a melody richer and deeper than any she had ever practiced on the *oud*. For her, there would be joy in a life at his side.

The past haunted and made her uncertain. If her father remained alive and knew of her fate, what would he say of her sinful longing for Yusuf? As a devout Christian, would he condemn her licentious thoughts worse than Fray Rufino could have ever done? Could he ever forgive her?

Yusuf interrupted her contemplation. "Since you will not give me the answer I wish for now, it is time for other truth telling between us. Why have you never acknowledged your former friendship with the slave Maryam? I have waited a month for an explanation of why she, not you, informed me of the connection."

His stone-faced visage took her aback. Where was the devoted man who pledged himself as her would-be lover a moment ago? Now the Sultan of Granada took his place.

"What did she tell you on that night, my Sultan?"

"Yusuf. I have oft repeated my name. You will address me by it or not at all, Butayna." His lips protruded in a pout, which made her long for his kiss.

Instead, she whispered. "Very well. What did she say, Yusuf?"

When he related the events of the night, Esperanza seethed and her hands tightened into fists. Maryam's blatant lies and half-truths would damn her to hell-fire in any religion.

Incredulous, she shook her head. "She told you that I abandoned her? I attacked her?"

"Did she make false claims? It is a grave offense to offer lies to the Sultan, treason punishable by death. Leila sat beside us, but she did not know the truth of your past."

"She's never asked for it! She's never cared before that night."

The Sultana Safa was also present on that night and defended Maryam, which meant she supported her version of events. If she did not know the truth, like Leila, Maryam had also misled her. If not, Safa had also lied to her son. Could he order the execution of his own mother just for her support of a lie? How would he bear the mark on his soul? Could she watch him suffer the recriminations, as he would heap on himself?

"Butayna, I am waiting for your explanation of these events."

She bowed her head. "I was angry with everyone after my father's death, including the Jewess who was once a dear friend." At least, that was true. They had quarreled on the *meseta* when Esperanza accused Maryam of abandoning Gedaliah.

She continued, "There is something else you should know. She blames me for the deaths of her daughter and the son she carried in her womb. I could not abandon my father although he demanded it. When the raiders stole us away, one of them bashed Palomba against a rock and raped her mother each day and night. She survived his abuses, but lost her unborn babe. I don't know if I would have maintained her courage."

"You admire her still, even with the distance of time and circumstance."

"Some bonds do not sever so soon."

When a tear trickled down her cheek, he wiped it away and kissed her skin. "Go to your rest. I have kept you here too long."

She turned to him. "I do care for you, Yusuf, more than I should if I wish to keep my faith."

He pressed his warm brow against hers. She breathed in the scent of him. The almond and rosewater on his breath from the last of the sweet *sukkariyya* dessert. Saffron, pepper, cinnamon, and lavender on his fingertips when he pulled apart the *dafair* loaves at dinner. The citrus infused in the fitted sleeves of his *shaya*, which followed the contours of his torso so well.

His eyelids were heavy as though he craved sleep, but she knew better. She cupped his cheek and nuzzled it. Some silent exchange passed between them.

His somewhat disheveled beard tickled her palm. "Butayna."

"Yusuf." When she slanted her head and pressed her mouth against him, he froze in an instant. Then his hands twined in her hair and a low moan rumbled his throat. Under the insistent pressure of his lips, she parted her own and tasted sugary sweetness at the tip of his tongue. His kiss turned hungry and unforgiving also, as if he sought to punish her for the delay. She clung to his waist while he pressed her back among the cushions and sustained his weight on one elbow. The other hand roamed lower and cupped her breast through the thin *qamis*. The pad of his thumb smoothed across a nipple. The sensation tingled and dipped down to her stomach. She dug her nails into his back through the *shaya* and deepened the kiss.

197

He broke away. Perspiration beaded at his hairline and trickled down his temple. She raised her head and licked at the salty wetness. His hoarse chuckle followed.

He asked. "Who kissed you before I did?"

A wave of heat warmed her face before she answered. "The arrogant merchant's son I would have married if not for the raid. After our betrothal, he said it was a formality. He told me we had promised our lives to each other, enough to try... certain things. Does the news displease you, Yusuf?"

He pressed his lips against her brow. "No one can change the past. Should I ask if he claimed more than a kiss?"

"I swear upon my father's soul, the boy just kissed me. I would never have permitted more although he desired it. It made him angry. Afterward, he told his parents I had demanded kisses from him. My father was ashamed, but the merchant saw no harm and believed we should marry as soon as possible. I never forgave that boy for his lie."

"But you enjoyed his attentions until he behaved like an eager fool?" His mouth hovered over hers. He had not removed his thumb from her chest either. In fact, it circled her nipple until she groaned and panted.

"Not as much as yours. Never...."

She held her breath as he dipped his head. His tongue traced the shell of her ear. Teeth nipped at her lobe. A groan filled her throat.

"Yusuf, please kiss me again," she whispered.

When he laughed at her, the sound was carnal, rich, and husky. She slid her fingertips up under his *shaya*. His stomach muscles clenched and he raised himself a little. His brows lifted and he froze above her.

She trembled. "Have I done something wrong? Am I not allowed to... to... touch you?"

He pressed faint kisses to her nose, forehead and temples, her cheeks and chin. "Oh, by the Prophet's beard, Butayna, touch me any place, anywhere, you would like!"

She raised her hands and captured his face between her fingers. "Then I would have your mouth upon mine again."

When their lips met again, Esperanza pushed the niggling doubts she had held aside. It felt right. She belonged in his arms. Her legs parted and she hooked one over his calf. Yusuf moaned into her mouth. When his hands dragged up the *qamis* and his fingertips skimmed her abdomen, she understood his earlier response. Pleasure surged through the length of her body. Nothing God fashioned, including the mutual ardor of two people, could ever be sinful.

His hands roamed higher and then stopped. She intended to offer some form of protest, but he broke the kiss first. "I need to look at you."

The hitch in his throat made her reach for him again. When he raised his head, she studied his expression. He seemed puzzled, as if uncertain where to begin. "Sit up."

When she obliged him, his hands shook as he pulled the *misha* from her shoulders. She subdued a little laugh while his fingers tugged at the tight strings of her garment.

"Yusuf, do not—"

Her objection faded as he ripped the cords in half and offered her a self-satisfied grin. "Now, lift your arms, please, so I can take off this shift."

Again, she indulged him. Cool air wafted over her skin as he tugged the sleeves halfway up and stopped.

"Yusuf?"

He palmed her stomach. "You are perfect."

She squirmed and giggled. "If you think perfect means having a boy's body, I must wonder for your sanity. My last governess said I would have difficulty in childbearing and rearing because my hips are too small and I have no breasts. Please help me take the linen off."

He pulled the cloth over her head and sat back on his heels. His hot gaze traveled from her shoulders to her stomach. Then his lips twitched and became downturned. "We have to stop."

"What? Why?"

He touched her inner leg. The *sarawil* clung to her there. He lifted his index finger, a red smear across the tip. "Your womanly time is upon you."

She looked down at herself, understanding at last the warm wetness she experienced. The bleeding had not occurred last week when she anticipated it. Why had it come tonight of all nights, in front of Yusuf? A flush crept across her skin. She stared at him again. Her gaze watered. He reached for the *qamis* and helped her with it.

"I know, Butayna. Do you understand this means you can have children?"

She gaped at him. "This is not the first time I have had my woman's blood! I know what it means." She pushed his clumsy fingers aside and made the best knot she could with the ruined cords at her throat.

His eyes widened. "You do not need to be embarrassed! When the bleeding is over, we can try again—"

"We should not! What if I bore you a child, eh?"

He compressed his lips together before they splayed in a wide smile. "Then I would be the happiest father on the earth! Our sons shall be strong like both of us, our daughters beautiful and spirited like you."

She rose to her feet. "Where I come from, bastards gain their spirited natures in defense of themselves against cruel taunts. I don't want to bear your bastards, Yusuf!"

She fled from his chambers. At the doorway of Leila's room, she realized he had not given her permission to go.

***

Esperanza toiled alone in the early morning. She hefted a wooden pail from the cistern filled with water and poured it into the lusterware jar on the ground floor. When she reentered the room, Ifrit looked up from her seat by the window. Esperanza offered her nod, which as usual, she did not return. Esperanza shook her head. Leila's body slave thought too much of herself.

Esperanza paused in the middle of pouring the water and focused on the woman's features. Ifrit reminded her of Juan Manuel's slave Binta.

Ifrit caught her staring. "What are you looking at, Butayna?"

"You. When did the Sultana purchase you?"

"Why does that matter?"

"I wish to know."

Ifrit's harrumph rose to the honeycombed ceiling, where voices echoed. "It has been two weeks. You are her mistress! You could influence her decision, Leila."

"You have just said you want the *jarya* willing! Why come to me to sway her mind?"

"She doesn't know what she wants! She's letting her religion guide her."

"As Islam guides you! What is good for you is good for her, Yusuf!"

Esperanza shivered and glanced at Ifrit. "Why is the Sultan here?"

"How should I know? Does he share his purpose with me?"

"Must you answer a question with a question?"

"Must you ask questions?"

Esperanza dropped the wooden pail. "Since I came from the House of Myrtles, you have resented me."

"Perhaps you should return there. Juan Manuel would find you another buyer."

"What do you know of Juan Manuel?" Esperanza paused and stepped closer to her. "You were with the Sultana when she first saw me at the House of Myrtles, but that was not the first time

200

you had been there, was it? What is your connection to Juan Manuel? Are you one of his spies?"

"Do not ask me questions! Why did you have to come to the Sultan's palace?"

"I never asked to be here! Your mistress claimed my freedom."

"I wish she had not!" Ifrit buried her face behind her hands. Her shoulders shook.

Esperanza stepped back and stared at the ground. Why would their disagreement have brought the woman to tears?

When Ifrit sniffled and swiped a hand across her nose, Esperanza said, "I do not ask you to like me and it's clear you never will, but we both serve the Sultana. You are very devoted to her. I can understand why. She... she reminds me of her brother. They are both good people, better than I expected of those who keep slaves. If you think I wish to replace you—"

"You could not! Look at you. Leila will always prefer me!"

Puzzled, Esperanza shook her head. She had never heard Ifrit use common address in reference to the Sultana. Some other meaning lay undiscovered in the slave's words, but she had no time to consider it when footsteps stamped across the wood above.

Then Leila's voice echoed atop of the stairs. "My Ifrit! Are you there, my loyal one?"

The body slave rounded Esperanza and stood at the base of the stairs. "*Nam*, my Sultana?"

"Why are your eyes red again? Never mind, we will talk later. When Butayna returns from the cistern, send her up to me."

"At once, my Sultana."

As Leila's footfalls retreated, Ifrit turned to Esperanza. "Butayna, our mistress wishes to speak with you."

Esperanza groaned and marched up the stairs. Halfway to the top, she glanced over her shoulder. "I am not finished with you. We will talk again of our differences."

Inside Leila's bedchamber, Yusuf sat cross-legged on a pillow. Dark shadows encircled his eyes. Had he not slept well?

He looked up at her and gaped. She bowed low. They had not seen each other for over two weeks, since the night she had left him without his consent. He had not summoned her again to break the fast of Ramadan, to play for him, or for any reason. When her resentment ebbed, there were long evenings in which she missed his company. Why had he come now? Would he punish her for disobedience or had he ordered his sister to do it?

Leila gave an impatient snort. "Do come here and sit with us, Butayna."

When Esperanza did so, Leila glanced at her brother, who nodded.

Ramadi slunk on his belly from Leila's side and purred next to Esperanza. She could not help her smile as she picked him up and settled him on her lap. She scratched behind his gray ears.

When she looked up, Yusuf clenched his fingers in his lap and released them. Her fingertips tingled as she stroked Ramadi's fur and the cat purred in satisfaction.

The Sultana rolled her eyes heavenward and muttered something in Arabic, which sounded like, "Traitorous little beast!"

Then Leila said, "My brother desires me to say, he wishes to claim you as his, but you must agree. He understands if you, as one of the *dhimmi*, have some concerns regarding children conceived in a union with the Sultan. In *al-Jazirat al-Andalus*, the children of a *jarya* and her master gain their freedom at birth, provided the father recognizes his children. They are legitimate, not slaves or bastards, but heirs entitled to a portion of their father's estate. It would be the same for the children of my brother. There is no question whether Yusuf would acknowledge the offspring born to any of his *jawari*. Any son of his and yours would be considered a candidate to succeed his father on the throne. Your concerns about bastardry are unimportant. Now, if you should give him offspring, Yusuf has promised to marry you. He will wed you upon the birth of his first living child, either a son or daughter. This is most unusual. I have advised against it, but he is a man of his word and will not forgo a pledge he has made. Do you understand what I am saying? He wants you in his life as his Sultana and mother to his heirs. If you go to him, you accept his ways and this life. Do you want him? *La* or *nam?*"

Esperanza's heart thudded. Her stare wavered between both of them. "What?"

Leila turned from her to Yusuf. "Must I repeat all I have said? You know how I hate repeating myself." When Yusuf scowled at her, she swung to Esperanza again. "What is your answer? Do you wish to be his *jarya?*"

"My Sultana, I did not understand your words. When you speak in all Arabic—"

"*La!* This is nonsense. You understood every sentence. Do you think I am ignorant of your deception? You do not have the talent for lies, Butayna, so stop your foolishness! You have lived in this harem for more than a year, with many opportunities to gain proficiency in our language. I've long suspected you had acquired a certain fluency last summer when we were at the

Jannat al-'Arif. You confirmed it on the night of your performance before the entire harem. You did not need anyone to translate what Maryam or Safa said. Your displeasure at their words was clear. I do not know what advantage you think you have gained by keeping this secret, but the time for idiocy is over! I will not repeat myself nor offer this opportunity again. I give you this one chance, a night's consideration. In the morning, you must decide whether you shall continue to serve as my maid, or become my brother's lover forever. Choose."

***

In the afternoon, while Leila slumbered after her visit to the *hammam*, Esperanza headed for the stable. She had found familiar comfort before among the horses while she bemoaned her losses. Bilal and al-Sagir never troubled or questioned her presence whenever she appeared.

Esperanza stumbled as the opened stable door came into view. Sultana Fatima sat in its recesses on a wooden stool without her attendant at hand. Al-Sagir slumped at her feet with outstretched legs. He drew on a glass pipe from a wooden mouthpiece. When he released it, white puffs of vapor almost obscured his face. His head lolled.

The Sultana smoothed her deep-veined, gnarled fingers over the hair close-cropped to his skull. "Rest now, boy. Soon you shall dream."

Esperanza shuffled, uncertain of her next move. When Fatima lifted a murky gaze to hers, she froze. Then she recalled the harem's rules and bowed low.

"Get up and come here. Sit at my feet."

Esperanza lifted her head and swallowed the knot in her throat. Fatima beckoned again her with a wave. She rose and did as commanded. A late frost covered the cold ground, but she paid it scant attention. Instead, her heart pounded while she waited for Fatima to speak again.

Bilal approached from the field south of the stable. He led a brown horse dappled with snowy spots. Esperanza nodded to him.

He wiped one muck-covered hand on his dirtied garments. "My lady! You have come. I am always glad to see you."

Esperanza did not answer him at first. She hesitated to reveal her secret understanding of Arabic, especially in front of Yusuf's grandmother. Still, the time for pretense had ended.

She whispered, "As I am pleased to see you, Bilal."

He nodded and flashed a gap-toothed grin. With some coaxing, he tugged the restive mount into the stable.

Fatima patted al-Sagir's head. He leaned against her leg, but she did not push him away from such a familiar gesture. Instead, she told Esperanza, "When my son Ismail was young, he would sit at my feet and listen to stories of our ancestors. My grandchildren are grown. They have heard my stories too many times. Now, I tell them to al-Sagir."

Esperanza hugged her knees. "The Sultan must still appreciate your past. He honors and loves you very much, my Sultana."

"You are the girl he loves now."

Esperanza blinked and stared at the ground. Her heart swelled at the Sultana's words, but she did not know whether they were true. Did Yusuf love her or did he only want her, another conquest for his bed? She shook her head at such mean thoughts. If he only desired her, he could have taken her on the night in his chambers, regardless of her woman's blood.

Fatima interrupted her musings. "I remember you. You are the one who serves Leila, but now Yusuf loves you. He looks at you in the way my beloved once looked upon me. I remember what it feels like to be the recipient of such regard."

Esperanza turned away and willed herself not to blush. "It would be an honor to have your grandson's love, my Sultana."

"You doubt you have it already?"

Esperanza's gaze flicked to Fatima's own again. A little smile lifted the corner of the Sultana's mouth and deepened the lines there.

"I do not disbelieve you, but I have never heard him speak of love, my Sultana."

"Do you have to? Can't you tell by the way he treats you? I can. Words are not enough. For those who matter to us, we show how we care."

Fatima focused on the boy at her feet. "Al-Sagir and Bilal's father was one of the guards at *al-Quasaba*. He used to beat his family, including his children, al-Sagir worst of all because he was always crying. His mother was a *henna* artist within my household. When al-Sagir was five years old and his mother could no longer hide her husband's handiwork beneath her own artistry, I intervened. Her husband never touched anyone in his household again. My eunuchs removed his hands."

A chill ripped through Esperanza's body and she peered at al-Sagir. He giggled, his red-eyed stare unfocused.

Fatima continued, "The damage this boy suffered could not be undone by such an act. His mother soon recognized he was not like her other children. He broke things and hurt his sisters. I thought *hashish* would calm him. At times, it as if he is two different people. The child who would never hurt anyone. Then he is someone else."

"What is *hashish*, my Sultana?"

"A drug derived from the cannabis plant and smoked in the water pipe. Yusuf does not like al-Sagir's dependence upon the drug. My grandson believes the *hashish* does more harm than good. Perhaps he is right."

At the audible hitch in Fatima's voice, Esperanza looked up. Tears streamed down Fatima's sun-browned cheeks. She closed her eyes and lifted her face to the cool wind.

Esperanza waited until Fatima's tears had subsided before she said, "Forgive me, my Sultana, if I ask an impertinent question. How is it you know so much of this drug? It does not seem like a thing in which you would indulge—"

"What do you know of me, girl, and the life I have lived? Nothing! Who are you to judge? You are a slave, yet you remain ignorant of the true fragility of life."

Fatima's cheeks darkened with a red flush. The large vein in her slender neck twitched.

Esperanza stiffened beneath the Sultana's cold regard. After a moment, she bent her head and her stare remained fixed on the ground. "Please, forgive me, my Sultana. I had no right to question you."

Silence followed, the lull sometimes broken by the snorts of horses in their stalls and al-Sagir's yawns. In time, he closed his eyes. His head bobbed.

Fatima bent and cupped Esperanza's chin. "*La.* You must forgive me." Esperanza could not stifle her soft sobs, even as the Sultana caressed her skin and continued, "I have never had the luxury of your naiveté. Perhaps I am jealous. I was born into this world, a daughter, sister, and mother of Sultans who have preceded me in death. Among them was my father, Muhammad *al-Faqih*, who gave his people a just rule. They never knew the truth of the last years of his life, spent battling an addiction to *hashish*, which his eldest son and heir forced upon him."

Esperanza dared look up at Fatima, but once again, she found herself unable to speak in the woman's presence.

Fatima withdrew her hand. "Not even Yusuf knows. I raised him in the image of his grandfather and meant for him to be wise and just like my father. I will never speak of this part of his heritage to him. I tell you now so you may understand the nature of our family and the legacy my grandchildren have inherited. You love my grandson. You would never deliberately hurt him, even with this truth."

"It is a great honor to be entrusted with such a secret. I would never betray you or harm the Sultan by repeating it, my Sultana."

"Despite your love, the past weighs upon you. Ease your burden and let love rule you. The past shapes us. The future is within your grasp. Only you can decide it."

Esperanza nodded. "If I might beg another boon, would you tell me more of your family?"

Hours later, she left the stable before Fatima did. Esperanza's mind swam with the knowledge she had gained of the Nasrids. A cruel, powerful, and complicated family. As she retired, the Sultana crooned softly to al-Sagir while he slept.

The noises of the industrial quarter intruded as Esperanza strolled, mired in thought, past the tanneries and kilns. Her nostrils flared at the stale stench of urine mingled with sweat. She had entered a complex world, at once strange and familiar, of people who were kind or cruel to those who served them. Powerful men and ambitious women. Above them all, Yusuf and his kinfolk, who relied upon and trusted the selfsame persons they had enslaved or domineered. In turn, those slaves or lifelong servants like Asiya remained loyal to the Nasrids. A strange world, yet one with familiar aspects. No differences existed between the patronage of the Cerdas and Yusuf's courtiers. If the Cerdas wished, at a whim they could ruin the lives of their dependents and shatter ties with them, as they had done to her father. If he had not lost his patrons and livelihood, she might not be here today.

Would Yusuf keep his promise to marry her and spare her from concerns about their children bearing the stigma of bastardy? All religions recognized marriage as a lawful union. While adherents of either religion would view the union of a Muslim and Christian as undesirable, any such marriage must be valid. Was she ready for such a future with Yusuf? A man with so many women, whose primary function revolved around his pleasure and heirs, had a bevy of choices. Yusuf would still have other women, even if he chose her for his companion in life. Muslim law allowed him up to four wives. Would he select others to share in his life? The precepts of her Catholic faith would not allow her to accept such an arrangement. How was that life any worse compared to those men who shamed their wives, abandoned their marital vows, enjoyed their mistresses, and sired bastards? If Yusuf married four times and sired children with each woman, the children would all be his heirs.

She shook her head at the direction of her thoughts. Would she accept any vagaries of life to justify her lust for him? Lecherous thoughts influenced her now, but were they so bad?

She released a loud sigh. Could she decide her own future in a day? She needed more time. The raiders had done it, altered her life in one bloodied hour, and taken her away from a perceived path into this ambiguity. She understood Leila's earlier admonition to her. This time, she would have to choose. The single certainty she held was in her regard for Yusuf. Her father once directed the course of her life and then, in some strange twist, Juan Manuel influenced it. Now, she must decide her own fate. A little tear splashed on her cheek. To embrace the future, she would have to relinquish ties to the past.

When she returned to the harem, Leila had woken and sat on her floor beside the bed. Ifrit knelt behind her and brushed the Sultana's hair, while Hamduna painted Leila's nails with *henna*.

The Sultana looked up when Esperanza entered. "Butayna, I wondered where you had gone."

Esperanza bowed before her. "*Al-salam 'alayka,* my Sultana. I went for a walk to the stable and considered the future."

Leila nodded, while the slack-jawed slaves beside her stared in amazement at Esperanza's easy address in Arabic.

The Sultana said, "Then you have made your choice."

"I have and I will never regret it, my Sultana."

Leila smiled and turned to Ifrit. "My loyal one, find Amat. Tell her I need suitable attire for Butayna to wear in Yusuf's chambers. Then fetch Zarru. She shall send word to the chief eunuch that there will be no request for another woman in my brother's bed tonight." Then she regarded Hamduna. "You will help us as well. I do not want garish paints. Instead, choose something simple and suited to Butayna's appearance. She must be beautiful for the Sultan."

***

Esperanza went with Zarru and Hamduna to the *hammam* tiled in blue, gold, and red along its walls. The stewardess demanded the bath attendants take special care of Esperanza with the *nura* while they removed any trace of bodily hair. Bathers came in and out of the rooms, moving through the vapors rising from the steam room to star-shaped vents. After a wash and rinse, Esperanza stretched out. The attendants dried her skin and hair and massaged her with rose oil. They also rubbed silk cloths infused with almond and jasmine oils on her hair.

Hamduna applied a mixture of pomegranate juice, rosewater, honey and crushed poppy seeds before she washed it away from Esperanza's face. Then she added a fine white powder. "This is *batikha,* which will ensure this porcelain skin of yours remains as the Sultan wishes."

Esperanza cleaned her teeth with *ghasul* paste and a *miswak.* Hamduna mixed some of the same paste with crushed rose petals and dabbed a little on her cheeks. "For color."

The women escorted Esperanza back to Leila's apartment. The Sultana ordered her to remove the robe and inspected her. Esperanza's heart throbbed. Leila's slaves stared at her, including Ifrit who remained at Leila's side and Amat, who had joined them. The Sultana circled her three times, fingertips tapping her lower lip at times.

Hamduna asked, "Shall I bring the *kohl,* my Sultana?"

"*La.* Yusuf has long admired her natural beauty. She will go to him as she is. Bring the *ghaliya* instead."

Hamduna gasped. "There is so little of the perfume left, my Sultana. It is so expensive."

Leila arched her eyebrows. "You think I do not know the cost? This night is special and Butayna will wear the fragrance."

"As you wish, my Sultana."

From an ivory vial with a stopper carved in the shape of a bird, Hamduna poured a fragrant perfume. She rubbed it across Esperanza's shoulders, from her breastbone to her stomach, at her wrists and behind her knees.

Esperanza inhaled. "It smells like musk and ambergris combined."

Leila nodded. "Mixed with a little camphor and oil of ben from the moringa trees of al-Maghrib." She signaled Amat. "Bring the amber stones to match her eyes. Turquoise as well."

Leila's women wound a long necklace of reddish-brown amber around her neck, the largest stone at the center suspended between her breasts, followed by another, shorter necklace of turquoise. There were bracelets and anklets of both stones to match. Over her *qamis* and a belted pair of *sarawil,* the slaves dressed her in a turquoise colored *misha.* Embroidered floral motifs in gold and turquoise edged the neckline and hem of the garment. Amat placed a gold ring on each middle finger, one topped with each of the stones. Then she brought Esperanza a pair of leather sandals.

Esperanza stared at the scars on Amat's hands. How had she received the little burns?

At some point, the call to prayer sounded, but Leila ignored it. "Allah will forgive if I observe *Salat al-Maghrib* a little later than usual."

While her women worked, she mused, "One day, you will let my Hamduna pierce those earlobes, Butayna."

Esperanza stared at the floor. "Is it painful, my Sultana?"

"No more than you can endure. Amat, the *barq* for her hair."

Amat remained while the other women withdrew to the fringes of the room. She brushed Esperanza's hair until it shone and then selected several strands, to which she snapped gold beads festooned with turquoise at the tips. Then Amat bowed and stepped back as well, leaving Leila beside Esperanza.

She sighed and ran her fingers over the smooth amber stones around her neck. "Will all of this please your brother?"

Leila smiled. "Yusuf could not be more pleased if you came to his chambers naked. *Nam*, this shall please him. The sun has set. Go to him now with my blessings."

Esperanza left with the well wishes of the Sultana's women. Even Ifrit murmured an invocation as she passed by.

At the edge of the alcove, Esperanza turned to Leila again. "Thank you, my Sultana."

Leila tilted her head. "*Wa-'alayka*, Butayna." Then she waved her on.

Chapter 15
The Kadin

Butayna

Granada, Andalusia
April 17, AD 1337 - August 1, AD 1337 / 20 Shawwal – 15
Ramadan 737 AH / 21st of Siwan - 15th of Iyar, 5097

Butayna went down the stairs and out into the cool spring
evening. Yusuf's guards stood in the shelter of the pavilion.

Their captain's black eyebrows flared as she approached.
Then he bowed. "My lady."

"Please tell the Sultan I have arrived."

"*Nam,* my lady."

She looked out to the other pavilions and the lamplight
dispersed from within. Some of the harem's women gathered in
their dormitories over a meal, gossiped and mused about their
brief time with Yusuf, schemed to gain his attentions or
wondered when he would send for them. This night would be
hers alone. As she surrendered the name of Esperanza Peralta
forever, so would she yield to her newfound desires. She could
not undo the past, only forge ahead for the future, and her place
at Yusuf's side.

"Butayna."

She turned at the sound. Dressed in gold and black, Yusuf
stood immobile in the doorway with his mouth agape. She
laughed. Color rushed to his cheeks.

"I did not think you would come to me tonight."

She teased, "Shall I leave you?"

"Certainly not." He grasped her hand and tugged her across
the threshold. The forgotten guards closed the double doors of
the chamber behind her.

Yusuf released her and strode further into the central
chamber between the chairs. He cleared his throat and froze
under the golden cascade of the lantern's light. "Are you hungry?
I had a little fruit and water to break the fast. I could summon
the slaves with dinner if you would like."

His resonant tone drew her to his side, where she shook her
head. "I don't think I could manage it just now. Perhaps later."

He turned and lifted the weight of her hair off her shoulders. "Beautiful."

The little gold beads tinkled and cascaded against her back again. "When I am with you, you make me feel beautiful."

When she linked her hand with his, a slight tremor passed between them. He trembled and his chest rose and fell beneath the *jubba* as if he struggled for breath. She guided his hand to the *tikka* tied at her belly. His fingers tightened on the knot.

"Butayna...."

"I am not afraid of what shall happen tonight."

He tugged her flush against him, his forearm hard against her back. They stood the same height. "I don't wish to hurt you. It may be unavoidable, but I promise there shall be pleasure in this night for you."

He smelled of musk. The scent made her ache to satisfy him. "And for you?"

"Haven't you guessed already? There is joy in holding you in my arms, in the knowledge of your trust in me. I know you would not have come to me tonight unless you wanted me, no matter what I had pledged. I will never give you cause to regret your choice, I swear it."

She pressed her palm against his chest, where his heart thrummed. "I believe you, Yusuf."

He grazed her lips with his own. She coiled her arms around his neck and kissed him as she had imagined doing all afternoon.

"So impatient," he whispered against her lips. "If... I... had known...."

"What... what would you... have done?"

"This!" He scooped her up in his arms without breaking their contact and took quick, determined strides into his bedchamber. He set her down beside the bed. She did not wait for his next move. She took the *misha* off herself and kicked off her leather sandals. Yusuf sucked in his breath, while he gazed at the outline of her body under the thin fabric. Then he cupped her cheek and stroked the curve with his thumb before he drew her close again. Wrapped in each other's arms, their breaths melded again and the kisses intensified.

Nothing mattered except the taste of his lips on hers, lemon peel on his breath. His groans filled her mouth. Her hands roamed everywhere, lost in his thick hair, at his nape. Nailo raked across his shoulders and left tiny indentations at the side of his neck.

He made short work of the belt around her waist and pushed her trousers down. The white silk pooled around her ankles. She allowed the briefest separation between them, while he removed the *qamis* and bared her before his turbulent gaze. She stood in the circle of his embrace, unabashed by her nakedness or the cool air across her back. Yusuf warmed her. His fingertips pressed into the small of her back, down her hip and cupped the underside of her thigh.

She unfastened his *jubba* and pushed it back from his shoulders. He helped her. Silk swished and cascaded to the floor, timed with impatient grunts from him. A rose-colored hue dappled his angular cheekbones and he reached for her again.

"Allah, you are magnificent," he whispered in a rough voice. His lips trailed a line across her collarbone and between her breasts.

Her hands stroked his heated skin, the puckered scar on his chest between the fine hairs and another jagged cut at his shoulder.

"How did you earn these, Yusuf?" she whispered. Her voice shook.

"Good lessons from... the master-at-arms. I didn't move out... of his way."

He pressed her shoulders and she sat at the edge of the bed. He knelt between her legs, grabbed her thighs, and draped them against his hips. His heartbeat throbbed in time with hers. He bent and his mouth closed on her rosy-tipped nipple, his tongue stiff and insistent.

She squirmed, her head thrown back and combed her fingers through his silky hair. The nails raked his scalp. His beard grazed her tender skin. When he lifted his head, he tongued and teased her other breast. Insanity drove her hips up to meet his. He groaned and raised his mouth to her neck. Teeth grazed the skin. The heat of his breath made her shiver. She stroked his back and traced the muscles bunched underneath the skin. His fingers skimmed the underside of her thighs and pressed her against his body. She could not ignore the hardness pressed between her thighs.

Yusuf raised his lips to hers once more. His heavy-lidded stare locked with hers. "You are certain of this?"

She smiled against his mouth. Once, she viewed him with such trepidation and thought him the most difficult man she had ever met. Now, she marveled at how her opinions had changed over time, how her perception of him had increased. Of course, he would have allowed her a final opportunity to consider the aftermath of her choice, but she would never regret it.

"I have never been more certain, Yusuf. I am yours this night. Forever."

***

The harem buzzed with gossip and speculation in the weeks after Butayna went to Yusuf's bed. He summoned her each night and she remained in his chambers until midmorning. On the days in which he did not hold public audience, she never left his side. By custom, she became his *kadin* in a month, although she still returned to Leila's apartment during Yusuf's absences from the harem.

She sat there now, among Leila and her slaves while they ate *dafair* bread, date balls soaked in rosewater, and stuffed eggs after midday. The women drank cold glasses of sweetened *sekanjabin*, licked sugar crystals from their fingertips, enjoyed the warm breeze from the windows of the first floor, and teased Butayna about her long nights with Yusuf.

"It is a wonder you can bear to leave the Sultan's bed each morning, my lady," Hamduna said.

Amat laughed and clapped her hands. "A wonder? Call it a miracle! The true wonder is that Butayna can walk from his chamber each morning. Light shines from the crack in his doorway at all hours of the night. If I had been abed with the Sultan, I would not possess the strength to stand, much less depart from him."

Leila shook her head and scooped up another sliced egg. "Is this what you do at night when I assume you are off with your lover at *al-Quasaba*? You peek under my brother's door instead."

The other women chuckled at Amat and Butayna's expense. Unlike Leila's slave who shared their amusement, Butayna's entire face, ears, and neck grew hot, even for this time of year. How much longer would she have to endure such taunts about her and Yusuf?

Leila advised, "Leave Butayna be. Can't you see she's blushing?"

Was it not enough for her to grow accustomed to his demands and be reconciled to her own lustful desires? Each morning Yusuf woke Butayna with kisses on her shoulder. She prayed to God for forgiveness, even as his lips closed on her nipple. With her hands in his hair and her ankles locked around his back, she forgot everything except the pleasure attained in his arms, coupled with his sighs and groans. She gained a portion of her joy in his satisfaction.

Mortification overcame her whenever she recalled her sinful behavior with the coming of dawn. No wonder God had abandoned her, for she lied to Him and mocked her Catholic beliefs each morning, while she rushed to Yusuf's bed at night.

The struggle to reconcile her former self with the woman she had become plagued her in daylight.

Ramadi slinked into view. He prowled the edges of the room and then dashed into a corner. Then he crept into their circle, a suspicious gray thread hanging from his mouth.

Butayna covered her mouth and suppressed her bile. Most of the slaves squealed while Leila shooed the cat.

"Disgusting! Get out of here with that filthy rodent at once, Ramadi!"

As the cat scurried away with his meal, Ifrit murmured, "You must admit, my Sultana. He's the best mouser we've ever had in the harem."

A eunuch begged entry. When Leila permitted him inside, he announced the arrival of the chief steward.

"Mufawwiz, you may come!" Leila brushed her hands free of crumbs and stood.

The chief steward's belly came into view through the door hanging before his face did. He bowed stiffly and a rough groan filled his throat. "*Al-salam 'alayka,* my Sultana. My lady Butayna."

"*Wa-'alayka,* dear Mufawwiz. You are just in time if you wish to eat with us. I saved some date balls just for you." Leila washed her hands in the rosewater bowl Ifrit offered and dried her fingers, before she reached for Mufawwiz.

He bowed and his fleshy lips kissed her hands. "You honor me with your kindness, my Sultana. I must decline for I have arrived at the Sultan's request. He has sent me to the *kadin.*"

Butayna's breath hitched inside her chest. "Is the Sultan well? Does he need me?"

Both Leila and Mufawwiz peered at her with upraised eyebrows, while Hamduna tittered behind her hand.

Mufawwiz released Leila's fingertips and inclined his head. "My master the Sultan is well, my lady. Before he attended public audience this morning, he asked me to provide for your comfort."

"My comfort?"

Leila nodded. "A *kadin* is entitled to a level of luxury unavailable in her former station as a *jarya.* She receives her own quarters and slaves. We begin with the slaves first."

Mufawwiz clapped his hands. "Jawla! Hafsa! Come now and greet your new mistress."

Two russet-haired young women, wiry and taller than any others she had ever seen, entered the room. Slave collars of black metal encircled their cream-colored throats. They bowed and held the position.

Leila moved beside them. "I found them in the *Qaysariyya* yesterday, when I looked for another slave to replace you. My quarters have suffered from neglect in your absence. Since Yusuf has robbed me of you, he offered recompense in the form of coin. I have purchased three slaves, one for myself and these two for you. Jawla, who stands beside me, will prepare your meals, taste your food, and keep your chamber tidy. She is trained in the detection of poisons."

Butayna's chest tightened. How did anyone learn how to detect poisons? She did not want to know what Jawla's training had entailed. "Is this a concern in the harem?"

Leila scratched at her temple. "Butayna, sometimes you ask the most peculiar questions. Would you rather let Maryam use the skills she will acquire from Safa against you? Do you intend to learn the hard way of some foolhardy *jarya* who wants to take your place as *kadin*? Your naiveté is unwelcome here. You have come to a dangerous place. Never forget this fact. It was one of my considerations when I chose Hafsa. She can attend you in the *hammam,* launder your clothes, and help you dress. She is also skilled with a dagger and will defend you with her life against the enemies you have already acquired."

Mufawwiz bobbed his head. "The Sultana Leila is right, my lady. You have attained a position many *jawari* will covet. You must be cautious."

Butayna rose to her feet and clasped her hands together. "The Sultana Leila bought me and made me a part of this harem. It is only now I receive warnings about my safety."

With a chuckle, Leila said, "Better a word of caution than none at all."

"True, for in such a circumstance I would be dead, none the wiser for my experiences. While I appreciate your... generosity, my Sultana, I must ask, why would strangers risk their lives for me? How can I depend on the loyalty of slaves, bought and paid for by you? What if there is someone else in the harem to offer these women more coin to betray me?"

"It's a chance you must take." Leila shrugged. "If you are lucky, these women will serve you for a lifetime."

"As slaves who do as they are told? I think not. There must be a greater bond between us." Butayna studied the pair of slaves. "Would you serve me well if the Sultan freed you?"

Leila demanded, "What are you doing?"

Butayna ignored her and focused on the new arrivals. "I do not have the authority to free you, but the Sultan does. If I spoke to him and begged a boon, he would do this. Would you pledge yourselves to the one who secured your liberty?"

215

Leila snorted and cut off any response either slave would have made. "You are a slave yourself and a laughable one at that! I give you women to serve you and you seek their freedom, when you do not even have your own?"

Butayna lifted her chin. "You have secured loyalty among your women by your own means, my Sultana. You have had years to ensure their trustworthiness. I must use other methods to safeguard my life, especially when the Sultana Safa has aligned herself with Maryam against me. I can perceive the danger there." She turned to Jawla and Hafsa again. "What say you to my offer?"

The pair looked at each other before they both bowed. "We will serve," they answered in union, a little lilt to their voices.

"I will never give you cause to rethink your choice. Do not give me reason to regret my offer."

Leila frowned at her. "Hmm, you are not so foolish after all. I will not misjudge you again."

"That was Maryam's mistake. She thought she could spin her lies for Yusuf and I would never know of them. I will safeguard myself from her future schemes. No one else can protect me from her cruelty, even the Sultan."

Then Butayna addressed the chief steward. "Mufawwiz, will you take me to the room chosen for me?"

"If you would follow me, my lady." He waved toward the staircase at the right, which Butayna had never taken.

She hesitated at the base of the steps and looked over her shoulder. "My Sultana, would you accompany me?"

Leila smiled. "I thought you would not ask."

They mounted the stairs together, Mufawwiz and Butayna's servants behind them.

***

Hafsa's insistent voice stirred Butayna from sleep. "My lady!"

She opened her eyes to the shimmery heat of the afternoon at the *Jannat al-'Arif*. Warm air blew in through the unfurled window and ruffled the edge of her *qamis*. She tapped her fingertips on her exposed abdomen, rolled on her bed, and sighed.

"What is it, Hafsa?"

The servant bowed at her side, red-gold tendrils plastered to her temple. "You must awaken, my lady, and go to the southern pavilion. The honorable *Umm al-Walad* has demanded your presence there. She is not alone. The slave who brought the message told me the noble Sultana Leila is with her, as is the chief eunuch Abdullah Hisham."

Butayna rose and swung her legs off the bed. A wave of nausea inundated her. She cupped a hand over her forehead, feverish and moist with perspiration. She squeezed her eyes shut.

Hafsa knelt at her side. "My lady! Are you unwell?"

Butayna's stomach fluttered. "*La*, just tired and thirsty. It is so hot. Please, some water."

Hafsa's long-legged stride crisscrossed the bare floor in an instant. Butayna took the cool water her servant had poured from a glass decanter and drank greedily.

She set the empty cup aside. "Did Sultana Safa give any reason for her summons, Hafsa?"

"*La*, my lady."

"Then she knows." Butayna breathed a ragged sigh and hung her head. "There is no reason Leila would be with her and Hisham, if she did not know. My God, have they already told Yusuf?"

Hafsa knelt at her feet and sat back on her heels. "It is possible they know, my lady. You must admit, you could not keep this secret to yourself forever. If my lady will forgive an unworthy servant, you should have told the noble Sultan weeks ago."

"You are right, but you knew why I could not. On the night I first planned to tell him, he received word of the Marinid conquest of Tilimsan. I have never seen my Sultan so angry in the long months since I have known him. He has been so preoccupied since then, with the journeys to Malaka and al-Mariyah. He ensures the Sultanate's defenses are secure. Leila says he fears no one will thwart Abu'l-Hasan Ali's ambitions to rule the whole of al-Maghrib. Yusuf will have to bend to the Marinids if their Sultan looks across the sea with covetous eyes."

"Our noble Sultan has grave concerns for the future of *al-jazirat al-Andalus*. You can cheer him, my lady, with this news."

Butayna nodded. "Bring my favorite *ridu*, the one Leila just gave me for my birthday."

Hafsa went into Butayna's trunks and retrieved an iridescent turquoise robe sewn with gold threads. At the back, a blue-green panel shimmered in the style of peacock feathers. Butayna slipped the ample robe over her shoulders, while Hafsa brushed her hair and braided it down her back. With brown sandals on her feet, Butayna left the chamber, Hafsa at her heels. At the doorway, Jawla bowed and fell into step beside her counterpart. Neither woman spent little time apart from Butayna, except when she went to the Sultan's quarters.

Butayna stepped out into the garden and walked south, aware of the intent gaze, which followed her progress. She went up the stairs and entered the antechamber, which led out on to the belvedere.

Leila sat just inside the doorway. Ramadi dozed in her lap. The chief eunuch knelt at her side, his pale hands encased in gloves as usual, despite the heat. The man's fastidiousness disturbed Butayna, but she avoided him wherever possible.

At a gesture from Leila, she sat. Jawla and Hafsa knelt on either side of her.

Sultana Safa came in from the balcony, her cheeks the same scarlet color as the *jubba* she wore. "Deceitful, willful girl! Do you think you can keep secrets in this harem? I know what you have done!"

Butayna glanced at Leila. She would not give Safa the satisfaction of the truth until she determined the extent of their suspicions.

Leila sighed and leaned forward. "Dearest, is it true? Have you concealed your pregnancy? Are you carrying Yusuf's child?"

Butayna released a drawn-out breath, a deep sigh of satisfaction.

Safa flung her bejeweled hands up in the air. "Of course, she is pregnant! What fool question is this? She has hidden the truth from us for months. She should be whipped for risking the life of the Sultan's child."

At her feet, Leila rolled her eyes heavenward. Her pinched expression tightened around the mouth and eyes. "Lest you forget, such an act would kill the child. Yusuf would not thank you for it. Besides, a woman who has never had a child before would not know at first if she had conceived, Safa!"

"A fact of which you are well aware, Leila!"

"Haggard, old bitch! It's a wonder you can remember the signs of pregnancy at all!"

Ramadi awoke and scuttled into Butayna's lap. She petted him while Yusuf's sister and his mother traded ruthless scowls.

Hisham fidgeted and batted his pale yellow eyelashes. "My Sultanas! Please! We are here to determine the truth. The midwife I have brought should examine Butayna."

"You did not summon her, Hisham! I did." Safa crossed her arms, stopped glaring at Leila, and shook her head at the chief eunuch.

"Of course, my Sultana. You were first to suspect the *kadin*'s pregnancy."

They were both wrong. Butayna believed Yusuf recognized the truth as well. He proved a passionate and tender lover, a hint of reverence and awe imbued his touch in the last in the last three weeks. He had bidden her to his bed every night for more than three months. Whenever they dined, he joked about her constant thirst and strange appetite. For the last three weeks, she craved nothing but eggplants. In the morning, his light pecks covered her stomach. Did he share her desire to leave the truth unacknowledged for the same reason? She could not share his bed after the official announcement occurred. She would lose him to other women who vied with her to give him an heir.

"Why does she not speak? Is she still so stupid? I thought you said she understood Arabic." Safa's frown fell on Leila again. Then the old woman's brow furrowed, as if she had just noted the presence of Hafsa and Jawla. "Which of you two can tell us the truth? Has your mistress had her show of woman's blood in the last two months?"

Butayna nodded to Hafsa, who said, "My lady has never bled in the months since I became her servant."

Leila looked down, focused on Butayna's abdomen as if she could saw the evidence through the folds of the *rida*. "You will allow the midwife to examine you now."

***

Butayna lay quiet on a pallet in Sultana Safa's room. The pompous queen would not permit anyone else in her bed. The midwife revealed the faint roundness of Butayna's abdomen for Safa and Leila's inspection. Both women hovered beside the bed and jostled each other at times. When the midwife placed her cool, clean hands on Butayna's breasts, she winced. She answered all of the questions put to her. Satisfied, the midwife declared the pregnancy viable.

Safa's brow crinkled. "Her hips are so small. Could the delivery kill her?"

Leila knelt beside the pallet and grasped Butayna's hands. "Try to sound a little less hopeful, Safa."

"I am not... I wondered because she is so tiny!" Safa bent and wagged her finger in Butayna's face. "You listen well to me, girl! You will eat everything placed in front of you. Do not starve the Sultan's child! Rest and ensure no harm comes to Yusuf's son."

"Or daughter," Leila murmured.

Butayna giggled at Safa's crimson-colored features, even when the Sultana sneered at her.

Huddled in the doorway, the chief eunuch stated, "The Sultan must be told when he returns from Wadi-Ash in the morning."

Safa swerved toward him. "I shall write to him today! I must be the one to tell him." She left the bedchamber. Green silk swirled behind her.

Hisham followed. "My Sultana, please, such news must be offered in private, in person." His sibilant tone followed Safa out into the antechamber.

"Oh, nonsense, Hisham! I...."

Leila peered through the door and then kissed Butayna's hands. Her gaze softened and watered as Butayna had never seen. "I am very pleased for you."

Warmth radiated from Butayna's head to her toes. She could not suppress a wide grin. "For your brother, of course, my Sultana."

"Do stop calling me that! I am pleased for you as well. I do not doubt you and your child shall be well, while I shall be the proudest aunt in all the land. I insist you call me Leila. I am a Nasrid and shall have my way."

Butayna sniggered. "You often do."

When Ramadi meowed at the door and joined them, Leila scooped him up. "You can keep this little beast with you from now on."

Butayna spread her fingers out in a fan against her breastbone. "My Sultana, I mean Leila, I could not! Yusuf gave him to you, he's your cat."

"He's as much yours as he is mine. Please, I want you to take him, Butayna."

Ramadi rubbed his head against Butayna's forearm. She patted him and fought against the tears. "Your generosity means so much to me, Leila."

"I have not always been so kind to you, especially when you first arrived in the harem." Leila looked at the floor for a moment and then regarded her again. "There is something I have wondered about, but never asked before now. The name your father gave you at birth, it means 'hope', doesn't it?"

"It does."

"You are Yusuf's hope now, the promise of a bright future, one which may dispel the demons of the past. We will wait for the court astrologer's pronouncement, but I do not doubt you carry Yusuf's son within you. I am pleased for both of you."

"Not just because everything has unfolded according to your design?"

Leila's chin dipped to her chest and she averted her stare. "I do not understand your suggestion."

"When you first saw me in the House of Myrtles, you wished to buy me. I saw the glint of interest in your eyes. You did not wish to reveal your intent for Sultana Safa, for she would have driven the bidding higher to thwart you. Then you waited until the right time and placed me within your household. You knew

Yusuf thrived on challenge and admired women who did not agree to his every demand. You planned all of this."

Leila laughed and threw her head back. "Such an imagination you have, Butayna. You should have been a storyteller instead of a musician." She sobered. "Butayna, a name you once loathed."

"I claim it now with joy. I have you to thank for it and for so much more."

Leila laid a hand on Butayna's stomach. "May your son be strong and magnificent, in the image of his mother and father. May you always know happiness and joy at my brother's side. I could not have chosen a better companion for him. You are his match in every way. You honor him by carrying his child."

She helped Butayna to her feet and paid the midwife before she dismissed her.

Arm in arm with Leila, Butayna left the southern pavilion. Her servants trailed a discrete distance behind them through the western walkway of the garden. Ramadi traipsed through the flowerbeds and chased the butterflies, the white tip of his gray tail flicking between the greenery.

At each footfall, Leila's smile faded until her lips thinned. Her shoulders slumped with a heavy sigh. Her chin trembled, as though she wished to speak and struggled with the words.

Butayna sighed. Did Leila feel some unease about the pregnancy because she did not have children of her own? Until now, Butayna would have never guessed the Sultan's sister wanted any heirs. She seemed so content.

Butayna turned to her. "You must not worry for the child, or for what Safa said earlier. I know my hips are small, but I am not afraid to carry this babe."

Leila paused at the central kiosk and looked out over the confines of the summer palace. She leaned against a marble pillar and Butayna joined her.

"What is it, Leila? I thought you were delighted for me."

"I am! I am."

"Do you resent it if I should have a child when you do not? You've never shown an interest in marriage or children of your own before now."

"Please, Butayna, please. You must not think I am jealous or anything of the sort. My heart is glad for you and for Yusuf because he has found a woman worthy of his love. I know you care for my brother. You would not have given yourself to him otherwise. Still, there are things you must know. There are rules, which govern the harem. Even Yusuf cannot alter them."

"What rules?" Butayna placed a hand on her arm. "Tell me! Please."

Leila glanced down at her feet. "Butayna, you cannot raise this child on your own."

Butayna's laughter pealed through the complex. "I do not intend to! I do not know the first thing about babies. I want to be a good mother, but I will need some guidance. There must be a governess to help...."

She trailed off as Leila shook her head and sagged beside the column. "*La*, you do not comprehend at all. You are a Christian and Yusuf is a Muslim. If a child is born of a Christian mother and a Muslim father, by our laws the child is raised as a Muslim."

"Oh." Butayna touched two fingers to her lips. "I suppose I understand. It does not matter to me. I would be gladdened to have my son or daughter raised in Yusuf's faith. I studied a little of it when I was in the House of Myrtles. I do recognize the reason for this rule and would accept such a course for my child's life."

"You will not like it when I tell you the rest. If your baby is a boy, he will be Yusuf's heir, the crown prince. He cannot be raised in the household of a Christian mother."

Butayna drew back and folded her arms across her stomach. "You do not mean it. You can't! No one will take my baby from me."

"*Nam*, Butayna."

"*La*! I won't allow it." Her vision clouded as she turned from Leila. She shook her head. It could not be true. Every muscle quivered and coiled. She readied to run from this barbaric place. Her mind scrambled for some explanation of the custom, but nothing made sense. Her voice exploded. "What sort of animals are you to take a babe from his mother just because she is Christian?"

"I am sorry you think we are animals. When you chose Yusuf, you also consented to live by the customs of his people. This is our way. You have no other choice."

Leila's monotone made Butayna's breath hitch. Her heart shriveled. She whispered, "Why?"

Behind her, Leila replied, "My great-grandfather Muhammad the Lawgiver had two wives. His first, Aisha, died a brutal death at the hands of his enemies. Then he married the Sultana Shams ed-Duna, daughter of a Marinid Sultan. Muhammad's heart beat for the *kadin* Nur al-Sabah, who was one of the most beautiful women of the harem. She became the mother of his four daughters and a beloved son, Nasr. The boy was not a candidate for the throne, but when his elder brother proved mad, Nasr became Sultan in his stead. Nasr drank wine in excess, dressed in the garments of Christians, and even kept Galicians, his mother's people, as his personal guard. The *khassa*, indeed all of the nobles, hated him for it. They said the influence of his Christian mother guided him. My father overthrew Nasr with the support of his own people."

Butayna flung her hand toward Leila. "What does any of this have to do with my child?"

"Afterward, the Sultan Ismail decreed any child born of a Christian woman at *al-Qal'at al-Hamra* should be raised by the relatives of the Muslim father. His mother cannot care for or educate him, lest she taint his upbringing with Christian ways."

"*La!* No one else will raise my child except me. Besides, Yusuf would never permit it once he knows my desire. He is Sultan. He can change the laws."

"Oh, Butayna, the circumstances are not so straightforward! You must acknowledge this fact."

Tears blurred Butayna's sight. She stumbled across the garden. Not even Ramadi's yowls stopped her. She refused to accept this cruel custom. No one would take a child of hers. Ever.

***

Yusuf's voice echoed through the harem and roused Butayna from a miserable slumber. In her dreams, Safa, Leila, even Yusuf wrenched her child from her arms.

"Butayna! Where are you?"

She rubbed at her swollen eyelids and sat up, bleary-eyed. When her feet touched the wooden floor, she winced at the cold sensation. Dawn's pink light filtered through the *shimasas*. Had she slept since the previous afternoon?

"She is here, my noble Sultan." That was Hafsa's voice.

A moment later, Yusuf burst into Butayna's bedchamber. The sight of his thick dark locks as they fell over his eyes and the wide grin shadowed by his trim moustache and beard should have filled her with such joy.

Instead, she collapsed with loud ad bitter sobs and buried her face in her hands. He dashed to her side and cradled her against him.

"Oh, my sweet love, I have returned early from my brother at Wadi-Ash to find you in tears! Why do you cry, my heart?"

She sobbed. "Please don't let them do this to me!"

He knelt in front of her and drew her hands away "Do what to you? Who is going to do what to cause my beloved such distress? Tell me why you are crying."

She reached for him, her brow against his forehead. "I am carrying your child."

He covered her mouth with his warm, wide one. "*Nam*! I know! I've presumed as much for some weeks now."

"Why didn't you say anything until now?"

"I waited for you to tell me. I too can count the days from the last time you bled until now. Your appetite has increased and there has been a little more of your breasts and belly to hold and caress at night. When you did not say anything, I thought of it as a little secret you and I shared with no one else. A childish notion, I know. I had planned to summon the midwife upon my return, to be certain of your health and our child's own. How could you ever be unwell? Look at the bloom upon your cheeks! How can you be in tears when you've been so cheerful of late?"

"Promise me you will not let them take the child just because I am Christian. Your sister told me of the custom. You would not allow anyone else except me to raise our child. I know it."

Yusuf lifted his head and drew back in the circle of her arms. He said nothing, just swallowed. Then a heavy sigh overcame him. His shoulders slumped, as Leila's own had done on the previous afternoon.

A chill crept up her spine. Her limbs shook and fell at her sides.

He rose from the crouched position and sat beside her on the bed. He cupped the back of his neck and rubbed it. "Butayna, you must understand the rules which govern the harem and children born into the Sultan's household."

She whimpered and sagged, her shoulders bent. "I do not have to understand! This is our child, created by our love. How can you permit anyone to take our baby from me? Please, leave me."

"Butayna, we have to talk about this—"

"I cannot! Not now. Please, I am asking you to go. I need some time alone, Yusuf."

"Do not push me away. We could always talk before this, Butayna. We have often shared our true selves with each other. I know this will be difficult, but if you would allow me to explain—"

"I know enough of your ways to be sure they are wrong. I do not accept them now and I never will. Your words cannot change my mind. So please, leave."

The bed creaked as he rose. "I am sorry you feel this way, Butayna."

"No more sorry than I am. If I had known this would be the result of conceiving your child, I would have never...."

Her words ended on a sob. She got back into the bed and rolled away from him.

"Never what, Butayna?"

She waved him away. "Go, Yusuf. Please leave me be!"

The tightness in her throat constricted her voice. She shriveled and curled her knees up to her chest. She grabbed a fistful of the damask coverlet and buried her face in it. Her sobs muffled, she keened her heartbreak and wept for the child inside her.

Chapter 16
The Doorway

Maryam

Granada, Andalusia
January 3, AD 1338 / 10 Jumada al-Thani 738 AH / 12th of
Shevat, 5098

Maryam drew her knees up and crouched in the corner near the
brazier at Sultana Safa's feet. She fingered the gold lace on a
damask curtain, which covered the closed window above her
head. Screams and cries echoed through the birthing chamber at
the western end of the harem. When would Butayna's travail be
over? If she wished, Maryam might feel some sympathy for the
girl, who panted and screeched in agony.

Maryam recalled Palomba's birth. Even worse, the memory of
Gedaliah's face lingered. He had visited her after the completion
of the ritual purification period. She would never forget his
words. "Next time, it will be a son." His statement held the
promise of dire circumstances for her if she bore another girl.

According to Yusuf's court astrologer and even the midwife,
Butayna would have no such concerns. Both predicted she
would bear a boy, ascribing their respective theories to the star
charts and the swell of her abdomen. Maryam rolled her eyes at
the thought. How either of them could have ascertained the truth
remained a mystery. Regardless of the sex of Butayna's child,
Maryam wished she would hurry and push it out. Then others
might find some rest tonight. The birth pangs had started an
hour after *Salat al-Asr* in the middle of the afternoon and
continued well into the evening. Sultana Safa dragged Maryam
with her to the birthing chamber after sunset to witness the
birth of Yusuf's first child. As night fell over the city, the midwife
and her assistant remained at hand. They coaxed and comforted
the expectant mother. Lines crisscrossed the faces of the trio.
Maryam did not doubt worry consumed each woman for the
same reason.

"*Dios mío*! He is fighting me!" Butayna gasped and clutched
her engorged abdomen.

She still appeared as thin and straight as a tree sapling, with an unappealing bulge in the middle. Perhaps the birthing would kill her, as it had done her weak mother. Countless women died in their travail each day. Still, it would not matter whether she lived or died. One son would not keep Yusuf beholden to her forever.

The Sultan's sister Leila knelt with her body slave beside Butayna's pallet and wiped her forehead with a cotton cloth. "The midwife says you are not ready. It won't be much longer now, I promise."

Seated on a stool beside Maryam, Sultana Safa thumped her carved walking stick on the wooden floor. "How would you judge her progress, Leila? A woman who has never given birth cannot know such things. She is too small. The birthing will kill her. It would be best to cut Yusuf's son from her womb and have done with her."

Butayna's lank hair clung to her temples. She sobbed and clutched Leila's hands. "Please, please, don't let them...."

Leila hushed her. "The midwife would have told us by now if she believed such a procedure necessary." She cast a sharp-eyed glance at the woman who knelt between Butayna's legs. "Is that not so?"

"It is, my Sultana. I still believe this Nasrid prince shall enter the world tonight by natural means and with my aid! My lady Butayna, you must hold fast to your courage. The pain is the same for all women. Do not think of it. Consider the joy when you hold your son in your arms."

Butayna wept bitter sobs against Leila's shoulder. The Sultana crooned and comforted her.

His mother leaned forward and thumped the stick again. Maryam hated the sound, for it occurred at all hours of the night through the Sultana's chamber when she could not sleep.

Safa called out, "Leila! You should not be here. A woman who has borne no children of her own should not see such things."

Leila lifted her chin from Butayna's hair. "Safa, for the last time, I am here at Yusuf's behest and in support of Butayna. Both have asked for my comfort and they shall have it."

Safa shrugged. "For my part, I cannot remember making so much noise when I birthed my own children."

Leila snorted. "Of course you can't, for it has been such a long, long, long time since you brought Yusuf and my younger sisters into the world. For one as old as you, a flawed memory is expected."

Maryam strove against her smile as Safa's cheeks reddened and matched the color of the room's scarlet curtains.

"You will regret those words, bitch, long before your life's ending!" Safa muttered under her breath so Maryam alone heard her.

Then Safa turned to Maryam. "Go to my chambers and tell Nazhun to bring my dinner here. I want my gloves as well. It seems this girl means to keep us waiting through the hours of a cold night."

"You could just leave, Safa," Leila said over her shoulder. "Ifrit can bring word of the babe's birth afterward."

"I will confirm the birth with my own eyes, Leila! Go and do as I have said, Maryam."

Maryam rose to her feet and bowed. "Shall I return with Nazhun?"

Safa looked at her askance. "What for? What do you care for the fate of this child?"

Maryam glanced at Butayna, who sweated and groaned. Her grip on Leila's fingers tightened and a spasm rippled along her belly. "You are right, of course. I shall attend to other tasks."

With another bow, Maryam left the birthing room. The chief eunuch turned to her from his position just outside the door. "What news?"

She averted her gaze from his spectral features. "Nothing yet. Butayna still lives as does the Sultan's child."

When he waved her away, she continued down the long corridor between rows of nameless women who sat in the doorway of their rooms or along the northern wall below latticed windows. The entire harem awaited the news. Maryam knew there would be more than one *jarya* who wished Butayna and her child dead.

At the end of the stairs, Maryam emerged under the honeycombed ceiling where Sultana Leila often took her meals. It seemed Butayna and Leila had developed quite a close bond. Maryam might have envied it, if she also did not know the vagaries of Yusuf's family. Would Leila turn on Butayna if she delivered a girl or a stillborn? Time would tell if the ties between the pair remained as strong. Maryam emerged into the harem's courtyard, ablaze in torchlight. A quick glance to the east affirmed Yusuf's doors folded back on their hinges, despite a frigid blast of air. A thrill coursed through Maryam's body. There would never be a better moment.

She pushed back her shoulders and ambled through the garden. The chill penetrated her leather cloak, but she ignored the sensation, like shards of ice knifing her skin. She sang as she went, a melody carried across the courtyard on the wintry evening wind.

"You there! Stop!"

She paused at the threshold of Sultana Safa's chambers and stilled her uneven breaths, as Yusuf dashed through the doorway. Lines etched under his eyes revealed his concern for Butayna. Maryam smiled and bowed before him. She knew just the means to ease his worry.

"Stand! Have you just come from the birthing room? What has happened? How is Butayna?"

Maryam straightened. "She fares well, my Sultan, though a first birth is often difficult. The midwife still believes you shall hold your son tonight."

He heaved a fatigued groan. "Ifrit brought me the same words over an hour ago at *Salat al-Maghrib*. Is Butayna in much pain? Does my sister still comfort her?"

"The Sultana Leila has not left her side, not even to touch the evening meal which her body slave brought. Butayna drank of the *sharbah* and the *sekanjabin*, but the midwife advised against any food. You must not be worried, my Sultan. Butayna does the best she can."

He offered her an assessing gaze. "You still speak well of her, Maryam, after you led me to believe she disdained your friendship."

She lowered her gaze and clasped her hands behind her. "How could I not be pleased for Butayna? Tonight, she will know the joy I once held in my own children, my Sultan."

Yusuf nodded. "She must be frightened. I wish I could be there for her now."

"Oh, my Sultan, a man should not see such things. If you are so concerned, would it please you to have me sing for you tonight and ease your troubles? Ease your cares while you await the birth of your son."

Yusuf studied her for a moment until she blushed under his scrutiny. "That is kind of you, Maryam. Thank you."

He ushered her to his quarters. She strolled beside him and hid her smile. An early success boded well for her plans. He closed the door behind him.

Inside the central chamber, she sat swathed in the glow of the golden lantern. Yusuf took one of two high-backed chairs. A brazier rested on iron legs between the seats. Though she wished he might have joined her on the carpeted floor, she would not press him.

Her voice rang through the air again, beginning with a sweet *cantiga* from a mother for her child. She stirred a dull ache at the back of her throat. Unanticipated thoughts of Palomba filled her mind. At the end of the song, she covered her face with her fingers.

Yusuf knelt beside her and drew her hands away. He said nothing, just looked at her.

She wiped her moist eyes and sighed. "I can no longer sing it without thoughts of my daughter and son. My husband wished for a boy so much, but I long for my sweet girl and think of her each day."

"Butayna told me you blamed her for the loss of them."

Had she? Maryam sniffled and looked away. Her mind raced. "It was wrong of me, my Sultan, but I no longer do. It is a mother's fate to love her children forever even when they are absent from her arms. I would do anything to have my daughter with me again."

He touched her chin and turned her to him again. "Your daughter must have been as beautiful as you."

"Oh, she was, my Sultan. She had my hair and eyes, very little of her father. I feel our son would have looked like him. Now, I shall never know."

He leaned toward her. She held herself rigid in anticipation.

"Sing to me again, Maryam." His sweet cinnamon breath washed over her.

She forced a smile just for him. "As you wish, my Sultan."

***

The Sultana

Butayna

Granada, Andalusia
January 4 – May 15, AD 1338 / 11 Jumada al-Thani – 24 Shawwal 738 AH / 13th of Shevat - 25th of Iyar, 5098

Butayna stirred with a groan, her eyelids heavy. The hard wood of the birth stool no longer pressed into her legs. Instead, she rested on something fleecy. She fingered the fibers beneath her. Wool. She reclined on a pallet. Her gaze drifted upward. The familiar cupola of the birthing room remained above her head, incised with gold and lapis lazuli, enhanced by glorious sunlight. The sun—but how could that be? Had she not given birth during the late hours of the night?

She palmed her rounded belly and lifted her hand from the wetness. Blood and clear mucus smeared her fingertips. Her heart raced. "Where is my baby? Where is my child?"

Leila's familiar features swam into view. "You have a son and he is here, dearest. The midwife and her assistant tend to him again. Do not fear. After dawn, we took him to his father while you slept. Yusuf has blessed the boy and whispered the *Shahadah* in his ear. He has ordered a celebration and summoned the wet nurse."

"Can't I be allowed to nurse my son?"

"You must know it is impossible."

Butayna closed her eyes and tears moistened her lashes. She recalled the sharp pain, the wetness as it gushed between her legs and then nothing more. She must have fainted just after the birth.

"What name–" she paused, her throat parched and her tongue swollen. "Water, please."

"Bring a cup for the *kadin* now," Leila commanded. In moments, her long fingers cradled Butayna's neck and she lifted her to offer the drink. Butayna sipped the cool refreshment and whispered her thanks.

Then she asked, "What name did Yusuf give our son?"

Leila kissed her brow before she fluffed Butayna's pillow. "He is Muhammad, a venerated forename in our family. Look, the midwife brings him now."

Butayna struggled to raise her head much less her arms, as a wave of lethargy still claimed her limbs. She did it for her son. As his small form settled against the crook of her arm, she peeled back the folds of the white linen with which the midwife had swaddled him. His eyes had opened. They were a dark shade of blue-gray. He peered at her from a mottled, rounded face. When he wriggled, she hugged him closer to the warmth of her body.

She inquired, "What day is it?"

"Is her mind addled? Perhaps the birth was too much for her. I have always warned she would be weak for it."

Sultana Safa's voice issued from the corner where she had sat near the brazier. Butayna had dismissed her presence from mind in her haze of pain.

"We are all aware of your opinions, for you have voiced them often and loudly!" Leila cupped her forehead and leaned toward Butayna. "It is the eleventh day of *Jumada al-Thani.*"

"*La, la!* That is not–"

"She wants to know the date according to the Christian calendar." Maryam appeared beside the pallet. Her stark features and the firm set of her mouth concealed all. Her widened gaze searched Butayna's face before she said, "It is the fourth day of January, a day of great significance to her."

Butayna closed her eyes again and blotted out the hateful sight of her. It appeared she had not forgotten their past in its entirety. Why, of all the people in the world, did Maryam have to be here on the most important of days?

Leila cajoled, "What does this day mean for you, Butayna?"

Her gaze still shuttered, Butayna fought past the lump in her throat. "Today would have been my father's birthday."

Leila's warm touch alighted on her hand. "How fitting it should be to have his grandson come into the world on the same day."

"A child he shall never know." Butayna held back her tears. She liked to think her father would have been proud on this day to hear of his grandchild, if he had lived.

"Oh, he knows him, dearest. He has seen the boy's spirit in the Christian heaven."

In the corner, Sultana Safa yawned and mumbled something about maudlin talk.

Butayna whispered, "Yusuf approved of him?"

"Oh, dearest, how could he not? The boy is a boon to him, an assurance my family's line will continue. When the time is right, Yusuf shall offer his gratitude in person, but for now, he knows you need time to recover."

"The Sultan was very worried for you last night."

Butayna looked up when Maryam spoke to her.

Leila glanced over her shoulder. "You talked with him then?"

"I did, my Sultana, after I left the birthing room."

Leila shook her head and clutched Butayna's hand again. "Yusuf adores you, as he will love your boy."

Butayna made no reply. She stared up at Maryam, who lingered beside her. Nothing about her sedate manner should be cause for concern, yet Butayna could not suppress a niggling doubt. Perhaps it was because she had not seen Maryam so calm, without a hint of her usual malice, in over a year.

Maryam said, "Your boy is beautiful, as I expected he would be."

Yusuf's mother moved beside the pallet. "With my son for his father, of course a Nasrid prince is perfection."

Leila sat back on her heels. "You're both kind and solicitous this morning, but I think we should leave Butayna to her rest now."

The door creaked and Ifrit entered the room. She bowed beside her mistress. "The wet nurse has come for Prince Muhammad, my Sultana."

Leila nodded. "Show her in. Let her feed the child here, so Butayna may see the woman chosen for her comfort. Then she should get some rest."

Butayna did not want to sleep, not when precious moments with her son ebbed away, but she could not deny how her eyelids drooped.

A short, olive-brown woman with a rounded face and high breasts entered the room, followed by Jawla and Hafsa. Butayna smiled for the first time at the sight of her servants. Both women bowed and congratulated her, along with the midwife.

She removed her *rida* and took a seat on a footstool, which Ifrit had placed beside the pallet. Butayna relinquished her child to Jawla's arms, the motion almost sapping the last of her energy reserves. The servant handed Muhammad to the wet nurse, who unlaced her *qamis*. The child wriggled in her arms. She cupped her swollen breast with a pink-tinged nipple and brushed it across his lips twice, before the babe latched on. She crooned while he nursed. Some other woman would nurse him, sing to him, and comfort him at night. Not his mother.

Butayna heaved a sigh. Leila reached for her hand again and squeezed it.

After the wet nurse finished, she rubbed Muhammad's back and settled him into the crook of his mother's arm again. "He did very well, my lady."

Safa cleared her throat and the fleshy wattle below her chin jiggled. She crossed her arms and stared into Butayna's eyes. "We should leave. The child comes with us."

While Butayna clutched Muhammad to her side, Leila nodded. Her shoulders slumped and she ran her fingers over her tousled hair. She looked to the midwife. "You will remain with the *kadin*?"

"I shall not leave her side, my Sultana. We will care for her and ensure she is well. The afterbirth is intact and though there was some bleeding, the lady shall be well with several days' rest. You may rely upon me."

"Good. You will send for me if she needs me at any hour. If anything should happen to Butayna, for any reason, I shall have you and your assistant executed."

The midwife's face turned ashen. "*Nam*, my Sultana. I understand."

Safa snapped, "We are wasting time!"

"Can you wait upon me, Safa? Asiya told me she heard the cries of a newborn, Yusuf's son. If this boy is of my line, then I wish to see this Nasrid prince."

233

Butayna turned, as did everyone else, at Fatima's resolute demand. The Sultana stood in the doorway, her long garment wrinkled and her hair disheveled. A sneer crisscrossed Safa's face, but she lowered her gaze as Fatima entered the room. Asiya carried a small silver cup and trailed her mistress. Fatima soon hovered beside the pallet and looked down at Butayna and her baby.

With a pained swallow, Butayna lifted Muhammad. Her arms quaked as she struggled to relinquish him, even for a moment, to Yusuf's treasured grandmother.

Fatima shook her head. "I will not take him now. If Allah grants me His enduring favor, I shall have many years to hold the boy. His mother should have the right now."

Safa's tremulous voice rose a little higher. "You know the Sultan's law regarding the children of nonbelievers!"

Fatima's grin exposed yellowed teeth and a gap where one had gone missing. "I should, for my Ismail wrote it! I remember a time when such a rule could have been used against you at Yusuf's birth."

Butayna glanced at Yusuf's mother, who clamped her mouth shut and averted her gaze. What did Fatima mean?

The aged Sultana knelt beside the pallet with a grunt. Asiya reached out a hand to steady her, but Fatima waved her away. "I am not so feeble that I cannot bless my great-grandson! Now give me the date syrup."

Asiya offered the tiny goblet, into which Fatima dipped and withdrew her forefinger. A dark brown liquid clung to her flesh. She glanced at Butayna.

"A child should have something as sweet as he is when he first enters the world. Will you permit it?"

Butayna nodded. Fatima rubbed her fingertip across the baby's rosebud lips. Then she accepted help to stand again. "May you know only joy as his mother."

As Fatima withdrew, she paused beside Safa. "For all your piety and devotion to Islam, you are a wretched woman! Does it give you joy to take a babe from its mother? How easily you forget the past and your humble beginnings. I have not."

While Butayna frowned in puzzlement after Fatima's departure, Leila crouched beside her and held out her arms. "Yusuf has decreed a place for Muhammad in my household. I shall look after him with the aid of my servants. The wet nurse is to enjoy a place in my household as well. There will be extra guards outside my chamber to ensure the little prince's safety. I shall love and nurture your son as if he were my own. I would give up my life in protection of his for more than Yusuf's sake. I do so for your sake also, Butayna, because I know how much he means to both of you."

Butayna's gaze swam and her chin trembled. The time had come. "Can't I hold him just a little longer?"

Her sadness mirrored Leila's own. The Sultana's face crumpled and contorted. After silent sobs, she sniffled and wiped at her nose with a handkerchief Ifrit offered.

"Please, dearest. Don't make this any harder than it has to be." Leila's tone lacked any vigor.

With a shudder, Butayna clutched her sweet boy and then placed him in his aunt's arms. When he squirmed a little, she fisted her hands at her sides. Then her fingers uncurled and went limp. Her heart thudded inside her chest. Would it stop beating now? Bereft of her son so soon after he came into the world, what happiness remained for her?

Fat tears streamed down Leila's cheeks while she cradled the newborn and arranged the blanket's folds around his face. Her clouded and red-rimmed gaze viewed Butayna again. "I promise you may see him at any hour of the day or night."

Butayna's gaze watered. "Care for him and love him well. My son is your son, Leila."

His aunt nodded and rose. She followed Safa and Maryam from the birthing room, Ifrit and the wet nurse behind her.

Jawla and Hafsa remained with the midwife and her assistant, both of whom turned away with little shakes of their heads. Jawla sniffed and wiped at the corner of her eye, while Hafsa focused a distant, empty stare at some spot on the tiled wall.

Butayna rolled on her side. She curled her fingers against her chest, her limbs too heavy to move. Her body quaked with silent tears. She closed her eyes and blotted the cruel world around her.

***

Butayna laughed and nuzzled the fat creases in her son's legs. He lay on Leila's bed, playing with his fingers, while she held his pudgy feet and kissed them. Then she bussed his rounded belly and trilled, "Ten little fingers, ten little toes. He shall be loved, wherever he goes!"

Muhammad chortled and batted her face with his hands.

Butayna pressed tiny pecks on his palms. "Look, Leila. See how well he loves my singing."

Beside her, Leila's upturned face took on a relaxed appearance. "And here I feared you would hate me for my part in raising him."

Butayna smiled at her. "How could I ever, when you've done so well with him. It has been four months since his birth and he is a wonder to behold each day. You have never kept me from him, never interfered when I wished to do something for him. How can I thank you, Leila?"

The Sultana placed her hand on Butayna's own. "By being the blessed mother you have been to him, for it is a joy to see."

Ifrit entered the chamber and bowed beside her mistress. "The Sultan is here, my Sultana."

Leila's gaze flicked upward. "Well, show him in, Ifrit! Do not make Yusuf stand at my door. Did you tell him Butayna is here?"

"He knows, my Sultana. He is here for her."

Butayna peered at Ifrit. "Not to see his son?"

"The Sultan was with him most of this morning until the little prince returned in time for your visit, my lady."

Butayna sighed and stood. "Then I shall determine what my Sultan wants."

Leila picked up Muhammad and placed him into the wood-carved crib. "Can Yusuf bear to be apart from you this evening?"

"We shall know soon."

"Join me again if you can. I wish to talk with you."

"As you like."

With a peck on the crown of her son's dark hair, Butayna left the room and exited through the alcoves. Yusuf stood on the landing, Mufawwiz and Hisham at the bottom of the steps among half his retinue of guards. Everyone else bowed while Yusuf grasped her fingers and kissed them. He wore a red, brocaded *jubba*. Black boots peeked out at the hem, the color of which matched her embroidered robe.

He asked, "You are well?"

She arched her eyebrows. "You saw enough of me last night to know I am in superb health."

He nuzzled her fingertips. "There is no such thing as enough of you."

Once, she would have blushed at the sensual tone he adopted. Instead, she leaned forward and brushed her lips against his. As her fingers threaded through his hair, his arms came around her and pressed her body flush against him. Her skin tingled wherever they touched. His lips caressed hers as if they stood alone in his chambers.

When he lifted his head, her hand smoothed his beard. She could not love him as she did, or adore their son while she remained ashamed of their lives together. Doubt and guilt plagued her less with each day. Muhammad's sweet visage and his eyes, which evoked memories of her father, chased away all qualms. When she held her son and her beloved, nothing else mattered.

"Come with me to your chamber. I have something to show you." Yusuf winked and interlaced his fingers with hers.

He led her down the marble steps. Jawla and Hafsa sat in a circle of the rest of Leila's women with Muhammad's wet-nurse. They ate date balls and drank mint tea. When her servants raised their heads from the meal, Butayna waved them off.

She and Yusuf took the stairs together. They entered her chamber, one-roomed but spacious with gossamer purple curtains arranged around the bed. Now, there was more in the room than when she had left it. Cloth of gold and varied silken fabrics piled high on the stools beside the bed. Two engraved brass lamps were on either side of the door, along with a silver tray decorated with mother-of-pearl. Turquoise, opal, amber, and gold necklaces spilled from a small coffer set at the base of the bed. A silver statue of two birds intertwined occupied the table beside her fruit bowl.

She turned to him, rendered speechless. Her stomach fluttered.

Yusuf brought her hands to his lips and kissed them. "Mufawwiz had the eunuchs bring these gifts all here while you were with Leila. I grant them in honor of my beloved *kadin*, who has borne my cherished first son."

She peeked past him at the chief steward, who smiled and bowed.

Yusuf drew her attention again. "These trinkets are nothing compared to my love for you. You are my heart and my life, Butayna."

Euphoria overwhelmed her at his pronouncement. He had whispered his love often in the darkness of their respective chambers, but never did she feel it more than today.

"I have another gift for you." With a wave, he beckoned Hisham, who knelt at his side and held out a rolled parchment with Yusuf's unbroken, red wax seal.

In turn, Yusuf handed the document to her. "This belongs to you, drawn up by the hand of my *katib sirri-hi* this morning. The *Diwan al-Insha* composes the most important proclamations on fine vellum. Break the seal and read the words."

As she did, her fingers flew to the pulse at the base of her throat. "You have freed me?"

"You are no longer a slave, Butayna. You are the mother of my son, a free woman with your own will to do as you please."

She clasped the precious words to her chest, while he continued, "No one shall ever call you a slave again. Read on."

Her tentative smile flourished as her gaze flitted across the delicate script again. "You have granted me the freedom to practice my Christian religion for the rest of my life."

Cheeks aglow, his radiant expression conveyed the depths of his emotion for her, even as his words provided confirmation. "I would never force you to convert, even for the sake of our son, my love for you, or my most fervent wish for us to share the same faith. Our religious differences shall never alter what I feel for you." He turned from her to the others. "Leave us, all of you. My next words are for Butayna alone."

"I hear and obey, my Sultan." Hisham bowed and departed in a bustle of white silk.

The footfalls of the others with him soon receded, until Butayna stood alone with Yusuf at the threshold. Her took her hand and guided her through the gifts scattered through the chamber to the table. A small, red leather pouch rested behind the fruit bowl.

He admired her again. "We will soon retire to the *Jannat al-'Arif*. When we are there, I wish us to celebrate an important occasion. To do this, I must have your consent."

She bounced on her feet. The lightness of her limbs made her glad for his hand. It kept her grounded. "You want my approval? My Yusuf, you may do as you please. You do not need my leave to commit any act."

He chuckled. "My sweet love, you are wrong in this instance. The learned men of my court would say I do require your permission." He knelt and looked up at her. "Is this how the *caballeros* of your *cantigas* pledge themselves, their hearts, to their ladies?"

Her eyes watered. "I have never known a *caballero*, Yusuf."

He kissed her fingers. "Then I have nothing to offer you except what a Christian knight would give his lady—my heart and my love. I ask you on this day to share a life with me, not as my *kadin*, but as my Sultana. You shall be my wife and my queen. You will sit by my side. You shall share in my joys and tribulations. I ask you to comfort me as I would comfort you. What say you to this, Butayna? Will you have me for your husband?"

When she would have answered, the breath caught in her throat.

He smiled. "Mufawwiz informed me it is customary among Christians for the prospective bride to receive a token from her bridegroom when their betrothal occurs, a sign of his intent to marry her."

He reached for the pouch and opened it. He drew out a gold band topped with a luminescent pearl the color of her skin, which he held up to the light. "For my pearl."

Tears streamed down her cheek.

He half-pleaded, "Shall you make me wait forever, my love, for your answer?"

She set the vellum on the table, crouched before him, and drew him into a long, deep kiss. When she released him, his Adam's apple bobbed as he swallowed.

"Does that mean you accept me? I must have the words, my sweet love."

"*Nam*, my Yusuf. I accept you and this way of life because I love you with all my heart. I will be your Sultana."

***

Yusuf missed *Salat al-Asr* and would have missed *Salat al-Maghrib* as well, if Butayna had not reminded him of his obligations. He left her chamber with his hair askew and a wide grin from ear to ear. She yawned and stretched catlike, before she clambered off the bed and rinsed her body. Still, his scent clung to her. She never wanted it to fade from her body.

She dressed again in a simple *misha*, a *qandara*, and *sarawil*. On an impulse, she wore the ring from Yusuf as well. In leather sandals, she walked down the corridor, past several of the *jawari* who offered her a deferential bow at each entryway. At times, she glanced at her finger and ensured the ring remained on her hand. She would treasure it forever.

Near the last door, peals of laughter echoed behind her. She turned, but saw no one in the hallway. She went down the stairs and found the chamber there empty. From the chatter above stairs, she guessed Leila resided with her women above. If the wet-nurse had already tended to Muhammad, perhaps Butayna might sing her son to sleep as she often did.

She leaned against the doorway and stared out into the courtyard. Sunset bathed the columns and roof tiles in a golden fire. Just over a year earlier, she once stood outside in the courtyard and marveled at her surroundings. So much had occurred since then. She was a mother and soon to be a bride. Moreover, the freedom she once despaired of would be hers again. She had wished to be free to leave. Now she would choose to stay and live among the Moors. Her son would grow strong and wise like his father and, God willing, perhaps next year he might have a younger brother or sister.

Movement across the courtyard caught her gaze. Maryam stood in the doorway in a green silk *rida*. Her dark hair fell in wavy ringlets around her hips. Her cheeks flushed pink. Butayna had never seen her so radiant. Maryam turned aside as Sultana Safa stepped to the threshold. The midwife who had tended Butayna during her pregnancy and after Muhammad's delivery passed between both women. She bowed to Yusuf's mother and departed. Safa cupped Maryam's lower abdomen through the garment, its rounded curves visible under the silk. Then both women turned and disappeared into the chamber again.

A small intake of breath rendered Butayna lightheaded. She gripped the doorpost and sagged against it. Her thoughts were a jumble. It could not be! She shook her head and squeezed her eyes shut.

"Butayna?" Ifrit stood at the top of the stairs. "Are you looking for Jawla and Hafsa? The Sultana called them to her side since you were... occupied with her brother."

Butayna released the door and flexed her fingers. "Where is she?"

"Who?"

"Your mistress!"

"Up here in her bedroom...."

Butayna took the stairs two at a time and knocked aside Ifrit in the process. "What are you doing? What is the matter with you?"

Her vision blurred, Butayna barged into Leila's bedchamber and found her on the bed beside the wet nurse, who cradled a sleeping Muhammad.

Butayna's fists shook. "You knew! You knew Maryam carried Yusuf's child and you didn't tell me. How could you betray me like this, Leila? I anticipated his unfaithfulness, but I expected better from you. I gave you my son, my trust and this is how you have forsaken me?"

Muhammad wailed at the sound of his mother's voice. Leila's slaves, along with Jawla and Hafsa, stared slack-jawed.

"Get out! All of you!" Butayna waved a hand to the door.

Leila stood. Her grimace compressed her lips. "Butayna, you have no right to order my slaves out of my room."

"A Sultana can do so! The wife of the Sultan can do many things."

The women scrambled until Butayna remained with Leila, who sighed and sat on the bed. "Indeed, she can. Yusuf has fulfilled his promise. He intends to wed you."

"He's forgotten his other vows!" Butayna paced the room. Her pulse pounded at the base of her throat. "He pledged his love–"

"Never his fidelity. Do you think he cannot love you and want other women?"

"Including her? Never her! She is–"

"A woman who fascinates him, who uses the wiles Safa has taught her, who plays upon his sympathy for her losses as a mother to gain her true desire. Not children. Not an empty triumph over you. Power. Yusuf has it and she wants it. That is all."

Butayna stopped and sank to the floor. She looked down at the pearl ring. Was it a meaningless bauble? How could Yusuf have betrayed her trust and love? He had taken Maryam into his bed again, the one person Butayna despised.

"When did she go to him? The pregnancy cannot be so many months along."

Leila would not meet her regard. "On the night of your labor, Safa sent Maryam out of the room. She never returned. I think she went to him then. I do not know if she and Safa planned her visit. The child would have been conceived on this one night."

Butayna drew her knees up to her chest and rested her chin on them. Where were her tears of heartbreak? How could Yusuf have done this to her? Of all possible nights, he chose the one in which she birthed their child to take another woman to his bed. Not just any *jarya*. Butayna's sworn enemy.

"So, she went to him while I gave birth to his son?"

"At first, I hoped she had betrayed him with a guard at *al-Quasaba*. Maryam has never left *al-Qal'at al-Hamra* or the *Jannat al-'Arif*. I have asked. She is pregnant with Yusuf's baby. She has done nothing wrong."

"She deceived Yusuf as to the source of the discord between us. She has lied to him too many times about me, to ingratiate herself with him, in his life and his arms at night."

Leila glanced at her. "What do you intend to do about it?"

Butayna threw up her hands. "What can I do? Whatever I say, Yusuf will deem it jealous lies, prompted by Maryam's pregnancy. He will think my Christian beliefs govern my words. He would be right."

Leila sniffed and twirled her rings. "My sisters have told me the first few months of pregnancy are the most dangerous. Anything can happen."

Butayna clutched her stomach. "*La!*"

"*La?*"

Butayna shook her head. "Leila, you will not suggest such a thing. Would you have an innocent child's blood on your hands?"

Leila's eyes glistened like hard emeralds in the lamplight. "*La*, since it seems you will not. A true Sultana would never hesitate to destroy an enemy."

"If that is so, why is Safa still alive in this never-ending rivalry you two share? Doesn't your love for Yusuf stay your hand?"

"It does not. The extent of Safa's spy network has kept her alive. She has many guards. I live for the day when she will not enjoy such protections. Then I will get rid of her, as I should have done years ago."

With a quiver, Butayna cupped her forehead. "She is Yusuf's mother!"

"I am his sister and she's tried to have me killed three times. One attempted poisoning resulted in the death of the slave girl Ishraq whom you replaced...."

"You told me she died in childbirth!"

"Ishraq ingested the poison meant for me by accident. It triggered the early delivery and loss of her baby. She bled to death, although my doctor tried to save her. The second time, Safa once had a eunuch attack me in the bath, but the superintendent and Mufawwiz saved me. The first instance occurred many years ago. Amat received some *cendal*, intended for a new *rida*. When she touched the cloth, it burnt her hands." As Butayna recalled the small burns dotting the slave's palms and fingertips, Leila continued. "Later, I went with palace guards to the royal draper's stall. Under torture, he admitted Safa paid him to taint the material with something which irritated moist, exposed skin."

"What happened to him?"

"My eunuchs donned chainmail gloves and covered his face with the same cloth. I'll never forget his screams."

Butayna sighed and shook her head. The unrepentant cruelty of Yusuf's family still startled her. "You have kept this from Yusuf? He cannot know how Safa has tried to hurt you."

"This is my fight. What choice could I ask Yusuf to make between the mother he cherishes and a beloved sister?"

Butayna could not speak. Leila leaned in her direction. "Safa will teach Maryam her tricks, be assured. I warn you, Butayna. For Maryam, this is nothing more than a game of chance, which she intends to win."

"Yusuf is not a prize for her gain!"

"He is not the prize she seeks. He is the pawn. If you do not stop her now, you will lose everything you have gained, even Yusuf's heart. There can be one victor. Are you willing to let Maryam win? Consider the cost. Sentiment and sympathy cannot guide you. Save them for her victims."

"I will stop her. Just not in the manner you have proposed!"

Leila's expectant gaze held hers. "What other ways have you considered?"

"I will find one of my own," Butayna insisted.

Leila mused, "The best move would be to kill her. I fear you shall never find the courage to do so, to your detriment."

Chapter 17
Another Heir

Sultana Butayna

Granada, Andalusia
October 2, AD 1338 – June 17, AD 1339 / 16 Rabi al-Awwal – 8
Dhu al-Hijja 739 AH / 18th of Tishri - 10th of Tammuz, 5099

Butayna sat on a carved wooden stool beside a window. Ten-month old Muhammad occupied her lap. Her son played with the strings of her *qamis*. A swift mid-morning wind ripped autumn leaves from the trees and scattered them into the fountains west of the harem. Clouds gathered and darkened the sky, a portent of sudden rainfall.

A newborn's cry rent the air and rose above the cries of his mother. Muhammad whimpered and buried his ruddy face in her chest. Butayna gathered him close to her and kissed his brow. "Hush, my little lion. Lions are never afraid."

Beside her, Leila bowed her head. "Maryam has delivered of a son." She cocked her head, as the squalls of the infant echoed throughout the birth chamber. "At least, we may be assured he sounds healthy."

At her feet, Ifrit reached up and pattered her mistress' hand.

"Listen to that voice! Another heir for my treasured Yusuf," Sultana Safa pronounced from her seat beside the birthing chair.

As one, she and Leila regarded each other with impassive features. Still, something inscrutable seethed between them, more than hatred or determination. Each had chosen sides in a battle for control over the harem and influence over Yusuf. Butayna feared she would remain a pawn between them, unless she chose for herself. What would be Maryam's role? She was not one to allow others to decide her fate.

The midwife knelt between her legs and ensured she delivered of the afterbirth. The midwife's assistant took away the child, long and lean like his mother. Mucus coated his trembling form. Maryam, aided by Safa's dwarf Nazhun, went from the birthing chamber into a small room beyond. She emerged anew in a black *rida* and went to a pallet. The assistant returned to her side with the swaddled boy and placed him in his mother's arms.

White linen encased his form. Puffed cheeks peeked between the folds of cloth and crammed between them, the nose flared with a reddened tip. The child quieted at once in Maryam's hold. She snuggled him close and kissed his forehead with her cracked lips.

Butayna did the same to little Muhammad, who wriggled in the security of her hold. He pointed his chubby finger at the newborn.

She murmured against his dark hair. "You have a new baby brother, my lion. You must be good to him, for he is younger and will depend on you to teach him all you shall learn. When the time comes, he shall support your ascension to the throne of your father. Take joy in your moments with him. You are blessed, for I never knew the delight of siblings."

Little more than ten months separated the sons of Yusuf. Butayna still could not fathom Yusuf's betrayal. They had never spoken of it, even after their marital ceremony. Despite his infidelity, she could not forsake her fervent wish to be his wife. Yusuf raised the topic of Maryam's pregnancy once after their marriage, but Butayna turned from him and refused to listen. Months later, the pain remained too fresh.

Now, faced with the reality of her husband's dalliance with a hated foe, she swallowed the heavy lump inside her throat. "What has my husband decided to name his new son?"

Sultana Safa looked at her askance, her gaze steady. Butayna returned the stare, while she wished the hated woman far from her sight.

Leila answered, "He shall be Ismail for our honored father."

Yusuf had chosen to honor Maryam's child with the forename of his beloved father. Butayna suppressed a shudder and silent tears, as another wound rent her heart. She murmured, "A blessed name to be sure."

Maryam lifted and held out her new son to the midwife's assistant. "Take him again. He must go to his father. Before he does, tell the midwife to bring a basin of warm water. I wish to be purified."

Leila tittered behind her hands. "Though I have no experience of childbirth, I do believe some time must pass prior to the ritual cleanse. Jews must observe similar beliefs."

Maryam's stare hardened. "As do all *dhimmis*." She fixed her near obsidian gaze on the midwife's assistant. "You will do as I command. I need the water for another purpose."

Safa snorted. "The blood of the Nasrid prince who grew inside her gives her pride. She forgets she is still a slave, not even a *kadin*."

The woman bowed and went to the midwife. Their exchange occurred in low tones Butayna could not overhear.

Leila stood. "Shall we go to Yusuf?"

Maryam said, "I need witnesses! Where's that damned water?"

Safa frowned and stood with the aid of her cane. "You need witnesses for what purpose? Speak sense, woman."

The midwife brought a metal basin of fresh water and a cloth draped at the copperware's edge. Maryam waved her away and washed her face, hands, and feet. The midwife took the child in her arms and idled beside her assistant. Leila frowned at Maryam and Safa grunted, while she tapped her walking stick. When Leila growled beneath her breath and stared at Yusuf's mother, the elder woman stilled the motion of her hands. The room became silent again, except for the swirl and swish of water in the basin.

"I bear witness that there is no God except Allah and the Prophet Muhammad, may peace be upon him, is His messenger." Maryam's recital of the *Shahadah* shattered the din.

Butayna expelled a ragged breath and closed her eyes. Maryam would not do as she had done. Instead, she chose to abandon the Jewish faith and prevent the loss of her son.

When Butayna opened her eyes again, Maryam regarded her. "As I once told you, Butayna, separate paths lie ahead of each of us. I accept Islam, the obligation of five daily prayers and all other duties. When the ritual of purification is completed, I wish to become a Muslim."

Leila advanced on her and halted when only a hand span remained between them. "A rinse and the *Shahadah* do not satisfy the requirements! How dare you mock my faith with perverse intent? You wish to become a Muslim so you may remain with your son and gain your freedom, as Butayna has done."

Behind her, Safa shouted, "That is a lie! Maryam has studied *al-Qur'an* for the last four months. She declared her intention to me in the weeks before she gave birth."

Leila rounded on her. "You are almost as terrible a liar as she! You did not know why she wanted the water, but now you claim she told you her plans beforehand. You could not even direct her on the proper method. The ritual wash comes after the declaration of the *Shahadah!* Both of you disgust me! I will warn Yusuf against this vainglorious attempt. He will never grant her freedom after this farce."

Safa shrugged. "He is Sultan, he will do as needed. Why do you care whether she is Muslim or not? It is a duty to maintain *jihad*. The struggle requires us to proclaim our faith and teach others of submission before Allah. Our laws and customs allow anyone to convert. Would you have Yusuf abandon such principles by your leave? I know why this conversion troubles you. Butayna gained her freedom through marriage. You do not want Maryam to obtain the same benefit and status as your former slave has."

"I care because Maryam is lying, Safa! If you're too ignorant to recognize her ploy, then you are the fool I've always known you were."

Safa raised her cane and aimed it at Leila. Yusuf's mother landed one wallop, before Ifrit rushed at her, grabbed the stick, and threw it into the corner. "Don't you dare touch her!"

All within the room gazed in shock. Butayna gathered her son even closer to her chest as he started to cry.

Then Safa swung her arm at Ifrit's head, but her momentum toppled her. "I'll kill you, filthy slave. How dare you put your disgusting slave hands upon me! You will die for this insult!"

Leila tugged Ifrit beside her and held her close. She kissed her cropped hair. "I am well, my Ifrit. Calm yourself now. It is over. She did not hurt me."

Ifrit pulled away and clasped hands with her mistress. "Are you sure you are unhurt?"

Safa struggled to stand with the aid of her beleaguered slave. As soon as Nazhun guided her to her feet and fetched the walking stick, the Sultana shoved her back. "Get away from me, you ugly beast!"

Nazhun bowed and scrambled to the corner.

Safa tapped the cane. Her stony gaze flitted from Leila to Ifrit, huddled together. "I shall have your head for this, slave."

"Do not count on it, Safa!" Leila lifted her chin. "When Yusuf learns how you struck me, he will not be so quick to summon the executioner."

Yusuf's mother did not say another word. She walked to the door, a little hitch at her stride. Nazhun trailed behind her, with the midwife.

Safa gripped the doorpost and peered over her shoulder at Leila. "Must I remind you of the custom? Yusuf's first son goes with us. Would you leave him with his Christian mother?"

"I would not deny you the pleasure of telling me so yet again." Leila's monotone voice belied her words. With a long exhale, she returned to Butayna's side and held out her hands.

Heaviness seeped through Butayna's limbs. She nuzzled her baby's forehead and pressed him close to her. "I shall see you later. Be good for your aunt, my little lion."

She stood and placed Muhammad in Leila's arms. He squealed, but settled against Leila, his tawny-colored eyes on Butayna's face. He reached for her cheek with a chubby hand. She kissed his tiny fingers and pressed them against her skin.

Safa bellowed, "The Sultan should not be kept waiting to greet his newest heir!"

With a small nod, Leila departed with Muhammad nestled against her hip and Ifrit beside her. Butayna clasped her hands together and stared in the direction they took out of the birthing room, long after their withdrawal. The midwife's assistant bowed and tidied the birthing chamber, but Butayna ignored her. She focused instead on Maryam, who sat on her pallet, a leer cast in Butayna's direction.

Butayna closed the gap between them and hovered beside Maryam. "You think you are so clever, don't you?"

"In comparison to you? Indeed, I am wiser than you have proven yourself. What did you believe would happen when you chose your faith over your own son, Butayna?"

"I did not choose–"

"*Nam*, you did. There are always choices, Butayna. You had a decision to make and you selected a choice, as I have. Jew. Christian. Muslim. Little difference exists among us. We prattle on with words before a God who does not always listen. I begged for the lives of my daughter and son. They are still absent from my arms. Today, I have a new son and I will never surrender him to anyone else. Not for the sake of a religion that has never aided me. What has your devotion gained you? Who wipes Muhammad's tears at night when he cries? Who shall be there for his first steps, his first words?"

"I could never be as faithless as you, not even for his sake!"

Maryam sighed and unfolded the blanket at the foot of the pallet. "You remain too foolish. Sometimes, a lie is better than the truth. Cling to your God, if you must. Does He comfort you when you are abed in the darkness of your room at night, unable to clutch your son to your chest?"

"Yusuf holds me to him. In his arms, I am never unhappy."

A flush colored Maryam's cheeks. Her fingertips gripped the edge of the blanket until the knuckles whitened. "This conversation leaves me wearied. I would enjoy some rest before they bring my son back. So get out."

"You are a *jarya*. I am a Sultana, beloved of my husband. You cannot order me to do anything!"

"We shall see how long those divisions between us remain." Maryam yawned, pulled the blanket up to her shoulders, and offered Butayna her back.

Butayna glared at her a final time before she stalked away.

Just when she reached the door, Maryam called out, "Two heirs to sit upon the throne when there can be just one Sultan to succeed his father. Some would say Yusuf is fortunate to have two sons. Others would think him cursed. Regardless, I do not doubt the news will please him, given your recent tragedy."

Butayna's nails raked the doorpost. Her other hand went to her empty stomach, where six weeks ago her second child had thrived for five months, until failure shattered her hopes. The court astrologer had predicted another boy.

Maryam added, "If you believe this is the last time I shall bear Yusuf a son, you are mistaken. I will not fade away, while you keep Yusuf at your side. He does not love me, not yet, but I will bind his heart with our children. If you think Muhammad shall inherit the throne just because he is the eldest, you are wrong."

A shudder coursed through Butayna. She fisted her hands at her sides before she turned to Maryam. "If you ever strike at Muhammad, no one, not even Yusuf shall save you from my wrath! I will choke the life from you with my bare hands. Do not mistake the measure of my love for my son."

Over her shoulder Maryam said, "Do not underestimate my ambitions for mine."

***

When Butayna knocked at her husband's door and entered at his command, Yusuf sat at his writing desk in the center of the room.

His shoulders hunched, he did not look up from the parchment. "A blessed evening! Give me a moment, my sweet love. I must finish this response to King Pedro of Aragon. He demands the return of a captive from Barcelona, a mariner named Macia Descarner."

Butayna clasped her hands together and stood behind him. She knew the travail this sailor faced all too well. "Do you have this Macia Descarner in one of your slave *corrals?*"

"I do."

"Will you free him?"

"There are larger interests at stake between Aragon and the Sultanate, Butayna. Things you would not understand."

"Because I am a simple woman, or one with whom you will not take the trouble to explain."

The reed snapped between his fingers. He raised his head. "You are angry with me over the birth of Maryam's child. Let us not pretend you were not determined to argue before your arrival."

"I do not plan to deny it. My reasons are valid. You just don't like them."

He swiped a hand over his dark hair and replaced the stopper atop the vial of ink. He turned on the stool and faced her. "What would you have me say, Butayna? In your Christian world, a man may enjoy one wife. If he beds another woman, he shames her. In my land, a man may have four wives and many concubines. There is no disgrace in such an arrangement. I cannot alter the differences between our customs. You knew them when you married me. Do you regret our union?"

She peeked at the carpet under the stool. "You know I do not, Yusuf."

His fingertips glided along her cheekbone. "I will not apologize for fathering another child under the laws of the Sultanate. I am sorry if my dalliance with Maryam has upset you. My love for you remains unchanged. I know there is some rivalry between you and Maryam. Can you both allow it to fade for the sake of the son she has borne me? He is guiltless in this matter between his mother and my wife."

She lifted her gaze to his and released a slow, steady breath. "I would never hurt a child!"

"I hope not." He rubbed the back of his neck and crossed his arms over his chest.

She flinched as though struck. "You doubt me?"

He sighed and reached for her hands. She shied away, but his fingers closed on her arms and tugged her to him. His embrace drew her against his body, but her limbs remained rigid at her side.

"Butayna, in my childhood, my father had three wives and they lived in relative harmony. I am aware it is not always possible for such compatibility among the women of my household. My mother and sister prove it every day. I can perceive the consequences of discord and must safeguard my sons against it."

"I am not the cause of arguments in this harem, Yusuf!" Her voice, though muffled against his *jubba,* rang through the otherwise silent chamber. She struggled against him, but his hold encased her. "I have abided every burden placed on my soul for love of you. I have learned to accept you will always take other women into your bed. But her? Why did it have to be Maryam, Yusuf? You know how she feels about me–"

"And I know your regard for her. Even if Maryam hates you, the sentiment is mutual. You cannot deny it."

She shook in his clutches. "I have good reason to detest her."

"She might say the same. Despite her attempts to assure me, I know she still holds you responsible for the deaths of her children. No mother who has suffered such pain surrenders her desire for retribution so soon, as Maryam would have me believe."

When his grip loosened, she drew back in the circle of his arms. "She has spoken to you of the loss of Palomba and her son?"

"She did so on the night she conceived Ismail."

Butayna bowed her head. Her lower lip trembled. "While I labored with our son."

His hands fell away. "I have told you already, I will not apologize for my behavior with a beautiful woman of my harem."

"You are Sultan, Yusuf. You do not have to justify your actions to me or anyone else." Breath hitched in her chest and she turned away from him. Her knees locked together. She could not leave, although she desired nothing more.

His fingers closed on her shoulders. "I cannot undo the past, Butayna. I can only promise nothing shall ever change between us. You have my heart! You will always have my heart."

"And Maryam will always have your son." She raised her head and looked at him. "You will not promise to keep from her?"

"She is the mother of one of my children! Would you have me abandon her and her boy for your sake?"

Her thoughts spun as her heartbeat slowed. What would she have done in a reversal of roles with Maryam? How would she feel if Maryam stood in her place and demanded Yusuf keep away from her and Muhammad? Would she not despise her even more?

She whispered, "You will never forsake them. You love our son. You will love Maryam's own, my Sultan."

Yusuf relinquished his hold, his hands frozen in midair. His face blanched and he stared at her open-mouthed. "So, that is the way of things between us? I am the Sultan again, not your Yusuf any longer?"

She blinked back her tears. "How can you be mine, when I cannot call you my own? Please, permit me to leave you. I promised to see Muhammad later. I would like to hold him before he sleeps tonight."

His eyes glazed over and he shared a quiet stare with her, until he pleaded, "Butayna, please do not do this! Do not seal your heart away from me. I love you! Just you!"

"If you think I could ever stop loving you, then it would seem you do not know me as well as you should. I do not doubt your

251

heart, or the likelihood it shall never be mine in whole. I'm sorry to say, but your love is insufficient."

***

At the *Jannat al-'Arif* in the following summer, Butayna guided Muhammad's furtive steps from the garden's southern edge. Her boy giggled, his ruddy cheeks aglow. He chased butterflies. Ramadi joined him and sprang ahead of his young master through the greenery and flowers.

Behind them, Leila laughed. "Dear boy, they are all faster than you including that fat cat! You'll need longer legs!"

Butayna grinned at her. "He shall have them soon. He's growing so fast."

He toddled off by himself between rows of violets and lilies. A light breeze stirred his dark, wavy curls. He called to the cat, which waited for him. "Madi! Madi"

Butayna paused beside Leila and clasped her hand. "I have you to thank for encouraging my son's curiosity. He is eager to discover everything around him."

Leila raised Butayna's fingers to her lips and kissed them. "*Nam*, often to my dread! He frightens at me times. My women adore him. He is a blessed boy, Butayna. He is my joy as well, but I know not as much as your own. You should be honored by his accomplishments as a child."

"I could not be more...."

She paused as Yusuf exited his room at the northern pavilion and stood outlined within the opened window. He held Ismail in his arms and pointed to the garden below, where Ramadi prowled and pounced at anything that moved. Maryam appeared beside him. Her belly jutted from the *qamis*. Yusuf had announced she carried another child for him a month before the family came to the *Jannat al-'Arif*.

When Butayna turned away from the scene, Leila touched her shoulder. "Shall I fetch the little prince? Perhaps he has had too much sun for today."

Butayna nodded. "Thank you, Leila. You are always so considerate of his needs."

From her peripheral gaze, she remained aware of Yusuf and Maryam as they stood side by side with their son nestled between them. By the time Leila caught Muhammad and twirled him in her arms before she brought him back to Butayna, Maryam held her son, tilted her head to Yusuf, and left him.

Butayna took her son and balanced him on her hip. She buried her face in his dark curls with the reddened tips. Over sixteen months, the color and texture became a perfect blend of her hair and Yusuf's own. He possessed his grandfather's eyes,

252

her pale skin and her nose, his father's limbs and mouth, all the best features representative of his dual heritage. Though he would always be a child of two disparate worlds, he belonged in the one she shared with Yusuf. The other would never accept him.

She lifted her head and found Leila regarded her with a tender smile, which crinkled the corners of her eyes.

Butayna said, "There are times I cannot believe my son is real, that God gave him to me. When I clutch him with such fervor, it is not only because I dread the moments in which we will be apart. I hold him close to assure myself he is truly mine. In the year before his birth, I often despaired at the trials placed in my path. I have lost a father and my former life, but gained so much more. Now, I know why I am here, to be Muhammad's mother and guide him through life. I shall never question God again."

Yusuf loitered at the window. Leila waved to him and he returned the gesture. Then she asked, "Shall we go in, Butayna? The wet nurse must be ready for him."

"I'm certain you are right."

As Butayna withdrew with Leila and Ramadi inside, she remained aware of how Yusuf's persistent gaze followed her movements until she disappeared from view.

Chapter 18
Rio Salado

Sultana Butayna

Granada, Andalusia
August 16, AD 1340 / 21 Safar 741 AH / 22nd of Av, 5100

In Butayna's bedchamber at mid-morning in the *Jannat al-'Arif*, Leila scanned the tunics, robes and veils scattered across the bed. "Where do you think you are going?"

Butayna shook her head. "With my husband, of course. I must be ready if he changes his mind. Where else should I be except at his side?"

A growl escaped Leila's lips. She grasped Butayna's arm and herded her beside the window. "What do you think you're doing?"

Butayna shrugged off her hold. "I am no longer your slave to do with as you please. Never touch me so again!"

Leila's sea-green eyes turned to slits in an instant. She drew herself up her full height and frowned. "I am left to wonder if you are still the naïve girl who entered the harem three years ago. Butayna, this is no pleasurable excursion as when Yusuf took us to Wadi-Ash to see Ismail last month. This time, he is going to war at the head of seven thousand cavalry. Have you ever seen a battle? Why would you want to place yourself in the midst of such carnage?"

"I am no ignorant simpleton, Leila. Lest you forget, I have seen blood on the ground before, my father's own!"

Fine lines deepened as they crisscrossed Leila's brow. She clenched her fingers and drew a deep breath. "The sight must have been terrible for you and I do not deny its impact. This is different, death on a scale of thousands."

"I shall remain within our encampment with a detachment of guards for my protection. Why do you act as if you care for my well-being?"

On a whim, Butayna turned aside and called out to Hafsa. "Pack another pair of the riding boots!"

"*Nam*, my Sultana."

One pair might not suffice for the journey. How many weeks would it take? Longer than the visit to Malaka after their wedding, for the distance to Tarif would be greater. When would she return? Would her husband and the Marinids be victorious?

Despite Butayna's intent to ignore her further, Leila pressed on. "Has it ever occurred to you that I might care more than you realize?" Her soft and plaintive voice reverberated through the otherwise quiet room.

With a deep groan, Butayna faced her again. "Leila, I do not wish to hurt you, but you cannot gainsay me in this. I am my own mistress. You no longer rule me."

"Then if you will not think of my feelings or worry for yourself, what of the safety of your unborn child?"

Butayna stared. She fisted her hands at her sides and stifled a natural inclination against cupping her lower abdomen. The gesture would give Leila the proof she needed.

"What are you talking about?" Her lower lip trembled and her cheeks warmed.

Leila crossed her arms over her chest. "Perhaps you think I have grown stupid this year. You have taken pains to hide the condition with your orders of cotton bands in this month. Your own body betrays you. The bloom of health upon your cheeks, the radiance of your skin and your increased appetite are all the same signs you exhibited as when you carried little Muhammad. You will bear my brother another child."

"You have no idea—"

"Three years here and you still haven't earned the talent for lies. All the signs of your poor attempt are there in the quiver of your lips and the flush blooming on your cheeks. You have forgotten my Sut often washes clothes at the same time Hafsa does. Your servant has not whitened the cotton bands from your menses for a month."

Butayna bit the inside of her cheek until she tasted blood. She refrained from offering Hafsa a furious glance at the other end of the room. The woman had likely not revealed a word, but Leila's servants remained vigilant in her service. "Damn your interference! Are there no secrets in this harem?"

She looked away. When Leila's warm hands settled on Butayna's shoulders, she allowed the familiarity between them. Her former mistress, now closer to her than any natural born sister might have been. The thread which bound them through the intervening years, mutual love of Yusuf, at times became frayed, neglected and in need of repair, but it never severed.

Leila whispered, "If my Sut is aware, how long will it be before Hisham notices? What of Yusuf? He would be displeased to discover you have placed another of his heirs in harm's way."

"I will be careful." Butayna turned and grasped Leila's fingers. "Don't you see? I must be at his side. What if something should happen to him on the battlefield and the last words between us were the cause of regret?"

"Does your impasse continue? What makes you believe he will change his mind then and let you go south with him?"

"Can no words pass between Yusuf and his wife in private?"

"You did not take pains to hide the argument, Butayna. No doubt, Maryam heard it. When Yusuf leaves, she shall remain behind. A woman so far gone with child for my brother cannot travel with the army. Your worry is not just for Yusuf's growing attachment to her."

Butayna sighed. "It is not. I do not doubt he will name her his *kadin* soon. Either one of us occupies his bed at night, despite his mother's attempts to send other women. I know the danger Maryam poses, but she is not my only concern. My husband does not always trust me. When I asked him if I could accompany him, he demanded to know why I wished to take the journey. He accused me of caring more for the fate of King Alfonso's men than his own."

Leila raised her eyebrows and withdrew her hands. "This surprises you as a Christian? As a person whose countrymen my brother shall face in pitched battle? You presumed your love would make him see beyond the differences between you. He intends to kill your people, Butayna. If it helps, please know my brother trusts no one in full. Not even me."

Butayna drew back. "I am the mother of his heir and by God's grace, shall bear him another child. How can he have married me and pledged his love without trust? Can there be genuine devotion between two people without an underlying faith?"

"It seems there can be. I do not doubt Yusuf's love for you. Remember, he is your husband, but he is also the Sultan. A man of his power and stature can never rely upon the motives of others. It is a brutal lesson, which Yusuf discovered at the death of our father."

"One I also found out when Maryam first betrayed me. I am still learning."

"Trust is not a Nasrid trait, but lack of it does not diminish my brother's emotions or his ability to care for you."

"Am I to never have the whole of him? Will there always be a portion of his heart hidden behind a wall no one can breach?"

"You know the answer better than I ever could. Perhaps a man free from obligation could give you his love in its entirety. The Sultan cannot."

***

After Leila left, Butayna helped her servants pack the trunks and satchels. Yusuf entered her bedchamber in the midst of the chaos. Butayna looked up from where she sat on the floor, folding her veils. Noonday sunlight streamed through her window.

Yusuf shook his head. "Jawla, Hafsa, leave us."

The women scrambled out of the room.

With a sigh, Yusuf sat beside Butayna. "You are a stubborn wife. Has any other man been as plagued by an insubordinate woman as I have?"

"My father was with my mother. I once heard my father threaten to beat the willfulness from her, but to my knowledge, he never did. Does Muslim law allow you to beat me? Would you?"

"Perhaps I should."

She quaked as he raised his arm. When he laid it over her shoulders and gathered her to his side, she laid her palm on his chest. "I never aim to make you so angry, my love. I take no enjoyment in your annoyance with me, but you must know how much I love you. I never wish to be apart from you. Please let me go with you."

"Is this why you have arranged your clothes for travel? You are so sure I will relent."

She peered up at him. "I am hopeful. Nothing with you is ever certain except your love for me. I believe in it."

He cupped her cheek. "My love for you would see you remain behind, where I know you will be safe and protected. Warfare is vicious and brutal. You understand I go to make war on your people, on Christians. I will slay them where they stand. Where does your heart lay, Butayna? With your Castillan countrymen or me?"

"Are you asking me to make a choice between you and my people? Can't you see I have decided? How many times, how many more ways will I have to prove my love? I have sacrificed so much of my former self to find contentment in your world, at your side. Do you still wonder whether I love you?"

When he did not answer right away, she laid a light peck on his forehead. "I love you."

Then her lips pressed against his temple. "I love you, Yusuf."

His forehead nestled against hers. "As I love you, Butayna. I always will."

257

She leaned back in his hold. "Does this mean you will let me accompany you?"

His barking laughter echoed. "You are relentless, woman."

"You would never wish for me to surrender too soon."

"Very well, you may come with me," he managed before she squealed in delight and hugged him. He pried her fingers from around his neck. "But I have rules, Butayna, meant for your safety. You will ride with a detachment of my guards and always appear veiled before all men, never without your handmaidens. You and your women will have protection at all times. If there is ever any danger to you, if I tell you to run, you will run. Otherwise, you will keep to the tent at all times. Swear you will do as I ask."

She kissed his chin and nosed his beard. "So serious at times."

"Butayna."

"*Nam*, I promise, Yusuf."

He cupped her hips and pulled her on to his lap. He made short work of the strings at her neckline and placed light kissed at her collarbone. A thrill surged through her body and she sighed against his hair. He tugged the *qamis* off her shoulders and revealed her breasts. She loved the way his gaze darkened whenever he stared at her skin.

"Why, Yusuf, it's the middle of the day. Shouldn't you be preparing for prayer?"

His tongue flicked her sensitive nipple. He murmured against her flesh. "I would rather worship at the temple of your sweet body."

She giggled and grabbed his chin. Her lips hovered over his. "That's blasphemy in any religion, husband."

His fingers raked through her hair. "I'll offer my penitence later. Now, all I want is you."

***

Near Tarifa, Andalusia
October 30, AD 1340 / 8 Jumada al-Awwal 741 AH / 8th of Marheshvan 5101

Butayna stood near the high banks above the Vega River an hour after dawn, her fingers on her rounded stomach. Beside her, Jawla and Hafsa looked into the distance at the plains below their hillside position. Half of Yusuf's guardsmen ranged in front of them, their gazes also on the enemy who gathered to the south. A sea of Christian knights in mail coats, with shields and swords readied to kill her husband and the Sultan of al-Maghrib el-Aska, Abu'l-Hasan Ali. At a distance, someone lifted a relic of the True Cross above the heads of those in the Christian vanguard. Pope Benedict XII even provided Alfonso XI with a crusader's banner. The men whom Yusuf and Abu'l-Hasan Ali's armies would fight represented two kingdoms united against the Nasrid Sultanate and al-Maghrib el-Aska. Castilla-Leon and Portugal put aside their trivial dynastic squabbles, intent on the destruction of Islam in the peninsula. According to Yusuf's spies, King Alfonso XI and the father of his wife, Afonso IV of Portugal had already decided how they would partition *al-jazirat al-Andalus* between them when they defeated the combined Moorish forces.

Butayna grasped a thick, fibrous rope, which secured the tent to the ground. The hemp cut into her hands, but she ignored the pain. What was minor discomfort, compared to a sword in the back or a lance through the belly? How could death occur on such a fair Monday morning, blessed by bright sunshine and a fair northern breeze from Tarif? What would become of her if Yusuf perished on the battlefield?

"My Sultana? Will you not join me for some tea? You must be hungry."

At the plaintive call from within the tent, Butayna sighed. Before she could answer, Sultan Abu'l-Hasan Ali emerged from his nearby tent. He stood beside the standard, which he called *al-Mankura* for 'the victorious', for he intended nothing less at the conflict's end.

Silken banners fluttered on the breeze between the Moorish encampments. Butayna read the epigraph inscribed on the closest one, a bright yellow flag with nine scallop points. "May victory be with our Sultan Abu'l-Hasan, *Amir al-Muslimin.*" The prince of the faithful, the same title Yusuf bore.

Her husband emerged from his ally's scarlet tent with Ibn al-Khatib. The minister's father and brother joined Yusuf. She darted inside the tent at her back. She doubted her sudden disappearance went unnoticed by the husband so furious at her deception, he had not spoken to her in weeks.

He had threatened to dispatch her home almost upon his discovery of her pregnancy at autumn's beginning. King Alfonso's swift movements down from Sevilla and raids from the south at Tarif thwarted Yusuf's intent. He kept her at his side, it seemed, to glower at her. Still, in the night he cradled her beside him with a protective hand on her stomach. When he noted the first stirrings of their child against his palm, his gaze misted and he kissed her hard. His fingers remained around her waist all that night.

Inside the tent, the first wife of Abu'l-Hasan Ali, Sultana Lalla Fatima looked up from her cup of mint tea. She held out her slim, olive-brown hands and gestured to the plush cushion beside her on the carpet. "Do sit with us, Sultana Butayna."

The daughter of the Caliph Abu Bakr of Ifriqiyah had married Abu'l-Hasan Ali as a peace offering. Her Hafsid people, who ruled most of al-Tunisiyah, Libya, and al-Jaza'ir, sealed a truce through her marriage with the Marinid Dynasty, which dominated the coast of al-Maghrib. Unlike Yusuf, Fatima's husband had brought many members of his household with him. His retinue included his children and their mothers. His sister, who only answered to the honorific title of Umm Alfat, scowled often at Fatima. The daughters of generals and commanders in the Sultan's army visited often. Even Abu'l-Hasan Ali's favorite, a fair-haired woman who spoke little and kept to the corner of the room, had a place among them. Her master called her Shams ed-Duna.

Fatima brushed black hair back from her shoulders and tucked it under her *hijab.* Butayna joined her and accepted a warm cup of tea.

Fatima rubbed at the mole on her pale brown chin. "Has my husband come from his tent? Does he believe *al-Mankura* and the relic of the Prophet, may peace be upon him, shall change his fate? Allah has already decided the course of this day."

Butayna replied, "The noble Sultan is likely aware of this fact, as is my lord Yusuf. Still, neither of them appear as men who will surrender to the whim of fortune."

With a warm smile, Fatima patted her fingers. "Indeed, they will not. How do you fare this morning? Your child?"

"We are both well. I am frightened for Yusuf. He has carried out raids before against my people at the fortress of Siles seven years ago, but this is the first major confrontation where he will lead his army into a fight with the Castillan forces."

"A battle to end all battles. *Insha'Allah.* My brother promised he would pitch his tents at the gates of Christian Sevilla before winter and avenge my brave nephew Abu Malik, may Allah preserve his memory." Umm Alfat stirred from beside her hookah. White smoke billowed from the pipe.

Fatima waved her hands in front of her face. "You will not live to see my husband's victory and his vengeance for Abu Malik's murder, if you insist on that pipe! Must you smoke opium? I told you, it is bad for the Sultana Butayna and her baby. If you wish to kill yourself, do it outside of my tent!"

Umm Alfat deepened the lines already incised on her brow and around her mouth. She stretched out and drew on the hookah again. Fatima groaned and buried her face in her hands. She muttered something Butayna recognized as one of the Berber languages.

"Do my fair, desert flowers fight again?" Sultan Abu'l-Hasan Ali parted the folds of the tent and entered. He towered at its center. A dark-skinned man in gray robes, he scratched his wiry beard accepted the homage of the occupants. Folds of skin sagged around his eyes and under his neck, hinted at his age. He could be Yusuf's father. Seated beside his favored wife, Butayna drew her lavender *hijab* over the lower half of her face, before he noted her presence.

Yusuf followed the Sultan into the tent. His gaze found her in an instant. He crossed the room and knelt beside her. His hands covered her abdomen. "Are you well? Is the child well also?"

She smiled at his insistence. "Sultana Lalla Fatima has offered the kind services of a trusted midwife, who promises I am well."

"I want our son or daughter born at home. We must prevail."

Abu'l-Hasan Ali clapped Yusuf's shoulder and almost sent him sprawling across Butayna's lap. "We will be victorious. The holy men have avowed it and, as you said to me in my tent, we must trust in Allah to secure this day for our cause against these Christian idolaters. Come, we must not linger. There is a battle we have to win."

When Abu'l-Hasan Ali kissed Fatima's hands and saluted each of his women, his daughters, and sister in turn, his *kadin* kept to the recesses of the tent. She turned her pale face to the wall and closed her eyes. He stepped over Umm Alfat, who cursed him in a vigorous protest. He grasped his favorite's chin. Forced to look at him, she glared at her captor with ice-blue eyes.

"You will be kinder to me when we meet again."

"I will not!" She jerked away from him.

The lilt in Shams ed-Duna's voice reminded Butayna of how Jawla and Hafsa spoke. Butayna understood the woman's reticence better than anyone else in the tent did.

With a snarl, Abu'l-Hasan Ali released her and left the tent.

Yusuf pecked Butayna's brow before he stood. "I shall return."

"Be safe, my love. May God protect you this day. Come back to me and our children." She clutched at his fingers and kissed them.

When he left her at last, she cupped her hand over her forehead. Fatima patted and rubbed her forearm, but the woman offered meager comfort. Yusuf was only twenty-two. Would Butayna become his young widow today?

***

While the majority of the women slumbered in Fatima's tent nearing midday. The battle raged south at the *arroyo* del Salado. Unable to sleep for the clash of swords and the screams of men and horses, Butayna sat with Hafsa who sewed a tear in one of the tunics. Jawla stood just outside. Abu'l-Hasan Ali's *kadin* leaned against the leather flap with her chin propped on her pallid hand.

Butayna asked her, "Are you from England?"

The doe-eyed woman raised her head. "How did you know?"

"My two servants, including Hafsa who sits here beside me," Butayna said as she waved a hand to her handmaiden who smiled and nodded to the woman, "are English also. Were you stolen away from your village as well?"

The woman nodded and bit back a sob. "I shall never see my parents or husband again! Not that they would want anything to do with me after so many years among these Moors."

Butayna rose and crouched beside her. "I endured life as a captive before I bore Yusuf his son and married. How long have you been in al-Maghrib el-Aska?"

"Six years, since I was twelve years old. Two as the favorite of the black Sultan."

"Do you despise him although he has made you his favorite?"

"He shames me. I have a husband, who must believe I am dead. I can never forget him or the life I had."

When Butayna would have comforted her and shared her own story, the snorts of horses echoed on the wind. A large number of mounts by the way the ground shook, too close to the encampment, while the sounds of the battle boomed from the south.

Jawla burst into the tent. "We have to leave, my Sultana! Now!" She grasped Butayna's hand and hauled her up.

A quarrel from a crossbow jutted through the flap, just shy of Shams ed-Duna's head. She screamed and backed away. Blood pooled around the protuberance.

Outside, Butayna's guards cried, "For the Sultan! Banu Nasr!" Metal clashed and flecks of blood sprayed the ground.

Jawla dragged Hafsa and Butayna after her, despite Butayna's resistance.

"*La*! What of these others here? Umm Alfat just awoke! What of the Sultan's children?"

"We cannot worry for them. We have to go, my Sultana. The Christians are pouring into the camp. They have slaughtered everyone who dared step into their path. What do you think they will do with the women of their adversaries?"

"*Dios mío*! What of Yusuf? Jawla! Where is Yusuf?"

"I don't know, my Sultana! You cannot worry for him now." Jawla drew a dagger from her boot and stabbed through the tent's leather hide. She ripped a jagged slit through the material with haste.

"*La*! I will not leave without Yusuf." Butayna looked behind her. The women and children awakened to a nightmare. Several gathered at Fatima's feet. She stood with a curved Damascene blade in her hand. Others grabbed daggers and food knives.

Fatima shouted, "Get away from the edges of the tent! Whatever comes through those flaps, we will not surrender without a fight! *Allahu Akbar*! Banu Marin! Banu Marin! Banu Marin!"

Butayna sobbed at the Sultana's words. Whatever the circumstances of her marriage to Abu'l-Hasan Ali, Fatima rallied his family and chanted their name rather than that of her Hafsid ancestors.

Jawla tugged Butayna's hand, but she stood her ground. Instead, she called out, "Fatima! Come with us!"

Over her back, the Sultana yelled, "*La*, Butayna! I did not run when the Marinids attacked my father's city. I will not flee before this enemy now. You must leave! I have had my children. My joy is complete! Go and find your Yusuf. Return home! You carry your husband's future inside of you. Go with Allah's blessing."

The first of the Christian warriors barreled inside with a savage roar. He brandished a mace. He swung it at the skull of a little boy at Fatima's feet. A second intruder stabbed with his spear. Fatima hacked at him and knocked the weapon aside.

Jawla pulled and screamed at Butayna. "You don't know if the Sultan is dead! He might be at our encampment. We have to get there. If he is dead–"

"Please, he can't be!"

"If he is, my Sultana, would you make Prince Muhammad an orphan? We have to go!"

Huddled between Hafsa and Jawla, Butayna raced through the encampment. A gurgled scream echoed. She knew the source, but turned anyway. Through the jagged rip in the tent, she glimpsed her last sight of Sultana Lalla Fatima, arms limp at her sides. She sagged to the ground. Dark curls spilled around her shoulders. Blood trickled from her mouth to her chin. A spear pierced her chest.

Chaos descended as people ran in all directions, some to their deaths on Christian swords. Others attained a temporary reprieve before their enemies dragged them from their tents and killed them where they begged for compassion in the dust. None received mercy. Butayna averted her eyes from the sight of the Castillan and Portuguese warriors who tore at the clothes of women and threw them down in the dirt. The enemies pilfered cloth of gold, saddles, bridles, daggers, and jewelry from the tents, even the silk from the tents themselves. Was this what the pope intended when he granted the papal banner?

Dust swirled and almost obscured Butayna's vision. Then red flags and pennons shimmered on the horizon. Butayna pointed. "It's Yusuf! Go!"

She raced with her women as fast as her legs could carry her up the incline. The ground shook behind them.

"Go, my Sultana! Hafsa, protect her!" Jawla skidded in the dirt and grasped an abandoned bow. Two arrows lay in the sand beside the weapon. "Don't stay here or wait for me! Just run."

Butayna and Hafsa grabbed each other's hands. A man's guttural scream echoed at their backs. The riders who bore the insignia of the Sultanate closed in on them. Yusuf led them. The noonday sun glinted off his golden helmet.

"Butayna! Butayna!"

She sobbed in relief as he reached her. Flecks of crimson covered his face and hands. He slowed his horse and leapt from it. They clutched each other before he hefted her up and on to the back of his mount.

She pointed across the encampment. "Yusuf, find Jawla!"

"I am here, my Sultana!"

The handmaiden ran to them. She cupped her waist. Blood seeped between her fingers. Yusuf signaled to the two riders closest to him, who each hauled one of Butayna's servants in front of him in the saddle. Jawla grunted and pressed her hand to her side.

Butayna asked, "Are you hurt badly?"

"Just a dagger wound, my Sultana, it's not deep. I turned my attacker's weapon on him and stabbed him in the throat."

One of the officers urged, "We must flee. They have reinforcements!"

Yusuf mounted up behind Butayna and spurred his horse. "We ride for Marballa! They are plundering our northern camp as well. We have to leave everything behind."

A jarred breath hitched inside Butayna's chest. She clutched his wrist. "The Christians attacked the camp without any warning. They slaughtered Fatima and others. Is Abu'l-Hasan Ali alive? Does he know what happened to his wives and children?"

Yusuf whispered against her ear, "Do not think of the battle now! It is over. You and I are safe. That is all that matters."

She nodded, desperate to believe him, but how could she ever forget all she had seen?

***

Granada, Andalusia
April 28, AD 1341 / 11 Dhu al-Qaʿda 741 AH / 10th of Iyar, 5101

Butayna stood in front of her window, which faced the south and overlooked the courtyard where the army gathered below. Leila sat on her bed and read verses of *al-Qur'an* to Muhammad, who was much more interested in Ramadi's antics. The cat scuttled back and forth, chasing some imaginary mouse. Muhammad's laughter pealed in the chamber.

"My little prince is content today. What of his mother?"

Butayna swerved when Yusuf's voice alerted her. The silk of her favorite *rida* swirled around her feet. Her husband entered the room, attired in black silk and boots, chainmail over his tunic. She bowed her head, as did Leila and Jawla. He set aside his gold helmet covered in swirling script on Butayna's table and halted beside her. When his light kiss landed on her brow, she closed her eyes and savored his familiar touch. To think, four years ago she would have shied away from him in trepidation. Now, no matter how many times he held her, she craved closeness to him and the reassuring warmth of his presence.

She sighed. "I am well, if only a little worried for you."

He fingered the folds of the blanket she clutched against her and revealed their daughter's miniature features. The child with a thick head of reddish-brown locks entered the world on Easter Sunday twenty days ago, after a labor twice as long as Butayna endured with Muhammad. Yusuf named her Aisha for the great-grandmother he never knew, a woman whom he said had influenced his grandmother's love for her family.

Yusuf nuzzled Butayna's hair. "I hate to leave you, her and our Muhammad."

She leaned against him. "I know why you must. King Alfonso of Castilla-Leon is a crafty adversary. First, he made you think he would attack at Malaga and then threatened north of this city instead. He intends to starve the people of *al-Qal'at ibn Zaide* by burning their wheat fields. Nothing can stop his bombardment of their walls, except your army. The town's residents have no one else to defend them against such aggression, but you. Go to them. Save them. I will be here when you return, as will our children."

Leila stood. "Yusuf, wait! Before you go, Muhammad has something to demonstrate for you."

She lifted the toddler on the carpeted floor. "Show your father just as we practiced."

Muhammad gaped at his aunt and then he executed a perfect little bow. While Leila clapped, Yusuf crouched before his son. He tousled his hair.

"You did that well, just as a prince should. Be good for your aunt or I shall hear otherwise."

Leila's dark brow lines knitted together and the little crease appeared that always betrayed her annoyance. "The little prince is always good, Yusuf. Why would you ever have cause to worry?"

Stiff-backed, she bent and lifted Muhammad on to the bed again.

Yusuf put up his hands in surrender. "I never meant to suggest it, dear sister."

Leila pursed her lips and rolled her eyes.

Butayna shook her head and walked with Yusuf to the door. He donned his helmet and looked at her. A warrior's eyes did not harden on either side of the noseguard. Those of her beloved husband glittered in the recesses of the helmet. Lover, husband, father, Sultan, the prince of the faithful and a majestic warrior, he meant so much more to her than all the titles he bore.

He murmured against her lips, "Wherever I am, I think of you and our children, Butayna. I shall return to your side as soon as I can. Think of me when I am gone."

"You are never far from mind or heart, my love."

When she kissed him, his fingers cupped her nape. They drew apart and he rubbed the tip of his nose against hers, before he turned on his heel and left her.

At the end of the hall, Maryam waited in the doorway of her chamber. With the birth of her second child, a daughter named Fatima for Yusuf's beloved grandmother, Maryam became the only *kadin*. The arrival of a third child one month after Yusuf's return softened the defeat at the *arroyo* del Salado. Maryam held the baby, Qays, up for his father's inspection while the wet-nurse carried the daughter Fatima.

Maryam's first son, black-haired Ismail huddled beside her in the doorway and clutched her leg. He shrank away even as his father approached.

Yusuf crouched and held out his hands. "Won't you kiss your father goodbye?"

Ismail whimpered and pressed his face to his mother's leg. Although she encouraged him to embrace Yusuf, the toddler clung to her even more desperately and refused to touch his father.

Maryam's face reddened. "Stop this foolishness this instant!"

Yusuf stood. "Don't upset him further. He does not recognize me in the armor. Come, I cannot linger."

He tipped her chin up and kissed her mouth. She pressed up against him, her hand on his cheek. Maryam's baby squirmed, trapped between his parents.

Yusuf laughed against Maryam's mouth and drew back. "Such passion."

"Please, beloved. Don't leave without a proper farewell to your children. Try again."

Despite Maryam's coaxing and pleas, the young children rejected her attempts. Fatima clung to her nurse and bawled even more than her elder brother did. Yusuf shook his head.

Butayna's lips quivered as she stifled a smirk. Her son had been unafraid. Yusuf went down the steps and disappeared from view. Then Maryam stared down the hall with a deep scowl at Butayna. The blood drained from her face. Butayna lifted her chin and returned to her window.

She did not have to wait long. Bilal held the reins of Yusuf's dappled gray mount. Soon, Yusuf appeared in the courtyard. Hafsa, who stood silent and unobtrusive between the window and Butayna's chests along the western wall, now opened each *shimasas*. Butayna cradled Aisha close to her and peered into the courtyard. When Yusuf sat in the saddle, he directed his men toward *al-Quasaba* with a wave of his hand. Behind him, hammers and chisels echoed as workmen opened up the walls to include a new southern gate.

Yusuf looked to her window. Her smile greeted him. He bobbed his head and she raised a hand in farewell. He wheeled his horse around and rode out of *al-Qal'at al-Hamra*.

Leila asked, "Have you told him of what the midwife said?"

Butayna blinked back sudden tears. "I have not."

"You would not be so foolish as to risk another pregnancy!" When Butayna gave her a sharp-eyed glance, Leila bowed her head. "I am not calling you a fool, Butayna. I meant you should not take avoidable risks."

"I am aware of what I should and should not do. I remember the midwife's admonitions. She fears another child will kill me. Yusuf has greater difficulties ahead of him without knowing of my disappointment. When he returns from *al-Qal'at ibn Zaide*, I will tell him the news."

Chapter 19
The Blood Bond

Sultana Butayna

Granada, Andalusia
August 13 - 20, AD 1346 / 23 Rabi ath-Thani – 1 Jumada l-Ula
747 AH / 24th of Av - 1st of Elul, 5106

At midday, Butayna stood beside a pillar of the southern pavilion the *Jannat al-'Arif*. Jawla accompanied her while she awaited Yusuf's arrival. He walked from *al-Qal'at al-Hamra* in the company of Ibn al-Khatib and his hunched chief *wazir*, Ali ibn al-Jayyab. The old man had served for over fifty years, from his days as a *talib*, an apprentice to the *Diwan al-Insha* during the reign of Yusuf's great-grandfather Muhammad II. After the disappointment at the *arroyo* del Salado, Yusuf had stripped Ridwan of his powers and imprisoned him for almost a year. In the meantime, Yusuf raised another short-lived appointee to the post, before he granted it to Ali ibn al-Jayyab again. Now Ridwan served on the council of ministers again.

Butayna believed her husband blamed Ridwan unduly for the failures in the battle, for the *hajib* also occupied the official post as leader of the army in Yusuf's stead. How could Ridwan bear the responsibility when he had ceded command to Yusuf on the battlefield?

She commented. "My Sultan looks tired. Does he have so much cause for worry these days?"

Jawla bowed her head. "If the Sultana will forgive an impudent observation from a mere servant, the Sultan sees enemies everywhere. His mind is troubled. My Sultana could always comfort him."

"In the past. Not now."

When Yusuf neared her, Butayna arranged the folds of the turquoise *rida*. She tugged her *hijab* closer to her mouth and bowed when the men stopped a scant distance away.

Ali ibn al-Jayyab bowed, stiff-backed. "... It is not what my noble Sultan would wish to hear, but it is the truth. I have not served the Nasrids since the time of your venerable ancestor the Lawgiver only to offer false hope now."

Yusuf spoke to his chief minister in a sharp tone. "I don't want excuses from my ministers! I need answers! Why do I employ spies to keep us apprised on Abu'l-Hasan Ali's actions along the coast if they can tell us nothing? The Sultan of al-Maghrib el-Aska has constructed new galleys. Eighty or ninety ships! Where will he deploy them? The Castillan admirals think he will sail for al-Tunisiyah. Others say he means to destroy Alicante. Find out!"

Butayna gasped. Alicante, home of the merchant family her father once chose for her. Ten years after the betrothal broken by her captivity, she recalled their name, Navas y Montilla. Were they still there? Had her betrothed married? Did his relations have any sense of the danger ahead of them? If eighty or ninety galleys attacked, how would the people defend themselves? She suspected many more captives might flood the slave markets of her al-Maghrib el-Aska and her husband's Sultanate, if Abu'l-Hasan Ali's ships reached the coast of Valencia.

Yusuf exchanged a few final words with his chief minister and personal secretary before he dismissed them. When he reached Butayna, he waved away Jawla as well. "Leave us. I wish to speak to my wife alone."

The servant bowed and left them. When she was gone, Yusuf tugged Butayna against him.

"I am wearied by responsibility. I would seek my bed and the comfort of the rest of the evening with you in my arms. Then I would be content."

She held him and wished she might ease his burdens. Her arms wound about his trim waist and she rubbed her cheek against his prickly beard. "You cannot forget your own plans. You have invited Ismail here. Your brother will join us at dinner."

He heaved a sigh. "*Nam*, there is the matter of Ismail. I had forgotten, or perhaps I wished to forget."

His obvious fatigue concerned her. Were the burdens of his position so grave? Butayna had never attended his court to know. In two months, his family would celebrate his twenty-ninth birthday. Nine years had passed since she came to the city. She celebrated her twenty-fourth birthday weeks ago with a garden party at the *Jannat al-'Arif*. Among her gifts, Muhammad gave her a wooden carving of an almond tree. He had inherited his father's talent with his hands.

She whispered against Yusuf's shoulder. "What ails you so, my love? Is there trouble with the *Diwan al-Insha* or outside the Sultanate?"

"*La*, it is other news you will not like."

He raised his head, but she held on to him. The announcement would not surprise her. She had expected it for weeks.

"Some think I should marry Maryam and make her my second wife."

She released a ragged breath. Despite her anticipation, the words still set her blood afire. "Who believes this? Maryam? Your mother? Why should you listen to their counsel on a choice of your own making?"

"Oh, Butayna, do not start this old argument again! There is no conspiracy between my mother and Maryam to usurp Muhammad's position."

"I do not intend to argue with you, my love. I will hold to my beliefs. You have yours. I expected you would marry Maryam this year. After all, she has given you six children with the birth of her daughter last month, while I am the mother of just two."

When her hands fell listless at her side, he clutched them. "I love our children. Their number does not matter."

"Do not tell me of the wishes of others. Speak your heart instead. Do you want to marry Maryam? You have no obligation to wed her. She could remain your *kadin* forever, as the beauteous Nur al-Sabah did with your great-grandfather. Do you love Maryam at last?"

Her scalp prickled while the silence between them lengthened. Her mind rushed headlong into myriad thoughts. Had Maryam replaced her in Yusuf's heart? Would one of her sons take Muhammad's throne? The Moors did not hold to the concept of primogeniture, where the firstborn son alone inherited. Any of Yusuf's sons might succeed him.

"Are you asking for my consent, my blessing?" She removed her fingers from his grasp.

The cords in his neck flexed. "I do not need it."

Her cheeks burned. "*La,* you do not, but you want it. You want me to accept your marriage to Maryam. Well, I will not. I will never accept her place in your life. I cannot alter your decision, I cannot ask you to dismiss her, but the one thing I can do is reject any attempt to make me accept her. Do as you like. My sentiments toward her will never change."

"You are too hard, wife, harder than marble."

"When Maryam blamed me for her children's deaths, when she forfeited a chance at escape, when she abandoned our years of friendship, I learned to rely upon myself, no one else. I had no choice except to harden my heart lest Maryam betray me again."

He shook his head. "I guessed as much. She rejected you, not the reverse."

"She's lied to you about our history, Yusuf, but I suppose none of it matters now when you have decided to wed her. She once told me she would bind you with the love of your children. She has succeeded."

He grasped her arms. "Do you believe I am unable to love both of you?"

"I do not doubt your capacity for love, only whether Maryam deserves it."

A desperate screech pierced the air and made them look toward the garden together. Muhammad scrambled down the eastern aisle, waving a cloth doll.

Aisha chased him, her tear-streaked face flushed. Long braids streamed behind her back. "Give it to me! It's mine."

"Catch me first," Muhammad taunted.

Yusuf grabbed him by the sleeve of his *shaya*. "What do you think you're doing?"

Aisha wailed, "He stole my doll, Father! I want it back, Muhammad."

She kicked at her brother's shin, while Muhammad held the doll just out of reach. Butayna grasped her daughter's wrists, while Yusuf shook their son.

"Is this how you think a Nasrid prince should behave? Teasing little girls."

Muhammad looked up at his father, wide-eyed. "I just joked with her, Father."

"What prince takes joy in mocking others? Especially his own sister. You are her elder brother. Whom shall she look to for protection and guidance when I am gone if not you?"

Muhammad's soft brown gaze watered. "I'm sorry...."

Butayna laid a hand on Yusuf's shoulder. "It was simple child's play, my love."

He shrugged her off. "Be quiet! The Sultan speaks. I am educating our son on the duties of a royal prince, of one who should expect to inherit responsibility for his household! Now, Muhammad, give the doll back and apologize to your sister. At once."

The boy held out the toy to his sister. "I'm sorry, Aisha. Take it."

Yusuf pointed to the family quarters to the east. "Go to your mother's chamber, now. Study *al-Qur'an* as you should be doing, not robbing little girls of their dolls."

Their son sniffled and bowed his head. He walked at first and then ran into the building.

Aisha tugged her mother's *rida*. "Why is Father so angry with Muhammad?"

Butayna bent and kissed her six-year old on the forehead. "I'll see you inside my chamber. Return to your play with your doll."

Aisha bowed before both her parents and followed Muhammad's footsteps. When she disappeared into the building, Butayna crossed her arms over her chest. "If it had been Ismail or Qays who teased Aisha, would you have been as harsh?"

"Of course I would have!" Yusuf raked a hand over his hair.

"I don't believe you. You single out Muhammad for criticism at every turn. You always find fault with him." He grabbed her arms again, but she slapped his hands away. "Do not tell me you treat Maryam's sons in the same manner! Muhammad sees your favoritism of his brothers as I do."

"Then neither of you understands the burden my eldest son faces."

"There is nothing to understand! He's just a boy!" She stomped across the marble.

"Where are you going? I did not give you leave to walk away from me, Butayna."

She maintained her furious strides. "Then send for your executioner! This is one instance where I do not care about your commands! I am going to comfort our son. Your man will find me in my bedchamber awaiting his blade."

Despite Yusuf's protests, she entered the building and went into her room. Aisha sat beside the window and trilled a meaningless song, while she brushed her doll's hair. Muhammad sat at the foot of the bed, *al-Qur'an* open on his lap. Butayna joined him and drew her knees up to her chest.

Her son raked a hand across his wet face. "Why doesn't Father like me?"

She draped her arm over his rounded shoulders. "Your father loves you, Muhammad."

He sniffled. "He doesn't show it."

She leaned toward him and kissed his curls. "He does, my lion. You must believe he does."

Her words were hollow. No wonder Muhammad turned to her and buried his face in her neck. She crooned to him.

Aisha stood before them. "Don't cry, brother. You can have the doll back if you want."

Butayna subdued her laughter and tugged her daughter on to her lap. She kissed her head and Muhammad's own. "My dear, sweet children. I am blessed to have you both."

***

During the evening, Butayna sat at dinner in Yusuf's chamber. Around the low table, he gathered Ismail, Leila, and Maryam for a meal. Safa declined the invitation and pleaded an ache in her head as the cause. Butayna did not miss her. Despite Maryam's presence, she relished an opportunity for the interaction of Yusuf with his family. They ate and talked of Ismail's good fortune with the redheaded daughter his *kadin* had borne him last spring. He brought both of his children and his favorite to the capital, but they remained at his house while he dined.

Near the conclusion of the meal, Leila patted Ismail's arm. "You must let me visit with your concubine tomorrow, dear brother, so I may see this newest niece of mine."

Ismail sniggered. "You wish to inspect my *kadin* and judge if she is worthy of a Nasrid prince, sweet sister."

Leila licked honey from her fingertips. "That too!"

Yusuf clasped his fingers together and placed his elbows on the table. He set his pointed chin upon his hands. His dark gaze lingered on Maryam's lush mouth, stained red with juicy pomegranates. "It is a delight to watch you eat. You are as enamored of food as you are of life."

Under the table, Butayna flexed her fingers. Yusuf's fascination with Maryam disturbed and embittered her, but she refused to let the mood turn sour.

Instead, she asked, "Is everything well at Wadi-Ash, Prince Ismail?"

He answered, "It is, my Sultana. How long have we known each other? Don't you think we should dispense with the titles by now?"

Yusuf said, "Butayna is a proper Moorish woman. She knows even this gathering does not follow our customs and behaves as she should."

Leila rolled her eyes and reached for another date ball. A eunuch begged entry. The slave bent and spoke to his master, who smiled and nodded.

Yusuf beamed at his guests. "My children are ready for bed. It is my custom to bless them each night before they sleep. Indulge me."

The pair of royal governesses entered with their charges. The young Sultanas Fatima, Khadija, and Shams rushed past them and launched themselves at Yusuf. He laughed and kissed each of their dark heads, so like their mother's own. One of the governesses carried the baby, Mumina. Three of Maryam's daughters resembled her, not their father, except for the eldest. Fatima favored her grandmother Safa, rather than her namesake. Butayna thought the resemblance a shame for the girl.

"Good night, my children. Go to bed when your governesses tell you. Do not stay awake all night, whispering to each other as you often do."

Aisha entered the room and placed a light peck on Butayna's cheek first. "Will you sing to me, *Ummi*?"

Butayna brushed thick locks away from her child's face. "Not tonight, my sweet girl."

"Oh! I never have bad dreams when you sing me to sleep. Please?"

"Aisha, I can't, but I'll be there when you wake in the morning. God's blessings upon you."

Aisha pouted and then skipped to her father's side. Yusuf hugged and kissed her as he had done with her sisters. "I love you, sweet girl."

"I love you too, Father, this much!" She wrapped her lean arms around his neck and squeezed until he groaned and begged for mercy. Whatever the cause of his reticence with Muhammad, at least Yusuf showed no reserve with his beloved Aisha.

She drew back once Ismail and Qays entered the room. Maryam sat up a little straighter as her sons strode to their father's side and bowed. Yusuf blessed them both. Then Muhammad approached with his gaze downcast. He executed a perfect bow, if a little stiff.

Ismail chuckled. "So formal! He reminds me of Yusuf at that age."

Yusuf blessed his eldest and asked, "Did you study *al-Qur'an* as I commanded, my son?"

"I did, all afternoon, Father. I want you to be proud of me when you hear all I have remembered."

"We shall see tomorrow. You will recite the *suras* you have learned after public audience."

"*Nam*, Father. As you wish."

Butayna nibbled her lower lip. "You forget Muhammad has his riding lessons with me at the same time."

Yusuf glanced at her. "What do you think I deem of greater importance, Butayna? He has started observing prayers, a duty for all Muslims. How else is he to learn *al-Qur'an* unless he studies?"

She clenched her jaws and nodded. How dare he speak to her as he would one of their children! She would let him know her opinion of his tone later in private.

Maryam reached for another slice of pomegranate and savored the fruit with a smirk on her face. "Pray forgive her, my Sultan. You cannot expect Butayna, as a Christian, would perceive the importance of Prince Muhammad's studies. The *dhimmi* cannot know the duty we undertake as true believers."

Yusuf nodded. "I suppose you are right, Maryam."

Leila speared a slice of pomegranate with her dinner knife and devoured it. She looked askance at Butayna, who shook her head. Leila growled low in her throat, but when Yusuf glanced at her, Butayna coughed and drew his attention.

"Do you need some water?"

"I am well. Thank you for your concern, my Sultan." Then she said, "Your *kadin*'s words surprise me. She discarded the Jewish faith of her forefathers with ease, while I cling to the Christian God. She uses the words 'true believers.' Those who trust in their religion can never abandon it, for any reason, no matter how advantageous."

Maryam observed, "In our youth, you did not cling to your idolatrous faith so much as now."

"After the experience of captivity and slavery, my mind can encompass devotion and sacrifice. One cannot remain a Christian in Muslim lands without some understanding of the power of faith. Likewise, I am satisfied with Muhammad's dedication to Islam. My son is dutiful in his studies, unlike others who pretend to espouse a certain religion for the sake of appearance alone. I do not have to become a Muslim to respect the tenets of Islam or the commitment of true believers."

Ismail slapped the table. "My Sultana, your wisdom, and honor are beyond compare! Brother, you have found a treasure in your wife."

Yusuf offered him a tight-lipped smile before his stare met Butayna's own. "I am blessed to call her mine, a fact I remember each day."

Maryam's grin did not fade, but her eyes narrowed to slits.

Yusuf dismissed his children and their caretakers for the night. The eunuch also withdrew from the room, bowing as he went. Butayna stared at Muhammad's rigid, straight back until he disappeared from view.

"My eldest son is lucky to have brothers as I did," Yusuf murmured. "Faithful brothers, whom I never thought would betray me."

His pronouncement drew everyone's stare to him.

Ismail sputtered, "It sounds as if you think you are no longer so fortunate."

Yusuf's brows knitted. "Am I? Did you think you could hide your treason with the Marinids forever?"

Butayna covered her mouth with her hand, while Leila looked from Yusuf to Ismail.

"It cannot be true! Yusuf, you are wrong. None of us would ever betray you."

He did not listen. "Men, seize him!"

The captain of the guards and some of his men rushed into the room. They grabbed Prince Ismail's arms and hauled him up. He did not struggle against them. Instead, he regarded Yusuf in silence.

Leila wept and clapped her hands to her head. "Yusuf! By the Prophet's beard, what are you doing?"

"Our brother has plotted with the Marinids to steal my throne. Ismail would take my place. My spies in Abu'l-Hasan Ali's court brought proof in the form of letters to the *Diwan*."

Leila turned to Ismail. "Speak for yourself. Tell him it is not true. It can't be!"

Ismail muttered, "Our brother knows me, Leila. He knows my capabilities, or at least, he used to know them. If he wishes to believe I am guilty, nothing I can say will change his mind."

Leila clutched the hem of his *sarawil*. "That is no answer. Please. These letters must be forgeries. Ask him to show them to you and we can see the proof...."

She stopped speaking and peered outside. In the doorway, a russet-haired woman huddled with a child in her arms. Both whimpered.

Yusuf shook his head. "Take them all to *al-Quasaba*, until I decide their fates."

Leila batted her breast and wailed. Butayna hugged her and whispered words of comfort, while she looked across the table at Yusuf. She could not reconcile her loving husband with the stalwart Sultan who sat in his place, his lips compressed, his stare inscrutable, while Ismail's *kadin* screamed.

"*La! La!* Not my daughter, too. Please! Please! Not my daughter. She is just a baby, she'll die in the dungeon. Mercy for my child, my Sultan, mercy!"

***

Soon afterward, Yusuf rose from the table and signaled an end to the meal. Maryam bowed before Yusuf, though he did not acknowledge her display with more than a little nod. While unobtrusive servants removed the remnants in silence, Butayna ordered one of Yusuf's guards to fetch Ifrit. The slave guided her tear-stricken mistress from the room. Leila's sobs resonated through the harem's walls.

"Butayna, I am tired. You may seek your rest." Yusuf waved her toward the door and turned to his bedchamber.

She stood and clasped her hands together. "*La,* husband. You will not get rid of me so soon."

He swerved to her. "What did you say to me? Did you just defy another command from your Sultan? Lest you forget, Butayna, I am master of this place and all within. If I tell you to go, you should go!"

She crossed the carpet and stood just in front of him. "You cannot dismiss me as you have done with the others. Lest you forget, I am no longer some poor *jarya* whom you can order about from here to there and back again! I am your wife, your Sultana. On the day you granted my freedom, you said my will was mine again."

"When I freed and married you, I did not grant you the will to disobey me!"

"*La*, only to love you, to sit by your side and be of comfort to you. If you think I shall ever forsake those duties, you are wrong. I will never abandon you, even when you think you do not want me. It is in such moments of crisis as these where you may need me the most."

He raked a hand over his lean features. "I am in no mood to bandy words with you tonight. Say what you must."

"We have to talk of what happened here. How long have you known of Ismail's betrayal. Why have you not shared such concerns with me until now?"

"You care so much for my brother, eh?" His gaze narrowed beneath a crinkled brow. "You have always been so solicitous with him over these years. Must I wonder at your loyalty as well?"

She waved a hand through the air. "Do cease this trivial, stupid jealousy of yours! You are my heart's desire! Next, you shall accuse me of wanting Leila as well as your brother Ismail. Both ideas are preposterous, as you already know. If I am concerned for Ismail, it is because I can never forget his goodwill when I first entered this harem. When your chief eunuch brought me here in chains, your brother greeted me with the peace of God. Later, he enlightened my knowledge of your family and explained a little of the observance of Ramadan. The first acts of kindness anyone showed me upon my arrival here."

After a loud groan, Yusuf tugged her into his arms. She burrowed her face in his neck and kissed him.

"Oh my love, I know how your heart must have cleaved in two with the knowledge of Ismail's actions. I was never so fortunate to have siblings, but when I first witnessed the bond between you, your brother, and your sisters, I envied the obvious closeness. I cannot fathom why Ismail has betrayed you now. The proof is undeniable?"

"There were details in the letters, which pertained to my court and events within the Christian kingdoms, information I shared with no one else, but Ismail as a trusted brother. It is not common knowledge, but Alfonso of Castilla-Leon intends to free the last of Abu'l-Hasan Ali's daughters whom he captured six years ago."

Butayna gasped. "I had no idea some of the Sultan's relatives survived the slaughter."

"The captives included Abu Umar Tashufin, one of the Sultan's sons. The Marinids discovered Alfonso ordered the surviving members bound with ropes and held in a *corral* in Sevilla. They did not wish anyone to know how the Sultan has pleaded for the lives of his children, for his adversaries in al-Tunisiyah would mock him for crying over his daughters. The Sultan is angered and embarrassed even before me, a man with daughters."

"Could Ismail have told this news to someone else whom he trusted? A person who betrayed Ismail's awareness of the truth to Abu'l-Hasan Ali's court in Fés el-Jedid?"

When Yusuf raised his head and peered at her, she rolled her eyes. "Just because I do not attend court, it does not mean I'm unaware of the capital of al-Maghrib el-Aska. These letters, are they in Ismail's handwriting? Could someone have forged them?"

"For what purpose, Butayna?"

"To weaken the ties I have spoken of, the blood bond between you and Ismail! You rely upon your family. Your brother, uncle, and cousins have all served you as governors. They are your pillars of strength and support. Those who seek to undermine you would need to remove those supports. If your enemies sowed dissent between brothers, your Sultanate would crumble. Can you not speak to Ismail and hear what he has to say? Find the truth before you condemn him. You shared a father and lives together as boys. Do not do something you may regret."

He nuzzled her forehead. "I know you counsel me with good reason, but I cannot choose either direction, to seek answers from my brother or leave him to his fate. My mind is too muddled."

"At least, Yusuf, do not leave your brother's child to wallow in the dank darkness of *al-Quasaba*. I have heard the screams and pleas from the prisoners and captives held inside those cells. They are not fit for a child or her mother, even if the woman is a slave."

"Then I shall send Ismail's *kadin* and her child to the fortress at Shalabuniya in the morning. We Nasrids have a tradition of keeping our troublesome relatives at the site. My grandfather Faraj died there after my father imprisoned him."

His wry observation did not diffuse her anxiety for him. She hugged him close. "If only I could do something to ease your burdens."

Yusuf drew back and clutched her hand. "Sing to me until I sleep, as you used to do in the early days."

She followed him to the bed. Atop its soft, silken comfort, she stretched outside beside him. He pillowed his head on her breasts, while she stroked his nape and sang to him until he surrendered his troubles in a deep slumber.

***

Maryam

One week after Yusuf arranged for the arrest of his brother, he announced the departure from the *Jannat al-'Arif*. The season would end soon, as would Maryam's time in the summer palace. She relished it, with the declaration of Yusuf's intent to marry her once they returned to *al-Qal'at al-Hamra*. At last, she would attain the power Butayna held.

In the usual manner, Sultana Safa organized a final garden party, which all the women attended, even Leila and Butayna. Like Maryam, she brought her children with her. For some reason, she also brought her horrid cat, which hissed and snarled at Maryam and Safa twice in the evening before it wandered off into the bushes.

Muhammad hovered beside his mother, his elbows pressed against her lap. She looked down at him with a gaze filled with the pride and devotion reserved for her precious prince, as if she alone possessed the capacity for a mother's love.

Maryam nuzzled Fatima's forehead and offered her sweet girl another date cookie slathered in honey. Fatima crammed the dessert into her mouth and demanded more.

"You have had enough."

Fatima's whine erupted. Most of the women seated in a circle rolled their eyes at her tantrum. Butayna raised her head for a moment, but her expression never altered. She returned her attention to her fat-faced son.

Maryam ignored the others and placed another cookie in her girl's grasp. "This is the last one. You cannot indulge too much."

Her daughter clutched her ill-gotten prize. "But why, *Ummi?* Date cookies are my favorite."

Fatima's puffed cheeks and pursed lips already mirrored the bloated features of Yusuf's mother. Maryam shuddered at the thought of the girl's appearance becoming even more her grandmother's own.

With a light peck on the child's brow, Maryam bent and whispered in her ear, "If you ate too many cookies, you would be fatter than Prince Muhammad. You don't want that, do you?"

The little girl shared a giggle with her mother.

Across the sunlit garden, Butayna's boy asked, "*Ummi*, why don't you ever pray with us? When we go to the mosque, you never come with us. The *imam* says all believers must pray five times a day. Are you not a believer?"

Maryam buried her nose in Fatima's dark curls and lowered her gaze, but not so much as to miss how crimson stains blossomed and billowed across Butayna's narrow features. Let her find an answer for her son now!

While Butayna hesitated, Sultana Safa lifted the porcelain cup to her lips and sipped a mouthful of *nakhwa* before she spoke. "Dear boy, your mother is a dutiful Christian. I have always wondered what sort of mother would cling to a false religion, one her husband and children do not share. If Paradise lies at a mother's feet, what of the mother separated from her offspring?"

"We have never been separated! You know that," Butayna insisted. "Yusuf permitted me to see my children every day and Leila has never kept them from me."

Safa continued as if Butayna had not spoken. "How should any of us who have known the joys and travails of motherhood consider one who abandons her boy to the care of others? Poor child, you are little better than an orphan. Your selfish mother would not relinquish her faith, even for your tender sake."

Butayna draped an arm around her son's shoulder and pressed him against her. She glared at Safa for a moment before her fingers cupped Muhammad's plump cheek. "That's not true! My lion, you must know I have never abandoned you. I never could, especially not for my religion. It is true your aunt Leila has raised you because I chose to remain a Christian."

Safa chuckled. "So, your faith did matter more than your son! Deny it, like the liar you are."

Muhammad drew back from his mother. His wide-eyed gaze glistened like morning dew. Maryam ducked her head for a moment and strove against a smile.

Butayna continued, "My son, you must believe me. I wanted to raise you and your sister within my household. The laws of the Sultanate forbid me from doing so, because I remained a Christian after marriage. It does not mean I have loved you or Aisha any less."

A little sob hiccupped in his throat. As red-faced as his idiotic mother, he questioned, "If Father is the lawgiver, why couldn't he make new laws to let Aisha and me stay with you?"

She framed his wet face in her hands. "Nothing is ever so easy, my lion. You will understand when you are older."

He wrenched from her grasp and stomped his feet. "I don't want to understand when I'm older. Teach me now!"

Butayna sighed and clasped her hands in her lap. "In my heart, I knew if I tried to surrender to Islam, my outward devotion would have been a lie. I shall always be a Christian in my soul. Better to be true to myself than tell falsehoods each day, kneeling before God and mimicking the devotion to a faith, which meant little to me."

Her gaze flicked to Maryam, who lifted her chin.

Then her rival returned her attention to the boy. "Christianity is not a false religion, as your grandmother would have you believe."

When Safa colored at the casual reference, Maryam bit the inside of her cheek and stifled a laugh. Where she had anticipated a dull, dreary time, mired in the presence of those whom she hated most, an afternoon's delight unfolded.

Butayna added, "Christians are a people of deep conviction, much like Muslims. We serve the same God, but whereas He is called Allah—"

Safa clanged her cup on the cedar wood table. The liquid inside sloshed and spilled over the rim. Nazhun scrambled and dabbed at it with linen, while her mistress stood. "You would not dare! You will not preach the idolatry of your prophet Jesus!"

"Nor would I let you defame me or my religion before my son! You go too far, Safa!" She rose and stared down the *Umm al-Walad*.

The fire in the depths of Butayna's gaze was unlike any Maryam ever beheld in the days since they came to live among the Moors.

Safa's bright gaze matched Butayna's own. "My son plucked you out of obscurity in the harem, because Leila pushed you into his bed!" She darted a heated glance at her rival before she continued, "By the Grace of Allah, you conceived a son and Yusuf honored you by calling you his Sultana. You could never be a Sultana. You do not possess the pride or heritage! No true Sultana of the Nasrids would have let anyone take her child from her arms and allowed another to supersede the role of mother. Ignorant child! You think to match wits with those who have played this game for years before you were born. You don't know, but you have already lost!"

"Life is no game, with people as your pawns to do with as you please! Your many years have addled your mind." Despite Safa's outraged gasp, she continued, "Yusuf made me his Sultana because he loved me. He also loved the child I carried before our bright boy entered the world. You can spread as many vicious lies about me as you wish, Safa, but you shall never force me from Yusuf's side. I am not afraid of you."

Safa clenched her fists. A swift kick aimed at Nazhun sent the slave on a hurried path out of her reach. Sandwiched between the women, Muhammad stared at both.

"Do not test me, girl!"

"You grow forgetful in your old age. I am no girl. A woman married your son. A woman bore his children. Perhaps you should not try with me, Safa!"

Just when the argument reached a crescendo, Leila interfered.

She reached for Butayna's hand and drew her back down to the stone bench again. "Hush, please, dearest Butayna. Be still. Do not let her goad you into idle threats you may come to regret. My brother would be displeased to hear of this argument. You have long known Safa's misguided views of you. They shall never change. It is an old argument, one you cannot win."

Butayna demanded, "Who would tell Yusuf we disturbed the peace of his home?"

Leila made no reply. Instead, she lifted her gaze and looked in Maryam's direction. Butayna followed Leila's stare, until she and Maryam regarded each other again.

With a sniff, Maryam turned to the platter of date cookies. She reached for one and bit into it. Sweet honey flooded her tongue. She licked her lips.

***

In the early morning, Maryam walked beside Safa as they went to the *hammam* together. A piercing cry shattered the stillness of dawn, followed by wails of despair. When both Sultanas halted with their slaves, Nazhun stumbled against her mistress. Safa turned and struck the dwarf across her face.

"Clumsy oaf! Go see what has happened," Safa ordered.

Maryam waited with her until the slave's swift return. "The Sultana Butayna is crying. She found her cat dead."

Maryam and Safa glanced at each other, before Maryam remarked, "A treasured pet for many years, but Butayna can always choose another."

"The Sultana thinks the cat was murdered, its neck twisted."

Safa sighed and yawned behind her hands, before she resumed the route to the bath. "All old cats die."

"Indeed, they do." Maryam fell into step behind Safa.

Chapter 20
The Price of Power

Sultana Butayna

Granada, Andalusia
May 19 – June 4, AD 1348 / 19 Safar – 6 Rabi al-Awwal 749 AH
/ 21st of Sivan - 7th of Tammuz, 5108

Butayna fled the court after the conclusion of public audience. Curious guardsmen observed her escape from the tower and out into the garden. The folds of her olive green *hijab* obscured her vision as much as the tears. She panted while she raced eastward and into the confines of the harem.

Jawla and Hafsa called after her. "My Sultana! Stop!"

She ignored them and darted into the southern hall. "Leila!" Her voice rang to the honeycombed ceiling.

She went out into the courtyard and asked a guard, "Where is the Sultana Leila?"

He averted his gaze. "In her chamber, my honored Sultana."

She ripped off her veil, reentered the hall, and raced up the narrow steps. She rushed through the doorway, past the alcoves and into the bedroom.

Leila moaned as Ifrit's hold tightened, both women naked from the waist up with their breasts pressed against each other, the slave's fingers lost in her mistress' curls. Seated on Leila's bed, low, almost desperate sounds issued between each feverish kiss.

Butayna backed away from the scene and bumped against a table near the entrance. The glass vase atop the wooden surface shattered into large shards.

The lovers turned as one. The slave scrambled to stand and attempted to cover her breasts with her hands. "My Sultana! What are you doing here?"

Leila sat unabashed as her chest rose and fell. "Butayna knows it is rude to burst into anyone's chambers unannounced. She is at fault here, my Ifrit. You should not feel ashamed."

Butayna shook her head. "I did not know...."

"How could you?" Leila chuckled. "It is not as if I have told the entire harem I prefer the touch of my slave to anyone else's own. Now you have embarrassed my Ifrit. Please, await me downstairs. I shall calm her before I get dressed and join you."

Dazed, Butayna turned on her heels and walked in a stupor down the stairs. Jawla and Hafsa awaited her at the base of the steps. Her mind struggled with the images she had encountered, as passionate as any she ever shared with Yusuf. Could two women share the ecstasy of a man and woman?

Jawla held Butayna's discarded veil in her hand. "Are you well, my Sultana?"

She nodded in distraction. "Please, await me in my chamber. I must speak with Leila alone."

Hafsa eyed her with a frown. "Are you sure, my Sultana?"

Butayna snapped, "Of course I am certain! Do I ever say anything I do not mean?"

Hafsa's wan cheeks colored under her mistress' scrutiny. "Forgive this humble servant, my Sultana."

With a groan, Butayna covered her face with her fingers. A dull ache throbbed at her temple. Then she reached for Hafsa's hands. "Excuse me. I know you sought to help. Please do as I have asked."

Her servants bowed and left her.

In a sea-green *rida*, which matched the shade of her eyes, Leila came down the steps. She padded across the marble in white kid slippers and waved Butayna to the carpeted alcove.

"Where are my children? Where are Muhammad and Aisha? I thought they would be with you."

"The rest of my women took them to the *rawda* for a picnic. The stories of our ancestors fascinate Aisha. As Zarru knows all of them from me, the stewardess is glad to tell her. Do not worry. Your children have never witnessed my... time with Ifrit. They remain as guileless as two children can be in a harem."

"I did not think such a thing was possible." Butayna leaned closer to Leila. "It is against your laws. What if Yusuf had discovered you instead of me?"

"That is why I must ask you to keep this secret. No one is above the laws of the Sultanate, not even the Sultan's sister. Do you understand a little of Ifrit's jealousy now?"

"What? She has been envious of me. Did she think...?"

"She did. She assumed at our first meeting in the House of Myrtles that I intended to replace her in my affections with you."

Butayna drew back. "Did you?" She remembered the spark of interest in Leila's eyes when she first appeared. Had Butayna misinterpreted her expression?

"You are a beautiful woman. I had considered it, but when I recognized Yusuf's interest, it seemed best to keep Ifrit at my side. Now, what made you come to me with such haste? Your eyes are red."

Butayna stopped gaping and answered, "I listened to the proceedings at public audience and heard the *Diwan's* reports afterward. The plague has reached the shores of the Mediterranean. No one knows the cause or can stop it. A coup has occurred in al-Maghrib el-Aska. Abu Inan Faris has claimed the throne of his father, Abu'l-Hasan Ali."

Leila rolled her eyes. "Another rebellion and another son. Perhaps the black Sultan wishes he had not sired so many children. Why should events across the sea concern you?"

"Afterward, Yusuf announced he is to be a father again before the whole court."

Leila mused, "Sultana Maryam is quite the prolific breeder. She had Zoraya just seven months ago and now she carries another child. Why should this upset you? She has given my brother seven children. Will one more make any difference to you?"

"The court astrologer says it is a boy! He has never been wrong. He predicted the births of Muhammad and Aisha. He knew the sexes of all of Maryam's children."

"Lucky guesses, Butayna."

"Nine times? He has been right nine times regarding the sex of each of Yusuf's children. If Maryam gives him another son, three sons to contend with my one.... I cannot allow it. She told me once she would bind Yusuf to her with their children. If she bears this one–"

"Muhammad will still inherit the throne."

"You can't know that."

"I do know how much care my brother offers his children. He provides for the education of his daughters and ensures his sons learn the art of chess. They study the bow and sword. They ride horses, all under their father's direction. Yusuf is attentive to Muhammad."

"You mean he is critical of him. Last week, he chided him about his stance with the bow in front of Ismail and Qays, who laughed at my son's expense. How would a boy who had not been trained in the bow beforehand know how to hold it?"

"Yusuf ensures Muhammad receive the training of one who lead armies into battle. He does not drill his other sons as he does with his eldest. While he has not revealed his intentions to me, I believe Yusuf has already chosen the heir, his son with you. Do not worry for the sons of Maryam. They shall serve their brother, or Muhammad will eliminate them. Never forget, he is a

Nasrid. We know how to deal with our enemies, even among family."

"I cannot have such blood on my son's hands."

"You would be foolish to hope they remain unblemished forever. If you do not wish to see your son take up such a burden, then you must accept it."

Butayna lifted her chin. Her heart pounded and she rubbed her breastbone. "I intend to, but I need your help."

Leila cocked her head and her lips formed a knowing grin. Her eyes sparkled in the lamplight. "Me? What could I do to aid you?"

"Don't. Not now. This is no time for your foolish games."

With a sniff, Leila examined the *henna* painted on her hands. "I cannot guess your meaning. Besides, games are for children. I have not been a child for many years."

"You know what I want. Maryam's child cannot survive."

As she spoke the words, which had swirled in her mind since the court astrologer's pronouncement, Butayna shuddered and leaned against the wall behind her. A tense knot in her stomach and the tightness contracting her throat would not turn her from this course.

Leila grasped her chin. "Speak of your wishes, do not feign intent now. I want to hear your wish from your lips."

Butayna slapped her fingers away. "Don't speak to me as you would a slave! I have not been yours to command for some time. I am Yusuf's wife. You will help me! I swear by the heavens if you do not, Yusuf shall know of this secret between you and Ifrit. I shall have my wish, the death of Maryam's child."

Leila stood and clapped her hands. "A Sultana at last!"

Butayna glowered at her. "You believe this is some farce, some jest of mine? Then you are wrong. I will tell him of your illicit love for your slave, Leila. Do not mistake me. I will do anything, even betray you, to have my way."

A bark of laughter from Leila filled the hall. "My dearest, I don't mock you. I congratulate you, for you have achieved what I long desired. The understanding of what it means to be a Sultana. To be stronger than you think you can be, to choose as you alone see fit regardless of the consequences for others. To seek advantage without guilt or doubt. It is a heady feeling, is it not? I feared you would remain frightened of your power forever."

Butayna winced. "I am well aware of how my position may change if Maryam should bear Yusuf another son."

"What of Maryam? This loss shall devastate her. You once cared for this woman. Can you rob her of a child? She already blames you for the loss of two others."

"It is all in the past, long before she attempted to usurp my position in Yusuf's heart and home with her children. Why should I be concerned for her worries or losses? She did not care for mine when she had one of her minions strangle Ramadi."

Leila nodded. "True, but a cat is not a baby, even one as cherished as Ramadi." When Butayna scowled at her again, she sighed and continued, "I have the means and method to rid Maryam of the baby, but you should be aware of the consequences of all you ask."

"I don't care as long as the child dies!"

Desperation drove Butayna. A nightmarish future evolved in her mind. Muhammad in pitched battle against his own brothers, the Sultanate mired in blood as brothers destroyed each other. If three stood against one, the odds could not remain in Muhammad's favor. To spare him, she had to eliminate one of Maryam's sons. Would it not be better to take the life of one whom Yusuf had never seen or held? The loss would pain him, but he would accept it.

"I have no means to prevent another pregnancy, another son, if you take this one from her."

"I will do what I must to secure the prospects for my son."

"Maryam could die also in the process. Is it just the child's life you would claim? Do you wish to see the mother dead?"

Kill Maryam? Butayna recoiled against the unyielding tiles at her back. She and Maryam had not been friends for over twelve years. Perhaps they never were and she imagined it all. She shook her head and remembered the last time bonds of friendship bound them, when she held Maryam's hands in the horse litter as they traveled across the *meseta* to the future Butayna once thought awaited her in Alicante.

Unbidden, the words of Juan Manuel spoken in the House of Myrtles returned to her, his admonition that she should never allow the women of Yusuf's household to change who she was in her heart and mind. How else could she survive without adaptation to ever-altered circumstances? Her son's future, his life, mattered most now.

"What is your answer?" Leila's sharp tone brought her back to the present. "I must have the words."

Butayna met her implacable stare. "Do they mean so much to you?"

"Power has its price. If you will use it, you must accept the consequences. Your request is no small matter. Such a thing may claim both lives and disappoint my brother. Can your soul bear all this pain?"

"My soul has borne so much already." What was one more death, Maryam's, or her child's own?

"Then say it, Butayna."

"I want Maryam's child gone from this world! I cannot allow its birth, for Maryam would use him or any other of her sons to supplant Muhammad in Yusuf's affections further. If she dies as well, so be it. For the sake of the son I have granted Yusuf, her boy cannot live. There. You have the words. Take them and go."

Leila stood and bowed. "I shall dress and go the *rawda* for the pennyroyal I will need. The first buds are coming into bloom. I could use doses of saffron or pomegranate seeds, but if we wish to be certain of the outcome, pennyroyal is best. Would you prefer a distillation of the oil instead? The oil would take a little longer to produce, but would cause certain death if Maryam ingested it."

"If you can gather the herbs and administer them, just do that! Please, hurry. My concern is the child's fate, not its mother's own."

"As you prefer." Leila went to the stairs.

"Leila? How will I know when you have done it? Leila?"

"Listen for the screams."

***

Six days later, Butayna paced the floor between the steady stares of Jawla and Hafsa, both of whom said nothing, but watched her with frowns and sighs. Butayna rubbed the back of her neck and patted her nauseous stomach. When she had vomited the mid-afternoon meal, her servants regarded her with questions in their taut gazes. She assured them she was not pregnant. After Aisha's birth, the bitter cassia, ground wild carrot seed, and ginger root brew from the midwife had kept Butayna from conceiving more children. She could not risk her life, even for Yusuf's pleasure in his children.

How would he bear the loss of the babe she intended to steal away from him? When Butayna had last seen Maryam unclothed in the baths, she appeared at least three months gone with her child, if not four. The last seven births prevented her from hiding early signs of her condition from the women in the harem. All of whom regarded her with envious eyes. Butayna did not wonder what they thought of her as well. Even as Yusuf's esteemed first wife, she remained the mother of only two of his children. How many of his *jawari* waited to give him more sons to rival Muhammad or daughters as beautiful as Aisha?

Her children's sweet faces came to mind. She recalled the day in which she first beheld each of them and knew the perfect love she sought lay not in Yusuf's arms, but in the love and trust of her children. She would do anything for them. Maryam loved hers as well. Whatever her faults, she devoted her life to her children, as attentive as Butayna had been to hers. How could she have done it, ordered a blameless life snuffed out with ease?

A sudden sound jarred her from thought. She looked to Jawla and Hafsa. "Did you hear it?"

Both women shook their heads and looked at each other.

Butayna trod the floor again. Ringed fingers cupped her forehead and rubbed at the ache, which still tormented her days after she last spoke with Leila.

"My Sultana, what ails you? What can we do to help?" Hafsa looked at her with a plea shining in her eyes.

"Oh, there is nothing...." She paused and cocked her head. She could have sworn she heard a cry, but it was nothing. Guilt mired her thoughts in worry and recriminations.

She muttered, "I have to stop her. We can't do this."

Jawla and Hafsa exchanged puzzled glances, before the latter asked, "Do what, my Sultana?"

Butayna ignored them and ran to the door. "Stay here. I'll return soon."

She raced down the corridor, past a group of *jawari* gathered around a hookah. In their torpor, surrounded by a haze of white smoke, they did not notice her when she sped by. At the top of the stairs, she heard it. The most terrified, awful scream, one an animal might make in agony, worse than the men in their death throes at the *arroyo* del Salado. She turned and caught sight of a slave who backed out of Maryam's chamber. Blood coated the linen in her hands.

The slave shrieked, "The midwife! Someone summon the midwife. The Sultana has fainted and she's bleeding between her legs! Sultana Maryam is bleeding...."

Butayna sank down beside the banister and cradled her head in her hands. She cried for the child lost to Maryam forever and the agony she knew Maryam must endure. Most of all, she wept for herself, for the cruel and merciless person she had become.

***

A quiet pall descended on the harem in the days afterward. Despite the bloom of spring outside and bright, sunlit days, a dreary mood encompassed of the occupants. Yusuf ordered palace eunuchs to find the royal midwife. They discovered she had gone to al-Mariyah for the month of her daughter's wedding. Yusuf engaged the services of another midwife, but she could not stop the copious blood flow or ease Maryam's intense cramps. The pennyroyal herb had worked too well. Maryam howled her grief for all to hear, as her child's life slipped away and soaked the linens on her bed.

Afterward, she became feverish. The Sultan demanded an explanation from the midwife, who could offer none. A third midwife went into the harem on the ninth morning. She pronounced the awful news. Maryam had an infection of the womb. The midwife tended to Maryam in her near delirious state, while at *al-Quasaba,* a distant, final cry shattered the silence of the afternoon. Birds scattered from the canopies. The second midwife died under the executioner's blade for her failure and incompetence with Maryam's care.

Butayna remained indoors despite the warmth. For the course of more than a week, she saw no one except her servants and her children. Leila preferred to avoid her as well. Perhaps it was for the best. Butayna refused Yusuf's invitations to dine and pleaded a furious ache in her head, which made her husband send his personal physician to her mid-week along with a portion of Yusuf's personal guards.

The young and handsome doctor, Muhammad al-Shaquri, stood in the circle of the Sultan's eunuch with their daggers at the ready, should he behave in an offensive manner. Al-Shaquri ignored them and concentrated on his duty to Butayna. He looked into her eyes and peered at the dark circles beneath them. He prescribed rest and told Jawla to make chamomile tea. "Ensure the Sultana drinks it each night before she goes to bed!"

Butayna knew no amount of chamomile tea or restorative would aid her now. She suffered for her sins, as she deserved. Innocent blood tainted her hands. She reclined on her bed at midday, while Jawla and Hafsa tended to her chamber.

At a knock, Jawla answered at the door. After an exchange of low murmurs, she bowed beside Butayna's bed. "The chief steward is inquiring after your health, my Sultana."

Butayna managed a faint smile. She admired Mufawwiz and often delighted in talks with him about his memories of their old home. Still, she shook her head. Jawla gave a nod and went to the door again. When she shut it, Butayna closed her eyes and willed sleep to come to her. It did, but in her dreams, Maryam's bloodied bedchamber ran red in her visions. She roused herself with a shake of her head. Hafsa appeared at her side.

"You were crying in your sleep, my Sultana."

Butayna fingered her wet cheeks. "It's nothing."

"Are you not hungry? You have eaten nothing except fruit since this morning. Such a meager portion of food cannot sustain you, my Sultana. The third call to prayer has come and gone. Perhaps the Sultan will wish to dine with you tonight."

"I would prefer he did not. Do not worry for me, Hafsa. Please, I am well and not hungry."

Another knock came. Butayna said over her shoulder, "I still wish to remain undisturbed, Jawla. Please apologize on my behalf. Perhaps tomorrow will be a better day for visitors."

"You will see your husband, my love."

Yusuf stood in the doorway. She recalled the first time they met, when he appeared as did now, dressed in white. He did not hold a kitten in his arms, but one of the white roses from the garden. He inhaled its fragrance and entered the room. Butayna's servants made their obeisance.

Yusuf sidestepped them, grasped a stool, and pulled it beside the bed. When she tried to rise, he shook his head. "Do not. Stay as you are."

She nodded and waved Jawla and Hafsa out of the room. "Go to Leila and see to my children."

Yusuf said, "I came to assure myself of your state. How do you feel?"

"I do not know at times, Yusuf." Better to answer him with words akin to the truth. He would perceive the lie if she responded that she was well.

He asked, "Is this one of those times?"

She cradled her brow in her hand and struggled to find the right words, to express some measure of sympathy and sorrow for the trouble she had caused, without damning herself. "My bewildered circumstances are nothing compared to your state. I am sorry for your troubles."

He waved his hand. "Do not speak of them."

"I have to, the pain cannot go... unacknowledged." Her voice cracked.

He leaned closer, his features inscrutable. "Why do you dwell upon this loss, Butayna? You do not suffer its repercussions."

She inhaled a deep, pained breath and closed her eyes. "I remember when I lost our boy."

How could she ever atone for her actions? Jealous fears resulted in the death of more than one victim and might cause Maryam's own before the week ended.

He tapped the rose petals against his lips. "Ah, *nam*. Still, your grief surprises me. You have hated Maryam for so long. Do you care whether she has lost one of her children and may be doomed herself?"

"You want to know whether I care if she has lost one of her children. I worry for your loss, Yusuf."

He tilted his head and smiled, but the manner of how his lips stayed tight at the corners caused her to gasp. Yusuf shook his head. "Now, you care for my pain. Did you ever consider how I might feel when you decided to murder Maryam's child?"

She covered her mouth with her fingers. *Dios mío!* He knew. Somehow, he had discerned her treachery.

Still, she murmured, "Yusuf, what are you saying?"

The stem fell from his fingers. "I am surrounded by liars, people who conceal and conspire. Have you become one of them, sweet love?"

"Yusuf...." Her voice wavered again. She could not draw breath without shudders passing through her.

"I have always admired your honesty, Butayna. It is your best trait. Leila is right. You have not earned the talent for lies. Do not start now. Maryam was well until the morning I informed the courtiers of her baby. Many saw you run from court to the harem afterward. Days later, blood, my child's blood, soaked Maryam's bed. I found the similarities between your behavior and Leila's own in the days afterward of particular interest. You both avoided each other, even me, despite your friendship. Why would you turn from each other, except to hide your guilt?

He held out his palms. "So, I have my sister who will not speak with me and my first wife who does the same. I have one woman with the means to destroy a life and another woman who, at least in her mind, has reason to claim a life. I wondered whether they could do it. Could they conspire to take my child from me? Did you forget the boy would have been my son? Did you have no further concerns beyond the wound you would inflict on Maryam?"

She whispered, "My love, please—"

He clapped a hand over her mouth. Her stare flew to his unwavering gaze. She whimpered behind his fingers.

He ordered, "Be silent. The Sultan speaks, not your husband. My mother and sister with their machinations have taught me more about cruelty than I ever learned at my father's death. I have watched them almost destroy each other over the years and ruin others in the process. Now, you and Maryam shall do the same. So many lives shattered by a foolish rivalry and stupid fears for a future I have already chosen. You are responsible for more than the death of my child and Maryam's suffering. I have ordered the execution of the midwife and Leila's accomplices in the kitchens, who aided her to taint Maryam's food. *Nam,* I found them as well. Did you think matters of such import occurred in the harem outside the knowledge of my spies? I condone much because I love my family. People are dead because you lacked faith in me. Your soul must bear the burden alone. How many more lives will your enmity with Maryam claim?"

Yusuf removed his hand from her lips and stood. "I thought you perceived my intent, Butayna, but I was wrong. That was my mistake. Yours was to think you could influence the course of the succession when I have long since decided it. No matter how many sons Maryam or any other *jarya* may give me, Muhammad will sit upon the throne after I am gone. My heir will be our son, no other. You believe I am cruel to him, but I have acted with purpose. Weakness and recklessness will not aid our son against his adversaries. He cannot allow a semblance of ineptitude to taint him in their eyes. He shall follow me because he has proven himself worthy, by his mettle and dedication alone. He does not falter when faced with a challenge. Instead, he fights harder for my approval. Muhammad is the brightest among my sons because he possesses the best traits of both his parents. His reign shall be glorious."

She stared up at him, unable to speak. How could she have been so foolish? Her thoughts returned to various instances where Yusuf appeared impatient and severe in his judgment of their son. At each episode, Muhammad never wavered or shrank from his father's lessons. Her son possessed more courage than she did.

Yusuf interrupted her reverie. "Maryam is very weak. She suffers bouts of dizziness and weakness. She hears voices when no one has spoken. The newest midwife has given her doses of a brew to expel the contents of her womb. Whether her aid will cure the infection remains uncertain. Pray Maryam lives, Butayna. Not for our son's sake, for I will never alter the succession. For your own."

Butayna reached for him. "Yusuf, I never meant...."

He slapped her hand away. "Do not! Do not touch me. For too many years, I have indulged you and allowed your willful tendencies and pride, but no longer. From this day forward, you will keep far from me. Never enter my presence again unless I command it. If you defy me, I shall summon the executioner. You have broken the trust between us and surrendered the best of part of yourself, which I treasured more than your wisdom or beauty. Your honesty."

She had forsaken more than Yusuf's trust in her. She had also betrayed herself.

***

Leila summoned Butayna via her servants. Muhammad had fallen from his horse while on a sunset ride with his father and brothers. He sustained a broken wrist and scrapes on his elbow. Yusuf's personal doctor, al-Shaquri, attended him in the afternoon along with a bonesetter. Now, the boy called for his mother. Butayna roused herself from her languor and dressed without the aid of Hafsa, who idled beside her counterpart.

Butayna asked, "Is my son in much pain?"

Jawla replied, "He does not complain for the swelling or pain much."

"Is the Sultan with him still? Does Yusuf know I am coming to our son?"

"The noble Sultan ordered the Sultana Leila to fetch you after the doctor had seen the prince."

"Where is Aisha?"

"The little Sultana is with them. She feared the doctor would do more harm to Muhammad and refused to leave the room, even while the bonesetter and al-Shaquri worked. She sang to her brother to keep his mind from the pain."

Butayna could not suppress a smile as she left the chamber. Her servants followed. In the hall, Yusuf's guards lined the doorway and the alcoves. Their leader blocked Butayna's access to the stairs.

She said, "I am here to see my son."

His stone-faced visage did not alter.

Jawla stepped in front of her mistress. "By Christ's blood, move, you overbearing arse! The Sultan sent for his Sultana. Now, get out of the way before I stab you between the ribs."

Leila appeared at the top of the steps. "Jawla! I did not give you to Butayna so you could threaten the royal guard. Come now, Muhammad is waiting to see his mother."

The captain stood aside with his head bowed.

Butayna bypassed him and said over her shoulder, "I knew you were fierce, Jawla, but I never heard such harsh language from you."

"Forgive this impudent servant, my Sultana," Jawla murmured at her back.

"I will, if you'll tell me one thing. What is the word you used, 'arse'?"

Hafsa chuckled. "A word the Sultana should not know."

On the landing, Butayna embraced Leila for the first time in days. "How is he?"

"Come see your son for yourself."

Butayna hesitated. "Yusuf is still with him."

Leila sighed and nodded. "He is... displeased with both of us, but he has relented in this instance. I regret nothing, but I suppose... neither of us considered the full repercussions of that morning. It is of little consequence now. You understand if Yusuf knows, Safa and Maryam will guess. They will move against you soon."

"I am prepared."

Leila sniggered. "*La*, I don't think you are. We will talk of it later. Come."

They entered the small chamber across from Leila's own, where Muhammad occupied the bed. Aisha sat at his right beside the window while Yusuf hovered over him. Despite the reddened, abraded skin on Muhammad's temple and the thick linen wound around his wrist, he smiled at his father.

Yusuf whispered, "My brave, brave boy. Before Al-Shaquri left us, he assured me the poultice of comfrey would aid you. You will heal soon and resume our evening rides."

"I'll be ready for them again, Father," Muhammad murmured. Then he looked across the room. "*Ummi!*"

After quick strides, she knelt beside his bed, aware of Yusuf's hardened stare focused on her head. "Oh, my lion. I came as soon as I could. How did you fall from your horse?"

Instead of their son, Yusuf answered, "The beast's foreleg buckled in a rabbit hole. Muhammad braced himself as well as he could. His quick action reduced the severity of the break. My guards brought him back. I was very proud of Muhammad today. I am proud of him."

She avoided her husband's rapt gaze and stroked Muhammad's tender cheek, which colored with his father's praise. She stated, "I am glad you are otherwise unhurt. Does the wrist trouble you so much?"

"Only when I try to move my arm, *Ummi*."

"Then do not. Whatever you need, you just have to ask."

He grimaced as a spasm crisscrossed his face. Her heart pitched at the thought of his torment. Yusuf was right. He possessed the best attributes of both of his parents, their courage, strength, and faith.

He begged, "*Ummi*, can you stay here with me tonight?"

Butayna lifted her head and gazed at Yusuf. His enigmatic stare told her nothing. "I believe the decision rests with your father."

Muhammad stared at Yusuf. "Please? Let *Ummi* stay. I know she does not remain with me in the evening, but I don't want anyone else with me tonight, just her."

His father's chest rose and fell. Despite his impassive features, he exuded a wearied and embattled appearance, in the slope of his shoulders and the hands listless at his sides. Butayna's eyes watered. He could not mean to be so cruel to their son.

Then he nodded. "It seems best. Your mother may stay for as long as she likes."

Leila stood beside Yusuf and said, "It appears I am not needed." She held out her hand. "Aisha, come. It's time to prepare for bed."

Aisha shook her head. "Please, Father, *Ummi*? Can't I stay here as well?"

Yusuf looked at his sister and sighed. "If she falls asleep in the interim, I shall bring her to bed."

Leila bowed to her brother. Her lips twitched before she turned and left the small room.

Aisha snuggled next to her father. He kissed her brow and stroked tendrils of hair back from her narrow face. "You're very good to keep Muhammad's company."

She looked up at him. "I would not want to be anywhere else except with my brother."

Butayna smiled at her children. Yusuf's cursory glance met hers, before both of them regarded their son, who closed his eyes.

Chapter 21
The Gate

Sultana Butayna

Granada, Andalusia
June 22 - 23, AD 1348 / 24 - 24 Rabi al-Awwal 749 AH / 25th –
26th of Tammuz, 5108

Muhammad tugged Butayna through the crowded southern
courtyard of *al-Qal'at al-Hamra*. A spiraling summer wind ripped
at her lavender *hijab*, but she gripped the folds. Aisha raced
ahead of them on coltish legs. Pearls glittered at the edge of her
silk cap.

She called out, "Hurry, *Ummi*, before it becomes too crowded
at the *Bab al-Sharia!*"

"Dear girl, I am moving as fast as I can in this *jubba*."
Butayna shook her head at her children's enthusiasm. What
could be so important about a gate? She had traversed them
many times over, here and at the approach to the *Jannat al-'Arif.*

The denizens of the palace complex crowded its inner walls.
Sentries stood along an ascending path to the stretch of wall,
which overlooked groves of almonds and olives. Below the wall
stood the former burial site of the Nasrids, where all but one of
the earliest members of the dynasty remained entombed.

Butayna smiled at Muhammad, who would inherit the
magnificent legacy of his ancestors someday. She hoped it would
not be too soon. Not before she and Yusuf reconciled. Their
strained relationship continued in the months after Maryam's
recovery. Though Yusuf did not speak of it, Butayna knew he
blamed her for the bouts of the falling sickness, which Maryam
endured. While al-Shaquri, who tended to Maryam, believed she
would recover in full and become her former self, Yusuf did not
share the same opinion. At night, Butayna often examined her
impulsive decision and adjudged herself a fool. Not only because
Yusuf had decided upon his heir beforehand, but also because
she had permitted her rivalry with Maryam to alter her heart. It
had turned her into a bitter, ruthless woman, a caricature of
Maryam. How could Butayna have become the very person she
despised? She vowed against ever treading such a dangerous

path again. She would protect her son by all possible means, but never do willful harm to Maryam or anyone else in the process.

Aisha and Muhammad found places among the crowd, which thronged around Ibn al-Khatib. Yusuf's personal secretary beamed while he stood at the inner facade of the gate, under the horseshoe arch of white marble. He peered through the crowd and then signaled to Muhammad, who released his hold on Butayna. Aisha took her brother's place beside Butayna.

Ibn al-Khatib bowed before Muhammad. "My noble prince."

Muhammad's broad smile revealed his dimples. "In the name of my noble father, the Sultan Abdul Hajjaj Yusuf, first of his name, the *Amir al-Muslimin,* and the seventh Sultan of the Nasrid Dynasty and lord of this land, I declare the *Bab al-Sharia* open. Gate master!"

At an adjacent door in the masonry stood the stout, wizened man charged with the gate's maintenance. He inclined his grizzled head to Muhammad. Then he grasped the iron ring handle of the wooden door. With a boisterous grunt, he opened the gateway to its southwesterly view of the *Sabika* hill and the old Nasrid gravesites beyond. The crowd dispersed to the surrounding countryside. Some stopped and admired its facade. Others rushed to an open-air market situated between the former *rawda* and the crest of the hill.

Butayna caught up with Muhammad and nodded to him. "Why didn't you tell me your father afforded you this honor? I am so proud of you, my lion. It's your first public duty."

"Of many, I am sure, my Sultana." Ibn al-Khatib approached and bent his back. Dark, curly hair fell over his eyes. "*Al-salam 'alayka,* my Sultanas."

Both Butayna and Aisha murmured, "*Wa-'alayka, al-katib sirri-hi.*"

Butayna placed her hands on her children's shoulders. "I remember when the work on this gate began, or rather my ears do, for all the hammering and pounding. It is a wonder to see it finished. Come, children, let us explore."

Ibn al-Khatib acknowledged them again and Butayna favored him with a little nod. She liked and trusted Yusuf's secretary. She paused before the foundation slab before the inscription.

She asked, "Can either of you read this?"

Muhammad peered at the two lines of script incised in the marble. He traced the lines with his uninjured wrist. "He ordered the construction of this gate called *Bab al-Sharia.* May Allah favor the law of Islam by it and make it a sign of the imperishable glory, our lord the prince of the Muslims, the Sultan, the champion of the faith and just, Abdul Hajjaj Yusuf, the son of our lord the Sultan, the champion of the faith and sanctified Abu'l-Walid ibn Nasr–"

Aisha interrupted him. "May Allah reward his virtuous works in Islam and receive favorably his actions in the *jihad*. It was completed in the month of the Birth of the Prophet in the year seven hundred and forty-nine. May Allah make it glorious and protective and inscribe it among the pious and enduring works."

Butayna fingered the double palm leaves carved into each corner. "The *Diwan al-Insha* honors your father with these words."

She turned and glanced at Ibn al-Khatib, who observed them with a little smile. She nodded her thanks, for the eloquence of his praise for her husband. Then she pointed to the top of the gate. "Look, my children."

Aisha smiled and reached beneath her *jubba* for the necklace worn against her skin. She held the pendant up to the glare of sunlight and aligned it with the shape of the hand carved into the masonry. "It's just like my *khamsa*. Father said mine belonged to his grandmother, may Allah preserve her memory."

Muhammad intoned, "The Hand of Fatima, daughter of the Prophet, may peace be upon him."

Butayna gathered her children to her. "Come, we'll walk to the old *rawda* and you can each tell me what you've learned of the Sultans buried there."

Muhammad's eyes widened. "The third Sultan was a crazed murderer, *Ummi*! Did you know that? He cut off the heads of his servants and left others to rot at *al-Quasaba*, where their ghosts still haunt the cells. Did Father name me for him? He was also called Muhammad."

Butayna said, "I like to think your father chose your name in tribute to his beloved elder brother or his great-grandfather the Lawgiver, or the Lawgiver's father, the first Muhammad who founded the dynasty. Many of your forbearers were men who defended their kingdoms. Have you both seen the inscriptions in the throne room of your family's motto? Do you know the reason why 'Only God is the victor' became the Nasrid maxim?"

When her children shook their heads, she continued, "I'll share with you a story the Sultana Fatima once told me, of the patriarch of the Nasrid Dynasty, the first Muhammad who captured this city. In his youth, he aspired to greatness as your father has done. Your ancestor's ambitions clashed with those of the Hud clan, who once ruled what is now Christian Sevilla...."

***

Butayna sat on the ground while her children chased each other in circles around the gravestones of the Sultans Muhammad III and his brother Nasr. She twirled the stem of a blade of grass between her fingertips and smiled while she watched them. Muhammad was eleven years old and Butayna had acknowledged the Christian date of Aisha's seventh birthday two months before. They belonged in their father's world, but sometimes, she wished she had something of their Castillan heritage to give them, more than blood ties to her father.

She drew up her knees and set her chin between them. A hot wind blew and scattered the flowers on the Nasrid sites. Her children knew the names of their Moorish ancestors, yet little of Efrain Peralta, whom she spoke of on rare occasions. Whenever Muhammad or Aisha asked of her parents, she told them adequate information to satisfy their desire for knowledge. Thoughts of her father still pained her, even after so many years.

She shook her head and stood. "Muhammad! Aisha! We should return to the *Jannat al-'Arif*. The day is too hot."

Aisha won the race to Butayna, who kissed both their cheeks and drew her *hijab* around her face, before they resumed the route back to the *Bab al-Sharia*.

Halfway there, Butayna stopped in her tracks. Yusuf stood beside Ibn al-Khatib with other ministers and spoke to them. Maryam lingered at his side with her handmaidens.

Butayna had not seen her rival for three weeks since her folly. Dark circles discolored the skin beneath Maryam's eyes and her gaze darted all around. She trembled and shied away from any woman who approached or acknowledged her. Self-recriminations made a tight knot in Butayna's stomach. Maryam was not the same haughty woman of the past. The pennyroyal poison had altered her. Butayna could only summon pity.

"Look. It's Father," Aisha cried.

Muhammad hushed her. "We should leave him be, sister. He's with the *Diwan al-Insha*."

Butayna swallowed past the lump in her throat. "Your brother is right, Aisha. We should not interrupt the Sultan and his ministers."

What could she do? Where could she go? Yusuf had ordered her to keep out of sight unless he requested her presence. With Maryam at his side and the evidence of her troubles still upon her, Butayna could not appear before Yusuf. It would just remind him of what she had done.

She asked, "Have either of you ever been to the *Qaysariyya*?"

"We cannot go there without guards," Muhammad whispered, though a gleam lit his gaze, which she could not ignore.

"We can do anything we want! Now come." Butayna snatched their hands and led them behind her.

Aisha's laughter made Butayna giddy, as she bolted down the *Sabika* hill with her children. They raced each other through the woodland, contented and joyous in each other's company. They needed no one else.

Butayna took them into the marketplace and kept a steady gaze on them among the crowded streets and dense pockets of activity. Curiosity overwhelmed her children, but she steered them away from baser sights at the slave market to the stall where the drapers sold their fine bolts of cloth. When the call for *Salat al-Asr* arrived, Butayna shuddered as she remembered Yusuf would have expected Muhammad to join him at this hour.

"Don't worry, *Ummi.* There are so many mosques in the city. I am sure I can find an appropriate one where no one will know my identity. I'll be safe in its walls."

Butayna and Aisha waited in the sunlight while Muhammad observed the ritual prayer. Then the trio returned to *al-Qal'at al-Hamra* via the *Bab al-Sharia.*

The guards on duty stared at Butayna as if she possessed an addled mind, when she answered their inquiries about her business by stating her relationship to the Sultan. "Get away from this place with your mad talk, woman!"

Muhammad stepped in front of her. "I am the son of the Sultan and my father shall have your heads on spikes atop this gate if you do not let us enter!"

"You men would do well to listen to the firstborn son of the Sultan."

Butayna whirled at the unexpected voice. A pale man, as short as Muhammad, stood at her back. Sunlight glinted off his baldpate. He bowed before Muhammad. "My noble prince."

"Master Ridwan."

Butayna had seen him twice before the battle at the *arroyo* del Salado. Ridwan, the disgraced minister whom Yusuf blamed for his troubles with the Marinids, brother of the chief eunuch, Hisham. There were no obvious similarities between the men to mark them as relations, except perhaps their matching height. Whereas Hisham stood ghostly white, at least the summer sun lent a little color to his brother. Ridwan's eyebrows were black and his skin the familiar olive-brown of the land's denizens. Even his demeanor and tight-lipped smile marked him as a different man from his brother, who never revealed his moods.

Ridwan called for the gate master, who then cuffed and cursed his men as stupid fools for not recognizing Muhammad as the prince who had dedicated the gate in his father's name. The minister left Butayna and her children at the outskirts of the chancery offices with little more than a nod. Butayna stared at his path long after he left it, until her children urged along the route to the *Jannat al-'Arif.*

Perspiration glided along Butayna's temple as she stepped inside. "Find your aunt Leila and have something to eat. I shall see you later at dinner with Leila."

She kissed and hugged them both before she entered her room. Jawla and Hafsa looked up from their floor with red-rimmed eyes. The latter sobbed behind her hands anew, while Jawla whispered. "Thank God! We had feared the worst. We didn't know where you were."

She shook her head. "There was no cause for worry. I'm starved! Please, fetch me something to eat and I need a bath. Gather my soaps and oils."

Butayna left her servants to do her bidding, while she went into her bedchamber and stripped. She removed the *jubba* and the thin cotton clothing underneath. Naked and unashamed, she stretched out on the coverlet.

"Where is she? Get out! I will speak to her alone!"

She jerked upright at the sound of Yusuf's voice. She grabbed the edge of the bed linen and pulled it up to her collarbone, just before he burst into the room.

His mottled face tightened around the eyes and his mouth became a thin seam. He reached down and hauled her up by her arms, dragging the cover with him.

"You have done some reckless and impulsive things in the past, but never this foolish! How dare you take my children where I could not find them?"

She gaped at him. "Your children? Are they not mine now?"

"A Christian woman who ventured out alone with the Sultan's heirs, without guards, not even your maidservants. If you ever do something like this again, I will forbid you to see those children! Do you understand me?"

She pressed her lips together and denied him an answer. How dare he behave this way? She had as much right to enjoy an afternoon alone with Muhammad and Aisha. His stupid laws denied her a mother's right to be with her children at all times and she refused to abide by it any further.

He shook her until her neck ached. His bellow blasted her ears. "Do you hear me?"

"I am not deaf! What did you think I would do with my children? Did you believe I would ever place them in harm's way? We went to the *Qaysariyya*, then Aisha and I waited while Muhammad observed his prayers. I would never risk their lives–"

"You did when you took them out the walls. I saw you returning to the *Bab al-Sharia* and then the three of you turned away. I thought you might visit to the burial sites of my ancestors or some other place, not the idiocy you undertook. They are yours as they are mine, but they are also royal children. You will never endanger them again! Why did you leave the grounds?"

"I did not anticipate your arrival at the gate! When Muhammad and Aisha told me they wanted to go there, I first ensured you had already been to the site. You have asked me to keep away from you and I have tried to follow your wishes–"

His hold tightened. "Now you care so much for what I say and want?"

"What do you want from me, Yusuf? I have tried to do as you asked! Now, you question why I have submitted! Do you even know what you want?"

"I want you!" His warm, wide mouth covered hers.

At first, her muffled protests died in her throat. His hands slid between their bodies and dragged the linen from her grasp, before he pulled her to him. Heated kisses traveled down her throat to her collarbone and across her shoulder, to the valley between her breasts. She clutched at his shoulders and inhaled the scent of him. It would be so easy to surrender. This abrupt change in him frightened and stirred her by turns. He still wanted her, but how long would his desires last until she did something to offend him, or worse, Maryam turned him against her?

She shuddered in his grasp and pushed at his shoulders, even as his ironclad hold crushed her to his body. "Is your desire for me only rekindled by the absence of Maryam?"

As she expected, he stiffened and raised his head. They stared at each other in silence, but for the ragged breaths both of them expelled.

Then he raked a hand over his contorted features. "Have you bewitched me in truth, as my mother often claims? What is the power you have over to me to make me forget my anger, even my own pride, for love of you? I should despise you for what you have done, but I cannot. I do know how. You have unmanned me, Butayna, made me a fool for you."

"If only it were possible. No matter how much you desire me, others will tempt you from my side, Maryam included. Have you come to my bed now because of her?"

"What are you asking me?"

She said, "Do not pretend. Neither one of us can bear deceit for too long. I want the truth from you. Why are you here now? Is it because you want me, or because Maryam is not available to you? Even before she revealed her pregnancy, you had not touched me for weeks. Why do you seek me out now?"

"Would you rather I bedded another of my *jawari*? I can do so, if that is your preference."

"You know I do not want another woman in your bed, not even your second Sultana. You have grown attached to Maryam. You love her as much as you love me. Perhaps more. Why do you need me?"

He released her. "Some would say I am blessed to have married twice for love. Is my love still not enough for you?"

Butayna turned away from him and blinked back sudden tears. Despite the warmth of the room, a chill stirred a shudder deep inside her. "It will never be. I can no longer accept the portion you would offer. I will have all or none."

His grip pressed her shoulder. "What you ask is impossible."

She shrugged him off. "You know we are at an impasse and there can be no bridge between your desires and mine. I have always understood that I would have to share you with others, but never accepted it. I do not have the power within me. For my part, I regret how the discord between Maryam and I has led me to rash behavior in the past, which I will never repeat again. Maryam does not matter, just our children. I must be content in the love of our son and daughter alone."

"You are rejecting me? You turn from me when I would have you at my side and forgive you for what you and Leila did to Maryam?"

Butayna turned and captured his hand in her. She kissed his fingertips and pressed his palm to her cheek. "I will never stop loving you. When I look upon our children's precious faces, all I see is you. The struggle with Maryam will never cease as long as I strive for another piece of your heart, which you cannot give. I long for your forgiveness, but even that is not sufficient. I must atone and relieve myself from guilt and burden. The one way I know how is to be a good and virtuous person, to be a devoted mother to our children for the rest of my days. I do not want to be the woman who fights with Maryam for your heart. I want peace now, Yusuf, just peace."

***

After dinner in the late evening, Butayna and Leila withdrew to the garden of the summer palace, once Muhammad and his sister went to bed. Leila strolled between rows of fragrant flowers and shook her head as Butayna related the earlier conversation with Yusuf.

His sister whispered, "Then it was all for nothing. You've let Maryam win his heart."

"The greater prize is the throne, which my son shall have."

"Will Yusuf declare his intent before the court? Will he acknowledge his chosen heir and place Muhammad's life in danger? I have warned you that Maryam shall discover the truth. She will learn of both of our roles in due time and retaliate. Whether she or Safa makes the connection first, Maryam will make you suffer."

"Whatever she does, I shall be ready for her. She is weak now, an injured snake. A wounded creature becomes dangerous and desperate."

Leila pursed her lips. "She could strike out against Muhammad. You claimed her child. She might try to take yours. She will be unable to control her impulses and become far more difficult to anticipate."

"*La,* I believe she will grow careless and imprudent. Without a plan in place, she will fail. I must keep pace ahead of her to ensure the safety of my children. I will find a way."

As they resumed walking through the shadows arm in arm, Butayna added, "You should not discount the hold I have on Yusuf's heart so soon."

Leila's brow crinkled and the thin, familiar seam formed between her brows. "What do you mean? You've all but given him to Maryam."

Butayna lifted her chin. "I have withheld myself from a man who is accustomed to deference to his wishes. Still, he has not changed, for he is the same Sultan who would not take a young, nubile *jarya* by force. Rather, he desired her consent and mutual enthusiasm for his lovemaking. When you placed me on the path to your brother's bed and heart, you knew he wanted a challenge. Not the *jawari* who have laid on their backs for him and uttered all the words Safa told them to say. Have you not seen his mother's frustration as he rejects her gifts week after week? Though she says it is unnatural to devote himself to two women, I believe Yusuf finds Maryam and I better suited to his tastes with good reason."

Leila snorted. "Good reason, you say. *Nam,* with you indeed, for you are exquisite. What is the source of his attraction to Maryam? She is beautiful like sweet honey, but as honey is a clever means to hide poison, so does she conceal the evil within her."

"Hence Yusuf's fascination, and another worthy challenge for him. She will never reveal the truth of herself. Some mystery will always remain hidden behind her eyes and he shall never stop trying to discover it. With me, he has found his true mate, but I have become too compliant and available. As a result, he has turned neglectful because he knows I will always be there. I forgot the first rule. My husband thrives on challenge. He never shrinks from battle. He never chooses the direct path. The journey fraught with peril and the chance of failure makes his victories even sweeter. With his women, he seeks the unattainable but desirable, the one who will not bend so soon before his power. It is time I reminded him of why he desired me first long ago."

After a moment, Leila's cheeks colored the same pale pink of roses in the garden. "It is a great hazard, but you are quite a clever woman."

"Nothing worth having in life comes without some risk. I will have Yusuf's heart or nothing from him."

"You may have his heart in whole someday. I have chided myself often against underestimating you. At each opportunity, you still manage to surprise me. You intended your ruse to bind my brother again?"

Butayna nodded. "I once told him I would never leave his side. If he should believe I have granted him freedom to do as he pleases, he shall not stray far from my side. Mark me. When I have him again, Maryam shall never interfere in our love and I shall have the peace I crave with my husband."

***

The Passing

Sultana Butayna

Granada, Andalusia
February 23-26, 1349 AD / 4-7 Dhu'l-Hijja 749 AH / 4rd -7th of Adar II, 5108

Butayna rose as soon as Jawla shook her awake. "Your noble husband, my Sultana, is here at your doorway."

Butayna planted her feet on the chilled floorboards. The brazier had died down in the night. "Has something happened to our children?"

"He did not say." Jawla bowed and stepped away from the bed.

Butayna rushed to the doorway. Yusuf stood alone at the entrance, his back turned to her. A green *jubba* covered him. She swallowed and reached for his shoulder. "Dreams of your brother have awoken you again? Shall I make your chamomile tea?"

When he shook his head and did not speak, she came around him. The glow of torches revealed his dampened cheeks. Her heart pitched. "Tell me of your sorrow."

He raked a hand over his haggard face. "It is Fatima. She is dying."

"Has al-Shaquri attended her?"

"I have not summoned my doctor yet. I last saw her yesterday after public audience. She looked better than she has in past years, but her memory of recent events has declined even further. I had to remind her I am a father several times over."

Butayna recalled how Fatima had blessed Muhammad at birth. Had the Sultan forgotten that day also? "Yusuf, how can you know—?"

"I have never questioned the knowledge of events beyond my understanding. Before my brother Muhammad died, I knew he would perish as a young man. I dreamt of his death. My grandmother is like me. I must go to her and I want you to come with me."

Without questioning his insistence, she reentered her bedchamber and dressed in the *jubba* she had discarded earlier, lavender brocade edged with pearls. By the time of her return, Yusuf had grasped a torch. In silence, they walked eastward and down the dimly lit stairs and corridors of the harem. Sentinels lined the walls, some hiding yawns behind their hands, or straightening at the sight of the Sultan.

When Yusuf and Butayna emerged at the southwest entrance under a sky filled with stars, she observed, "You did not ask your guards to join you."

"I do not need protection to visit my grandmother or when I'm with you."

Yusuf led her to the old palace of his ancestors, portions of its four wings dating from the reigns of his grandfather the Lawgiver and that man's warring sons, Muhammad III and Nasr. When she thought they would continue past its wide pool, Yusuf made a sharp turn to the west. Lights beckoned through shuttered windows from the second floor of a sienna-brown stone residence. Climbing roses almost obscured the doorway. Yusuf handed Butayna the torch. He pushed the greenery aside and his hand closed on the doorknob.

"My grandmother retreated here two nights ago. When I asked her why she had come, she said she wished to be closer to our ancestors."

Such sorrow laced his monotone, Butayna blinked back tears and whispered, "Thank you for allowing me to be with you at this time."

He looked over his shoulder, but said nothing. Instead, he pushed at the door. Its bolts groaned and the wood creaked. The torch illuminated paintings on the walls, one of a hunting scene with men on horseback who chased deer. Grateful to be indoors again, Butayna paused and stared, never having seen the like anywhere else in *al-Qal'at al-Hamra*. Yusuf brought her deeper into the house, to an almost bare room with cushions on three sides, except for the northern staircase. He took the steps two at a time and Butayna followed.

Lamps brightened the chamber where Fatima rested. Vapors of incense coiled from two burners. A fragrant mint flavor hung heavy in the air. Sheer red curtains draped the bed and the familiar figure of Asiya hovered beside the Sultana.

The servant parted the silk fabric and bowed before Yusuf. Black curls billowed around her puffy face and red-rimmed eyes. "My Sultan. She told me not to send for you. She said you would know when the moment had come."

She gestured to the bed.

When he stepped beyond the curtain and sank down, Fatima's head lolled on the pillow. She croaked, "I was right...."

Yusuf clasped her age-spotted hand and brought it to his lips.

Butayna shivered. Asiya approached and offered to take the torch, which she hung in an empty wall bracket.

The servant said, "I have brewed some tea, but my Sultana does not want any. Would you like some, Sultana Butayna?"

Butayna nodded and sat on a low stool below one of the lattice-covered windows. When Asiya brought the tea, she accepted it with thanks. The mint warmed her stomach. While Asiya folded several bolts of linen, Yusuf and his grandmother spoke in low murmurs Butayna could not overhear despite her proximity. Then Yusuf straightened and poked his head between the draperies. He nodded to Butayna.

"She wants to talk with you."

The teacup rattled in Butayna's hand. Asiya set aside the fabrics and took the vessel. She stated, "The leaves have clung to the bottom. The fortune-tellers say you can discover your future in the dregs of the tea."

Butayna shook her head. "I do not believe in such superstition."

Fatima rasped, "You should. Now come and sit with me. Yusuf and Asiya will wait downstairs while we speak alone."

At her easy dismissal, Yusuf led Asiya down the steps. Butayna stared until they disappeared from view.

"Do not keep me waiting forever. I do not know how much longer I may have."

At the sound of Fatima's voice, Butayna lifted the curtain. Fatima patted the space beside her with a limp hand. She appeared dwarfed by the pillows beneath her, clad in deep purple with her white hair splayed across the *cendal* cushions. Even the hollows around her eyes and the skin stretched across her furrowed brow like thin parchment could not detract from the almost ethereal grace of the smile on her lips.

She whispered, "I know your face. It is a little more careworn than when we first met, but I remember it. The life is of a Sultana is not as straightforward as that of a slave. Concerns burden your life. Worry for your son among them."

Butayna sat beside her. "Do not think of me. The Sultan is troubled by thoughts of you."

"While I have considered nothing else, but Yusuf, your children and you. Your son and daughter must think I am naught more than a little old woman who haunts the harem with her faltering steps, calling for her dead children. I remember them too."

"*La*, my children honor you!"

Fatima chuckled. "You mean the woman I once was, one with the strength to match the vigor of my heart and appetites. My only sorrow is in leaving this life before I see your son ascend the throne and know my line shall be blessed by his rule."

Butayna replied, "Nothing is assured."

Fatima's dry and rough hand pressed against hers. "Some things are."

The certainty in her voice stirred Butayna's curiosity. Was there something to Yusuf's beliefs about the strange abilities he and his grandmother possessed?

Fatima said, "You need protection, as does your son. For twenty-nine years, I have kept a tenuous peace in this harem. When I die, Safa shall resume her war with my Leila. Maryam shall fight you to claim a place for her son on the throne."

When Butayna gasped, Fatima chuckled and a light cough rattled her chest. "Do you think because I keep to my rooms that I am ignorant of strife in the harem? If I wished, I could still teach you a little something of intrigue. I tire of the deaths and long only for my own ending. As I said, you need help. A few years ago, Yusuf captured many Christian fighting men at Siles. They are in *al-Quasaba*. You should claim these men as your guards. Your son fast approaches the age where he must have his own household and *jawari*. He will require protectors. The request will not appear strange if you can convince Yusuf that Ismail requires the same upon his maturity. Naturally, if you have guards also, your rival will want her own."

Butayna sighed. Her son would soon reach his manhood and have dominion over his own servants. She had to safeguard him against any attempt on his life. Now, his great-grandmother offered a solution, but one problem remained.

"Eunuchs can be bribed with gold coins. My son could still be in danger."

Fatima responded, "Safa and Maryam cannot align themselves with the perspectives of Christians who remain captives, not when both women have abandoned their religions for Islam and expediency's sake." At Butayna's sharp intake of breath, a little smile tugged at the corners of Fatima's mouth. "You did not know, but Maryam and Safa made the same choice. Safa is an apostate, a slave who belonged to my son Ismail. She had the good fortune to bear Yusuf in her first pregnancy and gained a marriage. Why do you think Safa rails against you so? She sees herself in you. She remembers her climb from the depths. More importantly, she knows what it is like to have another powerful woman stand in the way of a mother's ambitions for her son's rule."

While Butayna absorbed the unexpected revelation, Fatima added, "As a Christian, you have something meaningful to offer these captives. You can grant them liberty in exchange for their unswerving allegiance. That is the right kind of coin any captive would accept without hesitation."

"It seems you have thought of everything."

Fatima laughed and coughed up flecks of bloodied sputum. Butayna reached for a handkerchief affixed to her belt. At Fatima's nod, Butayna blotted the old woman's lips. Fatima grunted and cleared her throat. "I have lain here on this pallet awaiting my death. What else is there to do, but think?"

Over the course of two nights, Yusuf sent word to Leila, his children and those closest among his courtiers of Fatima's declined health. All of the ministers of the *Diwan* came, Ibn al-Khatib and Ridwan the most frequent visitors. The family kept vigil throughout the late hours. Butayna had to insist Muhammad and Aisha returned to their beds before the sentries called midnight. Fatima blessed her grandchildren, even Maryam's daughters and sons, who shied away from the sight of her cadaverous features. If their behavior embarrassed Yusuf, he never said. He hardly left Fatima's side and al-Shaquri stayed with his master.

311

Butayna peeked out from the lattice on the third morning. A thin coat of snow had dusted the cobblestones last night. At dawn, pink light glinted off the pristine white.

She peered over her shoulder. Leila cradled her disheveled head and leaned against Fatima's bed. Ifrit snored beside her. The slave's head dipped low to her chest. Yusuf occupied a chair, where he propped up his chin on his hand. Al-Shaquri had taken the stool. Asiya stretched out on the floor by the windows, wisps of hair over her face.

Fatima stirred from the sleep that often claimed her and murmured something. Yusuf and Leila jerked awake. Butayna clambered over Asiya and approached the bed, where Fatima spoke so softly no one could hear her.

"Grandmother, what did you say?" Leila clutched at her hand.

The others opened their eyes. Yusuf pushed back the curtains. "Grandmother."

Fatima whispered, "You are all here."

Leila kissed Fatima's fingers. "*Nam,* we are here and we will never leave you."

Fatima looked upward. "Forgive me. I should have loved you more."

Yusuf said, "There is nothing to forgive, Grandmother. You loved us well."

Butayna touched his arm. "She isn't speaking to you." When he gave her a puzzled frown, she continued, "Upon my mother's death, she claimed to see the spirits of her father, the child she had just lost and others in our family."

Leila sobbed and Ifrit patted her shoulder. Butayna urged Yusuf's sister, "You must let her go. She is ready."

When Leila released her grandmother's fingers, Fatima stretched out her hand for a final time. "You have waited long enough, my heart."

Her limbs relaxed, her gaze still fixed on a spot above her that she no longer saw.

Al-Shaquri pressed his ear to her breastbone. He raised his head and met Yusuf's watery gaze. The doctor held his palms upward, closed his eyes and prayed for Fatima's soul. Yusuf cupped a hand over his face and Leila wailed. Only Ifrit could comfort her. Asiya bowed low and pressed her forehead against the floor in honor of her mistress. Butayna wrapped her arms around Yusuf and buried her wet face against him, all of them united in grief.

In the hours afterward, bells pealed to announce the passing of Fatima bint Muhammad. Yusuf sent word to Ibn al-Khatib to compose words befitting his grandmother's remarkable life and heritage. Ifrit brought word back to harem on Leila's behalf, while Asiya volunteered to wash the body alone.

Before she did so, Yusuf clasped the servant's hands. "You have been with her for forty-one years. Your devotion is beyond measure. Now, your life is your own."

Asiya managed a smile. "In a few days, I wish to leave Gharnatah for the last time. There is a promise I must keep."

"You go to Shalabuniya after all?" When she nodded, he vowed, "You will want for nothing there. Go in peace."

Butayna followed him with Leila from the room. Outside in the bitter cold, Safa and Maryam awaited them in fur-lined cloaks. Yusuf moved to them and spoke in low tones. Then he regarded Butayna and Leila. "I seek comfort in prayer. We shall dine together tonight, all of us, to honor Fatima's life. She would have wanted it so."

Yet Fatima had also perceived reality and the troubles among her family members.

Safa stood with her arms folded across her bosom, her glare fixed on Leila. With a wearied sigh, Leila pursed her lips and then bowed. She motioned for Butayna to do the same. When both women straightened, a wide smile smoothed Safa's features.

Leila held out her hand. "Come, Butayna, we must warm ourselves."

As they walked away hand in hand, heat swept up Butayna's spine. The war Fatima feared had already begun.

***

Butayna stood beside the *corrals*, little more than cramped holes in the ground, in the blistering afternoon sun at *al-Quasaba* while sentries watched her and Muhammad with Jawla and Hafsa. Butayna did not doubt their thoughts evidenced in their puzzled or hardened expressions, for no woman belonged in the citadel except for the prostitutes who plied their trade at its gates and in darkened alleys. A Sultana did not belong in front of the cells where Yusuf kept his prisoners.

Muhammad pinched his nose as the jailor forced a bedraggled lot out of the cell. The fetid smell of urine vied with other disgusting odors.

Butayna ordered, "You will lower your hand, my lion. These soldiers had no choice in their fates. You will show them respect by accepting them as they are. How can you command them and gain their respect if you scorn them?"

Although his lips twisted, her boy complied.

The men stumbled and covered their eyes against the harsh glare of sunlight. They had spent too many long years in captivity. Some struggled to stand upright, helped by their comrades. They ranged from young to old, all covered in grime and their own filth, gaunt, and sunburned. At least none had lost their hands. In total, a dozen men emerged from the dank opening in the earth.

The jailor barked at them to stand in a line, but Butayna waved him away.

"It is impossible for them to understand you. I am sure none of them speaks Arabic. Withdraw and let me talk to them."

When he coiled his leather whip and bowed, she strolled down the irregular line. Her black *hijab* swirled in the wind. The captives kept their gazes on the ground. Did they wonder about her intentions as the citadel's guards did?

"I greet you all in the name of God. When the warriors of King Yusuf of Granada raided Siles nine years ago, you were among the cavalry captured and gelded?"

The first among them propped up the dirtied, shaggy-haired man at his side. "We... were." His hesitance betrayed how he struggled with the first breath of fresh air in years.

She returned to his position at the forefront. "How many were taken at Siles?"

"Twenty-nine of us. Some did not survive the... the operation when these savages castrated them. The rest died from starvation, beatings, and exposure." He flicked a hardened gaze at the jailor.

She stared at the puckered, pink scar, which ran from the prisoner's forehead, across the left eye and midway down his cheek before she replied, "There will be no more of that. The sovereign who claimed your lives as his is my husband. I am Butayna, the first wife of Yusuf of Granada. When I was a girl, Moors captured me in a raid on the *meseta* and I became a captive before I endured the state of a slave. I once lived a very different life. My name was Esperanza Peralta, born at Talavera de la Reina in the year of our Lord thirteen hundred and twenty-two. I remain a Catholic Christian despite my marriage."

The men gasped and looked at each other with deep frowns.

Butayna clutched her son's shoulder. "This is the *Infante* Muhammad, my son and Yusuf's firstborn. By the grace of God, he shall follow his father on the throne of Granada one day. My son is a Moor as his father before him and an adherent of the Muslim faith. Through me, Muhammad also bears proud Castillan blood. Now, you know who we are. Tell me your names and the places from where you hail."

The man who had addressed her earlier said, "I am Alfonso Ruiz from Siles. This is my elder brother, Pero. He was the *adalid* and I served him as his second, the *almocaden.*"

Butayna glanced at the others. A chorus of answers followed. "I am Sancho Gomez del Monte, born in Arvas, Asturias. Pello Zabala, Bilbao. Javier Irugo from Biscay. Xurxo, born in a Galician vineyard, where my mother abandoned me. I am Don Nuño Enriquez Torres y Gordillo and I descend from a noble line of Toledo. Fernando Suarez Villar, also from Talavera. Antonio de Santiago, raised by the Grand Master of the Order of Santiago, Vasco Rodriguez de Coronado. Jose, a foundling from Madrid. Emilio Alvarez de Guzman, bastard-born of a noble mother in Cadiz. Alberto Jimenez from Moclin."

She nodded. "I will grant each of you independence if you agree to protect my son and I from any who would do us harm. You shall have the freedom of this place. There is good food, even wine if you wish for it. No one shall ever enslave you again for as long as Muhammad and I live. There will never be another day for any of you in the *corrals*. No one will harm you or obstruct your duties. In return, you must never abuse the authority my son and I shall grant you, or take your revenge upon those who held you imprisoned on my husband's orders. Serve us well and we shall reward you in kind. You will die if you betray us or exceed the limits of your duties. What is your answer?"

Antonio Ruiz looked at his brother, who grunted. The stooped man, crooked from the cramped conditions and low ceiling of his prison, grunted and straightened himself with an agonized groan.

"We... we will serve you and the... *Infante, mi... reina.*"

Butayna looked into the wide, glazed eyes of the jailor. "See to their food and comfort. They must take their time to eat. After captivity, it can be... a difficult adjustment to regular meals again. If they eat too fast, they will become sick. Take them to the bath in the Christian quarter and let them worship as they choose. Then they must go to the armory. In the evening, my son and I shall choose from among them to be our personal guards."

Then she glanced at the brothers Ruiz. "As the one called Pero is accustomed to command, he shall be the *adalid,* with the responsibility to protect my son. The younger Ruiz shall be the *almocaden.*"

Both men nodded their assent and the younger stated, "*Sí, mi reina.*"

Chapter 22
The Pestilence

Sultana Butayna

Granada, Andalusia
June 14, AD 1349 – March 30, AD 1350 / 26 Rabi al-Awwal 750
AH – 20 Muharram 751 AH / 27th of Sivan, 5109 - 20th of
Nissan, 5110

The guttural screams awoke Butayna in the middle of the night.
She had never heard such desperation in the sound of another
voice, even when Maryam lost her baby last summer. Butayna
slipped from her bed and raced to the door. High wails resonated
on the night air.

Jawla admonished her, "My Sultana, you cannot! You're not
wearing any clothes."

Hafsa rose from their shared pallet beside Butayna's bed and
offered her favorite *rida*. Butayna dressed and pulled the
rounded iron handles inward. Alfonso Ruiz bowed before her.

"*Almocaden*, what has happened?"

"I have sent Xurxo and Jose to investigate, *mi reina*. The
sound came from the *Infanta* Leila's room."

"Leila! *Dios mío*! Muhammad and Aisha share her quarters
tonight. Come with me."

Jawla and Ifrit followed as she and Ruiz went down the
corridor. Butayna met Xurxo and Jose. Both men backed away
from the light shining from Leila's chamber at the *Jannat al-'Arif*.

"What has happened? Are my children hurt? What of Leila?"

Ruiz's elder brother came out of the room with Muhammad
held aloft in his arms. Pello carried Aisha and set her at her
mother's feet.

"My sweet children, are you hurt?"

Aisha pressed her forehead against Butayna's thigh. "*La,
Ummi*, but Ifrit is crying. She says Aunt Leila will die. Please,
don't let her die."

The *adalid* bowed. "*Mi reina*, it is the plague. The *Infanta* Leila
has two blackened boils at her neck. She had a fit and bit her
tongue, which awakened the rest of her household. Then her
slave Ifrit noticed the swelling."

Butayna backed away a step. A quick jolt stabbed at her heart. She pressed her fingers to her lips. "Not Leila! She went to the market only three days ago with her women. Is she the first one who's shown signs of sickness?"

Her son's captain shook his head. "No, *mi reina*. The slaves Hamduna, Sut, and Zarru are also coughing. The woman Amat vomited blood on her pallet. I have sent the rest of my men to warn the Sultan. We must leave the summer palace and return to Alhambra palace."

She shook her head. "Take my *Infantes*! I can't leave Leila here to die...." She rushed to the doorway.

"Butayna, stop!" At the head of Muhammad's personal guard and his own, Yusuf pushed the rest of the men aside and grabbed Butayna's shoulders. He held her flush against him although she struggled. "*La!* Do you want to die as well? If it is the black plague, you cannot enter!"

She turned in the circle of his arms and sobbed. "But Yusuf... your sister...."

He pulled her close and kissed her forehead. "I know, sweet love, I know. I have awakened Mufawwiz and Hisham. We must go from this place tonight."

"But Leila's inside with Hamduna, Zarru, Sut, and Amat, who are also ill. Where is Rima? I haven't heard a word of Rima."

Muhammad said, "She ran out of the room crying when she saw Aunt Leila's neck."

Yusuf patted his shoulder and touched Aisha's forehead. "My children, are you well?"

Muhammad and Aisha nodded. The boy replied, "We do not feel sick, Father."

Butayna reached for both of them and cradled the children close. "They have spent so much time with me this summer, Yusuf, except at night when they bedded down inside. I would not let Leila take them to the *Qaysariyya*. Leila had a little cough and a feverish appearance when I saw her coming from the *hammam*, but Muhammad and Aisha have been well. Oh, merciful Jesus, receive the souls of the dead and dying. *Dios mío*, please protect my children."

Yusuf scanned the faces surrounding them. "What of everyone else? Is anyone here sick or ailing?"

The Christian guards shook their heads.

Yusuf's captain sneered at them and muttered, "The evil *jinn* have brought this plague on the wind from Christian lands. We should kill the Genoese traders and all the foreign dogs who...."

Yusuf glared at him. "I'll have no more foolish talk of spirits or the arrant slaughter of innocents! If this sickness comes from

Christian lands, why did it strike the faithful at Baghdad and Damascus before it arrived in Constantinople? I have spoken to my doctor al-Shaquri. The disease, for it is such, ravaged Al-Mariyah in winter and has claimed so many in Malaga during these past two months. Al-Shaquri has consulted with other learned doctors in Malaga, including the wise al-Hasan ibn Muhammad. My doctor also consulted the texts of the great physician, his former master Yahya ibn Hudhayl al-Tujubi. Al-Shaquri believes one cause of the rapid spread is the coughs of those who are infected. We must tie clean cloths over our mouths and noses. We must burn fires and incense day and night to purify the air. Al-Shaquri also said anyone who touches a plague victim would die, so we must be sure not to have bodily contact with an infected person. If you must do so, wear gloves and burn them afterward. If anyone has done so, you cannot come with us now. Have any of you touched the people who are already sick?"

Everyone replied in the negative or vowed they had not.

"I remind all of you, it is treason to lie to me, your Sultan. In this instance, it might also mean death to all of us, so I charge you not to hide the truth. We shall withdraw to *al-Qal'at al-Hamra*. Butayna and our children shall stay in my chambers. You men shall remain in the prayer room to the south. At the first sign of sickness, you must leave and return here. You will kill others if you do not. We must find the slave Rima! Allah alone knows if she is also ill, but even if she is not, she may soon be."

Butayna called out, "Ifrit! Ifrit! Please talk to me. Let me know you are still among the living."

Yusuf murmured against her brow, "She may not be able to answer, sweet love."

"We cannot just leave her here to die! She has to know we are not abandoning Leila, her and the others without warning."

A soft whimper alerted Butayna. Leila's faithful body slave crawled on her hands and knees across the woodwork. Yusuf stumbled backward, his arms around his family. He dragged them with him. The guards shielded all of them.

Yusuf's captain brandished his sword. "No closer, woman!"

Ifrit's brow and her torso glistened with perspiration. Like Butayna, she slept naked due to the oppressive summer months. She cupped her stomach where the ribs jutted underneath the flesh and sagged on the floor. Her arm outstretched, she revealed the inflamed, swollen flesh of her armpit. A black furuncle the size of an egg festered on her skin.

"Go... go... Butayna." Her tremulous voice cracked. "Don't... come back. Live."

Butayna turned away and buried her face in Yusuf's neck. Her first kind words from Ifrit came at the most terrible moment of their lives. This could not be happening. Was this God's punishment or the world's ending? A just reward for sins? How many more lives that are precious would succumb before God granted His compassion?

When Yusuf had first received word of the malady six weeks ago, he tasked al-Shaquri with the discovery of its extent. The awful truth reflected a grave and growing danger for the inhabitants of the city. The denizens of al-Mariyah, Malaga and Madinah Antaqirah died by the dozens, then more than fifty per day. No one knew the cause or cure for the rampage of sickness, which killed within a week. According to al-Shaquri, the few who survived had their limbs turn black with rot. They would die anyway without removal of the putrid flesh. The latest report arrived for Yusuf at the beginning of the week. Seventy dead per day. In fear of the pestilence reaching *al-Qal'at al-Hamra* via trade caravans out of the infected cities, Yusuf ordered the *Qaysariyya* closed. Leila had attended, fearing it would be the last time she would have access to her favorite *ghaliya* fragrance and precious silks from the drapers.

Butayna sobbed harder. If only Leila had not gone into the city, she would not have fallen ill.

Yusuf cradled Butayna close and then lifted his head. "My guards, awaken the rest of the household. Rouse my mother and her servants. Get Maryam, our children and her eunuchs. We are leaving the *Jannat al-'Arif* now! Take nothing from this place except the clothes on your backs, lest we endanger our lives. Afterward, clean your bodies and don fresh garments. Burn those you are wearing now. Make rags of some other cloth. Do not use the communal linens from the *hammam*! Bar against breathing in the sickness as al-Shaquri advises. Then send word to *al-Quasaba* and the ministers of the *Diwan al-Insha*. Close the gates of the royal *madina*, first at the *Bab al-Sharia*, lock them all! We must protect ourselves from this pestilence before it ravages the whole of the city and kills us all."

***

A large square of linen tied around her nose and mouth, Butayna pushed her way through the overgrown bushes and brambles, which lined the route to the *Jannat al-'Arif*. The epidemic spread through the city and took the lives of slaves, servants, and nobles alike.

Three days after Yusuf had ordered the swift return to *al-Qal'at al-Hamra*, Butayna feared the fate of Leila and her servants. The guards had found Rima on the morning after, afloat in the pool of the old palace where she had drowned herself. Yusuf would allow no one near the befouled waters in the wake of her death. As slaves dropped where they stood, the same boils on their bodies as with Ifrit, no one removed Rima's corpse or cut away the dense brush.

Hafsa and Jawla huddled behind their mistress. Where a fallen branch extended across the path, Ruiz moved past the women and sliced through the wood with his sword. He led them on a circuitous path to the summer palace. When he jerked to a sudden stop and muttered a muffled curse under his mask, Butayna did not doubt what she could see if she peeked around him. Still, she did not hesitate.

"Move, *almocaden*. You delay my purpose. I have seen death before."

"*Sí, mi reina*. Never like this."

She sidestepped him. A corpse crisscrossed the road to the Royal House of Felicity. A slave girl, perhaps of an age with Aisha. In repose, the child could have been sleeping, except for the dried blood crusted around her mouth and below her nostrils. The wind rustled her yellow hair and revealed the evidence of the blue-black pestilence at her neck and on her forearm. The scent of decay and clotted blood saturated the stale, hot air. The stillness overwhelmed Butayna. Never in all her years had silence pervaded the summer palace, until now.

With nimble steps, Butayna led the others around the body. She picked her way through others strewn across the grounds. When rats scurried away from an old man's body, his face contorted in agony, Hafsa yelped and grabbed Jawla's arm. Flies buzzed atop other cadavers. Butayna batted them with leather gloves. Up the stairs and beneath the southern pavilion, she found death in almost every corner. Another russet-haired young slave huddled with a dead eunuch, tumors all over his exposed calves. Ragged breaths and the slow rise and fall of her chest indicated she would not have much longer before the malady took her.

Butayna sobbed behind her hands. Ruiz shook his head. "You cannot help her, *mi reina*."

Even as he spoke, the death rattle sent a last, frantic gasp through the slave's chest. She shuddered and her head drooped a little on the chest of the black eunuch beside her, sightless eyes directed at the marble walkway. Had she loved him? Was he her friend? Had she just stumbled beside him, unable to move any further? No one would ever know of her last days or the countless lives taken by the black plague.

"Help... me!"

Hafsa screamed again, as Butayna turned to the steps at the western edge of the southern pavilion. The stableman Bilal stretched out across the marble stairs, one finger turned blacker than the rest of him. The open tumor on his neck oozed and appeared smaller than a *dirham*.

Butayna stated, "We can help him. The jailor came to the grounds this morning with the same sign, showed Yusuf the swelling in his armpit had reduced. Somehow, there are those who have survived the worst of it. We must send Bilal to the gatehouse where the jailor has withdrawn. Hafsa, run back to the palace and find two eunuchs. Tell them I order them to fetch come here and fetch Bilal. You must guide them back and ensure they take him. Go, now!"

As her servant scurried, Butayna edged closer to Bilal. "What of al-Sagir? Is your brother dead?"

"*La...* Sultana. Water!"

He gasped and slumped again.

"Live, Bilal! Fight this sickness. Help shall come, I promise."

With hope renewed, Butayna crossed the garden path. The door to the bedchamber of the summer palace swung back with a yawn and a thud. Jawla shivered and grasped Butayna's gloved hand.

Butayna patted her fingers. "Come."

Ruiz said, "Let me lead the way, *mi reina*."

Butayna followed him in the darkened hallway. The same stink reeked in the narrow confines. When they reached the entry into Leila's chambers, Butayna fell to the floor and wept.

Leila coughed behind her hand and shook, as she draped a woven blanket over Ifrit's shivering form within the doorway. Mussed, dirtied hair hung in hanks around Leila's pallid face. A black spot covered her left nostril. She looked up at the sound of Butayna's sobs. "You," she began, her voice croaking from disuse, "You... shed... those tears... for me?"

"You're alive!" Butayna clasped her hands in thanks as Jawla cradled her.

Leila swallowed. "Allah is not... not done... with me." She heaved a ragged breath. "Or, my... Ifrit."

She caressed the cheek of her favored slave, who whimpered. Tears rolled down Ifrit's cheeks.

"What of the tumors at your neck?"

Leila groaned as she lifted her hand. Her fingers brushed at her hair in a futile effort at first. She tried again and revealed the remnants of the tumors at her neck. "Do they... look smaller to your eyes as well? The pain... it... it hurts, but... not... as much."

Butayna turned and clutched at Jawla's fingers. "Go to *al-Qal'at al-Hamra* now! Tell Yusuf that Leila is still alive. He must summon Al-Shaquri. He must also send food, some broth perhaps. His sister needs clean water now."

"At once, my Sultana."

Ruiz remained beside Butayna. He covered his mouth and nose, despite the linen on his face.

Leila muttered, "The others... dead."

Butayna nodded and swiped at her eyes. "I know, I know. Rima is also dead."

"Ah. Pulled... the bodies... by the window."

"How? You haven't the strength for all that, Leila."

"I told... you. Allah is... not done. Now, I must... rest."

Leila collapsed on the floor beside Ifrit and clutched at her fingers, in the same state as those of Bilal.

"The blood has seeped beneath the skin and turned it black," Ruiz whispered.

Butayna nodded. "I know. Al-Shaquri believes the best treatment is to cut away the dead flesh. If Ifrit survives this, she will lose her hands. Leila will lose a portion of her nose, but at least, they will live."

***

Butayna remained with Leila, despite the odor. When she told Ruiz that he did not have to stay, he shook his head. "Everywhere, there is death. Where can I go, *mi reina?*"

"If you will stay, then help me. Find braziers and incense. We must purify the air and help drive the pestilence and stench away."

The call to prayer summoned worshipers at noon. How many remained at *al-Qal'at al-Hamra* to observe prayers and beg God's forgiveness?

After Butayna and Ruiz lit the braziers within the hall, they went outside with the same intent. Hafsa waved to them before she admonished the terrified eunuchs to be more careful with Bilal, as they placed him on a bier. Butayna whispered her thanks and set incense in a hot brazier near the door, while Ruiz went to the northern pavilion. The eunuchs carried Bilal away, while Hafsa led them around the bodies.

When Butayna and Ruiz had finished, dusk descended. Yusuf arrived, accompanied by Jawla and Safa's slave Nazhun. Both of the women carried ceramic bowls in their hands. Steam wafted from the smaller tureen Nazhun held in her hands. Yusuf waved them inside, while Butayna steeled herself for the encounter with him.

He stood before her and raked white-gloved hands over his hair. "You knew! You knew I had forbidden anyone from coming here! Still, you risked it. Why?"

Despite the muffled tone behind his mask, she did not have to guess at his anger.

"You know why. For your sister, who is a sister to me. You are lucky. You have had many sisters. I had none."

He hauled her against him. "My stupid, stubborn wife."

She slammed her fists against his chest. "You will not call me stupid! If I am stubborn, I am so because I love your sister as much as you do!"

He stilled her hands and crushed her in his arms. "I know you do. I cannot condone the risk you have taken, but I am blessed by your love for Leila."

"Did you bring broth and water as I asked?"

"I did. I have brought a good brown broth of lamb and herbs. There is also fresh water from the cistern. When Hafsa returned, she told me of Bilal. I could scarce believe it. Then Jawla arrived with news of Leila and her slave. It was more than I could have hoped for, but al-Shaquri has heard of survivors as well, at al-Mariyah. We have to begin the removal of these bodies. I have set slaves to the task. They wear falconers' gloves."

"What will you do with the dead? There are so many. Hamduna, Amat, Sut, and Zarru are inside."

"We will bury them all in mass graves. It would be sacrilege to burn the bodies."

She glanced at the opened door. "Why is Safa's slave here with you?"

"I told her to come. My mother was there when Jawla brought the news of Leila's recovery. I told Jawla to fetch water. My mother sent Nazhun to the kitchen for broth."

An agonized screech rent the air, almost as stark as the one that filled Butayna's throat. Her heart shattered into a thousand fragments. She clutched at the sleeves of Yusuf's *shaya* and shook her head. It could not be. Safa could not be so devious and heartless, could she? Butayna already knew the answer.

"*La... la!* Please, merciful Jesus... Leila!"

She raced indoors, Yusuf and Ruiz on her heels. She slid to a halt before the opened doorway. Jawla knelt on the floor. Sobs wracked her body. Nazhun backed away from the horrific sight.

Leila bent backward and clawed at her throat. Ragged nails abraded her tender skin. Her face purpled. She gagged and slumped beside an overturned bowl of the thin broth, spilled across the wooden floor. She gurgled once before stillness fell over the Royal House of Felicity again.

Butayna turned on Nazhun. She grabbed her collar and slammed her against the brick wall behind her. "What did you give her? What did you do to her?"

Yusuf tugged at her. "Butayna, your grief has made you mad! What are you doing?"

She closed her fingers around Nazhun's thick neck above the collar. "I know you must have followed your mistress' command. Safa told you to do it. Perhaps, you never even knew what she intended. She put something in the broth to kill Leila. Didn't she? Answer or I will choke the life from you!"

Yusuf wrenched her away. "Have you lost your senses?"

Nazhun bawled and fled the corridor. Her guttural sobs echoed through the grounds of the *Jannat al-'Arif.*

Butayna wailed and clenched her fists on Yusuf's chest, as he drew her into his arms. She could not summon the strength to pummel him just yet. Her last reserves of energy ebbed. She slumped on the ground. Yusuf's arms came about her again. Her hot tears soaked his neck.

He whispered against her brow, "She's gone, Butayna. We must accept."

She shook her head. "She lived! She would have lived, but for your evil mother!"

"Butayna...."

She wriggled in his hold. "*La...* let me go."

"I will not, until you see reason. This is the plague's effect. No one harmed Leila. She is at rest now."

She pushed at his shoulders. "You once told me, you condoned much for the love of your family. Will you permit the murder of your sister to go unpunished? Safa knew this would be her one chance. No one would question the sudden loss of an afflicted woman. No doctor would consider the possibility of poison as the cause of death. Except Safa."

"Calm yourself! We'll go back to *al-Qal'at al-Hamra* together."

"Let me go!" She fought him in earnest. After several of her bites and punches, he released her. On wooden legs, she stood and looked at Leila for the last time. A bloodied bubble formed between her pale lips. Safa had ensured her rival would never rise and walk the pathways between the palaces again. No more *ghaliya* wafting on the air. No shimmery silk rippling in the wind. No more peals of laughter.

Listless, Ifrit reached across the floor with her blackened fingertips. "Leila... Leila?"

Yusuf stood and held out his hand. "Come, Butayna. We must grieve together and tell the children. Leila raised them and they should know her fate."

"Tell them yourself! I do not have words to offer comfort. My words are gone with Leila's smiles."

***

Two months later, Butayna trailed Ifrit along the northern sentry walk to *al-Quasaba*, which faced the *Hadarro* River. A dying sun cast a gleam like burnished brass on the walls of *al-Qal'at al-Hamra*. The sight reminded Butayna of the dried blood around the mouths of some plague victims. Not the ones who coughed up black bile and died in less than three days, but those who vomited blood until they fainted from sheer exhaustion, waiting for death to claim them.

"You should be resting, Ifrit."

"I will." Ifrit led Butayna down the wooden access ramp.

With the stubs of her fingers still bandaged, Ifrit scanned the vicinity before she brushed aside the climbing vines and roses at the base of the wall. An iron-riveted door, half the height of a man, showed years of neglect in the splintered wood and rusted nail heads.

"Where does the tunnel behind it lead, Ifrit?"

"Just below the bridge over the *Hadarro*. This is the third exit I can show you today. What do you remember of the other two?"

"The first led to the old home of a former Jewish *wazir*."

"*Nam*. His descendants still live there, though they keep their Jewish faith a secret and worship in the mosque. They are prepared to guide and help you when the time comes. And the second path?"

"That route would take me into the woodland between *al-Qal'at al-Hamra* and the *Jannat al-'Arif*. I must not use torches at night, for watchmen might see them."

"Good. I have now shown you three means to leave this place in secret, as the Sultana Fatima commanded me. You once asked whether I came from the House of Myrtles. Sultana Fatima bought me when I was a child from that place. She told me of these hidden exits for Leila's protection. Fatima wanted you to know of them for your children's safety. You can flee through other underground locations. Still, I think if you tried to remember all of them, you would become confused. When the time comes, you must make a quick and certain decision. Failure and hesitation means death for your children."

"Where can I go if I must escape?"

"I think you know, my Sultana."

After the space of several breaths, Butayna nodded. She rearranged the foliage so the next patrol would never notice the disturbance. Then she turned to Ifrit. "He will help me when the time comes?"

"I believe he will. You must ask."

Butayna and Ifrit went up the short stairs and returned along the parapet. When the slave stumbled and gripped the rough, brick wall, Butayna steadied her. "Be careful or you will fall."

"You should not trouble yourself about me. Worry for your fate and the lives of your children."

Ifrit leaned against the low wall behind her. A nearby torch revealed her hollowed cheekbones and a stark, expressionless gaze. She stared at some point in the distance.

"You said I must ask for help. How do I request it? Through you?"

"Rely first upon Jawla and Hafsa. Mufawwiz can help as well. There are others, but those closest to you are best."

Butayna mused, "They are also targets for Maryam and Safa."

"Life is not without its perils. The Sultana knew." Ifrit groaned and swallowed.

"Does your chest still hurt? Should we return?"

"None of my aches matter. I must beg a last boon. Promise me you will not let Safa win. She thinks she has by poisoning the Sultana Leila."

Butayna pinched the bridge of her nose and closed her eyes before she pressed her hip against the wall beside Ifrit.

"I swear I will have vengeance against her for Leila's death. Yusuf refuses to acknowledge the truth of his mother's role."

"He had al-Shaquri's slave drink the same soup and the boy live."

"Yet, how difficult could it have been for Safa to have a kitchen maid add poison to the soup intended for Leila alone? Yusuf rejects this idea, although it is possible. He knows the terrible acts his sister and mother have committed against each other over the years, but he cannot accept how Safa schemed to poison his sister while the plague could have killed her. He believes my grief has overtaken me, but I know the truth. One day, Safa shall understand as well."

She lapsed into silence when a sentry approached. His stone-faced visage focused on an area to the west, not on them.

When he passed, Ifrit murmured, "The Sultana Leila loved you."

Butayna's eyes prickled with unshed tears. She looked out on the city of whitewashed houses and touched the neckline of her treasured *rida*.

"As a sister. She would never have chosen me over you. She loved you, Ifrit. You held her heart."

"Leila loved me as I loved her. I am not ashamed of the passion we held for each other."

"Was Safa aware of Leila's relationship with you?"

"I do not know. If she knew of it, she would have told Yusuf. It is against his laws for two women to love each other as the Sultana and I did."

"I believe my husband knew. He is generous to those whom he loves, even me."

Ifrit fingered the abraded line of her neck, as if she still felt for her slave collar. Yusuf had freed her in the aftermath of Leila's death. "The Sultana desired you for a time. Long before your marriage, she once told me she knew the Sultan would find you irresistible and you would desire him in equal measure. She saw no purpose in seeking a love long denied her by her brother's claims. I hated you for a long time, but the Sultana convinced me of the sincerity of her need. I never doubted her again."

Butayna laid a hand on Ifrit's arm and held her breath. When Ifrit did not flinch, Butayna sighed. "You will see Leila again. She awaits you in Paradise. Now, you are free to live."

"I do not want to be free of her. I am going to her now."

Ifrit offered Butayna her last, slight smile before she tipped backward over the wall. Butayna's shriek swallowed any cry Ifrit might have made as she plummeted to her death among the olive groves beneath the walls of *al-Quasaba*.

The watchman rushed back to Butayna's position and peered into the encroaching darkness. "What happened here? How did she fall?"

Butayna bit back a sob and turned from him. "She chose her ending, something few of us are ever able to do. That is all."

***

By Yusuf's command, Butayna occupied Leila's room in the winter after her death. Though Jawla and Hafsa feared the Sultana's uneasy spirit haunted the grounds, Butayna chided them for foolishness. Leila would never hurt those whom she loved. In the absence of their aunt, Butayna's children relied upon her supervision. If Yusuf held any objections, or his mother expressed them, Butayna never heard.

The children were gone with a portion of Yusuf's personal guard and Muhammad's own on an inspection of the site where their father resumed work on a new religious school. The frequency of plague outbreaks had lessened in the middle of the season and Yusuf's master builder recruited new workers from among survivors eager to resume their lives.

Jawla and Hafsa attended to their duties while Butayna stood by the lattice window, which overlooked the garden courtyard. It separated her chamber from Safa's own, where laughter echoed.

Butayna's jaw tightened. Ifrit had guessed the old Sultana enjoyed her triumph. "It shall be short-lived, I promise you."

Behind her, Hafsa asked, "Did you speak to me, my Sultana?"

"I did not."

She almost veered away from the window, when Yusuf's voice sounded below. She peered into the courtyard. He strolled from the direction of the *hammam*, beside al-Shaquri with the rest of the Sultan's guards behind them. Her husband wore the *taylasan* headcloth with short, black tassels, which signified his intent to pray. Of late, Yusuf adopted ostentatious garments rather than the simpler clothes he wore in the days of their first meeting. She remained skeptical as to whether she approved of his choice in attire.

A eunuch bowed at Yusuf's side and offered him a rolled parchment. He broke the seal. As he read the contents of the missive, his brow creased and color drained from his face.

She clutched the *shimasas*. Did his expression portend some disaster? Had the pestilence threatened to overtake the populace again? She clutched her chest. Her children were out there in the city. Despite Hafsa's pleas, she raced out of the room and down the steps.

Before she rushed into the courtyard, Jawla's hand closed on her arm. "Forgive this insolent servant, but you cannot go out there without your *hijab*! Would you have the Sultan furious with you for showing your beauty to al-Shaquri?"

Butayna scowled at her and donned the veil. "You always cloak your impudence in such polite words. You could tell a man he is a fool and have him believe it, just by the sound of your voice."

Jawla bowed with an impish smile on her lips. Butayna dismissed her. When she stepped out into the courtyard, Yusuf resumed the walk to his room alone. Her footfalls paralleled him until she met him at his doorway.

She greeted him. "What news? I saw you through the window. Is all well?"

His lips crinkled. "You worry too much, sweet love."

"How can you say such in this time of death and siege? Has something happened? Our children are at the *Madrasa Yusufiyya*. Are they in danger? Have we lost more to the malady today? Has Castilla-Leon taken Jabal Tarik at last?"

He shook his head. "I expect Muhammad and Aisha will return soon, in time for midday prayers. My people still die each

328

day of the plague, but less now than two months ago. The Castillans have no leader. My commanders at Jabal Tarik have sent word. King Alfonso is dead, a victim of the pestilence. He perished at Jabal Tarik five days ago. How do you feel about that?"

She groaned and eyed him. Still with these tests of her loyalty after so many years. "He used your alliance with Abu Inan Faris in the overthrow of his father Abu'l-Hasan Ali, as well as your seizure of some sheep and their shepherds as a pretext for the campaign. He has long desired Jabal Tarik. Why should I care if he is dead?"

Yusuf squeezed her fingers and brought them to his lips. "You are very harsh, wife. As it is, one of the ablest among my enemies has died, a man I despised and admired at turns. As such, I have sent word to my commanders. They will let the Christians leave Jabal Tarik without hindrance, in respect of their great warrior. I am not ignorant of the blessing Allah has granted me with Alfonso's death. His end is as fortuitous as the rise of Abu Inan Faris in Fés el-Jedid. The Castillans will anoint their new sovereign and I may once again turn my attentions south, to the Marinids. For years, they have interfered in the politics of this land and forced their holy warriors of *al-Ghuzat* on four generations of Sultans. No longer."

He released her and entered his room.

Butayna stared in his wake, aghast. "You cannot mean it! The Christian siege has only just lifted and you would strike against the Marinids."

He turned and winked at her. "Who said anything about warfare? Half of my men at Jabal Tarik considered conversion to the Christian faith, in the hopes plague might not destroy their lives. How can I trust them to fight for me now? The other half are dead. I must pray and give Allah thanks for His boons. Come to me tonight and bring my grandmother's *oud*. Sing me songs, some of your frontier ballads. Afterward, I shall tell you how I will rid my Sultanate of eighty years of Marinid intervention. When I have decided on a course of action, you will bring Muhammad to court. He must learn the duties of a prince of the faithful."

Chapter 23
The Bathhouse

Sultana Butayna

Granada, Andalusia
June 6, AD 1351 / 10 Rabi ath-Thani 752 AH / 11th of Sivan,
5111

Butayna and Muhammad shared a cushion edged with filigree in the throne room of *al-Qal'at al-Hamra*. They sat in a corner secluded behind a screen, while Yusuf concluded public audience and prepared to greet his guests.

A light breeze preceded the entrance of Maryam and Safa from the doorway at the rear, where a portion of Yusuf's guard stood in silent observation. Maryam maneuvered her eldest son Ismail to a nearby seat. He fidgeted with the sleeves of his *jubba* beside her although she chided in a soft voice. Safa pointed a cushion behind Butayna, which her slave Nazhun moved to the forefront. When Yusuf's mother sat down and blocked her view, Butayna glared at her back and imagined a knife stuck between Safa's ribs. It would be more than fair recompense for Leila's death.

When she looked up, Maryam's grin highlighted her cheekbones. "Your eyes betray you as usual."

Butayna met her regard. "What do they tell you now?"

Maryam giggled. "It is a blessing our husband does not allow weapons in the throne room, even among his guards. Otherwise, I would fear for my life at this moment."

"Perhaps you still should."

"You are no killer, Butayna. You do not have the temperament for murder."

Butayna stared at Safa again. "It would seem some others do."

Safa jerked around. "Be quiet! I wish to hear what Yusuf would say to the Marinid princes."

"I remind you, I am not afraid of you, Safa. I shall never be."

"Speak again to interrupt these proceedings and you will be afraid!"

Muhammad huddled closer to his mother. She patted his forearm and hugged him against her, before she looked through the screen.

The princes Abu'l-Fadl and Abu Salim, sons of Abu'l-Hasan Ali and the brothers of the new Marinid ruler, Abu Inan Faris entered the throne room. Both possessed the dark coloring of their father coupled with straight, pitch-black hair. Both appeared a little older than Muhammad, with little tufts of fuzz beneath their chins, which somehow reminded Butayna of goats. She stifled a laugh as they bowed in the doorway as the herald announced them and then midway to the throne room. Yusuf learned forward on the throne, his sandaled feet tapping on the marble.

Butayna perceived his impatience and nervousness. Her husband charted a course set to destabilize the Marinid regime and make an enemy of Abu Inan Faris. Yusuf held sound reasoning for his choice, but he knew the risk would not be without consequences. She despaired for him, but understood the profundity of his plan.

"You may rise, noble princes. Draw near." At a wave from Yusuf, the rebel Marinid princes took seats on brocaded cushions while the courtiers milled about, envy narrowing their gazes as Abu'l-Fadl and Abu Salim accepted water and slices of fig. Inside the throne room, the temperature soared. Even Ibn al-Khatib, who stood closest to the window behind Yusuf, mopped his brow beneath sodden curls.

After his guests had the fill of the small repast, Yusuf said, "Thank you for coming to me in this grave hour. I trust the journey from Runda was without incident."

Both of the princes nodded in assent.

Yusuf continued, "May Allah preserve the memory of your noble father, the *Amir al-Muslimin* Abu'l-Hasan Ali of the Marinids. A worthy warrior for Islam."

Yet, he had not always thought so. When the son Abu Inan Faris abandoned the governorship of Tilimsan and advanced on Fés el-Jedid, Yusuf supported the new government. Had he seen even then the path to throwing off the Marinid yoke, which had bound the Nasrids to a dangerous alliance from the days of their first Sultan?

"Great Sultan, you honor us with your kind words regarding our father. My noble brother Abu Salim and I remain at your service," Abu'l-Fadl said.

Yusuf nodded, as the corner of his mouth twitched. Butayna shook her head at her husband. How could he find humor at this dangerous time?

331

He replied, "Now, it is you who honor me. I am grateful for your... ah, service. However, I must relay, your brother the noble Sultan Abu Inan Faris would wish it otherwise. He has written two letters in the month since your father's death, begging for word of his beloved brothers in Runda. He wishes to know why Yahya ibn Umar, the commander of the *Ghuzat,* has not answered his inquiries about both of you and why you have not returned to al-Maghrib el-Aska in respect of your beloved father. This coupled with some strange demand for the services of Abraham ben Zarzar, who has emerged as one of the brightest young physicians in the Jewish community since the days of plague. The Jews have not fared well in al-Maghrib el-Aska of late. I would hate to have to worry for the fate of one of my most prominent citizens, as much as for your own fortunes."

The princes shot each other grave frowns, which belied their youthful appearances. Abu Salim cleared his throat and his brother beckoned for more water.

After a sip, Abu'l-Fadl said, "It is a wonder our brother can leave the bed where he keeps our father's concubine, Shams ed-Duna."

Yusuf settled back against the cedar wood throne, its arms covered in samite. "He's stolen a woman from your father's harem? If so, it would be a shameful act."

"The gossips say she is his English rose. He'll do no better with her than our own father did."

Yusuf propped up his chin with one hand and stroked the silk with the other fingers as if bored or stymied in idle thought, but Butayna knew him better. Were the rumors true? She had not known until now whether Abu'l-Hasan Ali's *kadin* had survived the brutal aftermath of the battle at the *arroyo* del Salado.

Beside her, Muhammad whispered, "Will Father send the princes home as Sultan Abu Inan Faris demands? Won't the Marinid Sultan just kill or imprison his brothers?"

Aware of Maryam's sidelong glance and the tilt of Safa's head as she listened in, Butayna murmured, "Your father will do as he sees best. A Sultan is responsible for many lives, even those who reside outside of the Sultanate. He must be prudent, yet remain aware of the opportunity to gain benefits for his people. The people are all that matter, my son."

Maryam pursed her lips. "You teach him means of governance as if the succession has already been decided. My Ismail is a worthy heir as well, lest you forget."

Right now, the boy whom his mother considered a suitable successor of his father proved himself a nuisance. He snapped the gold beads off the cushion beneath him and flung them at the latticework. When the beads clattered against the wooden screen, Yusuf lifted his head and peered behind him, as did Ibn al-Khatib.

At a sharp glance from Safa, Maryam grabbed the remainder of the pilfered beads from her son. Butayna rolled her eyes and returned her attention to the well-orchestrated spectacle in the throne room.

Abu Salim said, "Our brother would do well with the services of any notable physician. We have heard Fés el-Jedid remains in the grip of the pestilence, great Sultan. Abu'l-Fadl and I consider ourselves fortunate to have escaped its clutches. We are grateful to you for... allowing our presence in such a difficult time and we do not see any need to alter the arrangement."

Yusuf's chuckle echoed in the stillness of the throne room. Rapt gazes from every courtier concentrated on the subtle drama unfolding before their eyes.

With a nod to Ibn al-Khatib, Yusuf replied, "I am aware of the great risk I have asked my *wazir* to undertake. Ibn al-Khatib shall leave at the end of this assembly for Fés el-Jedid. He takes with him my letters of condolence to Abu Inan Faris."

Furious murmurs arose among the courtiers, but when Yusuf raised his hand in a bid for silence, the audience complied.

He said, "What shall Ibn al-Khatib tell Abu Inan Faris of his brothers in the Sultanate? Understand, my noble princes, the delicate intricacy required in addressing this matter. I have two paths set before me. One, to remain a generous host and support you, my noble... guests. I will earn the enmity of your brother the Sultan. The other path demands my agreement to Abu Inan's request. Even if I gained his favor, I would lose your generous opinions. I wish there could be some easy means to avoid this grave impasse, but such is my dilemma."

Perspiration beaded at the brows of both young princes. Butayna released a heavy sigh. She wished her husband would not extend the drama much further, for tears glistened in Abu Salim's eyes and Abu'l-Fadl appeared on the verge of an apoplexy.

Then Ridwan came forward and bowed his head. Yusuf tilted his head toward him. "Speak to us, learned *wazir*. Can you see a way out of this quagmire?"

The minister declared, "As we are all well aware, the Sultan Abu Inan is a younger son of the great Abu'l-Hasan Ali. He does not look with favor upon the rival claims of any of his brothers to the throne. Perhaps, we could ensure his understanding that these noble princes are not a threat to his rule."

Yusuf leaned on his hand again. "How would we convey such a message?"

"The faithful *Ghuzat* has served on Andalusi soil for over eighty years, since the progenitor of this illustrious dynasty accepted their gracious aid in the maintenance of our faith. The *jihad* will never be over, but perhaps the Volunteers of the Faith can serve another purpose. The noble princes, by virtue of their presence at Runda, have nominal power over these fine warriors for Islam. Perhaps a better use exists for them in the advancement of the claims of Sultan Abu Inan Faris to the west of al-Maghrib el-Aska. If the noble princes would cede the army under their control at Runda, their brother might perceive that they do not seek to use his own forces against him."

Butayna could have almost smiled at her husband's genius, if she did not hold some reservations about his plans for the Marinid princes. She had not anticipated how Yusuf would co-opt another minister besides Ibn al-Khatib into his scheme. The *Diwan al-Insha* and the courtiers had also been naïve, for crimson blotches colored their faces, beneath furrowed brows. Ridwan's former disgrace had haunted him for so long, no one might have presumed Yusuf would ever allow him influence at court again.

Yusuf nodded as if his minister had not repeated the words Yusuf trained him to say. "An excellent suggestion, but it would still leave the matter of the royal princes' safety unresolved. I am hesitant to consider such an approach without a plan for the safety of my guests."

He offered them a tight-lipped smile. An audible sigh from Abu Salim filled the court.

Abu'l-Fadl coughed in a vain attempt to cover his brother's indiscretion. "We would not wish to impose upon your hospitality further. I believe your minister's suggestion is a sound one and I thank him for it. For Abu Salim and I, perhaps it would be best after a detachment of the *Ghuzat* has left Runda, we should also withdraw as well."

Yusuf leaned forward. "But where would you go? How could I be assured of your safety?"

Abu Salim said, "My mother's Berber people hail from the southern region of al-Maghrib el-Aska. If the great Sultan would arrange for a boat for our sea crossing, we can assure our own safety. Moreover, we would be forever grateful to you for allowing us to depart in peace."

Yusuf waved his hand. "It shall be as you say. *Al-salam 'alayka,* my princes."

Both Marinids bowed their heads. "*Wa-'alayka, al-Amir al-Muslimin.*"

As the throne room erupted in applause and some notable sighs of relief, Muhammad tugged Butayna's sleeve. "*Ummi*, I don't understand what Father did."

Safa grunted and snapped at him, "Fool boy! This is how a Sultan plays the game of diplomacy. Never reveal your true intent. Let others believe your wishes are theirs. My son has manipulated the Marinids well. He has deprived the rebel princes of the services of the *Ghuzat* and necessitated their departure from *al-Andalus*. He has shown Abu Inan he will not support threats to the rightful ruler of al-Maghrib el-Aska and shall earn his favor as a result. Yusuf has also kept the friendship of the rebel princes, as they sought to keep his. If my Ismail had been half as shrewd as his son, perhaps my husband might still be alive."

Then she stood and glared at Butayna, who raised her chin. Safa observed, "You appear the least unsettled by these events. Yusuf forewarned you of his intent. He used to share everything with me."

Butayna shrugged. "It is the province of a wife to listen to her husband's concerns."

Safa snorted and clamped her walking stick, as she moved toward the exit. "Do not forget, Butayna, my son has two wives."

***

In mid-afternoon, Butayna went to the summer palace's *hammam*. The *jawari* frequented the baths at *al-Qal'at al-Hamra* during any hour of the day, but with a smaller number of occupants at the *Jannat al-'Arif,* Butayna relaxed on a marble slab beneath the ministrations of a masseur.

A sharp chin pressed against her hand, Aisha lounged at her mother's feet in *qabqab* bath sandals, unembarrassed by her naked state. An attendant wrapped in white linen around her waist brushed Aisha's hip-length tresses until they shone like bronze. No discernible differences existed between Butayna at her daughter's age or the mannerisms and appearance Aisha had developed. Straighter than a bow, with wit as sharp as a blade's edge, the little girl had inherited the best traits of her parents and little of their faults. Butayna had long accepted the truth. Muhammad belonged to the Sultanate and his father's people, but perhaps this daughter could be hers for some time.

"*Ummi?*"

"Hmm?" Butayna stirred from her languid haze. "What is it, my dear girl?"

"Do you think I shall ever marry?"

"Why would you not? You are a beautiful girl, but of equal importance, you are a Sultana. Your father shall have many suitors to choose from and I do not doubt he will make the best selection for your husband."

Hafsa, who kept a watchful eye on the attendant, now shooed her away and began braiding Aisha's hair. Hafsa affixed little gold beads of *barq* with amethyst stones to each plait.

Aisha said, "I will marry whomever Father says I must, because I know he will choose someone to make me joyous. Still, Sultana Safa said I have the body of a boy and no one will want me. She told me so last week, when Muhammad and I dined with our father and his mother in his quarters."

Butayna hid the fury broiling in her gut with a low laugh. "My governess once said the same of me. Now, I have you and Muhammad. You are just ten years old. Your father may not arrange your betrothal for two or three years. You have time to blossom into the woman you may become. Do not wish for a wife's burdens so soon. Do not dwell upon Sultana Safa's words. She does not know everything."

"I don't like her!" Aisha shook her head and the *barq* jingled in a melody almost as sweet as her lyrical voice. "I should respect her because she is my grandmother, but do I have to like her, *Ummi?* She is cruel to my brother and me. She calls Muhammad fat! He is, but she makes him seem horrid, although she must be more than twice his size!"

Butayna chuckled at her daughter's observation, although she seethed inside. "You are very astute, like your father."

"What does 'astute' mean, *Ummi?*"

"It means you are very wise, my child."

"Sultana Safa thinks I am an empty-headed fool like my mother."

"Does she?" As Butayna tensed, the masseur kneaded her shoulders a little harder.

Aisha replied in a soft whisper, "She said so, but she's a liar. You are... astute. Father says so. He often tells me, 'Listen to your wise mother, for she will always speak the truth.' He believes in you, *Ummi.*"

Butayna could not contain her grin. She ducked her head lest anyone witnessed the pleasure she took in Aisha's disclosure. After all the dreadful mistakes, to know Yusuf still held her in high regard meant more than anything did.

A cacophony of conversation and amusement heralded the arrival of Safa and Maryam with their slaves and Maryam's daughters. Aisha stiffened upon sight of them and Butayna raised her chin. The younger children, Khadija, Shams, Mumina, and Zoraya favored their mother's appearance so much, they hearkened back to a time in Butayna's childhood when she first knew Maryam. Only the eldest daughter Fatima had not received the blessing of her mother's beauty. She did not possess unpleasant features, just not as lovely as her younger sisters. In her visage were subtle hints of the beauty her grandmother Safa might have held in her youth. Still, Fatima would never be the image of her mother.

The women and their entourage began the bathing ritual, while Butayna turned away from them. Hafsa finished with Aisha's hair and summoned a masseur who would pamper the girl alongside her mother. Aisha removed her platform sandals and reclined on a heated slab next to Butayna.

"*Ummi*, why can't I have my hands painted with *henna*, as my sister Fatima does?"

"You need no enhancements, my little dove. You are already as sweet as need be."

Aisha's huff brought a wide smile to Butayna's lips, which she concealed behind her forearms.

"All of my sisters are pretty and plump. Fatima's hips are starting to show even though she is just a little older than me."

"Every girl grows into a woman at her own pace and in God's time. Why worry so much for what your sisters have that you do not? Are you not as lovely as they are?"

Aisha released a wistful sigh. "Not always."

Butayna sat up and regarded her child. "Well, you are beautiful to me and your father." She placed her hands on her slim hips. "You see these? They have always been too narrow. Yet, I birthed you and your brother." She lifted her legs. "My feet are too large, even your dear aunt Leila said so when she first met me. Have you ever seen a tiny woman with the feet of a giantess? Ridiculous. It is a wonder everyone in the harem does not see my feet before the rest of me arrives!"

Aisha laughed and Hafsa joined her. "Oh, *Ummi*, your feet are not so big!"

"Your father did not think so. He would rub them at night after we had dined."

"Doesn't he still?"

Butayna bowed her head. "I have not shared a meal with your father in some time, Aisha. We are not as we once were."

"Father still loves you, *Ummi*, I know he does. Otherwise, he would not say the kind words he often speaks of you. He is not often with the Sultana Maryam either. He prefers to dine with Muhammad, or sometimes my brother and I, or al-Shaquri, or Ridwan and Ibn al-Khatib. When I am with him and he talks about you, he always has a wide smile on his face. He must still love you, large feet and all."

Butayna placed her hand on Aisha's long forearm. "Thank you for your sweet words, dearest girl. They mean so much to me as you do. Never forget we are more than our bodies, my daughter. God fashioned them, so who are we to question Him? Inside the bodies with which we both find fault, we have strong hearts and minds, the desire to do good for others and the will to persevere in that struggle. This is why your father loves me despite these enormous feet. Never judge yourself by one standard alone. Be content with what God has granted you. He regards the full measure of us, our feelings, and our deeds."

"One of the *suras* of *al-Qur'an* says so. You are right, *Ummi*."

A cry shattered their mirth. They turned as one to the bathing fountain, where Nazhun clutched her cheek. Safa stood over her with her arm upraised.

"Go back to the harem and fetch it, you ignorant dog!"

The slave scrambled away from her mistress' side and fled the bathhouse. Butayna stared at Safa, who glowered and turned away, snapping at another of her women.

Tears welled in Aisha's eyes. "Why is she so horrible to everyone?"

Butayna kissed her daughter's cheek and brushed a finger over the girl's quivering lips. "No one is beneath you in God's eyes, Aisha, not even a servant or slave. Your ancestors built the wonders you have seen around you, even this *hammam* upon the backs of slaves. Remember that."

Butayna and Aisha still enjoyed their massages when Nazhun returned to the bathhouse with an ivory vial. A red streak slashed across her face where one of Safa's rings must have cut into her cheek.

The masseur indicated she had finished with Aisha first, who stood and slipped into her *qabqab* again. "*Ummi*, I'm cold."

Butayna nodded. "Go to the changing room and put on your *rida*. I shall come to—"

Safa's screech drowned out the rest of Butayna's words. "Go do it now!"

Nazhun fled as fast as her pudgy legs might take her and in her haste, she barreled into Aisha. The girl cried as she slid backward on the *hammam* floor. Her head hit the white marble with a sickening thud. Hafsa scrambled to her side and cradled the girl. Hafsa lifted her. Thick droplets of blood splashed on the tiles on the spot where Aisha had fallen. Butayna screamed and saw nothing, but red.

***

"I will have Nazhun's life for this!" Butayna's outrage echoed to the rafters of the small chamber. She knelt and wept beside Aisha's bed. Even an hour after sunset, the girl had not stirred despite the pleas of her parents of al-Shaquri's ministrations. When Yusuf heard of his daughter's troubles, he summoned his doctor at once.

Yusuf gripped Butayna's shoulders. "Hush, sweet love. You do not know what you are saying. It was an accident, a terrible accident. Maryam and all of my daughters have said so. Even Hafsa acknowledged it."

Butayna wrenched away from him. "I don't care what they saw. What if our daughter should die?"

Al-Shaquri stood opposite Butayna and Yusuf. "My Sultana, the girl will live. Her breathing is shallow, but there is life within her limbs. This is a common occurrence after a dreadful fall. You have faith!"

"I have every confidence that Nazhun will pay for her folly today, doctor. What if Safa told her to do this, to hurt my child?"

Yusuf withdrew his touch. "Butayna, my mother is capable of many things, but she would never harm a child. Not my child."

She swerved toward him. "And what of mine? Is she above harming one of my children? If she cares for yours so much, where is she now, eh? Where is this loving grandmother who calls our son fat and tells Aisha she is too thin to be a desirable wife?"

"I told *Ummi* to stay away, as it would only upset you more."

"You were right!"

"She will not keep away forever, Butayna. When you withdraw and seek your rest, I shall send word to her so she may visit the child and not disturb you."

"I am never leaving Aisha's side! What if she should awaken and I am not here? What if she needs me?"

"Can you do more than my doctor has?"

"I can be here for her. She is my daughter and I will never surrender her care to another for as long as I live!"

"I do not doubt your passion, or your love for our children. Still, you will need your rest, we both will. Al-Shaquri has promised to stay with her until she is well. He must go to his house this evening and fetch more medicines. You have posted your guards outside Aisha's bedchamber. She will never be alone."

"I would never leave any child of mine alone with your mother, not after what she did to Leila! I warned you, Yusuf, I warned you of how she poisoned Leila, but you would not listen.

You are always so willing to forgive, so bent upon believing those whom you love could never harm innocents that you do not—"

"If I did not hold to such beliefs, you would not be at our daughter's side today. Never forget, Butayna, you have claimed an innocent life as well in the murder of Maryam's baby. My baby."

She stiffened beneath his hard, merciless gaze.

Al-Shaquri lowered his eyelids and then said, "I should mix more of the poultice for the swelling. Do not let the little Sultana sleep for too much longer. Sleep can have a healing effect, but too much rest is bad for a person who has hit the head. If you will permit me to leave, my Sultan, I shall return to my house for the herbs. I shall not tarry a moment longer than necessary."

Without breaking his steady stare, Yusuf murmured, "You may go."

The physician bowed. "Thank you, my Sultan. My Sultanas." He patted Aisha's arm and bowed before Butayna. Then he withdrew from the room.

Just beyond the opened door, al-Shaquri revealed Ruiz. The *almocaden* stood alongside the wall, his hawkeyed gaze trained on all movement in the corridor. He nodded to the doctor and relaxed his tight grip on the hilt of a sharp sword. A swift summer wind dispersed the heady scent of ambergris through the room and buffeted the bright flames in two brass lanterns affixed to the wall.

The child mumbled something in her stupor. A thick linen bandage wound around her head and held in place the poultice of mint and other herbs al-Shaquri had prepared.

Butayna looked away from Yusuf and cradled her child's cheek. She shuddered with the memory of what she had done. Maryam suffered lessened bouts of the falling sickness over time, and al-Shaquri believed episodes would no longer plague her within a few years. Butayna's resultant shame and regret would remain for the rest of her life.

"Is this my punishment then? To have my child taken from me?" Her voice broke and her vision misted again.

Her words were the closest admission of her guilt in the death of Maryam's child she had ever uttered in Yusuf's presence. When his hand settled at the apex of her neck and shoulder, she trembled anew, a plea for mercy on her lips. Yusuf's fingers stroked her skin and she cried even harder at the oft-repeated demonstration of his capacity for compassion. He should have reviled her as much as she despised herself whenever she thought of her role in the cruel and needless murder of a baby. Perhaps God did seek to make her suffer now, to know another loss. He had already claimed one child from her. Was she destined to lose another now?

Yusuf whispered, "Neither of us can question the will of God, Butayna."

Muhammad entered the room, his cheeks flushed. Yusuf reached for his hand and drew the boy beside his sister. He looked down at her, his mouth in a wide O.

"Why didn't anyone send for me at the princes' school? Pero just told me what happened to Aisha. Is she going to die?"

Butayna clutched her daughter's fingers and shook her head, wordless. She did not know what to say to offer Muhammad comfort or herself. In her silent plea, she begged God for clemency and prayed He would not take Aisha from her. She would do anything, even forgive Nazhun's clumsiness, if her child lived.

Yusuf stood and gathered Muhammad to him. The boy buried his ruddy cheeks in his father's *jubba*. "Nothing is certain. We must wait and see. Al-Shaquri has done his best in tending to her. The rest belongs to Allah, as do all matters."

Muhammad sobbed in his father's clutches. Yusuf patted his shoulders and held him close. "My brave boy, she will need your strength in the coming days too, but weep for her now as you must. Pray for her as well. Through Allah all things are possible, even your sister's easy recovery."

Butayna struggled to share her husband's sentiments about the benefits of prayers. God had not listened when she cried out for justice in the aftermath of Leila's poisoning. Somehow, Safa had used her minion, the hapless Nazhun to perpetrate another heinous act. Butayna was certain of it. For so long after Leila's death, Butayna had struggled with her grief and rage. No one could convince that Safa had not claimed the life of Yusuf's sister. Now, the evil woman sought to destroy Butayna by taking the life of her child. If Aisha died, Butayna would not let Safa get away with the murder of another Sultana. Not this time.

Chapter 24
Recompense

Sultana Maryam

Granada, Andalusia
April 22 - 23, AD 1352 / 6 - 7 Rabi al-Awwal 753 AH / 7th – 8th
of Iyar, 5112

Maryam edged along the wall of the harem in the dimness.
Torches flickered at nightfall and incense burners in the corners
offered scant light. She crept closer to the sounds of the
disturbance, which echoed from Sultana Safa's chambers.
Something clattered against a wall and the slave Nazhun cried
out.

"*La*, my Sultana! Please, mercy!"

"You have ruined my *jubba* for the last time, you misbegotten
wretch! Mark me. This may well be the last night of your
miserable life. If I did not have to meet Yusuf for dinner, I would
strangle you with the silk myself!"

A heavy blow landed and the slave cried out again.

"Now, get out of my sight! Someone, fetch me my green and
silver *jubba* this instant. *Nam*, the one with the jade stones! Why
would you ask me such a foolish thing? Do I possess more than
one *jubba* with jade stones? Nothing except incompetent slaves
surround me! I should have all of you drowned in the *Hadarro*
for your stupidity! You're all a waste of precious coin."

Maryam withdrew into the shadows and waited, her fingers
clutching folds of silk around her. She gripped the fabric tighter
and willed her hands to stop trembling. Nazhun would be pliable
in her misery. Maryam had little to fear. Her stomach fluttered
although she had dined an hour ago with her beloved children.
Within moments, Safa raced out of her room and beneath the
northern pavilion. Her garments swirled behind her as she
headed for Yusuf's apartment. Her servants hurried and kept
pace with her, all except the beleaguered Nazhun. Maryam stood
silent until the door closed in Safa's wake. A quiet hush fell over
the garden courtyard, broken by the noise of a woman weeping.

With a hand pressed to her bosom, Maryam stepped into the
darkened room. Her shadow glided across the marble floor. She

took the wooden steps, which creaked with every footfall. She parted the silver damask curtain over the doorway and stood at the threshold.

In the Sultana's antechamber, the slave Nazhun sobbed behind her hand. Her squat form buried in folds of silk and her broad face contorted in agony, her other fingers rubbed her stomach where Safa must have kicked her. For years, Nazhun had suffered for her foolish mistakes at Safa's hands. Maryam had taken little notice of the woman's plight, for all of Safa's slaves had suffered her fiery rage, even Maryam before she became Yusuf's Sultana. What could those in misery and bondage have done to aid each other? Now, with her status as Yusuf's wife secured, Maryam could be of help to Nazhun, but such assistance would cost the woman something. Maryam would ensure she paid in full.

Maryam crooned, "Poor Nazhun! Has she hurt you again?"

As she approached with slow, deliberate steps, the slave shrank away from her.

Maryam paused between the doorway and the table where Nazhun sat. "You must not be afraid of me. I have not come to gloat, but to share in your misery. I remember what it was like to be a slave in Safa's dominion."

Nazhun mumbled, "What do you want from me? You've never spoken to me except to give orders in the past as the Sultana does."

Maryam crouched beside her and cupped the slave's cheek. The woman flinched, but she kept still. Maryam lifted her chin to the light and revealed the swollen, darkened area under Nazhun's left eye. She would bear a nasty, blackened bruise in the morning.

"I could not talk to you before, when I was not Yusuf's wife. Now I am his Sultana and there is no one who can stop me, not even your mistress. She is cruel to you—"

Nazhun pulled back. "You don't care! When you were the Sultana's slave, you stood by with the others and watched her as she almost kicked me to death many times."

"My dear Nazhun, you must have understood the danger I faced. Safa would have killed me too, if I had tried to intervene in her punishments. She treats you worse than anyone should treat a dog. You are lower than her footstool."

"And there is no person in the harem who can help me." Nazhun's thinned lips slackened. She clasped her wrinkled hands in her lap. Her tired and red-rimmed gaze lowered.

Maryam sat back on her heels. "I think it is the saddest thing in the world to be without a friend. I understood this pain when I endured slavery, but before that misery, I once had a friend in the Sultana Butayna. Before we became rivals for Yusuf's love and our sons had equal chance of inheriting the throne upon their father's death. Did you know of my past?"

Nazhun nodded. "I have heard you and the Sultana speak of it. I didn't mean to—"

With a shake of her head, Maryam patted the slave's lean-muscled forearm. What else had Nazhun overheard while she carried out her duties?

"You don't need to apologize, Nazhun. There are few secrets in the harem. *Nam*, Butayna and I were friends long ago, when she and I led different lives. She has hated me since I refused to join her in an ill-starred scheme to escape the Moors. I would have gone with her, but I knew how my life would unfold. My destiny would be at Yusuf's side. One day, my son shall rule and I shall have all I desire."

"You have what you want now with the Sultan's favor. You should be pleased and go from here, before the Sultana returns and finds you here."

"I am here for you, Nazhun. I want to help you. You say you have no friend. It is true Sultana Safa despises you, as does the Sultana Butayna. She wants you dead, for what you did to her daughter, for the Sultana Leila's sake."

Nazhun clapped her hands to her forehead. "I didn't do anything! I told the Sultan the truth. It was an accident in the *hammam*."

"It happened ten months ago and still the Sultana wants you dead. It is not only what happened to her daughter. She holds you responsible for the Sultana Leila's death as well. Did you know Safa intended to kill her with the bowl of broth?"

"I did not, I did not...."

"Ah, then. She used you, as she has used so many people. You did not know the message she sent to the kitchen contained instructions to poison Leila's meal. You have been the instrument of several of Safa's plans and still, she reviles you."

"What can I do, my Sultana, what can I do?"

Maryam reached for Nazhun's hand and leaned toward her. "I could help you against those who would harm you, the Sultanas Safa and Butayna. I could protect you, if you will help me."

Nazhun's fingers twitched. Her features appeared frozen before she asked, "How? Why? How could you help me?"

The quaver in Nazhun's voice, so like a child's own, would have tugged at Maryam's heart if she could summon the compassion. Maryam stared at her beneath half-lidded eyes. Slaves like Nazhun served a purpose and nothing more. For now, if the woman chose the right course, she would be useful. Otherwise she would die.

"I could protect you from Safa. I have learned much from her over the years, Nazhun. How to be patient most of all. I have endured her tyrannical rule of this harem and waited too long for its ending. She thought Leila interfered too much, so she had Yusuf's sister poisoned. Safa already considers Butayna a rival. If she succeeds in poisoning Butayna also, how long will it be before Safa does away with me or attacks one of my children? You could ensure she never harms anyone again."

From a watery gaze, Nazhun stared at her wide-eyed. "Please, tell me what to do."

Maryam looked toward the door and then said, "We shall use her means against her. She will be none the wiser for it. Allow her hot temper to cool tonight. When she awakens, beg her favor on my behalf, to allow us to share the morning meal together. If she agrees, I shall join her."

"And then?" Nazhun's nails raked Maryam's skin.

She bit back a curse at the slight pain and shook her head. "Safa still takes *nakhwa* and black seed brewed by your own hands in the morning?"

"*Nam*, she drinks nothing else."

"Excellent!" Maryam drew aside the folds of her *rida* and untied the handkerchief she had affixed to her *tikka*. She revealed the little brown seeds inside. "You will add this in the morning. These are hemlock seeds."

"They look familiar, a little like aniseed."

Maryam nodded. "Very good, Nazhun. As aniseed resembles *nakhwa*, so hemlock reminds some of aniseed. They soon discover theirs is a fatal error when they are unable to breathe. You will grind and mix the hemlock with the *nakhwa* and black seed in Safa's morning drink, but only if she permits me to join her tomorrow."

As Nazhun accepted the linen cloth with an unsteady hand, her tremulous gaze met Maryam's own. "But... but, why only then?"

Maryam rose and clasped her hands together. "I intend to drink the same brew. Safa would be suspicious if she extended the offer of a cup and I refused it."

"Won't it kill you as well?"

A soft chuckle filled Maryam's throat. "I don't plan to drink so much as to result in death, but a sip or two may sicken me if I am not quick to act. *La*, I must ingest an adequate amount to ensure Yusuf's suspicions. When he sees me and his mother, he will begin to wonder who would seek to poison both of us, but his ruminations won't last for long."

Indeed not, for he would see Butayna's hand in the foul murder of his mother and the poisoning of his second wife. Who else would have motive? A thrill ran through Maryam. Butayna would never guess at the cause of her undoing and even if she did, Yusuf would never believe her. He could not.

She sobered and gaze Nazhun a direct, probing stare. "You will do this and rid us both of the troublesome woman who has plagued this harem for far too long. If you do not help me or you throw the hemlock seeds away like a coward, I will tell Sultana Safa in the morning of your intent to murder her with them, which I discovered this night when I visited to request an audience. Be assured, she will believe me when I say I caught sight of you mixing hemlock with the seeds for her morning drink. After all, you are a resentful slave, weary of the proper chastisements you have received from your mistress. Bitter even, so bitter that you would resort to murder. Then this night will truly have been your last on this earth, as she promised."

Nazhun's soft gasp echoed. Her face turned pallid in the stark glare of the lamplight.

Maryam bent and cupped her chin. "So, as you see, you have little choice except to agree. Sleep well, Nazhun. You will find me a fairer mistress than Safa. I shall never be cruel to you. The difference between Safa and I is in my beliefs about slow torture. I do not engage in it. A waste of time. Better a quick death, than slow agony. Safa will soon learn this, when I see you both early in the morning."

Maryam rose again and went to the door. As she went, she stated, "I look forward to a cup of the brew, Nazhun. You will not disappoint me, I trust."

***

Maryam seated herself across from Safa just as dawn's glittering rays filtered through the *shimasas*. As Nazhun set down steaming cups of *nakhwa*, stuffed eggs, and flatbread perfumed with anise and sesame seed between the women at the table, Safa yawned.

"You surprise me, Maryam," she murmured.

Maryam reached for the cup and took a sip. After a soft sigh, she set aside the brew. "How so, my Sultana?"

"You told me upon your arrival this morn of how you wished to thank me. I have done nothing for you that I did not also do for myself. Your gratitude is unnecessary."

"How could I fail to offer it? You may not have intended to benefit me when you removed Sultana Leila from Yusuf's side, but now, Butayna is alone and isolated. She does not have a friend in this harem, whereas I have learned through you of the importance of alliances. The first of many good lessons."

Safa grunted and bit into an egg. "As you say." She speared a piece of flatbread and bit into it. "Mm, the baker has surpassed her usual effort today. Nazhun, bring olive oil and fresh butter. Maryam, you must have some of the bread."

"As you command, my Sultana." Nazhun flicked a quick glance at Maryam, who ignored her.

"Just a small slice, please." Maryam patted her belly, rounded after the births of her children for Yusuf. "My husband has not summoned me for some time. I fear he does not find me so beautiful after seven children."

Safa waved a dismissive hand through the air and handed Maryam the bread, before drinking from the cup again. "Nonsense! A woman who has birthed many children has a high stomach and marks upon her body as badges of honor and proof of the travail she has suffered. At least, he has not summoned Butayna either. I have heard rumors of her refusal of him, but how can that be? Why would my son, who can have any woman he wishes, allow a wife to reject him? As it is, he often dines with that odious son of Butayna's body or with al-Shaquri and his ministers. It is unnatural to restrain his normal passions."

"Does he prefer boys now?"

Safa sputtered. "Ignorant woman! How dare you speak so of my son and suggest such perversions?"

Maryam bit into the edge of the flatbread and set it down on her ceramic platter. "I do not accuse the Sultan of anything, but there are those among his ministers–"

"Yusuf would never indulge in pederasty! The idea of it is shameful. I will forgive your stupidity once, Maryam, but never again. If you think you have lost favor with my son, then you must make your body appealing to him. It is your own fault if he will no longer bed you. Perhaps, he grows tired of your whining children. Qays is hopeless. He follows Ismail like a Christian dog behind its master. Ismail will have much to learn if he ever becomes Sultan. Why don't you take him to court more often? Why let Muhammad and Butayna appear and absorb what they will of governance? You think Butayna's boy will have any trouble understanding the duties before him when the time comes. I promise you, he will not!"

"Yuouf will not choose his heir for some time. He is young, soon to reach his thirty-fifth year next month. There will be time for decisions on the succession. In such a period, many circumstances may befall Muhammad. Look at his sister. She almost died last summer. Did you arrange for her murder in the bathhouse through Nazhun's clumsy error?"

"Do not speak foolishness yet again! I despaired for Aisha's fate though her mother would never know the truth. I saw my granddaughter a few times in her sickbed, when her father permitted it. I may despise Butayna, but her children are my son's own. I would never kill my son's children."

Maryam jerked her head back at such unexpected news. She never anticipated compassion from Safa, but where Yusuf was concerned, perhaps his mother did have a softer side of her personality.

Maryam continued, "His sister though...."

Safa's ugly smirk widened her jowls and gave her appearance of a squat frog. "Another matter. Leila interfered where she should not have. She tried to influence the course of the succession and other matters. Her time is over. Now, I reign supreme over my son's harem. A fact Butayna shall soon accept or she will die like Leila."

She fell silent when Nazhun returned with butter and a jar of olive oil. The slave served her mistress and then withdrew to the corner.

Maryam sipped the *nakhwa* again and then took some of the stuffed eggs, enjoying lacy, green coriander mashed up with the egg yolks. Safa devoured her meal with such relish, could it be that she had not eaten at all the previous night in Yusuf's quarters? Maryam took great pleasure in her obvious enjoyment. When Safa bellowed for another cup of brew, Maryam snapped at Nazhun, "Well? Do not delay!"

Nazhun poured the brew and stepped back. Safa drank the last of it. When she gestured for more, Nazhun informed her that the pot was empty, which earned the slave a fearsome scowl.

Then Maryam said, "Butayna will be cautious. I believe one of her slaves has had some training in the detection of poisons."

Safa chuckled. "As did Leila's Rima."

"You were fortunate the plague descended when it did."

"Allah heeded my prayers for deliverance from Leila's interference. He will do the same with Butayna."

"Why do you hate her so? I have good reason, for she has had a hand in the fates of the beloved children I lost."

"She and Leila are of the same ilk. There is also the problem of her guidance of her son. While I would do nothing to hurt Yusuf's children, Muhammad will be more malleable when his mother no longer influences him. With his aunt gone and then his mother, who will he look to for direction except me?"

Maryam finished the last sip of the *nakhwa* and set the cup down.

As the vessel clanked against the wood, Safa looked up from her plate. "Have I said something wrong?"

"You act as if the reign of Butayna's son is certain," Maryam muttered.

"It is. You have not taken the initiative to train your spoiled Ismail. *Nam*, Muhammad shall be Sultan after his father and I shall dictate the course of his life, just as the Sultana Fatima once did for Yusuf. She eclipsed me and molded my son in the image of her father. I shall do the same for—"

Safa rubbed at her temple and shook her head.

Maryam raised her eyebrows and asked, "Did you mean to say you shall do the same for Butayna's son?"

Safa swallowed and her body heaved a spasmodic jerk. She looked at Maryam with dazed eyes. "What? I... *la*. Something is wrong."

Maryam smiled. "Not from my vantage. All seems well."

Perspiration edged Safa's hairline. Ragged breaths tore from her chest. She swiped her gnarled fingers over her forehead and back, across the grizzled curls on her head. She must have been a lovely woman in her youth, but now, her time was over.

"It occurs to me, Sultana Safa, I have not kept to my original purpose in coming to you. I wished to thank you and I have not finished."

Safa gripped the edge of the table. "I can't feel my legs! What have you done to me?"

Maryam shook her head and pursed her lips. "It's impolite to interrupt when someone wishes to express their gratitude—"

Safa screeched, "Yusuf!"

Maryam reached across the space between them and grasped Safa's chin in her hands. She pressed her nails into the flaccid skin until Safa winced. The older Sultana's eyes bulged and watered. Her breaths became raw and ragged.

"Now, you're being rude, while I have attempted to remain gracious. You will listen and let me thank you in the appropriate manner. Second, for the gift of entry into this harem, for without it, I would not be a Sultana. Third, for what you taught me of Yusuf, for I trusted he would prefer the opposite. He does not like women who surrender too soon, nor does he enjoy the little tricks you have imparted. They may have worked with Yusuf's father, but my husband is a far more passionate and inventive man. For instance, he prefers his women astride rather than beneath him in his bed. A woman on top seems best in his opinion."

Safa panted and pleaded, "Nazhun, help me!"

The slave remained in the corner with her head bowed.

Maryam giggled at her double entendre. "I cannot say I disagree with your son. I intend to remain on top outside of the Sultan's bedchamber as well. How dare you presume I would allow Muhammad to gain the throne? Why should his claim exceed that of my two sons Ismail and Qays? Fourth, I have taken well to the instructions you have provided since the morning I attacked Butayna. It proved a stupid move as you suggested. Afterward, I learned to be subtle and move in shadows. I discovered patience as you must have while burdened with Yusuf's grandmother. Are you proud of me, Safa?"

When the old woman did not answer, Maryam dug her fingernails into the flesh harder. "Are you proud of me? I demand to know."

Tears trickled down Safa's cheeks.

Maryam released her. "Oh, do not cry now. It makes you so ugly and vulnerable when you have always been beautiful and strong! Well, not beautiful as perhaps in your youth, but the latter is quite true. I have long admired your fortitude and your patience in dealing with your enemies, except as I explained to my dear Nazhun last night, I do not believe in the slow poison. Is that not what you said once? The slow poison and the blade in the back are the best methods."

Safa fell backwards against the floor. Her head hit the wooden planks with a heavy clunk. Maryam rose and crouched beside her. Safa's breaths came faster and she clapped at her chest as if might help.

Maryam mused, "While I do not subscribe to your ideas, there is some merit in the slow poison now. The particular one you have ingested is hemlock. It kills in a few hours and causes the victim's limbs to stop responding before breathing becomes impossible. The effects start in the legs and work their way up the body, much as you are feeling now. You did bring this upon yourself. You kept me from Yusuf and allowed Butayna to claim his heart first. A move I promised myself that you would pay for in the end. You need not worry about Butayna's fate. When Yusuf sees your dead body and the result of the dosage upon me, he will guess at Butayna's involvement."

Safa gagged. Bloodied spittle frothed and oozed between her pale lips.

Maryam shook her head. "Humph. Perhaps your death will be a little faster than I anticipated. I did not know whether my dear Nazhun would comply, so I had the baker add hemlock seeds to the flatbread as well."

When Nazhun whimpered, Maryam glared at her until she quieted again. Maryam said, "Do stop worrying! After the kitchen maids gave you the flatbread for Safa, my eunuchs strangled the baker at her house. Even if Yusuf connects all these incidents, no one else can tell him of my involvement. Except for you."

Then Maryam turned to Safa again. "Well, I have you to thank for a final time, for the introduction of various poisons. Poison is the work of women or eunuchs, so I suppose it is fitting you know so much. Here, my platitudes must end, but before I stop, let me share some favorable quotes of yours. Do I remember the words... ah, *nam!* You once said never reveal the intent before you strike at your enemy, but of all your words, I treasure these next the most. All old cats die."

With a smile, Maryam stood and turned to Nazhun. "It will be some time before she is incapable of any response. What of her other women?"

Nazhun mumbled, "They are asleep. They do not rise until the Sultana begins to bellow for them in the morning. She did not when she stirred and recalled your request for this morning. We are lucky."

"Lucky?" Maryam surveyed Safa's twitching body with great satisfaction. "Oh, Nazhun, how naïve you are. This farce is not over. We must wait a little longer for the poison's full effect on Safa. You had best pray the others do not awaken before then, or I shall have to let them know how you murdered the Sultana Safa."

She took her seat again and ate the rest of the eggs.

A wheezing gasp escaped Safa. Maryam stood again, as the death rattle signaled the passing of Yusuf's mother. Her last gaze lingered on the ceiling with widened eyes and upraised brows, as if surprised to have found her ending at Maryam's hands.

Maryam shuddered. The tingling began in her legs. She fell beside Safa's body and gripped the table's edge. "Nazhun!"

"*Nam*, my Sultana?"

"Run to Yusuf's chambers! Tell him someone has poisoned his mother and his wife!"

When the slave rose and darted past her, Maryam's fingers clamped on Nazhun's ankle.

"I remind you... of your promise to me. If you... betray me or if I should die, Yusuf will one day find a last note in my quarters, where I wrote of discovering you with hemlock seeds... and wondered if I should warn Sultana Safa...."

Maryam rolled on her side and stuck her index finger down her throat. She gagged and brought up the contents of her stomach.

Nazhun's cries rang through the garden courtyard. "Murder, my Sultan, murder! The Sultanas Safa and Maryam have been poisoned!"

***

Maryam broke free of the darkness, which gripped her. She blinked and opened her eyes to the sight of Yusuf and al-Shaquri's stark faces. She moaned and turned to her husband. "Beloved?"

His warm sigh washed over her. "Allah be praised! She is still alive, al-Shaquri! Maryam, my treasure! Can you hear me? I am here. No one will harm you again."

"Harm?" She lolled on something soft. A pillow on a bed. "Where... where's Nazhun? She found you?"

"I am here, Sultana Maryam. I did not leave your side except to summon the Sultan as you commanded before you buckled." Nazhun's voice penetrated the thick fog, which mired Maryam's awareness of her surroundings.

Yusuf grasped Maryam's hand. "She came to me, but you saved yourself by quick action. I found you in your own vomit. Someone poisoned you and killed my mother."

Maryam squeezed her eyes closed for a moment and willed the tears to flow. "*La*! Not Safa. It cannot be! We... we were just eating together in the morning."

Yusuf pressed his dampened forehead against hers. He sniffled. "There will be time to grieve for my mother. For now, I need you to rest and let my trusted doctor aid you. Al-Shaquri is here. He has summoned another who might be able to help us determine the circumstances that befell you and my mother. This is the doctor Hasan al-Qaysi."

Yusuf withdrew, though he held her fingers still.

A rounded, lined visage filled her gaze. "My Sultana, trust in Allah and in me."

She groaned and turned away from the stranger's fetid breath.

"*La*, my Sultana. You must remain still," al-Shaquri said at her right ear. "We are fortunate the good doctor Hasan al-Qaysi has visited us from Malaka this month. He has extensive knowledge of poisons and has developed an antidote for some."

"My great Sultan," Hasan al-Qaysi intoned, "I have collected the remnants of the meal in your honored mother's quarters. I believe this is the source of the foul murder. The flatbread contained crushed hemlock seeds. To the untrained eye, they would appear as aniseed, but I tell you this was the means of the honorable *Umm al-Walad*'s death. There are no other traces of hemlock, not even in the empty cups of *nakhwa*."

"My Sultana, what made you vomit?" al-Shaquri asked.

Maryam groaned. "I need to rest." Trust the doctor's sharp mind to inquire about such mundane elements. One day, he might prove troublesome and would have to go.

Yusuf inquired, "Truly, does that matter, al-Shaquri?"

"My Sultan, perhaps the Sultana Maryam recognized something strange in the meal, which made her take such action. It will help Hasan al-Qaysi and I to determine the full circumstances of this tragedy if she can tell us all she remembers."

"Forgive me, but I can do that." Nazhun's voice drew closer. "When Sultana Safa breathed her last, Sultana Maryam must have realized what happened. She pushed the flatbread away and begged me to summon the Sultan. Then she put her fingers in her mouth."

"I can give the Sultana a purgative brew to empty her stomach, if the learned al-Shaquri would assist," Hasan al-Qaysi said.

"It would be my honor."

Yusuf sighed. "I must depart for a time."

Maryam opened her eyes and clutched at his hand. "Don't leave me, beloved. What of our children? Do they know what... has happened?"

He patted her fingers. *"La,* and they can never know. I will never forget the fear on their faces when you lost that babe. Their governesses keep them entertained. Do not worry for them. Now, I must go, but only for a short time."

He kissed her forehead and released her. She stared at him beneath hooded eyelids as he crossed the room and spoke in low tones with both doctors. Then Yusuf went to the doorway, where his captain bowed.

Yusuf asked, "Have Butayna and Aisha returned from the *Qaysariyya* as yet?"

"La, my Sultan. They left just after dawn and it is almost mid-morning. *Salat al-Zuhr* will occur in an hour and the Sultana Butayna would never let the little Sultana miss her prayers."

Yusuf heaved a wearied sigh and swiped a hand over his face. "When Butayna comes, bring her to me in my chambers at once. Keep her guards at bay."

"As you command, my Sultan."

The warmth of contentment radiated through Maryam's limbs. She relaxed on the cushioning comfort of the bed. Despite grave risk, she had survived. Nazhun showed loyalty, though Maryam intended to keep a watchful eye on the slave's activities for the future. Yusuf would confront Butayna and then she would die by his command. Maryam smiled with certainty of her triumph. She had ruined both of her enemies in one day. It would not be so difficult to convince Yusuf of the merits of Ismail's inheritance with Butayna gone in disgrace. One day, Ismail would take his father's place on the throne and Maryam would be at her son's back as the *Umm-al-Walad*.

Chapter 25
The Second Betrayal

Sultana Butayna

Granada, Andalusia
April 23 - 30, AD 1352 / 7 - 14 Rabi al-Awwal 753 AH / 8th –
15th of Iyar, 5112

Butayna knelt on the carpeted floor of Yusuf's chambers. The
blood pounded at her temple. Heavy sobs wracked her body
while she wept behind her hands. "Yusuf! I swear I had nothing
to do with Safa's death or Maryam's poisoning."

How had this tragedy occurred? Only this morning, Aisha
woke her early after prayers and suggested they go to the
marketplace. They returned with an array of silks and the
ghaliya perfume Aisha loved only to find death and chaos in the
harem. Safa murdered with hemlock seeds baked in flatbread
and Maryam poisoned by the same method, but still clinging to
life. How was it possible? Who could have perpetrated such a
crime?

Butayna did not wonder why Yusuf accused her, for he knew
her hatred of both women. No one else in the harem had as
much reason to despise Safa and Maryam. Although she had
wished both of them dead countless times in the past, Butayna
always knew in her heart, she could never commit such
murders. Safa deserved her death, but Butayna would not have
killed in her.

Yusuf raked a hand over his hair. "I want to believe you, I do.
Yet how can I deny the circumstances of this crime suit your
desires for vengeance? Have you not hated my mother and my
second Sultana since you entered this harem? I remember how
my mother insulted you on the night of your performance before
the entire harem. You could not hide the fury in your gaze at her
vicious remarks. You hated Maryam's performance alongside
you. You hold more cause than any to have sought the deaths of
both women."

"I swear upon the lives of our children, who mean more to me
than anything, I did not do this! Perhaps some *jarya*...."

Yusuf waved a dismissive hand. "What could any of my *jawari* claim by disposing of Maryam and my mother? A place at my side whilst you are still alive? A son from another woman could not sit on my throne when I have three older boys. You would not confess when you took the life of Maryam's child. Now, I must wonder whether you have done something far worse. I know you did not do it to hurt me, but Safa was my mother, Butayna! Her murder cannot go unpunished!"

Butayna clasped her fingers in supplication and prostrated herself. "Please! Please! For the sake of my children, do not kill me! I have done nothing wrong. I admit it, I urged the death of Maryam's child long ago, but I had no hand in this! Yusuf, if you have ever loved me, you must know when I am telling the truth."

"I used to know, Butayna. I no longer do. Guards! Take her away. The rest of my men will keep her guards locked in her quarters, where they cannot interfere."

As Yusuf's eunuchs grasped her arms and hauled her up, Butayna struggled against them. Her heartbeat raced and she struggled to swallow with a dry mouth. She batted at the hands of her captors and jerked away from them.

Her pained stare found Yusuf's unabashed gaze. He sat in a high-backed leather chair, his hair disheveled and his clothing wrinkled. Darkness encircled his red-rimmed eyes. Even in her confusion and sadness, she ached for the agony etched into his fallen features. He would grieve alone for the loss of his mother, with neither of his wives to comfort him.

"Please, Yusuf. Do not consign me to *al-Quasaba*! I will die there in those cells. Don't do this to me."

Yusuf shielded his brow with one hand and waved his men away with the other. "Take her to *al-qasr Xenil*. She must have two guards day and night. I do not wish to see her face until I have decided her fate."

The eunuchs wrenched her backward, even as she screamed, "Yusuf! Yusuf!"

Butayna emerged into the glare of sunshine and the baleful stares of the occupants of the harem, who congregated in doorways at the hour of her downfall. From somewhere unseen, Aisha's screams rent the air. "Jawla, Hafsa, let me go this instant! I am a Sultana and I will have your heads for this! Where is *Ummi*? Why are you keeping me away from her? Where is my father? I want to see my father the Sultan now!"

From the window of Butayna's apartments, Ruiz yelled, "We will find you, my Sultana. We will never stop—"

He cried out as the butt of a short javelin struck his head. He disappeared from view, his place at the window occupied by one of Yusuf's men. Tears blinded Butayna and she had no choice except to submit as the guards dragged her out of the harem and into the street. Passersby turned and pointed at her, with low whispers among them.

"Stop!" Yusuf's captain directed his men. He glared at her. "Will you go to *al-qasr Xenil* without further commotion? I do not want to drag you to the citadel, but I shall put you in chains if you do not cooperate. You have the dignity of a Sultana about you still. Will you let others see it, or shall their last memory be of you kicking and screaming?"

She huffed and returned his fiery stare. "I will not give you and your men more trouble."

"Then come." He waved toward the citadel.

She arranged her *hijab* around her face before she marched in a circle of the warriors. Although tears blinded her and she tripped more than once on the hem of her *jubba,* she kept pace with them. She bypassed the *rawda* where Yusuf had buried their unborn boy and the row of houses between almond and orange groves. Through the gateway between the citadel and the royal palaces, the men led Butayna to waiting horses, which stomped and snorted. Their hot breaths issued as white smoke.

She mounted with the help of the captain, who grabbed the reins of her mare. She lifted her chin despite the curious gapes and murmurs around her. Her hands on the pommel, she leaned forward in the saddle as her horse trotted toward the *Bab al-Sharia.* The gate master opened the exit. She rode south and into the city.

Trapped in the confines of the marketplace, Yusuf's captain barked orders. "Make way! You there, boy, make way or I will have your head. Move!"

The crowds parted, but none offered Butayna more than a cursory glance. Anyone would have recognized her as a royal woman, a denizen of the palatine city upon the *Sabika* hill, by her rich silks and the escort alone. She stared at their faces. How long until they made the connection between her journey out of the city's walls and news of the death of Yusuf's mother?

Butayna straightened and her fingers tightened on the pommel. Tears coursed down her cheek and stymied her vision. She swallowed against the tightness in her throat and stared ahead as her horse approached the city gate. The familiar world of her life as Yusuf's Sultana faded. Whatever lay beyond these walls, she would survive.

***

Butayna's first sight of *al-qasr Xenil* sent a deep tremor through her belly. For the first time in fifteen years, she would be alone without anyone she knew in this place. A wide pool stretched across the golden-brown plains centered between fig groves. At the heart of the pool, a scalloped fountain bubbled up water, which flowed through a recessed conduit. The channel ran along a line into the whitewashed building of two floors just ahead of her. Guards stationed one either side of the doorway inclined their heads. A groom rushed forward, a blackened collar encircling his neck. He bowed beside the captain's horse and offered his back. The captain dismounted with a grunt, echoed by the boy's pained wheeze.

Butayna stared at the tower and the two buildings adjoining it. From behind the lattice woodwork over each window, she detected movement. Did some dark eyes watch her or had she only imagined the sensation?

The captain offered his aid, but she alighted from her horse without his help.

He lowered his hand. "This is *al-qasr Xenil,* home to the old wives and discarded concubines of previous Sultans. There are a few *jawari* from the harems of Sultan Yusuf's predecessors, his brother Muhammad and their honored father, may Allah preserve their memory."

"How long must I stay here?"

"Until the noble Sultan decides your fate."

"Am I allowed to receive visitors? Will my children know where I am?"

The captain bowed his head and averted his gaze. "The Sultan has not informed me of his intention as regards your children, my Sultana."

"How will I eat? Bathe?"

"There is a superintendent here. Mute, although he hears well enough. There are alcoves where the *jawari* sleep, but I believe you may have a chamber on the second floor. The superintendent will show you."

He waved her toward the small palace.

She looked around her, at the walled enclosure of the city and the mountains beyond. Water swirled and rushed nearby from some unseen source other than the fountain. Perhaps she heard the *Xenil,* which she could not see given the density of the fig groves.

Then she glanced at the eunuchs who had manhandled her. "When my son is Sultan, I will remember my treatment today."

She took some small measure of gratification in the whitened faces of the guards. Then she nodded to the captain. "Nor shall I forget the meager kindness shown to me in my deepest despair."

He inclined his head. "*Al-salam 'alayka,* my Sultana."

"*Wa-'alayka.*"

She strode past him toward the horseshoe arch set under a row of five latticed windows on the north-facing side. The guards bowed, but she ignored them and stepped into the tower. Her ragged sigh floated up to a honeycombed ceiling, which mirrored the one with the harem at *al-Qal'at al-Hamra*. A hunchbacked eunuch shuffled forward, whom she presumed to be the superintendent. He sagged beside her.

She stared at his baldpate. "I am the Sultana Butayna, wife to the Sultan Abdul Hajjaj Yusuf. You will show me to the room where I will sleep."

He flashed a lopsided grin and revealed wide spaces between rotted teeth and a jagged lump where his tongue should have been. She followed him eastward. Then he gestured to the stairs and led her up them. A doorway closed just as she reached the wooden landing. Dusty, speckled floorboards creaked under her feet. He pushed aside a somewhat tattered, orange door hanging. She stood on the outskirts of the room and peeked inside at the makeshift bed of one large cushion, draped in a dingy blanket and a chair beside a low table. A small basin rested under the table. Quite different from her spacious quarters at home. After the familiar comforts of the harem, the sordid appearance of the room dismayed her.

She eyed the eunuch. "Do you expect me to sleep in a place not fit for pigs? Where is the lantern or a lamp? Is there even a chamber pot?"

He went into the room and showed the basin to her. A small oil lamp was inside along with a stub of beeswax.

"And the chamber pot?"

He waved her over to the southern window and pointed to a lone building where two women entered.

"The latrine is beside the *hammam* in that building?"

He nodded with vigor.

"May I have something to drink? Even in the simplest home, there is water."

He pointed to the wood-covered well in the courtyard and then bowed beside her. She gritted her teeth together and gripped the windowsill. With a sigh, he left her.

When she stood alone at last, she sagged against the wall. Her weakened muscles would not support her. She collapsed on the ground, numbed and emptied of all strength by the turmoil of the day. She drew her knees up to her chest and clasped her arms around them. With her head against the wall, she closed her eyes and refused to let the tears fall. They would not help her now, just as pleas had not aided her with Yusuf. She had no one to guide her and nowhere else to turn for comfort.

The days and nights stretched and blurred in emptiness. Butayna spent most of her time at *al-qasr Xenil* alone in the chamber. She shook out the blanket every night, for on the first occasion when she grabbed it, a scorpion crawled from its folds. She wore her *qamis* and *sarawil* to bed and changed into the *jubba* alone during the day, except for when she had to wash her clothes in the basin. Her jailor brought her water in the morning and evening. He provided two meals, one at dawn, and another just after sunset. He showed no interest in whether she ate or peered with an upturned or wrinkled nose at the meager offering. Sometimes, the smell of a simple roasted goat drifting up from the inner courtyard stirred powerful longings for the meats she enjoyed at home.

Home. Yusuf's palace had been her dwelling for fifteen years this month. Once a spot she had never desired to live in, now it remained the only home she wanted. The foolish girl had become a woman, the frightened captive turned into a Moorish queen.

In the dim light of the sixth evening, she looked around the room. Despite the season, a heavy heat pervaded the space. It stank of unwashed bed linens and her fear of captivity once again. She could not stay in this place. This was not the abode of a queen, a Sultana.

How could Yusuf have believed her capable of such vile murder and imprisoned her here? He knew her better than this, didn't he? He had doubted her from the time she conspired with Leila against Maryam. She had disagreed with her husband and fought against him in numerous instances, but the divide between them never lingered for long. How would she ever find her way back to him after this?

Butayna awoke the next day with heavy, swollen eyelids. The superintendent stood in her chamber. She yelped and pulled the musty blanket up to her shoulders, despite the hideous smell of the wool. The eunuch moved beside the northern window and waved to her. She groaned and rose from the bed.

She looked down to the space between the pool and the building's façade. A rudimentary marketplace offered textiles, shoes, and spices to the eleven eager women domiciled in the small palace.

Butayna rolled her eyes heavenward. "I do not want anything. Leave me be!"

The perplexing man shook his head and then tugged her to the opposite window.

She slapped his hand away. "Do not think to touch me, you ignorant wretch!"

He opened the latticework and pointed down into the inner courtyard. She heaved a wearied sigh and joined him.

A hooded, robed figure stood beside the wall, back to her. Her heart pitched. Could it be Yusuf? Had he come to take her from this place? Had he forgiven her?

She raced out of the room in only the clothes she had slept in and no shoes, with the superintendent at her heels. He made those strange, gurgled noises in the back of his throat. She halted between the exit to the rear courtyard and the base of the stairs. He drew deep breaths and handed over her slippers, *hijab*, and *jubba*. She nodded her thanks and he bowed. After all, her visitor might not be Yusuf. Her shoulders slumped but she pushed them back and attired herself in suitable manner. She stepped out into the first full rays of sunlight.

She whispered, "*Al-salam 'alayka.*" Her voice warbled.

"*Wa-'alayka,* my Sultana." Ridwan removed his hood and exposed the thinning dark hair on his head. He bowed low.

She clutched the doorpost. "Ridwan! What are you doing here? Has Yusuf sent you... with his... decree?"

Her heart pounded anew. Would her husband summon her to the palace for her execution? Did Ridwan know the outcome Yusuf has chosen? She closed her eyes, a silent plea on her lips. Whatever he had decided, her children must not suffer from the consequences.

"My master is unaware of my presence here and he will never discover it, if the Sultana would assent."

She released an uneven breath and took a step backward. Had the minister come as an assassin in broad daylight? "Why do you keep secrets from my husband?"

He stretched out his arms wide and twirled once. The folds of his *jubba* billowed. "I will not harm you. I intend to help you return to *al-Qal'at al-Hamra*. It is the fervent wish of my brother Hisham."

"Hisham?" An ache gathered and pounded at her temple. "Why should the chief eunuch and a minister of the *Diwan* help me? Why do you care for my well-being?"

"In truth, my Sultana, we do not. We worry for the fate of the Sultanate. Your son is its future."

She nodded. "Then it is your belief that Muhammad will inherit the throne after Yusuf's death and your brother wishes to choose the right side. Is that it?"

"You have summarized our intent quite well. My brother and I will help you survive this disaster and return to your son's side where you belong. Muhammad is frightened distracted, even angry whenever he joins me for his daily lessons. He is furious with you and his father. He will not forgive Yusuf for your absence. He wants to know why you have abandoned him and his sister—"

She stifled a cry behind her fingertips. "I didn't abandon my children!"

"Muhammad says no one can make him believe the lies the courtiers and the *jawari* have said about you."

"What do you believe, Ridwan?"

"Does it matter what I think, my Sultana? I am but a servant."

She stepped down into the cobblestone courtyard. "A well-placed servant. You would not be here unless you knew something of the truth about Safa's death and Maryam's poisoning. You would not seek to align yourself with my interests in the throne for Muhammad, unless you were certain I could survive this debacle."

He shrugged. "I do not discern as much as my brother does."

Her hands clenched and fingernails dug into her palm. "What does Hisham know?"

"For years, my brother has spied upon the occupants of the harem." Despite her outraged gasp, he continued, "It is his province to remain aware of all matters. How else could he serve all interests, placing none above the others? In his capacity as chief eunuch, my brother is knowledgeable of many activities in the harem. For instance, he remembers the night before Sultana Safa died, where the Sultana Maryam went into the honorable *Umm al-Walad*'s quarters while she dined with Sultan Yusuf. Sultana Safa's slaves were with her except the little one, Nazhun. Your rival emerged some time later. In the morning, she sent a request to enjoy the first meal of the day with my lord's mother. Since then, Nazhun has joined Sultana Maryam's household. Maryam now occupies the apartment Sultana Safa held.

"On the same date Maryam took over the new rooms, eunuchs found a royal baker dead in her house. Stabbed in her heart, her hand still upon the knife. Kitchen maids confirmed the woman had last delivered one order of flatbread intended for Sultana Safa's table on the morning she died. My brother wonders why the Sultana Maryam met with the slave Nazhun alone and why the baker died. Hisham's primary concern is whether these singular events pertain to how Sultana Safa met her death."

Butayna did not share the same apprehension. She turned away from him and clapped her fists to the sides of her head.

Maryam! Maryam had done this to her. She had somehow inveigled Nazhun to join her in an elaborate scheme to kill Safa. Butayna would swear so upon the lives of her dear children. Despite all appearances to the contrary, of tolerance and even amiability between Safa and Maryam, Butayna knew two truths with certainty about both women. One, Maryam would never have been content to linger in anyone's shadow for too long. She had schemed with Safa to place herself foremost in Yusuf's heart. Two, Safa's pride would never have allowed Maryam to eclipse her. Leila had died because she tried to vie with Safa in influencing Yusuf's choices for the Sultanate and the succession. The death of one woman and the triumph of another had been inevitable. It would be the same for Maryam and Butayna.

She glanced at Ridwan. "You do not know how Safa died? Hisham does not?"

He waved his hand. "We have heard little except rumor. Do you know, my Sultana?"

"Al-Shaquri and another doctor believe she was poisoned with hemlock seeds baked into flatbread."

A charming smile twitched at the corner of Ridwan's lips. "Ah, hemlock. It could have been mistaken for aniseed."

"The doctor from Malaka said so."

"It might have been an accident."

"Not if Maryam was involved! A baker would have known the difference. Maryam gave her the hemlock to poison Safa."

"Let us assume the baker did not know the difference. Hisham has counseled your husband toward reason, away from hasty judgment. Yusuf could execute you on suspicion alone."

She shuddered. "I am aware of the possibility."

"Perhaps it is time Hisham took another approach, one which leaves this baker to bear the blame alone and permits for the consideration that this was all a dreadful accident. No one knows how the woman died, but any royal baker would have lived in fear after the announcement of Safa's death, especially if she had just baked poison by accident into flatbread served at the Sultana's table. Such a baker might have killed herself before the Sultan summoned the executioner."

"Or Maryam's minions killed her so she would not talk."

"You're not listening, my Sultana—"

"I have heard you! I listened to your words and heard no consequence for Maryam! Once again, she has betrayed me and does not suffer for it."

"Hisham will never move against Sultana Maryam. You must be aware of that."

"Why? If he seeks an alliance with me, he cannot be her friend as well."

Ridwan bowed his head. "My Sultana, nothing in life is ever so clear as friend or foe. Do not expect Hisham to choose between you and Maryam. Foremost, he chooses life for himself and to serve Prince Muhammad when he is Sultan."

"What of Maryam? Will there ever be justice for what she has done to Safa and I?"

"The Sultana will find her ending in due time, if you are patient." Ridwan edged closer to her. "One day, Muhammad shall inherit the throne upon his father's death. He is a fine young prince and you should be very pleased with him. His mother shall be the *Umm al-Walad*. In all the generations of Sultans, there have only been two women who ever bore the official title of Mother of the Sultan. The Sultana Fatima, Allah preserve her memory, and Sultana Safa. You will be the third, if you keep your wits about you. You shall rule your son's harem. Maryam shall live by your dictates or she shall die. The choice will be yours alone."

She shied away from him and circumnavigated the stone-built well. Could it be so simple? Could she let Maryam get away with this travesty only to triumph over her at Yusuf's death?

Ridwan asked, "What would you have me say to Hisham when I go to *al-Qal'at al-Hamra*? Shall he advise the Sultan to consider the possibility of an accident, one which would see all blame removed from your shoulders and placed upon the dead baker?"

She stopped pacing. "You must believe in Muhammad very much."

He inclined his head. "He is the best Nasrid prince I have ever served. Not even his blessed father can compare. In the reign of Muhammad, this Sultanate shall ascend again and its enemies shall quake with fear. For now, he is a boy who needs his mother's reassurance. Shall you return to his side and comfort him?"

"If Hisham can convince my husband, how soon will I be free of this place?"

"As soon as may be, my Sultana. It may take some weeks of convincing, for the Sultan has withdrawn to his rooms and permits a handful of visitors each week."

Did Yusuf miss her? Did he regret his anger already?

She questioned him, "How can I protect myself against Maryam? If she succeeded in poisoning Safa, she will try again with me."

"She will try, so you must be vigilant."

"Could she attack me through my children?"

"She can, but my brother and I shall remain watchful on Prince Muhammad's behalf."

"I have a daughter also."

"The Sultana Aisha will never sit upon the throne. You understand my sole concern and that of my brother is Prince Muhammad's well-being."

Butayna still struggled with such pragmatism and the manner in which everyone around her acted as if violent murders, deception, and ruthless schemes were simple tools to achieve one's goals or minor diversions from an overall plan.

She sighed and knuckled her forehead. "Will you carry a letter for me to my son?"

"*La.* I will not. Think of what would happen if anyone discovered it. No one must know of my presence here."

She nodded. "You are right, of course. How foolish of me."

"You are not a fool, my Sultana. I have seen many women take their place in Sultan Yusuf's bed for a night and leave it, never to join with him again. They die by Safa's orders and more women enter the harem, none more outstanding than those who have left its confines forever. The Sultan loves you for many reasons. He wants to believe you had nothing to do with his mother's murder. He will take Hisham's suggestion for truth because in his heart, he wants to judge it as so."

"He loves Maryam as well."

"A sad fact for you to accept, but it does not negate his plans for the future. Prince Muhammad shall be his heir. When the time comes, you will be the *Umm al-Walad.* First, we must have you freed from this place."

Ridwan bowed and she escorted him out to the improvised marketplace. The old *jawari* waved farewell to the merchants who bundled their wagons with anything they had not sold. The women went indoors. They chattered about the good silks and cheap perfumes they had bought to entertain each other with, but their jailor remained at the doorway. Butayna stood beside him.

The minister pulled his hood over his head, mounted a sturdy mule, and gave the order to ride out. The caravan turned in the direction of the city on the plains. At a crest, Ridwan halted his beast and raised his hand in salute to Butayna, who still watched him from the door. She returned the gesture.

The superintendent turned to her and bowed. She inclined her head, grateful for his help and discretion. Both of them entered the doors of *al-qasr Xenil* together.

Chapter 26
A Choice Made

Sultana Maryam

Granada, Andalusia
August 28 – September 10, AD 1354 / 8 - 22 Sha'ban 755 AH /
9th –21st of Elul 5114

Maryam stood in the shadows of the darkened stable in the late afternoon. As a mare snorted, Maryam peered from the back of a stall. Her gaze watered at the scene unfolding before her near the entryway.

Muhammad's rounded face, edged with tufts of hair at his cheeks and chin, lit up with an insipid grin. "I shall be the victor today, Father. What will you give me?"

Yusuf brushed his lean fingers over his son's mop of dark curls. "The prize is not your chief concern, my son. Bask in the joy of your success, if I allow it today."

Muhammad turned away. "It may be that *Ummi* shall best us both."

Yusuf nodded and followed the direction of Muhammad's gaze. "Your mother is the finest rider I have ever seen, even better than me."

The prideful Butayna never lifted her head in acknowledgment of Yusuf's undeserved praise. She tended to her horse while the slurring fool, al-Sagir, lifted the saddle on to the mare's back. Butayna stroked the Arabian's muzzle and tugged her forelock. Yusuf stared as a man with deep longing for one measure of the attention Butayna paid to the beast. How could he be so enamored of her after so many years? Despite their differences and the feuds of the past, his maddening attachment to the stupid woman remained and as usual, imperiled Maryam's interests.

She stifled a cry behind her hand and bit into the flesh to keep from screaming. She had come so close more than two years past to driving Butayna from Yusuf's heart forever. In less than four mere months after her departure to *al-qasr Xenil*, Butayna had returned in triumph. How had she accomplished the feat? Yusuf had believed her guilty of his mother's death, but inexplicably he restored her freedom when he should have condemned her to death. On a morning when a gray pall hung over the sky, she had entered the *Bab al-Sharia* again and hugged her children as if she never intended to let them go again. The petulant boy Muhammad pretended to hold some resentment of his mother's absence before he sobbed in her arms like a weakling. He and his father shared such faintness of heart and judgment in matters concerning Butayna. Maryam's own heart had almost stopped on the day of her rival's return.

Butayna's glare had hounded her in the weeks afterward whenever they chanced to share the *hammam* or passed each other in the harem's garden courtyard. Butayna's gaze had melted Maryam's calm exterior, for the fires of revenge glowed in the woman's eyes. Somehow, Butayna perceived Maryam's role in the troubles. Frantic, she had gone to Yusuf in fear that Butayna would put the evil eye on her from her vantage point across from Maryam's room. Yusuf had laughed at her and kissed her shoulders beneath the moonlight, before he drew her into his bed. She took no pleasure in his lovemaking after he dismissed her words and did not try to hide her displeasure. Soon, his summons had stopped.

Muhammad drew Maryam back to the moment when he said, "If *Ummi* should win again, what will be her reward, Father?"

Yusuf answered, "What could I offer your mother, which she does not already have? She possesses fine jewels and silks, even hunting hawks at her disposal. Of these things, she does not need more."

Butayna turned to him and led her mount forward. Her bland features mirrored those of her son. "Nor do I wish for the same. Of all the gifts my Sultan has granted me over the years, there is only one I treasure. His heart."

Yusuf said nothing. He stared at Butayna as if she alone existed in the stable, not al-Sagir, who now tended to Muhammad's mount, or his brother Bilal, who patted the Sultan's mount and proclaimed the stallion ready. Even Muhammad seemed to fade into the background for his parents, who held each other enraptured with their turbulent gazes. They would have embraced fervently if Muhammad had not been there.

Maryam viewed their renewed bond as a certainty. Had Yusuf returned to Butayna's bed? If not, it would only be a matter of time before she gained his heart again.

Then the spell broke and Yusuf patted Muhammad's shoulder. "We should go before we lose the light."

"Father, today's public audience lasted for hours. Are you not tired?"

"I am."

"Then why did you insist we keep to our afternoon ride?"

Yusuf replied, "When I am dead, you shall sit upon the throne and rule as I have. Take these simple moments with your parents and enjoy them while you can. You will achieve much in your lifetime, my strong son. Your people must always come first, but accept, other desires shall tug at your heart. The needs of your citizens will tear you from the arms of the woman you love and your children at play. A good Sultan must find balance between his private and public words. Whenever you are at council or at war, or if you are in the bed of the one who holds your heart, you will always feel as if you are in the wrong place at the wrong time. You cannot let such concerns lessen your joy or determination. Be a wise and blessed sovereign, do as you will for the good of your people and hold your loved ones close to you. Above all else, believe in Allah who ordains all. For who are we without Him?"

Muhammad nodded. "I understand your words, Father."

"Even about being with the one who holds your heart? Great God, have you been bedding *jawari* already?" Butayna gaped and her son reddened.

Yusuf gave a hearty laugh and led his mount out of the stable. He said as he went. "He is sixteen, Butayna. He is of an age and has his own princely household. You cannot have expected he would cling to his mother's skirts...."

As Muhammad and Butayna followed him out, Maryam stepped out of the shadows. They mounted their horses and left with a retinue of Yusuf's guards. Maryam's heartbeat raced and she swallowed in a dry mouth. Butayna had won. Somehow, she had secured the throne for her son.

Maryam leaned against a stall and closed her eyes. A shudder ran through her. How had her rival done it? When had she influenced Yusuf's choice? Yusuf had revealed nothing of his plans to anyone. Did he intend to name Muhammad as his heir before all?

Maryam jerked away from the post and paced the ground littered with straw. It clung to her silken *jubba*, but she ignored the chaff. Her erratic movements matched rapidly altering thoughts, as they cascaded through her mind.

Yusuf must have decided in recent weeks, as little as days. Did he no longer care whether Ismail played chess with him in the evenings? He had even postponed his walks with Qays through the complex. Maryam's beloved second son once delighted in such adventures, where Yusuf showed him all the city sights beyond their palaces.

With a growl low in her throat, Maryam clenched her hands. She had promised Butayna long ago that she would claim every moment of happiness the foolish woman ever held. One means remained open for her destruction now. Butayna's son would have to die.

Maryam lifted her chin and stared out of the opened doorway. Could she arrange Muhammad's death to appear accidental? Perhaps the saddle straps might give way if she sawed at them a little and let the motion of the ride do the rest. No one would perceive her involvement. They would blame al-Sagir and Bilal as-Sudan for carelessness. Their lives held no meaning.

Sour bile filled her throat and gagged. Tingling crisscrossed her chest and she crossed her arms over her breasts. She could not stop the rapid rhythm of her heart, the uncontrollable whimpers she tried to prevent. Despite her husband's continued folly with Butayna, Maryam loved him fiercely. Yet, she loved their sons even more than Yusuf. There had to be another way! How could she hurt him like this?

Still, she shook her head. There was no other course for her. Butayna had won. Maryam would exist at her mercy in the future, as Maryam's children might live or die by Muhammad's command.

Even at sixteen, Muhammad posed a great threat to her children and her plans for the future. The stout prince made no secret of his resentment of his brothers and sisters of the half blood. He would not claim their lives while Maryam lived. She would ensure their survival by any means. She knew what she had to do. For Ismail's sake, her actions would be well worth the cost. A future where her son sat on the throne remained the only viable outcome. Anything else meant death for her and her children. Butayna's poor choices had seen Palomba torn from her mother's arms and the long-awaited son of Gedaliah dead these past seventeen years. Yet, Maryam mourned those children as if she had lost them yesterday. She would not surrender another child, even to the eldest son of Yusuf.

"My Sultana?" Bilal found her as he appeared again in the doorway. "I thought you had left long before the Sultan and his family arrived."

She clenched her fists at her side. "I am part of the Sultan's family. Do not forget."

His mouth downcast, Bilal bowed. "Forgive me, my Sultana. Did you wish to ride as well?"

"I do not know how. Perhaps Prince Ismail can teach me. I could bring him by with me on another day. Would this time suit?"

"If you did that, I'm afraid you would have to wait for me to attend the Sultan and... the others."

"Does my husband always come here at this time with Butayna and Muhammad? Is Muhammad always with his parents?"

"The Sultan and his son come after public audience on the second and fifth days of the week. In the last few weeks, the Sultana Butayna has joined them."

Maryam nodded, as if she had not ascertained most of these facts beforehand. "Where is your brother al-Sagir now? He has disappeared."

Bilal's lips clamped together. She waited in silence for his answer.

Then he murmured, "He is resting."

"But I saw him only moments ago. He did not seem overtired, but enlivened."

"He needs sleep now. He becomes tired after he smokes the *hashish*."

Maryam raised her eyebrows. The rumors of al-Sagir's addiction were true. "What is this word? I do not know what the *hashish* is so you will tell me."

"May you never know, my Sultana. It is the only thing I have found to keep al-Sagir calm. A drug he smokes in the morning and at night."

She moved closer to him. "What happens if your brother does not have the *hashish*?"

"May you never see him then, my Sultana. His rages would frighten everyone. I fear he will kill someone, even me, if he does not smoke the *hashish* each day."

Maryam smiled. "I am not often afraid, Bilal, but I thank you for the warning."

She left him in the stable, her hands clasped together. She would have to learn more of this *hashish* and the effects of it upon al-Sagir. Ismail's place upon the throne depended upon it.

***

Thirteen days later, Maryam returned to the stable at the same hour. Yusuf, Butayna and Maryam's horses snorted in the distance. Maryam watched the riders as they dipped below the horizon along the *Sabika* hill. Then she entered the structure with two of her eunuchs. Her guard closed the doors.

Bilal peered from a stall where he tossed fresh straw into one of the empty enclosures. "My Sultana!" He bowed and straightened. His gaze darted behind her to the barred entryway. "How may I aid you?"

She clasped her hands together and smiled. "There are many ways you could help me, Bilal, but I have discovered only one will suffice."

"What do you mean, my Sultana?" He gave a slight shake of his head and swiped his dirtied hands over coarse linen garments.

She ambled toward him and crossed her arms over her chest. "Where is al-Sagir?"

Bilal swallowed. A lump in his throat bobbed. "He sleeps, my Sultana. It is the aftereffects of the *hashish*, as I told you before. You do not need him when I am here."

She mused, "*La*, you cannot serve my ultimate purpose. You will play your role, but it shall be short-lived."

He backed up against the post behind him. Faint lines crisscrossed his brow. A horse in the next stall whinnied and kicked the wood. Bilal jerked away.

Maryam paused before the stableman. "Do you enjoy your work, Bilal?"

"I do, my Sultana." He squeezed his hands into fists at his aide.

"Tell me, which is the fiercest horse in the Sultan's stable?"

"A Barb from al-Maghrib el-Aska, which my master keeps away from the others. The Sultan Abu Inan Faris gave the stallion as gift to my master a few weeks ago. The Sultan has never ridden him. It is not the horse for a Sultana, if you wish to ride."

"Hmm, he seems rather fierce. Will you show me this horse?"

Beads of sweat formed at Bilal's hairline. "I dare not, my Sultana. Sultan Yusuf ordered him kept in his stall away from others. I have just fed the remaining horses. This is not a good time to be near them."

"If my Sultan's prize is barred away in his stall, you have nothing to fear. You will show me the stallion, now."

Her lean-muscled eunuchs came up on either side of her.

Bilal groaned and his wiry shoulders drooped. "If you will follow me, my Sultana."

He plodded through the stable, past several rows of stalls. The majority stood empty. At the last row, a dark bay stallion whickered and pounded its tough horn hooves against the wood. A powerful mount, he carried his thick tail high and swished it from side to side. His smooth hindquarters met slender but solid legs. At their approach, the stallion lowered its head.

"This is it?" Maryam edged close to the stall.

Bilal waved her away. "Please, do not come any closer, my Sultana. This Barb almost kicked al-Sagir in the chest when he came too near to him at feeding time."

She turned to him. "You care very much for your brother, don't you?"

He looked down at his feet. "He is all I have in this world, my Sultana."

"You would do anything for him it seems; even sell your body to anyone who wishes to have you just to buy your brother the *hashish.*"

As the stableman's chin dipped to his chest, she studied him in silence. He shuffled on his feet and refused to raise his stare to hers.

Maryam circled him at a gradual pace. "I wondered how a mere servant who receives no wages for his work could afford supplies of *hashish.* It is not as if there is a steady source of *dirhams* and *dinars* available to you. I had my guards spy upon your activities in the evening, but it was unnecessary for one among them told me the truth. Anyone with a coin could have you for as long as he wished. A great sacrifice even for the sake of one's brother. Perhaps you enjoy the task as well."

Bilal's lower lip trembled. "I do what I must. No one else will help al-Sagir except for me. I am not ashamed of what I do for love of my brother."

Maryam gripped his pointed chin and lifted his face for her inspection. A heady thrill rushed through her as his eyes glistened with unshed tears. She uttered, "I have learned much of the power of sacrifice in this place. I will never forget yours."

"Mine, my Sultana?"

She stepped back and waved her eunuchs forward. "Take him."

The guards clamped their hands on Bilal and hoisted his body, flailing limbs and all He screeched, such a high-pitched note that the few horses in the stable neighed in response. The eunuchs heaved him over the top of the Barb's stall. The stallion snorted and stamped, ears pinned back against its head.

"*La!* Please do not do this to me! My brother needs me."

Maryam smiled at the poor, deluded fool. "Do not worry. I shall see to al-Sagir."

His fingers gripped the wood. One of Maryam's guardsmen peeled Bilal's fragile hold away, while the other batted the side of the stall. The Barb kicked and reared its powerful quarters, bucking hard against the enclosure. The stallion slipped sideways and Bilal screamed. Hooves flailed and a jarring thud against the wall silenced the cries from the stableman.

Satisfied, Maryam gestured toward the closest of her guards, who peeked over the stall. The horse snorted and the eunuch back away. With a shake of his head and a disgusted groan, he nodded. "It is done."

"Then we are finished here. Come, no one must find us."

***

Sultana Butayna

Butayna's mount slowed just outside the stable and she alighted without assistance. Winded from their furious race, Yusuf circled his horse beside her. "You cheated, my Sultana."

She flashed a grin at him. "I cannot help it if I have ridden horses since the age of four."

She loved the light banter between them, which had developed in recent weeks when they moved to the *Jannat al-'Arif*. Six months ago, it had seemed impossible for both of them to speak of anything except the simplest banalities. Yusuf had welcomed her from the *al-qasr Xenil* after her return and seemed desirous of a reunion. Her heart struggled with the act of forgiveness. There were days in which she despaired of their rapport, but in time, she found her resentment faded. Longing stirred inside her for the husband she had known for more than half of her life. Now, when her feelings surged, he behaved with reticence as if he held uncertainty about her attentions. She judged Muhammad's invitations to ride with him and his father as interference in his parents' relationship, but she appreciated his attempts to bring them closer.

Yusuf dismounted. "I wish to discuss an important matter with you. One of my governors, a close cousin through my father has broached a topic of interest to both of us. He proposes a marriage between our two families."

She gasped. "He has a daughter to whom he would marry our son? Isn't that rather presumptuous? Our son could marry a Sultana from al-Maghrib el-Aska, after all."

"*La*, Butayna. He does not inquire after my heir. He has a son whom everyone calls Muhammad the Red, for his hair and his... displays of bad humor at times. I consider him as a match for Aisha. She has your fiery temper."

"They might just kill each other. You want him for Aisha instead of Fatima, when she is your eldest. You will forgive me, Yusuf, if I say this Muhammad the Red sounds like a brute, your kin or not. If you wish for my opinion, I do not want him to wed Aisha. Let him wed Fatima instead."

"Fatima would certainly kill him first! She is arrogant, my eldest girl."

He moved and stood close behind her. "We don't have to decide the fates of any of my children now. Perhaps we could talk further this evening. Will you and Muhammad join me at dinner? Aisha should come as well. She should know the plans I have for her. It would be good for us to share a meal together as a family. We have not done so in some time."

The heat of his body warmed her. She inhaled the familiar, clean scent of him. A hot rush of wind blew her *hijab* back. He caught its trailing edge and rubbed the silk between his fingertips. When she turned and regarded him, his breath quickened.

"I had almost forgotten the softness of your silks, of you."

She whispered, "We are so different, my Sultan, than how we were before. We have been apart for some time."

"One thing has not changed. My love for you endures. It will never fade."

Her little fists tightened. For years, she had despaired of regaining Yusuf's heart. Now, she discovered it remained hers.

He sighed. "It may be that too much time has passed to undo the discord between us. I cling to a foolish hope. I have longed for a day in which we might stand before each other, just as Yusuf and Butayna, as husband and wife. You have often reminded me, I will always be the Sultan. Yet, I have never ceased to be yours. Perhaps, it is a dream I have of you and I. Nothing more."

She pressed her hand to the center of his tunic. "It is no dream, my Yusuf."

His heart pounded so fast beneath the cotton that its rhythm pulsed against her palm. He dipped his head toward her.

Their son joined them and slipped from his mare's back. "One day, I shall win against both of you."

Butayna drew apart from Yusuf and licked her lips. His gaze fell away.

She smoothed her hands over her garments and peered through the opened stable doors. "Bilal? Where is he?"

Yusuf tugged the reins and led his mount into the stable. "In the past, I have often returned and found Bilal asleep in the back of the stable. He is likely there now. I'll find him."

Butayna expelled a harsh breath and followed with her head bowed. Yusuf would have kissed her, in front of their son and the guards who waited nearby. She would have let him.

Yusuf handed the reins of his horse to Muhammad, who also took those tethered to Butayna's mare.

Yusuf said, "Wait here for me." He strolled through the stable. "Bilal! Bilal as-Sudan. Where are you? Surely, you know better than to leave the doors open. What if a horse had gotten loose from a stall?"

Butayna turned to Muhammad, who peeked at her with a sheepish grin. He mumbled, "I'm sorry I interrupted you and Father, *Ummi.*"

She clasped her hands in front of her arched her eyebrows. "Interrupted what, my lion?"

His plump cheeks flushed pink. "You know, back there. Out front between you and Father."

Her laughter echoed throughout the wooden building. "My lion, if I'm to understand your father, you have begun bedding your own *jawari.* You cannot mean to blush before me just because your father and I shared a quiet moment."

"I think it is the first you have had in a long time."

She smiled and nodded. "It is not a concern."

"It is for me and for Aisha."

"What has Aisha to do with anything?"

"She suggested these rides as a way to bring you and Father closer, since you have both always loved horses. You must know Aisha and I want you and Father to be content with each other again, as when we were children. Say you'll try, *Ummi.*"

"If it means so much to you, my lion."

"You still love Father, don't you, *Ummi?*"

She shook her head at his naiveté and leaned closer to him. She brushed her lips against his cheek. "I've never stopped loving your father. I do not know how to stop. I cannot."

Muhammad grasped her hand and placed it against his bearded cheek. "You have to believe he loves you also."

"I know he does. In the past, I often despaired whether love could sustain our bond. Yusuf and I have the rest of our lives to discover if this is true." She pinched her son's face. "You are far too concerned with your parents. You should look to your own happiness. One day, you must marry."

His loud guffaw startled the horses. "I am only sixteen! There is plenty of time to consider wives."

She crossed her arms over her chest and squinted hard at him. "If there are girls you can consider bedding, you can marry one as well. What if one of your *jawari* should give you a son? Would you dishonor her and keep her as your slave, the mother of a royal prince? I've raised you to do better than that, my lion."

He put a hand in surrender. "Very well, very well! By the Prophet's beard, *Ummi,* you have made your opinion clear."

"Never forget, I was once your father's *jarya*. I know something of the plight of the *jawari*. If I had not conceived you—"

"Allah! Bilal!" Yusuf's voice reverberated through the stable.

When Muhammad gasped and peered into the darkened recessed, she placed the flat of her hand on his chest. "Fetch your father's guards and remain outside with my captain and your own men."

"But, *Ummi*—"

She pushed him back. "Do as I say, Muhammad!"

She raced through the stable and at length, came upon Yusuf outside the stable of a dark bay horse. Between the wooden slats of the stall, she glimpsed a dark-skinned hand. She covered her mouth and stifled the scream.

Yusuf pulled her close to him and bellowed for his guard. He huddled with her. "Shut your eyes, Butayna."

She could not. She adjusted to the dimmed light with ease and made out the horrific scene within the enclosure. Between the jagged folds of a tear in Bilal's tunic, a massive purple bruise marked the center of his chest. A deep gash ran along his temple.

"I should not have accepted the gift of this wild beast from Abu Inan. Bilal tried to tame him once and I warned him against it. He must have gone into the stall to try again. Foolish man!"

She turned away and buried her face in Yusuf's neck. "Oh, this is a terrible accident. Have you seen al-Sagir? Where is Bilal's brother?"

"He is not here with him."

When Yusuf's guards arrived, he motioned to the body. "Get ropes. We must restrain the stallion. He may try to bolt or hurt someone else when we remove the body. Where is my son?"

Yusuf's captain answered, "He is outside with the horses your family rode."

"One of you, stay with those mounts. Another, run to the harem and fetch the chief eunuch and my chief steward. Come away from here, Butayna."

He shifted her backward, but she clutched at his arms. "Please, someone must find al-Sagir. What will he do without Bilal or his *hashish*?"

"Do not worry for that now, sweet love. I will find the young man. Come, come, I want you to return to the *Jannat al-'Arif* with Muhammad. Allah, you're shaking."

Yusuf drew her out of the stable at his side. In the evening light, she hugged him and shuddered. He framed her face between his hands and kissed her brow many time, as if he feared to part from her ever again.

"Please Yusuf, be careful with that horse," she whispered.

"I will be with my men. Go, my love, go." He raised his head and sought her captain. "Take her and my son back to the summer palace. Now!"

Ruiz bowed. "At once, my Sultan."

Muhammad clutched his mother's hand and led her away. Butayna kept looking behind her shoulder, even as Ruiz urged her on and Yusuf waved her away.

She did not rest or find comfort in her room, even when her servants tried to calm her. She related Yusuf's discovery and the women recoiled in horror. Aisha came to visit and discovered the truth as well.

She sagged beside Butayna on the bed. "That poor man. How can he be dead? Since I was a child, he's been so gentle with horses and so kind to everyone."

"We have no control over these creatures."

"What will Father do to the horse?"

"Your father is not an unkind man. I believe he will have his men free the beast on the plains. The stallion cannot be tamed."

"What will happen to al-Sagir now?"

"I shall arrange for his care through Mufawwiz, but al-Sagir must be locked up at night and watched during the day. He had no one except Bilal as-Sudan, may God rest his soul. Al-Sagir is addicted to *hashish*. The Sultana Fatima once told me Yusuf did not like this and Yusuf might try to put an end to it now. Your great-grandmother swore the drug was the only thing to contain al-Sagir's rages. Someone must ensure he remains calm. What will he do without his brother there to care for him?"

Aisha murmured, "I would be bereft without mine, but is al-Sagir... could he know the difference if Bilal is no longer with him?"

"The brothers have been together all of their lives. Al-Sagir will know. He will miss Bilal."

Before *Salat al-Asr*, a eunuch brought word of Yusuf's return. He still intended to dine with his family before the fourth prayer time of *Salat al-Maghrib*. Butayna and Aisha went to the *hammam*, though they did not stay long. While Aisha went to the oratory, Butayna returned to her chamber and prayed for the soul of Bilal as-Sudan.

At dinner in the northern pavilion, a subdued mood cast a pall over the meal. In the cool balm of a summer evening, Butayna sat with her children and husband at last. Yusuf never raised the topic of Aisha's marriage. Butayna resolved to discuss the matter further at another time. Butayna ate with her head bowed and said little, as did her children and Yusuf. At the end of the simple meal of flatbread, cheeses, chicken glazed in lemon sauce and a delicious *'tharid*, Yusuf raked a hand over his creased face.

Muhammad asked, "Did you find al-Sagir?"

"He was asleep in the loft above the stable. He did not see his brother's body. He has not asked for him, only *hashish*. There was a little left among Bilal's things. The rest of it will keep him calm tonight."

Butayna set down her piece of flatbread. "What will happen to him on the morrow?"

"Mufawwiz has promised to watch over him, but there will be no more *hashish*. It is time to wean al-Sagir from that particular addiction."

"But, Yusuf, he's dangerous without—"

He waved a hand through the air. She fell silent in an instant.

"Their mother believed so, as did my grandmother Fatima. Yet, even she abhorred the practice. She told me of its horrible effect, how *hashish* could change a person. When I asked her how she knew, she wept in her hands and never spoke of it, not even to me."

Butayna said nothing and reached between the food bowls and platters for his hand. She kept the confidence with which Yusuf's grandmother had entrusted her, even from her husband. Would he truly have been ashamed, as Fatima had suspected, if he knew of the addiction his ancestor suffered? Butayna would never know, for she would never burden Yusuf's heart. Secrets from Fatima's past would die with Butayna.

Yusuf linked his fingers with hers. Aisha strove against a smile she could not hide and Muhammad ducked his head.

Afterward, slaves removed the remnants of the meal. Butayna had not brought her *oud*, but the small family enjoyed the entertainment of a singing girl until the trio of Yusuf, Aisha and Muhammad observed the evening prayer. Butayna cast a *dirham* in thanks to the *jarya* and dismissed her for the evening. She bowed often as she backed out of the chamber. Butayna sat in silence at the table until her family finished their supplications in Yusuf's bedchamber.

Yusuf returned to her side with features as haggard as a man twice his age of thirty-six. "I wish you to remain with me tonight. I ask you to stay. I do not command it as the Sultan or even as your husband. Just one who would be at your side."

She grasped his fingertips and kissed them. "I will stay with you."

Soon, their children wished them well and departed with wide grins on both of their cherished faces. They went down the stairs and out into the night. The captain closed the door with a nod.

Butayna looked at Yusuf, who held out his hand. She placed her own in his.

He said, "I wish to keep you in my arms this night. I hold no expectations of you. I will not take anything you are unwilling to give. Just allow me to be near you and I shall be satisfied."

She crept closer to him and nuzzled his hands again. "What if what you propose is inadequate for me?" When he gasped, she whispered against his flesh, "We have spent so much time apart. I do not intend to ever leave your arms again after this night, if you will have me."

Yusuf tugged her against him. His sweet visage filled her vision before he bent his head and captured her lips with his. Her arms wound around his and she sought a deeper, richer closeness with him than she ever had. In swift motions, he removed her veil and the lavender *jubba* she had chosen for tonight.

Yet, he placed the silk on to the bed with something akin to reverence. "My favorite color, Fatima's color. I love to see you in this garment."

"Not only out of it?" When he chuckled, she added with a husky sigh, "Why do you think I have worn it so often this summer?"

His mouth hovered over hers. "Butayna. My Butayna."

She laughed and nuzzled his lips. "Always, your Butayna."

***

On the next morning, Butayna met Ridwan by chance, as she ventured out to the garden early. He came up the steps under the southern pavilion and greeted her.

She inquired, "You are meeting with Yusuf so early?"

"He requested it, my Sultana."

In a low whisper, she asked, "Has your brother questioned whether Bilal was alone in the stables before he died?"

"Bilal was not alone, Sultana. Your rival was seen leaving the stable that afternoon."

She clenched her fingers and then flexed them. Someday soon, Maryam would pay for her treachery. "Why did she have him killed?"

Ridwan pursed his thin lips. "Why indeed."

Chapter 21
The Little One

Sultana Butayna

Granada, Andalusia
October 18 - 19, AD 1354 / 30 Ramadan – 1 Shawwal 755 AH /
1st - 2nd of Marcheshvan, 5115

On a cool autumn evening, Butayna knelt beside Aisha's bed.
She stroked thick locks away from her daughter's brow and
marveled at her beauty. Already thirteen, one day she would
become someone's wife. At least she would not become the
property of Muhammad the Red, whom Yusuf had accepted as
the future husband of his eldest daughter, Fatima. Butayna
never asked how Maryam reacted to her daughter's marriage.
Butayna did not care for Maryam's opinions. She would follow
Yusuf's dictates, as they all did.

A soft knock came at the door. Butayna asked, "What is it,
Ruiz?"

Instead of her captain, Yusuf entered with two white roses in
his hands. Butayna recalled the last time he had brought a
flower into her chamber, just before he revealed the knowledge of
her hand in the death of Maryam's baby. Butayna shook her
head, scarce believing how imprudent and ignorant she had once
been. Now, Yusuf took every opportunity to show her his love
and unending devotion.

He sat on the bed and placed the rose on Aisha's hair fanned
out across the silk pillow. "I should have named our daughter for
Leila."

Butayna smiled. "That would have been confusing while her
aunt raised her. You chose the name for your grandmother's
mother, as you told me. A woman who sacrificed her life for the
daughter she loved. May our Aisha never face such a choice."

He smoothed petals of the second rose across Butayna's
cheek. "I should never have let anyone take our children from
your arms. You are a devoted mother and though you may not
be a Muslim, you have respected my faith and encouraged
theirs."

She clutched his hand against her skin. "As you have done for me. Who would have ever thought there could be such contentment between a Christian and a Moor?" When he laughed with a throaty sound, she continued, "Together we might have something to teach this King Pedro of Castilla-Leon. Does he still bluster about tribute owed to his kingdom?"

"He does."

"Will you renew the tribute?"

"I will." At her gasp, he added, "If only to give my people a measure of peace. A decade ago upon a cool spring day, we established a truce for ten years with Pedro's kingdom. Now, he demands two hundred and fifty thousand of his gold coins or he shall attack my cities. I grow weary of the bloodshed and maneuverings. All I want is peace now with you, my heir, and the rest of my children."

"Maryam as well," Butayna murmured.

He shook his head. "She's turned cold toward me for two years now, since your return from *al-qasr Xenil*. We are not as we were. Maryam remains part of my family. She has granted me the blessing of children as you did. For these and other happy memories, I will never shun her if she chooses to return to my side."

Butayna mused, "One of her sons did not seem so pleased with you after the evening prayer."

"Ismail resents my commands, but he shall follow them. I have insisted he and Qays will attend the *Madrasa Yusufiyya* with Muhammad. When Muhammad takes the throne one day, the *muftis* and scholars of my court will aid his reign. He should have strong brothers who have studied *Sharia* law at his side."

"Will they be at his side or against him?" Butayna placed her palm in Yusuf's lap. She held no reason to hope Maryam's rivalry with her had not stirred some resentment in the woman's sons. Ismail and Qays always sneered in Muhammad's presence, though they tried to hide it whenever Yusuf appeared.

"They are Muhammad's brothers, sweet love."

"Your brother languishes in a jail for treason." When he groaned, she rushed on, "I no longer question your judgment in the matter, my love. Please believe I do not. Only heed the lesson of your generation."

"Ismail and Qays are my sons, Butayna. Would you have me send them to Shalabuniya as well? You despise Maryam. Must you hate her children?"

"I do not hate them. I am devoted to mine."

"As every mother should be." He stood and held out his hand. "Come to bed, sweet love. Our daughter sleeps under the watchful protection of your guards. She is safe."

She accepted his aid as he helped her rise from the floor. She sighed and rubbed her lower back. "I should have had Hafsa massage my back before I dismissed her for the evening."

"Would you deny the pleasure of your supple flesh beneath my hands?"

She cupped his cheek and kissed him with a light peck. "I cannot deny any of your wishes, my love."

"Then it is my wish to please you tonight. Come."

He led her away, fingers interlaced with hers. Outside of Aisha's room at *al-Qal'at al-Hamra*, Ruiz bowed in acknowledgment. Butayna followed Yusuf down the stairs and out into the courtyard.

Maryam had just returned from the *hammam* with a train of slaves behind her. Wet, dusky hair clung from her shoulders to her waist. Her bathing robe hugged her curves under the garment.

Butayna met the sleepy-eyed stare from Maryam. Butayna's hand tightened on Yusuf's own. Maryam's gaze swung between the pair of them. She shrugged a little before she offered Yusuf a slight nod and withdrew into her apartment.

As Butayna strolled beside her husband, she shook her head. "Did you see the way Maryam looked at us?"

"Think nothing of her jealousy." He ushered her before him into his chambers.

As the doors closed behind him, she said, "I do not think Maryam was jealous at all. She seemed... indifferent."

A baleful scream echoed and made her shudder. She clutched her throat.

Yusuf moved behind her and rubbed her shoulders. "You would think after three weeks, you might have grown accustomed to al-Sagir's screams. His body still craves the *hashish*, but his mind fights for control."

"Shall his mind or body win?"

"Only he can decide, sweet love."

***

The next morning, Yusuf awoke Butayna with kisses on her stomach. They made love once more before he rose for his bath and prayers. She remained in his chamber at his request after he visited the *hammam*. He returned and kissed her one more time, before he drew back.

"Stay as you are in my bed. I wish to find you this way when I return."

382

She sighed and gave a languid stretch. The coverlet fell away to her waist. He sucked in his breath and she giggled.

"I cannot spend all morning naked in your bed, husband."

"You have delighted in reminding me over the years. I am the Sultan. I shall have you naked in my bed as often as I wish."

"Your memory is convenient and unpardonable."

"I am going to the mosque before you rob me of my original purpose. Wait for me. I promise I'll return to you." He stole another kiss and left her.

She remained in his chamber for another hour. Slaves came to retrieve last night's bedding for the laundry, so she rose and put on her favorite *rida* from the previous evening. Others offered her fruit and water, which she accepted while she sat at Yusuf's table. After another hour, her fingertips tapped on the top of the wood. She looked behind the bed and chests for her veil, but she must have bundled it with the bedclothes. With a sigh, she rose and ventured to her own apartment.

The guards who remained under the pavilion bowed with their eyes averted. Had they never seen a woman's hair before? She smirked at their discomfort and raced through the garden courtyard, tresses billowing around her face. She found Jawla and Hafsa awaiting her. Both bowed and greeted her with smiles.

"I want you to make me beautiful for Yusuf today. Find my lavender *jubba*. I will wear it again for him."

Hafsa followed Butayna, who went to the *hammam*. She met Aisha in the changing room while she spoke with her younger sister, Maryam's second daughter Khadija. The girls drew apart and Khadija darted out of the bath.

Butayna stared in her wake until she addressed her daughter. "Did I interrupt something between you and Maryam's daughter?"

"She's my sister! I like her!"

"You should be more cautious, Aisha."

"Khadija isn't like her mother. You and Maryam have kept us away from each other, but Khadija and I wish to be friends. She has invited me to Fatima's *henna* night whenever it occurs before she marries Muhammad the Red. I want to go."

"You will not."

"Khadija's my sister! You can't keep me away from her."

Butayna clamped a hand on her daughter's arm. "I'm trying to keep you safe, you insolent girl."

"I'm not a girl. I have bled and Father considers other possible suitors for me. One day soon, I will marry and if I choose to have a relationship with all of my sisters, you can't stop me!"

Aisha wrenched her arm away and fled the *hammam*.

Butayna swallowed and clapped a hand to her forehead. Hafsa shuffled on the tiles and said nothing.

Later, when Butayna returned to the harem, she inquired with the first guard she met about Yusuf's whereabouts.

"He has not returned, my Sultana."

She nibbled at her lower lip and proceeded into her chambers. The first prayer had finished at least two hours ago. In the room, Hafsa dressed her in the *jubba* Butayna had selected and painted her eyes with a little gold dust, despite objections.

"Yusuf prefers me as I am."

"He wants you beautiful—"

Heavy, booted footfalls drowned out Hafsa's voice. Ruiz knocked and entered the chamber. He inhaled, grabbed his chest, and regained control over his erratic breathing.

Butayna rose from the stool. "*Dios mío!* What is it, Ruiz?"

"The minister Ridwan sends word. The Sultan was alone in the mosque. Al-Sagir burst in and he stabbed the Sultan!"

A heavy weight settled on Butayna's chest. She stumbled backward and righted herself in an instant. It could not be true. He had left her just this morning with promises of his return. Hafsa burst into tears and Butayna snapped at her. "Be quiet!"

Butayna knelt at her captain's side. "Is it certain? Is he still alive?"

Tears trickled down Ruiz's cheek. She drew back. He had never cried, not even when Xurxo, one of his most trusted men, died of the plague in its last weeks. Now, he wept for her husband, a Moor.

"Ruiz, tell me!"

"I do not know, *mi reina*. His guards are bearing him back to his chambers."

"Where is our son?"

"At his lessons with the weapons master. I have sent discreet word to my brother to bring the *Infante* Muhammad here now."

"Come with me."

Butayna left Hafsa behind and did not concern herself with a *hijab*. Her hair unbound, she swept out of the harem and into the garden, just as Yusuf's men disappeared into his apartment. Rivulets of blood trailed in his wake across the white marble floor. She covered her mouth with a shuddering hand.

"Please, oh please, God. Do not take him from me now that we have found each other again. If it is Your will, I shall... I shall try to be strong for our son, I shall bear the loss, but please do not let him go where I cannot follow for Muhammad's sake. Not yet."

Ruiz cupped her elbow. "Come, *mi reina.*"

He escorted her as she plodded through a gathering crowd of eunuch guards, who had stood by in amazement when Yusuf reentered the harem. She went into his rooms. His men had placed him on the bed. Crimson stains coated his bed and the black *jubba.* Blood spurted from two wounds at his neck and stomach, despite how his captain and another man pressed them with their fingers.

The captain looked at her with a tortured gaze. "We have called for al-Shaquri! He was visiting the burial site of his father, but he will come, my Sultana."

Butayna moved beside her husband. She cupped his cheek. Blood matted his beard and chin. She bent close to him. "I'm here, my heart. I will always be at your side."

His watery gaze found hers. "Butayna?" Blood trickled from his mouth.

She nodded and pressed her hand to her lips. A dull ache throbbed inside her throat. She could not speak, only trembled as he raised his bloodstained fingertips to her face. Her tears flowed and she did not try to stop them. Instead, she clasped his hand. "Rest, my Yusuf, you must rest. Don't try to talk. Only rest. Your doctor will come to you. He will save you! You must believe this, my dearest heart. Yusuf, do not leave me! Not now. Please, please stay with me. Please!"

Tears spilled from his eyes. "My... sweet love."

His touch against her cheek slackened. Still she held his fingers close, callused as they were, from his hours with the sword and bow. His gaze remained on her face, though he no longer saw her.

Horrific screams erupted from the doorway. She looked up from Yusuf's body and found Maryam and her eldest daughter, Fatima. Ismail stood behind them with a pallid face, whiter than even Hisham's appearance, framed between thick strands of waist-length hair.

"*La,* Father!" Fatima wailed and fell at her brother's feet.

Maryam joined her child on the floor. Maryam batted at her breasts. She tore her *hijab* from her head and ripped it apart, before she buried her boisterous sobs in the material.

Could she have been so sadistic? Had this been her plan all along? She had killed Bilal or he died on her orders somehow in that stall. She removed the one person who could have controlled al-Sagir. Then he turned mad for lack of the *hashish* and attacked. Why had he chosen Yusuf as his victim? Did he perceive Yusuf's orders had denied him the drug he craved? Had Maryam conveyed the truth to him or directed him somehow in Yusuf's death? In doing so, had she directed the murder of their husband?

Maryam did not care who died in her quest for power. To get her Ismail on the throne, would she have done this to Yusuf? Maryam could not be so heartless as to kill the father of her children.

The vicious words she had hurled at Butayna years ago outside the bathhouse returned now with startling clarity.

'Every happy moment you may ever discover shall be mine! Do you hear me? I will never rest until I have ruined you....'

Butayna gazed at Yusuf. His skin still felt warm upon her cheek. She bent and kissed his lips. Their familiar touch evoked so many memories of hours spent with him, and all the time they had lost in misunderstanding and futile arguments. She banished those recollections and dwelled on those in which he had simply kissed her.

Then she summoned her courage and placed his hand on his chest. With a sigh, she reclined beside him for a moment, her head against the heart that no longer pulsed with vigorous life. Bereft of his sweet touch forever, she sang a portion of the words Yusuf had offered during their first meeting.

However far you may be from me, have faith.
Your love has ruined me for another.
God in heaven, never let me leave this life,
Ere I see your sweet, fair face again.

"Move back! I said move back in the name of the Sultan!"

Butayna raised her head as Ridwan and Ibn al-Khatib preceded Muhammad's entry into the room, with his Christian guards at his back. The sight of her son's stark features brought a fresh round of tears, flooding Butayna's cheeks. Still, she rose from the bed and moved on stiff legs toward him. She collapsed before him and clutched his knees.

He demanded, "Is it true? Has al-Sagir murdered my father?"

Yusuf's captain answered, "It is so. My men and I stood at the entryway while the Sultan made the last *rak'ah*. Al-Sagir burst in, raving as he has done for weeks. He grabbed one of the daggers my men carried. He must have escaped the eunuchs the chief steward had assigned to him. We could not reach al-Sagir in time before he stabbed the Sultan in his neck and back. He was a wild creature, stronger than any I have ever fought. We wounded him many times, but still he plunged the blade into the

Sultan's stomach a third time before we stopped him. If you wish it, my men and I shall kill ourselves for this shame."

Butayna sobbed harder. If Fatima had not given al-Sagir the drug, Yusuf might still be alive today. Still, deep in Butayna's heart, she believed al-Sagir alone did not bear the full blame for the tragedy of today.

Muhammad murmured, "Your deaths won't bring my father back to life. Nothing can. Where is his murderer now?"

"The rest of the Sultan's guards have him, my prince."

Ibn al-Khatib stepped forward. "He is not your prince. Kneel in the presence of the Sultan Abu Abdallah Muhammad ibn Yusuf, the *Amir al- Muslimin* and lord of the land!"

As one, the occupants of the room prostrated themselves with bowed heads, except for Maryam. She jerked to her feet, her eyes wild. She shook her head and held out her hands.

"How can this be? Yusuf never chose an heir. Why should it be Muhammad? You have no right to do this, Ibn al-Khatib. None! By what right have you, Muhammad's childhood tutor and Yusuf's secretary, proclaimed the heir in my husband's stead? I will not allow it! What of my sons?"

Muhammad bent and whispered, "*Ummi*, release me."

When she would not, he pried her fingers away and then strode across the room. He raised his hand and swung wide, smacking Maryam across the face. She cried out, clutched at her cheek, and fell beside her son. Ismail raised his head and stared wide-eyed at Muhammad.

Muhammad stabbed a finger at Maryam. "Did I give you permission to rise or speak in the Sultan's presence? You will kneel before me and remember your place as a second wife to my beloved father!"

She looked at Ismail, who bowed his head. "Are you going to let him do this to me? To us? Where is your pride, your Nasrid pride?"

With a snarl, Muhammad bent toward her and backhanded her a second time. "Be silent and submit! I swear by the Prophet's beard if you do not kneel, I shall cut off your head myself!"

A soft sob in her throat, Maryam prostrated herself beside her children.

Muhammad's gaze swept over the room until he found Butayna again. "My honored mother shall rise."

Butayna sniffled and swiped a hand across her nose. Her limbs quaked and refused to cooperate. She struggled to rise, and when she could not, sobbed behind her hands.

A second time he said, "Rise, *Ummi*. You are stronger than this trial, as am I. You have made me so."

When her knees buckled again, Muhammad dashed to her side and supported her. "You are the mother of the Sultan. You will never kneel in the presence of others. Now stand." He released her and drew back a pace.

She stood in the center of the room and whispered. "Thank you, my... my Sultan."

He kissed her brow and then declared, "My loyal ministers may also rise."

Ibn al-Khatib and Ridwan stood. Ridwan said, "I shall summon the *ghasil* to wash... my lord Yusuf."

How Butayna wished that she, not some stranger, might bathe her treasured husband's body, but the Sultanate's laws deemed such an act unclean. Her son would never have permitted it, though she would have undertaken it as an honor, the duty of a beloved wife for her murdered husband.

Muhammad squeezed her hand. "*Ummi*, there is blood on your clothes and your face. My father's blood. Go to the *hammam*. Aisha must learn of this day's treachery later. She went to the *Qaysariyya* with three of my guards, in the company of our sister, Sultana Khadija."

Butayna nodded, too numbed to speak.

"Aisha should not see you with our father's blood upon you. Wash and dress yourself again. We will be together soon. I shall comfort my sister and we will comfort you, *Ummi*. Go, go now."

She followed his instructions and passed from the apartment. Ridwan and Ibn al-Khatib bowed as she departed. Ruiz fell into step behind her.

At the doorway, she paused and looked over her shoulder. "What does the Sultan intend to do with al-Sagir?"

Muhammad stated, "He shall have the justice all murderers deserve."

She peeked at him, saw Yusuf's visage and heard his voice in their son. She bowed her head and nodded. Al-Sagir would find no comfort in a swift and merciful death. She wanted to believe he deserved no compassion, but she could not draw such a conclusion, having known al-Sagir for so long.

Her gaze flitted over Maryam, still prostrate at Muhammad's command. It would be so easy to speak the words, which would condemn the rival Butayna once called her friend. Whether Maryam directed al-Sagir's final choice or not, she influenced it by the murder of Bilal as-Sudan. Wouldn't it be better for everyone if she died?

Then Butayna glanced at Maryam's children, who wept and cowered beside their mother. The death of their mother would ensure some form of retribution, unless Muhammad killed them as well. Butayna shook her head. She could not allow her son to bear the burden of his brothers and sisters' blood upon his hands. For the sake of her children, Maryam had to live.

The guards and eunuchs drew back in mute horror as Butayna resumed her stiff walk and bypassed them. Yusuf's precious blood cooled on her cheeks, and marred the sleeve and breast of her *jubba*. The eunuchs who guarded the inner sanctum of the harem bowed their heads. Tears shone in the eyes of most of the men, which they would not shed. Others made furtive touches upon the arms of their companions.

Peace, her heart pleaded. For how long would her cries go unanswered?

When she approached the bath superintendent, his mouth gaped in a wide O before he moved from his post at the doorway and recalled his courtesies. He offered her a rigid bow.

"My Sultana, your husband's *jawari* remain within the *hammam* at this hour."

He fell silent as the chief eunuch Hisham, Ridwan's secretive half-brother, glided beside Butayna. His face ashen and his bloodless lips pressed together, he could have been another corpse in the palace instead of a snake.

"Get rid of them!" Hisham spoke with clear purpose for the first time. "Would you have the *Umm al-Walad* usher them out herself? She would cleanse her body of the blood of our master, murdered this day by the traitorous fool al-Sagir. Dismiss the women and do not speak of the Sultan's death to anyone. They will know soon enough."

He turned his heavy-lidded gaze on Butayna. "If the *Umm al-Walad* would permit, we may wait in the superintendent's chamber."

She turned away and blinked back a fresh round of tears she would not permit him to view. Must he call her by the title so soon? Could she not remain Yusuf's beloved, his Sultana, for a moment longer?

The superintendent fled, the heels of his sandaled feet clacking on the tiles.

Butayna turned to Ruiz. "Await me here."

She wrapped her arms around her torso and retired with Hisham to the antechamber. She stared at the room's fixtures without truly seeing them. Such a small space for a large man. Yusuf would have admired the austerity of his apartment, with one long, narrow bed and a chest for furnishings. Her Yusuf, gone forever from her arms. How could it be possible? Just a little longer, a moment's strength required of her before she could cast off this day's violence and be safe from prying eyes, where she might weep in silence for her beloved. How could he have left her so soon, with their son and daughter bereft of him? Muhammad would rule and Aisha would marry, but Yusuf would never know.

His absence, so fresh and new, seemed almost unfathomable. Her ability to stand upright, even to breathe, came from some inner strength she had not known she possessed. Leila's words came back to her, of how the deepest sorrow summoned the greatest power inside a person. Fortitude alone would help her survive and remain strong for her children. They needed her now more than ever, especially Muhammad. Even as Sultan, he would never be safe from Maryam's ultimate desire to see her son on the throne in Muhammad's stead.

The chief eunuch bowed before her. "I expect no gratitude from you, my Sultana. I have done little to earn it before the hour of my master's death."

He spoke Arabic this time, as if he had not disdained to do so with her for years. Did he fear her now? She could have laughed at the thought if regret and sadness permitted her such an empty gesture.

Still, she inclined her head. "You have my appreciation all the same, Hisham."

A flurry of feet and chatter beyond the antechamber almost swallowed up her last words.

When the superintendent returned, he bowed again. "The *hammam* is yours."

She moved past him through the archway into the changing room. At a muffled gasp behind her, she faced both men. The floor bore reddened stains. She had tracked her beloved's blood inside. She looked up. Her glance encompassed both men. The superintendent spoke first.

"Do not fear. I shall remove all traces of al-Sagir's treachery in the *hammam*."

If he could just sweep aside the horror from her mind and heart, Butayna mused. Under his watchful gaze and the intent stare of the chief eunuch, she bent and took off her dirtied slippers. She set them beside a low stool against the wall and walked barefooted across the tiles, past *al-bayt al-barid, al-bayt al-wastani* and into the hot bathing room.

All the while, the superintendent trailed her and cautioned, "My Sultana! You cannot! The heated tiles would burn the soles of your feet."

She smiled at his concerns and plodded on. Two pairs of click-clacks moved in unison behind her. The deepest desires of her heart for peace and solitude would remain elusive today. She would have to be strong for Muhammad and Aisha, for love of Yusuf.

Muggy heat, warmer than an Andalusian summer, and a haze of white vapor obscured her vision until she became acclimated. Ruined fabrics clung to her skin even as she stripped them off, one by one. The *jubba* of lavender damask Yusuf loved so much, his favorite color. The gossamer tunic clung to her breasts, a sight to stir her husband's passionate gaze if he yet remained alive. Her fingers slipped beneath the gold waistband as his own often had, whenever he tired of her teasing and wanted her under, astride or beside him, but always naked in his bed. The *sarawil* fell and pooled around her ankles, revealing the limbs she used to drape around his waist, always eliciting a hoarse groan and the whispered demand for her to keep him in her clutches forever. In the sweet, but all too brief days of the last three weeks, where she had held his heart and his love again. When she once believed nothing and no one would destroy their lives together. A time now gone forever. She would cling to the memories until her death.

When the tears came again, she smiled at her remembrances. "I promise, my Yusuf, you shall live on in my heart."

The warm water enveloped her. She immersed herself, even ducked her head below the surface. A moment's panic ensued before she relaxed and cleansed her skin of the day's violence.

After some interminable time, she rose and crept to the edge of the water. The chief eunuch and bath superintendent each held aloft the bath linen. She emerged and they enveloped her in its folds. Droplets cascaded from her saturated hair and coursed down her cheeks. Surely, even the sly Hisham could not discern the difference between the bathwater and her tears.

Chapter 28
The Bargain

Sultana Maryam

Granada, Andalusia
December 1 - 14, AD 1354 / 15 - 28 Dhu al-Qa`da 755 AH / 16th - 29th of Kislev, 5115

Despite the cold of the frost-covered ground, Maryam knelt beside Yusuf's grave and wept most of the morning. Her eunuchs stood apart from her and safeguarded her privacy. She sobbed until her throat ached and her vision blurred. Then she laid her head against the marble tombstone.

"Please forgive me, beloved. I never meant to lose you. I thought the consequences would have been so different. I meant Muhammad to suffer, not you. Never you! You would have grieved for him, but my Ismail would have been there to comfort you. Allah! What have I done?"

Self-recriminations would not change her grievous mistake or bring her husband back to life. Despite how he had betrayed her by choosing Muhammad over Ismail, she never doubted her ability to alter Yusuf's heart. He would have loved her again and in the tragic, sudden loss of his heir to al-Sagir's blade, he would have found joy again at her side. She would have comforted him, while paving the path for Ismail's ascendancy. Now he would never be Sultan in his father's stead.

With a weary sigh, she raised her head and raked her frozen fingers over her face. She smoothed the folds of her *hijab* and covered the lower half of her feature. In a leather cloak trimmed with ermine fur at the edges, she stood on wobbly legs and brushed the snow from her clothing and boots.

"Wherever you are in Paradise, beloved, know that for a time, I did love you almost as much as I love our children. They shall never cease to remember you with pride. For my part, please forgive me for how I have wronged you. It should have been Muhammad, it should have been him."

Her icy fingertips skimmed the cold, marble gravestone. "Goodbye, beloved."

She turned away and walked out of the *rawda*. She turned south and went to the *Bab al-Sharia*. In the cold, she waited in the recesses of the gateway. The gate master stood nearby and he gave her a stiff bow. She ignored him and looked across the eastern *Sabika* hill. Out of the woodlands enshrouded in a white haze, a band of ten emerged.

In their lead, Muhammad the Red peered from beneath a leather hood. He pushed it back and revealed the hair, which had partly earned him his sobriquet.

She inclined her head and they exchanged the traditional greeting. Then she said, "I am the Sultana Maryam, beloved of Yusuf, may Allah preserve his memory."

Muhammad the Red peered down his nose at her from atop his mount. "The gossips say the Sultan preferred you over his first wife at times. I can see a little of why in this lovely, dark gaze."

She ducked her head and pretended to smile, so the appearance of mirthful little crinkles around her eyes might lull him. Beneath her veil, she grimaced. How dare he speak so to the mother of the girl whom he would marry? Yusuf had informed her of his age. Twenty, brash and bold as many of the Nasrid princes, but this one also held a vicious temper. His intended bride Fatima had proved she possessed the fiery passion of her mother and her paternal grandmother. If Muhammad the Red thought he would gain a docile wife, he would soon discover the error when he wed Maryam's daughter.

He dismounted and tossed his reins to the closest of his men. "Wait for me."

She raised her eyebrows at his easy command. Did he expect his men would stand idle at the *Bab al-Sharia* for untold hours while he shared her afternoon meal? What gave him such confidence in his power over those who served him?

Still she waved him into the courtyard and through the secondary gate. He strolled beside her, his dark green *jubba* a perfect complement to his ruddy skin and fiery hair. He turned and studied her beneath abundant eyebrows.

"Why do you stare, my prince?"

"I am wondering whether my future wife possesses your eyes."

"Fatima has the beauty of her father's mother."

"May I see for myself?"

She stopped and drew herself up her full height. "You will see Fatima in full after the wedding. I have agreed she may welcome you before we eat the noonday meal, but she will not remain in the harem. The chief steward shall escort her and her sisters to the drapers' stalls in the *Qaysariyya*, as soon as you have met Fatima."

"Does Sultan Muhammad know you will share a meal with me alone in your quarters?"

She disliked the innuendo laced in his tone almost as much as his heated gaze upon her face. "The Sultan does not have to grant his approval of everything I do. His mother is aware and she sees no difficulty in the arrangement, not when my guards shall remain with us."

That should be enough to deter him lest he had planned to do something foolish and untoward during their meal. His lips tightened into a taut smile. She shared the same reaction under her veil.

They entered the harem by the doors to the southwest and went through the western portico to reach her rooms. Her slave girls awaited them and bowed as she entered. She preceded Muhammad the Red up the steps and into the chamber where her daughters stood beside a table laden with rich food. The girls bowed.

Fatima and Khadija wore their veils, as they had reached marriageable ages and endured their monthly cycles. Shams, Mumina, and Zoraya remained too young for such concerns. Still Muhammad the Red peered at their glistening black hair and dark eyes first.

Then he looked at Maryam. "Which one shall be mine?"

She despaired of his coarse manners, especially when Fatima and Khadija exchanged wary glances, reflected in wide-eyed stares between the folds of their veils.

Maryam said, "Fatima, my love, come and present yourself before your future husband."

Fatima greeted him as her mother trained her to do. When she lifted her head, he stared hard at her face, as if he could discern something of her features from within the opaque cloth.

"It is ridiculous that I cannot see her face until I bed her!" He clapped his thigh.

Maryam's hands fisted at her sides. "It is tradition." She turned to her children. "Girls, go the courtyard. Mufawwiz said he would collect you before noon. A portion of my guards shall be with you."

Her daughters lined up and she kissed each of them upon their forehead. She tickled and poked her youngest, Zoraya, in the belly until the little girl laughed. Then she dismissed them. "Be well, my daughters."

They went down the steps. Muhammad the Red's stare followed little Zoraya until he caught sight of Maryam's steady glare.

She gestured toward the table and enjoined him to partake in the meal. When she tugged aside her veil to join him, his harsh intake of breath both thrilled and reviled her. He nodded to himself, perhaps made more comfortable with his choice of one of her daughters in marriage.

While her guards stood silent in the corners of the room, more than once she considered whether it might not be best to poison her guest or have her eunuch strangle him. Could she trust the Sultan to seek another husband for his younger sister? He tolerated his younger siblings, no more. He would not provide a better man. She could not rely upon Muhammad for anything, least of all the improvement of her children's lives. He would just as soon kill them all before he allowed them to prosper.

Maryam sipped her *sekanjabin* near the conclusion of the meal. The water clock almost marked the time for *Salat al-Zuhr*.

Muhammad the Red asked, "Does the Sultan pray in the same building where his father died?"

Seated across from him, she stiffened. "How should I know what the Sultan does?"

"You live in his palace—"

Her glass clinked on the tabletop. "This was Yusuf's abode before it became his son's own!"

A smirk lifted the corner of his mouth. "You do not favor your stepson's rule, do you?"

"I have no idea what you could mean. I am a loyal citizen of the Sultanate."

"Not loyal to the Sultan Muhammad, I think." He stuffed a *hais* pastry into his wide mouth.

She eyed him. "What you speak is treason."

"It is also the truth. I have learned your eldest son Ismail is little more than a year younger than the Sultan, whom his minister Ibn al-Khatib declared as the rightful heir. Your husband, Allah preserve his memory, never chose a successor."

"He did not." She knew otherwise, but as long she perpetrated the belief, others would think the same and question Muhammad's claim.

"He might have easily chosen your son had he lived."

She nodded. "Indeed, but Sultana Butayna's son rules over us now."

"That does not mean his reign will last forever."

She took the last sip of *sekanjabin* and patted her mouth with a pristine linen cloth. She waved a *jarya* over with the basin of rose water. After Maryam dipped and dried her hands, she ordered the girl away. She gripped the edge of the wooden table's surface.

Muhammad the Red said, "You must know the Sultan will die sooner or later. Why must it be later?"

She flicked a look at her guards who stared at unseen spots along the wall. "Why do you have any interest in this matter?"

He leaned toward her and rested his fingertips on the tabletop, near her hand. "I would gain your favor."

She pulled away as if burned by his touch. "That is all you shall gain!"

"There are others who do not approve of how the new Sultan ascended the throne." He withdrew his hand and sipped from his glass.

She gritted her teeth and glared at him. These Nasrids were the most fickle and mercurial people she had ever known. She would have to be cautious with Muhammad the Red. "Strange, for I remember how the *khassa*, all of the provincial governors including your noble father and the *Diwan al-Insha* swore oaths of loyalty to the Sultan. I did not witness or hear of this disapproval you have just mentioned."

"It exists. As I recall it, you and your household took those oaths as well upon the Sultan's ascension."

"What is an oath delivered under duress?"

"Who is the lawful Sultan when one of his ministers alone chose him?"

She leaned back and studied him. "Why should I believe your words? Perhaps you seek to trap me in some ill-starred venture."

"Perhaps I wish only to gain the favor of the mother of the next Sultan, the mother of my future wife."

His intentions aside, she would require help to secure the throne for Ismail. Could she rely upon Muhammad the Red? Would he betray her? She did not doubt he would, given the opportunity. She must safeguard her son's claim and her life against this man.

She tapped her nails on the table. "If you want me to trust you, I will require proof of your abilities for discretion and preparation."

He leaned toward her. "Command me and I shall fulfill your every wish."

One desire of her past remained unsatisfied. In time, she would deal with the Sultan and his mother Butayna, but for now, she would gain vengeance against the remainder of those who had wronged her.

She picked at fuzz on the cushion where she sat. "I want your men to search for two people for me. Both of them are slavers. One would be a man of my age and the other older than me, his uncle. Their names are Fadil and Ahmed al-Qurtubi. If you wish to pledge your faithful devotion to my cause, find these men. Bring them into the city. Not to this place! Somewhere private, where the Sultan will never know."

"Why do you require these two men?"

She avoided his intent gaze. "My purpose does not concern you now, but you shall discover it in time. Do as I have asked if you expect to earn my trust. Find the slavers. I shall deal with them. Then, I shall have my revenge upon Butayna in due course. She shall suffer for how she and her son have wronged me. When my Ismail is upon the throne, Butayna and her children shall kneel at my son's feet and know the power he possesses over their lives. I swear it."

***

Maryam stood in the center of a windowless room at the outskirts of the city with Muhammad the Red beside her, some two weeks later. Her guards surrounded them in the space, occupied by two filthy and bruised men. Strong fibers of hemp bound their hands behind their backs. The elder and burlier of the two had a vicious gash crisscrossing his face from his right eye to his left cheek. Blood still seeped from the cut and splashed on the dusty floorboards. The other had a broken arm and a blackened eye. He groaned and could not lift his head.

She glanced at Muhammad the Red. "Where did your men find them?"

"In *Al-Bayazin*, in the nephew's house. They put up a valiant struggle. Are you certain you wish them both dead?"

She moved closer to the prisoners and nodded. "I have never been more certain of anything in my life, more sure than even of my determination to have Ismail rule this Sultanate in his father's stead. These men will die today."

She grabbed a hank of the elder man's hair and raised his bloodied face for her inspection. "Do you remember my face? The years have not been so kind to you, Ahmed al-Qurtubi."

He opened his remaining good eye, the other clotted with blood. "Who are you?"

"Do not pretend. You know me."

"I do not know you, woman! Why have you brought me here?"

She released him. "Almost eighteen years ago, you took three captives on the border with Castilla-Leon. A young girl of fourteen, along with a woman of nineteen and her two-year old daughter. The woman was pregnant with another child. You sold

397

two of the captives as slaves, but not before this vermin beside you," she said as she waved her hand at his companion, "raped the woman every day and night, and killed her child. Have I refreshed your memory?"

His frown lines deepened. "I have taken many captives over the years! Why should I remember you?"

She shook her head and signaled to one of her guards. "Show him what I can do. Perhaps that will stir his recollections."

The eunuch grasped Ahmed's ear and slashed it before he flung the piece of skin in the corner. Ahmed screamed and howled, as blood poured down the side of his face.

"Stop! Stop, woman! I never hurt you."

She waved the guard away and bent close to his unblemished ear. "You did not, but you permitted it. That is why you will die first and soon. I was Miriam Alubel, the Jewish woman whom you took captive on the plains, reborn as Maryam, the wife of Sultan Yusuf."

He stared at her. His mouth gaped. "It cannot be! I... I... n-n-never harmed you! I tried to be kind."

"Kind? Kind!" Her barking laugh echoed to the rafters. She almost choked on her bile. "You call enslavement a kindness? The murder of my daughter! My rape, night after night!"

"That was Fadil! He did all of that!"

"You never stopped him."

He shook his head vigorously and babbled, "It wasn't me, it wasn't me! I didn't do it. He did. He did it all. I am an old man, just an old man. My father was a warrior, a great warrior, like his father before him and he wanted me to be one too—"

"Silence! Your past does not matter to me, Ahmed. The present should concern you now! As for the future, you have none." She flicked her gaze to the guard again. "Stab him in the heart and let him die."

"*La!*"

Ahmed's final cry occurred before the dagger plunged into his chest three times. He slumped on his side and blood poured out of his mouth.

Maryam clasped her hands together and turned to Ahmed's nephew, Fadil. Her chief tormentor. The murderer of her sweet first daughter. "Shall you pretend you do not know me as well?"

He raised his head and spat on her boot. "You were not the first bitch I took, but you were the sweetest. Do what you will to me now! Kill me. I won't plead and cry as my uncle did."

She chuckled and stepped back from him. Another of her eunuchs wiped the spittle from the leather and kneed Fadil in the face. Copious blood flowed from his nose.

She pushed the guard back. "Do not touch him! *La*, he will suffer in other ways." She bent and cupped between Fadil's legs. "Start here. Cut off his manhood first, for he has savaged others with it. Do it slowly, as he did with those whom he ravaged, letting them die piece by piece each day."

Muhammad the Red grasped her elbow. His fierce stare roved over her face. "Did he do these things to you as you have claimed?"

She shrugged off his hold. "Do not presume! I am a Sultana. Do not question me or my men will slay you as well!"

A scowl etched across his features and made him appear older. She almost backed away. She had to tread warily with him. This one might prove dangerous, a man she should not cross.

She sighed and asked, "Why do you care for my past?"

"I have told you, I would gain your favor. Let me slay your enemy on this day."

She surmised his earnest gaze. He had become biddable again, so unpredictable as the rest of his family, but at least the danger had receded.

She waved her guards away. "Then do it, Muhammad. After you have castrated him, break his fingers and toes before you cut them off. Slice off the tip of his nose and remove his tongue. Save the ears and eyes for last. I want him to know everything that happens to him."

Muhammad the Red bowed and nodded, before he turned to Fadil. For the first time since Maryam had seen her persecutor again, tears gathered in his gaze. His lips formed a silent plea, which ascended to a howling screech as Muhammad the Red reached for his *khanjar*. The dagger's tip gleamed in his hand.

Chapter 29
Mother of the Sultan

Sultana Butayna

Granada, Andalusia
July 2 - August 15, AD 1355 / 20 Jumada al-Thani – 5 Sha'ban
756 AH / 22nd of Tammuz - 7th of Elul, 5115

At the *Jannat al-'Arif*, Butayna retreated indoors with her children and dined in the Sultan's chambers. The trio sat at the low table covered in red samite, where ten months before they had sat with Yusuf. Beyond the door, Muhammad's coffers, chests, and clothing occupied the bedroom of his father. Tonight, he would sleep in his father's bed.

Some of the scrolls Muhammad brought from his earlier council meeting littered the cushions arranged at dinner. He maintained a rigorous schedule, which began an hour before dawn each day and ended sometime in the late hours of the night. Butayna sent *jawari* to him in the middle of each week, but of late, the girls often returned to their dormitories early, too soon to have spent any substantial time in their master's bed. Butayna inquired whether Muhammad found the choice of women disagreeable, but he always assured her, the duties of a Sultan took precedence, as they did now when they dined together.

"A letter from the court of King Pedro of Castilla-Leon has arrived." Muhammad scanned the contents while he chewed and swallowed a mouthful of apricot chicken. "We should expect a new *alfaqueque* at the slave *corrals* within the month. A Fray Antonio Navas y Montilla, who journeys from the Trinitarian chapter house in Murcia. King Pedro expects the usual guarantee of his safety in this ransoming expedition."

Navas y Montilla. A friar who traveled from the east. Muhammad's mention of the name sent a tremor through Butayna's body in response. She hid her hand under the table until the quiver subsided. She licked her dried lips and pushed the half-eaten food away. A trickle of perspiration glided along her temple below the *hijab*.

"King Pedro may presume anything he pleases, but you will do nothing to stop the enslavement of others within the Sultanate, will you, my son?"

Muhammad's jaw tightened before he swallowed. Aisha held the glass goblet to her lips, but she never sipped the water. Her dark brown gaze flitted between her brother and mother. "Must we have the old argument again, *Ummi?*"

Butayna scowled at her daughter. "This does not affect you, child."

"How can you say so? Am I not a part of this family? Your concerns and those of my brother are my own. You dwell upon the past. Even now, you refuse to accept a way of life you shall never understand."

"You are Nasrids. I am not. I could never share your beliefs."

"Then do not ask Muhammad to go against his nature or attempt an abrupt change, which would alter more than just our lives. Do not blame my brother for what Father could not do."

"Could never permit himself to do! There is a difference, Aisha, whether or not you or Muhammad will acknowledge it."

He cleared his throat. "The past cannot be changed. If it could, Aisha and I might not exist. If the slavers had never captured you, my father would not have known your love. When will you accept these facts, *Ummi?*"

"I can never deny them, my son. I have no regrets regarding Yusuf, or the beloved children at my side. If you think I shall allow this city to rob its neighbors of their most precious possessions, the lives of their people, you do not understand me well."

"What are you planning, *Ummi?*"

Without an answer, she discarded her table linen next to the plate. Jawla bent at her side and offered another bowl of rosewater, with which Butayna washed her hands.

"Will you give me leave to retire, my son? This afternoon's heat is oppressive."

"I do not permit you to go! Is it just the heat you cannot bear? Would you withdraw from my company as well? Is this how you behaved when you and Father quarreled? Like a stubborn child denied her wish. Do you forget Christians hold Muslims captive on their side of the border? Or is your sympathy still reserved for those among your countrymen?"

"Muhammad!" Aisha placed her slender fingers upon his forearm. Her nails indented the black silk. "Please, do not shame *Ummi*. Her opinions are her own. We do not share them, but my Sultan, she does not deserve your anger."

He shrugged off his sister's hold. "I have earned her censure! Tell me, *Ummi,* what did you think would happen when I became Sultan? Did you expect our laws, our society would change? Don't you know by now? Nothing can ever be as simple as we may imagine it."

Butayna closed her eyes. She heard Yusuf's voice in his son's own, a shadow of the not so distant past. Nasrid cruelty and arrogance had shaped him more than her devoted care.

"*Ummi?*" Aisha clutched at her hand.

With a sigh, Butayna looked at her daughter. The girl's eyes glittered.

Muhammad shook his head and gave a dismissive wave. "You may leave us."

Butayna bowed her head. "*Al-salam 'alayka.* Daughter. My Sultan." She pulled her fingers from Aisha's grasp and went to the door. Jawla and Ruiz's murmured requests to depart followed, as did Muhammad's gruff response.

When Butayna clasped the door handle, her son called out. "The burdens upon me are numerous, but I try to manage them as best I can, *Ummi.* If you will not support me, I am lost. There is no else I trust more in this world."

Her fingers closed on the metal. She paused before the door and made no response to his version of an apology, the only one his Nasrid dignity would allow him to offer. Then she turned her head so his image entered her peripheral gaze. As strong and stalwart as Yusuf had been. Her heart ached in the absence of the man who had been her loving husband.

She whispered, "You shall always have my love and loyalty, my Sultan."

He remained silent, as did Aisha.

Butayna left Muhammad's chamber. Ruiz's near silent footfalls echoed at her right shoulder. Jawla kept quiet.

"*Almocaden.* I need you to do something for me."

"*Sí, mi reina.*"

***

A little over six weeks later, Alfonso Ruiz herded the hooded brown-robed Trinitarian and his similarly attired companion up the stairs and into the southern pavilion, where Butayna resided. The captain forced the new arrivals to their knees. Butayna relaxed in the doorway of the belvedere on the Persian carpet, a lavender pillow behind her. Hafsa knelt beside her and offered a tray of dried dates and figs. Jawla poured cold pomegranate juice into a silver goblet and brought it. Butayna waved both of them away.

"It would be impolite to eat anything further before I have seen to the comfort of my guests."

Her servants bowed their heads and shuffled to the corners of her receiving room. She tugged the gossamer folds of her veil over the lower half of her face.

Ruiz deposited two dusty saddlebags on the marble floor. He sketched a bow, his short red mantle thrown back from his broad shoulders. "I have done as you bid, *mi reina.*"

She smiled at him. "You have done your duty well, *almocaden.* Remove their hoods and the ropes around their wrists."

As he did so, the noonday sunlight glinted off the ruddy, broad faces of the pair. The Trinitarian gaped wide-eyed at her for a moment before he turned to his companion. "Nephew! *Dios mío!* I had feared the worse. Are you hurt?"

The young man at his side bore a strong resemblance. Same crinkled golden curls, tonsured as well. "No, Fray Antonio, they did not harm me."

Butayna pressed against the pillow. "My guards received precise instructions. No matter how you resisted, they were not to harm you. Thank you for seeing me today."

"I was not aware we had a choice, *señora.*" The Trinitarian rubbed at his reddened wrists. "Your men abducted me and my clerk in broad daylight from the slave market. The members of my order will discover my capture and submit protests to the lord of this land. My name is Fray Antonio Navas y Montilla. I represent the Crown of Castilla-Leon in the ransom of captives held in Andalusia. Among my personal property, I carry letters signed by King Pedro, which guarantee my safety."

"You mistake my aim, Fray Antonio. I do not intend to keep you here for longer than is necessary. Indeed, you may thank me for our introduction in the end, for I can be of great help to you. I am *la reina* Butayna, mother of King Muhammad, lord of all Granada, the prince of the faithful among his people."

Both of the Trinitarians gaped, but the friar mustered the courage to speak. "Then, *la reina,* you must know the rules regarding the treatment of royal ransom–"

She raised her hand in a bid for silence. "Fray Antonio, you're not listening. Perhaps you will allow me to explain, after I have seen to your ease and comfort. Please, rise and be seated in the chairs. Will you take some pomegranate juice or water and dried dates? Or would you prefer something else?"

Fray Antonio regained his composure. "No. No. I thank you for your generosity."

He and his nephew took seats in the high-backed chairs between Hafsa and Jawla's positions. The servants offered the platter of dried fruits and cups of pomegranate juice. Ruiz kept a watchful eye upon them, while Butayna waited for them to finish the small repast. She did not eat anything.

Fray Antonio sniffed everything before he put a morsel of food or a drop of drink to his fleshy lips. Then he caught sight of the captain's glare. The friar stared almost catatonic across the chamber at the jagged path of the pink scar across Ruiz's left eye.

Butayna glanced at him. "Your fearsome visage disturbs the friar's digestion, *almocaden.*"

"N-n-no," Fray Antonio sputtered.

"Better a little fear than nothing at all," Ruiz muttered.

Butayna chuckled. "You'll have to ask for absolution if the friar agrees to all I shall ask of him."

At the end of the meager meal, Fray Antonio gave the empty silver goblet to Hafsa. His meaty hand still shook and his lower lip trembled. Ruiz's sour-faced regard for him had not improved.

Jawla brought water to wash the Trinitarians' hands. When they were finished, Butayna dismissed her servants. They took the remnants of food and left her with Ruiz and her reluctant guests.

Butayna began, "In the winter of the year of our Lord one thousand three hundred and thirty-seven, a Castillan doctor, Efrain Peralta and his daughter Esperanza traveled from Talavera de la Reina across the *meseta* to Alicante for the girl's marriage." Despite the friar's gasp, she continued, "They never arrived. The Moors ambushed Doctor Peralta's party and killed him. His daughter survived a difficult transition from captive to slave within these walls. In time, she became the favored concubine and the first wife of Sultan Yusuf. Have you guessed why I brought you here, Fray Antonio?"

His Adam's apple bobbed. "I believe so. Are you the girl from Talavera?"

"In my youth, I bore the name Esperanza Peralta."

"My elder brother Fernan was betrothed to you in his youth."

She clapped her hands. "Fernan! *Sí,* I had forgotten and could not remember it in all these years! I recalled the family name, but not his. When my Sultan received the letter from King Pedro regarding your duties, I knew your patrimony and origin could not be coincidence."

He wiped his feverish brow, aghast. "Have you been here all this time?"

"Moorish raiders sold me into Yusuf's harem. I became his wife and mother of his heir, though I have remained a Christian."

"While my brother married another, with whom he remains besotted to this day. He thrives as a merchant in Alicante still." He clapped the shoulder of his companion. "This is my nephew Fernando, the youngest of Fernan's five sons given to the service of God."

The clerk nodded and Butayna made the same gesture.

Then she said, "My experiences have left me desirous to help others. No one should undergo such horrid circumstances. I could say Juan Manuel Gomero, the merchant who purchased me, exhibited some kindness. He is a rarity among others of his ilk. I know better than to plead with my son to forbid this practice. He is Sultan and has the pride of his forefathers. The death of his father has terminated the last ten-year truce between the Sultanate and Castilla-Leon. I cannot wait until the ministers of both governments negotiate new peace treaties. The flood of human booty into Andalusia will continue. Slavery is this country's lifeblood. I am willing to pay for the ransom of any captives, including their costs for food and lodging, and the taxes imposed. I can provide them with Granadine escort by land or galley, to ensure their return home. It is my wish to help ransom captives, but I will never know if they reach their destinations without assistance."

The young man beside the friar coughed and his face reddened like a ripe pomegranate. Fray Antonio clapped him hard on the back until the fit subsided.

Fray Antonio stated, "Some captives do not return home, *la reina*, before they find themselves enslaved again along the border with Castilla-Leon or claimed by pirate galleys, which descend upon the shores. Some of those pirates come from Andalusian cities."

Butayna asked, "Do the mendicants still require former captives to serve the Order for a time? Must they still accept indenture, swear oaths, and beg for alms?"

"They do so of their own free will to help us bring awareness of the plight of all captives. The faithful who give alms benefit from the Church's indulgences. We must not discourage this practice or there would be few who gave."

"I have the means to lend significant financial support to your cause. The lives of those ransomed by my coin shall be theirs again, not given to the Order. See these people to their homes and let them rebuild their lives. I will have your oath in fulfillment of my wish."

"*La reina*, yours is a worthy, Christian aim and I support your effort. The redemption of captives is merciful work. You cannot hope to obtain the release of so many, even with your obvious wealth."

"Still, I will retrieve as many as I may entrust to your care. I shall arrange for their comfort over the next three days, but on the fourth, I wish to begin the task. If you will accept my aid, I must have your promise. Any captives within your charge will have no obligation to the Trinitarians."

"You must permit me to send word to my superior in Murcia."

"You may do so, but I will gain your compliance or seek another to advance my purpose."

"*Sí, la reina*. I shall send a message to you by my clerk once my superior has given his opinion."

"Thank you, Fray Antonio. If the Trinitarians agree, I shall send my Ruiz to you and he will bring you to the slave merchant's house."

"I must ask, *la reina*, why you would risk your son's anger in such a venture? The Sultan might view your attempts as treason. You are a generous woman, but even I must caution against threats to your safety in this enterprise."

"Muhammad will do nothing to stop me because of my faith. He respects my long-held Christian beliefs though he will never share them. Now, you know my intentions and I await your decision. You are free to leave the palace at any time. No one will hinder or harm you. Before you leave us, I ask another boon. My personal protectors and I remain fervent in our Catholic beliefs. Will you hear our confessions now? Before you leave Granada with those you have ransomed, will you return here of your own free will and allow us to take Holy Communion?"

The friar bowed his head. "I have received the sacrament of ordination. I have the authority to hear confessions and offer Holy Communion, *la reina*. It would be my honor and privilege."

"Excellent. There is a room across the garden path where we may have privacy. I use it for my prayers. Ruiz will stand watch outside so no one may interrupt. Then he and his men may offer their confessions as well." She stood and approached Fray Antonio. "I have lived in this harem for more than half of my life. There is much to confess."

The friar spoke to his clerk, who retrieved one of the saddlebags. From it, he withdrew an embroidered purple stole of fine silk, which Fray Antonio draped over his hefty shoulders. He and Ruiz followed out of the chamber and down the steps. They walked north to reach the chamber where Butayna observed her prayers. Ruiz guarded the entrance, while she and Fray Rufino went inside.

At a gesture from her, the friar stood by the window and made the sign of the cross. "In the name of the Father and of the Son and of the Holy Spirit."

She knelt before him and bowed her head. As she crossed herself and clasped her hands, a sudden tear splashed on her cheek. "Bless me, for I have sinned. It has been eighteen years since my last confession...."

***

At dawn five weeks afterward, Butayna pressed a hand to the iron-riveted door and rapped the lion-headed knocker, coated in rust. Almost twenty years before, a young girl stood in her place and wondered at the dire future awaiting her behind the walls of this house.

"*La Reina*? Forgive my inquiry, but are you certain he is awake at this early hour?" Fray Antonio shuffled his ponderous weight on the cobblestones beside his red-faced clerk. "Such a vile man as he may be expected to be indolent."

Butayna chuckled. "Vile? You are quick to judge the slave merchant. You do not know him and would do well to set aside ignorant assumptions. I assure you, while he is a man of many moods, laziness is not among them."

"*Sí, la reina.*"

Footsteps echoed through the heavy wood. Butayna pressed her ear to the door. Her eunuchs hovered, but she shooed them away with a wave of her hand. "No harm shall ever come to me in this place."

She stepped back as the door creaked. Deep creases in the rounded features of a black woman filled the iron grille. The inner bolt groaned.

"Oh, it's you." An obsidian gaze fell on Butayna, who smiled and shook her head.

"I am pleased you remember me, Binta. Your disposition has not improved."

"Master does not complain." Binta crossed her arms over her full breasts. She stood before Butayna, as sour-faced as she had ever been. Her fat lower lip jutted beneath the upper one.

"If your master did complain, would it alter you? I think not. I wish to see him."

Binta peered past Butayna to her entourage. "Who are these men you bring into his house?"

Butayna's gaze swept over them. "They are in the service of the *Amir al-Muslimin*, the Sultan Muhammad ibn Yusuf, who is my son."

407

Binta's scowl deepened. She did not move from the doorway. "And the priest in his robes and the boy with him? Do they serve the Sultan also?"

"Fray Antonio Navas y Montilla is a Trinitarian of the mendicant order. The boy with him is his clerk. They are here to redeem captives on behalf of King Pedro of Castilla-Leon." When no glimmer of recognition lit Binta's churlish gaze, Butayna sighed and added. "You will permit his entry, Binta, as you will allow mine and those of my son's household."

Despite her frown, the slave stepped aside. Butayna preceded Fray Antonio and her guards into the courtyard. She sat on a wooden bench under a myrtle tree and inhaled the fragrant scent of new spring buds. "Your master shall come to me, Binta. I await him here."

Binta muttered something unintelligible under her breath and reentered the house.

"Shall he keep us waiting for long, do you think, *la reina*?"

"He may delay for as long as he likes. This is his domain."

"He must do better than to have the mother of Granada's ruler linger for his sake."

"When he knew me, I was not yet the mother of the Sultan."

"True, you were not. A young and fulsome girl left the House of Myrtles on a frigid day, the opposite of this one." Juan Manuel strode into the courtyard dressed in a yellow *pellote*, the pride in his footfalls no less diminished by the frail legs or his hunched back. "Now, a summer queen of Granada returns in her place."

The gray hair had receded from his forehead. He bent with a groan, his shoulders hunched. A visible shudder coursed through him. "The mother of the Sultan honors me with her presence and remembrance."

She stared at the *dirham*-sized scar on his neck before she answered, "I am here to do more than that, Juan Manuel Gomero. Among my plans for today, I seek to enrich your coffers."

He straightened at the mention of money. Butayna could not conceal a peal of laughter. "You have not changed in all these years."

His rheumy-eyed gaze crinkled at the corners. "You are as kind as ever, my Sultana."

"Bring out all of those whom you hold captive. I am here to purchase their freedom and Fray Antonio shall escort them to their various homes, wherever they may be."

Juan Manuel's lips pursed. "All?"

"All. Do not delay, Juan Manuel. The friar has a long journey ahead of him and I would ensure he begins it as soon as possible."

"There are thirty-three women, twelve men, and seven children under the ages of thirteen in my cells. If you mean to have all, then you must intend to pay several thousand gold coins today, my Sultana."

She chuckled again. "Do not seek to bargain with me. You will accept my offer, the first and only one I intend to make, because you know I am a fair person. You have perceived the truth of me since we first met. Moreover, you accept that money today in your coffers exceeds the possibility of money tomorrow from any other buyer. I do not doubt the slavers shall bring you still more captives. I mean to have them all. You will never sell another captive into slavery. I will buy every one of them from the House of Myrtles in an exclusive arrangement with you. You shall be rich beyond your dreams of avarice and I shall have some of the peace of mind I desire at last. I cannot stop the slave trade in Andalusia, but I shall ensure others do not face the peril I once did."

Juan Manuel bowed before her. "Come to my garden courtyard and we may conclude the details."

He waved her toward the opened doorway and followed her into the house, her guards with Fray Antonio among them. Soon, Butayna stood in the garden of shrubs and marble columns where she once endured a beating with the bastinado. Juan Manuel motioned to a stone bench, but she declined the offer.

Instead, she said, "Perhaps Fray Antonio would wish to sit instead. Indeed, friar, you look as if you would faint."

The Trinitarian stopped staring at the opulence of the garden and took the stone bench. He mopped his face with the linen square his clerk offered. After some time, Juan Manuel's eunuchs led a line of unkempt captives out into the sunshine. Many covered their faces and shielded them from the first glare of light they might have seen in some time. Others wept as their bleary-eyed gazes fell on the robes of Fray Antonio and his clerk.

Butayna addressed the Trinitarians. "Speak to these people of their fates and offer them what consolation you can. When we leave here, they shall first go to an inn I have designated for their rest and comfort. They will eat and receive suitable clothes for the journey. Let them know they shall see their families in the coming months."

"Shall you speak with them as well? After all, your coin will grant their freedom."

"Keep your promise to me and relieve them of obligation to the Trinitarians. Let them go home and rebuild their lives. Their freedom is the reward. I desire no more than this, not even their appreciation."

"But why, *la reina*? You should be proud—"

"I am proud to be a Sultana, the mother of Muhammad, son of Yusuf. I am content in my life here."

Chapter 30
Heritage

Sultana Butayna

Granada, Andalusia
August 15, AD 1355 / 5 Sha'ban 756 AH / 7th of Elul, 5115

Butayna left Fray Antonio to his grateful company in the garden. The captives thronged around him and cried tears of happiness, as he explained his purpose. Some of them shot curious, even wary glances at her. She sensed the direction of their thoughts, for what purpose could a woman in Mohammedan dress and veils serve in their release from the House of Myrtles? To them, she was just another Moor, but she would take no trouble to correct them now. After more than half her life spent in Andalusia, she belonged in this world as much as her children did.

She gestured to Juan Manuel. "Will you take a stroll with me through the garden? It is a cool morning and I promise the walk shall not strain you too much."

He nodded and fell into step beside her. Her armed escort followed at a scant distance.

She halted and looked around at Ruiz and his men. "I have told you I am safe here. You will not follow this time."

Ruiz stiffened and colored. She eyed him until his stare fell away and he replied, "*Sí, mi reina.*"

With a nod, she left her ardent protectors.

Juan Manuel commented, "They are dedicated. Christians all?"

"*Sí*, as is the rest of Muhammad's royal guard."

"A bold choice...." His voice trailed off. His chest rumbled before a coughing fit overtook him. He turned from her and covered his mouth from his brown-spotted hand.

She waited until his convulsions subsided. From the *tikka* around her waist, she offered him an embroidered handkerchief, which he accepted with thanks.

When he quieted in full, she asked, "Are you unwell?"

He cleared his throat. "I am not. It is a remnant of the plague's effects and a reminder of my good fortune for having

411

survived the pestilence. Sadiya perished soon after it struck the city."

She sighed. "I am sorry she did not live."

"Do not think upon her final days. The agony ended when she died at peace in her bed. She would have been joyous upon this day to see how much you have achieved. You found the freedom you sought and regained a family, dreams you might have thought lost to you forever. Were you contented for a time with your Sultan Yusuf? Did you love him?"

She answered his questions with one of her own. "Did Ifrit never tell you when she reported on life in the harem to her former master? Was she not one of the best spies you planted at the Sultan's palace?"

He glanced at her and shook his head. "She did not write to me of such things. How did you guess she was one of my spies?"

"I suspected such long before her death. Binta should be gratified by her daughter's faithfulness." When he gasped and paused beside her, she added, "The connection was not so difficult to make. For one, their sour moods matched. Ifrit told me of three others, my husband's chief steward Mufawwiz, and my own servants."

They continued the walk. "Ifrit was a loyal servant of the Sultanate." She pitched her voice lower. "Before her death, she showed me three of the secret passages. How did you learn of them?"

"Sultan Yusuf's grandmother told me. She often feared for the safety of her grandchildren in the presence of the Marinid rebels and Volunteers of the Faith. She once made me swear if anything occurred within the palace that I would get her grandchildren to safety outside the Sultanate. For more than twenty-two years, I have maintained my promise to her. My spies observe day and night for any sign of trouble."

"I suppose you will not reveal the rest of them, just as you hid Ifrit's role."

"Another choice might imperil many lives."

Butayna bowed her head. "As you decide. I may require you to extend the promises made to the Sultana Fatima for my benefit. The harem is as divided as it was in the days of Safa and Leila. Maryam's faction gives all the outward appearance of loyalty to my son. I do not trust them, with cause. Maryam remains above certain suspicion for now. Still, she desires Muhammad's throne for Ismail and has no reason to alter her thoughts. She would rule the Sultanate through her son. When she moves against me and mine, I may not be able to foil her, but I shall ensure the safety of all my family."

He stopped for a third time. "I did not know things were so bad."

When she nodded, he bobbed his grizzled head. "Call upon me whenever you have need. You have always held my loyalty. I will do all I can for the protection of those whom you love."

"I'll hold you to the vow, Juan Manuel."

"You may rely upon it and on me." When they continued, he said, "You still have not told me of your feelings for your husband. Did you find joy and contentment at his side?"

Her mind recalled the tender man who had knelt at her feet and asked her to share her joys and sorrows with him. The father who had blessed Muhammad and proclaimed him a worthy heir in the weeks before his death. The passionate lover who pleasured her in the long hours of the night. She chose to remember her beloved, not the arrogant and mistrustful Sultan.

"*Sí*, I found what I had sought with Yusuf for too brief a time. Treachery ruined our joy, but my feelings are unchanged. Yusuf remains my heart and my husband. I loved him well."

Juan Manuel paused and gripped a column. He sagged against the white marble, his mouth set in a grim line. "Your words are pleasing. I am glad for your happiness and pained by your losses. On the morning of your departure from this house, I faced two choices. To sell you into the Sultan's harem or accept the ransom the Cistercians at Calatrava offered. You will remember there was some delay in my visit with you on that morning. The *alfaqueque* arrived an hour before Hisham did. The monks offered a payment on behalf of your father."

A sudden coldness closed tight as a fist around her heart. A tremor passed through her. "My father? What cruel jape is this? You must be confusing me with someone else, another captive. The raiders killed my father on the *meseta*."

The fleshy wattle below his chin sank to his chest. "Ahmed al-Qurtubi thought he had murdered your father. He did not. Efrain Peralta survived his wounds, though they pained him for the rest of his life. A strong man, much like the daughter he raised. I lied to the Cistercians and told them you had been sold to the Sultan already."

Heat blossomed and tingled throughout her body. "You had no right! How could you keep me from my father?"

"My heart told me you belonged here."

"Not your heart! Greed alone governed you in those days. It still does!"

She flung her hand toward him and turned away. Muscles under the skin coiled and quivered. She hugged her torso lest she strike out at him. How could he have done this, denied her a chance to see her father again? They could have been so blissful in each other's arms again and made a new life together. A little voice in her head warred with her heart. The happiness she had gained as a mother and a wife meant more to her than the past. She had been exultant in Yusuf's love, even for so short a time. She also adored their son and daughter. Would her staunch Christian father have wanted to know her small family, the Muslim ruler she had married, and the Muslim children she bore him?

Juan Manuel spoke and a quaver filled his hoary voice. "Greed held no sway over all of my actions while I considered your future, my Sultana. The Order offered twice what Hisham paid for you. When you gave Sultan Yusuf his heir and married, I knew I had made the right decision."

"It was not yours to make! You robbed me of a reunion with my father."

"True. Would you have gone to him and left your new family behind? Would your Sultan have let you bring your father to Granada?"

She had no answer for him, so instead she demanded, "Tell me why I should not have my eunuchs slay you for this treachery."

"I did you a kindness—"

"By keeping my father's survival a secret all of these years? That was cruel, even for a slave merchant such as you."

"I was not always so cruel." He turned from her and summoned Binta. "Bring the letters." Then he spoke to Butayna again. "After your wedding, I wrote to your father in care of the Order. I informed him that you were still alive, the wife of the Sultan and mother to his heir. Within months, the doctor's reply came. He thanked me for news of you. In thanksgiving, he pledged his life to the Cistercians and became a monk in their chapter house until his death during the pestilence."

"He lived for so many years after the raid?"

Binta returned in haste and bowed beside Juan Manuel. He accepted a thick wad of folded parchment tied with yellow cord and dismissed her.

He offered the bundle to Butayna. "Your father sent letters to me intended for you. They arrived twice a year, always after Easter and Advent. He asked me to deliver them after the Cistercians sent word of his death. He understood the brutal choice you would face if you knew he yet lived. He could not forsake his vows. You could not abandon your husband and children. I have never broken the seal of his letters. You should read them now."

She snatched the sealed missives from his rickety hand and tore open the first. Her gaze watered as she stared at the writing as familiar as her own, a letter dated six weeks after Easter in the year of our Lord one thousand, three hundred and forty-one, two months after Aisha's birth.

The letter began, '*My sweet hope, today is a joyous day. My vows compel me to keep silent, when I would tell the world of my happiness. Today, I learned I am a grandfather twice over, made so with the birth of your daughter, the Infanta Aisha. I do not doubt she is a babe who shall grow in the beauteous image and strength of her mother. Watch over and protect her, as you must also do with your dear son, the Infante Muhammad. You must have found it difficult to maintain the Christian faith you have held. Continue to trust in God, for through Him you have endured and kept your last vow to me. When you read these words, do not be saddened or disheartened by my long absence from your side. You and your children are forever in my heart. Though I shall never see them, know they receive my blessing each day, as you have. Do not think of the past and all we have lost. Consider the life and family you have regained. Keep God in your heart and survive as you once promised me. Live, mi hija, live for the future and for your children. With kind felicitations and enduring love, your devoted father. Efrain.*'

She laid the parchment on her lap and wept for the father she would never see again. Her tears were joyful. He survived the raid and knew of her life with Yusuf and their children. His fate had been more than she could have ever hoped for and her appreciation exceeded words she could express.

Juan Manuel cleared his throat. "I shall leave you to your correspondence. Stay as long as you like, my Sultana."

He bowed at her side and with a groan, stiffened, and shuffled away.

She called out to him. "Although I shall never forgive you for keeping my father from me, I shall never cease to be grateful for your exchange with him and the gift of his last words."

Juan Manuel never turned to her, but he gave a stiff nod. With a hitch in his step, he reentered the House of Myrtles.

Butayna found another empty stone bench and sank down on it. She tore open half of the letters, each word made more precious by her father's evident pride in her. He counseled her on the duties of a parent, of a spouse and always cautioned her against abandonment of her Christian faith.

She read another missive. '*Mi hija, so many are dead or dying at this desperate hour. Has our Lord and Savior deserted us? I do not believe so, for in our despair, God hears all prayers and answers in His due time. I do not know how much more I can write today. The great mortality has struck down so many of my brothers in the chapter house. If the tumors on my thigh and neck are any indication, I shall soon be among the dead. Now is the time for truth between us. I hope when you read these words, you will understand why I kept the past hidden from you for so long.*

'In the year of our Lord one thousand, one hundred and ninety-five, a terrible calamity struck Toledo and resulted in the massacre of hundreds of Jews. At the time, my great-grandfather was a boy of seven and he had an elder brother of twelve. They were Jews, Simenon and Naphtali Esra, the sons of Abraham Esra. We are among their last living descendants, mi hija, from a line of Jews killed in the purge of Toledo's court, when the courtiers sought to destroy the family of Rahel la Fermosa. Simeon and Naphtali escaped for a time to the great city of Granada, but our ancestor did not remain there. He knew his family would never be free from persecution. Thus, he converted and started a new life in our birthplace of Talavera.'

Butayna gulped ragged breaths. Her family had been secret Jews. They descended from the family of a king's mistress. The name struck a chord deep within her. Rahel *la Fermosa*. Juan Manuel had told her of the woman before she left the House of Myrtles of his connection. Butayna's heart lurched as she devoured the rest of the letter's contents.

'There, Simeon took the family name of Peralta and severed all ties to his brother Naphtali, who took the appellation of Gomero and remained a secret Jew. Simeon also took a new given name, Esteban. He forced the lie of a strong Christian heritage on his son, my grandfather. When my own learned father came of age, he discovered the truth. As a trained physician, he once encountered a young merchant who required his services in the city of Pamplona. This merchant had your grandfather's eyes, eyes he had seen nowhere else except among his ancestors. When the merchant revealed himself as a member of the Gomero line in Granada, my father knew the truth. Naphtali's descendants lived in Granada for subsequent generations and I tell you with great confidence, your benefactor Juan Manuel Gomero is among them. He is your kinsman. I suspect he must have some inkling of the truth as well, for why should he have aided you with such devotion? Trust in him, for his missives have been a comfort to me in these last years.

'You will remember how much I loved your mother. She was always so willful and determined. She bequeathed you two of her greatest gifts in your compassion and strength. She also gave you another link to your Jewish past. Before we married, she

converted at my wish, so I might perpetuate the myth of our
Christian lineage and keep the suspicions of the Cerdas at bay.
By now, you must have guessed why they dismissed me. I have
never been ashamed of the past. I go to my death now in the
knowledge that, at least in Granada, some measure of our proud
heritage shall continue in your children. Teach them of their true
lineage when it is right, mi hija. Even while you keep the Christian
faith, remember there is another part of you, which hearkens to a
time before the Moors, the Goths, and the Romans. Always with
loving pride and blessings, your devoted father, Efrain.'

Butayna stood and scattered the folded pieces of parchment
in her lap. Ruiz and Binta rushed across the garden and helped
her collect each letter. She accepted them in a stupor. Her mind
could not fathom the revelations among her father's words. A
secret Jewish heritage derived from her mother and her father's
family. The discovery of her link to Juan Manuel Gomero. It all
seemed too much to encompass all at once. She recalled the
words he had spoken during her captivity, which she once
dismissed. He told her God had led her to his house and life
among the Moors. He was right. She had not lost all of her links
to the past with her father's death. One vital connection
remained.

She asked, "Binta, where is your master?"

"In his counting room, my Sultana."

Butayna nodded. "I shall see him now. Wait for me here,
Ruiz."

"*Sí, mi reina.*"

She went into the residence and upon her inquiry, a
maidservant directed her to the counting room. Juan Manuel sat
at his low table beneath the window, where he once tutored her
in Arabic. He lifted his gaze from the words etched on
parchment, bound between leather covers. She sat across from
him and placed the stack of letters between them.

"This *siddur* belonged to my father Simeon." He set down the
Jewish prayer book. "The pages of my father's prayer book are
faded, but I keep it for sentimental value."

Without any preliminaries, she said, "You knew I had other
family left in the world when you discovered my name. That was
why you told me of Rahel *la Fermosa* all those years ago."

When he nodded, she knuckled her forehead. "How could you
have kept the truth of our blood ties from me? Knowing I was
your kinswoman, no matter the distant ties, how could you have
sold me into slavery?"

"I did not think you wished to know the truth at the time, my
Sultana. You were unprepared to hear of it as a captive. If I had

told you of our connection, of the heritage long denied you by four generations, you would not have accepted it. I knew you would have survived the harem. Esra women have always possessed great courage. Now that line remains unbroken in the Sultan and his sister the Sultana Aisha. As I have said, you belonged in the harem, where you may serve a greater good."

"What greater good?"

"*El Dio* shall reveal it in due time."

"You did not know Yusuf would have loved and married me, or whether I would have given him heirs. You gambled with my life on uncertain odds."

A grin split his wizened features and made him appear youthful again. "It is a good thing I guessed well."

She did not share his humor. "This is too difficult for me to fathom. In my youth, I struggled with the Christian faith and then clung to it after my captivity. Today I find my heritage heralds another past and a different religion. I will have to tell my children someday, but not now."

"As you prefer." He lifted his age-spotted hand and set a weapon between them, its golden handle encrusted in precious gems. Her fingers flexed before she touched the flat of the blade.

She whispered, "My father's dagger. You kept it all of these years."

"I told you I would have." He also produced her brooch, carnelian, and sardonyx, set in gold. A gift from Maryam. "This belongs to you as well. I told you I would return these items when we saw each other once more. I have always known we would."

She gazed into his glistening, wet eyes and remembered when they sparkled like hers. "Keep the mementos a little longer. The hour will come in which I shall take them forever."

She held out her hand across the table. His gnarled fingers linked with hers. "From this day forth, we are bound together, Juan Manuel. Nothing shall ever part us again."

***

Butayna returned to the summer palace before midday and went to her chambers in its southern pavilion first. She left the letters received from Juan Manuel in a chest in her bedroom. There would be time to discuss the contents of her father's correspondence.

She went north to her son's chambers. Muhammad rose from his writing desk and enfolded her in his arms.

"You have returned, *Ummi*. No one knew where you had gone."

She gazed into his shimmering eyes, her father's eyes. Efrain Peralta should have done more than receive letters about his impressive grandson. Her father should have known Muhammad.

"I am here now." She cupped his chin. "What is this frown? Are you displeased with me because of my long absence?"

"I have been lost in thought for most of the morning. Thoughts of Sultana Maryam."

Butayna's heart thudded. Did he know? "Why her of all people?"

"She is a concern to me, as are her sons and her relationship with Muhammad the Red. He dines with her at least once a week."

"He is to marry her daughter Fatima. There is no more than that. Your spies would have told you if she dishonored your father's memory." She withdrew from him and went into the alcove. She took a seat by the wall.

Muhammad followed. "She does not concern you further, *Ummi*? You do not suspect Sultana Maryam's involvement in Father's death as I do?"

She shuddered and coughed to hide the loud gasp in her throat. "What are you talking about? Al-Sagir is dead, my Sultan. He acted alone."

Muhammad chuckled, as his father would have done. A chill settled deep within Butayna's heart. She rubbed at the imaginary ache.

Her son sat beside her on the cushion and grasped her fingers. "You do not expect me to believe al-Sagir bears sole responsibility, *Ummi*, not while Maryam looks with covetous eyes upon my throne and thinks how well it would suit her son Ismail."

When Butayna gasped and drew back, Muhammad's hand closed on her wrist. The strength inherent to his touch evoked the power of his father. His stare held her enthralled. He lifted her fingers to his lips and kissed them. A sigh coursed through her. Yusuf should have been here to see the formidable Sultan he had made in the image of himself and his ancestors.

He continued, "Mark me, *Ummi*, somehow Maryam is involved in Father's death. I do not know how, but I feel it. I can feel it! As surely as the hot blood coursing through my veins when I think of how she enticed Father for so many years, lies about love on her lips. All she ever wanted was power for her son and my throne."

"If you believe this, why haven't you arrested her?"

"Despite what the courtiers may whisper of me in the shadows, I am no tyrant to take a life on suspicion alone, not even Maryam's own. No protestations of innocence shall haunt me until the end of my days."

Butayna sagged against his shoulder. To his credit, he neither scowled nor found fault with her weakness. Instead, he bolstered her and drew her close with his arm around her waist.

She rested her forehead in the crook of his neck. "What will you do, my Sultan?"

"For now? Nothing. Yet, I vow if I ever discover the proof of Maryam's involvement in the murder of my father, her pretty swan's neck shall run red. Blood shall stream across those pretty shoulders my father once caressed in the moonlight."

She raised her head and stared at him. "I beg you, for my sake—"

"Maryam's children shall join her in death. Then the courtiers may speak of Muhammad the mad despot."

His gaze reflected the torchlight above them. A golden fire smoldered at the center of those doe-like eyes now, silent fury engulfing him.

She once imagined he might possess the gentle nature of her father. For all the gifts her Castillan ancestry had granted him, dignity and self-determination chief among them, the pride and blood of Nasrid generations flowed in his veins and bound him to a legacy of revenge. She had already lost her beloved to violence. Must she lose their son?

He kissed her brow, his lips a tender caress before he stood and retrieved the rolls of parchment at his writing desk. He went to his bedroom.

Over his shoulder, he issued a final command. "Send me a *jarya* tonight to warm my bed and my heart. She must sing me to sleep."

She stood and cleared her throat. "Your usual preferences, my Sultan?"

"Of course, *Ummi,* as you know them."

With a shake of her head and a wry smile on her lips, she went down the stairs. "A *jarya* of wit and beauty in equal balance. No black hair, lest she sour your mood."

Beneath the pavilion and along the garden courtyard's walls, Butayna strolled past stalwart guards and slaves, who each bowed upon her approach. A bark of laughter warned her of Maryam's presence, just before she emerged from the family rooms to the east.

Maryam paused in the doorway between her eldest daughter Fatima, who still favored her grandmother Safa, and the girl's intended husband Muhammad the Red. Handsome and of a height similar to the Sultan's own, the young man bowed beside the women and left the *Jannat al-'Arif* via its exit under the southern pavilion. Fatima bussed her mother's cheek and retreated inside, while Maryam remained framed in the doorway. She looked across the harem.

The garden of summer wildflowers and fragrant orange trees separated Butayna and Maryam as they stared at each other in silence. After some time, Maryam inclined her head in a deferential nod, a tribute to Butayna's status as the *Umm al-Walad*. Maryam's inscrutable visage never wavered or revealed any emotions. Butayna acknowledged the sign and did little more than incline her head in return. What would Maryam say if she learned of the secrets Butayna had discovered of her family's heritage? Perhaps Maryam had always known and reviled the Peralta family for betraying their pasts. Butayna would never know.

As Maryam withdrew from sight, Butayna shook her head and proceeded into her chambers. Despite any servile gestures from her rival, Yusuf's death and Muhammad's ascension had not ended her struggle with Maryam. Their war would never be over, not until one of them met her death at the hands of the other.

THE END

Author's Note

When I first wrote about the Nasrid Dynasty, I had not planned further books beyond the stories told in *Sultana* and *Sultana's Legacy*. As I delved into the history of the protagonists in those two books, the lives of their descendants captured my imagination. For the next novel, I knew the story of the Nasrid Dynasty was not enough. The plight of millions of captives stolen from their homes across the Mediterranean, as represented by the experiences of the slaves Butayna and Maryam, became the subject of *Sultana: Two Sisters*.

Inspiration for this novel also came from the relationship that Sultan Muhammad V, Yusuf and Butayna's son, fostered with the Jews. The Jewish community of Granada gave Muhammad V a spectacular gift in the twelve marble lions whose figures now adorn the *Patio de Leones* in the Alhambra. Each of the lions represented a tribe of Israel and came from the house of a Jewish vizier, Samuel ha-Levi Ben-Yusef ibn Nagrela, who served the 11th century rulers of Granada. Today, the lion figures still surround the same 14th century basin installed during the reign of Muhammad V. While Spanish Christians throughout Castile and Aragon persecuted the Jews, Muhammad V offered the beleaguered Sephardic people Granada as their haven. I wondered whether a personal connection could explain his behavior. My speculation about his having had a mother of hidden Jewish origins is pure conjecture, but not outside the realm of possibility.

The Moors

The Moors were Islamic people of Arabian and Negro descent, who invaded the Iberian Peninsula, which encompasses modern-day Portugal and Spain, beginning in the Christian eighth century. They called the conquered land *al-jazirat al-Andalus*, but in later years, the term referred to the south of Spain and became Andalusia in modern times.

The Moors penetrated the interior and brought three-fifths of the peninsula under their control. They gave their unique culture, rich language and the religion of Islam to a land that welcomed them at first, for the valuable riches and social order they brought. Where superstition and ignorance once pervaded all elements of life, the Moors brought intellectual pursuit and reasoning. Their blood mingled with that of the Visigoths and produced a mixed race of individuals.

By Islamic law, Muslim men could marry or have sexual relations with non-Muslim women. Periods of zealous anti-Christian and anti-Jewish views occurred and resulted in forced conversion, but mostly, Christians and Jews enjoyed religious tolerance under Moorish rule. Some families chose to convert willingly, for all the requisite benefits including the avoidance of certain taxes and the gains of political and social advancement, while others practiced their former religion in secret.

Spurred on by religious fanaticism, bigotry, and jealousy of the Moorish achievements, the people of the northern half of the peninsula began the *Reconquista*, a determined struggle against the Moors. Beginning in the Christian tenth century, the rebellion spread slowly southward, until one Moorish kingdom remained, Granada, nestled within the Sierra Nevada Mountains.

Islamic dates in this novel approximate the equivalent periods of the Hijri and Julian calendars. The Julian calendar was in force in this period, rather than the Gregorian calendar in use after AD 1582. Any errors in the relevant dates of the Hijri calendar are based on the Julian dates. The sighting of the crescent moon determines dates in the Hijri calendar. The term AH refers to events occurring in numbered periods after the year of the *Hijra* or the emigration of the Prophet Muhammad from Mecca to Medina in September AD 622.

The Jews

The Jews of Sephardic Spain had various names for their language, known today as Ladino; Judezmo, Judyo or Spanyol. Jews inhabited Spain for millennia. They lived varied, but oftentimes marginalized lives in the Christian kingdom as gold and silversmiths, artisans and moneylenders. Islamic rulers considered them like Christians, Hindus, and Buddhists as *dhimmis*, non-Muslim citizens of Islamic states and as People of the Book, one of the groups who received the word of God.

Still, Jews faced persecution throughout Spain's Christian and Muslim kingdoms. Jewish people worked in the trades the

Catholic and Muslim rulers of Spain permitted them to engage in, such as the work of silver and goldsmiths, and as moneylenders. Others became trusted physicians and court officials. Some even developed deep personal relationships with rulers, such as Rachel Esra, better known as Rahel *la Fermosa*, who became a king's mistress until a violent purge brought about her death.

Hebrew calendar dates in this novel approximate the equivalent periods of the Hebrew and Julian calendars. The Hebrew calendar, like the Hijri, is based on lunar sightings.

Yusuf I entered the world on June 29, AD 1318 or 28 Rabi al-Awwal 718 AH, likely as the second son of Sultan Abu'l-Walid Ismail I. Yusuf's father died after his cousins murdered him in a dispute over a slave girl when Yusuf was seven years old. His elder brother Sultan Abu Abdallah Muhammad IV succeeded Ismail. Both boys and their two younger brothers submitted to the tutelage and care of their grandmother the Sultana Fatima; reputedly, the four princes exercised only the power to choose the dishes they ate during meals. Muhammad IV died on August 25, AD 1338 or 7 Safar 739 AH at eighteen, purportedly at the hands of Uthman ibn Abi'l-Ula. As one of many Marinid princes from Morocco living in Muslim Spain and the commander of the Volunteers of the Faith, Uthman had allegedly conspired in the death of Ismail. After Muhammad's men interred his body at Malaga, Yusuf ascended the throne at the age of fifteen.

Chronicles of the period left a detailed description of Yusuf as 'dark-skinned and naturally strong' with 'large eyes and dark straight hair, a thick beard, a handsome face and a clear voice that was a pleasure to hear.' Yusuf became an enlightened ruler and a warrior. Chroniclers also claimed he could perceive the future. He had two constant companions, considered alternatively as concubines or wives by historians. The women Butayna and Maryam were the mothers of Yusuf's three sons and six daughters. Butayna and Maryam existed as slaves in the harem before they became Yusuf's companions. By all accounts, he favored Maryam and her children more than he did Butayna and hers. He might have considered his second son Ismail as the favorite and a possible heir for a time.

While another son occurs in one primary source, a prince named Ahmad, I have found nothing beyond a poetic reference in 1343 to him along with Muhammad and Ismail as the sons of Yusuf. The author of the poem, the chief minister Ibn al-Jayyab incidentally does not mention Yusuf's third son, Qays, in his verses. All other sources have specified Yusuf as the father of one named son and daughter by Butayna, and two named sons and five daughters by Maryam, without mention of Ahmad as a possible son of either woman. Therefore, I have not included Ahmad in the narrative. If he existed, his mother also remains a mystery. While there are no other named partners indicated for Yusuf, there is a brief mention of another unnamed wife of Yusuf from within his own family, likely a cousin of his as the Nasrids often married their cousins. Perhaps this anonymous woman mothered the equally mysterious Ahmad, but lacking more details, I did not make her a part of this story.

Throughout Yusuf's life, troubles within his family also plagued him. He jailed his brother Ismail on suspicion of treason. In addition, Yusuf's brother Faraj died on the orders of either Muhammad IV or Yusuf, but not before Faraj's son, another Ismail, escaped to live in Morocco. Without further knowledge of Faraj or the circumstances of his death, I chose to exclude him and his son from the narrative as well. Among Yusuf's named sisters, there were Fatima and Maryam, whom I have omitted to avoid confusion with other important characters. Leila is a fictionalized character. Yusuf's mother lived for some years during his reign. A former captive according to one primary source, she converted to Islam and became noted for her piety. Historians like the famous Ibn Battuta who visited Granada during the time of the Black Death, though she was a charitable woman. Apparently, she provided some financial support for Ibn Battuta's extended stay, for which he was very grateful.

In AD 1340, Yusuf allied with Sultan Abu'l-Hasan Ali of Morocco in armed conflict against Castile and Portugal, which the Muslims lost on October 30, AD 1340 or 8 Jumada l-Ula 741 AH at the Battle of Rio Salado. Abu'l-Hasan Ali suffered great personal tragedies as a result, when his first and favorite wife Fatima, the daughter of the caliph of Tunisia, along with other wives, children, and at least one of his sisters suffered attacks from the soldiers of Castile and Portugal. Many of the women and children in the encampment died. The Christian warriors confiscated gold, silver, and luxurious silk banners, the latter of which still exist in Lisbon's museums. The surviving captives endured confinement in Seville until AD 1346.

After the battle, Yusuf returned to Granada and the comforts of his home. He made occasional raids through Christian Spain and interfered in the turbulent politics of Morocco. He maintained the rebel princes Abu Salim and Abu'l-Fadl in Andalusia, despite demands for their return from Abu'l-Hasan Ali's successor, Abu Inan Faris. Yusuf later provided passage for the princes to Sous in southern Morocco, where they fueled rebellion against Abu Inan Faris into the reign of Yusuf's heir.

The kingdom of Castile considered Yusuf a vassal like many of his ancestors and demanded a yearly payment of between 30,000-40,000 gold coins from him, which Yusuf did not always pay, for example after the defeat at Salado. Still, in a magnanimous gesture, Yusuf allowed the cortege of his lifelong enemy, King Alfonso XI of Castile, to depart from the siege of Gibraltar in March AD 1350 and gave orders that none in his kingdom should attack the king's men.

Yusuf made additions to the Alhambra, his family's palace. He enlarged the Comares tower, which served as the throne room of the Sultan, and built the *Bab al-Sharia* (incorrectly known today as the Alhambra's Gate of Justice). He also built a religious school, the *Madrasa Yusufiyya* in Granada in AD 1349. He also worked on the gates, towers, and walls at Malaga, including the citadel at the Gibralfaro. His ministers Ridwan (a Christian convert), Ibn al-Khatib and the elderly public official Ali ibn al-Jayyab (who served from the time of Yusuf's paternal great-grandfather Sultan Muhammad II) created literary works and poems, which still decorate the walls of the Alhambra today. Yusuf benefited from the treatment of his personal physician Muhammad al-Shaquri, a wise man despite being nine years younger than the Sultan. Al-Hasan ibn Muhammad ibn Hasan al-Qaysi, another doctor from Malaga developed new antidotes for poisons in AD 1352.

Under Yusuf's regime, the Marinid Volunteers of the Faith, which had controlled parts of Andalusia since the time of Sultan Muhammad I in the 1260's, began their withdrawal, and later allowed Yusuf's heir to begin the reclamation of territories at Ronda, Marbella, and Gibraltar. Yusuf was a remarkable man, whose life ended too soon in tragedy. He died at the age of thirty-six on October 19, AD 1354 or 1 Shawwal 755 AH, on the morning of the feast to celebrate the end of fasting during Ramadan. A demented black slave from his stable stabbed him to death with a dagger, as Yusuf made the last prostration in his mosque. Yusuf's servants carried him into his palace, where he died almost immediately. He was buried the same afternoon in the graveyard next to his father Ismail. After the fall of the Nasrids in AD 1492, Yusuf's bones along with the relics of his family left the Alhambra forever.

Sultan Abu Abdallah Muhammad V

Sultan Abu Abdallah Muhammad V, the eldest son of the then twenty-year old Sultan Abdul Hajjaj Yusuf I and the Sultan's concubine / wife Butayna, was born on January 4, AD 1338 or 11 Jumada al-Thani 738 AH. Muhammad had a younger, full-blood sister, Aisha, and seven siblings of half-blood. He became the eighth ruler of the Nasrid Dynasty, ascending to the throne in October AD 1354 when he was just sixteen upon the violent murder of his father Yusuf. The former Sultan's ministers proclaimed him the heir; Yusuf never publicly designated one. The minister Ibn al-Khatib composed the oath of loyalty, which the nobility, court dignitaries, Muhammad's family, and the governors swore on the new Sultan's ascension. Muhammad assigned his half-siblings and their mother Maryam to a palace within the Alhambra complex. He depended on the Christian convert Ridwan, who became his prime minister as in the days of his father Yusuf.

Learned like his father, Muhammad established treaties and a personal relationship with King Pedro I of Castile, who was four years Muhammad's senior. He even renewed the tribute his forefathers had paid. Because of their friendship, both rulers had a great deal of influence on the policies and cultural flowering of their two kingdoms. Muhammad retained a corps of two hundred Christian guardsmen, derived from former captives, throughout his lifetime.

Sultana Butayna

Butayna, the Christian mother of Sultan Muhammad V and the concubine / first wife of Sultan Abdul Hajjaj Yusuf I, left no record of her life in the Alhambra. I do not know her original name, the date or location of her birth, or her age when she bore Yusuf his heir. The only certainties are her harem name Butayna, which meant 'one who possesses a young and tender body,' her status as a slave in Yusuf's harem by at least AD 1337 prior to her first pregnancy and her belief in the Christian faith. She was one of apparently five Christian women who became mothers of the Sultans of Granada. Chroniclers of the period learned miniscule details of her life through the deep-seated rivalry she and Maryam shared. Both women sought the throne of Granada for their sons after Yusuf's death. Butayna became the mother of two of Yusuf's children, including a younger daughter Aisha.

Period sources referred to Butayna as either a concubine or wife of the ruler Yusuf. As a Christian concubine, she became the first in his harem to bear him a son. Since history most often refers to her as a slave, it is unlikely she ever converted to Islam. Muslim law sanctioned the freedom of all persons who converted. It also recognized the concept of freedom for the slave mothers of children born to Islamic rulers, but the practice was not universal. Most of the Christian West relied on primogeniture (the inheritance by the firstborn). The Muslim West never followed such strict rules. Sons vied with each other for their inheritances, even the throne of Granada. Yusuf's apparently favorable disposition toward Maryam and her children meant Butayna's son, even as Yusuf's firstborn, should not have expected to inherit the throne automatically.

Life altered forever for Butayna on October 19, AD 1354, when Yusuf died. Records indicate she was still alive at this time. Then, Butayna set aside the label of slave forever and became a queen, the mother of the Sultan Abu Abdallah Muhammad V. Islamic law recognized the manumission of slaves upon the deaths of their masters. Butayna's role in the harem would have changed. She might have influenced her son's decision-making and perhaps, the course of Spanish history. I often wonder whether her gains at Muhammad's side compensated for the trials she must have endured as Yusuf's slave.

Sultana Maryam

Maryam, the concubine / second wife of Sultan Abdul Hajjaj Yusuf I, and the mother of two of his sons, Ismail and Qays, and five of his daughters, Fatima, Mumina, Khadija, Shams, and Zaynab, also left no record of her life. One secondary source indicates the modern day understanding of her name as Maryam might be an error in transcribing the original Arabic; instead, the name might have been Rim. Her origins and date of birth are uncertain. A slave like Butayna, she seems to have enjoyed greater influence over Yusuf than her rival did. Maryam gave Yusuf his second son, a boy named for his grandfather Ismail, born on October 2, AD 1338 or 16 Rabi al-Awwal 739 AH. His elder brother Muhammad preceded him by ten months. It is highly likely Maryam conceived Ismail within a short span of time around the birth of Butayna's first child. Maryam would have enjoyed the same luxuries as her rival in the Alhambra, including close access to the Sultan. In time, her eldest daughter married a red-haired cousin, Muhammad, more commonly known in Castilian Spanish history as *El Bermejo*. He descended from Yusuf's grandmother Sultana Fatima through her second son, also named Muhammad, the father of Ismail, who became *El Bermejo*'s father.

When Yusuf died, Maryam and her children lived under the dominion of Sultan Muhammad V and his mother Butayna would have controlled Muhammad's harem. Muhammad gave his stepmother and her family quarters in another part of the Alhambra complex. What was life like for Maryam at this time? She went from having influence over one Sultan, her husband, to likely none with her stepson Muhammad V. A step down, just when her star seemed to be rising. It is interesting to consider the possibilities and problems faced by a woman in Maryam's position. I have portrayed her as greedy and ambitious, just as the sources indicate, but one detail in my characterization is different from the historical record. For dramatic purposes, I have described Maryam as a Jewish woman, but chroniclers of the period indicate she began life as a Christian like Butayna. Whatever the truth of their circumstances may have been, Maryam and Butayna were sisters in faith, through their belief in the same God, as well as sisters in bondage within the palace of Alhambra. Each played her part in shaping the future of Muslim Spain.

Until the near completion of this novel, I had once believed Fatima, the heroine of *Sultana* and *Sultana's Legacy* died in the early years of Yusuf's rule. It was a pleasurable shock to discover that she lived throughout most of her grandson's reign, dying on February 26, 1349 at more than ninety years old. Fatima was the matriarch of the Nasrid Dynasty and as one of the sources put it, "Of all the descendants of Muhammad II, Fatima was the most prominent, not only for being the mother of his grandson Sultan Ismail, but also for her unusual participation in Nasrid politics for generations of rulers. It is therefore possible to say that she was one of the most significant women with historical repercussions for the entire dynasty."

As Yusuf's grandmother, Fatima not only reared him after the premature death of his father; she tutored and nurtured his love of the arts and sciences. Their bond influenced the course of Yusuf's life. I do not know the nature of her relationship with her son's chosen companions Butayna and Maryam, or with Yusuf's children. The end of her remarkable life inspired Yusuf's minister Ibn al-Khatib to write of her, "... she was Fatima, daughter of Muhammad II. She was the cream of the kingdom, the central pearl of the dynasty, the pride of the harem women, the height of honor and respect, the link that gave the people the protection of the kings and her life was a reminder of the legacy of the royal family."

The Black Death

An epidemic of bubonic plague arrived in the shipping ports of Moorish Spain by late December AD 1347. Rats in European towns and ports, aided by general filth and poor sanitation, advanced the spread of the disease through the fleas gathered on their dying bodies. The rats and fleas encountered people. After a fleabite, lymph nodes developed into painful buboes, which turned the skin black and appeared on the groin, thigh, armpit, or neck of infected person. Within three to five days in which these signs of infection manifested, victims spat blood, had seizures and terrible coughs, or watched their limbs turn black with rot. Eighty percent of them died within a week. The Catholic Church interpreted the spread of plague as a curse from God, spurred by the presence of heretics. Jews suffered particular persecution.

On the eve of this great pestilence, there were 7.5 million persons living in the Iberian Peninsula, throughout the Christian kingdom of Portugal, Castile, Aragon, Navarre, and Granada to the south. Beginning in May AD 1348, the Black Death claimed the lives of at least seventy persons per day in the Muslim city of Almeria, until the epidemic died down in February AD 1349. The first death in Malaga, further down the coast, occurred during April AD 1349. A month later, plague began ravaging Granada. It crossed into Spain's northern territories, reaching Toledo in June AD 1349 and Seville in September AD 1349. It claimed old and young, peasants and kings, Christians, Jews and Muslims. It devastated the population. King Alfonso XI of Castile died from the Black Death on March 22, AD 1350, during the siege of the fortress at Gibraltar. I have no information on how plague affected members of Yusuf's family personally, but the dynasty's rulers and their dependents would not have been immune to the effects. Arab doctors in the Middle East advanced the methods discussed for dealing with the plague in the narrative. There is a current theory that the descendants of Europe's plague survivors have a gene that enables their resistance to virulent diseases like HIV. The Black Death may have claimed thirty to forty percent of the population of Spain before it ran its course in AD 1350. Ibn al-Khatib would later write a treatise on the course of the plague in AD 1374. The plague reoccurred in Spain in later years, most notably in the 16th and 17th centuries.

Thank you for purchasing and reading this book. I hope you found the period and characters fascinating. Please consider leaving feedback where you bought this book. Your opinion is helpful, both to me and to other potential readers.

If you would like to learn more about the Alhambra and Moorish Spain during the Nasrid period, visit Alhambra.org or Patronato de la Alhambra y Generalife. Learn more the *Sultana* series at my website. You may also email me at lisa@lisajyarde.com or join my mailing list for more information on upcoming releases at http://eepurl.com/un8on. I love to hear from readers.

Butayna and Maryam's story is not over. The power struggle between them has larger consequences for Sultan Muhammad V and his first wife in *Sultana: The Bride Price*, available winter 2013-2014.

Islamic Regions and Modern Equivalents

Al- Andalus: Andalusia
Al-Bayazin: Albaicin
Al-Jaza'ir: Algiers
Al-Jazirah al-Khadra: Algeciras
Al-Jazirat Al-Andalus: Spain
Al-Maghrib: Northern Africa
Al-Maghrib el-Aska: Morocco
Al-Mariyah: Almeria
Al-Qal'at ibn Zaide: Alcala la Real
Fés el-Jedid: new city of Fez
Gharnatah: Granada
Ishbiliya: Seville
Jabal Tarik: Gibraltar
Madinah Antaqirah: Antequera
Malaka: Malaga
Marballa: Marbella
Martus: Martos
Munakkab: Almunecar
Qirbilyan: Crevillente
Shalabuniya: Salobrena
Tarif: Tarifa
Wadi-Ash: Guadix

Glossary

Addahbia: bridal trousseau

Adar: the twelfth Jewish month, which during leap years has 30 days, rather than 29 days

Al-Andalus: the southern half of Spain

Al-Bayazin: the Albaicin neighborhood north of the Alhambra

Al-bayt al-ma': latrine

Al-bayt al-barid: the cool room in a Moorish bath

Al-bayt al-maslakh: changing room in a Moorish bath

Al-bayt al-wastani: the tepid room in a Moorish bath

Al-Ghuzat: the Volunteers of the Faith, the Moroccan soldiers billeted in Granada

Al-jazirat al-Andalus: the Iberian Peninsula

Al-Qal'at al-Hamra: the Alhambra, a complex of palaces, residences, shops, mosques, etc. that served as the royal residence in Granada. Begun in AD 1237 under Sultan Muhammad I, each of his successors made improvements, especially Muhammad III, Ismail I, Yusuf I, Muhammad V, and Yusuf III

Al-Qasr Xenil: a Moorish palace built near the Genil River before the founding of the Nasrid Dynasty. It served as the residence of foreign rulers and dignitaries, but after the reign of Sultan Ismail I, the palace primarily became the residence of discarded harem women from the Alhambra

Al-Quasaba: the citadel within the royal residence in Granada

Al-Qur'an: Muslim holy book

Al-salam 'alayka: the traditional Muslim greeting, 'may peace be upon you'

Adalid: captain in medieval Castile

Alfaqueque: a royal official appointed to ransom captives

Aljama: the Jewish neighborhood as a minority in Spanish cities

Allah: God

Allahu Akbar: God is great

Almocaden: infantry commander or sergeant in medieval Castile

Amir al-Muslimin: prince of the faithful

Arroyo: brook

Av: the fifth Jewish month

Bab al-Sharia: the Gate of the Esplanade (incorrectly called the Gate of Justice) on the southwestern side of the *Sabika* Hill, built by Sultan Yusuf I and commemorated in June AD 1348. Today, it serves as the main entrance for visitors to the Alhambra complex.

Ballesteros: Castilian crossbowmen

Barq: little gold beads for hair decoration

Batikha: fine white cosmetic powder for maintaining a porcelain appearance

Bint: daughter of

Caballeros: Christian knights

Camisa (Spanish) / Qamis (Arabic): long shirt of white cotton or linen, worn as an undergarment by both sexes, in all social classes

Cantar de mio Cid: 'the song of the Cid', which is one of the oldest Castilian epic poems, centered on the life of Rodrigo Diaz de Vivar, Spain's national hero

Cantiga: medieval Spanish song

Cendal: a type of silk

Corrals: slave pens

Cristianos Nuevos: 'New Christians' in Castilian Spanish, a somewhat derogatory term most often associated with Jewish converts to Christianity

Dafair: loaves of bread, made from white flour, leavening, salt, eggs, and saffron, shaped like braids, browned in a frying pan with oil, and sprinkled with honey spiced with pepper, cinnamon, Chinese cinnamon and lavender

De bona guerra: the incessant conflicts between Christian and Muslims along the borders of the Christian and Moorish kingdoms of Spain, during which both sides allowed the taking of captives

Dhimmi: a non-Muslim living in a Muslim territory, allowed to retain his or her religion

Dhu al-Hijja: the twelfth Islamic month, a period of pilgrimage to Saudi Arabia

Dhu al-Qa`da: the eleventh Islamic month

Dinar: Islamic coin bearing a religious verse, commonly made of gold or silver, or rarely, copper. They were minted in Granada with the Sultans' motto, "none victorious but God" and could be round or square shaped. Gold *dinars* weighed 2 grams, contained 22 carats of gold, and were widely used for internal and external trade. Their value fluctuated over the centuries. Silver *dinars* were square and had a fixed value. Copper *dinars* were used for internal trade in the Sultanate and had a fixed value

Dios mio: My God in Castilian Spanish

Dirham: Islamic coin bearing a religious verse, commonly made of silver or other base metal. In Granada, they were minted with

the Sultans' motto, "none victorious but God" and weighed 2-3 grams
Diwan al-Insha: the Sultan's chancery of state
Duenna: governess in Castilian Spanish

El Dio: God in Ladino
Elul: the sixth Jewish month

Ghaliya: a perfume of musk, camphor, oil from the moringa tree and ambergris
Ghasil: man who washes the Muslim dead
Ghasul: a paste with a variety of cosmetic purposes

Hadarro: modern-day river Darro that flows through Granada
Hais: pastries filled with ground almonds and pistachios, dusted with crystalline sugar
Hajib: Prime Minister
Hammam: bathhouse
Hashish: cannabis
Henna: dye or paste prepared from a plant and applied to various parts of the body
Hijab: a veil
Houri: virgins in Paradise
Hud: enemies of the Nasrids

Ibn: son of
Imam: the male prayer leader in a mosque
Infanta / Infante: a royal child in Castilian Spanish, plural *infantes*
Insha'Allah: God willing
Iyar: the second Jewish month

Jannat al-'Arif: the Generalife, the summer palace of the Alhambra, constructed during the reign of Sultan Muhammad II and enlarged mainly by his grandson Sultan Ismail I
Jarya: concubine, plural *jawari*
Jihad: the struggle; a personal commitment to maintain the Islamic faith, to improve Islamic society and to defend Islam and an Islamic way of life against its enemies
Jinn: evil spirits
Jubba: Moorish floor-length robe with wide sleeves, opening at the neck, worn by both sexes of the nobility
Jumada al-Thani: the sixth Islamic month
Jumada al-Ula: the fifth Islamic month

Kadin: favored Moorish concubine, who has also had children for her master
Katib: secretary
Katib sirri-hi: the Sultan's personal secretary
Kehilla: the Jewish community
Khamsa: the Hand of Fatima, an amulet in the shape of a hand, meant to convey patience, abundance, and faithfulness to the wearer, attributed to the daughter of Prophet Muhammad
Khanjar: Moorish dagger
Khassa: collective Moorish nobility
Kislev: the ninth Jewish month
Kohl: black eyeliner
Kursi al-mulk: seat of power, the throne

La: No
La frontera: 'the frontier' in Castilian Spanish

Madina: a city
Madrasa: religious school of higher education
Maravedies: Castilian gold coinage, singular *maravedi,* originating with the Islamic conquest. When the Castilians incorporated the coinage in their use, it eventually fell in value from silver to copper coinage. The Castilian government stopped issuing *maravedies* in the 1850's when the Spanish currency changed to the decimal system
Marcheshvan: the eighth Jewish month
Marinids: rulers of modern day Morocco AD 1248-1548
Masjid: mosque
Mayordomo: 'majordomo' in Castilian Spanish
Meseta: the tableland of La Mancha, Castile, which served as a frontier between Castile and Granada
Mezuzah: a parchment inscribed with Hebrew verses from the Torah
Mi hija: 'my daughter' in Castilian Spanish
Mi querida: 'my dear' in Castilian Spanish
Misha: a long garment with wide sleeves
Miswak: stick for cleaning the teeth
Muger fermosa: 'beautiful woman' in Castilian Spanish
Muharram: the first Islamic month

Nakhwa: aromatic seeds, ground into powder form and drunk as a tea
Nam: Yes
Nasrids: rulers of Granada AD 1232-1492
Niña: 'child' in Castilian Spanish

Nissan: the first Jewish month
Nura: a depilatory

Oud: a pear-shaped musical instrument similar to the lute

Pellote: a Castilian Spanish surcoat
Purim: commemorates the day of Jewish deliverance from a plotted massacre, as discussed in the Biblical Book of Esther

Qabqab: platform sandals with wooden soles
Qadar: pre-destiny
Qandara: a short shirt
Qur'an: the Islamic holy book as revealed to the Prophet Muhammad
Qaysariyya: the central marketplace in Granada

Rabi al-Awwal: the third Islamic month
Rabi al-Thani: the fourth Islamic month
Rajab: the seventh Islamic month
Rak'ah: prescribed series of movements and words during Muslim prayer
Ramadan: the ninth Islamic month, a venerated period of abstinence and fasting from sunrise to sunset
Rawda: cemetery
Reconquista: the struggle to remove the Moors from Spain
Rida: a Moorish housecoat for women

Sabika: the hill where the Alhambra was built
Safar: the second Islamic month
Salat al-Asr: third Muslim prayer time, obligatory at afternoon (about four hours after *Salat al-Zuhr*)
Salat al-Fajr: first Muslim prayer time, obligatory at sunrise
Salat al-Isha: fifth Muslim prayer time, obligatory at nighttime (about an hour after *Salat al-Maghrib*)
Salat al-Maghrib: fourth Muslim prayer time, obligatory after sunset (about three to four hours after *Salat al-Asr*)
Salat al-Zuhr: second Muslim prayer time, obligatory at noon
Sarawil: Moorish trousers
Saya: a Castilian Spanish dress
Sekanjabin: a sweet and sour Moorish drink of Persian origins, made of vinegar and honey
Sha'ban: the eighth Islamic month
Shabbat: the Jewish day of rest
Shahadah: the Muslim Profession of Faith
Sharbah: sherbet

Sharia: the religious law of Islam
Shawwal: the tenth Islamic month
Shaya: functional short garment with fitted sleeves
Shimasas: the latticework screen over a window in the harem
Shevat: the eleventh Jewish month
Siddur: a Jewish prayer book
Siwan: the third Jewish month
Suftaja: a letter of credit between merchants
Sukkariyya: a Moorish dish of crushed almonds cooked in sugar and rosewater, with sugar sprinkled on top.
Suras: verses of the *Qur'an*

Tabaq: tray
Talib: apprentice or student
Tammuz: the fourth Jewish month
Taylasan: a tasseled headcloth worn at Muslim prayer times or by supreme judges
'*Tharid*: Moorish dish of crumbled pieces of bread served in a meat or vegetable broth
Tikka: belt
Tishrei: the seventh Jewish month
Toca: Castilian headdress

Umm al-Walad: mother of a child
Ummi: my mother

Vega: the fertile lands of southern Spain

Wa-'alayka: traditional response to the greeting of *Al-salam 'alayka*
Wa-la ghalib illa Allah: the Nasrid motto, 'Only God is the victor'
Wazir: Moorish minister

Xenil: modern-day Genil River

Zapatas / zapatos: short, leather boots in Castile
Zabarbada: a Moorish dish of melted cheese, mixed with onion, coriander and pepper, and thickened with flour and eggs
Zirbiya: a Moorish dish of hens, doves, pigeons or lamb, cooked with salt, pepper, coriander, cinnamon, vinegar and saffron, boiled down in a sweet, thick paste of mashed almonds and sugar soaked in rosewater

About the Author

Lisa J. Yarde writes fiction inspired by the Middle Ages in Europe. She is the author of two historical novels set in medieval England and Normandy, *The Burning Candle*, based on the life of Isabel de Vermandois, and *On Falcon's Wings*, chronicling the star-crossed romance between Norman and Saxon lovers. Lisa has also written three novels in a six-part series set in Moorish Spain, *Sultana, Sultana's Legacy,* and *Sultana: Two Sisters*, where rivalries and ambitions threaten the fragile bonds between members of a powerful family. Her short story, *The Legend Rises*, which chronicles Gwenllian of Gwynedd's valiant fight against English invaders, is included in Pagan Writers Press' 2013 HerStory anthology.

Born in Barbados, Lisa currently lives in New York City. She is also an avid blogger and moderates at Unusual Historicals. She is also a contributor at Historical Novel Reviews and History and Women. Her personal blog is The Brooklyn Scribbler.

Learn more about Lisa and her writing at the website www.lisajyarde.com. Follow her on Twitter (**@lisajyarde**) or become a Facebook fan (**Lisa J. Yarde**). For information on upcoming releases and freebies from Lisa, join her mailing list at http://eepurl.com/un8on.

CPSIA information can be obtained at www.ICGtesting.com
Printed in the USA
LVOW10s1101061113

360240LV00010B/134/P